DEDICATION

To those who dare to step beyond the glass

GIRL OF GLASS

Book One

CHAPTER ONE

Nola dug her fingers into the warm dirt. Around her, the greenhouse smelled of damp earth, mist, and fresh, clean air.

Carefully, she took the tiny seed and placed it at the bottom of the hole her finger had made.

Thump.

Soon the seed would take root. A sprout would break through to the surface.

Thump, bang.

Then the green stem would grow until bean pods sprouted.

Bang, thump!

The food would be harvested and brought to their tables. All of the families would be fed.

"Ahhhhh!" the voice came from the other side of the glass. Nola knew she shouldn't look, but she couldn't ignore the sounds any longer.

It was a woman this time, her skin gray with angry, red patches dotting her face. She slammed her fists into the glass, leaving smears of red behind. The woman didn't seem to care as she banged her bloody hands into the glass over and over.

"Magnolia."

Nola jumped as Mrs. Pearson placed a hand on her shoulder.

"Don't pay her any mind," Mrs. Pearson said. "She can't get through the glass."

"But she's bleeding." Nola pushed the words past the knot in her throat.

The woman bashed her head against the glass.

"She needs help," Nola said. The woman stared right at her.

Mrs. Pearson took Nola's shoulders and turned her back to her plant tray. "That woman is beyond your help, Magnolia. Paying her any attention will only make it worse. There is nothing you can do."

Nola felt eyes staring at her. Not just the woman on the other side of the glass. The rest of the class was staring at her now, too.

Bang. Thump.

Families. The food she planted would feed the families.

Bang.

Pop.

Nola spun back to the glass. Two guards were outside now. One held his gun high. A thin spike protruded from the woman's neck. Her eyelids fluttered for a moment before she slid down the glass, leaving a streak of blood behind her.

"See," Mrs. Pearson said, smoothing Nola's hair, "they'll take her where she can't hurt herself or any of us ever again."

Nola nodded, turning back to the tray of dirt. Make a hole, plant the seed, grow the food. But the streaks of blood were burned into her mind.

The setting sun gave the greenhouse an orange-red gleam when the chime finally sounded.

"Students," Mrs. Pearson called over the sounds of her class packing up for the evening, "remember, tomorrow is Charity Day. Please dress and prepare accordingly. Anyone who doesn't come ready to leave the domes will be sent home, and their grades will be docked."

"Thank you, Mrs. Pearson," the students chorused as they drifted down into the hall.

"Magnolia."

Nola pretended she hadn't heard Mrs. Pearson call her name as she slipped in front of the group leaving the greenhouse. She didn't want to be asked if she was all right or told the sick woman would be cared for. And she didn't want to see if the glass had already been wiped clean.

Lights flickered on, sensing the group heading down the steps. Hooks lined the hallway, awaiting the gardening uniforms. Nola pulled off her rubber boots and unzipped her brown and green jumpsuit, straightening her sweater before shrugging out of the dirt-covered uniform. The rest of the class chatted as they changed—plans for the evening, talk of tomorrow's trip into the city. Nola beat the rest of them to the sink to scrub her hands. The harsh smell of the soap stung her nose, and the steaming water turned her hands red. But in a minute, the only sign of her time in the greenhouses that remained was a bit of dirt on the long brown braid that hung over her shoulder.

"Nola." Jeremy Ridgeway took his place next to Nola at the sinks, shaking the dirt from his light brown hair like a dog. It would have been funny if Nola had been in the mood to laugh. "Are you ready for tomorrow?"

"Sure. It's our duty to help the less fortunate." She sounded like a parrot, repeating what their teachers said every time Charity Day came around. Nola turned to walk away.

Jeremy stopped her, taking her hand.

"Are you okay?" Wrinkles formed on his forehead, and concern filled his deep brown eyes.

"Of course." Nola forced herself to smile.

"Do you want to come over tonight?" Jeremy asked, still holding her hand. "I mean"—his cheeks flushed—"my sister and my dad are off-duty tonight, and she hasn't seen you in a while."

"I've got to get home. My mom leaves tomorrow. But tell your dad and Gentry I said hi." Nola pulled her hand away and half-ran down the hall. More lights flickered on as she sped down the corridor. She made herself breathe, fighting her guilt at running away from Jeremy. She liked being in the greenhouses better than the tunnels that dug down into the earth. There might only be a few feet of dirt on top of her, but knowing it was there pressed an impossible weight on her lungs.

The hum of the air-filtration system calmly buzzed overhead. The solar panels aboveground generated power so she could breathe down here. She pictured the schematics in her head. Lots of vents. Great big vents. The air would be filtered, cleaned and purified, and the big vents would bring oxygen down to her.

Blue paint on the wall read *Bright Dome* above an arrow pointing to a corridor on the left. Nola ran faster, knowing soon she would be aboveground. In a minute she was sprinting up the steps. She took a deep, gulping breath. The air in the tunnels might be the same as the air in the domes, but it felt so different.

The sun had set, leaving only the bright lights of the city across the river and the faint twinkle of the other domes to peer through the glass. Nola squinted at the far side of Bright Dome. The other homestead domes glowed gently, but if she tried, she could almost make out a few stars. At least that's what she told herself. It might only have been wishful thinking.

Tall trees reached almost to the roof of Bright Dome. Grass and wildflowers coated the ground around the stone footpaths that led from house to house. Nola followed the path through the buildings to the far side of the dome. Twelve families shared Bright Dome, each of them lucky enough to have been granted independent housing units.

The trees in the dome hung heavy with crisp, green leaves. The flowers had begun to close their petals for the night. A squirrel darted past Nola's feet.

"A little late getting home, buddy." Nola's pulse slowed with each step closer to home.

The birds were all flying back to their nests. Bright Dome had been assigned robins and blue jays this cycle. The birds and the squirrels shared their home to be kept safe from contamination. The domes provided them all protection from the toxic air and tainted water.

The lights were on in Nola's house as she swung open the door.

"Hey, Mom," Nola called.

"Mmmmhmmm." The sound came from her mother's office in the back of the kitchen.

"How was your day?" Nola pulled the pot of steaming vegetables from the stove, knowing they would be overdone without having to lift the lid.

"Fine," her mother said, running her fingers through her shoulder-length, chestnut hair, which had been graying quickly of late. "We've been running samples in the lab all day."

"You'll figure it out." Nola didn't ask what the problem in the lab was. Her mother, Lenora Kent, was one of the heads of the botanical preservation group. It was their job to decide what plants from the outside needed to be preserved and how to take care of those plants once they were safely inside the domes. Whatever her mother was working on was for the good of them all. Beyond that it was all vague answers about classified projects.

Nola pulled bowls down from the cabinet, dishing out steamed beans and broccoli, adding spices to make the food taste like something real.

Nola pushed the bowl in front of her mother. Only when she put the spoon in Lenora's hand did her mother seem to notice Nola was still in the room.

"How was your day, sweetie?" Lenora looked up at her daughter.

Nola's mind flashed to the woman. Pounding on the glass, shattering the serenity of the greenhouse.

"It was fine." Nola smiled. "Don't forget to pack for the conference. It'll be colder at Green Leaf, so pack your sweaters."

"Of course." Lenora nodded, but she was already looking back at the charts on her computer screen.

Nola carried her dinner up the narrow stairs to the second floor. She crept into her mother's room and found the duffel bag under her bed. Nola pulled clothes out of the tiny closet. They were lucky. The residents of the domes hadn't been forced into uniforms outside of work and school. Yet. That would come when there was no one left on the outside to work in manufacturing.

When she had counted out enough blouses and slacks for her mother's week-long trip, Nola moved the suitcase to the head of the bed, where her mother would have to see it if she went to sleep that night. A picture in a carved wood frame sat on the nightstand. Six faces beamed out of the photo. A ten-year-old version of herself sat in a tree above her mother and father. Kieran sat on the branch next to her, and below him were his parents.

Nola touched her father's face, wishing the photo was larger so she could properly see his bright blue eyes that had matched her own. But her father was dead, killed in the same riot as Kieran's mother. And now Kieran and his father had been banished from the domes. The photo blurred as tears pooled in Nola's eyes.

She slid the picture into the top of her mother's bag. Lenora would need a bit of home during the Green Leaf Conference—even if their family had broken.

Nola snuck across the tiny landing at the top of the stairs and into her room. She climbed straight into bed, leaving her dinner forgotten on her desk. She pushed her face into her pillow, hoping sleep would come before the face of the woman desperate to get through the glass.

CHAPTER TWO

The scent of stale vegetables filled Nola's room when her lights flickered on the next morning. A faint beeping came before the computerized voice that said, "Reminder: today is Charity Day. Please dress in uniform, remember sun protection, pack I-Vent..."

"Yeah, yeah." Nola rubbed her eyes.

"Remember," the computer continued, "charity must be done to ease the suffering of those on the outside, but protecting yourself means the salvation of mankind."

"I said, I got it!" Nola tossed her shoe at the wall.

Her mother's bedroom door was open, and the kitchen was empty. "Have fun at your conference, Mom," Nola muttered to the empty house as she ran out the door.

It was easier to go through the tunnels in the morning, when she knew sunlight filled the domes above, but still, Nola walked as quickly as she could without being glared at by the people she passed.

The bus into the city would leave from the atrium, the only place in the domes with an exit to the outside world. Five-minute walk underground, then in the outside for four hours, then class, then to the greenhouses. Nola made the list in her mind.

Not too bad. I can get through today.

"Nola!" a voice called from behind her.

Nola slowed her step without looking back.

A moment later, Jeremy walked at her side.

"You ready for this?" Jeremy's voice bounced with excitement.

"Yep." Nola held up her wide brim hat and gloves before patting the I-Vent in her back pocket. "Ready for a trip into the dangerous world. How could I not be with PAM's help this morning?"

"So, your computer got a little snarky with you, too?" Jeremy smiled. "I love how it gives us the 'greater good' speech before we go out and try to help people."

Nola shrugged. She wanted to say, *How much good do you think doling out one meal a month to the people we deem worthy of our assistance really does?* But Jeremy looked so hopeful she couldn't bear to disillusion him before they had to look the outsiders in the face.

"If we get on the bus soon enough, we can call the good jobs." Jeremy took her hand and pulled her, running down the corridor.

Nola laughed as she tried to keep up, her voice echoing through the hall. People turned to stare at them, but that only made Jeremy run faster.

Nola's step faltered as she tried to keep up with Jeremy's much longer stride. She laughed through her panting breath as they rounded a corner and darted past a group of their classmates.

"Last one to the bus scrubs the pans!" Jeremy shouted.

The green bus waited for them in the atrium. Mr. Pillion shook his head but didn't bother hiding his smile as they skidded to a stop in front of the bus.

"Morning." Nola pinched the stitch in her side.

"Good morning, Magnolia. Jeremy." Mr. Pillion's puffy white hair bounced as he nodded.

Nola bit her lip. He always reminded her of one of the snowy white sheep from the Farm Dome. Images of the farm workers sheering Mr. Pillion's hair floated through her mind.

"I'd like to take ladle duty." Jeremy turned to Nola.

Nola didn't really care what job she had. Being out there and seeing the outsiders was terrible. Did it really matter if she scrubbed pans, too? But Jeremy stared at her, eyebrows raised.

"Ladle for me, too, please," Nola said.

Jeremy smiled and moved to pull Nola onto the bus.

"Wait," Mr. Pillion said, holding out a hand. "One dose each from the I-Vent before we get on the bus."

"But we don't use them till we're on the road," Nola said.

The I-Vents cleared their lungs of the smog that hung heavy over the city. There was no reason to use them in the pure air of the domes.

"There was a riot last night." Mr Pillion's usually cheerful face darkened. "There's still smoke in the air, so we need to be more cautious."

Nola pulled the I-Vent from her back pocket. Holding the metal cylinder to her lips, she took one deep breath, letting the vapor pour over her tongue. The medicine tasted metallic and foul. She shivered as the mist chilled her throat. Nola pictured the drugs working. Finding all of the impurities in her lungs and rooting them out. Forming a protective layer to keep the toxins from seeping deep into the tissue.

"Good." Mr. Pillion nodded, lowering his arm and allowing them onto the bus.

A line of other students had formed behind them now.

"Everyone. One puff of the I-Vent before you can get on the bus," Mr. Pillion called to the crowd. "No, Nikki, you cannot get on the bus without your hat."

"That girl is going to fail again this year," Jeremy whispered as a girl with bright blond hair ran back to the tunnels.

A few of their classmates had beaten them onto the bus. Their class was for ages fifteen through eighteen. Some aged into the next group before others, but really they had been together since they were little, the younger ones rejoining the older ones when they moved to the next age level. They had all split into groups of friends years ago, and nothing had changed besides their heights. Until Kieran left.

"Nola," Jeremy said, offering Nola the seat next to his.

She should be sitting next to Kieran.

If he were still here.

Lilly, Nikki's best friend, raised an eyebrow and tilted her head toward the open seat next to her.

"Sure." Nola smiled at Jeremy.

Lilly winked, giving Nola a sly grin before turning back to her book.

Nola sat down next to Jeremy. He leaned casually against the wire-laced window, watching the other students loading onto the bus. Nola's chest hummed. She kept her gaze on her hands, afraid Jeremy would hear her heart racing. How could he look so calm and handsome when they were about to leave the domes?

"Everyone ready?" Mr. Pillion asked.

"Yes, sir," the class chorused.

"Good." Mr. Pillion took his seat. Eight guards in full riot gear loaded onto the bus, sitting up front by the door.

"Umm, Mr. Pillion," Lilly said, "are you sure we should be going out there if we need eight guards?"

They always had guards when they went out for Charity Day. But usually only four, and never in full riot gear.

"We cannot allow the unfortunate actions of a few to dissuade us from helping the many," Mr. Pillion said as the bus pulled up to the giant, metal bay doors. "We must show the population we are here to assist and protect them as long as they remain law-abiding citizens. I promise you we have done everything possible to ensure your safety."

A low rumble shook the bus roof as the atrium ventilation system prepared for the bay doors to open. Nola's ears popped as a *whoosh* flowed through the bus. She pinched her nose and pushed air into her ears along with the rest of the class.

The metal door scraped open, and unfiltered sunlight poured in. Guards in uniforms and masks stood at attention outside the dome doors, their gaze sweeping the horizon for unseen threats.

"What happened last night?" Nola whispered to Jeremy.

"A bunch of Vampers," Jeremy muttered. The people in the seats around them leaned in. "They're ridiculous. They take a bunch of drugs that make them crazy then cause trouble for the poor people who are just trying to survive."

"I've heard the Vampers are invincible," Rayland said, his pudgy face pale with fright.

"They aren't invincible." Jeremy shook his head. "My dad's Captain of the Outer Guard, so I've heard more about the Vampers than you could come up with in your nightmares. And my dad's people have taken them down before."

"But what about last night?" Lilly said.

"The Outer Guard went in to raid one of the Vamp labs," Jeremy said. "It got messy."

"I heard," Lilly said, shivering as she spoke, "Vampers actually drink blood. I don't think I could fight a person who drank blood. It would be like offering them a buffet of you."

"Vampers aren't people." Disgust twisted Jeremy's face.

"Why would they drink blood?" Nola swallowed the bile rising in her throat.

"Because they're a bunch of sickos," Jeremy spat. "And they're taking the city down with them. The rest of the neighborhood around the Vamp lab freaked out, like the guards were stealing food from orphans, and the riot started. They burned down a whole block before the guards could stop it."

"Were any of the guards hurt?" Nola's balled her hands into tight fists, hiding their trembling.

"No." Jeremy took her hands in his. "All of our people are fine."

"I get that life out there is a nightmare," Lilly said, sliding back to her own seat, "but why would they try to make it worse?"

Nola looked out the window, watching as they crossed the long bridge into the city. Children ran barefoot on the sidewalks, their heads exposed to the pounding sun. Garbage had been tossed along the curb, bringing insects and wild animals to feast on the refuse. Even with the ventilation system on the bus, the stench of stagnant water and the sickening sweetness of rotting fruit tainted the air.

Jeremy squeezed her hands tighter as he followed her gaze out the window.

It was easy to forget the world was ending when you lived in the safety of the domes.

CHAPTER THREE

When they were only a few blocks from the Charity Center, a video screen folded down from the ceiling at the front of the bus.

"Are you ready for this?" Jeremy snuck past Nola to kneel in the center of the aisle, facing the rest of the students.

Jeremy coughed as the screen blinked to life.

"Jeremy," Mr. Pillion said in a warning tone.

"I'm word-perfect, sir," Jeremy said. "They will receive all the dire warnings accurately."

A man appeared on the screen, and Jeremy turned back to the class, plastering a somber look on his face to match the man in the video.

"Good morning, students," Jeremy said with the man on the screen.

"Good morning, Jeremy," the class echoed.

Jeremy smiled and nodded in perfect sync with the man.

"As we near the Charity Center, please take a moment to utilize your I-Vents." The man lifted a shiny, silver tube to his mouth and took an exaggerated breath.

Sounds of squeaking seats and pockets unzipping floated through the bus as the students dug out their I-Vents to follow suit.

"Good," Jeremy said with the man on the screen. "Remember, it only takes one day of soiled air to begin contaminating the lungs." Jeremy faked a cough before continuing with the video. "Your work today is important. While we within the domes work hard to live a healthy life, the people in this city do not have the opportunities for safety and security that we do. Poverty is rampant, and sometimes even simple things like food are unattainable."

Jeremy dropped face-first onto the floor as the screen switched to a video of orphans, sitting at a long table, their young faces sad and drawn. Even as they ate, hunger filled their sunken eyes.

The screen changed back to the man, and Jeremy popped up to his knees.

"Poverty can induce desperation." Jeremy placed both pointer fingers on his chin, his hands clasped together. "To ensure your safety while helping the needy, here are a few simple rules to follow: First, do not leave the Charity Center or the perimeter secured by the guards."

The guards at the front of the bus waved, earning a laugh from the students.

"Second, do not partake in the food we are here to provide the less fortunate. The food provided is for them, not for the people of the domes. Third, an unfortunate side effect of living in the sad conditions of the city is an insurgence of drug use among the desperate." A new face appeared on the screen. The man's eyes were bloodshot almost to the point of his irises being red. Red splotches marked the pale skin of his cheeks. "Everyone who enters the Charity Center must submit to testing to ensure no drugs are present in their systems. However, should an addict—"

"Vamper!" the students shouted together, laughing at their own joke.

But the image of the woman beating on the glass flew unbidden into Nola's mind. She dug her nails into her palms as the man on the screen, and Jeremy, kept talking.

"—attempt to enter the Charity Center, approach the bus as you enter or exit the Charity Center, or in any way harass you, alert the guards immediately. Though a user may seem normal and calm, they could become violent at any moment. While helping those who live on the outside is important, above all, we must consider—"

"The safety of the domes!" the class chanted together as the bus rumbled to a stop outside an old stone building.

The doors opened, and the eight guards piled out. The students stood, all cramming into the aisle, ready to get off the bus.

"Did you like my dramatic interpretation?" Jeremy asked.

Nola nodded, pulling on her sunhat and trying to stay in step as everyone moved off the bus.

The Charity Center was dark gray, almost black stone. But in a few places the black had been worn away in long tear-like streaks, showing the rosy brown color the building had been before years of filth had built up on it. Iron bars strong enough to keep rioters away from the charity supplies crisscrossed the closed windows.

The class filed up the chipped stone steps. The guards flanked the stairs, their gaze sweeping the streets.

How terrible was the riot to make the best of us afraid?

Jeremy leaned into Nola and whispered, "Two more."

"What?" Nola said, trying not to gag as the smell of harsh cleaners and mass produced food flooded her nose.

"I turn eighteen in two months." Jeremy smiled as they filed into the changing room. Aprons and gloves had been laid out for each of the students. "Eighteen means I graduate and go to trade training. Eighteen means no more Charity Days. I only have to do this two more times."

Nola counted. Eleven months. Eleven more times she would have to look into the eyes of hungry people and know that, though she was feeding them today, tomorrow they would be hungry again. And while they suffered, she would be locked safely back in the domes. With fresh food and clean air.

Jeremy pulled on his gloves with a sharp *snap*. "Let's do this."

It took an hour to heat all the food in the giant kitchens. Old stoves and ovens lined one wall, their surfaces covered in years of built up grease and grime that refused to be cleaned. Shelves of chipped trays and bent utensils loomed over the giant sinks that hummed as the dome-made filters cleaned the water before the students were allowed to wash their hands.

Years of repetition had trained the class in how to get the work done as quickly as possible. One group prepped the giant pots and pans as another group pulled great sacks of flour and milled corn down from the shelves.

Nola and Lilly went into a hallway in the back.

Large cans of food lined the corridor. In the dim, flickering light, Nola had to squint to read the labels to find the cans they needed.

Stewed beets and black beans.

"Can you believe they think this is food?" Lilly shook her head, loading as many cans into her arms as she could carry. "How old is this stuff?"

Nola watched Lilly's silhouette waddle awkwardly down the hall before loading cans of processed fruit into her arms and following.

An iron-barred window bled light into the back of the kitchen. Nola peered through the soot-streaked glass. The line of people waiting to be fed wound around the block.

"What's out there?" Wrinkles formed between Mr. Pillion's white eyebrows as he squinted out the window.

"I've never seen that many people waiting before." Nola tightened her grip on the cans as they slipped.

"A good number of people lost their homes last night." Mr. Pillion shrugged before turning to the rest of the class and shouting, "We open the doors in five minutes!"

The trays and pots of food were moved to the serving room as the doors opened.

The first in line was a woman with two little boys behind her.

"Hand," the guard said, though the woman already had her hand held up as though she were carrying a tray.

The guard held a small black rectangle over the woman's palm. She winced as the needle pierced her skin. The device glowed green, and the woman lifted her older son, who bit his lip as the black box tested his blood, immediately flashing the green light. The smaller boy couldn't have been more than three. He buried his face in his mother's shoulder as the guard tested him for the drugs that ran rampant in the city. The little boy pulled his hand away and held it close to his chest as the guard waited for the light.

Nola hadn't realized she was holding her breath until the guard said, "Enjoy your meal," as the light flashed green, clearing the small boy.

The mother handed each of the boys a tray before picking one up for herself. Nola watched as they came down the line. Each of the ladle workers doled out portions of whatever was in their pot. Nola looked down at the green and brown slop as she scooped it onto the small boy's plate. She didn't even know exactly what she was serving him.

He paused in front of Nola. Purple rings marked his face under his big brown eyes. His lungs rattled as he took a breath to mutter, "Thank you."

A fist closed around Nola's heart. She wanted to stop the line. To find a way to help the poor boy with the bad lungs. But he had already walked away, pushed forward by his brother, and his mother, and the long line of other hungry people wanting food.

Nola worked mechanically, staring at the little boy until his mother took him out the heavy wooden door at the far end of the room, clearing seats so more could eat. But the line still hadn't stopped. Nola's ladle scraped the bottom of the pot.

She'd run out of food. And judging by the angry murmurs rising from the front of the line, she wasn't the only one.

"Go get more cans," Mr. Pillion whispered in Nola's ear. "I don't care what it is. Get cans, mix it together, and put it in a pot."

A man at the back of the line shoved people out of the way, trying to get to the food before it disappeared.

With a *hiss* and a *pop*, one of the guards shot the man in the neck with a tiny needle that disappeared into his flesh, leaving only a glint of silver at the top of a trickle of red.

The crowd screamed as more people began to push.

"Go. Now." Mr. Pillion scrambled up onto the counter. "Please remain calm! We are going to start making more food immediately. Everyone in line will be fed, but we must ask for your patience."

Nola slipped into the kitchen as the crowd began to shout over Mr. Pillion's voice.

CHAPTER FOUR

T he darkness of the storage hall had never bothered her before. But the echoing shouts from the dining room, from people who could have been a part of the riot, transformed each shadow she passed into a person waiting to attack.

"Get it together, Nola." She grabbed cans down from the shelves.

She stumbled under their weight as she ran back to the kitchen and shoved the armload of cans onto the counter. Shouts carried from the serving room. The angry voices of the crowd drowned out Mr. Pillion. Nola sprinted back into the storeroom, reached up to the top self, and pulled down giant cans of beans.

"Nola."

Pain shot up her leg as the heavy can dropped onto her foot.

"Careful now," the voice came again.

Nola spun around.

A pale boy with dark hair and green eyes flecked with gold smiled at her.

"Kieran," Nola gasped, running to him and throwing her arms around his neck, all thoughts of food and riots forgotten.

He had changed since the last time she had seen him nearly a year ago. Muscles had filled out his lanky frame, and his hair had grown longer, hanging over his ears.

"What are you doing here?" Nola stepped back, looking into his face.

"It's Charity Day." Kieran shrugged, his smile fading.

Nola's stomach dropped. "Are you here for food? Are things that bad?" She thought of Kieran's father, a man so brilliant simple things like eating had always seemed trivial to him.

A man like him shouldn't be on the streets.

Kieran shook his head. "Dad and I are fine. I know this may shock you, but getting kicked out of the domes didn't kill either of us."

"Kieran—"

"Dad's still working in medical research, but now instead of being told only to help the elite and getting thrown out for trying to help people who really need it—"

"That's not—"

"People out here love him," Kieran said, his voice suddenly crisp and hostile. "Out here, he saves people."

"He's brilliant," Nola said. "He's been saving people as long as I've known him."

A smile flickered across Kieran's face. "We're doing good." Kieran took Nola's hand. Calluses covered his cold palms.

"If you're doing well, then why are you here?" Nola asked. She had been in the storage room for too long. Someone would come looking for her soon.

Unless the dining room's turned into a riot.

"I came to see you." Kieran brushed a stray curl away from her cheek. "I don't need contaminated food dished out by Domers."

"The food isn't contaminated," Nola said, trying to ignore her racing heart and Kieran's tone when he said *Domers*.

"Then why aren't you allowed to eat it?" Kieran asked.

"Because it's for the poor."

"Someday you won't be able to believe that."

He reached across the few inches between them, sliding his hand from her shoulder to her cheek.

"I need your I-Vent," he whispered.

"You're sick?" The butterflies in her stomach disappeared, replaced by the sting of panic.

"I'm fine," Kieran said. "It's not for me."

"I can't give medicine out." Nola took a step back, shaking her head. "I'm not allowed to distribute resources."

"They have stores of medicine in the domes," Kieran said. "I only need one."

"If I give you medicine and they find out..." Kieran's father was important, a savior to the domes, and they cast him out for giving away the community's food.

I'd be banished before sundown.

"I can't do that."

"Tell them it was stolen." Kieran stepped forward, closing the distance between them. "Tell them I did it." He wrapped his arms around her, pulling her close.

Nola's heart pounded in her ears. His face was a breath from hers. His hands on her waist. The cold of his fingers cut through her sweater as he traced the line of her hips.

He pressed his lips to her forehead. "Thank you, Nola."

She raised her lips to meet his, but Kieran stepped back, holding out his hand. Her I-Vent rested in his palm.

"You're saving a life."

He turned and strode away, disappearing into the darkness before the tears formed in her eyes.

Nola stood alone in the dark.

She could scream. She *should* scream. She should shout to the guards that an outsider had stolen dome medicine. But would they be able to hear her over the chaos in the dining room? And what if they caught Kieran? Would they shoot a tiny, silver needle into his neck?

She grabbed a few cans without reading the contents and ran back to the kitchen. Her whole class stood in the back of the room, craning their necks to look out the window.

"I can't believe they thought they could get away with that," Jeremy growled. He was taller than most of the class and had a clear view of the street below.

"What happened?" Nola stood on her tiptoes, trying to see over the heads of her classmates.

"After they neutralized the first guy, people got crazy," Jeremy said. "More people started shouting. Then people were pushing to get to the food. Mr. Pillion got knocked off the counter. Then the guards took a few more people down, and everyone else just sort of ran away."

"It was terrible." Lilly's voice wavered. Marco wrapped an arm around her, and Lilly turned to cry into his shoulder.

Mr. Pillion burst through the doors to the kitchen. "Everyone back on the bus, now."

Nola turned to go back to the hall to put the cans away.

"Leave it, Magnolia!" Mr. Pillion said.

Jeremy grabbed the heavy cans from her and tossed them onto a table before grabbing Nola's hand and dragging her back through the door they had come in less than two hours before.

Only two guards joined them as the students scrambled to their seats. The door shut, and the bus jerked forward.

Nola stumbled and Jeremy caught her, holding her close as they drove away.

Groups of people lined the sidewalk. Whether they had been in the Charity Center or only come to see what the commotion was, Nola didn't know.

A terrible *crunch* sounded from the front of the bus as a brick hit the windshield, leaving a mark like a spider web in the glass. The bus accelerated as the shouts of the crowd grew.

They reached the outskirts of the city. The domes rose in the distance, shining across the river, high in the hills.

"Class," Mr. Pillion said, holding a hand over his heart as he spoke, "our world is falling apart. It has been for a long time. The greatest trial of those who survive is to watch the continuous decay that surrounds them. As the outside world grows worse, so too does the plight of the city dwellers. We witnessed the desperation that plight is causing today. Let us not dwell on the harm they might have done to us. Rather, let us be grateful for all we have. For if our roles were reversed, I promise you each of us would be as desperate as those we saw today." He took his I-Vent from his shirt pocket and held the silver tip to his lips, taking a deep breath. "We must be grateful for even the simplest of things."

Mr. Pillion sat, and the students dug through their pockets for their I-Vents.

Jeremy took a deep breath from his before turning to Nola.

She stared down at her hands, willing Jeremy not to look at her. There were scratches on her fingers. How had she gotten them?

"You need to do your I-Vent." Jeremy nudged Nola.

"I lost mine," Nola whispered, "I—" Jeremy had known Kieran. They had been friends. But Kieran wasn't one of them anymore. "I think it fell out of my pocket when things got crazy."

"Use mine." Jeremy pressed the silver tube into her palm.

Nola stared down at it. Kieran had come to find her for a tiny tube.

To save a life.

"Look, don't be nervous about asking for a new one," Jeremy murmured into Nola's ear, wrapping his arm around her. "I'll go with you. And after what happened today, I don't think anyone is going to blame you for losing it."

"Right." Nola gave a smile she hoped looked real before holding the tube up to her lips and waiting for the metallic taste to fill her mouth.

CHAPTER FIVE

Nola flopped down in bed.

It had taken hours to get a new I-Vent from the medical department. There were forms to fill out and questions to answer. Jeremy had wanted to stay with her to keep her company, but the doctor kicked him out. A quick "See you tomorrow!" was all he managed to say before the door *swooshed* shut in front of him.

They drew blood and performed a chest scan to be sure she hadn't been skipping her doses. Nola was too tired to argue that she hadn't been skipping anything. That she had used Jeremy's I-Vent on the way back from the Charity Center.

After a few hours, the doctor finally declared her lungs undamaged and gave her a new I-Vent. None of them seemed to suspect the old one had been stolen. And no one mentioned Kieran Wynne.

Nola lay on her back, staring at the new I-Vent in her hand. She held it up, watching the light reflect off its silver surface.

Such a simple thing.

Medicine in a tube. But Kieran needed it to save someone. Nola dug her fists into her eyes, trying to wipe away the thoughts of Dr. Wynne ill. Or Kieran himself.

It's just a little tube.

She had been carrying one in her back pocket every time she left the domes for as long as she could remember. Was that why Kieran had come to her, because he knew where she kept her I-Vent? Or had he simply been waiting in the darkness for one of the students to be alone?

Her skin tingled where he'd held her hips, pulling her close. All he had wanted was a chance to steal the I-Vent.

How had she not felt him take it? Was she that mesmerized by seeing him again?

Nola shoved her hand in her back pocket. Her fingers found something crisp. She pulled out a piece of yellowed, folded up paper.

Nola

Her name was written on the paper in Kieran's untidy scrawl. She recognized the careless way he swished his pen. Her hands shook as she unfolded the note.

Dear Nola,

I'm sorry I had to get you involved in all this. I needed the medicine, and I had a feeling you wouldn't turn me in. If you knew the girl who needed it, you wouldn't be angry at all. She's sick, Nola. Lots of people out here are. I know I can't save everyone right now, but I need to start with her.

I wish you could meet her. I only hope the I-Vent can buy her some more time. I wish I could repay you. If you ever need me, the folks at 5th and Nightland know how to find me.

I miss you, Nola.

Please forgive me,

Kieran

Nola buried her face in her pillow. He had planned to see her. He had written a note for her.

He came for me.

She couldn't breathe. The pure air of the domes crushed her lungs. Nola's heart raced. The energy pulsing through her veins begged her to run away or break through the glass. She opened her bedroom window and climbed up onto the sill. With a practiced motion, she grabbed the groove at the edge of the roofline and, using the wall for support, pulled herself up onto the soft moss that covered the roof. She lay down, taking deep, shuddering breaths. Her arms stung from pulling herself up, but she was grateful for the ache. The sting took her mind off her racing heart. And Kieran.

If you ever need me.

What would she need him for? He was an outsider. A city dweller. She had everything she needed in the domes.

Everything but him.

She dug her fingers into the moss. The thin layer of dirt beneath still held the heat of the day. Kieran had known her better than anyone. He had been her best friend. They had held hands, supporting each other at her father and his mother's funerals.

He was the only boy she'd ever kissed.

Three faint beeps echoed throughout the dome. Then there was a little *pop* and a *hiss* as the rain system turned on.

The cool water spattered her skin. Nola didn't move as it soaked her. If she lay there long enough, would she disappear into the soft moss of the roof?

The dome-made rain drenched Kieran's letter, washing the ink away. Nola tore the letter into sopping pieces and let them dissolve with the rain. No one could see that letter. No one could know she had seen him.

5th and Nightland. That was all she needed.

* * *

"One of the most elementary lessons farmers learned early on was crop rotation." Mrs. Pearson drew the words on the wall with her silver pen. "Why is crop rotation so important?"

Nikki's hand shot up in the air.

Mrs. Pearson's eyebrows arched high. "Yes, Nikki?"

"You have to change what crops you grow where so you don't exhaust the soil," Nikki said.

"Very good," Mrs. Pearson said.

The concept of crop rotation was something they covered every year. Just like studying the importance of the ozone when the summer heat scorched the city beyond the glass—an inescapable measure of the passing of another year.

Mrs. Pearson slid her hand on the wall, and the words she had written flew away. She began to scrawl out equations. Tapping the corner of the wall, pictures of plants and soil sprung up around the border of the screen.

Nola let her mind wander, staring out the tiny window in the corner. She knew the equations. She knew how to test the soil and how to make it fertile again. Her mother had been training her to join the Botanical Preservation Group for years. Some kids got to choose which branch of the domes they wanted to work in once they turned eighteen and finished school. Nola had known her path since she was a little girl.

Her eyelids grew heavy. She hadn't been able to sleep last night. Hadn't been able to keep thoughts of Kieran from racing through her mind. What if he needed her?

What if I need him?

The bell beeped softly in the corner. As one, the class stood, putting their tablets back into their bags.

"Nola," Mrs. Pearson called as Nola reached the door to the hall.

Nola gritted her teeth and turned around.

"I wanted you to know I spoke with your mother over the com system yesterday," Mrs. Pearson said, her tone serious as she folded her hands in front of her.

"My mother?" Nola asked. "What happened? Why did she call?"

"We were discussing the progress of the Green Leaf Conference, and the topic of the incident at the Charity Center came up," Mrs. Pearson continued. "You reacted so poorly to the unfortunate woman outside the Green Dome, and then to have another shock so near after..." Mrs. Pearson pursed her lips, giving Nola a pitying look, like she was ill. Like there was something wrong with her, Nola, for being upset.

"I'm fine." Nola pushed her face into a smile.

"After losing your father—"

"That was three years ago," Nola cut across. "I'm fine."

Nola turned and walked out of the room, ignoring Mrs. Pearson calling after her.

As she turned into the hall, a hand caught her arm. Nola gasped as Jeremy fell into step beside her. "Don't scare me like that."

"You all right?" he asked.

"Why does everyone think I'm not okay today?" Nola twisted her arm away from Jeremy.

"Maybe it's the full moon." Jeremy took Nola by the shoulders, turning her to face him. "Maybe you're a member of one of the new packs."

Nola caught herself smiling a little. "Pack of what? Did the wildlife department bring in coyotes?" Nola rubbed a hand over her face. "I mean, I get we're the new Ark and we're supposed to preserve living creatures in a dying world and all, but I still think the insect habitats are creepy. And now they want to bring in coyotes?"

"I never said anything about coyotes. It's the new big thing in the city. I was talking to my dad about it."

"So, pack of what then?" Nola asked.

Jeremy draped an arm around her shoulders and started walking slowly down the hall. He spoke in a low voice as though telling a frightening bedtime story. "Werewolves. It's the new drug craze. Lycan. Outsiders have started injecting it."

"Isn't Vamp bad enough?" Nola shuddered. "Exactly how many drugs do people need? And why would they risk taking something that dangerous?" The woman outside Green Dome flashed through Nola's mind. Fighting to get through the glass, seeking out flesh to tear with no thought left for anything else. A zombie.

Jeremy shrugged. "This one is different. It makes you stronger, faster. You heal more quickly."

"Just like Vamp," Nola murmured.

"But Lycan changes your pheromones. The riot two nights ago. The guards tried to arrest a man for prowling around during the raid on the Vamp lab. Turns out he was the alpha of one of the packs."

"Like wolves."

"Just like wolves," Jeremy said, his voice shifting from conspiratorial to angry. "And when the pack found out the guards had their Alpha, they attacked. They're the ones who lit that building on fire. It destroyed a whole block, and the guards had to kill a few of them just to get away."

Vampires, zombies, and now werewolves.

A thousand horrible images of blood and fear tumbled through Nola's mind.

"So, they're still out there?" Nola asked, wishing she were aboveground, not just so she didn't feel like she were being crushed by the earth, but to be able to see out the glass—to be able to see if the wolves were coming.

And to escape.

"For now," Jeremy said.

Nola stared at Jeremy's face, trying to see the color of his eyes instead of streets painted red with blood.

"How do you know any of this?" Nola asked.

"My father," Jeremy said.

"Why did he tell you?" Nola asked. "You're always complaining he doesn't tell you anything about what he does outside."

His father was the head of the Outer Guard who patrolled the city. What they did, most people didn't want to know about.

"Because"—Jeremy paused, stepping forward to face Nola—"I just found out that, as of my birthday, I'll be training to join the Outer Guard."

"What?"

"Dad told me." Jeremy beamed. "It's everything I want."

"That's amazing!" Nola stood on her toes and threw her arms around Jeremy's neck. He pulled her in close, his chest rumbling against hers as he laughed.

"He's been telling me things so I'll be up on all the business of the city when I start training," Jeremy said. "Just don't tell anyone. About the Outer Guard or the wolves. The 'guard' thing won't be announced until next month, and my dad doesn't want people freaking out about the werewolves."

"Why would they want to be called that?" Nola shivered.

"When I get one, I'll ask." Jeremy winked. "But don't worry about them."

Jeremy took Nola's hand, pulling her more quickly down the hall, almost running in his excitement. "We're safe here. No one can get into the domes. There isn't a way in or out of this place not covered by guards."

Nola stumbled, but Jeremy didn't notice.

There is a way out.

It had been pouring outside the domes that night. Dark sheets of rain that roared as they struck the glass. Nola's mother had gone to a conference at the domes on the far western side of the country. Dr. Wynne had been charged with watching Nola. Not that she needed it. She was fourteen. But it meant more time with Kieran. And Dr. Wynne had been too distracted to pay Nola or Kieran much mind anyway.

His research had been keeping him in the lab until all hours. His face had been growing paler and thinner for months.

"There has to be a way," he would mutter over and over as he wandered through the house. Kieran cleaned and made supper as he had done since his mother died. But there was something more to Dr. Wynne's ramblings now. More than his brilliance-bordering-on-madness, more than missing his wife. He had a secret.

Nola had spent many nights lying out on the roof of her house. She liked it up there. If she squinted, she could pretend there was no glass between her and the stars. More than once, she had seen a shadow coming out of the Wynne's house and disappearing into the night.

The last night Nola was to stay at the Wynne's, there had been a riot in the city. Nola had curled up on the couch, covering her ears, trying to block out the sounds that were too far away for her to hear. She watched as fire sprang up around the city. Flames danced on the glass. A fire so large, even the pounding rain couldn't douse it. The flames sent shadows swaying in the orange glow of the burning city.

"There won't be anything left if they keep burning sections of the city down," Kieran had said. "Don't they know they're destroying their own homes? Once the city is gone where will they live? Build huts and tents?"

"The rain will burn them like the fire," Nola had muttered, burying her face on Kieran's shoulder.

"Not tonight. The rain won't burn tonight. The clouds were white. There are still good days to bring hope. But they're hungry," Dr. Wynne spoke softly, the red glow of the city reflecting in his eyes, giving him the look of the mad scientist he had always threatened to become. "The rain didn't come this year. And the clean water that fell wasn't enough to feed the plants. If you were starving, if you were watching your child starve, your anger would outweigh your reason. Their homes have been on fire for years. Only tonight, we can see the flames."

Tears streamed down Nola's cheeks. There were guards out there trying to protect the city dwellers, but the outsiders wouldn't see that. They would only see attack... never help.

"It's okay, Nola." Kieran wiped the tears from her face with his sleeve. "We're safe here." He laced his fingers through hers. "There are guards at every entrance and exit. No one could get in here without the guards stopping them."

"No," Dr. Wynne snapped, lifting his son by the collar.

Kieran staggered, his eyes wide with shock.

"There is no such thing as safe when the world is descending into madness. When the people burn the city, the palace will fall, too." Dr. Wynne clung desperately to his son. "One day, the outsiders will have had enough, and they will find a way into our paradise."

"But we can't have them all here," Nola said. "We don't have the resources."

"They will not come to join us." Dr. Wynne grasped Nola's shoulders, forcing her to look into his face. "They will come to destroy us. You have to know the way out."

Dr. Wynne grabbed Kieran and Nola by the hands and ran from the house, dragging them both behind him. He ran down the stone walkway and under the great willow tree. When they were nearing the far corner of the dome, he pulled them onto the grass and into a stand of trees.

Nola wanted to shout at him to stop, to scream they were safe. But something in the doctor's madness swept through her, and she followed, running as quickly as her feet could carry her. Dr. Wynne stopped inches before hitting the glass of the dome. They stood, staring into the darkness for a moment. Watching the rain stream down the outside. Nola pressed her face to the glass, looking to the west, where the fire was slowly beginning to die.

"When the time comes, and the only chance for survival is to go into the dying world, you must take the only way out," Dr. Wynne murmured.

Terror filled Kieran's eyes as his father knelt in front of the glass. Slowly, Dr. Wynne dug his fingers into the top corner of the bottom pane. With the tiniest scraping noise, the pane inched forward enough for him to squeeze his fingers in, pushing the panel to the side. The second layer of glass was still there, blocking them from the rain, but Dr. Wynne didn't hesitate. Pulling a penknife from his pocket, he shoved the blade into the crack where the pane met the metal beam, and the glass fell silently into his waiting hands.

"This is the way to salvation." The gleam of victory dancing in Dr. Wynne's eyes frightened Nola more than fires and riots.

Dr. Wynne crawled out of the passage he had created and into the rain. Spreading his arms wide, he gazed up into the storm. Lightning split the sky, silhouetting the triumphant form of Dr. Wynne.

Nola hadn't spoken to anyone about that night or the way out through the glass. Not even to Jeremy. Not even when the guards couldn't figure out how Dr. Wynne had been smuggling food to the city.

This is the way to salvation. And the way to Kieran.

CHAPTER SIX

Nola sat alone at the kitchen table, poking at the food on her plate and trying to do her reading for school.

The medicinal applications of plants must be weighed equally with their nutritional value. Also included in the assessment must be other species that would be required to maintain a proper habitat, and their accessibility—

There was a tap on the kitchen door.

"Coming," Nola called. Her heart dropped when she saw a giant shadow through the window.

Captain Ridgeway stood outside her door, his face somber.

"What happened to my mom?" Nola asked before Captain Ridgeway could speak. "Is she sick? Did she get hurt?"

Green Leaf is too far away. I don't know how to get to her.

"You're mother's fine." Captain Ridgeway stepped into the kitchen. As tall as Jeremy, Captain Ridgeway's well-muscled frame overwhelmed the tiny kitchen, leaving Nola no room to breathe.

"Oh." Nola clasped her shaking hands together. "What happened? Is somebody dead? Is Jeremy okay?"

"There was an incident in the city last night," Captain Ridgeway said. "There was a fight between two groups that accelerated to the point where the Outer Guard had to become involved."

"But everyone's all right?"

"There were a few injuries," Captain Ridgeway's voice dropped.

"Gentry?" Nola knew she was right before Captain Ridgeway nodded.

He's not just an Outer Guard. He's Jeremy and Gentry's father.

"Is she going to be all right?" Nola pictured Gentry, tall and strong with short, blond hair framing her round face. Always laughing, but now she was hurt.

"She'll recover," Captain Ridgeway said. "But there were a few deaths. The packs that were attacking each other dragged in bystanders that shouldn't have been involved in their fight."

"Werewolves," Nola breathed.

"Nothing travels faster than rumors in the domes," Captain Ridgeway said without surprise. "When we searched the casualties for identification, we found dome medicine on one of the deceased."

The room swayed.

"You lost your I-Vent?" Captain Ridgeway continued.

Nola nodded, not trusting her voice.

"Is there anyone who stood out to you at the Charity Center? Anyone who tried to get close to you?"

Nola shook her head.

"If someone is stealing dome medicine, we need to know," Captain Ridgeway said, his eyes searching Nola's face.

"I just lost my I-Vent," Nola said, her voice shaking. "I think I..."

Kieran dead. Killed by werewolves.

"I dropped it. The person who had the medicine—"

"Is dead. But that doesn't mean there isn't someone out there trying to steal dome supplies. If a black market for our medicine is creeping into the city, it needs to be stopped immediately. Did you see anything suspicious? Anything at all?"

"I don't know," Nola said.

Captain Ridgeway nodded, his eyes still locked on Nola's face. "If you remember anything, please come to me immediately."

"But—" Nola stepped in front of the Captain as he turned toward the door. "No one we know, none of our people died?"

"No. All the guards will recover."

He stepped outside and shut the door behind him with a sharp *click.*

Nola slid down the wall, her head in her hands.

All the guards will recover.

But what about Kieran?

Had he been trapped between the wolf packs?

What if someone had stolen the I-Vent from him? What if he had lied, and he was the one who needed the medicine? What if he was the one they had found the medicine on?

He could be dying. He could be dead, and she would never know.

Nola pressed her palms together, trying to stop her hands from shaking. Her breath came in panicked gasps.

Kieran torn apart by wolves.

I have to know.

Nola sprang to her feet, willing herself to move quickly enough she wouldn't have time to change her mind.

There was only one way to know if Kieran was alive.

5th and Nightland.

CHAPTER SEVEN

The damp chill of the night air cut through Nola's coat. The wind had pushed the stench of the city all the way up to the domes. Nola crouched just outside the glass, like a child reaching for something dangerous with the certainty someone would snatch it away before she could get hurt.

A night bird soared overhead, cawing at the darkness. Nola jumped at the sound, flattening herself against the glass. The bird kept flying into the distance, not caring that Nola stood alone in the dark. She waited for a moment, counting each breath of outside air. She pulled out her I-Vent and took a deep breath of the medicine. But still, no guards came charging toward her.

I'm alone.

Carefully, she knelt and slid the outer glass so it was nearly in place. No one passing would see anything amiss, but there was enough space to squeeze her fingers in to push the pane aside.

She stood and turned toward the city. Lights glowed through the haze that hung over the buildings. She wanted to turn and crawl back into the dome and into her warm bed where she could pretend Captain Ridgeway had never come to the kitchen door.

Kieran.

She took a step forward. And then another. She would do this. She would find Kieran.

One road ran from the domes to the city. The only path with lights and guards. Nola stayed away from the road, cutting through the old forest.

She had seen pictures of what the forest had looked like before, when her mother had been young and the founders were still building the domes. The trees here had been thick and lush, their branches so dense the sunlight could barely peek through to the forest floor.

But the trees had begun to die a long time ago. A few still had leaves clinging to them. Most now stood like skeletons—dead and barren.

The moon peered through the clouds, and the naked branches cast strange shadows onto the ground.

Keep moving, Nola. Just keep moving.

One foot, then the other. A single step at a time. Moving deeper into the woods.

Did animals still live in these trees? Or worse, had people too poor to live in the slums of the city dared to make the dead forest their home?

Nola moved as quickly and quietly as she could. Every now and then, a rustle in the distance would send her sprinting for a few minutes, fleeing from the unseen danger.

Soon she neared the edge of the woods, and the city rose above her. She cut to the left toward the bridge that led into the city. The river roared beneath her. The foul stench of chemicals and rot sent bile into her throat. How many times had the bus taken them to the city, and she had never smelled the river like this. She had always been sheltered from the worst of it by the technology of the domes.

Shadows stalked across the bridge. Some in groups, some alone. Nola clenched her fists in her pockets, wishing she had thought to grab a heavy stick or rock from the woods. Anything to defend herself with.

She quickened her pace, trying not to walk so fast as to seem scared. The metal of the bridge gave a dull *thunk* every time she took a step. Nola kept her eyes forward, moving with purpose, pretending she belonged.

She was halfway over the bridge and could see the streets in front of her. The Outer Guard patrolled the city at night. If she had to call for help, would she be banished from the domes?

A group of people near Nola's age had bunched together at the city end of the bridge. Talking and laughing like the reek of the river and danger of the night meant nothing. Both the boys and girls wore torn up leather clothes. The girls' tops were ripped in deep Vs, letting their pale skin gleam in the night as they hung from the boys' arms. The pairs all stood under one man, bigger and older than the rest. He perched on the railing of the bridge, holding court over those beneath him.

Nola turned her gaze away from the group. She was almost off the bridge. She could see the seam where metal met concrete.

The man who stood on the railing turned to look at her. His cheeks sunk into his pale face, a scruffy beard covered his chin, and in the glow of the city lights, the man's eyes gleamed a deep, blood red. He smiled, and a sound like a wolf growling rumbled from his throat before he tipped his head to the sky. Flinging his arms to his sides, the man howled. The group around him threw their heads back, joining him.

Nola ran, not knowing if they would follow or where she was going. Her feet pounded on the concrete as the howling rent the night.

Werewolves.

Jeremy hadn't been lying. Lycan changed people. Wolves filled the city.

She turned a corner and pressed herself into the shadows of a building.

5ᵗʰ and Nightland. Just get to 5ᵗʰ and Nightland.

A sign on the corner that appeared to have been painted over and over again read *12ᵗʰ Street*, the other read *Rotland* in an untidy scrawl. Nola's hands trembled. She closed her eyes, picturing the maps of the city in her mind. The number was right, but the name was wrong. Who had renamed the streets of the city, and why had she never known?

North. Go north to find 5ᵗʰ.

Staying close to the buildings in the depths of the shadows, Nola walked, keeping her head down, trying to picture what the city would have looked like when it was still prosperous. When the river water was clean, and people rode in boats on its glittering surface.

11ᵗʰ Street. 10ᵗʰ.

What would it have been like to live in a city in the open air, with parks to play in and a whole world to explore?

Nola passed a dark stairway leading down to a basement.

A hand reached out, grabbing her leg.

"Please," a woman's voice came from the shadows, low and crackling. "Please, do you have any change?"

"No." Nola stumbled back, wrenching her leg from the woman's weak grasp. "I don't have any money."

It was true. They didn't use money in the domes. Currency had always been a vague concept—numbers on a screen, not something to be kept in a pocket.

"You're strong," the woman muttered, crawling up the stairs. "Vamp. Do you have Vamp?" The woman dragged herself into the light of the street lamps. Wrinkles covered her thin face. Cracks split her dried lips, and the skin under her eyes hung loose in horrible bags. "I'm dying!" the woman shrieked, trying to push herself up but crumpling to the ground. "You have Vamp. I know you do!"

"I don't." Nola shook her head, backing away from the woman. "I'm sorry. I can't help you."

"Lycan, ReVamp. Please!" the woman screamed after her as Nola ran down the street. "I'm dying. Murderer!"

Nola ran from the woman, not caring who saw her, her only thought to escape from the echo of the woman's voice.

Murderer!

In her haze of panic, she almost ran right past the sign that read *5th Street* and *Blood Way*.

Turning her back to the river, Nola walked west down 5th. There were lights in the windows here. And the farther she walked, the more people there were on the streets, some walking on the cracked pavement, some sitting in doorways. The scent of the river had disappeared, replaced by the stale smell of humans and animals living too close together.

The back of Nola's neck prickled with the feeling of a dozen people staring at her back.

"You," a voice called from behind her.

Nola quickened her pace.

"Don't bother trying to get away," the voice said. A moment later a hand had locked around her arm.

Nola clenched her fists, ready to punch whomever had grabbed her, but the man already had her by both wrists.

"Please, I don't have—" Nola began.

"Anything but a dome jacket?" the man said, eyebrows raised.

Nola glanced down at her coat. It was plain black, made for warmth, not protection from the sun or acid rain. But the man's coat was tattered and dirty, like everything else in the city. Nola's looked brand new.

"Why would a Domer be out on the streets this late at night?" the man asked, tightening his ice-cold grip on her wrists. "A little thing like you clearly isn't an Outer Guard."

"I'm looking for someone." Nola tipped her chin up, staring into the man's eyes.

His irises were black, leaving voids where color should have been.

"Who?"

"That's none of your business," Nola said, trying to sound confident the man wasn't going to kill her in the middle of the street.

"Look, sweetheart," the man whispered in her ear. His breath smelled of iron as it wafted over her. "I don't care if you're here to buy Vamp or get laid. But this is my territory. If a Domer gets killed here, we'll have the Outer Guard after our heads, and the last thing I want is a riot getting all my people killed. Believe it or not, I'm probably the only thing standing between you and getting your throat ripped open."

Nola gasped as the man squeezed her wrists so tight she thought they might break.

"Tell me who you want to see so I can make you somebody else's problem to clean up."

"Kieran," Nola said, "Kieran Wynne. I'm supposed to be able to find him at 5th and Nightland."

The man cursed under his breath. "I love it when the hero sends a pretty girl to die."

"He's my friend."

The man took her by the shoulders, steering her roughly down the street.

"Friends don't send friends into Vamp territory," the man said.

Fear shot through Nola's body, setting fire to every nerve.

"What, sweetheart?" the man hissed. "You didn't know you were being saved by a monster?"

He smiled, showing two long fangs in the front of his mouth.

Nola swallowed her scream.

The man gripped her tighter, shoving her down the street. "The better to eat you with, my dear."

"That's the wolf's line," Nola said. A Vamper was steering her through the dark. What would people think when she wasn't in the domes tomorrow? How long would it be before they noticed?

They'll never find me.

"Be glad a wolf didn't grab you," the Vamper laughed. "They like to fight and die. And if you think all this shit with vampires and werewolves is going to work out like a fairytale, this really is your first time in the city. Here"—the Vamper pushed her up onto the curb—"5th and Nightland. Have your friend get you out, if you make it that long. The next time you cross through my territory, I'll let them have you. They'll dump your dried up body into the river before the Domers know you're gone."

The man turned and strode away, leaving Nola alone under a flickering street lamp.

She looked up at the sign. 5th Street and Nightland. But there was no one in sight. No one waiting to give her help, no sign reading *find Kieran alive and healthy here.*

Where are you, Kieran?

Nola closed her eyes. A very small, very foolish part of her thought when she opened her eyes Kieran would be there. Or maybe if she called his name he would appear.

When she opened her eyes, there was nothing in front of her but an empty street. Maybe the Outer Guard had raided the area? Why would they need to raid a place where Kieran would be?

Muffled voices came from nearby, but Nola couldn't see anyone. No lights on in the houses, no people roaming the streets.

A thumping pounded from below her feet. A strong, steady rhythm. Like music. Nola studied the ground. Trash, dirt, and soot covered the cracked sidewalk.

Something white twenty feet away caught her eye. The thumping grew louder as she approached. Voices became distinct, and a melody broke through the noise. A metal trapdoor had been built into the sidewalk, a single word painted across its surface. *Nightland.*

Nola reached into the hole in the metal door just big enough for a hand and tried to lift. She gritted her teeth against the weight of the metal, but the door didn't budge.

She took a breath and tried again, pulling until pain shot through her shoulders. Panting, she let go of the door and staggered back a step.

Go to Nightland, find Kieran. I have to find Kieran.

"I have come too far to get turned back by a door."

Taking a deep breath, she stomped three times on the metal. The sound echoed through the empty street, and the noise from below changed.

The music still thumped on, but the voices were different. Their tones loud and urgent.

Nola jumped back as the metal door flew open with a *clang* that shook her ears. Four people leapt onto the sidewalk.

Each of them held a weapon in their hand—a pipe, a sword, a staff, and a knife. The four glared at Nola. She took another step back, missed the curb and fell into the street.

A woman with bright purple and scarlet-streaked hair stood over Nola, twirling a knife in her hand.

"Such a pretty little thing to be knocking on our door." The woman grinned.

A dark-skinned man with scars dotting his face stepped up next to her, digging his staff into the pavement beside Nola's neck. "Did someone order dinner?" The man had fangs, like the one who had brought her here.

"Bring her inside," the man with the sword said.

"Not worth the risk," the man with the pipe said, staring at Nola with frightening hunger.

"Then we kill her out here." The woman raised her knife.

"Kieran!" Nola shouted, covering her face, waiting for the blade to strike. Even if he heard her scream she would already be dead.

"What did you say?" the woman said.

"Kieran," Nola said, uncovering her face. "I'm here to see Kieran Wynne."

"How do you know Kieran?" The woman lifted Nola to her feet by the collar of her coat.

"F-from the domes," Nola stammered.

"But how did you find out about Nightland?" The man with the pipe sneered, showing his frighteningly white teeth.

"He told me," Nola said.

The woman lifted her higher so her toes barely reached the ground.

"He came to the Charity Center. He stole my I-Vent and left a note in my pocket. It said to find him at 5th and Nightland."

The woman let go of Nola's collar, and she fell back onto the pavement, cracking her head against the stone.

"You're the one." The man with the staff tilted his head from side to side as he stared at Nola. "If the boy wants her..." He shrugged.

"Is Kieran alive?" Nola asked as the man with the sword lifted her to her feet and clamped a hand firmly around her arm.

"If you don't mind"—the man ignored Nola's question. His tone and accent sounded strange, like he wasn't from the city—"I would suggest you not try and run away. I'm sure it was quite a feat for you to make it here from the domes alone, but I promise, if you go off on your own, you won't survive Nightland."

The man with the staff struck the metal door four times, pausing for a moment before repeating the four beats. The sound echoed through the streets. The Outer Guard would hear.

They'll save me.

The door swung open, and the pounding rhythm of the music drifted up into the night. Kieran could be down there. Nola didn't know if she wanted to be rescued by the Outer Guard or not.

The man with the sword bowed, still keeping a grip on Nola's arm as he gestured down the steps. "Welcome to Nightland."

CHAPTER EIGHT

The metal stairs vibrated under Nola's feet, but the music ate the sound of her steps.

The woman with the scarlet and purple hair waited at the bottom, knife still drawn. Once all of them had descended below the street, two men appeared from the shadows and closed the door. It was thicker than Nola had realized. At least three inches of heavy metal, as thick as the doors to the outside in the atrium. But the two men lowered it back into place as if the weight were nothing and bolted the door shut.

Nola's heart raced.

There's no way out. I'm trapped underground.

Even if there weren't guards, she would never be able to lift that door.

"If you please," the sword man said, sliding his blade back into the sheath at his waist. The sword looked new, and its embossed leather sheath shone with fresh black polish.

Who makes new swords and sheaths?

The woman walked in front, leading them down another set of stairs. The music grew louder with each step, and flashing lights bounced across the landing below.

Nola's gasp was lost in the music as the room came into view. Hundreds of people in a seething mass, all moving to the same rhythm. Arches were carved into the walls of the room, some leading nowhere, some disappearing into darkness. The smell of sweat, metal, and dust permeated the air. It was different from the stench of the city. A scent as primal as the dancers, all swaying to the music, some alone, some wound tightly around their partners.

The woman walked into the crowd, and the dancers parted, leaving a path as though frightened of the woman. A few of them stared at Nola, speaking loudly to their fellows, but Nola could only make out one word over the music: *Domer*.

They drew near to the speakers, and the sound vibrated in Nola's chest, sending her heart sprinting. She balled her fists tightly, letting her nails bite into her skin, willing herself not to panic. She could hear now that there were words in the music, but she couldn't tell what they said.

The woman turned left, heading toward an arch that was blocked off by another heavy metal door.

A woman as tall as any man Nola had ever met stood beside the door, her arms crossed and her face set in a grimace. She nodded at the woman with the knife and opened the door. The scraping of the metal against the concrete floor cut through the music, slicing into Nola's ears.

As soon as they entered the dark passage, the door screeched shut behind them, dampening the music. Nola glanced back. Only the four who had been aboveground accompanied her now.

The woman led on, and the man with the sword didn't let go of her arm. Dim lights were set into the ceiling of the tunnel, leaving shadows for them to pass through every few steps.

"What is this place?" Nola asked, half-choking on the damp smell of the tunnel, panic squeezing her chest.

We're twenty feet underground. Maybe thirty. Far enough for the weight of the earth to crush us.

"Nightland," the woman said.

They walked in silence for a moment. The pounding of the music faded, and the walls muffled the sounds of their footsteps.

The ceiling here was short, barely above the sword man's head. The woman at the door to the tunnel would have needed to hunch to walk down it.

The walls swayed, closing in around them. Smothering Nola in dirt.

Nola blinked, willing the walls to hold still.

"You all right?" the sword man asked, raising a sculpted black eyebrow at Nola.

"She's fine," the man with the pipe said. "She's from the domes. If the air bothers her, she can just use her I-Vent."

"Not the air," Nola said. Her voice sounded faint even to her own ears. She took a deep breath and tried to sound stronger. "I don't like being underground."

The woman with the knife laughed, her voice bouncing down the tunnel.

"And Kieran asked you to come here? And I thought you must be an old friend of his."

"I am," Nola said. "What is this place?"

"Nightla—"

"What is Nightland?" Nola cut the woman off.

It was the man with the staff's turn to laugh. "Nightland is exactly what it sounds like, Domer. It's the land of the night dwellers, and you just wandered into it."

Night dwellers. Impossibly heavy doors. People in the city who roamed the night. All of those people were dancing, not coughing, not sick. Dancing underground in the night.

Vampers. Kieran led me to a Vamper den.

Nola stopped walking and almost toppled over as the man continued. But his grip on her arm was so strong she couldn't fall to the floor. He held her up without seeming to notice.

She should run away or shout for help. But there was nowhere to go and no one to hear.

"What are your names?" Nola swallowed hard. "I'm Magnolia." Maybe if they thought of her as human, like them, not as a meal. But were they human? If a drug changed you that much....

"Raina," the woman said, looking back at Nola. The turning of her head sent her purple and scarlet hair dancing in the dim light.

"That's Julian."

The man with the sword and the dark shining hair bowed his head. "It's a pleasure."

"Desmond."

The dark-skinned man with hundreds of tiny scars gave a jerk of his head.

"And Bryant."

The man with the pipe didn't acknowledge Nola.

"Those are great names," Nola said.

"What were you expecting?" Desmond asked, his voice a low grumble.

"Something along the lines of Fang, Shade, Bloodlust, and Satan I expect," Julian said.

"I-I meant," Nola stammered, hoping accidentally being rude wasn't enough of a reason to eat a person, "that it is lovely to meet all of you. And thank you for bringing me safely to Kieran."

"Don't worry, Domer," Bryant said from behind. "We won't hurt you. Not before you get to see Kieran."

"So, he's alive?" Nola's heart leapt into her throat. "Kieran's fine?"

"I don't think our definitions of *fine* would match." Raina sneered, baring her teeth.

Nola tensed. Kieran was alive. He would protect her. Kieran wouldn't let them drink her blood. He had told her to come here.

He wouldn't lead me here to watch me die.

They walked in silence. Every once in a while, there would be a metal door in the wall, or another tunnel twisting away into the darkness.

Nola tried to remember each time they turned. But there were no arrows on the walls like in the domes. No signs pointing the way. And even if she could remember the path, there was no way she could get back the way she came. Not unless they wanted her to go.

"How big is this place?" Nola asked, more to break the endless pounding of their footfalls than because she actually wanted to know.

"No idea," Raina said. "I don't own a measuring tape."

"Then how much longer until we get there?" Nola asked. She didn't know how long it had taken her to find Nightland or how long she had been down here.

If I'm not back in the domes by sunrise . . .

"We'll be there soon," Julian said as the tunnel began to widen and slope downward.

"Where is *there*?" Nola's voice shook. How far underground were they now?

The tunnel widened even more, and the doors along the walls became more frequent. Soon they were passing people in the hall. Some nodded, others averted their eyes, but all of them gave the group a wide berth.

Brick and stone replaced the dirt of the walls. The lights were evenly spaced, giving the hall a more populated feel. The doors were still made of metal, but they didn't look as though they were meant to withstand a bomb blast.

Two boys a few years younger than Nola ran down the hall, laughing, only falling silent as they passed the group. Nola could hear their laughter begin again behind her.

A sudden jerk shot pain through Nola's arm. Raina had stopped in front of an antique-looking, intricately carved wooden door, and Julian held Nola in place.

Raina knocked, and the sound echoed through the hall. Shadows passed behind a small piece of glass set in the door.

Slowly, the door opened. Nola had hoped Kieran would come running through and tell Julian to let go of her arm where she could feel bruises forming. But instead, a tall man whom she had never seen before stood in front of her, his arms crossed as he stared at the group. Young and handsome, he had curling black hair down to his shoulders. His skin looked as though it should have been a deep olive but had grown pale without the sun. And the man's eyes were dark with black irises the same as the man who had led her to Nightland.

Nola glanced at Julian. His eyes were black as well.

"Emanuel." Raina bowed. "This Domer showed up at the gate. She said Kieran Wynne told her to find him here."

Emanuel examined Nola, starting from her feet and ending with her brown hair. "She looks like the right one. Nola?"

"Yes." Nola nodded. "How do you know my name?"

"Kieran told me about the girl who gives Eden breath." Emanuel smiled. "I'm glad you decided to brave the outside world. Bring her." Emanuel turned and walked away.

Julian steered Nola through the door, and Bryant closed it behind them. The inside of the door had been built of the same heavy metal as the door that led to the street. The intricate wood was only a façade.

Nola turned to Emanuel but gasped at the space around her. They were in a chamber larger than Nola's whole house. But instead of bare walls, beautiful art decorated this room.

Paintings, like the ones Nola had only ever seen on computer screens, adorned the tops of the walls. In the center of the ceiling hung three large crystal chandeliers, bathing all the paintings in their warm light. In one corner sat a piano and in another a harp. Below the paintings, the walls were covered with bookshelves, six feet tall and packed with books.

"Wow," Nola whispered.

"It's beautiful, isn't it?" Emanuel said. "These things would have been destroyed aboveground. Burned in the riots or for warmth, but we decided to protect them. You see, the Domers care about protecting the genetics of the human race. But down here, we want to protect what it is to be human. Sometimes, things have to change in order to survive. It all depends on which part of ourselves we're willing to give up. Some choose the body, others choose the soul."

Nola's mind raced, trying to take in everything in the room and understand what Emanuel was saying at the same time. She wanted to ask them to stop and let her look at the paintings or touch just one of the books, but they led her on and out through the far side of the room. They entered what appeared to be a home. Dark and, Nola shivered, underground, but a house nonetheless.

An older woman hovered over a stove, and a little girl clung to her skirt. She reached up to Emanuel as they walked by, but he shook his head at the child and kept walking. Hurt filled the little girl's big brown eyes as the group moved past the kitchen. Open doors to rooms filled with beds came next and then a steel door. Emanuel pushed the door open, and they all stepped through.

CHAPTER NINE

Nola caught a flash of scrubbed metal tables and brick walls draped in clear plastic before a voice shouted "Nola!" and Kieran's arms were around her.

"You're not dead," Nola breathed, burying her face in Kieran's jacket. "I thought you were dead."

"I'm fine," Kieran whispered. "I told you the medicine wasn't for me."

"But Captain Ridgeway found dome medicine on a dead body. After a riot." Tears streamed down Nola's face. "I thought it was you. I had to see if you were alright."

"I'm fine." Kieran pressed his lips to her forehead. "I'm fine. And you're safe here."

"Safe?" Nola half-shrieked. "There was a werewolf pack on the bridge. A sick woman was begging me for help, and I didn't have anything to give her. And then a Vamper almost killed me. He dragged me out of his territory and told me not to come back. I don't know how I'm going to get home, if I even have time before they find out I'm gone and decide they don't want me in the domes anymore."

"Are all Domer girls this hysterical?" Raina asked from her place by the door.

"Oh, no." Dr. Wynne appeared behind his son's shoulder. His hair stuck out at strange angles and had turned almost completely gray now, and his skin was nearly translucent in its pallor. "Nola is usually quite calm and reasonable. She is simply not used to our element, so you'll just have to be patient while she adjusts." He gave Nola a fatherly pat on the shoulder, muttering, "It is good to see you," before wandering back to his worktable.

"If it's good to see me"—Nola rounded on Kieran—"then why didn't you warn me what was at 5th and Nightland?"

"No one asked you to come here," Raina said. "I certainly didn't ask for a Domer to ruin my night."

"Raina," Emanuel said, silencing her. "How could we have known if you would turn us in?" Emanuel stared intently into Nola's eyes.

"Or that you weren't dumb enough to get yourself killed your first trip outside the domes." Raina shrugged as Emanuel turned his gaze to her.

"I'll make sure you get home before dawn." Kieran took Nola's hand. "I won't let them find out you're here. I won't let them banish you."

"I thought you were dead," Nola said to Kieran, keeping her voice low though she knew the rest of the room could hear. "You stole my I-Vent, left me a note telling me how to find you, and now I'm in a den full of Vampers."

"We prefer the proper name: *vampire*. Vamper is a rather nasty term. Rather like us calling you Domer. But I should give you some credit. At least you're smart enough to have figured that part out," Julian said in a genial tone. "Although Desmond's fangs do rather give it away."

"Kieran, why are you here?" Nola gripped Kieran's hand, hanging onto the one thing in the room that didn't terrify her.

"I think it's time we had a talk," Emanuel said, gesturing for Nola to sit at the large metal table.

The table looked like a slab for a corpse, not a place to sit for a pleasant chat.

"Emanuel—" Kieran began, but Emanuel silenced him with the wave of a hand.

"It is providence that you traveled to us tonight." Emanuel pointed again for Nola to sit.

Nola nodded and took a seat at the table. Kieran sat next to her, his smile disappearing as his brow furrowed.

"Raina, if you could—" Emanuel started.

"Get the Domer some refreshments?" Raina said, her tone barely polite. "Of course. The woman will go to the kitchen and get some snacks for the guest." She spun and walked out of the room.

Julian shut the door, leaving Bryant and Desmond standing on either side like guards, neither putting away his weapon.

"I must admit, Nola," Emanuel said, "we did have a courier that was caught up in the unfortunate incident last night. And he had an item with him. Something we need very badly. Where do we begin?" Emanuel took a seat across the shining metal table.

"With Fletcher," Dr. Wynne said. "If you want her to understand, you have to start with Fletcher."

Emanuel sat for a long moment. "Before you were born, before even Dr. Wynne was born, the Incorporation started building the domes. Forty-two sites around the world. To be filled with the best and the brightest. Not only to encourage research, but also to protect the gene pool. People were sick, dying. Cancer had become a plague. Clean water was scarce, and food supplies were in danger. But that wasn't what the people who created the domes feared.

"Fertility rates were dropping, and birth defects were becoming more common. The Incorporation had to protect the future of the human race by making sure it could breed. That's what the signs read, what was spouted at every conference. *To protect our children.*" Emanuel spat the last sentence. "But soon, the people realized it wasn't all the children the Incorporation were trying to protect, just the chosen few who lived in the domes. The rest of the population was left out here to watch their children suffer and die. The sicknesses became worse. But all of the researchers were in the domes. The brilliant minds were gone, and we were left with Fletcher."

"I've never heard of a researcher named Fletcher," Nola said.

"You wouldn't have," Kieran said. "They don't talk about him in the domes."

"People were in pain, and Fletcher came up with a new medicine. A drug that could stop tumors from growing. Make lungs impervious to the filth in the air. The medicine made people strong and slowed the natural aging process."

"That's amazing," Nola said.

"But the cure came at a price. Sensitivity to light. The inability to metabolize normal food, the reliance on blood for nutrition. Anger, violence, bloodlust. It changed you to the very core. But it was a way to survive. At first, the drug was only given to a few people. The ones who were very ill, on the brink of death. But soon, others outside Fletcher's control began to manufacture the drug, and it spread like wildfire."

"Vamp," Nola said, studying Emanuel's black eyes. "Vamp was made to be a medicine?"

"Not all vampires set out with the intent to wander the night. We were trying to survive. Vampires are what we had to become. There was no other choice," Emanuel said.

"But the wolves," Nola began.

"Someone tried to improve Vamp. To alter the way Vamp affects the ability to eat food."

"So, it is true." Nola swallowed the burning in her throat. "Vampires drink blood."

"Animal blood," Kieran said, reaching for Nola and pulling his hand away when she flinched.

"Nightland does not allow vampires who hunt for human blood," Emanuel said.

"But there are some who do?" Nola asked.

"You met one tonight," Julian said. "The man who showed you here, he was from a group who drink from humans. Almost all those who live aboveground do."

"Wolves are able to eat but suffer pheromone changes that alter the way they interact with each other," Emanuel said.

"Packs," Nola said. "It makes them run in packs."

"Yes," Kieran said, "which makes them more dangerous than any of the vampires."

"Ours is the only real community of vampires," Emanuel said. "Most prefer to roam and hunt on their own. There are turf lords, and territorial groups, but they would kill each other without hesitation for fresh blood. We have banded together in Nightland because we want something more. More than injecting Vamp and living to breathe another night. We want a chance for the children on the outside."

"And that is where I come in." Dr. Wynne spun his chair around and faced the group as though he had been waiting for his cue. "Vamp has a tendency to alter the user's moods. With the increase in strength comes increased aggression. With the need to drink blood comes a taste for violence."

"And the eyes, and the teeth," Nola said, her gaze darting to Emanuel's eyes.

"The eyes, yes," Emanuel said.

"The teeth are prosthetic," Desmond said from behind Nola. "If I'm going to be called a vampire, I might as well embrace it. Besides, it makes hunting easier."

"Desmond," Dr. Wynne said, flapping his hands as though fangs were trivial, "lived as a roamer for a long time and has no personal aversion to human blood." He paused, scratching his head for a moment. "But if there were a way to create a new formula of Vamp, one that would make people strong and healthy without subjecting them to the unfortunate side effects, we would have essentially found a cure. A way for people to live healthily on the outside without constant fear of contamination and death."

"That's what he's working on. ReVamp," Kieran said. "It would keep people healthy and keep the streets safe."

Nola ran through it in her mind. The woman who had begged her for help. The little boys at the Charity Center. All healthy.

"You could save everyone," she breathed.

"Not everyone," Emanuel said softly before looking to Desmond. "Fetch Eden."

"What's Eden?" Nola asked.

"Eden isn't a what," Emanuel said. "Eden is a who."

Emanuel nodded, and Desmond opened the door, disappearing into the hall.

"Before you meet her, I want to thank you," Emanuel said. "Without you, we would have lost her already."

Desmond returned, holding the small girl from the kitchen in his arms. As soon as the little girl's big brown eyes found Emanuel, she reached out, wanting him to hold her. Emanuel stood and took the child, kissing her gently on the cheek before kneeling next to Nola.

"This is Eden," Emanuel said. Eden hid her face on his chest. "She is my child."

"She's beautiful," Nola said.

"Eden," Emanuel said. The little girl turned her eyes back to her father. "Can you say thank you? This is the nice girl who gave you your medicine."

"Thank you," Eden said so softly her words could barely be heard.

"Good girl." Emanuel kissed her black curls that matched his own.

He handed Eden to Desmond, who slipped back out of the room.

"That's why I stole your I-Vent," Kieran whispered. "She needs the medicine."

"Eden has tumors in her lungs," Emanuel said. "They were getting bad enough she couldn't breathe. Your I-Vent bought her more time."

More time for a little girl with big brown eyes. Someone so small shouldn't be so sick.

"I'm so sorry. An I-Vent can't cure tumors," Nola said. "But when Dr. Wynne finishes ReVamp, he can cure her."

"Vamp, Lycan, ReVamp"—Emanuel gripped the table. The shining metal bent under his grasp—"they all have consequences."

"You just said—"

"If you're too sick or too young," Julian said, "all of the drugs can kill you. Or worse."

"What's worse?" Nola's heart raced as though she already knew the answer.

"Zombies." Julian glanced at Emanuel. "If the body rejects the drug, the body will start to decay. Beginning with the mind. All that's left is a craving for human flesh. Zombies would eat their own family without a thought. They know no pain. No fear. Only hunger. You've probably never seen such a thing."

"I have," Nola said, swallowing the bile that once again rose in her throat. "The zombies come to the domes sometimes. The guards drug them and take them away for treatment."

"There is no treatment," Emanuel said, his voice breaking. "There is no medicine that can cure a zombie. There is no medicine in the outside world that can save Eden."

"But there is in the domes." Dr. Wynne placed a hand on Nola's shoulder.

"I had a contact from far outside the city," Emanuel said. "He had managed to procure the medicine Eden needs."

"But he didn't make it all the way to Nightland," Kieran said.

"And somehow," Emanuel said, his black eyes studying Nola's face, "you did. And you have brought hope with you."

"We would only need a vial," Kieran said, "and that little girl could live until she's old enough—"

"To become a vampire," Nola said.

"To live to see twenty," Emanuel said. He reached across the table and took Nola's hand. His fingers were colder than the metal surface. "It's such a small thing in the world of the domes, but it's my daughter's life out here."

"You want me to steal medicine from the domes?" Nola pulled her hand out of Emanuel's reach.

"I am asking you as a father to save my daughter's life. I'm not asking as an outsider, or as a vampire. I am asking as a human, a man who is terrified. I am no different from you."

"You are." Nola stood up. "And not because I'm from the domes and you're an outsider. You are a vampire. You're asking me to help vampires."

"We are all humans." Julian spread his arms as though reaching out to every person in the city. "We've done what we had to in order to survive. But we are still humans. Can't you try to see us that way?"

"If you want to be seen as human, why would you name yourselves after monsters?" Nola asked. "Why would you choose to be called something so evil?"

"We've been forced to live in the dark for years. Is it so strange we would name ourselves after children of the night?" Raina asked as she pushed open the door, carrying a tray of tea. "We are living the nightmare. But we didn't choose it. We were abandoned out here. We're just the ones that have become strong enough to survive."

"Nola," Dr. Wynne said, "that little girl will be dead within the month. We need one vial. One tiny tube to save her. And you're the only one who can get it."

"But you know how to get into the domes." Nola shook her head. "You're the one who showed me how to get out."

"The medicine is in medical storage. You have to get to the lower levels to get near the room," Dr. Wynne said.

"And your mom works right down the hall from medical storage," Kieran said, his voice low and steady as he took Nola's hand in his. "All you have to do is visit her and then take a detour. No one will ever know."

"And if I get caught?" Nola said. "If they banish me for stealing from the domes?"

Forced to live in Nightland, stuck in a living tomb for the rest of my life.

"Tell them I broke in," Dr. Wynne said. "Tell them I came to your room and threatened to kill you if you didn't do it. They already believe me insane. I'm sure they can believe I could become violent."

"They would send the Outer Guard after you." Nola's mouth went dry in her panic.

"A worthy risk to save a child's life." Dr. Wynne shrugged and went back to his work.

"You won't get caught." Kieran took both of Nola's hands. "I know how you can do it. All you have to do is trust me. Please, Nola. For me."

Nola found herself nodding before she knew she had made a choice.

CHAPTER TEN

Nola clutched her hot tea, afraid her trembling hands would give away her fear if she lifted the cup to her mouth.

Dr. Wynne spoke first, explaining to Nola exactly what medicine he needed. Then Julian appeared, bringing with him maps of the domes.

"How did you get this?" Nola reached for the map. Bright Dome was there with her house drawn in the far corner.

"All the domes were built the same," Julian said, "and the Wynnes aren't the only ones who have left."

Nola's shoulders tensed at the word *left*. *Left* didn't seem to describe it.

"Under the circumstances, I would think you would be grateful for the breach in dome security as it will make your job that much easier. Medical storage is here." Julian pointed to a small square space. "It's environmentally controlled."

"Cold storage," Dr. Wynne said. "It'll be in the back cage."

"Isn't medical storage locked?" Nola asked.

"It is," Dr. Wynne said, "but seed storage isn't. And they share a vent system."

"All you have to do is go see your mom," Kieran said. "You're still planning on going the botany route?"

"It's not like I have a choice," Nola said.

"Head into seed storage," Kieran said. "No one will question why you're there. Go through the vent."

"Go through?" Nola pushed away from the table, her heart racing at the mere thought of entering such a small, dark place. "You want me to climb into a vent!"

"Only for a minute," Kieran said. "And then once you have the vial, you walk out the door and back to your room. I'll come into the domes tomorrow night and get the medicine from you." He took Nola's face in his hands. "You can do this, Nola."

"You shouldn't risk coming back into the domes," Nola said. "If they catch you..."

"They won't," Kieran said.

"When your mother returns from Green Leaf tomorrow," Emanuel said, "will she be going back to her lab?"

"She will." Nola nodded. "She'll go straight to the lab to check on her samples before she comes home. She'll make a guard bring her bag to our house. It's what she always does."

Kieran nodded to Emanuel.

"Then go see your mother as soon as you can," Emanuel said. "Eden is depending on you."

The room fell silent for a moment. Nola wanted to say something brave, or hopeful, but her mind buzzed with fatigue.

"Your walking into Nightland was providence, Nola," Emanuel said. "Even in the darkest of places, hope can appear."

"We should get you home," Kieran said, standing up and laying his hand on Nola's shoulder.

"I won't make it back before dawn," Nola said. "How long have I been down here?"

I should have brought a watch.

Kieran looked at Emanuel who nodded to Desmond and Bryant. Both men stepped aside, and Raina opened the door.

"There's a shortcut to the domes," Kieran said. "I'll take you."

"Raina, Julian," Emanuel said, "make sure Nola gets home safe."

Kieran's hand tensed on Nola's shoulder.

"This way." Raina led them back past the kitchen, but Eden was nowhere to be seen. They went through the gallery and back into the halls, going in the opposite direction of where the people had been dancing.

"How long have you been here?" Nola asked Kieran softly, though she had no real hope Julian and Raina wouldn't hear.

"Since the night after we were banished from the domes." Kieran rubbed the back of his neck. "My father had a few friends in the city, the ones he'd been helping."

"The starving children he had been feeding with the overabundance of the domes," Raina said.

"We went to them," Kieran said, "but I suppose word travels fast out here. In the middle of the night, Emanuel showed up where we were hiding."

"It's not every day a brilliant medical researcher ends up on the streets," Julian said. "Emanuel has been looking for an alternative to Vamp for a very long time." He opened a door and bowed them into a narrower corridor that sloped farther down into the earth.

"He asked my dad to come down here. Promised food, shelter, protection, and all my dad had to do was try to find a way to help people."

"By giving them better drugs?" Nola said. "There has to be a way to make people healthy without making them vampires."

"And what's so wrong with being a vampire?" Raina rounded on Nola. "Is hiding behind glass really better than living underground?"

"Raina," Julian warned.

"If she's going to be around, she should learn how to not insult people who could break her in half." Raina's black eyes gleamed.

A low growl came from Julian.

Raina shrugged and continued down the tunnel.

"I'm not going to be around," Nola said. "One vial. I'm getting one vial to help a little girl, and then I'm done."

Kieran squeezed her hand. "Then you're done."

Raina had stopped walking again, and Nola, too busy looking at Kieran, almost ran into her. His dark hair had fallen over his eyes, but it didn't hide their hurt and fear.

"Kieran—" Nola began, but Julian stepped forward.

"No time for teenage angst, I'm afraid. Cinderella must get home." Julian took Nola by the shoulders, steering her out of the corridor and down a small tunnel with a dead end.

The air in the tunnel was thick and damp. Nola squeezed Kieran's hand, willing herself not to panic at the sheer wall of blackness.

Raina pulled out a heavy key attached to a long chain that had been hidden inside her black leather top. In the darkness of the tunnel, Nola didn't notice the door until Raina reached for the keyhole.

The lock gave a heavy *thunk* as Raina turned the key.

Where she had only been able to see shadowed wall before, cracks of moonlight now split the darkness. Cool, crisp air flooded the hall as the door opened.

"Up you go." Julian pointed to a set of metal stairs.

Nola glanced at Kieran who nodded, and began climbing the metal steps. She expected the stench of the river, or the haze of the city to greet her, but instead, the air smelled like wood and decaying leaves.

A pool of light bathed the top of the steps. Nola reached her hands out, expecting to feel metal or concrete, but her hands met wood. Light crept in through a crack large enough for her to climb through. She turned sideways and slid out into the forest. She looked behind to see Raina climbing out of the tree after her.

No leaves clung to the branches. There would be no reason to look at the tree twice. Kieran climbed out of the vertical slash in the trunk. It looked like the tree had been split by lightning or time. The gap in the bark didn't seem large enough for a person to fit through until Julian emerged from the opening.

"Onwards?" Julian asked.

Nola's gaze followed him as he started up the hill toward the glittering domes, rising just above them.

"What?" Nola said, her feet not moving as she glanced from the tree to her home.

"I know, I know," Julian said, shaking his head, laughter bouncing his voice. "It is a bit passé to have a secret entrance hidden in a tree. However, I find when one becomes the stuff of legend, one might as well embrace the whole fantastical existence. I prefer to write myself into an unlikely fairytale rather than accept my fate is a horror story."

"But it's right here. There's an entrance right here!" Nola shouted before clapping a hand over her mouth.

They stood silent for a moment.

Nola listened for the sounds of guards coming to search the night but couldn't hear anything beyond the pounding of her own heart.

"I was almost killed getting to Nightland tonight," Nola finally whispered. "And you mean to tell me I could have just climbed into a tree and found out Kieran wasn't dead in twenty minutes? Skipping entirely over nearly being killed three times?"

"We couldn't allow that." Raina grabbed Nola's arm, dragging her up the hill toward the domes.

"Why not?" Nola yanked her arm from Raina. "You want me to sneak around and steal things for you, but you couldn't let me use a short cut?"

"It may be hard for you to understand"—Raina tossed her hair, her fingers twitching as though aching to reach for her knife—"but it's just as hard for a vampire to trust a Domer as it is for a Domer to trust a vampire. We couldn't just let Kieran tell his little girlfriend all our secrets, even if he did think you had an actual soul."

Julian hissed, silencing Raina.

"Fine," Nola said. "But if I had died, how long would it have taken you to find someone else who could get you the medicine?"

"If we'd known you would be more useful than the I-Vent, perhaps we could have arranged a parade to escort you to Nightland." Raina took a step toward Nola, her hand draping over the hilt of her knife. "Then again, showing someone who is going to betray you the second they get inside their cozy little domes an easy way into the only safe place you have is a sure way to get all of Nightland slaughtered."

"Enough," Kieran said, stepping between Raina and Nola. "I'll take her the rest of the way."

Raina opened her mouth to argue, but Julian spoke first. "We'll wait for you here, Kieran. Shout if you need us."

Kieran put a hand on the back of Nola's waist, guiding her up the hill.

"This is crazy," Nola said.

"You can do it," Kieran said. "I know you, Nola. You'll be all right."

"No, not just the medicine." Nola ran her hands through her hair, her tangled curls snagged on her fingers. "Vampires, and werewolves, and zombies. This isn't how the world is supposed to be."

"The world is broken," Kieran said. "We broke the planet. Is it so hard to believe the planet broke us right back?"

"But it's all legends, story stuff." Nola tripped over a root.

Kieran wrapped his arm tightly around her waist, steadying her.

Nola looked away from the worry creased on his forehead, blinking in the darkness, trying to focus her tired eyes on the uneven ground. "All I wanted to know was if you were alive. And now..."

"I'm fine," Kieran said. "And now you have the chance to do some real good. Don't forget, Nola, people living in domes was once story stuff, too. We can't choose which stories come true and which stay stories. None of us are that strong."

They were almost to the domes now. The sun had barely begun to paint the night sky gray. Soon the workers would be up, and then the new shift of guards would take up their posts.

Kieran stopped at the last of the trees in the forest. "I don't think I should go any farther."

"They might catch you."

"I might not be strong enough to leave." He touched the ends of Nola's hair and then her cheek. "Be careful."

"I'll see you tomorrow." Nola nodded. She walked out into the field, forcing herself not to look back, knowing Kieran would be watching her.

She half-expected guards to be waiting by the loose pane of glass. Or an alarm to sound as she crawled inside. She crept through the trees and back out onto the stone path as the gray light from the sky turned orange.

She peered through the glass, down over the forest and thought she saw a flicker of movement, but there was no way to know. Back into the empty house and up to her bed. She pulled the I-Vent from her pocket and took a deep breath, letting the metallic taste fill her mouth as her eyes drifted shut and she tumbled into sleep.

CHAPTER ELEVEN

The faint ringing of PAM's bells dragged Nola from sleep. Her head pounded as she tried to sort through everything that had happened the night before. The scent of the damp tunnels clung to her tangled hair. Her shoes were still on, and she clasped her I-Vent in her hand.

It wasn't a dream. There is a tunnel in the woods that leads to a den of vampires living under the city. Kieran is with them.

I've agreed to help them.

"Good Morning," PAM's voice said as soon as Nola climbed out of bed. "Reminder: Today, Dr. Kent will be returning home. Morning lessons will be in the Aquaponics Dome. This evening—"

"Thank you, PAM," Nola said, cutting the computer off. She didn't care what was happening in the domes that evening. Her mind couldn't move past the medical storage unit three stories underground.

Nola went to the shower, turned the water on as hot as she could stand and scrubbed the filth and stench of the city off her skin.

Does Kieran have hot water or soap?

Nola shut off the water, pressing her face to the cool ceramic wall. The shower, the warm fluffy towel. It all suddenly felt too extravagant to be allowed.

"You can't save everyone. Just get the medicine."

She turned the water back on and rinsed her hair. Normal. She had to look normal. Like this was any other day.

Mr. Pillion droned on, his voice dulled by the moss and heavy tank glass in

the Aquaponics Dome. He spoke in a soothing, calm tone about the effects of
algae blooms on fish populations.

Nola hated the Aquaponics Dome. The class was seated in the dug-down
section of the dome, eye-level with the tanks of fish.

Mr. Pillion coughed loudly.

Nola sat up straighter, aware of his eyes on her.

"As the fish waste feeds the plants, the plant waste feeds the fish," Mr. Pillion
continued. "What we really need to think about is what plants and fish mesh
best together in this type of symbiosis, and which plants and fish can best
contribute to the dietary, medicinal, and preservation goals of the domes."

The fish smelled terrible, but it was dark and warm by the tanks—a nice
place to sleep. The fish swam in slow circles under the roots of the plants.

Nola didn't feel herself slipping into sleep, but her eyes flew open at a sharp
kick in the shins from Jeremy.

"Magnolia," Mr. Pillion said, his eyebrows furrowed in concern, "are you
feeling quite well?"

Nola sat up straight and smiled. "I'm fine. Just tired. Sorry, Mr. Pillion, it
won't happen again."

"Perhaps we should send you to the clinic." Mr. Pillion frowned. "Just in
case."

Nola chewed the inside of her lips. Being sent to the clinic would take hours.
And if they thought she was sick, they would place her in isolation. She would
never be allowed to visit her mother in her lab if the doctors thought there was
any chance of her being contagious.

"Really," Nola said. "I just couldn't sleep last night." Her mind raced for an
answer. "I don't like being by myself in the house."

Mr. Pillion gave her a sympathetic look. "Of course." He nodded and turned
back to the screen where he was working through a list of extinct ocean species.

Some of the students still stared at Nola. She kept her eyes on the board. She
never would have been left alone before her father was killed. Before Kieran and
Dr. Wynne were banished. She could feel their sympathy radiating toward her.
Nola bit the inside of her lip hard, blinking back the tears stinging the corners of
her eyes.

"Unfortunately, some species such as Blue Whales were too large for an
attempt at their preservation even to be made," Mr. Pillion said.

The whales had been left out in the ocean to fend for themselves. The tiniest
algae killed the largest mammal. The injustice of it burned hot in Nola's chest.

But where could we have put a whale?

The end of lesson chimes sounded in the hall. Nola threw her things into her
bag and was first to the door. Her mother should be here by now. If her mother

behaved as she always had, she would already be in her lab, carefully checking each specimen and experiment to be sure everything was perfect.

"Nola." Jeremy caught up to her and took her hand, easily matching her quick pace. "Are you sure you're okay?"

Jeremy twined his fingers through hers. Nola's heart caught in her throat. Last night she had been walking with Kieran through the dark in a place she should never have been. And now she was going to steal from the domes. She looked up into Jeremy's eyes. Brown eyes as dark as Eden's.

"I'm fine." Nola pulled her hand away, pretending she didn't see the hurt in Jeremy's eyes as she stepped back. "I'm going to go say hi to my mom. Will you let Mrs. Pearson know where I am if I'm late?"

"Sure."

Nola turned and walked down the hall before Jeremy could say anything else.

Her mother's lab was located three floors below the normal tunnels. The research labs were some of the most important parts of the domes, so they were buried deep underground, far out of reach of storms or riots.

Nola went down the first flight of stairs. Offices branched off in either direction, all lit by sun-mimicking bulbs to make sure no one suffered from lack of light while they worked through the day.

There were no lights like this in the vampire tunnels.

Are sun-lights enough like the real sun to make Raina suffer?

Nola shook her head, banishing thoughts of places she should never have seen. But the clearer her thoughts became, the more the pressure of the earth weighed down upon her.

She descended another flight of stairs to where the food and supplies were stored and where those deemed fit for only menial tasks labored.

Then down the final flight of stairs. Nola's chest tightened, even worse than it had breathing the outside air the night before. Guards stood at either end of the hall, protecting the researchers behind their shiny white doors.

One of the guards nodded at her, not bothering to ask the reason for Nola's visit. She came down to the labs often. If she was going into botany, she needed to know as much as possible, even if the depth of the labs made her ill. She had almost begged to go into transportation just so she would never need to descend the steps to the laboratory. But choosing a path outside botany would have killed her mother. Nola would study plants and how to save the world. It was the only path her mother could accept.

Her mother's figure moved on the other side of the frosted glass of the laboratory door. Nola knocked lightly.

"Yes." Her mother's brusque voice cut through the glass.

Nola peeked her head into the lab. "Hey, Mom."

"Magnolia," her mother said after pausing for a moment, as though trying to figure out who would be calling her *Mom*. "What do you need?"

"I just wanted to say hi, see how the conference was." Nola stepped into the room as her mother began typing away on the computer.

"The conference was fine." Her mother moved toward a tray of cooled samples on the table. "We agreed to institute a new policy that will double food production."

"That's amazing," Nola said. "With that much food, we could actually bring produce to the Charity Center."

"Don't be foolish," her mother said. "The excess space in the greenhouses will be used for further plant species preservation. Just because you can't eat a plant doesn't mean we should allow it to be wiped off the face of the earth."

"I'm sorry," Nola murmured.

"No." Her mother sighed, running her hands through her short hair. "I didn't mean to snap. The conference was good." She sank down into her office chair, massaging her temples. "We're going to be converting one of the domes for tropical preservation this year. We're bringing in a new batch of rain forest species, which is truly exciting. Something I've been fighting for since I got this job."

"Then, what's the matter?" Nola perched on her mother's desk.

"Something went wrong with the seed samples while I was gone." Her mother waved a hand at the tray.

Nola leaned over, examining the dishes of seeds. The outsides had cracked where tiny stems had tried to break through, but the green had faded, replaced by withered brown.

"I was trying to see how short the cold simulation could be," her mother said. "The heat at the end of the cycle was too high and fried the seedlings. And I have no idea what went wrong with the program."

"I'm sorry." Nola pulled her mother into a hug.

"It's fine, I just need to—"

"Get back to work," Nola finished for her mother. "I'll see you at home."

Nola walked back out the door and into the hallway. The guards didn't even look to see who had come out of the lab.

Sweat slicked Nola's palms, her heart pounded in her chest.

I won't even make it to the door before they know something is wrong.

Two doors down. All she had to do was enter two doors down. She exhaled and willed her shoulders to relax.

She wiped her palms on her pants and pushed the seed storage door open.

She glanced at the guards, but their backs were still toward her. She slipped inside, shutting the door silently behind her.

Nola's breath rose in a cloud in front of her. Even with the adrenalin pumping through her veins, she began to shiver. The room had been built to keep the rows upon rows of seeds hibernating. Saving thousands of species from extinction.

It had always seemed strange to Nola that the Dome Council didn't place more guards on seed storage. To the Kents, this was the greatest wealth of the domes.

Someday, years from now, when the water had begun to clear and the air was pure again, people would leave the domes. They would spread out around the world to begin again. And these were the seeds they would take with them.

Nola wanted to stay, read every name on every tray and picture what the plants would look like when they had grown. But this room was not where the answers for Eden lay. Blowing heat onto her hands, Nola walked to the end of the room before turning and heading to the back corner.

There it was, just where Julian had said it would be; a grate at the base of the wall, as high as Nola's waist and just as wide. It was bigger than she had thought it would be, and the faint light of the medical storage room filtered through from the other side. It was only three feet. Less than that really.

Nola knelt and pulled out a thin strip of metal, sliding it into the crack at the edge of the grate, gently prying it away from the wall. She stopped every few seconds, listening for footsteps or the *whoosh* of the door swinging open. But as the grate slid into her hands, no sound of panic came—no running feet, no alarm. Taking a deep breath, Nola crawled into the wall. Her hands trembled. She could leave the other side of the grate off. Leave an exit from the cramped darkness. But if someone came in, they would spot the hole in the wall.

Nola grasped the slats of the grate, feeling them cut into her skin as she pulled the metal into place. Her breath came in shallow gasps. The airshaft opened above her, leading to the next floor. Cold air blew on her, coming from stories above, going through filter after filter to get down to her. Nola turned to the other grate, her whole body shaking from cold and panic. She pushed against the metal, but it didn't budge. She leaned her body into the grate, but it refused to move.

"Please, please just open," Nola whispered, twisting to push on the grate with her feet. A whine of metal on metal echoed around the vent as the grate moved a fraction of an inch. Nola froze, waiting for one of the guards to come running into the room, searching for what had made the noise. But the hum of the air system was the only sound.

"Open dammit." She gave the grate two kicks, and it popped out, hitting the floor of the medical storage room with a clatter.

Nola dragged herself into the room and lay on the ground, gasping at the dim ceiling lights overhead. Again, she waited for the pounding of guards' boots as they ran to arrest her. To throw her out into the world. But there was nothing.

She pushed herself to her knees, searching the room. Where there were rows of shelves in seed storage, here there were glass-fronted cabinets, each labeled with its contents. Nola pictured where Julian had pointed on the map. She pushed herself up onto her shaking legs and walked along the back wall. The vials were classified by type. Names Nola didn't understand.

It should be Kieran down here, climbing through airshafts and stealing medicine.

He would know what all the names meant and be brave enough not to fear the guards.

She reached the cabinet in the far corner. Nola didn't hesitate as she opened the glass door. Fog blossomed on the glass at the heat of her hand.

Pataeris. Sitting right on the shelf. Nola picked up the vial. She expected an alarm to sound. Or for PAM to reprimand her loudly. But there was no noise. No hint of danger.

Nola slipped the vial into her pocket and sprinted back to the grate. Back through the darkness and into seed storage. She could be aboveground in ten minutes. She would see the sun. Nola crawled into the shaft and jammed the grate shut behind her, ignoring the sting as the metal dug into her fingers. With a grind and a tiny *thunk*, the grate was back in place. Nola twisted to the other grate as a familiar voice said, "What the hell was that?"

CHAPTER TWELVE

Nola froze as footsteps came closer to the grate.

"It sounded like the ventilation unit," a man's voice said.

There was an angry murmur before Nola's mother's voice came loud and clear. "I lost an entire tray because the computer mishandled the climate settings on my experiment. That same computer also monitors the climate settings in this room. Correct?"

Nola could picture her mother's face. Eyebrows raised, nostrils flared.

"Yes," the man said. "PAM monitors both systems."

"And PAM is malfunctioning," Nola's mother growled. "So go get every climate control and computer tech down here and get this fixed before we lose every seed we have!"

Angry footsteps pounded away toward the door. Nola could see a pair of thick black boots through the slats of the grate. She held her breath. If he bent down, he would see her.

After a few seconds, the man walked away. Straining her ears, Nola heard the door *whoosh* shut behind him. He would be back. Back with people who needed to inspect the vents. Nola looked at the other grate. She could go hide in medical storage, but for how long? They would need to check the temperature in there, too.

I'm trapped.

Nola leaned against the metal inside the shaft. She could crawl out now, tell them what she had done, and beg for mercy. They would want to know who the medicine was for.

What if they trace it back to Kieran? And Eden. Wide-eyed little Eden.

Nola opened her eyes. There was another way.

She looked up into the darkness above her. How far up was it to the next floor? Ten feet, maybe twelve? And how long before the man came back?

Nola swallowed and took a deep breath. It was no different than climbing onto her roof. Except for the darkness, metal walls, and tight space. Not to mention the possibility of being banished from her home.

She placed her hands on either wall. Her sweaty palms slipped on the smooth metal. But the walls were close. Close enough for her to balance her weight as she lifted one foot and then the other onto the walls. Although the metal of the airshaft moved with a heavy clunking sound as she pressed against it, Nola didn't stop. It didn't matter if a guard heard. If she stopped, she would be caught. Her pulse thundered in her ears as she climbed, gaining mere inches in height with each step. Her arms shook, her legs cramped, but she couldn't stop.

Kieran.

She took a step.

Kieran will come tonight, and he'll take the medicine to Eden.

Another step.

Once Eden is well, she can grow up strong.

Another step.

Then she'll take ReVamp.

Nola's grip faltered, and she slid down an inch. She jammed her arms into the walls as hard as she could.

Shadows moved above. A foot higher, and she would be to the next level. Nola inched up to the grate. Through the latticed metal, she could see rows of bunks. The guards' housing. And on the other side an office, with the only visible chair empty.

Her fingers shaking, Nola dragged herself onto the ledge by the office, and with the last ounce of energy her legs could muster, kicked the grate away. Gasping and shaking, she threw herself onto the office floor.

Nola lay on the carpet, her eyes closed, trying to convince her heart it should try to keep beating. She waited for a voice to yell—someone to scream at the girl lying on the floor. But there was nothing.

After a minute, Nola opened her eyes. The office was small and empty. A desk and a chair sat in front of a tower of drawers. A faint humming filled the room. Still shaking, Nola pushed herself to her feet, searching for the source of the sound. It couldn't be an alarm. Not with a noise that steady.

A picture of Captain Ridgeway with Gentry and Jeremy perched on one corner of the desk. The Captain wore civilian clothes, and all three of them smiled broadly. Jeremy was shorter than Gentry, so the picture must have been a few years old at least. Nola reached for the picture, wanting to study the normality of it.

The humming stopped her. It came from the drawers. Nola placed her hand on the metal tower. It was cold, like the cabinets below.

Glancing at the office door, Nola quietly fitted the grate back into the wall and opened the buzzing cabinet.

Tiny vials lined the cold drawer. Like the one in her pocket but filled with deep black fluid.

"I don't think it's the vents." The voice traveled up the shaft.

Nola snapped the drawer shut, tearing toward the door. She turned the handle and pulled the door open just a crack. There was no one in sight, though she could hear voices in the distance. Nola ran her hands over her hair in a hopeless attempt to smooth down her curls, and stepped into the hall.

She walked slowly and deliberately, hoping no one would notice the dust on her clothes.

Two men came out of the barracks. They looked Nola over before one elbowed the other and winked at her. The two men laughed softly as they went down the hall.

Nola blushed. They thought she was down here with a guard.

At least they haven't arrested me. Yet.

Half-running, she sped down the hall and up the stairs. She turned a corner and slammed into a group of terrified looking people.

"Sorry." Nola reached for the vial in her pocket before she could stop herself.

If the three she'd run into noticed anything strange, it didn't show as they murmured their apologies and continued toward seed storage. All three wore maintenance uniforms and anxious looks on their faces. They should be worried if Lenora blamed them for the lost seedlings. Nola waited until the workers were out of sight then sprinted the rest of the way up to the atrium.

Nola staggered at the bright light and fresh clean air of the atrium. She wanted to sit on the floor and cry. She was out of the dark and aboveground. The bright green leaves on the trees rustled as the vent blew out air. They were running harder than usual, probably testing the system. That was good. Nola nodded to herself. The more air through the vents, the less likely anyone would notice sweaty handprints.

"Nola!" a voice called across the atrium.

Nola froze, unsure whether to run or not, then finally settled on turning to see who had shouted for her.

"Nola!" Jeremy said again as he ran toward her.

The people who had been enjoying the calm of the atrium scowled at him as he passed.

"Where have you been?" he said as he reached her. He wasn't even out of breath. All of his preparation for guard training was paying off.

"Nola?" he said again, this time with concern in his voice as he took her shoulders.

"Yes?" Nola said.

"You missed our time in the greenhouse," Jeremy said.

She had been gone longer than just lunch. Mrs. Pearson would want to know where she had been.

"I went to see my mom," Nola said. "One of her experiments went wrong, she was upset..."

"And you ran for it?"

That was right. More or less.

Nola nodded.

"I'm sorry," Jeremy said, brushing the sweaty hair from Nola's face. "It must have been some run."

Nola tried to smile at his joke.

Jeremy took her hand and led her down a side path, away from the still glaring bystanders. He stopped under the low-hanging branches of a tree, out of sight of the rest of the atrium.

"Are you sure that's all that's wrong?" Jeremy said softly. "Because you could tell me. Whatever's wrong, whatever's bothering you, you can trust me. You know that, right?"

"I do."

"It's just," Jeremy began, looking down at Nola's hand clasped in his, "I'm here for you. If you were worried about being alone when your mom was away, I could've, I mean, we could've spent time together. Because I want... I want to be with you, Nola. All the time."

Jeremy's hand stroked her hair, then rested on the back of her neck. And he was kissing her. Gently, he pulled her in close, lifting her up so she stood on her toes. His heart pounded so hard the beats resonated through her chest. Nola froze as something in her pocket pressed against Jeremy's hip.

She gasped and took a step back.

"Nola." Jeremy reached toward her.

She pulled her hand away from him without knowing she had moved.

"I'm sorry," Jeremy said, his face red and his eyes filled with hurt. "I thought, I thought you felt the same as me."

Nola's mind raced as she tried to think of feelings beyond fear. The vial in her pocket burned her leg as though it were on fire. Surely Jeremy could see the flaming vial, the proof of her betrayal.

He knows what I did.

"Just forget it," Jeremy said. "Forget I ever... It won't happen again. But I meant what I said. If you need me, I'm here." He turned and walked down the path.

She should let him go, get the vial back home, and wait there for Kieran. Jeremy was disappearing through the branches.

"No." Nola ran after him, taking his hand.

He turned to look at her, his eyes bright and brow furrowed.

"Forget this happened," Nola said. Her mouth had gone dry. She didn't know what she was saying as the words came tumbling out. "Forget you kissed me and I was a sweaty mess who can't manage to think right now."

Jeremy nodded. Pain still filled his face.

"But try it again," Nola said. "Not today. But sometime."

Nola turned and ran through the atrium. She needed to get away before Jeremy asked questions she couldn't answer.

Back through the tunnel and into Bright Dome. She had already missed class. There was no point in going back. There would be no more trouble for missing evening lessons. Up the walk and into her home, Nola shut the door behind her, leaning against it and panting.

She closed her eyes. She had the medicine. She'd finished her job. Now all she had to do was wait for tonight and Kieran would come for the vial. But Jeremy had kissed her. Nola slid down to sit on the floor, trying hard not to think of Jeremy kissing her. Of his warm arms around her.

There were more important things to worry about than if she wanted to be kissing Jeremy in the atrium right now. She slipped her fingers into her pocket and pulled out the tiny vial. She held it up, and the light shone through the orange liquid. There was so little in the tube.

Is this really all it takes to save a little girl's life?

Nola pushed herself to her feet and climbed the steps to her room, absent-mindedly grabbing a bowl full of fruit along the way.

Setting the vial on her desk, Nola popped a sweet grape into her mouth. How desperate would you have to be to take Vamp and give up food like this? Nola pulled her drawer out from her desk and set it on her bed. Vial in hand, she reached all the way to a tiny recess at the very back. Carefully, she slid the drawer back into place. It was as though the vial had never existed.

Nola curled up in bed, staring at the drawer. The sun hadn't set yet. It would be hours before Kieran came. Her arms and legs burned. Fatigue muddied her brain. Slowly, her eyes drifted shut.

Darkness filled her room when she woke up. The sun had gone down, and the house was quiet.

The dim clock in the wall read well after eleven. Her mother must have been home for a while. Nola moved to sit up but froze as a shadow shifted.

"It's me," Kieran whispered, taking a step into the pale strip of light that came through the window. "I didn't want to startle you."

"It's okay," Nola whispered, pushing herself to her feet. "I got the vial."

Kieran took a deep breath, catching Nola's hands as she reached for the drawer and pulling her to his chest.

"I thought they'd caught you." Kieran pressed his lips to her forehead. "I was watching the domes. People were coming in and out, looking at the air vents."

"There was something wrong with the climate control." Nola rested her cheek on Kieran's chest. "I had to climb up the vent. I ended up in the Guard barracks."

Kieran pulled away to look into her eyes. "I'm so sorry, Nola. I never should have let Emanuel get you involved."

"He wants to save his daughter." Nola shrugged. "He needs the medicine."

"*Eden* needs the medicine." Wrinkles formed on his forehead. "I won't let Emanuel ask you to do something like that again. It's too dangerous."

"It's fine." Nola laid her fingers on his lips. They were soft, and his breath was warm.

"Nola." He took a step forward. And he was kissing her.

Her knees went weak, but his arms locked around her, holding her tight. Her heart raced as he gently parted her lips with his own.

"Kieran," she murmured, lacing her fingers through his hair.

Kieran froze and backed away, leaving Nola swaying on the spot.

"I have to go," Kieran said, his voice hoarse.

"Now?" Nola stepped in front of the door.

"I live on the outside," Kieran said. "You live in here. What are we supposed to do?"

"I don't know." The rush of heat drained from Nola's body, leaving a cold numbness in its wake.

Kieran took her hands in his. "The hardest part about leaving the domes was losing you." He ran his fingers over her cheek. "But I can't have you. I can't come in here. And I won't"—he cut Nola off before she could speak—"let you leave the domes to find me."

"I miss you." Tears spilled from her eyes, leaving warm tracks running down her cheeks.

Kieran brushed her tears away with his thumb. "I have to go. You know I'm right."

"Stay," Nola whispered. "Just for a little while." She lay down on the bed, pulling Kieran down with her.

She curled up next to him, resting her head on his chest. His heart beat slowly under her ear.

"When will I see you again?" Nola murmured.

Kieran tightened his arms around her, and she knew his answer.

Never.

Nola clung to his shirt, willing time to stop passing so he would never leave.

"Sleep, Nola," he whispered. "Just sleep."

Soon, she had drifted away to the slow rhythm of his heartbeat.

The sun streaming through the windows woke Nola with a gasp the next morning. She sat up, looking for Kieran, but her room was empty. There was no mark on the bed where he had been—if he had even been there at all.

"Kieran," Nola whispered, opening her closet. Her clothes hung in an undisturbed row. She turned back to her room. The fruit bowl sat empty on her desk.

Nola yanked the drawer free, letting it clatter to the floor. She felt into the back corner. The vial was gone. But something small had taken its place.

A slip of paper wrapped around something hard. Nola unfurled the paper and found a little charm. A tiny tree, delicately carved out of wood. Nola held the charm up to the light. A barren tree with a split on one side, a perfect copy of the tree that hid the forest entrance to Nightland.

Nola looked down at the paper. At the note in Kieran's untidy scrawl.

I'm always yours. Be well.

Nola sank to the floor. He was gone. Kieran Wynne had left the domes. Again.

CHAPTER THIRTEEN

"Nola," her mother's voice came through the door. "Are you awake?"

"Yeah," Nola said, forcing her voice to sound normal, like she hadn't just lost her best friend.

Again.

Nola's mother poked her head through the door. "Good. I was worried when I came home last night and you were already asleep."

"I'm fine," Nola said. "Just tired, really tired."

"Well, come on down. I brought some treats from Green Leaf." Her mother winked and left.

The attendees of Green Leaf always brought food with them—rare fruits that were only grown in their own domes. Nola's stomach rolled in disgust.

Kieran had stolen a bowl of grapes. She could picture him, Dr. Wynne, and Eden sharing the fruit. They were probably the only people in Nightland who could eat it. And they would sit in the kitchen, savoring every bite. While she ate papayas and pomegranate seeds.

Nola went to the bathroom and looked in the mirror. Her curls surrounded her face like a tangled lion's mane. The dark circles under her eyes made her look as ill as an outsider.

Her hands shook as she splashed cold water onto her face.

She swallowed the scream the smell of the soft, clean towel sent to her throat.

Gripping the edge of the sink, she stared into the mirror. "You've done your part, Magnolia. It's over."

She picked up the comb and tore it through her hair on her way to the kitchen. She didn't care about the pain as she brushed away the last of the filth from the vents. Had it not been for the tiny tree in her pocket, it would have been as though it had never happened at all.

Nola ate her breakfast silently as her mother griped about the subpar maintenance of the cooling system.

"It's pathetic really." Lenora sipped her tea. "We're trying to preserve the resources the world has given us, and they look at me like I'm overreacting when they endanger our seed supplies. Like I'm worried *I* might overheat."

"Right." Nola nodded.

Has Eden taken the medicine yet?

"And I'll be busy enough as it is without having to worry about faulty cooling systems." Lenora took the empty plates from the table and set them in the sink. "We're going to have to start working on the greenhouse consolidation within the next few days if we're going to get the rainforest dome prepped for planting by the end of the month."

"Right."

How long will it take for the Pataeris to take effect?

"Well, I'll see you tonight." Lenora walked out the door without looking back.

"Have a good day, Mom," Nola murmured to the empty house. "I kissed two boys yesterday and stole dome medicine to save a vampire's kid. See you tonight."

Nola grabbed her tablet and headed out of the house. Dark clouds loomed over the horizon. A deep green tint shaded the sky. Acid rain would be falling on the city in a few hours, burning anyone who strayed outside. Destroying any hope for unprotected crops.

"First acid rain of the year," a voice came from over Nola's shoulder. Gentry Ridgeway limped toward her. "It'll make things worse in the city. A few people had managed to grow a bit of food but—" she shrugged.

The growers would have to start over again.

"How are you?" Nola asked, looking from the cut on Gentry's forehead to the brace on her leg.

"I'll be fine." Gentry blew a bit of her short, blond hair away from her eyes. "Busted leg and a cut-up head. Dad just likes to overreact and tell everyone in the domes I got banged up."

"He worries about you."

"And I worry about Jeremy." Gentry limped a step closer to Nola. "Look, I try not to get involved in my baby brother's life. He's a good kid. He'll be a great guard. And for some reason, he's decided he's head over heels for you."

Heat leapt into Nola's cheeks.

"I don't know what happened between you two yesterday, and quite frankly I don't care," Gentry pressed on, "but I think we can both agree Jeremy is the nicest guy you're going to be able to find in this place. Right?"

"Jeremy's great," Nola said.

"Add that to the fact that he actually likes you, and I see you as one really lucky girl." Gentry pulled herself up to her full height, seeming to tower over Nola. "So, whatever you said that got him all confused yesterday, fix it. I don't care what you have to figure out, or how you have to do it. That boy would walk through fire for you."

"I didn't—I never," Nola pressed her fists to her temples, trying to squeeze all her thoughts together into something that made sense.

"I know you never tried to get him to go all crazy for you, but it happened," Gentry said. "And I don't want to see him hurt. So, make a choice and stick to it. You're a nice girl, Nola. You should get a nice guy. This isn't Romeo and Juliet. This is the domes. You pick someone, and you build a life."

"I'm seventeen," Nola said. "Jeremy is wonderful, but I just—"

"Don't explain anything to me. If you don't want Jeremy, that's your deal. But tell him. And don't wait forever to do it."

Nola nodded, tears stinging the corners of her eyes.

"Now get to class before Jeremy freaks out and thinks you're avoiding him."

Nola nodded and walked down the stone path.

Jeremy would be waiting for her in class. Waiting to make her laugh. Wanting to hold her hand. Offering a world of safety and sunlight, far away from the darkness of Nightland.

CHAPTER FOURTEEN

It had taken nearly three weeks to rearrange the plants in the Amber Dome to make more room for the crops from the Leaf Dome. Classes had been cancelled since all the students were needed to help transfer the fragile plants. If something went wrong and the crops were lost, the food supplies of the domes would disappear with them. All nonessential workers had been assigned to the delicate task.

The days were a blur of work—digging, sorting, and planting until the light became too dim. The domes had become a frenzy of chaos, perfect for avoiding all the Ridgeways.

Nola's mother had begun work on modifying the Leaf Dome two days before, preparing for the shipment of trees and animals that would arrive from the south domes later in the month. The soil content needed to be altered. Different fertilizers, different acidity. Everything the new rainforest would need to grow.

Sweat beaded on Nola's forehead as she hauled another bag of soil up the stairs to the dome. The air hung heavy with the scent of perspiration and fertilizer. The temperature had been turned up to mimic a tropical climate. The only one who seemed to be enjoying the heat was Nola's mother, standing in the middle of the Leaf Dome, new schematics in hand, shouting orders as plant and seed trays were loaded out of the dome.

"You know," Jeremy grunted, sending Nola stumbling as he lifted the bag she'd been dragging up the last few stairs, "there are, what, ten thousand people living in the city? Don't you think we could pay them to haul the dirt? I mean, we could do the planting, but I'm supposed to be going through the training material before I start guard training. Instead, I'm hauling glorified cow poop."

"We can't have outsiders in the domes." Nola searched for a clean place on her sleeve to wipe her forehead.

"Not even once?" Jeremy smiled cautiously.

"No," Nola said, more forcefully than she had meant to. She took a breath. "It wouldn't be fair to show them everything we have and then kick them right back out into the city." She reached up to the little tree charm that hung around her neck. It would be wrong to show Eden the clean air and bright lights of the domes. Her father couldn't live in the light anyway.

"I'm sorry." Jeremy's brow wrinkled. "It was a joke."

Nola arranged her face into a smile. "I know." She pushed out a laugh, but it sounded tinny in the humid air.

"Do you want to get some water?" Jeremy asked, holding out his dirt-covered hand, reaching for Nola's equally filthy one.

"Sure." Her stomach fluttered as she took his hand.

Water stations had been set up along the sides of the dome. Nola's mother's eyes flicked to them every few minutes, making sure no one dared slack off during the planting.

Dew clung to the outside of the water vat, and dirt from the planters' hands had turned to mud on its surface. Jeremy poured two cold glasses and, holding them both, walked away from the others in line for water.

"Here," Jeremy said, passing the glass to Nola. His fingers closed around hers. A shiver ran up Nola's arm.

She didn't know if it was from the cold of the glass or Jeremy's touch. Nola pulled away, taking a drink and turning to watch the planters.

"Are we okay?" Jeremy asked after a long pause.

"What?"

"I kissed you," Jeremy said.

Nola's breath caught in her chest as she remembered Jeremy holding her tight. The warmth of his body flooding into hers.

"And for the past three weeks you've barely spoken to me."

"I'm sorry." Nola shook her head, not knowing what else to say. She couldn't explain she hadn't been talking to anyone because all she wanted to do was scream. And she couldn't stop obsessing over not knowing if the medicine had saved Eden or if the whole thing had been pointless. And she most definitely couldn't tell Jeremy she was terrified of talking to him because if she said something wrong, Gentry might murder her.

"It's all right. I know," Jeremy whispered, taking Nola's hand in his.

"Know what?" A buzz of panic started at the back of Nola's mind.

He turned her hand over, running his thumb along the lines on her palm. "It's Kieran."

"Kieran?"

He knows. He saw Kieran come through the glass. He saw him come into my house.

"You love him." Jeremy let go of Nola's hand.

"I—what?" The buzzing vanished, leaving Nola blinking at Jeremy.

"You two were together. He got banished. You still love him," Jeremy said. His face was set, not with anger, but determination.

"We were friends," Nola said.

"You dated."

"Only for a few months."

"When they made him leave," Jeremy said, "it was like you broke."

Nola remembered. Crying in her room for days. Barely eating. Not speaking to anyone. Until Jeremy made her, forcing her everyday to become a little more human again. Making her laugh when she thought it was impossible.

And they were back there again.

"He was my best friend," Nola said, "and they took him away. But he, we, it's not like we were going to get married." But was that true? If he had stayed, would they still be together? Would they have been together for years, or for their whole lives?

A life in the sunlight with Kieran by my side.

"He was my friend, too," Jeremy said. "And I don't expect you to forget him."

"He's not dead," Nola snapped.

The workers standing by the cooler glared at her.

"He's not dead," Nola whispered. He was just outside the domes. Through the tree. She gripped the charm at her throat without thought.

"He's gone," Jeremy said. "And he's never coming back." He stepped forward, raising a hand to caress Nola's cheek. "But I'm here. I'm right here, Nola. And I'm not going anywhere."

"Jeremy," Nola whispered.

His hand smelled like soil and life. Like the domes and everything they protected.

"I think we could be something wonderful," Jeremy murmured. "I think we could be happy."

Nola looked into his eyes, and the fear that had clung to her heart for weeks faded away. She raised her hand to hold his as it rested on her cheek. "I think so, too."

Standing up on her toes, she leaned forward and brushed her lips gently against his. Her heart fluttered, and her stomach danced. But the world stayed upright. There was no rabbit hole for her to tumble through like with Kieran.

"Magnolia," an angry voice came from behind her.

Jeremy looked over Nola's head and jumped away from her as though burned.

Nola spun around to see her mother's rigidly angry face.

"Magnolia," Lenora said. "I would have expected you to show a little more respect for work that is so important to the domes. And Jeremy"—she rounded on Jeremy, who suddenly looked smaller than Lenora—"if you expect to join the Outer Guard like your father and your sister, you will have to learn some discipline. Priorities need to be respected. Especially where my daughter is concerned."

Lenora grabbed Nola by the arm and dragged her away. Past the water station, where the people now openly gawked at the Kents, through the planting lines, and to an empty section of the dome.

"Mother," Nola said as the men carrying the planting trays stopped to stare, "I can walk on my own."

"And I can see exactly what you walked into," Lenora spat.

"I'm seventeen," Nola said, yanking her arm away. "I kissed a boy. I shouldn't have stopped working, I'm sorry. But you like Jeremy."

Lenora stopped and glared at her daughter. Nola could read the battle raging in her mother's mind, warring between what she wanted to say and what she knew would be most effective.

"Jeremy has his path, and you have yours," Lenora said, her tone clipped. "You have an obligation to the domes. Above all other things, the domes come first. And *we* believe the best way to preserve the domes is by preserving the plants and people within them. Nothing more, nothing less. Jeremy Ridgeway does not fit into that plan."

Lenora took her daughter's shoulders and steered her to the far corner of the dome. A line of trays lay next to the glass, filled with spinach plants that were past their prime and tomato vines that had stopped bearing fruit for the season.

"Harvest the dirt," Lenora said.

"Dirt?" Nola examined the last few stunted carrots that had been pulled from the soil.

"Get the plants out of the dirt," Lenora said. "Put the plants on the carts for compost. Save the soil in the bins. It's still fertile. It can be used in the new Amber Dome beds once the roots from these plants are gone. When you've done that, you come straight home. You do not speak to anyone. You do not stop anywhere. You are—"

"Grounded," Nola finished for her mother.

"I'm glad you have enough sense left to figure that out." Lenora turned and stalked away, leaving Nola alone with the aging plants.

Darkness had fallen before Nola finally limped up the steps up to Bright Dome. Her back throbbed from spending hours stooped over the plants. Choosing each bit of edible food and sorting it from the dead plants to be composted, laying the food neatly on trays to be sent down to be distributed to the residents of the domes.

The lights blazed in her house as Nola walked up the worn stone path. Nola flicked her eyes up to the stars, giving a silent plea her mother wouldn't want to talk about Jeremy again.

She rubbed the dirt from her hands onto her pants before opening the kitchen door. Holding her breath she counted three seconds of silence. Maybe Lenora had fallen asleep, or better yet, was still locked in her office down in the tunnels.

"Magnolia," Lenora's voice came from the corner, "how long can it possibly take to finish a simple task?"

Nola chewed the inside of her cheek, her fatigue telling her to argue with her mother, her common sense telling her to keep quiet and hope it ended soon. Nola stepped into the bright kitchen and closed the door behind her.

"I asked you a question," Lenora said, stepping in front of Nola and blocking her path up the stairs. "Why has it taken you so long to get home?"

"I came home as soon as I was finished." Nola took a step forward, watching the dirt fall from her clothes onto the polished kitchen floor.

"Why on earth did it take you five hours to sort the trays?" Lenora snapped. "It would have taken a ten-year-old two."

"Then you should have asked a ten-year-old to do it," Nola growled, knowing it was a mistake to have spoken as soon as she saw the lines form around her mother's pursed lips.

"I asked you," Lenora said. "Did you stop to see Jeremy?"

"No." Nola dug her filthy nails into her palms. "I sorted the edibles from the scraps. Got rid of the compost, prepped the food for distribution, and labeled the soil trays for transfer. And yes, that was a lot of work, and yes, I just finished."

Lenora raised an eyebrow. "I never told you to salvage any food. Those plants were past their prime."

"There was still good food," Nola said.

"And it will do just fine as compost." Lenora waved a hand. "If I had wanted it for distribution—"

"You're just going to throw that food away?" Nola asked.

"No, we're going to compost it," Lenora said.

"But it could be eaten." Nola's mind scrambled to grasp her mother's meaning.

"We don't need it," Lenora said, walking back to her computer at the table.

"But the people in the city do," Nola said. "We could send it to them."

"There isn't enough to feed the whole city. It isn't even enough for an afternoon at the Charity Center. I appreciate your extra effort, and your coming straight home, but next time I suggest you pay closer attention to instructions."

"But the food could go to the city." Nola followed her mother to the table. "There are hungry people who need to eat."

"There isn't enough to go around." Lenora didn't look up from her computer. "Besides, the outsiders can take care of themselves. They aren't our concern. They've invented enough drugs to keep themselves plenty occupied without our getting involved."

"Mom, those people out there are dying." Nola shoved her hands through her hair, feeling the dirt crumble into the dark strands. "Even the little kids, all of them are sick. Those drugs they take are the only way they can survive."

"I know that, Magnolia." Lenora lifted her hands from her computer and folded them in her lap. "The people in the city are suffering. Their lives are filled with hardship, want, and pain, which is why we have a moral obligation to help them however we can. The Charity Center is more than enough—"

"Feeding them, what, a few times a month? Each age group only goes to the Charity Center once a month, and we call that helping? That isn't enough. We have good food here you're going to get rid of. We have clean water. We have medicine that can help them. It could save their lives!"

"We don't have enough for all of them," Lenora said, her voice growing sharp. "I know it is a difficult truth to accept. But we don't have enough resources to feed everyone. The greenhouses can only produce enough uncontaminated food to feed the population of the domes."

"Then grow more." Nola paced the kitchen. "Build another greenhouse, get rid of the new tropical plants, increase food production."

"We're trying." Lenora stood and took her daughter by the shoulders, stopping her mid-step. "What do you think the Green Leaf Conference is about? We are trying to secure the future of the human race. We have to preserve our resources—"

"But what about preserving those people?" Angry tears formed in Nola's eyes.

"We're doing our best. Everyone here is working to find a way to save what's left of our planet."

"But what if the person who could figure out how to save us all is stuck out there? What if there's some kid in the city who's smart enough to figure out how to grow enough food that no one will ever be hungry again?" Tears streamed down Nola's face.

"We'll never know." Lenora picked up her napkin and wiped her daughter's face. "I know it's terrible. I wish we could feed everyone, but we can't. The domes aren't about saving this generation. The domes were built to preserve the human race—to protect our DNA and the ability to produce healthy children. So that when we find a way to get rid of the toxins in the air and the water, there will actually be healthy humans left to carry on."

"And what about the people out there dying right now?" Nola choked through her tears.

"If a life boat isn't big enough to save everyone on a ship, that doesn't mean you let all the passengers die. You save as many as you can, and you head for shore." Lenora stared into her daughter's eyes. "It is the only way."

Nola turned away. She couldn't stand to look at her mother anymore.

"Hate me if you want," Lenora said. "It's a terrible truth. But it's one we have to live with. It's the only way we can survive."

"I don't know if I can do that." Nola didn't wait for her mother to say anything. She walked back out the kitchen door, letting it slam behind her.

Rain pounded down on Bright Dome in fierce sheets, the water tinted brown in the dim light. The rain would burn everything in its wake tonight.

How acidic would rain need to be to leave marks like the ones on Desmond's skin?

Nola wanted to run out into the rain. To scream and cry and let the world burn her for living hidden from its pain for so long. To tell the outsiders there was food and medicine waiting inside the domes.

Nola walked to the gurgling fountain at the center of the dome. Its noise was barely audible over the rain that grew harder by the minute.

Nola stuck her hands into the water, washing away the dirt before splashing her face. The cold water gave her goose bumps wherever it touched her skin. It was cleaner than any of the water they had on the outside. She stood and ran to the stairs, not wanting to be near the fountain anymore. It was too lavish, too selfish.

Her feet carried her down into the tunnel before she could even think where she wanted to go.

CHAPTER FIFTEEN

The Iron Dome was near the very center of the compound, beside the atrium, directly above the barracks. All of the Outer Guard with families lived in that dome with the barracks beneath for unmarried guards. The Iron Dome and the barracks were the only residences where weapons were kept, the only place where metal could shield the glass walls in case of attack.

A guard waited at the top of the stairs to the Iron Dome.

"I'm here to see Jeremy Ridgeway," Nola said before he could ask, hoping the darkness would hide her tear-streaked face.

The guard stared at her for a moment before nodding and letting her pass without another word.

The homes were smaller here. Utilitarian units meant to house soldiers. There were no trees here that could block sight lines. Only low-lying plants were allowed in the Iron Dome. Nola's skin tingled with the feeling of being watched.

Jeremy's house sat on the outskirts of the dome. The only hint that the home belonged to the head of the Outer Guard was its being shaped like a slightly larger shoebox than the others.

Light streamed through the windows of the house, and voices came from the kitchen.

Nola ran a hand over her face as she tried to think. Captain Ridgeway wouldn't like her crying at his door this late at night. Nola crept around to the side of the house, hoping no guards would be lurking in the shadows, ready to shoot her with one of their shiny needles.

Nola knelt, tracing her fingers through the edge of the garden bed, searching for a few pebbles. Carefully, she tossed the handful of stones at Jeremy's window. Nola tensed at the faint clatter of the rocks against the glass. She held her breath, waiting in the dark.

Please don't be in the kitchen, Jeremy.

Jeremy's window slid open and he popped his head out, looking around. He smiled as his gaze found Nola. "Aren't I the one who's supposed to be throwing rocks at your window?"

"I just..." Nola began, but she didn't know why she had needed to see Jeremy, only that she hadn't known where else to go.

"Are you okay?" Jeremy asked, his tone shifting from light to concerned.

Nola shook her head.

She gasped and stumbled back as, in one swift movement, Jeremy vaulted out of his window and landed next to Nola with barely a noise.

"You've been training," Nola said, her voice shaking.

Jeremy didn't answer as he wrapped his arms around her. She laid her head against the hard muscles of his chest. She had never noticed them there before.

He's already becoming one of the elite.

Her breath caught in her throat as she began to cry again.

"Shh," Jeremy hushed, petting her hair. "You're okay. I've got you." He held her for a moment in the darkness. Both of them flinched as a barking voice carried from the kitchen.

"Come on." Jeremy threaded his fingers through Nola's, leading her away from the house to a stand of ferns near the wall of the dome. Jeremy dropped down to his knees, hiding his height in the shadows, and pulled Nola to follow.

"What's wrong?" He pushed Nola's curls away from her face. "Is your mom that upset about us?"

"Yes," Nola said before shaking her head. "She is, but that isn't what's wrong."

"Then what is it?" Jeremy took Nola's hand and pressed her palm to his lips. "You can tell me, Nola. Whatever it is, you can trust me."

Nola's mind raced back. The I-Vent, ReVamp, the break in the glass, Kieran. She could tell Jeremy everything.

You wouldn't have to be alone anymore. You wouldn't have to lie anymore.

Jeremy would understand why she couldn't stand her mother or the idea of only saving the chosen few.

"I do trust you." Nola swallowed, tightening her grip on Jeremy's hand.

Light splashed out of Jeremy's front door as five Outer Guard in full city uniform poured out of the house.

Jeremy dove to the side, pulling Nola out of the light and clamping a hand over her mouth.

They waited, frozen and silent until the group disappeared down the dark path.

Nola pulled Jeremy's hand from her mouth. "Why were there Outer Guard in full city uniform in your house?"

"My dad's their boss," Jeremy said, his voice tight.

"Guards only wear those uniforms when they leave the domes," Nola said. "Why would they be hanging out in your house like that? If they're going on patrol, they should be leaving from the barracks."

Jeremy looked to the house. The kitchen door was closed. "My dad doesn't trust the Dome Guard right now."

"Why?" Nola asked. "The Outer Guard and the Dome Guard are the same. They're just an extension of each other."

"You can't tell anyone," Jeremy said. "My dad wouldn't have told me, except I'll be in training next month. And Gentry has been going out with the patrols lately. I started figuring out something was going on."

Nola nodded.

"The Outer Guard have found a den. It's a bunch of Vampers all living underground together." Jeremy glanced back at the house. "The Dome Guard think it's not our business. That the Vampers should be able to do what they like on their side of the river. But the Outer Guard, they're out there on the street every night. The wolf packs running around are bad enough, but that many Vampers, if they decided to come after the domes…"

"We couldn't stop them."

Raina and Julian breaking through the glass. The people from the club coming in search of blood.

It would be a massacre.

"But why would they want to attack us?" Nola said.

"They don't understand what we're doing in here." Jeremy swept his hands up to the glass of the dome. "We're trying to save the world. We live trapped in here for the good of the species."

Trapped in a lifeboat while the rest of the world drowns.

"It's okay." Jeremy pulled Nola to his chest, pressing his lips to her hair. "They're close to figuring out where the den is. Once they do, the Outer Guard will go in—"

"And what?" Nola's mouth went so dry she could barely form the words.

"Neutralize the threat." Jeremy looked deep into Nola's eyes. "I won't let anyone hurt you."

Eden. Tiny little Eden couldn't hurt anyone if she tried.

"What if they don't want to hurt us," Nola whispered, her voice trembling.

"What if all they want is to survive? And they have to live underground to protect themselves?"

Jeremy leaned in, brushing his lips against Nola's. "You always want to believe in the good in the world. I think that's why I love you."

Nola forgot how to breathe as Jeremy kissed her, holding her close to his chest. Nola pushed away, falling back onto the grass, her heart racing as her body remembered she needed air.

"Jeremy—"

"Don't say anything now." He stood and reached down, pulling Nola to her feet. "I know it's a lot. But it's true. I love you, Nola." He took her hand, turning it over to kiss her wrist.

Her knees wobbled as tingles ran up her arm.

"And I can wait." Jeremy smiled. "I can wait till you're ready."

A bubble of pure joy washed away all thought. There was nothing in the world but his brown eyes and his smile meant only for her.

The lights in Jeremy's living room flicked off.

Jeremy cursed. "I have to go." He kissed Nola on the top of the head. "I'll see you in the morning."

He ran toward the house and vaulted through his window before Nola could remember why she had come to the Iron Dome.

The food.

She was angry with her mother for not wanting to share the domes' food with the people the Outer Guard were going to attack.

Nola's hands trembled as she reached for the tree pendant at her throat.

Kieran.

If the guards went into the tunnels, they would find Kieran. Nola looked up at the sky. Rain still pounded down on the glass. Did the guards already know about 5th and Nightland? How long would it take them to get there?

Keeping her eyes front, Nola walked back to the guard at the stairs. His helmet and coat hung on the wall next to him.

"Captain Ridgeway wants you at his house," Nola said. Her voice sounded far away as though someone else were speaking. "He heard someone prowling around."

The guard nodded stiffly before running toward the Ridgeway house. Grabbing the coat and helmet from the wall, Nola bolted down the stairs, not bothering to wonder what the guard would think when Captain Ridgeway told him there had been no prowler.

CHAPTER SIXTEEN

The oversize coat hung down over Nola's hands. But she would need the protection from the rain. She'd already tucked the inner glass to the side. Nola's fingers slid across the outer glass, slipping on the condensation.

"Please just move," Nola whispered. What had been such a simple plan when she took the guard's jacket now seemed impossible.

What if I can't find the tree in the rain? What if the door is locked from the other side?

Gripping the glass, she pulled with all her might, not letting up as she felt a jagged edge slice into her fingers. Finally, the glass moved and she pushed it aside, sucking on the cut. She would have to be more careful putting it back when she came home.

Nola shoved the helmet onto her head. The stench of someone else's sweat flooded her nose, overpowering the acrid scent of the night. Wrapping her hands tightly in the coat, she crawled out into the rain, twisting carefully to replace the glass before standing up and running down the hill.

She didn't bother searching for guards. She wouldn't be able to see them coming through the rain, which pounded down on her coat. She could feel the weight of each drop as it struck the fabric. She had never dreamed rain could have such weight—that each drop would have individual definition.

The sound of her breathing and the rain striking the helmet matched the pounding of her heart as she ran down the hill toward the forest.

Her heel slipped out from underneath her, and before she could try to right herself, she slid down the hill. She screamed as something struck her spine.

Digging her bare hands into the mud, she finally stopped, lying on her back. The helmet had somehow stayed on. Rain and mud smeared the visor.

Nola pushed herself up. Tears flowed from her eyes as pain shot from her spine. The skin on her hands burned from the rain. Nola wiped them on her pants, but it was no good. Her hands still stung. She looked back over her shoulder. The dim lights of the domes were barely visible.

Her bed and her shower were at the top of the hill. A doctor who could make the pain in her hands stop was at the top of the hill.

She turned back to the trees, scrambling to her feet. Her ankle throbbed as she walked into the forest. She searched the darkness for a barren tree with a slit she could climb through. But in the rain, all the trees looked the same. Nola glanced back at the domes. She had been able to see Bright Dome when she came out of the tree with Kieran. Squinting through the visor, she tried to make out which dim light was Bright Dome. It was hidden behind the Amber Dome with its wide stance and low ceiling. Nola walked left, closer to the bridge into the city, studying each tree as she went.

A shadow passed in front of her. Nola dove behind the nearest tree, pressing herself into its shadow. Her breath came in quick gasps. The Outer Guard. If they had found the tree, they would find Nightland.

If they find me...

Nola peered around the side of the tree, searching for the moving shadow. And there it was, fifty feet in front of her. The tree that hid the entrance to Nightland. Nola waited for a moment, holding her breath, searching for an Outer Guard in the night. Nothing moved.

Run, Nola, you need to run! the voice inside her head shouted, but her feet wouldn't move.

Ten seconds, Nola. Her father's voice echoed in her memory. *You get ten seconds to panic. Then you're done. That's all you're allowed.*

Nola nodded.

Ten, nine, eight, seven...

What if the Outer Guard were already through the door?

Six, five...

What if they had already found Dr. Wynne's Laboratory?

Four, three...

Kieran.

Nola ran toward the tree, ignoring the pain that shot through her back and the grip of the mud as it tried to steal her shoes. Her fingers closed around the edge of the bark as she pulled herself through the opening.

Crack!

Pain shot through her head before burning cut through her ribs. Blackness overtook her before the scream left her mouth.

CHAPTER SEVENTEEN

Her mouth tasted like dirty cotton. She tried to lick her lips, but her tongue cracked with the movement. She tried to take a breath, but pain shot through her lungs, and a cough caught in her sandpaper-like throat.

She opened her eyes. Spots danced in her vision, blocking out the scene around her. The lights in the room were bright—much, much too bright.

The medical wing. I must be in the medical wing.

But the skin on her hands still burned.

Nola tried to lift her hands to look at them; it felt like sand had filled her arms, making them too heavy to move properly. The skin on her hands was red against the white light.

"Nola," a voice breathed.

Footsteps pounded across the floor, and Dr. Wynne and Kieran hovered over her, their faces blurred.

"Nola." Kieran knelt, taking Nola's hand. The cold of his fingers soothed her skin.

"What—"

"Don't try to speak." Dr. Wynne disappeared from view, coming back with a cup in his hand. "You need to drink."

Kieran lifted Nola's head. She gasped as pain shot through her skull. "Sorry," he whispered before tipping cool liquid into Nola's mouth. It tasted metallic and stale, but it coated her throat and made it easier to breathe. Kieran sat on the bed, lifting Nola to lean against his chest before giving her more of the foul fluid.

"Where am I?" Nola asked after a few sips.

"Nightland," Kieran said.

Nola's mind raced. Back to the tree. To the pain. "But the Outer Guard. They found me."

Dr. Wynne looked at Kieran before speaking. "It wasn't the Outer Guard. It was our guard."

"Why in Hell were you wandering through the woods in a guard's uniform at night?" Kieran said, anger creeping past the concern in his voice. "They thought you were trying to break in. They almost killed you. If they hadn't recognized you, they would have."

"I had to tell you," Nola said, remembering her urgency and coughing in her haste.

Kieran lifted more water to her mouth.

"There's no time." Nola pushed the cup away. "I only have a few hours."

Kieran glanced to his father. "Nola, you've been here for two days."

The bed swayed. Her head spun, blurring the room around her.

Two days. Nola tried to reason through the words. *I've been here for two days.*

"That can't be right." Nola shook her head and the world danced in bright spots.

"Careful." Kieran steadied her as she tipped toward the edge of the bed. "We patched you up as best we could, but you need to be careful."

"They'll know I'm gone." Nola pictured her mother calling for her when she didn't come out of her room in the morning. Did she think Nola had snuck out to be with Jeremy? And Jeremy. What did he think when Nola's mother came searching for her? How long did it take them to figure out she was gone? Had she already been banished in absentia?

"Why on earth did you come out in the rain?" Dr. Wynne pressed something cold and metallic against Nola's forehead. "You could have gotten lost in the storm, or sick from the rain, you aren't used to the toxicity. And then being stabbed on top of it all."

"Stabbed?" Nola asked, remembering a searing pain in her back.

"They thought you were trying to infiltrate Nightland," Kieran said. "They didn't mean to hurt you."

"The Outer Guard." Nola pushed away from Kieran to seize Dr. Wynne's hands. "I have to talk to Emanuel. I have to see him right now."

"Why?" Dr. Wynne said. "I know it must be frightening to be away from the domes for so long, but you're safe here."

"No one is safe here." Nola twisted to throw her legs off the bed. Every muscle in her body ached. "The Outer Guard. They know about Nightland. They're trying to find a way in. They might already know how. You have to get everyone out."

Dr. Wynne and Kieran exchanged silent glances.

"I'll go," Kieran said, lifting Nola and laying her back on the bed. "Stay. Let him take care of you. I'll be right back." He disappeared behind the head of the bed, and the slam of a door shook the room a moment later.

"Well," Dr. Wynne said, sitting next to Nola's bed, "you have a concussion. But you're awake, so a good rest is all we can do for that. The knife didn't go too deep, and thankfully it missed all the really important bits or you would have bled to death before they got you to me. You've been stitched up, and I've given you everything I can to make sure you don't get an infection."

"There's a hole in me?" Nola said, bile burning her throat at the thought.

"Yes, and no." Dr. Wynne took off his glasses and cleaned them on his shirt. "I may have tried something a little... experimental."

"Experimental?"

"I needed to heal the wound as quickly as possible, and we have such limited resources." Dr. Wynne's hands fluttered through the air.

"What did you do?"

"Well, after doing as much as I could"—Dr. Wynne looked at the ceiling—"I gave you a few tiny injections of ReVamp."

Nola's heart raced as though trying to prove its lack of humanity.

"It was all very localized," Dr. Wynne added quickly. "You should have no long term effects. Your body temperature and heart rate are still very normal. And I must say the wound has healed exquisitely. Once you're rehydrated and can get up and moving, I would say you should be just fine in a few days. Maybe less. As I said, it was an experiment. And the rate of healing has been extraordinary."

"So, you didn't make me a..." Nola couldn't bring herself to say the word.

"Vampire?" Dr. Wynne shook his head. "No. Though if you hadn't woken up soon, a full injection may have been the only choice. But it seemed, under the circumstances, that your return to the domes would be infinitely more difficult if you had become a vampire."

"I don't think they'll take me back." Nola stared at her red hands. "I left. I went outside, without permission, to help vampires. I don't think that's the sort of thing the domes will take me back from."

"Don't give up hope yet," Emanuel's voice came from behind the bed.

Nola struggled to sit up, and in a moment Kieran sat beside her, supporting her weight.

"Emanuel," Nola began, the words tumbling out, "the Outer Guard. They know about Nightland. They know there's a huge group of vampires living together underground. They think you're all working together, planning to attack the domes. And they're looking for you. They want to destroy you. And they're getting closer to finding you. They could be at 5th and Nightland right now, trying to break in. You have to get everyone out of here. It's not safe anymore."

Emanuel considered Nola for a moment, his black eyes narrowed. "How do they know about Nightland?"

"I have no idea," Nola said. "But they do."

"How do you know?" Emanuel asked.

"Jeremy Ridgeway." Nola's face flushed.

Emanuel's eyes flicked to her cheeks, and more heat flooded her face.

"His father is the head of the Outer Guard," Nola said. "I saw guards coming out of his house in full uniform. I asked why, and Jeremy told me."

"Why?" Emanuel asked. "Is it common knowledge in the domes?"

"No." Nola shook her head. "Jeremy's father told him about Nightland because Jeremy is joining the Outer Guard next month. And Jeremy told me because"—Nola thought of Jeremy sitting with her in the dark—"because he trusts me."

Kieran stiffened by her side.

"And why did you come to tell us?" Emanuel turned his gaze to the ceiling. "Why did you place warning us over the trust of Jeremy?"

"Because," Nola said, balling her red, scarred hands into fists, "you are good people. It's not your fault you have to live out here. You're doing the best you can. You aren't going to attack the domes, so how could I let the guards attack you? It would be a slaughter. They have weapons—"

"We are well guarded." Emanuel knelt in front of Nola, taking her hands in his own. "We have more protection than the guards can comprehend. But knowing they are coming, we can ensure that when they arrive we can turn them away without unnecessary violence. You have saved lives in coming here, Nola. You were incredibly brave."

"Thank you." The words caught in Nola's throat.

"I will make sure you are not punished for your bravery," Emanuel said. "We will find a way to get you home."

"They won't want me."

"There may be a way. A way that will get you home and save lives in Nightland." Emanuel stood to leave. "Kieran, please see that she has food and fresh clothing. I'll go speak to the others and see what we can think up to save our hero." He nodded to Nola and left.

"I'll be right back," Kieran said, gently squeezing Nola's hand before following Emanuel.

"Well," Dr. Wynne said after a long moment. "Let's check your bandages, shall we?" He pushed his glasses up on his nose. "Lean forward."

It wasn't until that moment Nola realized she wasn't wearing her own clothes. She had been changed into an old hospital gown. It was worn, soft, and tattered around the edges.

Nola winced as Dr. Wynne pulled the sticky bandage from her skin.

"Hmmm," Dr. Wynne murmured as he ran his fingers across her back.

"What?" Nola asked. "Is it infected? Am I becoming a vampire?"

"Not a bit," Dr. Wynne said. "It's even better than I expected."

Nola pushed herself to her feet, tottering for a moment before stumbling to the cracked mirror in the corner of the room. Pulling the robe down over her shoulder, she twisted to see her back in the mirror.

"Careful," Dr. Wynne warned. "You don't want to tear anything that's newly mended."

Then her eyes found it. A red, raised, jagged mark three inches long right under her left shoulder blade.

"You're very lucky you were wearing the guard's coat. Otherwise the knife would have penetrated your lungs. And that"—Dr. Wynne spread his hands —"would have been a very different story."

"It looks like it happened months ago," Nola said, trying to touch the mark.

"She shouldn't be standing," Kieran said as he came back through the door, balancing a plate on top of a pile of clothes.

"I feel better standing." Nola studied her face in the mirror. She looked pale, like she hadn't slept for days, but otherwise healthy. The only marks on her were the scar on her back and the red of her hands.

"You should feel better the more you move." Dr. Wynne smiled. "I gave you another tiny bit of ReVamp this morning." He waved away the frightened look on Nola's face. "You needed it to heal. And as I said, no lasting effects. And the more the drug is circulated, the better you'll recover."

"That's remarkable." Nola rubbed her fingers over the tight red skin on her hands.

"It seemed a bit much," Dr. Wynne said, his brows furrowed, "to give you localized ReVamp injections in your hands just to fix the inflamed skin. The chance for infection is so small, it's really only cosmetic damage, and they can mend that in the domes."

If I ever get back into the domes.

"Thank you." She pushed her face into a smile. "Thank you for saving my life. ReVamp...what it can do is amazing. We don't have anything that can do this in the domes."

"You need to eat," Kieran said, pulling out the desk chair and setting down the plate of food.

"Right." Nola swallowed the lump in her throat. Her stomach rumbled at the sight of food. She hadn't eaten since the domes.

She looked down at the food on the plate. Some sort of chopped vegetables she had never seen before lay next to a hunk of bread and a small bit of meat.

"I know it's not what you're used to," Kieran said, handing Nola a fork as she sat down at the desk, "but it's not bad."

"But will," Nola said, glancing between Kieran and Dr. Wynne, "will it make me sick?"

"This is good food," Dr. Wynne said. "It's the best we have."

"I'm sorry," Nola said. "I didn't mean—"

"It would take years for you to get sick from this," Kieran said. "It may not be dome-pure, but Nightland spends a lot of time finding the best soil we can. We work hard to keep the irrigation water clean. This is better than anything you'll get on the streets."

"Thank you," Nola said. "For sharing." She took a bite of the vegetables, trying not to wrinkle her nose at the metallic taste of the food.

"That's the ReVamp." Dr. Wynne perched on the edge of the desk. "The unfortunate taste should dissipate as you metabolize more food. The meals here really aren't that bad."

"Why do vampires grow food?" Nola choked down another bite.

"For the kids," Kieran said. "For the people in the city who don't have anything to eat."

"Vampires feed people?"

"The ones in Nightland do," Kieran said. "Emanuel doesn't want to keep everyone in Nightland forever."

Dr. Wynne stood, clapping his hands together. "I'm sure Emanuel will be back any minute with a plan to get Nola out of here, and she should be dressed." He walked out of the room, holding the door open for Kieran to follow.

"I'll be right back," Kieran said.

The door shut behind them, leaving Nola alone. She took a bite of the bread, hoping the tinny taste would be different. It wasn't.

She picked up the clothes that had been left for her. Thick black pants and a stitched-together black leather top. Both were worn and patched in places.

Nola dug the heel of her hand into her forehead. She was alive, that was good. They wanted to get her back to the domes, also good. Dr. Wynne was hiding something from her. Badly. Not so good.

CHAPTER EIGHTEEN

S he pulled on the clothes without letting herself consider the rough texture of the leather against her bare skin. They had been made for someone larger than her, with muscle and curves Nola lacked.

A knock sounded on the door.

"Are you dressed yet?" Kieran called.

"Yes?" Nola said tentatively, staring at her pale face and leather-clad body in the mirror.

I look like I belong in Nightland.

Kieran came in, not bothering to suppress his laugh as he saw her.

"Thanks." Nola grimaced, taking another bite of the bread and instantly regretting it as the metallic taste flooded her mouth.

"You look great." Kieran ran a hand through his hair. "Just not like you. It's going to take them a while to figure things out. Emanuel has a grand plan, but they still have to iron out the details."

"What kind of grand plan?" Nola pushed the food around her plate, searching for an appetizing bite.

"Emanuel doesn't usually share his plans with me," Kieran said, his face darkening for a moment, "but I trust him."

"What were you saying before, about Emanuel wanting to get people out of Nightland?" Nola looked into Kieran's eyes, seeking a real answer.

"Nothing."

"Then why did your father make you leave?"

Kieran grinned. "You know him so well."

Nola waited in silence.

"There's a lot of land, other places away from the domes," Kieran whispered, his words flowing more quickly as he spoke. "There are places where the soil isn't as bad. Where there isn't a polluted river in the backyard. The domes were built here because they needed the city for laborers. But they abandoned the city as soon as the domes were ready. Why should we sit here waiting to die if there's something better out there?" He stretched his arms to the sky through the dirt above them.

"Why didn't your father want me to know?"

"Emanuel doesn't want the domes to know." Anger crept into his voice. "He's worried they won't want us to build a good place of our own."

"Aboveground?"

"For Eden," Kieran said. "The vampires can't stay in the light."

"But the food," Nola asked. "Do you grow it underground?"

"I was sort of hoping you'd ask." Kieran's eyes gleamed with excitement. "I think you'll be amazed with what we've done." He stood, walking toward the door before reaching a hand back to Nola. "Come with me?"

Nola stood and took his hand, not caring where he led her.

They were in the same part of Nightland where she had seen Eden. They passed the kitchen, but the little girl with the big brown eyes was nowhere to be seen.

"Eden," Nola asked as they slipped into the gallery, "is she—"

"She's fine." Kieran beamed. "The medicine helped. She can breathe now. I actually had to chase her this morning. We had a hard time keeping her out of your room."

"Why?"

He led her out into the tunnel and in the direction of 5th and Nightland.

"You're her hero, Nola," Kieran said, stopping and turning to face Nola so quickly she ran into him. "Literally. You saved her life." He ran a finger over her cheek. "You are braver than even I imagined." He turned and continued walking down the hall. "And now you've come to save all of us."

"The Outer Guard," Nola said as Kieran pushed through a heavy metal door and into a narrower tunnel. The low ceiling left only a few inches of clearance over Kieran's head. "Emanuel may think they can't get into Nightland, but they could. They're..." She searched for a less cowardly word than *terrifying*. "You know them. They aren't like everyone else in the domes. If they decide to come in here, they won't stop because they're destroying your home."

"Or killing people," Kieran growled. "I know. *We* know. But they don't know us. And when they try to come after us, they'll see. This isn't their city. It's ours."

They walked in silence for a moment, the tunnel becoming narrower and the lights dimmer. Sweat beaded on Nola's palms, burning the raw skin. She could feel the anger radiating from Kieran, overpowering her panic at being in the tunnel. He stopped at a dead end. Crumbling concrete and dirt had caved in the wall in front of them.

"What happened?" Nola asked. "Did a cave-in cover the garden?"

"We found our own way up." Kieran pointed at the ceiling above him to a narrow hole and a thin metal ladder. "You first."

Nola reached above her head to the ladder, but this was more than climbing out her window or even up the vent. Her fingers only grazed the bottom of the first rung.

Kieran's hands closed around her waist, and he lifted her up over his head. Nola grabbed for the ladder, gasping. "Thanks." Her arms shook, and the skin on her palms stung as she began to climb.

With a ringing *thunk* that shook the ladder, she felt Kieran launch himself onto the bottom rung. She closed her eyes for a moment, taking a breath before continuing to climb. Soon, even the dim light from the tunnel had disappeared. Nola groped the air in front of her, feeling for each rung to pull herself up.

"How far up are we going?" she asked after a few minutes when her muscles burned in protest.

"About 124 rungs," Kieran answered.

"Was I supposed to be counting?" Nola puffed.

"Nope," Kieran said, adding slowly, "but you should start watching your head... now."

Nola froze, waiting for something to swoop out of the blackness at her face.

"Reach up," Kieran's voice drifted through the darkness.

Hesitantly, Nola reached one hand overhead. Cold, flat metal blocked the path above her. She pushed, and the metal lifted easily, letting in a flood of outside air and the faint glow of the moon through the haze of the city. Giving the door a heave, she flipped it open with a loud *clang*, then climbed out into the night and onto a roof high above the city.

Rows of plants stretched out in front of her. Scraps of every kind had been used to make raised beds for the garden. A row of beans was surrounded by planks of an old painted sign for *The Freshest Oxygen Bar in Town*. An apple tree grew in the broken bed of a truck. Rows of melons sprouted from the base of an old shipping container.

"How?" Nola breathed, running her fingers along the leaves of a plant. The texture was perfect. No damage from the acid rain, no signs of blight.

"It takes a lot." Kieran leapt onto the edge of the old truck and pulled a red apple down from the tree. "We had to get miles away to find soil that wasn't contaminated by the old factories. It took a few months to find the right spot.

By then, we had found enough planting containers, though getting them up here was a chore. We had to make sure none of the Outer Guard saw us hauling old truck beds up the side of the building."

"But they could have helped." Nola leaned in close to the apple tree and smelled the earth. The scent was different from the dirt in the domes, less pungent in its fertility, but still clean and fruitful. Free from the chemicals that flowed through the river.

"I don't think they want to help vampires." Kieran tossed the apple to Nola. "Even if the vampires are growing food for starving kids."

Nola ran her thumb along the smooth red skin of the apple. "But the forest, the trees there are dying from the rain. The chemicals burn them."

"These plants aren't watered with rain. Stay here." Kieran ran down the rows of strange planters.

Nola held the apple up to the moonlight. The fruit didn't match the size of those grown inside the glass, and the skin lacked the luscious, vibrant color expected of Lenora Kent's crops. It couldn't match the perfection of the domes.

This food can still save people's lives.

Nola looked out over the city. Only one building stood taller than the garden, blocking the light of the domes from view as though her home didn't exist at all.

The *buzz* of a rope being pulled quickly came from the direction where Kieran had disappeared. An odd flapping sound pounded all around the roof as long sheets of fabric unfurled from the sides of the plant beds. Hung from wires so dark Nola hadn't noticed them before, the cloth rose up high, floating into the sky like sails before, with a shuddering *whine*, they all turned at once, making a patchwork of fabric that covered the whole roof.

Before Nola could really begin to think through what she had just seen, Kieran had returned to her side.

Nola moved her mouth for a moment, searching for the right words.

"I designed it." Kieran beamed. "It took Desmond and Bryant a long time to find the material, but it works."

"How?" Nola gaped.

"The material is waterproof and coated against the rain. It's what the old triage tents were made of, back when there were doctors on the outside. They scavenged all of this, and then we built the pulley system. We put the fabric up to keep off the midday sun and any rain, but the rest of the time, we leave it open."

"But the water?" Nola climbed up onto the truck bed to feel the fabric. It was light and thin, but coated in something that felt rubbery, like the Outer Guard's jackets.

"The rain runs off of the tent and into a filtration system." Kieran shoved his hands into his pockets, looking every bit the proud genius Nola had known him to be. "It's rudimentary, but it gets the water for Nightland and for the plants clean enough to be used. And this is just one rooftop. If we could find the materials to farm on other roofs, we could feed the city. And if we could take all this with us, we could build a home somewhere without the smog of the factories and the stink from the river." Kieran grabbed Nola around the waist, sweeping her into his arms. "We could help people, really help them."

His dark eyes stared into hers, his gaze so intense she flushed and looked away.

"It's brilliant." Nola tucked her hair behind her ears and took a step away from Kieran.

"And it's all because of you," Kieran said. "All that studying in botanicals your mother was always making you do. It gave me the idea. I came up with the plan and built the pulley system. My dad did the chemical testing and pretty much everyone else in Nightland helped with the rest."

"And the guards never noticed?"

"We're still here." Kieran shrugged. He lifted Nola's hand that held the apple up in front of her. "Take a bite."

Carefully, Nola bit into the apple. Her teeth pierced the skin, and juice flowed into her mouth. Through the bitter metal tinge of the ReVamp, she could taste the sweetness of the fruit. "It's amazing," she whispered. "It's real food."

Kieran smiled. "I know."

Nola held out the apple for Kieran to take a bite.

"No, it's for you." Kieran shook his head, his gaze fixed on the juice dripping onto Nola's finger.

"But it's wonderful." Nola took a step toward him. "You should enjoy the fruits of your labor."

"No." The light of the moon caught the corner of his eyes. No color broke through the shadows. Only black where emerald green should have been.

Pain ripped through Nola's chest as the apple tumbled from her hand. "Kieran, you're a vampire."

CHAPTER NINETEEN

"Nola," Kieran said, reaching toward her.

Nola took a step back. Pain shot through her leg as something sharp cut into her calf. She didn't dare look away from Kieran as warm blood trickled down her ankle.

"Nola, you're hurt." Kieran stepped forward.

"Don't touch me." Nola felt for the truck bed behind her. She stepped sideways, gasping in pain as she put weight on her leg.

"Let me help you." Pain flooded Kieran's eyes. "Nola, I would never hurt you."

"You're a vampire," Nola spat.

"So, is Emanuel—"

"That's different."

"And Raina, and Desmond. You came out here to save vampires."

"But not you!" Nola shouted. "You weren't supposed to be like them." Tears streamed down her face.

"Why?" Kieran asked. "Why does it matter?"

"You drink blood?" Nola's voice quaked.

"Yes."

Nola choked on a sob.

"But not human blood, never human blood." Kieran took a step forward.

Nola tried to run, but her leg gave out under her, sending her tumbling to her knees.

"Nola," Kieran whispered.

She could hear his heart breaking as he said her name.

"I've never attacked a human," he said, his voice cold and dead. "I only drink animal blood."

Images of Kieran sucking the life from a poor animal's neck seized Nola's mind.

"We have a farm for the animals," Kieran said. "It's no different from eating meat."

"Yes it is." Nola tried to stand, but her leg couldn't bear any weight. "I thought you were trying to save the vampires. Find a way to make them human."

"You can't go back," Kieran said. "Once you're a vampire, the change is permanent. Either inject the Vamp or die. It's a one-way trip, Nola."

Nola sobbed on the ground. Kieran's green eyes were gone.

I'll never see them again.

"I had no choice," Kieran said. "I was running out of time."

"What?"

"After three months out here, I got sick," Kieran said. "I had been giving out food, there was a cough going around. It didn't do anything that bad to most people. But I didn't have the same immunities. After a few days, I couldn't breathe. My dad didn't know what to do. He had been working on a new kind of Vamp. One that didn't change people's personalities. It wasn't ready, but he didn't have a choice. I was drowning. Drowning in my own body. I was terrified. I was dying."

He knelt next to Nola, and she didn't back away.

"He gave me a small injection of ReVamp like he did for you, trying to get the disease out of me, but it didn't work. He had to give me a full dose. It felt like my lungs were on fire. I thought I would boil in my own skin. Then my lungs filled with ice. And then my whole body was filled with ice. I was sure I would freeze to death. But eventually, I stopped shaking, and I got used to the cold. It took a few days, but I woke up." Kieran looked into Nola's eyes. "I'm the first of the new vampires."

Nola looked down at Kieran's hand in hers. She hadn't realized she had reached for him. His cold skin sent chills up her arm.

"Does it feel different? Touching me?" Nola said.

"I can feel the blood flowing through your veins like lava," Kieran said. "But the heat doesn't hurt."

"They said in the domes that vampires hunt people, that they attack them and drink their blood."

"The ones on the streets do," Kieran said. "But not in Nightland. They only take blood they pay for."

"Pay for?"

"There are desperate people in the city," Kieran said. "They sell their blood to vampires. But most of us take the blood from the farm animals."

"So, even though—" Nola glanced down at her bloody leg, her wanting to know warring with her fear of Kieran.

"I can smell your blood," Kieran said before she could speak. "It smells sweet."

"I smell like candy?"

"A little. But I'm still me. And you know me, Nola. You know I would never hurt you. I would do anything to protect you."

Nola nodded, not trusting her voice.

Kieran placed his hand on Nola's cheek. A tingle ran down her spine, leaving goose bumps in its wake.

"We should get you back to my dad," Kieran said. "I think you need stitches."

"I don't know about that ladder," Nola said. "I can't even walk."

"Do you trust me?" Kieran grinned mischievously.

He looked like the old Kieran. Her Kieran, who she knew better than anyone, planning something that would scare and excite her. The Kieran who had taught her to climb onto her roof. The Kieran who would save a city with a garden.

"Absolutely."

In one swift movement, Kieran lifted Nola onto his back. "Hold on tight." He ran to the open trap door.

"You can't carry me all the way down," Nola said as Kieran twisted onto the ladder, taking two steps down and shutting them into the darkness.

"Just trust me, Nola," Kieran said before taking both hands off the ladder and launching them into the void.

The air rushing past them stole the scream from Nola's throat. Kieran laughed as they sped through the darkness.

Nola tightened her grip, holding onto Kieran with every bit of strength she had. And just when she began to fear the ground, Kieran landed as light as a cat on the tunnel floor.

Gently, he pried Nola's arms from his neck, pulling her around to cradle her as though she weighed nothing.

"I told you to trust me." Kieran smiled.

"Mmmmhmmm," was the only noise Nola could manage as she pulled herself closer to Kieran's chest.

Kieran pressed his cheek to her hair, rocking her gently for a moment.

"I didn't mean to scare you," he said.

"Of course you did. You always liked to scare me." Nola let go of his neck and smacked him on the chest. "But I'm not mad. It's nice to know—" Nola paused for a moment, searching for the right words. His heartbeat pounded through his chest and into her hand. Its rhythm beat slower than hers, pumping the cold blood through his body in a rhythm she didn't recognize. "It's nice to know your sense of humor hasn't changed."

Kieran beamed down at her. "Never. I'm still me, Nola. Just me with super strength... and a different appetite."

His smile disappeared, and his eyes begged her to understand.

"You're Kieran," Nola said. "You're still my Kieran."

He leaned down and brushed his lips against hers. The cold of his touch tingled her skin.

"I will always be yours," he whispered.

A door rasped open down the hall. Kieran cursed under his breath. "We need to get you back to my dad."

"It's not bleeding that badly." She didn't want to go back to the others. Back to the worn hospital gown and cold tools. If she could just stay here with Kieran for a few minutes.

"It's bad enough." Kieran walked down the tunnel.

Nola felt his muscles tensing as though he were preparing for a fight.

"I don't want to freak you out, but the other vampires will scent your blood."

"Scent my blood?" Nola looked down at her red-stained leg.

"You smell like fresh baked brownies," Kieran said, his voice tight.

"Do you need to leave me here?" Nola's voice came out as a squeak.

"I told you before, I would never bite a human." Kieran rounded the corner.

A dark shape waited for them in front of the door to the main corridor.

"But some of our people are recovering human biters," Kieran said. "We don't want them to relapse."

"What happened to her?" a deep voice called from the shadow.

"Cut her leg," Kieran said, his voice steady and calming as though he were trying to soothe a frightened animal. "I'm taking her up to my father now." Kieran took a step forward. "You know my father. Dr. Wynne."

"ReVamp." The man leaned out of the shadows. The scars covering his face twisted as he frowned. "He made ReVamp."

"Yes," Kieran said. "Have you had ReVamp?"

"I turned long before the good doctor decided to save us all." The long white scars cut through his skin as though something had clawed his face over and over again.

"Then you are one of the strongest to have joined Nightland," Kieran said, still walking forward. "It takes a special vampire to understand how we must change to survive."

"I did change to survive." The man tossed his bald head back, displaying more scars coating his neck. "I changed because my lungs were rotting. I came down here to be safe from the Outer Guard."

"Nightland is about more than being safe from the guards," Kieran said. "Nightland is about hope. It's about creating a better future."

"Nightland is about rules." The man took a step forward. "It's about protecting one man's vision while the rest of us hide underground."

"We aren't hiding," Kieran said.

Nola clung tighter to Kieran's neck as he shifted her weight in his arms.

"Every night we are working to make things better," Kieran said.

"Better for the ones who haven't been turned."

"Better for all of us." Kieran had stopped moving forward.

"Then why won't you let us eat?" the man roared.

Nola flew from Kieran's arms, landing on the ground behind him, knocking the wind from her. The thumping of fists on flesh came from behind her. The sharp crack of breaking bones and muffled yells echoed through the tunnel. Pain shot through her as she gasped, forcing air back into her lungs.

She rolled onto her side, trying to see who had been hit, but they were moving too quickly for her to know if either was hurt. The man lifted Kieran, tossing him into the wall with a sickening *crunch*. Dust from the ceiling fell into Nola's eyes as the walls trembled.

The man took Kieran's head, slamming it back into the wall.

"No!" Nola screamed.

The man turned to her. His eyes were pitch black. He opened his mouth, hissing and showing two long, bright white fangs.

CHAPTER TWENTY

The vampire ran his tongue along the sharp tip of his left fang, coloring its point with his own blood.

Nola watched in horror as the vampire's blood dripped down his chin, making him look more animal than human.

"Leave her alone." Kieran launched himself onto the man's neck, sending him face first into the dirt. He grabbed the man's head, slamming it into the ground again and again until the man's screams of rage stopped.

Kieran let go of the man, standing up and jumping over the blood pooling on the dirt floor.

He reached down to Nola. Red coated his palms.

Nola tried to reach for him, but she couldn't make her arms move. The crimson pool seeped toward her.

"Nola," Kieran whispered. "He was going to kill you."

The man's bloody fangs flashed through Nola's mind as tears ran down her cheeks.

"He'll wake up in a few hours," Kieran said. "But I'll make sure Raina's found him before then."

"He's dead." Nola's voice cracked.

"He's a vampire. He'll heal. But I won't let him hurt you. Not ever." Kieran reached down for Nola again. "Can I touch you?"

Nola nodded, clinging to Kieran as soon as she was in his arms. She buried her face in his chest, squeezing her eyes shut as Kieran leapt over the man's body. She could feel the uneven pounding of the floor under Kieran's feet and the air flying past them and knew he was running. She wanted to look, to watch the tunnels fly by, seeing them as Kieran did. But she kept her eyes closed, afraid if she opened them, another pair of bloody fangs would be waiting.

Soon, Kieran slowed to a walk.

A door *clicked* open in front of them.

"What happened?" a voice with a lilting accent said.

Nola opened her eyes, and Julian was staring at her, his face tense. They were in the gallery. Julian held an open book in his hand.

"She cut her leg in the garden," Kieran said, not stopping his stride as Julian joined them. "I was trying to get her back here, and we were attacked."

"Someone thought she was a dinner bell, eh?" Julian said. "Did you kill them?"

Kieran shook his head. "Just smashed his head in. He'll wake up in a bit. He's in the last tunnel on the way to the garden."

"I'll get Raina." Julian held open the door to Emanuel's home before leaving them and walking back out through the gallery.

"What's Raina going to do to him?" Nola asked.

"Nothing more than he deserves," Kieran said.

The old woman in the kitchen looked up as they passed but didn't try to follow.

"What's going to happen?" Panic clenched Nola's chest.

"Raina will execute him," Kieran said. "We all make the deal when we choose to live in Nightland. No violence within these walls. No attacking humans. No attacking each other. That man is a monster. We can't keep him here. We can't let him out in the world, or he'll leave a string of bodies behind him, and we can't give him to the Outer Guard—"

"Or he'll tell them exactly where to find us," Nola said as Kieran swung open the door to Dr. Wynne's lab.

"What on Earth?" Dr. Wynne said, pushing up his glasses as he stared at Nola. "Was she stabbed again?"

"No, she cut her leg." Kieran lay Nola down on the cold metal table. "The apple tree truck."

"And your hand," Dr. Wynne said, glancing at Kieran as he cut away the bottom of Nola's pants, exposing the jagged gash.

Nola's stomach turned at the sight of her own ragged flesh.

"Broken," Kieran said. "Foot, too."

"What?" Nola tried to sit up on the table to look at Kieran, but he grabbed her shoulder, holding her down.

"Do you need it set?" Dr. Wynne asked, seemingly unconcerned by his son's broken bones.

Kieran flexed his hand and stomped his foot a few times. "Just the hand."

"Pardon me, Nola," Dr. Wynne said, disappearing behind Nola's head. There was silence for a moment, and then a sharp *crack* and a muffled groan.

"Thanks," Kieran said, coming around to Nola's side, keeping his right hand by his chest and gripping Nola's hand with the left.

"Are you all right?" Nola asked.

Dr. Wynne fluttered around the laboratory, gathering tools.

"Fine." Kieran smiled down at Nola, only the corners of his eyes betraying any pain. "It'll be healed in an hour or so. One of the vampire perks."

"Speaking of vampire perks," Dr. Wynne said, placing a tray of tools next to Nola, "I'm afraid your food is going to be distasteful for longer than anticipated. I can stitch you back together, but you've lost a fair bit of blood, and with the rust and filth on that truck bed, the risk for infection is too significant. I'm going to stitch you back together and give you another localized dose of ReVamp."

Dr. Wynne raised a hand as Kieran began to protest. "She will be at no risk of being changed, but I don't think her mother would like her returned to the domes sans a leg."

"You're sure it won't change her?" Kieran asked. "Dad, you have to be sure."

"I am quite sure." Dr. Wynne picked up a threaded needle. "ReVamp will only affect the brain and circulatory system if it is injected directly into the blood stream. Think of this as a localized anesthetic."

Kieran opened his mouth to argue again, but Dr. Wynne waved him away. "You must trust me, Kieran. I did invent the stuff after all." He turned to Nola. "You might want to take a deep breath, dear, I have nothing to numb you with."

Nola squeezed Kieran's hand, shutting her eyes tight as the needle pierced her leg.

Her stomach seized at the tugging of the thread pulling through her skin.

"Prison," Nola said through gritted teeth, searching for something to distract her from the nauseating sensation of her flesh being violated by a needle and thread. "The man who attacked us, why can't he go to vampire prison?"

"There's no such thing as vampire prison," Kieran said with a touch of laughter in his voice.

The needle pierced Nola's leg again, and she redoubled her grip on Kieran's hand. "But we're underground. With all the tunnels, why can't you make a prison? Then you could lock him up instead of just killing him."

"We barely have the resources to keep Nightland safe from the outside," Dr. Wynne said, his voice low and slow as he continued to work on Nola's leg. "And if the Outer Guard really are going to try to break in, well, we can't afford to have people guarding someone who attempted to kill a Nightland guest."

"Put him in a steel room and deliver him meals," Nola said, trying hard not to think of the fact that *she* had nearly been the vampire's meal.

"He's a vampire, Nola," Kieran said, stroking her hair as she bit her lip, trying not to pull away from the pain.

There was the *tink* of metal on metal and the sound of footsteps walking away.

"If we left him alone, he could try and dig his way out or tear through the stone," Kieran said. "There aren't many things an angry vampire can't break through given enough time. And we only have enough of that kind of metal for the door to the outside. There isn't a way for us to lock him up."

"Silver doors all around?" Nola said.

Kieran chuckled. "Vampires can touch silver."

"So, it's not like the sun allergy *going to get lots of blisters and die* type thing?" Nola asked as Dr. Wynne's footsteps returned.

"Well," Dr. Wynne said, "I wouldn't recommend wearing silver as some irritation can occur. A bit of discoloration and some nasty swelling in rare cases, but if you're afraid of a vampire, I wouldn't suggest trying to kill them with a silver cross. It could take hours for him to be bothered with it at all. This will sting a bit."

A needle pierced Nola's skin again. Pure ice poured into her flesh, freezing the wound on her leg. Nola groaned as cold unlike anything she'd ever felt before seared her skin.

Keep breathing. You have to keep breathing.

Opening her eyes, she glanced down at her leg. The skin around the wound had become stark white, while the cut itself turned a violent red.

"Don't watch it," Kieran said, taking Nola's face in his hands and turning her to look into his eyes. "It's better if you don't watch it."

Nola let out a deep, shuddering breath. "What about stakes through the heart? Is that true? Should there be a ban on wood in Nightland?"

"If you destroy a vampire's heart, he will die," Dr. Wynne said.

The sound of metal instruments being laid on a metal tray came from the end of the table, but Nola didn't look away from Kieran.

The ice in her leg had changed now, from something stagnant to something squirming as though worms crawled under her skin.

"It's about the only thing a vampire can't heal from," Dr. Wynne continued. "Well that," he paused, "and decapitation. But I see hardly any of that in here. It is very hard to cut an entire head off without meaning to. And if you meant to cut a person's head off, I don't know why you'd bother bringing them to me for help. At that point, it's really a matter of hiding the body where it won't smell too terribly and the Outer Guard won't find it. I suppose that's what makes the river so popular for those things. But there must be lots of other choices—"

"Thanks, Dad." Kieran cut his father off just as Nola began to wonder how many bodies had been dumped in the river and if there were any bones left or if the toxicity was so high everything had been eaten away.

"You can sit up now," Dr. Wynne said, pushing himself backwards on his rolling stool.

Nola opened her eyes a crack to look at her leg. The squirming had stopped. Now it felt like someone was holding a bag of particularly cold ice on her calf. The skin around the cut was still pale, but the cut itself was what made Nola sit up to examine her leg more closely.

There were twelve stitches in her leg, holding together a cut that looked to be at least a few days old. Shiny new skin had bridged the gap between the two ragged sides.

"The stitches will make sure everything heals in the right place, and the scarring should be minimal," Dr. Wynne said, his brow furrowed and lips pinched as though afraid Nola might not approve of his handiwork.

"That's incredible." Nola poked the cut before Kieran lifted her hand away. "If they had this in the domes—"

"They'd never use it," Dr. Wynne said. "ReVamp alters you at a genetic level. Not badly for you. In a week, you won't notice you were ever injected. Still, the whole point of the domes is to preserve a genetically healthy human race. ReVamp changes the way DNA works. It alters your body at the most basic level. Why do you think they despise the vampires so much?"

"Because all the ones they deal with are violent." Nola's voice rose in excitement. "If you could show them this—"

"Then they'd still kill us all if they had the chance," Raina said as she slunk into the room. "A drug is a drug, impure genes are impure genes, and a vampire is a vampire. They don't see differences. It's all black and white, and they don't give a shit how many of us die out here."

Nola opened her mouth to argue, but Raina held up a finger.

"Please don't fight me on things you don't understand, little girl. You'll make me sorry I didn't manage to stab you through the heart."

"You're the one that stabbed me?" Nola said, looking at the knife tucked into Raina's belt.

Raina followed her gaze. "Did you expect me to throw my knife away in remorse? You were sneaking around."

Nola opened her mouth to explain, but Raina cut her off with the wave of a hand.

"I know you were coming to save us from the big, bad guards. And I do appreciate the sentiment. But the way I see it, it wasn't my fault you were in a very bad place at the wrong time, and I did lend you some of my very fine old clothes. And since you'll apparently be needing to borrow yet another pair of pants, as you can't seem to keep from bleeding all over the place even if I didn't cause it, I would say we're pretty even."

"Pants versus stab wound," Kieran said, one dark eyebrow raised. "That's a rough trade to call."

"It's a cold, cruel world. You take what you can get." Raina glared at Nola. "We're good, right?"

Nola nodded. "We're good."

"Excellent." Raina flashed a smile that made Nola more nervous than the knife had. "Because we've figured out a way to get you home. And any trust issues could definitely get a few people killed."

Nola looked to Kieran who gave the slightest shrug.

"Emanuel wants us all to meet in the gallery." Raina turned back toward the door.

"It must be a grand plan if he wants us in the gallery," Dr. Wynne said, moving over to a sink in the corner to wash his hands. "He always likes to make big announcements in there."

Kieran took Nola's hand and helped her off the table. Her leg still felt shaky as she put pressure on it, but the unbearable pain and terrible weakness had gone.

"Thank you, Dr. Wynne," she said, taking his hand in hers as he moved for the door. His skin was warm to the touch.

"Of course, dear." Dr. Wynne smiled. "You are family. And, well, it is my job, I suppose."

"I'll help her." Kieran wrapped an arm around Nola's waist. "You go on ahead."

"Your dad," Nola whispered as soon as Dr. Wynne was in the hall, "he hasn't taken ReVamp, has he?"

"No. He hasn't needed it yet. He had more immunities than I did from sneaking in and out so much, and he doesn't think people should take it unless they have no other choice. How did you know?"

"His hands are still warm," Nola said, sinking into the cold of Kieran's hand cutting through the leather that separated their skin. "And his eyes are still green, like yours used to be."

"Very observant," Kieran said as they walked into the hall, him supporting most of Nola's weight. "He'll have to take it soon, though."

"What wrong with him?"

"He's started losing weight. He can't focus. He goes on tangents even worse than usual."

"Maybe being underground is getting to him," Nola said. "Maybe, if he got out—"

"He's too valuable," Kieran said. "They won't let him go where they can't protect him."

"Even if he wants to?" Nola stopped walking and nearly toppled over as Kieran continued forward.

"This is about saving people, thousands of people. He understands that," Kieran said. "He's starting to show signs of toxicity poisoning. If he takes ReVamp, he'll get better. And when we get out of Nightland, he'll get all the fresh air he wants."

Kieran pushed through the heavy, wooden door into the gallery.

Bryant and Desmond sat stone-faced on one of the large couches. Raina sat next to Dr. Wynne while Julian leaned on a bookshelf, and all of their eyes were fixed on Emanuel who stood in the center of it all.

"Nola." Emanuel spread his arms to her. "I see you've recovered nicely from your accident."

"Yes," Nola said, suddenly aware that everyone's attention had shifted to her. "Dr. Wynne is brilliant, and the garden was amazing."

"I'm glad you appreciate what we are trying to accomplish here"—Emanuel's brief smile vanished—"as I am afraid we need to ask for your help once again."

CHAPTER TWENTY-ONE

"What kind of help?" Nola asked, resisting as Kieran tried to guide her to a chair.

Emanuel paced across the carpet. "The only way to get you home is for the domes to believe you were brought here against your will. If we are operating under the guise that vampires broke into the domes and kidnapped you, then, and I mean no offense, we must also maintain that we wish to give you back. I am sure we can all agree it would be a very unlikely story that we in Nightland kidnapped sweet Nola and she managed to escape us and arrive home undamaged."

The group in the room nodded.

After a reluctant moment, Nola nodded, too. "I don't think I could escape a few hundred vampires in an underground lair alive."

"Good." Emanuel's shoulders relaxed. "We've contacted the domes and informed them of your kidnapping and made our ransom demand."

"What did you ask for?" Nola's said.

If the domes have to give something vital, it could put the whole system in danger. The life boat could sink, and it would be my fault.

"We asked for things that will be very valuable to us and can be easily replaced by the domes," Emanuel said. "Common seeds of plants that no longer grow on the outside. A few doses of medicine for the children. Nothing the domes will even miss."

Nola nodded.

"We've asked them to meet us on the bridge tomorrow, an hour before dawn," Emanuel continued. "That should make them feel secure while giving us ample time to get back underground. By daybreak, you'll be cozy in the domes, and Kieran will have some new seeds for the garden."

"But if they think you broke in and kidnapped me, won't that give the Outer Guard a reason to come after you?" Nola asked.

"They don't need a reason to come after us," Desmond said. "They'll come no matter what we do."

"And you have to be back in the domes when the Outer Guard bang on our door." Raina's hand rested on the hilt of her knife as though expecting the Outer Guard to run into the gallery as they spoke.

Nola reached for Kieran's hand. "But what will I tell them when they ask me what happened?"

"That's where I come in," Julian said. "We've worked it all out so you can give them enough details to be believable without telling them anything that could endanger Nightland. I'll coach you on all of it. Dr. Wynne and Kieran won't be involved. As far as the Outer Guard will know, we broke through the glass in Bright Dome to get you."

"They'll seal it," Nola said. The squirming knot of fear in her stomach disappeared, leaving her hollow. "I won't be able to get back out."

"I think," Dr. Wynne said, looking down at his hands, "that will probably be for the best."

"You almost died out here, Nola," Kieran said, turning to face her. "Next time, you might not make it through the woods."

"So, I'll just never see you again?" Nola's voice was tight, higher than usual. "I'll just go back to the domes—"

"And live the life you're meant to have," Dr. Wynne said. "You can't keep going back and forth, and you can't stay out here."

"Why?" Tears crept into Nola's eyes. "Why can't I stay? You need me. I could help with the garden. I know more about agriculture than any of you."

"You'd get sick," Kieran said, his voice barely a whisper as he brushed the tears from Nola's cheek. "You'd get hurt. I won't let you die out here."

"What about ReVamp?" Nola said, remembering the bitter taste of metal in her mouth. "It saved you."

"You could never go home." Pain filled Kieran's eyes. "You would never see your mother again. I want to keep you more than anything, but I won't take the sun away from you, Nola."

He pulled Nola into his arms, and she buried her face in his shoulder. "How many times are we going to have to say goodbye?"

"Not to be completely insensitive," Raina said, "but a few of us still have to risk our lives to get the princess back to the castle. So, rather than focus on true love lost to circumstance and the bad luck of her going back to Jeremy my-father-wants-to-destroy-Nightland for comfort—"

"Raina, don't," Kieran muttered.

"Don't tell the truth? I think we all know why Jeremy gave Nola the info that sent her here. And we can be sure the Domer will take care of her once we make the trade."

Nola's cheeks flushed in anger and embarrassment.

"Let's stop pretending this is *Romeo and Juliet* unless you both want to end up dead. Why don't we give Nola to Julian to make sure she doesn't get herself caught for being a traitor, and once they're done, you two can go feel each other up in a dark corner."

The room froze for a long moment.

Bryant moved first. "Gonna go make sure we have enough vamps on board for the swap."

Desmond followed him out into the tunnels.

"I'll take you to the kitchen to work on your story," Julian said, awkwardly patting his hands on the sides of his legs. "I think we have something that resembles tea for you to drink."

"Anyone want to help me bury the guy who tried to kill Nola?" Raina asked, looking at Kieran.

"Just go, Raina," Kieran said, his face stony and impossible for Nola to read.

"All the dirty work for me. How kind." Raina stepped forward, baring her teeth.

Julian's hand closed around Nola's arm, and he led her from the gallery.

The door muffled Kieran's shouted response.

"Does it all make sense?" Julian asked as Nola finished her third cup of what was not really tea.

"Yes." Nola traced a jagged line that had been carved into the wooden kitchen table with her fingertip.

"It's about more than being able to repeat the details to me." Julian sipped from his dark mug.

Nola had closed her eyes when he had poured something from the refrigerator into it. *Knowing* he was probably drinking blood and actually *seeing* him do it were two very different things.

"You have to understand the story you're telling," Julian said.

"I get it." Nola kneaded the point of pain that pierced her forehead. "You kidnapped me to find out whatever you could about what my mother had learned at the Green Leaf Conference. I got hit on the head and stabbed a bit. Told you what you wanted to know since it didn't really matter anyway. You made the trade."

"Good girl." Julian tapped his knuckles on the table.

Nola dug her fingers into the wood, watching the white of her knuckles blossom through the red scars on her hands. "What if I don't want to?"

"Want to what?" Julian cocked his head to the side.

"What if I don't want you to make the trade?" Nola said. "What if I want to stay in Nightland? Help with your work."

"Kieran's already explained." Sympathy crept into Julian's voice. "If you stay here, you'll end up a vampire. Perhaps not right away, but eventually it would be either ReVamp or death."

"But being a vampire doesn't seem so bad."

"It's not," Julian said. "It took me a few years to get off the human blood and a decade more to forgive myself for all I'd done. But once you get used to blood and darkness, it's not such a bad life."

"Then let me stay," Nola said. "I want to be here. I want to help you save people."

I want to be with Kieran.

Julian studied his pale hands for a long moment. "I'm afraid that's impossible."

"But you just said—"

"I said being a vampire wasn't that bad. I didn't say you could be allowed to stay in Nightland."

"But—"

"They know you're here, Nola," Julian said. "We've told the domes we kidnapped you. If we don't give you back to them, it could start a war. And if the domes decided to fight the vampires in earnest, I don't even want to begin to imagine how terrible the damage to both sides would be. You have to go back. There is nothing else to be done."

"I could tell them it was me. That I ran away. Then they'll banish me."

"Think, Nola. Between the story we've written for you and the truth, which do you think they're most likely to believe?"

"But if I only tell them the truth, your story won't matter."

"They know the beginning of our kidnapping tale," Julian said. "That will be enough. They'll claim brainwashing or coercion. We have to give you back in the trade. It's the only way."

"The only solution is a lie," Nola said.

"A lie, yes." Julian patted Nola's hand. "And a hope you might eventually forget how wonderful the truth you lost could have been."

Nola closed her eyes, hating the sympathy on Julian's face.

"We can work on your story again tonight," Julian said, taking Nola's cup to the sink. "It's late. You should get some sleep."

"By late you mean early?" Nola's head spun from fatigue and trying to keep everything straight in her mind. What had happened since she left the domes, what she had to say had happened, and what could never happen.

"The morning is rather new." Julian washed both of their cups.

"Do vampires sleep?"

"Yes." Julian gave a half-shrug. "Most sleep at least an hour or two a day, mostly out of habit. We can go for a week or more without really feeling the physical need to sleep. But when days don't end, it takes a toll on the mind."

A door in the back of the kitchen opened, and a tiny girl emerged, her curly hair still rumpled from sleep.

"Eden." Julian swept the little girl into his arms.

Eden's face split into a grin, and she giggled as Julian rocked her back and forth.

"How are you this fine morning?" Julian said.

Eden bit her lips together, her brown eyes on Nola.

"Don't be afraid," Julian said, following Eden's gaze. "You know Nola. She's the one who got you your medicine. Can you say *thank you, Nola?*"

"Thank you, Nola," Eden said in a voice barely loud enough to be heard before burying her face in Julian's neck.

"Why don't we take Nola someplace she can get a bit of sleep, and then you and I can go find your father?" Julian asked.

Eden nodded.

Julian led Nola into the hallway and toward the room lined with bunks. Nola expected him to lead her to one of the metal bunk beds, but instead, he walked farther down the hall than Nola had been before.

"I'm sure no one will mind." Julian stopped at an unmarked door and gave it a cursory knock before swinging it open. "Sleep well."

Nola stepped into the room, not turning as the door closed behind her.

It was Kieran's room. She could tell without him even being there. He and his father had barely been able to take anything with them when they left the domes. A few pictures hung on the wall. Kieran with his parents all smiling at a party. Kieran and Nola high up in the willow tree in Bright Dome.

There were sketches of plants and animals. And Nola. She stared back at herself from the wall.

But the drawing was a perfected version of herself. The shape of the face was right, and so were the eyes. The pale freckles that dotted her nose and the tiny mark near her eye were all there. Still, she looked different. Calm, beautiful, and angelic.

A version of me I could never hope to be.

Nola reached up for the picture, wanting to study it, to see what Kieran's idea of her could teach her, but the door opened again.

"Julian said he was done for the morning," Kieran said, glancing from Nola to the sketch of 'perfect Nola.'

Heat rose in Nola's cheeks. "We're done."

"Sorry," Kieran said, running a hand through his hair, "if that's weird." He swept a hand toward the sketch. "You weren't supposed to see that."

"It's beautiful," Nola said.

"Not as beautiful as the original."

His words hung in the air for a moment.

"I haven't seen you draw anything since—" Nola paused.

Why am I making this worse?

"Since my mom died." Kieran picked up a pad of paper from the desk. His mother's face gazed up at them, a smile caught on her lips. "It took a while."

Nola took Kieran's hand, squeezing it tightly.

"You should get some sleep." Kieran lifted a small pile of clothes from the bed and tossed it onto the ground.

Nola laughed.

"I know," Kieran said. "Even down here where I hardly own anything I still can't keep my room clean. Dad comes in here every day to stare at the mess."

"Some things don't change."

"Maybe," Kieran said, his eyes locking with Nola's for a moment before flicking away.

"Kieran, Jeremy and I," Nola said, willing herself to get the words out before she lost her chance, "we're not together."

"Yet."

"No."

"You've kissed him," Kieran said. It wasn't a question. "You've kissed him. And even if you're not together yet, even if you're not in love with him yet, you will be."

"No, I won't."

"He's a good guy, Nola." Pain etched Kieran's words. "Hell, he's probably a better guy than I ever could have been even if I'd stayed in the domes. He's steady and strong. When you get home, he'll take care of you. He'll be with you every day while you try to forget what you saw down here. And then one day you'll realize he's the best thing you've got. And in a few years the Marriage

Board will tell you it's time to pick someone as your pair, and you'll pick him. You'll get married, have kids, and forget all about Nightland—"

Nola cut off his words with a smack. Her hand throbbed from hitting Kieran's face, but she couldn't see more than his blurred outline through her tears.

"How dare you," Nola said. "How dare you decide what my life will be, what Jeremy's life will be?"

"I didn't decide. The domes did."

"What if that's not what I want?" Nola yelled. "I don't want to be with Jeremy just because—"

"Because it's the way things work for Domers."

"Because I can't have you." Nola sank down to her knees. "You say I have to go back to the domes to survive, but what kind of life will I have?"

Kieran knelt, wrapping his arms around her. He smelled like he always had, the scent she had known for years.

Are vampires supposed to smell so human?

"That's the problem with trying to save the human race," Kieran whispered. "You lose humanity."

Nola swiped her tears away with trembling hands.

Kieran lifted her onto the bed. "Sleep, Nola."

Nola shook her head as more tears streamed down her face. "I can't. If this is it, if I never get to see you again, I want to be with you. I don't want to sleep. I don't want to miss it."

"You aren't going to miss anything," Kieran murmured. "I'll be right here. I'll hold you close. And when you wake up, you'll still be in my arms. Won't that be a thing to remember?"

He lay down next to Nola, and she put her head on his shoulder in the place where she fit so perfectly.

"Goodnight, Nola," Kieran whispered. "I love you."

His words ran through her, filling her up before shattering her.

"I love you, too."

CHAPTER TWENTY-TWO

I ce surrounded her. But something deep in the back of her mind told her to hold the ice closer even as she shivered. That the cold she was feeling was precious and not to be let go.

"Nola," a voice whispered as the cold began to move away. "Nola, you're shaking." Lips brushed her forehead.

Nola's eyes fluttered open, and Kieran was gazing down at her. She pulled herself closer to his chest, not looking away from his eyes. Their black was still rimmed in a thin band of gold-speckled green.

"I don't mind the cold." Nola traced her fingers along Kieran's chin. A strong chin. A man's chin. Bits of stubble caught on her fingers.

When did we become grownups? Did it happen before the world got this dark or after?

Kieran wrapped both arms around her, pulling her to his chest. Nola closed her eyes, relishing the feeling of being held so tight he could not possibly let go.

"It's time to get up anyway," Kieran said, again pressing his lips to her forehead. "Bea will have breakfast waiting for you, and Julian will want to talk through your story again."

"Can't they wait?" Nola gripped Kieran's t-shirt with her fingers.

"Probably not."

Nola's stomach squirmed at the regret in his voice.

"How long before it's time?"

"Eight hours until you leave Nightland. Nine until the exchange."

Nola's ribcage turned to stone. She couldn't breathe. Her lungs had no space to expand. "That's not much time."

"Let's not waste any of it." Kieran tipped Nola's chin up. Softly, gently, he kissed her.

Nola's heart raced. She pressed herself against him, memorizing the feeling of his body next to hers.

With a creak, the bedroom door swung open.

Nola gasped as Dr. Wynne stared down at them, his face a mix between confusion and disappointment.

"Nola, you're needed in the kitchen." Dr. Wynne's voice was brusque and businesslike, something Nola had rarely heard from him.

Nola awkwardly struggled to climb over Kieran without looking him or Dr. Wynne in the face.

The bed springs creaked as Kieran stood.

"Nola, to the kitchen," Dr. Wynne said. "Kieran, stay here."

Nola walked out into the hall without looking back.

The door slammed behind her. She squeezed her eyes shut and took a shuddering breath.

They'll let me say goodbye to Kieran.

They would have to or...

Or what?

She would refuse to go back to the domes in the exchange and let the Outer Guard destroy Nightland?

A laugh shook Nola's chest. A high hysterical laugh she wouldn't have recognized as her own if she hadn't felt it ripping from her throat.

"I like it." Raina's voice pulled Nola from her frenzy. "A little insanity. It'll help sell the kidnapping story to the Domers."

"A *little* insanity perhaps." Julian peered over Raina's shoulder, his dark cup already in his hand. "But if she really has lost her mind, she might not be able to remember what to tell them, and then where would we be?"

"I remember," Nola said. "I remember all of it. I know the coat and trying to escape. I know I was dropped and there were lots of voices. I know all of it." Nola tugged a hand through her knotted hair. "I'm a quick learner. Just let me go back to Kieran."

"Really? You've already been in there all night," Raina said.

"And I'd really like for you to shut up!" Nola growled.

Raina smiled and tossed her purple and scarlet hair over her shoulder. "Is that what you want?"

"I think Raina should go back to practicing killing things," Julian said, stepping around Raina, "and Nola should come and brush up her details with me. Raina will get to stab things, which always makes her more cheerful, and the sooner Nola and I are done, the sooner she can be swept back into young love's tender throes."

"Fine." Raina turned and sauntered back toward to gallery. "See you in a few." Julian gave Nola a tight smile. "After you."

The old woman was already standing over the stove in the kitchen, poking at something in a pan with a wooden spoon.

Nola sat down in the same seat she had taken the night before, willing herself not to start tracing the scratch with her finger again.

The *clink* of a plate being pulled from the cupboard brought Nola's attention back to the present as Bea shuffled over with breakfast—grilled vegetables and a little hunk of meat.

"Thank you," Nola murmured, deciding not to ask what sort of meat it was. She sniffed the plate, her mouth beginning to water. Carefully, she speared a green vegetable onto her fork. It tasted earthy and pungent, but like food.

"No more tinny taste?" Julian asked.

"It's gone," Nola said. She watched as Julian took a sip from his cup. "Do you miss food?"

"Me?" Julian chuckled. "No." He paused for a moment. "No, I really don't miss eating. But then, I was so ill before I became a vampire, eating had ceased to be a real option for me, so I suppose I am a terrible judge."

"Right."

"Now, down to business." Julian rubbed his hands together. "Who moved the glass?"

The next few hours passed slowly, Julian asking Nola the same questions in slightly different ways until her head spun.

"Well," Julian said when Nola had explained how she had gotten out of the Iron Dome for the twelfth time, "I think that's as good as we're going to get. And just remember, if you get confused, tell them you hit your head and all you remember is darkness and fear. Hopefully they'll feel sorry enough for you to leave you alone until you can sort out what you're supposed to say."

"You know the Outer Guard," Nola said as real fear clawed at her stomach. "They aren't known for their kindness and compassion."

"Careful, Nola," Julian said, "you're starting to sound like a Nightlander. I think our time here is done." Julian looked over Nola's shoulder.

Nola turned to find Kieran leaning against the doorframe. His dark hair stuck out at odd angles, and anger marked his face.

"I tried to keep things as swift as possible."

"Thanks, Julian," Kieran said, stepping into the kitchen and taking Nola's hand.

"Get our Cinderella back here by three. We don't want her to be late for the party being held in her honor." Julian nodded to them both and left the room, still holding his cup.

"How did it go?" Kieran asked after a long moment.

"Good," Nola said. "At least I think it went well. I've never been prepped to tell a giant lie before. What did your dad say?"

"Nothing." Kieran pressed his palm to his forehead. "Everything I already knew and had decided to forget. Dad's great at that."

Nola took Kieran's hands in her own, tracing the calluses that marked his palms with her finger.

"What do we do now?" Nola asked, studying Kieran's face, trying to memorize every line, even those formed by anger.

"If we were in the domes," Kieran said, twisting his hands so their fingers laced perfectly together, "I would say we should climb onto your roof and look at the stars."

"Or go lay under the willow tree," Nola said. "How many hours do you think we spent under that tree? Not talking or doing anything really. Just being together."

"Not nearly enough."

Nola laid her head on his shoulder. "We could go back to the garden."

"It's raining again," Kieran said. "Besides, I don't think Emanuel will let me take you aboveground until it's time. It's too risky."

"I can't just sit here." Nola stepped away from Kieran, her body telling her to run from the room. To keep running and running so the world couldn't catch her. "I can't just sit and count down the time. I need to do something."

"You've never been good at waiting." Kieran caught Nola around the waist, pulling her back into his arms.

"Never." Nola wound her arms around him. Her stomach purred.

If Dr. Wynne hadn't walked in, where would we be right now?

"I have an idea." Kieran swayed side to side with Nola as though they were dancing. "Let's go to Nightland."

"We're in Nightland." Nola laughed in spite of herself as Kieran twirled her under his arm.

"5th and Nightland. Let's go dance. We'll forget morning is ever coming."

Nola leaned in and kissed him. "Promise you'll hold me?"

"Until the sun comes up."

Kieran took her hand and led her out to the gallery.

Nola expected there to be someone at the door to make them stay in Emanuel's house, but Kieran led her into the tunnel without interruption. Whatever Dr. Wynne had said, he wasn't keeping Kieran from 5th and Nightland.

They didn't talk as they walked. What was there to say?

The closer they got to the club, the more Nola worried she wouldn't fit in with the other revelers.

I'm wearing Raina's old clothes. I can't get much more vampire than that without ReVamp.

Every few hundred yards, a vampire stood against the wall. They didn't wear any sort of uniform, but something about their posture, the way their gaze followed her and Kieran, made Nola certain they were guards.

"Did Emanuel put the extra guards on watch?" Nola whispered as they passed another guard, this one a boy not much older than herself with flaming red hair. "Because of the Outer Guard?" The red-haired boy's neck stiffened at the mention of the Outer Guard.

"Yes," Kieran said. "The housing tunnel is under strict watch. The club can defend itself, and so can the working areas. But this tunnel is where the kids are. The ones who can't fight. It's where Eden would be if Emanuel weren't her father."

The hairs on Nola's neck prickled at the thought of Eden hiding from the Outer Guard.

"Don't worry." Kieran kissed Nola's hand. "We're safe down here. You warned us, and we're better protected than we have ever been before."

A thumping noise echoed in the distance. A low, rhythmic buzz that shook the floor under Nola's feet.

Nola's heart began to race as they grew closer to the music of Nightland. Two tall guards stood, arms crossed, knives in their belts, in front of the metal door.

One of them lifted his head as Nola approached as though sniffing the air.

"That her?" he said to Kieran who nodded.

The other guard turned and swung open the door. The music flooded into the hall so loudly Nola could barely hear herself call "thank you" as the guards ushered her past.

Flashes bounced down from the ceiling, throwing lights so bright into Nola's eyes, she was blinded when she tried to look into the shadows.

Vampires filled every corner of the club. The music thumped into her very bones. Each vibration shook her lungs, making it impossible for her to get a deep breath.

Kieran laced his fingers through hers, leading her out into the mass of surging bodies to find a place on the dance floor. Every time they passed a group of revelers, their eyes locked onto Nola.

"They're all staring at me," Nola whispered.

"Huh?" Kieran shouted above the music.

"They're all staring at me." Nola pressed her lips to Kieran's ear.

Kieran looked around the crowd, giving a nod to a group of vampires with dark red and black tattoos etched into their skin. "No one here will hurt you." He wrapped his arm around Nola's waist.

"Because they're all nice vampires who don't believe in eating Domers?" The question caught in Nola's throat.

"Because you're with me." Kieran smiled and swayed with the music. "Because they know you're the Domer who came here to help us."

The people around them began to dance again, surging as one massive unit. Kieran held Nola tightly, swaying gently. "Ignore them," he said. "Let it just be us."

Nola looked into Kieran's eyes. The green was almost gone now, replaced with black. But the darkness didn't frighten her. In his eyes she could see his soul pouring out to her with every glance.

Kieran smiled and took her by the hand, spinning her under his arm. Nola tossed her head back and laughed. The music swallowed the sound of her laughter, but it didn't matter. Kieran was laughing with her. He pulled her back into his chest, one arm wrapped around her waist, holding her tight.

He brushed the loose hair from the sweat on her forehead. He ran his fingers over her curls as though hoping to memorize each strand. The music changed, and the crowd around them cheered. This song was faster, with shouted words Nola couldn't understand.

Kieran didn't sway with this song. He only gazed at Nola, sadness filling his eyes.

"Nola..." his mouth formed the word, but Nola couldn't hear the sound. She laced her fingers together around his neck, leaning up until their lips met.

She tightened her fingers in his hair, pulling him even closer. His heartbeat thudded through her chest, overpowering the music until there was nothing left but him. His hands traced the skin from her waist to her ribs. She gasped at the ice of his fingers.

Their eyes met for a moment before he was kissing her again, wrapping his arms around her so her feet left ground. She disappeared, lost in a haze. There was nothing left in the world but her and Kieran. Cheers and shouts glided past, but she cared for nothing except Kieran and her hunger for him. She teased his lips, reveling in his taste.

A loud *clang* shook the air, and Nola looked up. Her feet still hovered above the ground as Kieran held her, but they were in a tunnel away from the crowds of 5th and Nightland. The thick stone walls muffled the thumping of the music. Lamps dotted the corridor, leading off into the darkness, but no shapes moved in the shadows. They were alone.

CHAPTER TWENTY-THREE

"Nola," Kieran breathed, pressing his lips to hers gently at first, then with growing desperation.

This is it. All we'll ever have.

Kieran lifted her against the wall and pressed himself to her as his hands explored the bare skin of her back. Nola pulled herself closer to him, as though they could melt into one and the bridge would never come. She moaned as Kieran's fingers grazed her ribs, sending pulses of pleasure trembling through her.

"Kieran," she breathed, wrapping herself around him.

This is perfect. This is right.

"No." Kieran stepped away.

Nola crumpled to the ground, hitting her head on the stone wall.

"What?" Nola said, blinking to see Kieran past the stars that danced in front of her eyes.

"I want you, Nola," Kieran said, his voice desperate and sad. "I want to keep you here. I want to make you mine."

"Then do it." Nola swallowed the lump of fear in her throat as her words hung in the air. "I'm not afraid."

Kieran stepped forward, taking Nola's hands and helping her to her feet. She swayed as pain shot through her head, but the ache did nothing to shadow the longing that filled her. Kieran traced her lips with his finger, then placed his hand over her heart.

"You have to get to the bridge." Kieran turned and walked down the tunnel.

"Kieran," Nola said, forcing her feet to move as she ran after him. "We have time."

"A few hours," Kieran said, not slowing his stride.

"One night. You said we could have one night. I thought—"

"I want you, Nola." Kieran turned to face her. He took both her arms, holding her tight. "More than anything, I want you. But the whole point in giving you back to the domes is to make sure you have a life."

"I can have a life tomorrow."

"And what would you tell Jeremy?" Kieran said. "Would you lie? Never mention it happened? Or would you admit you gave yourself to a Vamper in a filthy tunnel?"

"It's none of Jeremy's business."

"You belong with him!" Kieran pulled away from Nola and paced the tunnel, tearing his hands through his hair. "I lost my chance with you when I got banished from the domes."

"That wasn't your fault—"

"It doesn't matter." Kieran punched his fist into the wall. Tiny bits of rock clattered to the ground.

Nola ran to him, taking his hand in hers, expecting to see blood and broken bones. But his hand was perfect. The skin unharmed.

"See," Kieran panted. "I'm not who I used to be." He took Nola's face in his hands. "I love you, Magnolia Kent. I will always love you."

"Kieran, please don't." Pain dug into her chest.

"But I love you too much to let you stay down here in the dark." Kieran kissed her cheek. "And I love you too much to give you one night in a tunnel and send you away. You deserve the world, Nola."

He took her hand and turned down the tunnel, but Nola couldn't make her feet move.

"Kieran," she whispered, not waiting for him to turn back to her. "I love you, too. And I should have a choice."

His fingers tightened around hers, and together they walked down the tunnel toward 5th and Nightland.

Say something. There has to be something you can say to stay here. To stay with him.

They had nearly reached the metal door when a loud *thunk* echoed through the hall.

Nola stepped away from the door, expecting a burly guard to walk through. But the metal door stayed shut.

There was another *thunk*, and the noise from the club changed. The music silenced, replaced by frightened voices.

Thump.

The ceiling shook, sending a rain of dust down onto Nola and Kieran. More *thumps* came, breaking over the screams of the crowd. The door to 5th and Nightland swung open, and people poured out into the tunnel just before—

Bang!

The sound pounded into Nola's ears, blocking out the cries of the people around her.

Kieran grabbed her, shoving her against the wall and covering her with his own body as chunks of the ceiling came tumbling down.

There was more shouting and the sound of people running away down the tunnel.

Soon the shouts of fear vanished, replaced by roars of anger.

"Shit," Kieran muttered.

Nola looked up in time to see red beams of light darting through the dust of the ruined club.

Faint *pops* echoed through the air, and Nola watched the shadow of a vampire fall before Kieran knocked her over, pinning her to the ground.

"Get out of our home!" a voice roared.

The screech of metal on metal wailed through the hall, followed by the sound of splintering wood and howls of pain.

The vampires were fighting back.

"Nola, I need you to run," Kieran said just loudly enough for Nola to hear his deadly calm voice. "I need you to run down this hall and not stop until you find where it meets up with the big tunnel. Go left from there, and you can find your way back to Emanuel's."

"You want me to get help?"

Another series of *pops* punctuated the shouts, but the vampires had armed themselves. This time, a guard fell to the floor. Another figure in a black uniform leapt into view, bringing down a heavy baton onto a vampire's neck.

"Help is already coming, but they can't see you here."

A *bang* shook the floor.

Nola watched in horror as the wall between the tunnel and Nightland began to collapse. Before Nola could gasp, Kieran had lifted her and was sprinting down the hall, carrying her in his arms.

He rounded the corner and held Nola to the side as a dozen vampires armed with swords, knives, and weapons Nola didn't recognize, ran past.

"Go," Kieran said. "Get where it's safe."

"Come with me!" Nola clung to Kieran's hand.

"They're invading my home, Nola," Kieran said. "I have to fight."

"I'll fight with you," Nola said, searching the floor for a rock, anything to defend herself.

"There are vampires in there," Kieran said, cupping Nola's face in his hands. "If you bleed, they could attack you. The guards can't see you. Just go. I'll meet you in the gallery when it's over." He kissed Nola, quickly, urgently as shouts and the grinding of metal on metal came from the fight. "I love you, Nola. Now go!" he shouted over his shoulder as he disappeared into the dust.

Nola wanted to run after him. To shout at the guards to stop. These were people, too, and they had a right to protect their home. But if they saw her, they'd know she was a traitor, and the war with the domes would begin.

She stifled a sob and ran down the hall, half-blinded by her tears. Another group of vampires tore down the passage, knocking Nola off her feet. Pain shot through her wrist and ribs as she hit the ground. Spitting dirt from her mouth, Nola pushed herself to her feet, staring down at the hot sticky blood that covered her palm.

"Shit." She glanced up and down the tunnel. There was no one in sight, but a vampire would come soon. A vampire that could smell her fresh blood. Pulling with all her might, Nola tore the sleeve from her shirt. Grabbing a handful of dirt in her bleeding hand, she wrapped the leather around the soil, hoping it would be enough to cover the scent of her blood.

Nola ran down the hall, but the sounds of the fighting didn't seem to get any farther away. The guards had gained ground, delving deeper into Nightland.

How many guards had they sent that the vampires still hadn't—Nola couldn't stop herself from thinking—*killed them?*

Finally, she reached a door. It was metal but thankfully light enough for her to move on her own. Pain seared through her palm as she gripped the handle with both hands, forcing the dirt deeper into her wound.

As soon as she was through the door, she shoved it closed behind her. There was a lock on the inside of the door, a heavy metal bar that could be slid into place. It could block the Outer Guard from the hall—maybe only for a minute, but it would be something. But it would lock the vampires in with the guards. Shouts came through the metal door.

"Stay in formation. We don't leave without the girl."

Nola slammed the metal bar into the lock and stared at the door.

They were searching for her. If she let them find her, maybe they would leave. The fighting would be over. They had fought their way this deep into Nightland. The Outer Guard were stronger than Emanuel had thought.

But if they found out Emanuel had lied, they could destroy everything.

You can't be seen! Kieran's words pounded through her mind as the door shook.

Nola ran left down the corridor.

Please let me be right. If Kieran is hurt...

She pushed the thought out of her mind. He was a vampire. He only needed to protect his heart.

A woman stood in a doorway, clutching a sweater to her chest as she looked up and down the tunnel.

"Get inside," Nola shouted as she ran past. "The Outer Guard are here."

The slam of a door sounded behind Nola.

Her legs burned. How much farther until she reached Emanuel's house. Would she even be safe there? A group of vampires running in ranks, dressed all in black, charged past. Nola recognized Desmond's scarred, bald head as he ran in the lead.

Nola raced farther down the tunnel, where vampires still stood in the hall with no apparent concern for the attack.

"What's got the guards riled?" a man asked, stepping out in front of Nola. His long white fangs peeked over his bottom lip.

A human drinker.

"The Outer Guard," Nola panted, keeping her wounded hand clamped tight at her side. "They got into 5th and Nightland. They're coming."

The lights overhead flickered as though confirming her words.

"And the human runs," the vampire sneered. "Bloody and weak." His eyes moved from Nola's panicked face to her injured hand. "I could protect you. The little girl lost in the dark."

He stepped closer, and the vampires around him shifted, forming a ring around Nola.

"Beautiful, weak, and so sweet," the vampire said, his black eyes gleeful. "You need protection. I could protect you. Make you mine." He leaned close to Nola, his fangs mere inches from her neck. The stench of sweat and stale blood wafted off his skin. He leaned closer, his nose brushing her neck. "You smell so pure, so clean."

"I am a guest of Emanuel," Nola said. "I am here under Emanuel's protection. And if you so much as touch me, Raina will have your head." Nola stepped back and stared unflinching into the vampire's black eyes.

"Raina." The vampire straightened.

"She owes me," Nola said. "Now get out of my way before the Outer Guard come."

The vampires stood frozen for a moment before, as a unit, they stepped back and out of her way.

Nola sprinted down the hall, the scent of the vampire still caught in her nose.

Soon, the doors became nicer, and she found the carved wooden door that led to Emanuel's home. Five guards stood flanking the entrance to the gallery.

"Nola." Bryant stepped forward as Nola skidded to a stop. "Where's Kieran?"

"At 5th and Nightland," Nola said as quickly as her panting would allow. "He stayed to fight. The Outer Guard made it through the doors. They're in the corridor."

"We know." Bryant opened the door to the gallery. "Get inside. They'll take you someplace safe."

Nola stepped into the gallery, and a cold hand closed around Nola's arm.

"And here I thought you might have run into the waiting arms of the guards," Julian said, dragging Nola through the gallery and to the living quarters.

"I thought about it," Nola said, her breath still coming in short gasps, "but I didn't know if it would make them stop. And Kieran said to stay out of sight."

"Kieran is a very smart lad." Julian led her through the kitchen and the narrow door in the back. There was a wooden door on the right and a heavy, metal door straight ahead.

Julian pounded on the metal door with his palm. "Dr. Wynne, I have Nola."

A shadow flitted behind a tiny piece of thick glass in the door. A creaking came from the other side before the door, even thicker than the entrance to 5th and Nightland, ground slowly open.

"Oh, thank God," Dr. Wynne said, beckoning Nola into the room.

"Reseal the door." Julian turned and ran away.

Dr. Wynne put his shoulder into the door and slid it shut before turning a thick metal wheel in the center that closed the lock with a heavy *clunk*.

"Where's Kieran?" Dr. Wynne asked as soon as the door had been secured.

"He's fighting," Nola said. A horrible stone of guilt settled in her stomach. "He told me to run. But there are others there. He'll be fine. He has to be."

"Nola dear," Dr. Wynne said, his voice unusually tired, "I gave up on my son being safe the moment I turned him into a vampire. It was my fault we were banished from the domes and my drug that turned him."

"To save his life."

"I saved his life by making him a part of a very dangerous community." Dr. Wynne took off his glasses and kept his gaze down as he slowly cleaned the lenses on his shirt.

Nola didn't miss the glimmer of tears in his eyes.

"Every day I have with him is an extra gift I don't deserve. Kieran is a brave man. He would never sit idly by while others are in danger. Of course he's fighting. And he won't stop until everyone is safe."

"But he'll be okay," Nola said, unable to keep a trace of question from her voice.

"He's a vampire, Nola," Dr. Wynne said. "And a strong one at that. That is the best assurance we have that he'll be back in a few hours. Beaten, bloody, maybe missing a few fingers. But he'll still be Kieran, and he'll heal."

"Because you made him that way." Nola turned to the door, wondering how long it would be until someone came for them.

"Because I made him that way."

CHAPTER TWENTY-FOUR

Nola scanned the room where she'd been trapped.

No. Protected. They're keeping you safe.

She had expected concrete, weapon-lined walls. But instead, a pattern of bright blue clouds decorated the eggshell-white walls. Along one side sat a small bed with a soft pink comforter, and in the corner Bea rested in a rocking chair, apparently unfazed by the commotion around her. Eden huddled at Bea's feet, clutching a ragdoll.

Of course Eden sleeps in the safest room in Nightland. Emanuel wouldn't have it any other way.

He's keeping me safe, too.

"How are you?" Nola asked, sitting on the floor.

"Good," Eden muttered, crawling over and planting herself firmly in Nola's lap. "Did you get a booboo?"

"A little one," Nola said, shaking her head at Dr. Wynne's startled look. "I fell and cut myself. It's not that bad. I just wanted to hide the smell."

Dr. Wynne pulled a wash basin and jug down from the dresser in the corner and sat on the floor next to Nola.

The walls shook, and Eden clung to Nola's neck. "It's okay," Eden whispered into Nola's ear. "My daddy made this place safe for me, and he'll come get us when he gets rid of the bad men."

"He sure will." Nola pushed Eden's curls behind her ears with her good hand, trying not to flinch as Dr. Wynne began washing the dirt from her other palm.

The walls shook again, and Nola swallowed hard, trying not to show Eden her panic. Trapped underground. What if the tunnel collapsed? They would be buried forever.

Nola tried to picture herself in the domes, full of light and air.

Far away from Kieran.

"Why did the bad men come?" Eden asked, standing up so she was eye to eye with Nola.

"They aren't bad men," Nola said. "You know how you're afraid of them? They're afraid of you, too. And sometimes when people are very afraid, they do things they shouldn't, and they hurt people."

"Why are they scared of me?" Eden tipped her head to the side and scrunched up her forehead.

"Because they don't understand how wonderful and precious you are," Nola said. "They don't understand your daddy is just trying to make a safe home for lots of people."

"If they did, would they go away?"

"I think so."

"When I get big, I will teach them we are nice, and my daddy is nice," Eden said, lifting her pudgy chin in determination.

"I'm sure you will."

"All done," Dr. Wynne said, tucking a bandage around Nola's palm. "While I admire the ingenuity of using dirt to try and cover the blood odor, I wouldn't recommend using tunnel dirt for that purpose in the future. It's not really sanitary. Although if it's either that or be considered a snack, I suppose the chance of infection is worth it."

"Right, desperate times only." Nola stood and sat on Eden's bed. The mattress springs creaked under her weight.

Eden followed her, curling up and tucking her head on Nola's lap. Another *boom* echoed through the walls, this one more distant than the last.

Were the guards being driven back, or simply coming at them from another direction?

Eden whimpered and covered her face with her doll.

"Hush," Nola said, stroking the girl's silky, black curls. "We're safe here. Just close your eyes and relax."

Nola hummed a song her father had sung to her when she was very little. She couldn't remember the words anymore. Only that she had liked the tune—the song had made her feel happy, safe, and sure her father would always be there to fight the demons away.

Nola kept humming as Eden's breathing became slow and steady, hoping Eden would fare better than she had. And Eden's father would come home.

Loud banging on the door shook Nola from her stupor. Eden clamped her hands over her ears. Dr. Wynne ran to peer through the glass slit in the door. Even Bea sat up straight in her rocking chair, the first sign she had given that she had noticed anything strange.

"Emanuel," Dr. Wynne said, opening the door and tripping over Eden as she streaked past him into her father's waiting arms.

Emanuel swept Eden up, holding her to his chest. "It's all right," he murmured. "You're safe, Eden. Daddy would never let anyone hurt you."

He had been in the fight. A long cut marred his cheek and blood matted his hair. The cut already appeared days old.

"Kieran?" Dr. Wynne said, before Nola could form the word.

"He's alive," Julian said from behind Emanuel's shoulder.

"Alive?" Nola clung to the door.

"He was hurt," Emanuel said. "Badly. But he'll heal."

"They didn't get his heart?" Dr. Wynne lifted a trembling hand to his glasses.

"No," Julian said, "though they tried their damndest. He's unconscious now, but I think if you give him another dose of ReVamp—"

"He shouldn't need anymore. Not for weeks." Dr. Wynne's voice sounded thin, like there wasn't enough of him left to contemplate the injuries of his only son.

"He needs to heal more quickly," Emanuel said. "Stitch him up, and give him an injection. Then we can wake him and get him to the bridge."

"Bridge?" Nola said. "What happened to Kieran that he needs more ReVamp? He's supposed to be able to heal."

"He will," Julian said.

"But—"

"Kieran needs to be fit for the exchange," Emanuel said. "We're moving forward."

"But they attacked us!" Nola said so loudly Eden covered her ears again. "They came in here and ruined everything, and you think they'll go through with the deal?"

"They'll have to," Emanuel said. "They won't leave you standing on the bridge."

"And you're just letting them take me?"

"They only sent in a handful of guards." Julian spread his hands in a helpless gesture. "If we tried to keep you here, it would be a rallying cry to start an all-out war."

"We can't protect Nightland if they decide to do that," Emanuel said, handing Eden to a waiting Bea who shuffled past them into the kitchen. "They could blast down from the city."

"It would be catastrophic, and not just for Nightland. For the humans who are still trying to survive aboveground," Julian said. "But after tonight, I can't find it in myself to believe the Outer Guard wouldn't do it."

"So, we go to the bridge." Nola's voice sounded far away as she said the words.

"I'll try and wake Kieran," Dr. Wynne said.

"Don't." Nola gripped his sleeve. "Let him sleep. He needs to heal."

"He would want to be there," Julian said.

Nola shook her head, wincing as the pain of heartbreak cracked in her chest. "I don't know if I have the strength to walk away from him." Her voice came out barely louder than a breath.

"Is there anything you want me to tell him?" Dr. Wynne asked, squeezing Nola's hand.

"Nothing that will make it hurt less."

CHAPTER TWENTY-FIVE

The tunnels had collapsed in places. Bits of stone and piles of dirt littered the corridor. Some of the light bulbs had blown out, and those that remained flickered feebly.

Raina maintained a viselike grip on Nola's arm as she steered her though the halls, half-lifting her over the ruble.

"I'm not going to try and run," Nola said as Raina's fingers dug painfully into Nola's arm when they passed a vampire lying in a pool of his own blood. The man's breath rattled though his wounded chest. "Should we help him?"

"He'll heal," Raina said. "And I'm not worried about you running. We have a lot of pissed off vampires who don't know if the Outer Guard are going to try and attack again. I'm supposed to get you to the bridge, and I'll be damned if I let someone snatch you before trade time. Sorry, you'll just have to live with the bruises."

Sour bile rose in Nola's throat as Raina led her past a woman mumbling and crying as she clasped her bloody stump of an arm.

They reached 5th and Nightland, but if Nola hadn't known their destination, she wouldn't have recognized the club at all.

No music pounded through the air. No dancers writhed to the pulsing beat. The bright flashing lights had been replaced by pale moonbeams creeping in through the giant hole that led to the streets above. Lined up along one wall lay five vampires, their hands crossed gently on their chests. Nola tried not to look at the horrible wounds that covered their bodies. One woman had a hole larger than a fist in her chest. One man's head was barely attached to his neck. All were too far gone to heal.

Under the hole where the trap door to the street had been lay six guards, their bodies torn and beaten, their faces still hidden by helmets. The body of a tall, broad shouldered male lay farthest down the line. His boots were shiny and new, his uniform hardly worn aside from the tears from the fight.

"Jeremy." Nola wrenched her arm away from Raina and ran to the end of the line. She knelt next to the body and cradled his head, trying take off the helmet. Her hands shook too badly to manage even its slight weight.

"Let me," Raina said, lifting away Nola's trembling hands.

Raina pulled off the helmet, and tears streamed from Nola's eyes as a head of bright blond hair emerged.

Nola had seen this man before. He was just old enough to have always been in the class above her. Lying in the dirt, he looked like a child.

A surge of guilt flooded through Nola.

Not Jeremy. It's not Jeremy.

He hadn't been lost to Nightland. But someone would mourn when the blond boy didn't come home.

"Not him?" Raina asked after a moment.

"Not him." Nola pushed herself back up to her feet. "What are you going to do with them? They're Domers. They should be burned and scattered to the wind."

"After we get you traded back, we'll figure that out," Raina said, taking Nola by the waist and lifting her high into the air, passing her to hands that waited at street level. "If they play nice and give us what we asked for, we might give the remains back as a peace offering."

Desmond set Nola down on the cracked pavement.

"And if not?" Nola asked, giving a nod of thanks to Desmond.

"We put them in the river," Raina said. "It's where all the death around here comes from anyway."

"It's time," Bryant said from his place at the head of the pack of vampires that had assembled as Nola's escort.

Nola nodded, feeling more like she was being led to the gallows than sent home.

Bryant led them through the city. A haunting *clang* echoed down the empty streets every time he struck his pipe on his open palm.

The journey to the bridge seemed much shorter than the first time Nola had made the trek alone in the darkness.

As the bridge rose in the distance, a lone figure in a long, black coat emerged from the shadows. A silver sword peeked out from under the coat's trim.

"Nice of you to join us," Raina said.

"I was scouting the bridge, if you must know," Julian said as he matched step with Nola. "And they do seem to be playing nicely."

A strangled cough came from Raina. "We'll see."

The first gray of dawn peered up over the hill.

The shadow of the Outer Guard caravan waited across the river.

Nola stood flanked by vampires. Julian and Raina each held one of her arms.

"Just stay calm," Julian said in a low voice. "They want to get you home safe, and so do we. If we all stay calm, we'll be in the tunnels before daylight and you can have a nice breakfast with your loving mother."

Nola nodded, not trusting her voice.

"Don't play the victim just yet," Raina said. "Keep your big girl panties on until you get back to the domes. Then you can curl up in a ball and tell them how badly we abused you."

"I won't lie," Nola said. "You're not monsters. You never hurt me."

"They have to believe we kidnapped you," Julian said. "Don't worry about our image. Keep the story believable, just like we practiced."

"Besides, I stabbed you," Raina said, a glint of laughter in her eyes. "Use that for your inspiration."

"Right," Nola said. "That *did* really hurt."

"It's time," Desmond called from his perch on the side of the bridge.

"Forward ho," Julian said, pushing Nola in front of him and Raina as though using her as a human shield.

"Can't I walk next to you?" Nola said, fighting her instinct to run as guards piled out of the trucks.

"I want to get you home safe, dear," Julian said, "but I'd like to get home, too. And they're much less likely to shoot you than me. So, you first."

"Right." Nola put one foot in front of the other. But somehow the distance between her and the trucks never seemed to lessen.

I'll have to walk until dawn. We'll still be walking across this bridge when the sun rises and burns the vampires.

With a bright flash, all of the trucks turned their lights on as one, shining them directly at Nola. The hiss of the vampires echoed behind her. She tried to lift a hand to cover her eyes, but Julian and Raina kept her arms pinned to her sides. She squinted, trying to see past the lights. Spokes of bright white emanated from the sides of the glow that blinded her.

Shadows moved in front of the lights, and red beams joined the white ones.

"Lower your weapons," Desmond's deep voice boomed from far behind her. "Lower your weapons, Domers, or Magnolia Kent goes into the river."

The flashes of red lowered toward the ground.

"Magnolia, are you all right?" A magnified voice came from the far end of the bridge.

"Yes," Nola said, her voice stuck in her throat. She swallowed. "Yes!" She shouted.

"Bring the package to the middle of the bridge," Desmond called. "Once we confirm you've given us what we asked for, we'll give you the girl."

Lights bounced across the bridge as three guards ran forward, two with rifles pointed at the vampires, one with a box in his hands.

"That's it?" Nola asked. "That's all you wanted?"

"It's a lot." Julian let go of Nola's arm and took a step forward. "I'm coming to inspect the package."

Nola held her breath as Julian ran toward the rifles all alone.

"He shouldn't be out there by himself," Nola said. "What if something goes wrong?"

"Careful, Domer," Raina said, "you almost sound like you care."

The guards placed the package in the middle of the bridge and took three steps back.

Julian bowed to them as he reached the box before kneeling over it.

A minute ticked past and then another as Julian examined the package.

"It's all here," he finally called over his shoulder.

"Here we go." Raina pushed Nola forward. "Try not to end up in Nightland again."

"In case you stab me a little too well next time?" Nola asked, trying to sound cavalier as her knees wobbled with each step.

"If you hadn't been wearing an oversize protective guard coat, I would've gotten you in the heart. And then what would we have to trade?" Raina said.

Nola turned to see a smirk on Raina's face.

"Hooray for oversized coats," Nola whispered, unsure if any sound had really come out.

Julian stood, hands behind his back as he faced the guards.

"I'll pick up the box," Julian said. "Then Magnolia walks to you."

"The girl comes to us first," the guard said.

"Funny how I know our prisoner's name, and you call your citizen *the girl*."

"Julian," Raina hissed.

"Anyway," Julian said, "I pick up the box, then you get *the girl* whilst we run away. If you don't agree"—Julian pointed over his shoulder, and instantly cold hands wrapped around Nola's neck—"one flick of my dear friend's wrists, and Magnolia is no more."

Silence hung over the bridge. Raina's fingers around Nola's neck drained the warmth from her body, leaving her shivering.

"I like that," Raina murmured. "Keep it up."

"Take the box," the guard said.

"Thank you." Julian lifted the box that seemed to weigh hardly anything, at least to a vampire.

"Now the girl," the guard called.

"Good luck," Raina said, shoving Nola forward.

Nola stumbled before her legs remembered how to walk. The bridge echoed with each step under the heavy boots Raina had given her. In two steps, she was past Julian. A moment later, a guard lifted her into his arms and sprinted back across the bridge, carrying her like a child.

Roars spilt the night as the Outer Guard's trucks started.

Nola twisted, trying to look back at the other end of the bridge to see if the vampires had made it to safety. In the glare of the truck lights, she could almost make out two figures running away across the bridge.

"You're safe now," the guard who carried her said.

"Is she hurt?" Lenora jumped out of the back of a truck and ran toward them.

Someone pushing a gurney sprinted forward.

Lenora grabbed her daughter's hand as the guard lowered Nola onto the gurney. Nola gagged as the smell of medicine and cleaner surrounded her.

Lenora gasped, looking horror-struck at Nola's red, scarred hands. "What did they do to you?"

"Out of the way, ma'am," a doctor said as two guards lifted the gurney into a truck. Lenora clambered in after, and the truck sped up the hill.

A guard waited in the corner of the truck. He reached out, placing a hand on Nola's shoulder before taking off his helmet.

Sweat covered Jeremy's forehead, and tears welled in the corners of his eyes.

"You're alive," he whispered, lifting Nola's hand to his lips. "Thank God you're alive."

CHAPTER TWENTY-SIX

The slow, steady beeping marked the minutes they forced Nola to lay in bed. After the Outer Guard raced her back to the domes, the doctors had made Lenora and Jeremy leave. They ran tests and scans, drawing her blood and searching her entire body for signs of harm.

"I'm fine," Nola said, so many times the words seemed to lose all meaning.

They put a mask over her face and made her breathe in medicine that smelled like soured fruit, then stuck needles into her arm to pump in antibiotics. Each of her bruises had to be recorded. Kieran's finger marks showed purple on her arms. The doctors all spoke in low voices about the horrible abuse she had suffered.

Nola bit her lips until they bled, fighting the need to scream that Kieran had been saving her life when he bruised her—he would never ever hurt her. But then they would know where Kieran was, and they would never believe her anyway.

Finally, when the sun had fully risen, the doctors left.

Before Nola could take a breath, more people invaded the bright white cell. Jeremy's father walked stoically into the room followed by a man with a bald head and thick black eyebrows, wearing a Dome Guard uniform. The embroidered rectangle on his chest read *Captain Stokes*. Lenora and Jeremy followed close behind, Lenora leaning on Jeremy's arm for support.

"How are you, Magnolia?" Captain Ridgeway asked in the softest tone Nola had ever heard him use.

"I'm fine," Nola said for the hundredth time that hour.

Captain Ridgeway nodded to Lenora and Jeremy, and they parted ways, taking up posts on either side of the head of Nola's bed as though guarding her.

Jeremy reached out to take Nola's hand, but it was heavily bandaged in thick foam. They had to heal the imperfections the rain had left on her skin.

Nola wanted to tear off the bandages and throw them to the floor.

Why does it matter if I'm not dome perfect?

"Magnolia," Lenora said, "did you hear him?"

Nola looked to Captain Ridgeway. He stared down at her with mixed concern and anger on his face. Nola hoped the anger wasn't for her.

"No," Nola said. "Sorry."

"I need to ask you what happened when they took you," Captain Ridgeway said. "The more we know, the sooner we can act."

"Act?" Nola tried to sit up in bed, but Jeremy's hand on her shoulder held her down.

"We need to know how they got in and what happened to you," Captain Ridgeway said, his eyes boring into Nola's as though he hoped to watch the events unfold within them. "The more we know, the better we can protect the domes and make sure the Vampers don't get in here again."

"All right," Nola said.

"They've said we can stay, if it'll make it easier for you. If you'll feel more comfortable," Lenora said, brushing a hair from Nola's face. She hadn't done that since Nola was very little.

"But if you would rather speak to us alone," Captain Stokes said, his glare darting from Lenora to Jeremy, "then I am sure they can wait outside and see you when we've finished."

Will it be easier to lie with them in here, or to say it all again later?

Jeremy's hand warmed Nola's shoulder. He was there, protecting her from his father and Captain Stokes.

"They can stay," Nola said.

"Fine." Captain Ridgeway nodded. "Now, start from the beginning."

"The beginning..." Nola's mind raced back to kissing Jeremy under the bushes. "I had a fight with my mother."

Lenora gave a sharp exhale. Nola looked up and found tears welling in her mother's eyes.

"I was upset, so I went to see Jeremy," Nola said. "I know it was late, and I shouldn't have been there—"

"I should have walked you home," Jeremy said, his voice a low growl.

"No." Nola laid a mittened hand on Jeremy's. She should have made them leave. She had only thought of making it easier on herself, not protecting them. "They wanted me. If you had been there, they would have hurt you."

"What happened when you left Jeremy?" Captain Stokes stepped forward.

"I was leaving, and then two people came out of the dark," Nola said, remembering the words Julian had taught her. "A man and a woman. The woman had a knife. She told me to send the guard at the stairs to Jeremy's house. She said she would kill me if I didn't. Her eyes were black. I knew she was a vampire and I wouldn't be able to run away, so I did it."

"What happened next?" Captain Stokes asked.

For the first time Nola noticed the recorder sitting in his palm.

"They made me put on the guard's hat and coat. We went back to Bright Dome, and in the back there was a loose section of glass. We crawled through it and into the rain."

"Did you move the glass or did they?" Captain Stokes asked.

Fingerprints. Julian had warned her once she told the guards how she had gotten out, they would check for fingerprints.

"I did," Nola said, "mostly. The woman told me to, and I tried, but it was heavy. The man ended up moving it in the end."

"What then?"

"We went outside. Down the hill toward the bridge. The rain was so thick, I could barely see. I got scared. I didn't know where they were taking me. So I ran. I barely made it ten feet. Something sliced into my back, and I fell. I think that's how I hurt my hands." Nola glanced down at the thick bandages that hid the red scars. "My head hurt, and when I woke up I was locked in a room. There was a doctor who took care of me. Then he came to ask me questions."

"Who's *he*?" Captain Ridgeway asked, a fire brewing in his eyes.

"Emanuel." Nola whispered the word. Julian had told her to say it, said to give the name, that the Outer Guard already knew who commanded Nightland, but the hatred in Captain Ridgeway's eyes frightened Nola.

Jeremy's hand tightened on Nola's shoulder. Had he heard of Emanuel, too?

"What did Emanuel want to know?" Stokes asked.

"About Green Leaf," Nola said, her stomach throbbing as her mother gave a tiny sob. "They wanted to know what seed groups you had brought back and if we were expanding the domes to accommodate planting the new crops. I was scared, and it didn't seem important, so I told him."

"Good girl," Lenora said. "Why on earth would they think you knew anything worth all of this?"

"I don't think they really cared," Nola said, keeping her words steady. "I answered Emanuel's questions, and he left. I didn't see anyone again until they came to tell me they had given you a ransom demand and you had agreed to the swap. A few times, they gave me food. But the next time Emanuel came to see me was for the trade. They put a bag over my head and took me to the bridge. I didn't see anything until the bridge was in sight." Nola looked to Stokes. "I'm sorry I can't be more helpful."

"You've done very well, Magnolia," Captain Ridgeway said.

"Dr. Kent, Jeremy, why don't you give us a few minutes?" Captain Stokes said, his tone brusque and hard.

"Why?" Jeremy tightened his grip on Nola's shoulder. "You've asked your questions. She needs to rest."

"I'm afraid there are a few things left unanswered," Captain Stokes said, "and I think perhaps it's better to leave Magnolia on her own to answer them."

"I'm not leaving my daughter," Lenora said. "Ask your questions."

"As you wish." Stokes nodded. "The doctors found traces of drugs in your system. A version of Vamp."

Lenora gasped and seized Nola's face in her hands, staring into her eyes.

"I'm fine, Mom." Nola sat up, trying to push her mother away with her mittened hand. "The doctor gave it to me. Just a tiny bit. He was saving my life."

"By trying to make you a Vamper?" Jeremy sat on the bed next to Nola, examining her eyes as though searching for a monster behind the blue.

"Vamp helps you heal faster," Nola said, touching Jeremy's cheek with her bandaged hand. "They don't have a hospital like we do in here. I was stabbed in the shoulder. I would have died. And I'm fine. I can eat food and everything."

"And your leg?" Stokes asked.

"I don't know how that happened," Nola said. "But the doctor said he did the same thing as with my shoulder. Is that all?"

Nola stared at Stokes who glanced at Captain Ridgeway before responding. "No. There are bruises on your arms."

"And they matter more than me being stabbed?" Nola said.

"They're hand prints," Captain Ridgeway said. "Marks like that, someone pinned you down."

Lenora grabbed Nola's arm with shaking hands and pushed back her sleeve. "Oh God."

Jeremy wrapped his arm around Nola, pulling her close to him. His angry breaths rattled against her cheek.

"What's your question?" Nola didn't let herself flinch as she met Captain Ridgeway's gaze. She had been pinned down. Kieran was trying to protect her from the Outer Guard's attack, but that had been after Julian had taught her the lie.

"How did you get those marks, Magnolia?" Captain Ridgeway asked. "We need to know who pinned you down. Did someone hurt you?"

"Did one of the Vampers attack you?" Stokes asked, stepping in front of Captain Ridgeway. "Did Emanuel force himself on you?"

"What?" Nola screeched. "No, why would you think that? I told you they kept me in a room."

"Where Emanuel visited you," Captain Ridgeway said. "It's not your fault, Magnolia. No one would blame you."

"Emanuel never hurt me," Nola spat. "He would never lay a hand on me."

"You were stabbed." Jeremy's face was ice white, pain wrinkled the corners of his eyes where laughter should have lived. "They *did* hurt you."

"Yes," Nola said. "No. Yes, I was stabbed. No, Emanuel never raised a hand to me. He never would. You talk about him like he's some kind of monster—"

"He's a Vamper."

"He's a leader!" Nola shouted, shoving her mother and Jeremy away. "He is a leader of a lot of very desperate people. Emanuel doesn't want to hurt anybody. He's just trying to help his people survive!"

"Then where did you get the bruises?" Captain Ridgeway asked, the angry lines between his brows the only sign he had noticed Nola's outburst.

"When your guards tried to destroy Nightland," Nola said. "When you decided to blow your way into the tunnels when you had already agreed to a deal. Emanuel had come to get me. There was an explosion nearby, and part of the ceiling in my room fell. Emanuel saved me. He knocked me down and pinned me to the ground, out of the way of the falling rocks. He didn't want me to get hurt."

No one spoke as all four stared at Nola.

"Magnolia," Lenora said when the silence had begun to pound in Nola's ears, "you should rest. I'm sure any other questions they have can wait until later."

"Yes, Dr. Kent," Captain Stokes said, "I'm sure we can speak more after Magnolia has regained her composure."

Nola laughed. "I'm sure we can."

"Come on." Jeremy took her elbow, guiding Nola to lie back on the bed.

"Dr. Kent, if I could have a word," Captain Stokes said, still not pocketing his recorder. "In my office."

Lenora looked down at Nola.

"Go, Mom. Get it over with so they can leave us alone."

"I'll be back soon," Lenora said, tucking the sheets in around Nola before following Captain Stokes from the room.

"You'll be safe here," Jeremy said. "I won't let anyone hurt you. Not ever again." He leaned down and kissed the top of Nola's head.

"There are guards in the hall," Captain Ridgeway said, his face softening. "You can sleep. The domes are secure."

"Thanks," Nola said.

Captain Ridgeway turned to leave, but Jeremy sat down next to Nola.

"Can I stay with you?" he whispered.

His father had stopped outside the door, standing guard, feet planted apart, one hand on his weapon.

"To see if I drool?" Nola asked. Her eyelids weighed as heavy as lead as she laid her head down on the pillow.

"To see that you're safe," Jeremy said, taking Nola's bandaged hand in his. "I almost lost you, Nola. I could have lost you forever." He kissed the inside of Nola's wrist. "I can't risk that again."

"I'm not going anywhere." Pain tore at the edges of Nola's heart as she said the words.

I have nowhere to go.

She couldn't leave the domes. Her future lay inside the glass prison. But as she drifted off to sleep, her mind flew to Kieran, lying in a hospital bed deep underground. And she knew he would be thinking of her, too.

CHAPTER TWENTY-SEVEN

Hurried whispers lured Nola back out of sleep. It took her a moment to realize the voices came from the shadows beyond her door.

"This is my fault, Dad." Jeremy dragged a hand over his short hair. "I should have protected her. I should have made sure she got home safe."

"You should have." Captain Ridgeway took his son by the shoulders. "You *should* have walked her home. You *should* have made sure she wasn't alone in the dark. Every day for the rest of your life you'll wish you had walked that girl back to her mother."

Jeremy clutched his chest as though someone had punched a hole straight through him.

"But it's still not your fault. There was no reason you should have thought Vampers would have found a way into the domes, let alone targeted Lenora Kent's daughter. Just because you *should* have walked her home," Captain Ridgeway said, still gripping Jeremy's shoulders, "that doesn't make what those monsters did your fault. That's on them, not you."

"It *is* on me," Jeremy said. "I could have stopped it. All of those scars are my fault. If one of those monsters raped her—"

"She says they didn't."

"She says they would never hurt her." Jeremy turned away from his father, and light fell across his face. His eyes were wide with madness and pain. "She thinks they're good people, Dad. What if they brainwashed her?"

"They didn't," Captain Ridgeway said. He turned to look in at Nola, and she clamped her eyes shut. "She's confused, but she's still her. It happens sometimes. Kidnap victims start to sympathize with their kidnappers."

"So, what do I do?" Jeremy said.

"Let her heal," Captain Ridgeway said. "Give her time to sort out everything those monsters put her through."

There was a long pause.

"And keep a close eye on her, in case she sorts things out the wrong way."

"Thanks, Dad."

"I always thought you'd be a good Outer Guard, Son," Captain Ridgeway said. There were two soft thumps of Jeremy being patted on the shoulder. "Between your mother's blood and mine, I knew you'd have what it takes. But now, I'll be damned if you don't turn out to be the best guard we've ever seen."

"Why?" Jeremy asked. His voice sounded closer, and his shadow fell across Nola's eyelids as he stood next to her bed.

"Because you've got that girl to fight for."

The doctors swarmed Nola as soon as she woke up. More blood to be drawn, more drugs to be administered. Lenora sat by her daughter's bed the whole time, asking questions about everything they were doing until Nola asked her to stop. She didn't want to know what the needles were for. She just wanted them to finish their work and leave her alone.

She hadn't seen Jeremy since she woke up. Every time she thought of him, the guilt rushed back. He blamed himself for her being kidnapped, but that wasn't what had happened at all.

"Where's Jeremy?" Nola finally asked her mother when they took the horrible breathing mask off after a half-hour treatment.

"I sent him away." Lenora pinched the bridge of her nose. "He didn't sleep last night. He stayed awake, watching you. He's terrified you'll disappear again. I am, too."

"Mom—"

"I'm sorry we fought." Tears shone in the corners of Lenora's eyes. "You are a good and kind girl. You have a bigger heart than I am capable of, and if I had lost you—"

"You didn't."

"I know. And I am so very grateful for that." Lenora patted Nola's hand. The thick mittens had been replaced by green silicone gloves filled with goo that didn't seem to warm up no matter how long it touched her skin.

"And Jeremy," Lenora said. "He's a good boy. It's difficult for me to admit, but

I was wrong about him. And his father. I don't think either of them slept while you were gone. If it hadn't been for Captain Ridgeway and the Outer Guard, I don't know if we would have gotten you back alive."

"Right. You're right."

Julian had taught her the lie.

He didn't teach me how to live with it.

"How's Sleeping Beauty?" Jeremy appeared at the door.

"I'm fine," Nola said.

I'm never going to get to stop answering that question.

"I thought *you* were sleeping," Nola said.

"I did." Jeremy smiled. "I'm bright as a daisy."

"If you're going to sit with her for a while..." Lenora said, standing.

"Go to your lab, Mom." Nola shooed her mother away.

"I'll check in later." Lenora gave a quick wave and slipped out the door.

"Wow," Nola said. "For her, that was downright clingy."

"She was worried about you." Jeremy sat down on Nola's bed, holding out a cup of foamy green sludge. "Terrified actually. We all were."

"So, now you want to poison me for scaring you so badly?" Nola sniffed the cup. It smelled like a mix between fungus, chlorophyll, and fertilizer.

"It's a detox shake." Jeremy grinned. "It's what the guards who go outside the domes regularly drink to help purify their systems."

Nola took a sip, and gagged on the thick froth.

"I never saw my dad with this." She tried to push the cup away, but Jeremy lifted it back to her mouth.

"He would have had it in the barracks, not at home. Drink up."

Grimacing, Nola took another sip.

"You'll be having this for meals for a few days."

"Lucky me." Nola took a gulp and regretted it instantly.

"You *are* very lucky." Jeremy took her face in his hands, leaning in so his forehead touched hers. "And I am very lucky to have you home."

"Jeremy."

"I thought, when the raid didn't get you"—Jeremy's hands shook—"I thought we'd lost you for sure."

"The Outer Guard," Nola said, freezing with the cup halfway to her mouth, "were they sent down to the tunnels to get me? Only to get me? Emanuel had already made a deal."

"We didn't think they'd show at the bridge, and we couldn't leave you with the blood suckers."

"But the guards. Six guards died." The air vanished from the room. From the domes. "And vampires. Vampires died, too. Because of me."

Her glass shattered as it hit the floor.

"No. Because of the Vampers that took you," Jeremy said. "They took a citizen of the domes. We had to get you back. Those guards knew what they were getting into."

"Dead." The line of guards, their bodies torn and twisted, flashed through Nola's mind. "Bloody and dead because of me."

Sobs broke over her words. Gasping breaths racked her lungs, sending pain shooting into her heart. She had tried to help, and now there was blood on her hands.

Jeremy bundled her into his arms. Hushing softly, he lay back on the bed, cradling her to his chest. "It's all right, Nola. It's over now. I'll keep you safe. I love you."

CHAPTER TWENTY-EIGHT

It took two days for the doctors to allow Nola to go home. Two days of smiling sweetly and hoping no one looked too close. Jeremy stayed with her all the time, only leaving when Lenora came by for a few hours here and there.

Three times the doctors had retested her blood, making sure the level of Vamp had decreased. Making sure she hadn't been turned.

A full set of guards came to escort Nola home. Lenora held onto Nola's arm the whole way to Bright Dome, as though terrified Nola might crumble and fall. What Lenora should have been afraid of was the voice in the back of Nola's mind screaming, *Run!*

But how could Nola run when she was flanked by guards?

Nola could sense Jeremy's eyes on her back as they walked. He hadn't said anything about her breakdown in the hospital. Only sat with her as she stared at the ceiling, wondering if the bodies of the guards had been returned to the domes or dumped into the river. He'd made small talk about the planting and had given regards from classmates. But mostly he had just held Nola tight as though he feared she would shatter into a thousand irreparable pieces. He didn't know how right he was.

"Here we are," Lenora said when they approached the house, as though Nola might have forgotten what her home looked like in a week.

"Thanks for walking me," Nola said to the guards, looking at their boots instead of their faces.

"You're welcome, Miss Kent," one of the guards said.

Nola glanced up to the man's face. He was broadly built with a square jaw and bright blond hair.

"Your brother," Nola forced the question out. "He was at Nightland?"

"He was a brave man, miss," the guard said, the sudden crease between his eyes his only show of grief. "He died a hero's death."

"He did," Lenora said, taking the guard's hand. "And we are so very thankful."

The guard nodded to Lenora and looked back to Nola. "Welcome home."

Lenora kept her hand on Nola's back as she guided her into the house.

"Well," Lenora said as soon as she had closed the kitchen door, leaving only herself, Nola, and Jeremy in the house, "I guess I should make dinner. A nice welcome home meal."

"You don't have to," Nola said. "You can go back to the lab."

"No." Lenora shook her head, straightening Nola's braid over her shoulder. "I want to make you a welcome home dinner. Jeremy, you'll stay of course."

"Thank you, ma'am," Jeremy said.

"I think I'll go to my room for awhile," Nola said.

The clanging of the pots and pans drilled into her ears as she climbed the steps.

Nothing should be this normal. This calm.

Jeremy's footsteps followed her up the stairs.

"I'm fine," Nola said as she opened the door to her room. "I can find my..." but her words trailed off as she stared at her desk. A beautiful orchid waited for her.

"Do you like it?" Jeremy asked. "It's an old tradition. To bring your girl flowers."

"Where did you get it?"

Bright purple speckled the white petals.

"I have an in with the head of Plant Preservation," Jeremy said.

"It's beautiful." Nola turned to face Jeremy, feeling a genuine smile flicker across her face.

"Not as beautiful as you." Jeremy pressed his lips to the top of Nola's head. "I love you."

He had said it a dozen times since Nola came back. She still didn't know how to answer.

"Jeremy, I—" How could she begin to break his heart?

"Don't," Jeremy said, wrapping his arms around Nola. "I don't need you to say it back. I don't need you to tell me you want to spend the rest of your life with me."

Nola's heart stopped as Jeremy tipped her chin up to meet his gaze.

"But I need you to know that I love you. I've loved you for years, Nola, and if I hadn't told you before they took you, if you hadn't come back..."

"But I did," Nola whispered.

"And now I have the chance to tell you every day," Jeremy said. "I won't lose that."

Nola pulled her gaze away, looking back at the flower. The bloom seemed so strong, so sturdy, but a fierce wind could break its stem. Damage it beyond repair.

"I know you need time," Jeremy said. "You need time to sort through everything that happened. But I'll be here. I'll help you any way I can. I love you. I want to spend the rest of my life with you."

Nola's heart skipped. For a moment, she wasn't sure it would start beating again. For a moment, she didn't want it to.

"I'll wait for you, Nola. As long as it takes."

"But what if I'm not here?" Nola said.

Better to make a break. A clean break.

Jeremy froze his arms still around Nola's waist. "What you do mean *not here?*"

"I can't stay here. I can't stay in the domes." Now that she'd begun, the words tumbled out. "Eleven people died because of me. I can't stay locked in here and pretend it didn't happen. If I go out there, I could help people. There are gardens, ways to grow food out there. I could help people have food to eat. I could save lives. And then maybe those eleven deaths would mean something."

"They do mean something," Jeremy said. "Those guards who went down after you were trained. They were doing their jobs."

"They should have left me!" Nola clamped her hands over her mouth. "But they didn't. I'm here, and they're dead. And the only way I can live with that is to make my life worth it."

"You can do that here," Jeremy said, taking Nola's hands in his larger ones, making her newly healed skin disappear beneath his grasp. "You are brilliant, like your mother. You can join botany, help with the work of the domes."

"That's not good enough." Tears stung her eyes. "There are people dying out there right now, and I can't just pretend it isn't happening. I've seen it. I can't ignore it."

Jeremy studied Nola for a minute as though searching for a crack. "Fine. We'll leave the domes."

"We'll? Jeremy, no you don't understand."

"I lost you out there once. I won't do it again. I love you, Nola, and love means finding a way to stay together. You go out there, I go, too."

"Jere—"

"But not yet. You say you want to help people, and I understand that. But you haven't even finished school yet. You finish school and do your apprentice-ship, then we'll go."

"An apprenticeship takes a couple of years. I can't stay here that long. There are people out there who need help now."

"There will always be people who need help, Nola. But how much more good will you be able to do when you're fully trained?"

Nola buried her face in Jeremy's shirt, shutting her eyes as tightly as she could bear.

"Once your training's done, we'll ask to be released from the domes." Jeremy held her tight, his broad shoulders surrounding her, blocking out everything else in the world. "I'll have a few years as a guard by then. I'll be able to protect you."

"Jeremy," Nola said, not taking her face from his chest. "I can't let you do that."

"You're not *letting* me do anything," Jeremy said.

"And when we get sick?"

Jeremy stepped back so Nola had to look at him. "I won't let that happen."

He meant it.

He would leave the domes for me. Leave everything he knows to follow me.

"I should go down," Jeremy said. "I don't want your mother to get worried about my being up here. She made a whole list of rules for me."

"She did?"

"Yep," Jeremy said. "And I'll follow them to a T. I don't want to lose my 'Nola privileges.'"

Nola took Jeremy's hand before he could leave. "How are you so good?"

"Because"—Jeremy leaned down, brushing his lips against Nola's—"I've spent a long time trying to become the kind of man you deserve." He smiled and disappeared through the door.

Nola went to the head of her bed, sinking down onto the floor. She took deep breaths, staring down at her perfect hands, trying not to let panic take her.

Jeremy loved her. He was perfect and good. He would do anything to keep her safe.

Kieran.

They had said their goodbyes. She should leave him alone. He didn't want her to be a part of Nightland, didn't want to make her a vampire.

Nola dug her fists into her eyes. Being a citizen of the domes meant making sacrifices to build a better world.

The figures of the dead eleven swam into her mind. The people who would morn for them, the days they would never get to live.

Nola reached into the desk drawer for a piece of paper. Her fingers closed around the tiny wooden tree Kieran had left for her.

Her hand shook as she found a pen and began to write.

Dear Jeremy,

I'm sorry. I'm sorry I'm not the girl you need me to be. I have to go now. I can't wait. I can't survive it. Please don't try to find me. More people will get hurt, and I can't survive that either.

Thank you. Thank you for being there even before I knew it was you holding me up. Please find another girl to love. Someone who can give you the life you deserve.

I love you, Jeremy. You are good, and brave, and everything wonderful. I will always love you.

Please forgive me,
Nola

She folded up the paper and tucked it under the orchid. He would find it first. He would tear apart the domes searching for her. Nola tugged on her work boots and pulled her thick coat from the closet, hiding the tree charm in her pocket. She could sneak out now while they thought she was resting. She would go to the atrium. Sneak onto a truck and find a way out from there.

Nola's mother's laugh rang up the stairs. She hadn't heard her mother laugh like that in years. The urge to run to her mother and hold her close froze Nola in place. But if she went down the stairs, she might never find the courage to leave.

Nola slipped the note back out from under the flower pot.

Please explain to my mother. And tell her I'm sorry.

She scrawled the words quickly and tucked the note back in place.

Taking the I-Vent from her drawer, she slipped it into her pocket. Eden might need it. Sitting on the windowsill, she swung one leg out the window.

BANG!

CHAPTER TWENTY-NINE

The sound shook the glass of the dome as brilliant orange flames lit the night. Nola tumbled backwards into the room, hitting her head on the floor. The ceiling spun as shouts shot up from the kitchen.

"Nola!" Jeremy shouted.

"What's happening?" Lenora screamed.

Jeremy threw open Nola's door.

"Are you hurt?" He knelt by her side.

"I fell," Nola said, shaking her head and sending her vision spinning again, "but I'm fine."

Flashing red light poured through Nola's window as the emergency siren blared to life.

"Is she all right?" Lenora ran into the room.

A piercing *beep, beep, beep* cut in between the siren's wails.

"We're under attack." The color drained from Lenora's face. "The domes are under attack. I have to secure the seedlings." Lenora looked down at Nola.

"I'll get her to the bunker," Jeremy said, yanking Nola to her feet. "You go."

Lenora nodded and ran out the door.

"Who's attacking us?" Nola screamed as another explosion shook the house. A fresh burst of orange lit the night, coming from the direction of the atrium.

"I don't know," Jeremy said, pulling Nola's arm. "But we have to go."

He ran down the stairs and out into the night, half-carrying Nola as she struggled to keep up.

Other figures dashed through the dark, heading for the tunnel. Nola couldn't recognize the people in the flickering shadows of the fire that blazed in front of the atrium. There were two bunkers for catastrophes in the domes. Nola had always thought they were for natural disasters—a hurricane strong enough to destroy their home—but now the Domers ran from monsters in the dark.

Tiny *pops* and *bangs* pounded through the glass as the guards added their weapons to the cacophony. At the base of the stairs Jeremy turned right, away from the atrium. The entrance to A bunker was there, under the vehicle site. But all the Domers ran away from the fighting, fleeing to the same hope of safety: the B bunker under the seed storage area.

Nola sprinted next to Jeremy, her feet pounding as quickly as they could. She stepped on something soft and tumbled to the ground.

"Nola!" Jeremy screamed, lifting her to her feet before she could see what she had tripped over. A man lay face down on the ground, blood pooling around him.

Jeremy pushed Nola against the wall as another group came running by, barely missing trampling the man.

"He's breathing." Jeremy hoisted the man over his shoulder. "We can't leave him here."

A *pop* sounded in the hall behind them.

"Go!" Jeremy pushed Nola in front of him.

Down more stairs and past the Dome Guard's quarters. The doors to the empty barracks sat open. All of them had gone to the atrium.

Nola ran flat-out, Jeremy keeping up even with the added weight of the man.

They sprinted down another hall. A knot of people ran toward them. Nola moved to the side, letting them pass on their way to the atrium. The red lights flashed overhead, lighting the corridor and glinting off a head of scarlet and purple hair sliding out from under a hat.

"Raina!" Nola screamed.

Raina glanced back then picked up speed, running to the head of the knot of vampires, each wearing a heavily sagging pack.

"Stop!" Nola turned and tore back up the hall after the vampires.

"Nola, no!"

She heard Jeremy's shout but didn't slow down.

She sprinted up the stairs, ignoring the pain in her lungs, reaching the top just in time to see the last of the vampire pack round a corner toward the atrium. Nola pounded after them. People fled from the fight up ahead. Wounded guards were being carried into the hall, but there were still sounds of fighting coming from the atrium.

"Stop them!" Nola shouted to a group of guards that ran past her down to the tunnels Nola had just run out of, but the guards kept moving, their eyes focused front. Just before the atrium, the vampires turned left into the entrance for the small Grassland Dome.

Nola followed, barely hearing the shout of "Nola!" behind her.

The Grassland Dome had always been quiet and peaceful, filled with the rustling of grass. But tonight, screams rent the air. The explosion that had shattered the atrium had broken apart the glass here as well. A wide swath of the dome wall had shattered.

The vampires ran toward the break in the glass. In a moment, they would be outside. Nola couldn't catch them.

A group of guards ran in from the night, weapons raised high, blocking the way out.

Something hit Nola hard in the back, knocking her to the ground before a series of pops blasted over the bedlam.

"Stay down." Jeremy pinned Nola to the ground.

"Their bags." Nola shoved Jeremy off of her, trying to stand. "Their bags are full. They stole from us!"

Nola looked around wildly, half-expecting Emanuel to appear out of the dark and explain what was happening.

"I'll warn the guards." Jeremy leapt to his feet and charged toward the fight.

The guards battled hand-to-hand with the vampires now. Knives and clubs flashed in the night.

"Jeremy!" Nola screamed after him. The vampires would tear him apart. "Jeremy."

Nola ran after him, ignoring the sting as the tall grass tore at her legs. More vampires and guards had joined the fight, with more appearing from the darkness every moment. Jeremy charged toward the middle of it.

Nola ducked as a pipe flew from the hand of a fighter, whizzing only a breath away from her skull. A cold hand grabbed Nola's wrist, jerking her back.

Before Nola could look at the face of the man who had grabbed her, he knocked her to the ground, planting a knee in her stomach. The man smiled and bared his glistening white fangs that were already stained red with blood.

"Help!" Nola screamed.

The man laughed. No one could hear her over the chaos.

He leaned down, pinning Nola's arms to the ground. She screamed as his fangs pierced her skin.

"Get off of her," a woman shouted, and the man was torn from Nola and tossed aside like a ragdoll.

Nola grabbed the place on her neck where the man's fangs had been ripped from her flesh. Hot blood streamed down her collar bone.

Raina stood over her in the dark.

"That one is to be left alone!" Raina shouted at the man. "It's his orders."

But the man had already reached for his knife. Holding it high in the air, he threw the blade at Nola, bloodlust glinting in his eyes.

Nola saw the knife. Watched it flying end over end toward her heart. There was nowhere to run, nothing to do.

Raina leapt to the side, and the sharp point of the knife disappeared into her chest.

"No!" Nola shouted as Raina collapsed to the ground.

The man looked down at Raina's body and ran, cutting through the fight and out into the night.

"Raina." Nola crawled over to her.

The knife stuck out of Raina's chest, moving as she fumbled for the hilt. Raina coughed, and blood trickled out of her mouth.

"You're okay." Nola lifted Raina's head into her lap, pushing the scarlet and purple hair away from her face.

A trail of blood dripped from Raina's lips to her chin. She coughed again, and a horrible gurgling sound came from the wound.

"You can heal from this." Nola pushed her hands down around the blade, trying to stop the bleeding. "Should I leave the knife in or take it out?"

A shrill whistle came from outside the domes.

"It's too late for me, kid," Raina said, her voice crackling as she spoke. She coughed a laugh and smiled. "Funny that a knife stopped me."

"I'll get help," Nola said, laying Raina's head gently down. She stood, searching for a vampire who would know what to do. But all the vampires were running out through the glass. The guards who were left standing were still trying to fight, but there were too many vampires.

"Stop please!" Nola shouted. "She needs help! Raina needs help."

Only one of the fleeing pack turned to face her. He wore a dark hood, but as the red light hit his face, she saw him.

Kieran.

His eyes were coal black, no hint of green or gold left at all. He carried a heavy box in his arms and was surrounded by vampires holding weapons.

"Go!" a voice shouted. Bryant lifted his pipe and charged at the guards.

Kieran looked at her for only a moment longer before racing after him.

"Kieran," Nola whispered, sinking to the ground. There were more shouts of pain and a visceral scream.

"Jeremy!" Nola shouted.

He was in the center of the fight, trying to stop the vampires.

Nola turned back to Raina. Her eyes were closed, but she would heal. She had to. Nola wrenched the knife from Raina's chest and ran into the fight.

Jeremy's left arm hung limp and bloody at his side. In his right hand, he held a guard's club, which he swung at a boy with brilliant red hair.

Nola had seen the red haired boy in Nightland. He had looked so young and helpless in the tunnels beneath the city. Now he bared his teeth, violent hatred twisting his face. He swung his broken sword at Jeremy's neck. Jeremy jumped backwards, dodging the jagged strip of metal, and swayed sideways. He had stepped on a guard who lay face up on the ground, her eyes wide open and blank.

The red-haired boy lunged again, taking advantage of Jeremy's stumble. Jeremy tried to duck, but his wounds slowed his reflexes.

Jeremy!

Nola couldn't make her mouth form the word. She raised Raina's knife high in the air and sank the blade into the boy's back. The sword fell from his hand as he screamed in rage and pain before dropping to the ground.

He lay still next to the fallen guard, his eyes as blank as hers.

"Nola." Jeremy scrambled toward her.

"I know where the heart is," Nola said.

"Nola," Jeremy said, "are you hurt?"

"I know where the heart is." Nola turned away from the red-haired boy. He wouldn't wake up.

"We have to go," Jeremy said, pushing Nola to move with his good hand that still clutched the club.

They ran back out of the Grassland Dome. Blood slicked the corridor floor.

"We need to get you to the bunker." Jeremy turned toward the corridor that led to seed storage and safety.

Nola ran to the atrium instead, grateful that Jeremy's heavy footfalls followed her.

Most of the glass on the city side of the atrium had been shattered. Shards of it covered the ground. The vampires had fled into the night. Guards stood at the break in the glass, trying to secure their ruined wall, shooting at the vampires that fell behind the rest of Nightland's retreat. Bodies lay twisted and broken on the ground. A blond girl lay by the door.

"Nikki." Nola knelt next to her, not caring as the glass sliced her knees.

She placed a hand on Nikki's chest. Blood coated her pale pink shirt. Her throat had been torn out, and terror filled her unmoving face.

Nola kept her hand pressed to Nikki's chest, waiting for a heartbeat she knew wouldn't come.

"She must have tried to come to the atrium bunker." Jeremy lifted Nola's hand away.

The sounds of the fighting had ended, replaced by cries of fear and pain mixing with shouted orders.

"Guards on the break, keep watch!" a voice bellowed in the darkness.

"Dad." Relief flooded Jeremy's face.

"All others to the armory." Captain Ridgeway stood in the middle of the rubble. Blood covered half of his face, a gash still dripping on his brow. The stoic man who defended the domes had disappeared; a raging warrior now commanded the Outer Guard. "We're going after the Vamper scum."

Jeremy nodded and stood.

"What are you doing?" Nola grabbed his good arm as he moved to follow the others.

"Going with the guards."

"But you can't." Nola held tight to his hand. "You're hurt."

"I have to, Nola." Jeremy's voice was low, filled with an anger she had never seen in him before.

Nola wrapped her arms around him as he tried again to walk away. "You said we had to get to the bunker, so let's go. We'll go together."

"Gentry and my dad will both be out there," Jeremy said.

"They're both Outer Guard."

"So am I. I was sworn in the day they took you," Jeremy said. "It was the only way I could help find you. Nola, I have to go."

"What if you're hurt? What if—"

Jeremy leaned down, silencing her protests with a kiss. Nola wrapped her arms around his neck, pulling herself closer to him, desperate to keep him there with her.

"I can't lose you," Nola whispered as he pulled away.

"Never." Jeremy smiled. "I love you, Nola. I'll be home soon." He was gone before Nola could stop him.

CHAPTER THIRTY

Nola stood frozen in the sea of chaos, unsure of what to do. The guards would be going to Nightland soon. She knew more about the tunnels than any of them.

I can't let anything happen to Jeremy.

Nola ran to the front of the atrium. The shattered glass crunched beneath her feet with every step. Blood pooled on the floor in places. Boot prints smeared the red, leaving designs of death in the battle's wake.

Had the blood spilled from Domer or vampire veins? Was there even a way to tell?

The engines of the guard trucks had already rumbled to life.

"Wait!" Nola shouted as the guards loaded into the back. "I have to go with you!"

"Not a chance," one of the guards said, blocking her at the break in the glass.

"But I've been in Nightland. I can help." Nola watched the stream of uniforms filing out of the domes, wishing she could catch a glimpse of Jeremy.

"Miss, you're injured. You need medical attention."

Nola's hand flew to her neck, sticking to the blood that covered her skin.

"The guards," Nola said. "Some of them are hurt, and they're going."

Gentry ran past, jamming on her helmet.

"Gentry!" Nola sprinted after her, catching Gentry's arm as she climbed into the truck. "I have to go with you."

"No citizens are to leave the domes, no exceptions," Gentry said. "Get to the bunker. Your mother will be there."

Nola took a breath, trying not to scream. Her mother waited below, guarding the seeds. But Jeremy would be in the tunnels.

Jeremy fighting Kieran.

"I can help. I know about Nightland!" Nola shouted desperately as Gentry turned away.

"If you think you have important information," Gentry said, "go to the Com Room. The operation is going to be controlled from there. Maybe they'll talk to you."

"Thank you," Nola shouted, already running for the far end of the atrium.

In the back of the atrium stood the tower, the only concrete structure to rise above the domes. Two guards flanked the doors to the staircase.

"I have to get up there," Nola panted, trying the push past the guards, who easily shoved her away.

"I'm afraid not, miss," the guard said. "Go to the medical unit. They can help you there."

"I'm Magnolia Kent. I was held in Nightland, and I have information that can help them. Please, you have to let me help."

One guard nodded to the other before raising his wrist to his mouth. "Magnolia Kent is here. She says she has information that can help."

There was a pause before a voice crackled out of the man's wrist. "Send her up."

"Thank you." Nola slid through the door before it had fully opened. She sprinted up the staircase.

This area hadn't been touched by the attack. The vampires hadn't bothered to break into the Communications Center.

Nola pounded up the flights of stairs, adrenaline pushing her to run faster. *How long until Jeremy reaches Nightland?*

A guard waited at the top of the stairs, punching the code in to open the door only when Nola stopped, gasping for air, on the top landing.

"In here." The guard ushered Nola into the wide room.

She had been in the Com Room only once before. Years ago. Her entire class had been brought up here to see how communication with the other domes and the rest of the outside world worked. That day, the room had been a place filled with wonder, where she could see the face of a person on the other side of the world as they spoke. That day the world had seemed infinite and wonderful.

Today, chaos filled the tower.

Happy faces weren't smiling back from the screen. Instead, a live feed of the guards on their way to Nightland took up the whole wall. The Outer Guard poured out of their trucks onto the street at 5th and Nightland.

"Magnolia." Captain Stokes limped toward her. "They said you have information."

Nola's mind flickered back to her lessons with Julian. Sitting at the table, learning the things she was allowed to say.

The lie doesn't matter anymore. Nightland destroyed my home.

"I know where in Nightland Emanuel lives," Nola said. "I can tell your men how to get there."

Stokes stared at her for a moment. "Do it."

"But there's a little girl," Nola said as a man strapped a headset on her. "You have to promise me you won't hurt the little girl."

"We aren't the monsters here," Stokes said. "We don't hurt children."

The Outer Guard were in Nightland now.

"Tell them which way." Stokes fixed his gaze on the screen.

Nola squinted at the picture, trying to make sense of the shadows. "The second tunnel on the left, the one with the door blown off. Go that way."

The guards all moved in formation, slowly and methodically sweeping their lights in the tunnel. As the beams flashed over the rubble, Nola remembered the last time the guards had been in Nightland. Kieran had protected her, and now she was sending the guards after him.

"How far down?" Stokes asked.

Nola swallowed and looked out over the atrium. Smoke still billowed from the fire below. Through it she could barely see the dome helicopters taking flight. The helicopters had no sides. No defense against attack. But the brave pilots would fly over the city to try and aid their compatriots. They were going to help Jeremy.

"They'll hit a bigger tunnel. Follow that left until they find the wooden door," Nola said, her voice a harsh whisper. "It's old, and the wood has carvings in it. Go through there to the gallery. It's like an old library." Nola waited, watching the screen.

Screams carried through the feed.

"Behind you!" a man's voice shouted.

"I've got him!" a woman answered.

A *pop* and a scream of rage flooded Nola's ears as the screen flashed and went black.

"There are more behind him!" a voice shouted. "Keep going. We'll cover you."

The sounds of labored breathing and more shouting pounded into Nola's ears.

"I think I found it," the voice said after a moment. "Yep, this is it."

"We're clear," a different voice said.

"Where now?"

"Go through the door at the end," Nola said. "There's a kitchen on the right. In the back, there's another door. Through there is a heavy metal door. It's the safe room. That's where Emanuel will be."

"How do you know?" Stokes turned to Nola, his eyes sharp even though blood dripped from his leg.

"That's where his daughter will be," Nola said. "He wants to keep her safe."

"We're in the kitchen," the voice came through the headset. "The room is empty. The room with the metal door is open."

"Emanuel left." The words felt hollow in Nola's mouth.

"What?" Stokes said.

"Emanuel left," Nola said. "If Eden is gone, he will be too."

"How do you know?" Stokes asked, his forehead so furrowed his eyebrows had become one angry strip of black.

"The garden." Nola pointed out the window to the skyline of the city. "On the roof above Nightland, the second tallest building in the city, there should be a garden on the roof." Just because Emanuel left didn't mean all of Nightland was gone. Maybe Kieran had stayed behind in the city, saving the poor and the hungry.

The guard barked orders for a helicopter to circle the building.

Nola watched the light of the helicopter circling in the air. It looked like a fairy, far away over the city. Barely even a speck in the distance.

"There's a bunch of trash on the roof, sir," the pilot's voiced crackled in her ears. "It looks like there was something here, but whatever it was, it's gone now."

Nola's heart crumpled. The static of the screen swayed in front of her. "They're gone."

The garden, Dr. Wynne, Kieran.

"He's gone."

Nola's knees buckled. Arms steadied her and lifted her to a chair. But she couldn't think, couldn't move beyond Kieran.

Gone.

CHAPTER THIRTY-ONE

They sat her in a chair in the back of the Com Room. A doctor came up and cleaned and wrapped the wound on her neck.

"You're a lucky girl," the doctor said. "If you'd torn your jugular, there's nothing we could have done."

"Raina saved me." Nola stared at the dried blood that still covered her hands. *Mine, Raina's, the red-haired boy I killed, Nikki's. Who else's?*

She couldn't even remember.

"Magnolia." Stokes came over from the giant screen. He had been shouting into the com a few minutes ago. Vampires had been hiding in the tunnels, waiting to ambush the guards. The guards kept talking about Emanuel leaving traps. But Emanuel would be out of the city by now, finding cover before dawn.

"Magnolia," Stokes said. "I need to ask you some questions."

"She needs to rest," the doctor said, planting himself in front of Nola.

She wanted to thank him, but Stokes had already pushed the doctor out of the way.

"I have guards risking their lives in the city," Stokes said. "She can rest when they do."

The doctor looked as though he might argue for a moment before shaking his head and walking through the metal door to the stairs.

Nola wanted to follow him. But where would she go? Had her mother made it home yet? Was her house even still standing? Had Bright Dome been destroyed?

"How did you know the path through the tunnels?" Stokes asked.

"He walked me from 5th and Nightland, from the Club to the gallery," Nola said. "He wanted me to see where he lived."

"And the garden on the roof?"

"He took me up." Tears burned in the corners of Nola's eyes. "He wanted to show me what they had built. He said they were finding a way to feed the city."

"Why didn't you tell us?"

"He said not to," Nola said. The burning had moved to her throat. "He said you would destroy the food, and people would starve. I thought they only wanted the ransom. I thought it was over and I would never see him again. He said they wanted to be left alone. I didn't want more fighting." Tears streamed down Nola's face.

"Sir," a man shouted from the front of the room. "We have a problem. The convoy's been attacked at 10th and Main."

Stokes cursed and ran back to the screen.

"We have wounded!" a voice echoed over the com. "We need emergency medical assistance."

Guards tore around the room, calling everyone they could for help. Nola pushed herself to her feet and stumbled to the door, running from the room before anyone tried to call her back.

Guards sprinted up and down the stairs. What had happened on the street? Sour rose into Nola's throat.

Wolves. There are still werewolves on the streets.

Back in the atrium, guard trucks drove in and out of the break in the glass, ignoring the place where the ruined door had been. Doctors rushed to the injured.

Nola watched as uniforms ran past, searching for Jeremy in the throng.

She shoved her shaking hands into her coat pockets. Her fingers closed around the tiny tree.

A truck rolled in, and gurneys were pulled from the back, but the doctors walked straight past. Those guards had been covered in white sheets. The doctors couldn't do anything for the dead.

Nola stood still as the chaos moved around her, her eyes constantly searching for Jeremy in the crowd. Every time a gurney passed, her heart stopped.

Not Jeremy. Please, not Jeremy.

Her nails dug into her palm as she gripped the tree. The wood cracked in her grasp. She pulled her hand from her pocket to stare at the broken and blood-covered charm. Tipping her palm, she let the tree tumble to the floor. The wood disappeared in the sea of shattered glass and blood.

The sky had turned from gray to pale orange as the sun began to rise, then back to gray as dark clouds coated the horizon. Trucks scrambled back out to the city. They had to get the rest of the guards inside before the rains began.

Lightning split the sky in the distance. The rumble of thunder shook the broken glass.

Another truck pulled into the dome. There were no gurneys this time. Only guards carrying their injured fellows.

"That's the last one!" the driver called just as the rain began to patter against the dome.

Nola ran toward the truck. Jeremy had to be in there. He had to be in the back of the truck. Nola scrambled into the truck bed. Blood stained the empty seats. "Jeremy."

She jumped down from the truck, stumbling before running through the crowd. "Jeremy! Jeremy!"

The bodies draped in white had been lined up against the wall, waiting for the families to be notified and the grieving to begin.

"Miss, you can't be over here," a guard said as Nola swayed staring at the bodies.

"Jeremy Ridgeway." Her mouth was dry. She could barely form the words. "Is he—"

"Nola," a voice called from behind her.

Nola turned to see Jeremy running toward her.

"Jeremy." Before she could remember how to move she was in his arms. She wrapped her arms around his neck so her toes barely touched the ground, pressing her cheek to his, feeling his warmth pass into her.

Tears streamed down her face as she sobbed, the exhaustion and pain of the horrible night finally flooding through her.

"Shh," Jeremy whispered. "I'm here."

"I thought," Nola coughed, "I thought I'd lost you. I waited, and I looked for you, but you didn't come back in the trucks. I thought you were gone."

Jeremy pulled away, looking down into Nola's eyes. "I would never leave you, Nola."

She leaned in, pressing herself to him as she kissed him. The world spun, but he held her close, keeping all she had been from slipping away.

Thunder shook the air again.

The rain pounded down on the dome, pouring through the break in the glass in solid sheets.

"What are we going to do?" Nola asked.

The guards backed away from the break, watching helplessly as contamination violated their home. But there was no way to fight the rain.

"We salvage what we can," Jeremy said, still holding Nola close. "Then we rebuild, we move on."

"We move on."

Jeremy took Nola's hand, and she didn't argue as he led her away from the atrium. Through the broken dome and past the broken bodies. Down the corridor to Bright Dome. Back home. There was nowhere else to go now.

BOY OF BLOOD

Book Two

CHAPTER ONE

Drops of bright red streaming and swirling into nothingness. Deep red from someone.

Someone's veins had been split open. Were they dead or still clinging to life? The blood didn't care as it was washed away. Swept down the drain by the pure water of the domes.

Nola's sobs echoed off the shower walls, blocking out the sounds of the outside world. She knelt on the floor, watching the blood turn from crimson to pink as the burning water removed all traces of the battle. Someone knelt beside her, washing her, murmuring comforting things she couldn't hear. They combed their fingers through her tangled curls, removing bits of glass and dirt.

She should look. See who was taking care of her. But what did it matter? As soon as they knew what she had done, they would disappear. Or she would. They would learn the truth. Then Nola Kent would vanish.

Strong arms wrapped her in a towel and carried her to her bed. Outside the window she caught a glimpse of the rain pounding down on the dome. But the storm wouldn't taint Bright Dome. Nola's home hadn't been harmed. They had destroyed her world but left her home. A poor attempt at pity.

Something sharp pierced her arm.

"Hush," Jeremy whispered. "It'll help you sleep."

Before Nola could say she didn't deserve sleep, darkness took her.

Her mouth tasted of cotton and blood when she woke. Her arms and legs were heavy, like someone had buried her alive. But they hadn't. She lay in her bed as though nothing had happened. A beautiful orchid sat on her desk. Jeremy had brought it for her.

A flower for his girl.

It might have been a century ago.

Nola bit the inside of her mouth, willing herself not to scream. Footsteps on the stairs finally made her sit up in bed. Someone had dressed her in her mother's robe. It smelled like Lenora Kent. Fresh flowers, earth, and strong cleaner.

She rubbed her hands over her face. Her fingers found the bandage on her neck as her bedroom door swung open.

Jeremy walked in, balancing a tray of food. A smile lit his tired face when he saw Nola.

"You're awake." Jeremy set the tray down and sat next to her on the bed. "I wasn't sure you would be yet."

"You gave me something to sleep?"

"The doctor did." Jeremy brushed a dark brown curl from her cheek.

"Doctor?" Nola thought back, trying to find where in the blood and tears a doctor had come near her. "I don't remember a doctor being here."

"Two days ago," Jeremy said. "He put the patch on your neck, too. He said you should be okay now. No permanent damage."

She kicked free of the covers and stood, tipping sideways and knocking into her desk.

Jeremy grabbed her around the waist before she could take another step toward the mirror. "Careful."

"I want to see it." Her fingers trembled as she pulled off the pale-pink patch on her neck. Two thin, white marks showed on her skin. Shaped like teardrops and barely raised at all, they were the only trace that a Vamper had bitten her, tried to kill her only two days ago.

"The doctor can work on it some more," Jeremy said, his deep brown eyes meeting Nola's in the mirror. "He'll get rid of the scars."

Nola studied her reflection. The dark curls belonged to her, but the face had changed. Paler and harder. She looked more like someone from the outside than a girl who'd spent her life in the safety of the domes.

"I don't want him to fix the scars." Nola turned away from her reflection and didn't fight as Jeremy drew her into his chest. He was so tall, and his well-muscled shoulders so broad, it felt as though he could fold her into his body and protect her from the sun itself.

Safety is just another myth.

"It happened," Nola said. "The domes were attacked, I got bit, and people died. We can't make it not true, and I don't want to pretend we can."

"Okay." Jeremy kissed the top of her head. "If that's what you want, we'll make the doctor leave the marks alone."

She stood in Jeremy's arms, waiting for something to happen. For a siren to sound or fire to rip through the Kents' tiny house. But no crashing danger came. No screams, no flames. Just Jeremy. His smell of fresh earth that matched the domes mixed with the starch in his new guard's uniform. Jeremy, warm and steady, holding her up even when she couldn't find the strength to hold him.

"What's happened?" Nola asked, when the silence grew too loud to bear. "Since...since I fell asleep."

"Not much." Jeremy guided her back to the bed. "The rain stopped for an hour that first night, and we scrambled to get the places where the domes were shattered fitted with temporary covers. But that's about all. The wounded are all out of the medical wing and back home except for the worst few. And the dead—"

"They can't be burned until the rain stops." Nola's empty stomach churned at the thought of the line of dome dead waiting their turn.

"With this much acid rain, we haven't been able to go into the city to see if any of the Vamper scum who did this to us are still there, but on the plus side—"

"They'll be stuck wherever they are, too." She tried not to picture Kieran hiding underground with the others from Nightland, packed into dark holes, desperate not to get burned. But Kieran had betrayed her, had betrayed the domes. He had led the Vampers into her home and stolen from the domes. Innocent people died because of him.

Because I trusted him.

Her hands shook, and her breath came in ragged gasps.

"Nola, we're safe here." Jeremy kissed her palm. "No one is going to get back in here to hurt you. I won't let them."

"Jeremy," Nola said, fighting to keep her voice steady enough for her words to be understood. The time had come to tell the truth, to rip open the terrible wounds before they had more time to heal. "When I was with the Vampers from Nightland—"

"Jeremy," a voice called from downstairs. "Is Sleeping Beauty still out?"

Jeremy smiled at the sound of his sister's voice. "Nope, but you would've just woken her up anyway."

Footsteps sped up the stairs, and Gentry Ridgeway stepped into Nola's bedroom. Her eyes lingered on the robe Nola wore for a moment before she spoke. "All people able to move and not on guard duty are to report to the Aquaponics Dome in twenty minutes. There's a meeting about the plan for moving forward with..." Gentry gestured to the walls around her as though to say *our existence.*

"I'll be there soon," Jeremy said.

"Nope." Gentry shook her head. Her dark blonde hair she wore barely longer than Jeremy's ruffled around her face, making her, for a moment at least, appear softer than the fierce Outer Guard she was. "You *and* Nola will come now." Gentry held up a hand when Jeremy began to argue. "She's awake and can move, she has to come to the meeting."

"It's fine," Nola cut Jeremy off when he opened his mouth to argue again. "I'm fine. I'll come to the meeting."

"Good," Gentry said. "We need everyone who's left to work their asses off to get this place put back together. Every single one of us will have to give our all for the domes to survive." Gentry said the last words to her brother, giving him a hard look before walking out of the room.

Nola waited for the sound of the kitchen door closing before looking back to Jeremy. "Does Gentry not think you're doing your part? I mean, you're not even eighteen yet, and you're already an Outer Guard. Why would she—"

"That's not what she said." Jeremy took her hand, carefully helping Nola to her feet. "And that's not what she thinks. We lost a lot of people and a lot of supplies. The domes have to be repaired, and now there are a bunch of rogue Vampers who've declared an all-out war on us. The domes were built to help us survive in this broken world, and now the world is trying to break us. But there is no way in hell I'm going to let them." Jeremy leaned down, brushing his lips against Nola's. "I promise."

It took Nola longer than normal to pull on clothes. Every muscle ached as she dragged her shirt over her head. Her fingers burned as she tied the laces on her work boots. She didn't have the will to force her curls into a tight braid, so she let her hair hang wildly around her shoulders. Just another thing knocked out of place in the strict order that preserved the domes.

She let Jeremy lead her down the stone paths that cut through the grass and wildflowers, weaving past the willow trees and tall maples that made up the green spaces of Bright Dome. Even the roofs of the houses had been planted with thick moss. Every detail had been planned to make the most of the precious space within the glass.

Dome perfect.

But not anymore. Bright Dome had changed since she stumbled through it after the attack. Sleeping bags and boxes of food hid beneath the dangling tendrils of the largest willows. Neat piles of clothes nestled next to the bubbling fountain.

"Some glass in Low Dome and Canal Dome got cracked." Jeremy followed

Nola's gaze. "The rain isn't getting in, but the Council doesn't want people sleeping in there. We moved most of the singles into the Guard barracks, but the families had to find other places."

"So, they're sleeping on the ground?" A knot formed in Nola's throat. "They're sleeping in the dirt like the homeless in the city."

"Not like in the city." Jeremy led her away from the makeshift camp, down the stairs and into the tunnels that were the paths between domes. "In the city, the people who sleep outside aren't safe. Here, they are. They're fed and guarded, and it's only for a few days. As soon as the rain stops, we can get Low Dome and Canal Dome fixed, and everyone can go home."

She nodded, not trusting herself to speak.

The cleaning crews had been busy in the tunnels. There was no glass from shattered lights left to crunch beneath their feet. All traces of blood had been scrubbed from the floor. The normality of it, the cleanness, was worse than the blood had been. Horrible things had happened. Mopping the floor wouldn't make it go away. It would have been easier to see the horror. To point to it and scream *this is why I am broken!* But the halls were scoured to perfection.

People packed the Aquaponics Dome by the time Nola and Jeremy arrived. Half-buried with the fish tanks sitting below ground-level, the dome was dark at the best of times. With the storm raging outside, it was impossible to tell if it was night or day down by the meeting, where the department heads stood in a line in front of the fish.

Hundreds of people crowded together. Some in work uniforms, others in normal clothes. The sight of them all jammed together like animals set Nola's nerves on edge. But worse was the fact that they all fit. There should have been more of them. Enough people to spill up onto the stairs. There should have been chatter and laughter bouncing off the glass. But the only sound was the dull hum of the fish tank pumps. The people stood silently as if the funerals had already begun.

"People of the domes," Captain Ridgeway, Jeremy's father and the head of the Outer Guard, addressed the crowd, "we have come upon a dark and terrible time. Our mission has always been, will always be, to protect the people, plants, and animals that are in these domes. We do not do this for our own survival but for the survival of the human race. To protect our children's children. Since the domes were founded, those who live on the outside have coveted the resources we hold, right down to the clean air we breathe. But never before has a group maliciously tried to destroy mankind's best chance for survival." Captain Ridgeway paused, surveying the crowd. "They tried to destroy us, but what they don't understand is that we learn. We have learned where we were weak, we have learned the depths to which they will sink to annihilate us, and we will never allow them the opportunity to attack the domes or its people again."

The crowd clapped and cheered. Shouts of "For the domes!" and "Destroy the Vampers!" carried over the din.

Captain Ridgeway held up a hand, and the moment of celebration faded. "We have a lot of hard work ahead of us. Sacrifices must be made to push forward for a better, stronger future than the domes have ever dreamed of before. Together we will stand strong. Together we will push forward. Together we will become the future the world needs us to be!"

The shouts of the crowd echoed off the glass, drowning out the sound of the thunder beyond.

CHAPTER TWO

"I just want to help," Nola said for the hundredth time as she followed her mother through the seed cold-storage room.

"Magnolia, I don't have time for this," Lenora snapped, moving to the next row to check the temperature of the seed trays.

"You would have more time if you let me help you!" Nola let her voice ring off the walls.

Lenora stopped moving and pinched the bridge of her nose. "I know you want to help. You are a wonderful girl who wants to help the domes, and I appreciate that more than you will ever know. But right now, the most important thing is to protect these seeds. Without these seeds, the people in the domes could starve, and even if we managed to survive on corn, we would leave nothing for future generations to bring back out into the world. The Vamper scum stole three boxes of my seeds, and now with the dome repair, I can't trust the air system to be reliable. I'm sorry, Nola, but the most helpful thing you can do is leave me to my work."

Nola stood for a moment, teetering on the verge of shouting again. "Right. Sorry, Mom."

She turned without giving her mother a chance to say another word and stalked past the shelves upon shelves of seeds, not stopping until the cold-storage door *whooshed* closed behind her. Nola leaned against the concrete wall of the hall, letting the panic of being three stories underground take her. Her vision swam and her heart raced. Every nerve in her body told her she would be crushed to death at any moment. The panic at being so far below the surface was

MEGAN O'RUSSELL

better than the terrible fear and self-loathing that filled her aboveground, surrounded by the blatant signs of attack.

The seeds were stored deep under the earth in the safest place the domes had to offer, but still the attackers from Nightland had gotten into seed storage and medical storage right next door. More than thirty feet of hard-packed earth above and the Vampers had gotten in and out. They had known where they were going and exactly how to get past the guards. Nola's hands shook. She dug her nails into her arms, willing herself not to scream.

Footsteps came toward the door of medical storage. Nola pushed away from the wall and hurried down the hall, past the guards, and up the stairs.

"Miss Kent," the sharp voice sounded as soon as she reached the landing on the next level.

She froze for a moment before dashing up the next flight of stairs.

"Miss Kent, I need to speak with you immediately."

Nola turned slowly, not needing to see his face to know Captain Stokes was the one calling her, his black eyebrows pinched at the center as he glared at her.

Captain Stokes was the head of the Dome Guard, the ones who protected the domes themselves. Just as Captain Ridgeway was the head of the Outer Guard, the elite unit that patrolled the streets of the city across the river, fighting on the front lines when riots overtook the decaying slums.

It was Captain Stokes' men who should have stopped the attack from ever happening. His Guard who had failed five days ago.

"How are you, Captain Stokes?" Nola's voice wavered as the powerfully built man approached her.

He limped, still favoring his right leg after the battle, but that didn't make him any less intimidating.

"My fallen guards are up next for burning, the ones who are still alive are protecting the shattered side of the domes, and the damned doctors can't set my leg properly," Stokes said. "How well do you think I'm doing, Miss Kent?"

"About as well as the rest of us," Nola said. "Everyone's lost something, Captain Stokes."

"But was everyone surprised by the loss?" Stokes narrowed his eyes. "I need to talk to you about your time as a prisoner in Nightland."

Though she had been expecting his words, her heart began to race.

"You told us you had only seen the inside of your cell when you first came home, but when the attack came, you became a fount of information." Stokes leaned closer, backing her into the wall.

The knowledge that Captain Stokes had every right to glare at her like he knew each horrible thing she had done didn't make it any easier to not run away.

"How to navigate the tunnels of Nightland, how to find their leader's home, even where they had been storing things aboveground. I'd like for you to explain to me how you knew all those things if you never left your cell, Miss Kent." Stokes' face was only inches from hers, but something in the foul stench of his stale breath emboldened her.

"What happened to me in Nightland was outside the domes," Nola said. "What happens outside the domes is Captain Ridgeway's concern, not yours. If Captain Ridgeway wants to talk to me, he knows where to find me. In the meantime, why don't you go check on your guards? Make sure no more of them end up in line for burning."

She sidestepped Stokes and darted up the stairs, not breathing until she had reached the lights of the dome two stories above. Sunlight touched her face as she gasped for air. Even through the glass of the dome the sun warmed her skin.

Her feet carried her toward Amber Dome, away from the workers with their heavy boots and noisy tools that toiled frantically to fix the side of the atrium before the rains returned. Back down a flight of stairs and into a short tunnel. Heavy panes of glass leaned against the wall, waiting to be used in the atrium. But the steel had to be fixed first. It would take days for the wall to be in place, and no one knew how long for decontamination to be complete.

The steps leading up into the Amber Dome were empty, and the few people tending the crops in the low, wide dome didn't pay Nola any mind. The vents blew in clean air, and the fans lifted the scent of fresh, moist earth and vibrant leaves. Rows of leafy green vegetables ran along the outer edge of the dome, closest to the glass, but she headed straight for the center, to the middle of the wheat field that swayed in the breeze. She ducked her head low as she walked so no one could see her path, and when all the walls were out of sight, she lay down on the warm soil, letting the green and amber stalks surround her.

Thick, gray smoke cut through the dazzling blue sky above. Ten would be burned today. Ten of the seventy-two fallen Domers. A list had been read over the com that morning. PAM had displayed their faces on all the computer screens for ten minutes, one last memorial to those who had died. This was the third day of burning, and they hadn't even made it to the fallen guards yet. They would be burned last, their sacrifice in protecting the domes given the highest point of honor.

Twenty-seven guards had been lost.

Nola rolled onto her side, covering her head with her arms. Twenty-seven guards who wouldn't be there to defend the domes if Nightland attacked again.

But the Vampers from Nightland had fled the city. Taken everything they had and vanished. They could be hundreds of miles away by now. Or only a few. Kieran had never told her where it was Emanuel, the leader of Nightland, wanted to take his people.

She took a shuddering breath. Pain shot through her, but there were no tears. How could she cry for herself when she knew what was to come?

She had thought before that Nightland would never attack the domes. She had been delusional enough to believe she knew Emanuel and Kieran. That they were good people who would never harm her or her home.

Seventy-two dead.

Her home had been shattered. She had to pay the price, but she would be damned if she was going to wait for Stokes to come for her. Nola looked back up to the bright sky. The smoke had started to fade. Another body gone. Scrunching her eyes, she tried to memorize the bright blue. She might never see the noon sky again. But the blue held no thrall. No lightness or joy. All that was left for her was justice and darkness. She stood and, walking tall, headed straight for the Iron Dome.

CHAPTER THREE

Two Dome Guard flanked the steps to the Iron Dome. Neither of them attempted to stop Nola from passing. Neither of them called her a traitor or tried to haul her away. It would have been simpler if they had. It would have spared her from having to tell the world herself.

I don't deserve for this to be easy.

The Iron Dome was wide-set with low bushes instead of trees to ensure sightlines in case of attack. It was the only dome where metal could be lowered to shield the glass from destruction and the only dome where weapons were allowed. But Nightland had attacked the exact opposite side of the complex, leaving the Iron Dome completely untouched.

Nola approached the largest of the shoebox-shaped houses. A shadow moved past the kitchen window as she climbed the steps to the Ridgeways' door.

Good. Better to get it over with. You've made up your mind. Now do it.

Her hand didn't shake when she knocked. Almost instantly the door swung open, and Jeremy stood in front of her.

"Nola." He beamed down at her as though finding her at his door was the most wonderful thing he could imagine. "Come on in." He took her hand and led her into the kitchen, pulling her into his arms as soon as the door closed.

His heart pounding quickly in his chest couldn't compare to the speed at which Nola's raced.

"What are you doing here?" Nola stepped the foot away from him the tiny kitchen allowed. "You're supposed to be on duty."

"I got switched to night patrol for today, so I got sent home to rest," Jeremy said. "But you must have—"

"I need to talk to your dad," Nola said. "I need to see him right away."

"So, you didn't come to say hi to me?" Jeremy gave her a joking smile.

She couldn't find it in herself to smile back. This wasn't how it was supposed to go. She was going to tell Captain Ridgeway, and have it done. All at once. No more complications.

"Where's your dad?" Nola asked.

"He's not here." Jeremy stepped forward, taking her face in his hands. "He's out in the city. There was some trouble, and he wanted to check it out himself before tonight."

"Dammit." Nola scrunched her eyes shut. She needed to do it now, but there was no way they would let her go out into the city to find Captain Ridgeway.

"Nola," Jeremy said, wrapping his arms around her, "you're okay."

"Don't!" She shoved Jeremy away and started for the door, but Jeremy was faster. He stepped in front of her, blocking her way out before she could even reach for the handle.

"Nola, what's—"

"Get out of my way, Jeremy."

"Nola, what do you—"

"I said get out of my way!"

Jeremy flinched as though she had hit him. Strong Outer Guard Jeremy, who fought Vampers without fear, flinched because she had yelled at him.

"Please," she whispered, dragging her fingers through her tangled hair, relishing the pain it caused. "Let me go."

"No," Jeremy said. "Not until you tell me what's going on. Nola, I love you. I know you're hurting and scared. After what you've been through in the last few weeks, anyone would be. So I can't just let you leave if you're this upset. I love you, and I'm scared for you. It's my job to protect you."

"Please don't say that." Her words barely squeezed through the tightness of her throat.

"But it's true. I love you, and whatever you need to talk to my dad about, whatever has got you so upset, I'll do whatever it takes to help you." Jeremy stepped forward, wrapped his arms around her and kissed her. "I love you, Nola Kent."

"Please don't." Tears trickled down her face.

"I can't help it." Jeremy brushed away her tears. "I love you."

Nola looked into Jeremy's brown eyes. He loved her. He truly did.

Her heart shattered, like a physical blow to her chest, bending her in half with the pain of it.

She sank to the ground, willing herself to stay present, to not slip away into the terrible agony of it all. The hard way would be better for Jeremy. Breaking him now would allow him to heal.

"Nola, are you all right?" Jeremy's eyes went wide with fear. "I'll call a doctor."

"I'm a traitor." The words rushed from her as though they had been waiting for their chance for weeks. "I betrayed the domes, and everyone that died is dead because of me."

Jeremy's brow wrinkled, but she didn't stop. He needed to know everything. She had been selfish in wanting to tell Captain Ridgeway. It was Jeremy her betrayal would hurt most. He deserved to hear the horrible truth first.

"I didn't mean to. It didn't start that way," Nola pushed on. "It started at the Charity Center the day of the riot. Kieran Wynne was there. He stole my I-Vent. He told me if I needed him, I could find him at Nightland."

Jeremy turned away, but Nola grabbed his face, forcing him to look at her, making sure he heard every awful word.

"I wasn't going to go after him, but then someone with dome medicine was killed on the streets. I needed to know if it was him. I broke out and went into the city. I knew the way through the glass—one loose pane. One stupid, loose pane I had known about for years. Kieran was alive, but I met Emanuel, the leader of Nightland, and his little girl. She was dying. A little girl was dying, and they needed more medicine. I stole it for them. I thought I was done. I thought she was saved and it was over, but then you said the guards were going to raid Nightland, and Kieran, Emanuel, and his daughter would all have been killed. So I left through the glass again to warn them. I was never kidnapped. I went to warn them."

"They stabbed you, Nola." Jeremy latched onto the one thing that could prove her innocence.

"They thought I was a guard. I stole a coat to stay safe in the rain. They thought a guard was attacking. They didn't mean to hurt me. But by the time I woke up, it was two days later. Emanuel said the kidnapping story was the only way to get me home. I didn't even know if I wanted to come home, they all seemed so good. Trying to feed the city, trying to build a new world for everyone, but Emanuel said it was the only way to prevent a war, and they had to send me back. I trusted him. I trusted Kieran."

Nola spoke through her sobs, feeling Jeremy's anger growing, but it wasn't over. Not yet.

"They taught me a lie. What to tell you had happened. That they had taken me and locked me up. But they didn't tell me how horrible living with the lie would be. Being here in the sunlight and knowing how many good people were trapped in the dark. I wanted to go help them. That's why I wanted to leave. I would have gone. But then they attacked. I didn't know they were coming. I swear to you I didn't.

"I never thought they would attack my home. But they did. Kieran was here with the others. I saw him. He was stealing from the domes while the Night-landers were murdering our people. I didn't know, I promise I didn't know that they were going to attack. But it doesn't matter. I betrayed the domes. I betrayed you and my mother, and everything the domes are supposed to stand for."

She took a breath, her body hollow now that the flood of words had left her. Hands trembling, she let go of Jeremy's face, wiping away her tears before speaking again. "I have to tell your dad. I'm a traitor, and I have to face the consequences. I am so sorry, Jeremy."

He looked away at the sound of his name. She couldn't blame him for never wanting to see her again.

"I did terrible things, but I never ever wanted to hurt you," Nola whispered as she pushed herself to her feet. "I'll go wait in your dad's office till he comes back. Please don't tell anyone till I talk to him. I just want to get it done."

"Don't," Jeremy said, pressing his palm to the door so she couldn't open it. "Don't you dare walk out of this house, Nola."

She froze as Jeremy sprang to his feet, not taking his hand from the door.

"I have to go," Nola said, her voice barely above a whisper. "I have to tell—"

"Don't you dare tell me what you have to do." Jeremy took Nola by the shoulders, pinning her against the counter. Fury flashed in his eyes.

She didn't blame him. She couldn't. She was a murderer standing in his home.

"Your father will turn me in to the Council." An eerie calm filled Nola. "They'll decide what to do with me."

"No, they won't, because you aren't going to tell any of them a damned thing." Jeremy's face was inches from hers, but she didn't look away. "We lost seventy-two people in the attack on the domes and six when we tried to rescue you."

"I'm sorr—"

"Don't!" Jeremy shook her. "Seventy-eight people are dead. Don't you dare tell me you're sorry! The domes lost more than a tenth of our people. A tenth of our carefully-calculated population designed to save the world. And now you want to strike out one more? Because you feel guilty?"

"I have to tell them! Stokes knows I lied. He knows I saw the tunnels in Nightland!"

"Stokes is a moron! Stokes is one stupid man, and you're just going to have to keep lying to him, because we are already losing too much! Look at this." He dragged her to the window, making her look out at the fresh waves of dark smoke blooming in the sky. "There is too much grieving and too much loss here, Nola. You don't get to add to it. We need you, and if that means you have to live with the guilt of hiding what you've done, so be it."

"You don't need me," she said, grasping for the words that would make him understand. "You would all be better off without me."

"You're being trained in plant preservation." Jeremy spun her to face him. "We need you to keep feeding our people."

"There are other people who can do that job."

"And what about when your mom cracks up? She can't lose you, Nola." He gripped her shoulders. "I can't lose you. I won't."

"People are dead because of me." A fresh wave of tears tumbled down her cheeks at the look of horrible desperation in Jeremy's eyes. "I am no good to anyone. Least of all you!"

"Did you ever want to betray the domes?" He shook her. "Did you ever for one minute do something that you thought would hurt us?"

"No. I thought I was helping. I just helped the wrong people."

"I won't lose you because you made a mistake." He pulled her to his chest, his strong arms surrounding her like a steel vise. "There is too much at stake to lose you, too."

"But I have to pay for what I did." She leaned against Jeremy's chest, certain if he let go for an instant she would fall.

"Pay for it by helping the domes survive." His breath was ragged as he whispered. "Pay for it by making the world a better place."

"But Stokes wants to talk to me."

"Lie." He lifted her chin and stared straight into her eyes.

"I can't."

"You aren't allowed to say you can't. Promise me you'll lie."

"How can you even want me here? How can you even stand to look at me?" She laid her hand on his cheek, willing him not to slip away. For him not to be a part of a terrible dream.

"Because I love you," he said. "I love you because you are good and kind and want to help everyone. Those Vamper scum, they lied to you. They manipulated you. Whether you see it or not, they hurt you and used you. But I won't let their abuse take you away from me. I fought too hard to get you back."

"I don't deserve for you to love me." Nola pressed her lips to his cheek. "I'll never deserve it."

Jeremy turned his head, his lips brushing gently against hers. She pulled herself to him, wrapping her arms around him, willing herself to believe that this was real. He was there, holding her, protecting her. After all the blood and pain, he still believed she was worth saving.

Nola's heart raced as his fingers found the skin at her side, tracing a line toward her ribs. She deepened their kiss, stumbling when he pulled away.

He took her hands in his, staring at them for a moment before kissing both her palms.

"Promise me one thing," Jeremy said, still looking at her hands. "Promise me you aren't still in love with Kieran Wynne."

She took his face in her hands, staring deep into his brown eyes. "If I ever see Kieran Wynne again, I'll kill him myself."

CHAPTER FOUR

R eport to the Amber Dome at 0800 for planting. You have been assigned a supervisory role. Report to Lenora Kent for further information.

The message started blinking on Nola's bedroom wall at six in the morning. PAM woke her up, beeping as the words lit the darkness.

Magnolia Kent. You have received an assignment from the Dome Reconstruction Committee. Please tap your screen to confirm receipt.

Nola climbed out of bed and tapped the screen in her wall before PAM could continue. It was the first assignment she had received since the attack. Everyone else who wasn't in the hospital had been given a task but her. She had assumed the Council had deemed her too broken or too much of a liability. But there it was, blinking on her bedroom wall. The domes wanted her to work. Or at least her mother did. Dressing quickly, she popped her head out of her bedroom door, listening for the sounds of her mother. Silence filled the house. Lenora had been sleeping in her office for the last week, coming home only to shower.

Grabbing two apples from the counter, Nola started toward the door. She could go down and see her mother and still make it back to the Amber Dome in time to work.

She froze with her hand on the doorknob. She'd been summoned to the Amber Dome. One of the domes that hadn't been damaged by the attack. Whose walls were still solid with no cracks to the outside world.

The air in there would be clean. It was safe to work on plant preservation. There was no chance of acid rain contaminating the workers. But there would be no chance of her trying to run either.

Mom doesn't know. Only Jeremy knows.

Nola exhaled, forcing her lungs to remember how breathing was supposed to work. She wouldn't let the panic that floated right under her skin take control, not when there were useful tasks to be done. She was alive and in the domes. She had a chance to be productive and people were counting on her. She had lost the luxuries of fear and self-loathing.

She opened the door and walked slowly out into the bright morning sun. The vents above pumped in fresh, cool air, their low humming a battle cry against the heat of the outside world.

This is part of my punishment. Living with the lie. I'll never be sure if someone knows what I've done.

She reached the bottom of the steps to the tunnels and instinctively headed, not toward her mother's lab or even the Amber Dome, toward Jeremy's house. He should be home from his night's work in the city. He was probably asleep. But he wouldn't mind Nola waking him.

Nola smiled to herself, her first real smile in weeks. Jeremy would be happy to see her even if she only had a minute.

She ran the rest of the way through the tunnels, waving at the Iron Dome guards as she passed. One of them smiled and waved back, not bothering to hide his chuckle. She stopped below Jeremy's window, her panting from running so long swallowing the laugh that bubbled in her chest.

She reveled in the foolish feeling of standing under his window in broad daylight.

"Jeremy," Nola called up softly. "Jeremy!"

The window opened a moment later, and his face appeared. Though his cheek was marked with lines from his pillows, his eyes were alert the moment he saw her.

"Nola, what's going on?" he asked.

"Nothing." She shrugged. "I just wanted to see you."

In one swift movement, Jeremy jumped out his window, landing silently in front of her.

Without a word, Nola wrapped her arms around his bare stomach, laying her head on his chest.

"Are you sure you're okay?" He held her close, pressing his lips to the top of her head.

"I'm—" She stopped herself before speaking the comforting lie. "I have a work assignment today, in the Amber Dome."

"That's good." He leaned back just enough to look Nola in the eye. "You'll be helping."

"I know, and I want to, I do. But everyone else is working in the atrium or in the Grasslands Dome where the real damage is. What if my mom knows? What if..." All the happiness Nola felt at seeing Jeremy faded away. Her hands shook at the thought of her mother knowing what she had done. Lenora wasn't like Jeremy. She wouldn't forgive the way he had.

"Shhh, you're okay." He took her trembling hands in his. "I talked to your mom."

"You what?"

"I told her she needed to stop treating you like you couldn't help," Jeremy said. "She'd been keeping the Council from giving you an assignment because she thought you needed more time to heal. I told her you would be better off helping."

"But not near the breaks in the glass?" Nola's throat tightened.

"You aren't medically cleared for it." Jeremy's brow wrinkled. "You were with the Vampers and in the open air too long. The Council is worried about people getting contaminated with the outside air coming in, and you're at the top of the list of people who have been overexposed."

"But you and the other guards have been going out every day. If you can go into the city—"

"That's different. It's our job." He tucked Nola's hair behind her ear. "And they make sure we're okay. They take care of us."

"But why not do the same for me? I want to help, I don't want anything with Nightland to stop me from doing what I can—"

"They won't let you, Nola." He grimaced, resigning himself to something very unpleasant. "You're a girl."

"What?"

"You're a really smart girl, with really great DNA," he said quickly, as though ripping off a bandage. "The doctors are worried about birth defects in the next generation if the young women are exposed to the outside air. So, they're pushing all the women away from working on the breaks in the glass to *protect future generations*. It's not just you, I promise."

"Well," Nola began slowly, "at least it's not because they think I'm a liability or a traitor."

"There is that." Jeremy gave a tight smile.

She glanced at the house. "Does the ruling go for guards, too? Are they going to try and keep the female guards in the domes?"

"Yeah."

"And how does Gentry feel about that?"

"Not good." Jeremy wrapped his arms around Nola. "She's furious, and I can't blame her."

"Can she fight it?" She pressed her cheek into the warmth of his chest.

The Outer Guard were the elite. The ones who had chosen to risk their lives every day for the protection of the domes. Nola's father had been an Outer Guard and had died in service to the domes. If anyone had ever tried to keep him inside, they would have had one very angry, very skilled man on their hands.

"How can you fight what's for the good of the domes?" Jeremy said.

"You can't," Nola said. The weight of the truth hung heavy in the air. "So, I guess I should get to the Amber Dome. Where the young women go to work." She leaned up to kiss him.

Jeremy brushed his lips against hers. "Thank you for waking me up." He kissed Nola again. "I think you should do it more often."

"Me, too." She kissed him on the cheek and walked away, holding onto his hand until their fingers couldn't touch anymore.

CHAPTER FIVE

Six guards flanked the steps to the Amber Dome, all wearing full riot gear. Nola hesitated in front of them, unprepared to meet a full complement of guards in her brown gardening jumpsuit. But the first guard nodded at her to pass. She hurried up the steps, finishing the braid in her hair as she entered the vast space of the Amber Dome.

Lenora stood with three guards on a high platform in front of the patch of wheat. Nola's shoulders tensed at the sight of guards in the middle of the garden.

Amber Dome housed most of the domes' edible crops. Rows of vegetables bordered trellises that supported vines bearing heavy tomatoes and gourds. The placid greenery held no threat for the guards to defend against.

"Magnolia," Lenora called as Nola approached. "How are you?" Her mother looked her over from head to toe as though searching for a sign that even being asked to work was enough to make Nola crack.

"I'm good." Nola forced a bright smile. "I'm happy to have something productive to do."

"Good." Lenora reached down to help her daughter up onto the waist-high platform. "And you won't just be working, you'll be supervising. We are going to have to move more plants in here. We lost animal feed from the grasslands, and we can't let the stock starve."

"Right," Nola answered, still trying to listen to her mother as movement at the stairs caught her eye.

"It's not desperately complicated, and with the men in the department working in the Grasslands Dome, the muscle trying to rebuild the walls, and everyone in the technical departments trying to purge toxins from the domes' systems, we've had to get a little creative with the workforce."

A dozen people emerged from the staircase. People Nola had never seen before, dressed in the worn clothes of city dwellers.

"I'll be up here supervising the operation, and you'll be down there making sure none of the outsiders damage our plants. They've all been cleared and seem competent, but I doubt they know much about agriculture."

Guards herded the outsiders toward the center of the dome. A look of something between amazement and fear showed on each of their faces.

"Mom, we aren't supposed to have outsiders in the domes," Nola said.

"Desperate times, Magnolia. The Incorporation couldn't send help from any of the other domes, so this is what we have to work with," Lenora said. "They build sets of domes all over the world to ensure future generations of children have a shot at living. They meddle in every decision we make from how much iron we get in our diets to what plants I should grow. But ask the Incorporation for some extra help after you've been attacked by thieving murderers, and this is their solution."

She turned to the outsiders who now stood at the foot of the platform. "Thank you all for joining us." Lenora spoke in a bright voice that sounded nothing like her usual tone. "You will be broken up into four groups for planting tasks. With any luck, we can get all of this done over the next few days. We genuinely appreciate your assistance during the domes' time of need."

Lenora ignored the stony looks the outsiders gave her as she issued instructions. Nola was one of four who had been chosen to supervise the outsiders. The other three Domers were also women, all under thirty. Jeremy had been right. They hadn't assigned her here out of fear she would run. They were trying to protect the women.

Disgust mingled with relief as Nola led her group of three workers to the lattice side of the dome. Past the tall stacks of pots where the leafy greens grew and the coated pipes with tiny sprigs of herbs peeping out the side, to where vines bound with thick twine wrapped around metal poles.

Trays waited at the end of the long line of vines. She didn't need to ask her mother what task they had been assigned. The tomatoes were ripe. They needed to be harvested and sent down to food collection. Then the vines that weren't useable anymore would be trimmed away, making room for newer plants to join the lattices. Nola had been doing the same job for years. Only the workers were new.

"Right," Nola said, trying to sound more confident than she felt as she turned to face the outsiders. "Thank you for coming to help us today." She realized how horrible the words were as soon as they left her mouth.

The three people that stood facing her hadn't come to the domes out of the goodness of their hearts. They'd come because the domes were paying them, or maybe even forcing them.

And now it's my job to make them help me harvest food that's better than anything they've eaten in their lives.

"I'm Nola." She held out a hand to the worker closest to her—an older woman about her mother's age, but with bright white, thinning hair.

"Catlyn." The woman's voice was low and soft as she took Nola's hand for only the briefest moment.

"Beauford," the only male in the group said, clasping his hands firmly behind his back as though daring Nola to force him to shake hands.

"Nice to meet you, Beauford." Nola nodded.

Beauford looked strong, healthy, and barely older than Nola herself. Aside from the wear on his clothes and faint rings under his eyes, he could have been from the domes.

For a moment, Nola forgot to breathe. What if the man was on Vamp? What if he had been injecting the drugs that were so popular in the city in order to stay healthy? But the domes would have blood-tested everyone they let in to work for illnesses that could be spread.

They must have checked for Vamp and Lycan as well.

"I'm T." The last worker's words pulled Nola back to the conversation, or lack thereof.

"T?" Nola asked.

The girl nodded with a forced and fleeting smile. Her long, auburn hair shimmered with the movement. Freckles covered the girl's face, and though she wore a long-sleeved, baggy shirt, Nola was sure that the freckles covered T's arms as well.

"I appreciate all of your help." Nola smiled as convincingly as she could. "First thing we need to do is harvest the tomatoes. Just pick the nice red ones—"

"We know what tomatoes are supposed to look like." Beauford grabbed a cart. "Just 'cause we're from the outside doesn't mean we're stupid."

"I never meant—" Nola began, but T shook her head.

"Don't worry about it, Miss. We know what we're here to do, let's just do it."

Without another word, the three outsiders began picking the tomatoes and laying them out on the carts. Nola moved far enough down the row to be able to glimpse one of the other work groups. The Domer in charge of the only other group in sight stood, hands on her hips, as she watched the outsiders work. Lording over them as though they were animals that couldn't be trusted.

Nola walked back to her group and knelt on the sun-warmed earth, picking tomatoes and laying them on T's cart. T eyed her for a moment before continuing her work, carefully removing each good fruit.

It took hours to work their way down the line. By the time all the tomatoes had been harvested, they had five full carts, and the time for lunch had come.

A table had been brought out near the side of the dome, filled with food and vats of water.

"Right," Nola said, dusting her hands on her pants and hoping she was giving the right instructions. "We need to take the carts to the stairs, and then it'll be time for lunch."

At the word "lunch," all three outsiders turned toward the table laden with food. Nola's chest tightened at the look of hunger in their eyes.

A simple meal to us is something unbelievable to them.

Nola grabbed a cart and started pushing toward the stairs, not sure how to explain they would only be fed a simple work lunch.

Two of the other groups had already moved over to the food table. The supervisors sat off to one side, watching their charges eat the trays of fish and fruit they had been given.

Nola pushed her cart into line with those that held squash, beets, and kale. "I'll go back for the last cart." She turned to her crew.

They had formed a chain, Catlyn leading, Beauford in the middle, and T in the back, moving four carts between the three of them.

"Or...not," Nola said.

"We've got it," Catlyn said, her eyes on the table of food. As soon as the carts were in place, the three descended on the table, each taking a tray without looking at what was on them and settling onto the grass.

Nola surveyed the leftover trays. All had seared fish. It was the most abundant meat in the domes, so of course that's what they would feed the outsiders. Each piece of meat was accompanied by a handful of string beans and an apple, pear, or plum.

Nola chose a tray with a plum and sat down with her group. Each of them immediately stopped their ravenous eating to stare at her.

"May I join you?" she asked.

"Of course." Catlyn smiled then went back to eating at a slightly slower pace than before.

Beauford glanced at the other Domers in the corner with a look that clearly said he wished Nola had chosen to eat with her own kind.

Nola crunched a string bean, trying to think of something to say. She shouldn't ask about jobs. If they had those, they wouldn't be working in the domes. She shouldn't ask about family. With the child mortality rate on the outside so high, at least one of them would have lost a family member. "So how did you get chosen to work here?" was the first thing she could think to say that didn't seem too terribly offensive.

"You're right," Beauford said. "We were *chosen*. It is such an honor to harvest food we'll never eat."

"We are eating it." Catlyn glanced fearfully at Nola.

"They came around the city looking for folks," T said, looking Nola square in the eyes. "People who didn't have jobs and were still healthy, or at least not contagious. There weren't very many to choose from. I don't think anyone they found hasn't been brought to work in some capacity. Hauling glass for the walls or working on planting at least."

Nola froze, a string bean halfway to her mouth. "You're it? The ones who came to work are the only healthy ones left?"

"The ones who haven't turned to Lycan or Vamp," Beauford said.

"We're the only ones without jobs," T corrected, giving Beauford a hard look. "The healthy ones like us all work in factories or the few shops that haven't been trampled. Workers who won't cough blood on the machines or die on the floor are in huge demand."

"Then why aren't you working somewhere out there?" Nola tried to rid her mind of the image of a human coughing blood. She understood the reality of illness, but hearing T speak of it in such a matter-of-fact way somehow made it worse.

"There won't be factories in the city much longer." Catlyn reached over and squeezed T's hand. "Between the fires and the city falling to the Vampers and the wolves, and with those poor zombie folks attacking people in the streets, there isn't really a way for people to buy things."

"The only factories left are the ones making those nice uniforms you wear and extra glass for your walls." Beauford took a violent bite out of his apple.

"And even those are starting to shut down." T glanced sideways at the guards. "The fires a while ago took out a factory, and then the fighting at Nightland took out another. That's how we lost our jobs. You'll still have new glass and machines, but don't expect clothes to be coming in from the city for much longer. Destroying Nightland hurt the city, too."

"Nightland," Nola said, focusing hard on T's eyes to keep her head from spinning. "Getting rid of Vampers hurt the city?"

"It hurt a lot of people," T said.

"There were some factories that were damaged," Catlyn said. "We were right above the tunnels, and when the guards went in, part of our floor collapsed. The machines stopped working, and we didn't have the parts to fix them."

"But Nightland was in a Vamper neighborhood," Nola said. "How could a factory have been hurt?"

"Nightland reached under the streets and touched more of the city than you would ever know, Nola Kent." T leaned in, her eyes boring into Nola's.

The sound of her last name echoed in Nola's ears.

She knows. She knows who I am! The voice in her head screamed. Wouldn't stop screaming. Her breath hitched in her chest as panic set in.

No. No, stop it. She dug her fingers into the grass, willing the world not to slip away from her. *Someone said my name in front of her. My mother, another Domer. They told her I would be in charge of her group.*

"It is an honor to help the domes." Catlyn's voice reemerged as the pounding in Nola's ears quieted.

Catlyn smiled brightly and put a hand on T's shoulder, pulling her away from Nola. "They are offering us good pay and a good lunch. I've never actually eaten a piece of fruit like this." Catlyn held up her pear. "It really is delicious."

"I'm glad you like it." Nola stared down at the food on her plate, suddenly too disgusted to eat.

"We should get back to work." Beauford stood, his plate already clean.

Nola nodded, leaving her mostly full plate on the ground.

"Aren't you going to eat that?" Catlyn eyed Nola's food.

Nola shook her head. Before she could say she really wasn't hungry, Catlyn had snatched the plate, pushing the extra food onto T's.

"I don't need—" T began.

"You'll eat and be happy about it," Catlyn said.

"Yes, ma'am," T murmured, eating Nola's leftover lunch in a few quick bites. The whole thing was over before Nola could think.

"Time to move the plants?" Catlyn gave Nola a bright smile as she pulled T to her feet. "What sort of plants are they going to be adding in? Something exotic maybe?"

"I don't know." Nola looked up at her mother who still stood on the platform in the middle of the dome. "They'll let me know when we get that far."

CHAPTER SIX

Trimming back the dead plants took another hour. Then the delicate process of digging up the roots began. The living vines had to be cut loose from the trellises. Once the roots were free, everything had to be shifted down the row.

Nola lifted the first of the root bases, her arms burning with the weight of it. T crouched down to lift the next one.

"Don't," Beauford said, taking T under the arms and lifting her to her feet. "You keep the vine part from dragging."

"I can do it," T said so softly Nola almost couldn't hear.

"But we won't let you," Catlyn whispered, looking at the ground as soon as she noticed Nola watching them.

"Coming," Beauford said, easily lifting the root bundle and following Nola the twenty feet down the row to where the plants needed to be transferred.

Nola settled her roots into the freshly dug and perfectly sized hole. T trailed behind her, supporting the delicate vine.

"Are you hurt?" Nola asked, glancing around to make sure none of the other Domers heard her. If Lenora knew T couldn't lift, she would be taken out of the domes and sent back to the rubble of the factory Nightland had destroyed.

"No, Miss," T said.

"Because if you are," Nola said, reaching out and taking T's sleeve, her body making the decision before her mind could reason through her action, "you can tell me. I won't tell them, they won't get rid of you."

"It's got nothing to do with you," Beauford said, stepping in front of T.

He bumped Nola backward, but she still had a grip on T's sleeve. Her slight tug on the fabric lifted the waist of the shirt, revealing T's swollen stomach.

"I-I'm," Nola stuttered, letting go of T's shirt. "I'm sorry. I didn't know."

"You weren't supposed to." T pulled the baggy shirt down, covering her stomach.

"But if you're pregnant, you shouldn't be doing this kind of work," Nola whispered, searching the rows to make sure no one could hear.

"If I don't work, how am I supposed to eat?" T said.

"Women on the outside do heavy work all the time while they're carrying," Catlyn said, taking Beauford's arm and moving him out of the way before he could speak again.

"But you need to be careful," Nola said.

"Don't you think the Domers who brought us in here knew?" T asked. "They're willing to let me work, so let's just get to it before they think I'm slowing things down."

T held the vines up, waiting for Nola to tie them to the trellis.

"Fine," Nola whispered, pulling thick twine from her pocket and carefully attaching the vines, "but you don't do heavy lifting, and if you start feeling sick, you tell me."

"I'm an outsider," T said, her face unreadable. "*Sick* is a very relative term for us."

Nola opened her mouth to argue, but before she could think of anything to say, a wail rent the air, shaking her lungs and stinging her ears.

The domes' sirens blared, and red lights flashed overhead.

Nola ran toward the glass, stumbling over the freshly dug holes in the ground. Heart racing, she searched the world outside for explosions and attackers. But there were no Vampers charging the domes. No bright orange flames destroying her home.

"Everyone evacuate now!" Lenora's voice carried over the siren. "Nola!"

She turned to see her mother running toward her, arms outstretched. "Nola!"

"We have to go!" Nola shouted to Catlyn, Beauford, and T. "Come with me!"

The three hesitated for only a moment before following Nola as she ran toward her mother.

"Nola!" Lenora grabbed her hand, and together they ran down the stairs. The other work groups had beaten them down the steps, leaving only the guards in the dome.

"What's going on?" Nola asked as soon as they were down in the concrete corridor. The sound of the siren was different here, echoing down the hall in a more menacing way than it had sounded in the open space of the Amber Dome.

"Trouble in the city," one of the guards said. "All civilians are to report to the bunkers."

"What?"

Before the guard could answer Nola, her mother had dragged her down the hall.

"This way!" Nola turned to call to her group, but the guards had stopped them in the hall, herding them with the other outsiders.

"Where are they taking them?" she asked. "Mom, where are they taking the workers?"

"Not our problem." Lenora sped up to a run as they joined the throng of Domers heading toward the bunker.

Two bunkers had been built to protect the people of the domes. One underneath the atrium and one underneath seed storage. While the atrium had been badly damaged in the Nightland attack, the bunker was buried too deep to have been harmed. Even still, instinct and fear drove all the dome residents toward the seed storage bunker.

The scream of the sirens didn't lessen as Nola followed the crowd deeper underground. The weight of the earth above pressed down on her lungs, stifling her breath.

"What's happening?" Nola repeated the question to everyone she got close to, hoping one of them might have an answer. If there was trouble in the city all the way across the river, why should the Domers have to hide? There were fights in the city all the time and riots every few weeks. But never before had the residents of the domes been sent into the bunkers.

Nola had only ever gone into the bunkers during the biannual emergency drills. She hadn't made it down that far when Nightland attacked.

But this was no drill. Panic permeated the air. When they reached the barracks level, a long line of Outer Guard ran past in full riot gear. Thick jackets with armored vests, screened helmets, and shining pistols made the guards one congruous, and terrifying, unit.

Jeremy would be with them, racing toward whatever terrible thing might be happening.

"Jeremy!" Nola fought to free herself from the ever-moving crowd. But she couldn't escape the throng. "Jeremy!" Before she made it to the hall where the Outer Guard had been passing, they disappeared up the steps, the gap closing behind them.

Nola let the crowd sweep her the rest of the way to the bunker. Guards held the thick steel door open, waiting for the last of the Domers to make it through.

"Keep moving in!" the guard shouted as Nola passed.

The crowd had stopped right inside the doorway, leaving no room for the rest of the people to file in.

"All the way to the back!" a voice ordered, and the crowd began to move.

A man much taller than Nola stood right in front of her. The people behind her forced her forward, pressing her face into the man's back.

She tipped her head up toward the ceiling, focusing on the caged light bulbs and flashing red beams.

Breathe in. Breathe out. Breathe in.

Jeremy will be going into the city.

Breathe out.

Jeremy will be fighting, and I'll be locked underground.

Tears crept into the corners of Nola's eyes as the thick metal door slammed shut.

CHAPTER SEVEN

"Find a place and calm down!" a gravelly voice shouted. The crowd spread, moving toward the benches and tables that lined the walls. Above the tables hung metal rectangles that could be folded down into makeshift beds.

Please don't let us still be trapped here when it's time to sleep.

As people began to sit, she scanned the crowd for her mother. Lenora glowered by the door, grilling the guard who had shut them in.

"Has seed storage been locked down?" Lenora asked, her tone reflecting the importance of protecting the seeds. Without the seeds, there was no point in hiding in the bunker. The Domers would just starve to death.

"We told you last time," the guard said, "seed storage was locked down before we even came down to the bunker. The seeds are as safe as we are."

"I should be allowed to stay with my seeds," Lenora spoke through gritted teeth.

"All dome residents have to come to the bunkers," the guard said. "I'm sorry, Ms. Kent, but the Council made that quite clear. They are unwilling to take any more chances with dome citizen lives. If you want them to change the rules, you'll have to talk to the Council about it. Which should be easy since you're on the Council."

"Don't take that cheek with me," Lenora said. "Why have they put us down here in the first place?"

Nola inched closer to her mother, gazing aimlessly around the bunker while listening to the guard speak, afraid if he caught her eavesdropping he might not tell Lenora the truth.

"There's a fight in the city," the guard said, his voice low. "A big one. And it's not just in one place, it's all over. The radio said it was like an all-out street war."

"War between whom?" Lenora asked. "It's daylight, and the Vampers of Nightland all fled. The filthy, thieving, murdering cowards."

"I have no idea, ma'am. I honestly don't," the guard said. "I'm only doing as I'm told. I only know what the radio's told me. The only thing any of us in here can do is wait for word and try to keep everyone calm. So please, Ms. Kent, sit down and relax. As soon as I hear anything, I promise you'll be the first to know."

"I'd better be," Lenora growled before turning to Nola.

"Come along, Magnolia." Lenora took Nola's elbow and led her to the front bench.

Every seat had already been filled by fearful people who spoke in hushed tones.

"I'm so sorry, but we're going to need to sit here," Lenora said. "I need to stay by the door." It was a sign of how frightening Lenora was that all five people on the bench stood without argument and walked down the bunker without so much as an angry look over their shoulders.

"We could have gone farther back." Nola sat next to her mother. "The guard could have found you."

"But here I can watch him," Lenora said, her eyes fixed on the guard. "If he hears anything in his earpiece, I'll know."

Nola nodded, though she knew her mother couldn't see her.

Two little girls sat across from them with their mother and father. Nola studied the children, hoping that memorizing the blonde curls on the girls' heads would keep the horrible nightmares from coming.

It doesn't count as a nightmare if I'm awake.

That one errant thought allowed the images to whirl into being. Her father, dressed in an Outer Guard's uniform, going to stop a Vamper riot in the city and coming home covered in a plain white sheet Nola wasn't allowed to look beneath.

She hadn't understood the fighting then. Hadn't known what the screaming and terrible banging would sound like. In Nightland, she had heard the screams when the Outer Guard had blown their way in. The dust roughly coating her throat, and the horrible wailing ringing in her ears.

When Nightland attacked, it had been worse. So much worse. Glass had shattered, and blood slicked the floor. The world stained red, breaking every promise of safety. Maybe that's why they had all been sent so far beneath the surface. With the Outer Guard in the city, the domes were vulnerable. The domes couldn't afford to lose any more people. There had already been too much blood and death.

Nola's breath caught in her chest.

"You're all right, Magnolia." Lenora squeezed her daughter's hand. "Take a deep breath. That's all you have to do to stay calm."

I wish that were true.

Five hours passed before the guard at the door lifted his hand, pressing his fingers to his earpiece. His brow wrinkled for a moment, and before it looked like he had finished listening, Lenora shot to her feet, ready to question the poor man.

Nola glanced back at the rest of the bunker. Some people had already pulled beds down from the walls, but most still sat on the benches, talking quietly to their neighbors or staring silently at the walls.

Lenora's movement drew the attention of those nearest her. Silently, Nola followed her mother.

"What's going on?" Lenora asked in a hushed tone.

"They're coming back from the city." The guard held up a hand when it looked like Lenora was going to ask another question. "That's really all I know."

"Is anyone hurt?" Nola asked, dropping any pretense she wasn't listening.

"Yes." Fear touched the guard's eyes. "All medical personnel please come to the front of the bunker!" the guard shouted, his voice resonating through the concrete space. It was big enough to fit all the residents of the dome, but the hard walls allowed his voice to reverberate loudly enough for everyone to hear.

The medical personnel sprinted to the door. Sound burst out around the bunker, people shouting to know what had happened, who needed help.

"Silence!" the guard bellowed. "Only medical personnel will be allowed out now. That is the only information I have. Everyone else, please stay seated."

He punched a code into a panel at the side of the door, and the metal bolt slid aside. The medical personnel ran up the hall, but Lenora stepped in front of the guard when he tried to close the door.

"If it is safe enough for them to work on patients, it is safe enough for me to check on my seeds."

"Ms. Kent—"

"Dr. Kent," Lenora corrected.

Neither of them noticed Nola standing only a foot away. Without any thought of consequences, she darted through the door and up the stairs, following the line of medical staff.

Jeremy had gone out into the city. If he was hurt, she had to be with him.

She slowed to a walk.

Be with him and do what? You aren't a doctor.

Nola took a breath, letting the calm of the hall fill her. The sirens had stopped blaring. The only noise was the fading sound of footfalls as the doctors ran toward their patients.

You need to get to Jeremy, because he would find a way to get to you.

She didn't run up the stairs. Instead, she looked carefully around each corner, making sure she didn't meet anyone who would try to send her away.

She didn't see another person until she reached the tunnel level. Guards tore through the halls, carrying stretchers that bore their injured comrades. Doctors ran between patients, assessing the ones who needed the most immediate treatment.

Dome Guard were mixed in with Outer Guard.

They took all of them into the city.

Nola pressed herself to the wall, trying to catch a glimpse of Jeremy. Or better yet, hear his strong healthy voice giving an order. But she didn't see him. He was tall enough that his dirty-blond hair should have been visible above the crowd. Unless he was one of the ones who kept their helmet on.

Gentry Ridgeway came into view, carrying a stretcher with an older black-haired man lying unconscious on it. Trying to walk as though she was meant to be there, Nola started out into the hall, following Gentry, hoping she would know where her younger brother might be.

"Out of the way," a guard barked as he ran past the others. The guard on his stretcher gasped rattling breaths. Blood stained one side of his chest, and the mark grew wider every second. One of his arms had been severed at the elbow. The sight of raw flesh sent bile into Nola's throat.

Jeremy. Find Jeremy.

Nola staggered down the hall, following Gentry, ignoring someone's warning of, "Miss, you need to get out of here!"

Most of the gurneys had been brought into the largest medical room. Screams of pain and shouted orders filled the air. Nola staggered as the stench of blood and chemicals slammed her in the face.

No longer caring about being caught, Nola tore down the row, searching for Jeremy. But none of the people in the room wore Outer Guard uniforms.

"Where are the Outer Guard?" Nola grabbed the arm of a Dome Guard. "Where did they take them?"

"Next level down, to the barracks," the guard said, not seeming to care that Nola shouldn't be there. Even though the guard had been carrying others, blood seeped out of a gash on his thigh.

"You need help." Nola reached toward the guard.

"We all need help." The guard limped back out to the hall.

Running the length of the room, Nola went out the far door, cutting down the corridor to avoid the doctors and taking a longer route to the stairs.

The sounds coming from the lower level were different from those of the medical area. There were no screams of pain or panic. The Outer Guard were groomed to stay calm no matter what, but the lack of sound shot more terror through Nola than the screaming had.

She ran down the stairs, but before she was three steps into the hall, a hand reached out and grabbed her.

"Nola, what are you doing here?" Blood streaked Gentry's face and matted her blonde hair.

"Jeremy," Nola said. "Where is he? Is he okay?"

Gentry's eyes flicked to the door behind Nola for a split second. "Nola, he'll be fine. They're taking care of him."

"Is he hurt?" Panic surged in her chest. "What happened?"

"Nola, you have to get out of here."

Two women carried another stretcher down the stairs. The guard at the front pushed Gentry and Nola aside, not seeming to care if she knocked them over. Gentry's grip on Nola's arm slackened for only a moment, but it was enough. Nola yanked her arm free and ran toward the door Gentry's eyes had flicked to, hoping it would be the right one.

Nola shoved open the swinging door and froze.

Jeremy, lying on a table, covered in blood. His own blood. Doctors moved around him, one of them giving orders to the others.

One ripped away the tattered shreds of uniform that covered Jeremy's stomach.

"No!" Nola screamed without realizing the word had left her mouth, but the doctors didn't notice the noise.

Ragged gashes cut deep into the flesh of Jeremy's stomach. Blood poured from a bullet-shaped hole in the center of his chest.

Jeremy's face was untouched; his helmet had protected him. His eyes were closed, he could have been sleeping.

"What the hell are you doing in here?" A doctor knocked Nola aside, a needle filled with black liquid held in her hand. "Someone get her the hell out of here!"

An arm seized Nola around the waist, lifting her out of the room. She didn't turn to see who it was. She couldn't look away from Jeremy as the doctor rammed the needle into his chest.

"Nola, I told you to get out of here!" Gentry grabbed Nola by the shoulders and shook her. "Nola! You have to leave!"

"Jeremy." Nola swayed on the spot. "Not Jeremy, please not Jeremy."

Sympathy flickered in Gentry's eyes. "He'll be fine, I promise you. My brother can make it through this. But you have to go before more people notice you're here."

"I can't leave him." Nola tried to go back through the door. "He stayed with me in the hospital, I have to be with him."

"Later." Gentry dragged Nola away, dodging between stretchers and shouting guards. "If you care about my brother at all, you will run as far away as you can and pretend you were never here. If anyone asks you, lie." Gentry grabbed Nola's chin and looked straight into her eyes. "Nola Kent, you have to lie. Now go!"

Without another word, Gentry ran down the hall toward the stairs to the atrium. There were still more wounded coming down the steps. Most of them were on their feet now, being helped along by other guards. How many had been hurt?

All of them. All the guards.

Nola turned and ran down the hall in the opposite direction of the stairs. She couldn't bear to pass them. To look at their faces and not know if they would survive.

The Guard barracks made up the rest of the hall. She would find a place to hide, a place in the dark. A few of the wounded had been brought into the barracks, the ones who weren't as badly ripped and bleeding as Jeremy. Nola's breath hitched in her throat, and she ran farther, down to the end of the hall.

There was a thick door she had never thought to look at before, but she didn't hesitate as she reached for the handle. Didn't wonder when the heavy handle turned easily. Didn't stop to think until she had entered the long hallway that shouldn't have existed.

CHAPTER EIGHT

The hallway was narrow. Nola noticed that first. It was long, too. Over a hundred feet. One hundred feet of tunnel that shouldn't exist. That *didn't* exist on the domes' maps. The Guard barracks should have been the last thing on this level. But the long corridor stretched out in front of her.

With a *swish*, the door to the barracks closed. The noise of the guards disappeared. Nola stood frozen for a moment, waiting for Gentry to grab her and shout that she wasn't supposed to be here either. Even without Gentry yelling at her, the air told her this wasn't a place she was allowed to be. Doors lined the hall. Thick, metal doors with tiny windows at the top.

Fists clenched, Nola took a step forward, then another, walking toward the nearest door.

The window was nearly too high for her to see through. Rising up on her toes, she peered into the room beyond. Six bunks hung along the back and side walls. People rested on the bunks. Nola ducked as Catlyn pushed herself up on her elbow, staring toward the window.

Carefully, Nola reached for the door handle and tried to turn it. The door was locked tight.

They left the workers locked in.

Fear mingled with rage in her chest. Those people were from the city. Their families might have been hurt, and they were locked up.

But they locked all the Domers up, too.

Slowly, Nola peered back through the window. Catlyn lay back on her bunk. T had taken the bed beneath her, lying on her side, one hand draped across her stomach. Beauford was nowhere to be seen. Only women had been locked in this room.

Nola tiptoed across the hall, peeking into the cell opposite. Men filled this room, but they weren't lying on their beds. The men sat on their bunks, talking to each other, saying things she couldn't hear. One of the men glanced toward the window, making eye contact with Nola for a split second before she dodged out of sight. The sound of fists banging on the door echoed through the hall.

"Let us out of here, you filthy Domer!" The thick metal muffled the angry voice. "We didn't agree to be your captives! You're worse than the monsters on the streets! At least they don't lie about what they are!"

Nola leaned against the wall, her heart racing in her chest. They would let them out as soon as the threat was over, they would have to. Nola wanted to look back through the glass, to explain the domes meant them no harm, but she couldn't risk him recognizing her later.

What if I'm wrong? What if the guards don't let them out of the cells as soon as the danger is gone?

She crept farther down the hall. There were two more rooms on either side, all four the same size as the ones closest to the door, all four holding six outsiders. Six more closely spaced doors waited beyond the filled cells. Nola stayed on one side of the hall, looking through each of the windows as she passed. These rooms were empty. In each of them a single ledge of stone, which looked as though it were meant to be a bed, stuck out of the wall, and a crude sink and toilet were securely set into the concrete.

"At least they didn't lock you in there," Nola whispered, wishing the man who had screamed at her could see the guards had put him in the better place.

Moving across to the other side, she glanced into each cell. When she finally got to the last window in the hall, she sighed at the unoccupied bed, relieved for a moment the guards hadn't been cruel enough to lock the outsiders up with only stone to sleep on. But then her eyes caught a glimpse of color on the floor.

Scarlet and purple atop a figure dressed all in black lying curled up on the ground. Slowly, the figure moved.

Run.

Her body shouted at her to flee, but her feet clung to the concrete as a pair of black eyes met her gaze.

Raina.

Her face was paler than even a vampire's should be. She'd been stripped of the leather clothes Nola had always seen her wear and dressed in a black cotton hospital gown that hung open in the back.

Raina's hair hung limp around her face as she pushed herself shakily to her feet, her eyes not drifting from Nola's face. Mouse-brown roots showed through the streaks of scarlet and purple in her hair.

Raina lurched toward the door, stumbling and thudding against the metal. She was taller than Nola, tall enough that she could look easily through the window, her face only inches from Nola's.

"You're alive," Nola whispered, fear and relief mixed in her voice.

Raina stared at her.

"I thought you were dead," Nola said as loudly as she dared.

Raina rolled her eyes. Even that slight movement looked as though it cost more energy than Raina could spare. "You would think that, wouldn't you?"

"You were stabbed in the chest." Nola's hands trembled at the memory of it. The man trying to drink from Nola's throat, Raina saving her. Raina jumping in front of a knife to save Nola...again. "I thought it killed you."

"He didn't get my heart, Domer." Raina sneered, swaying as she continued. "Though if I'd known this would be my fate, I would have stabbed myself in the heart. Or cut off my head. I'm not too picky."

"How long have you been in here?" Nola glanced down the hall. She still couldn't hear anything from the barracks beyond. What if they had more people they wanted to add to the cells?

"How long ago was the rebellion?" Raina asked.

"Rebellion?" Nola's voice rose in anger. "You mean the time you broke into the domes and murdered innocent people?"

"Innocence is in the eye of the beholder." Raina gave a weary shrug, like the thought of dead Domers meant nothing to her.

"You destroyed our home," Nola said. "You stole from us!"

"We took what we needed to survive."

"Well, I hope you have a great time surviving in here." Nola turned to leave.

"Because I got captured after getting stabbed to save your damned life?" Raina's crackling voice echoed through the hall. "Yeah, I'll try."

"Don't pretend you saved me because you actually like me." Nola smacked both hands hard against the door, taking pleasure in Raina's flinch. "You saved me because Emanuel told you to. And I don't even know why he bothered to do that. Did it make him feel better about destroying my home?"

"If you think this is what a *destroyed home* looks like, you know even less than I thought you did, little girl." Raina turned and sagged back to her spot on the floor. "And it wasn't Emanuel who cared enough to want you to stay alive. It was Kieran. Your precious Kieran. I guess I deserve to be locked up in this florescent-lit, concrete hell for listening to a lovesick kid. Now leave me the fuck alone. I saved your life, at least let me die slowly in peace."

Raina curled back up, her face hidden beneath the curtain of her hair.

Nola slid down the door and pressed her forehead into the cool metal, taking deep, shuddering breaths, willing herself not to panic.

Kieran had protected her. Told the others not to hurt her. She jammed her hands in her hair, pulling hard against the roots. He had wanted to keep her safe. She had to be safe, but everyone in the domes that she loved could die. Her home could be shattered, her family killed, but he wanted her alive.

It was cruel.

"He wanted to torture me." Nola viciously wiped away the tears on her face. "That is not love, Nola Kent. If Kieran loved you..." She choked on the words. It didn't matter if Kieran had ever loved her. His betrayal was too much to ever forgive.

And Jeremy...wonderful, steady Jeremy who had forgiven her, or at least wanted to, was hurt and bleeding and she couldn't help him. She couldn't help anyone.

Shaking so hard she could barely stand, Nola fought her way to her feet. She wouldn't stay near Raina. And there was no point hiding in here anyway. She would have to leave the hall eventually, might as well be caught now. She would lie to the guards, say she had never seen Jeremy's terrible wounds.

Another lie to add to the ever-growing list.

Slowly, she walked down the hall. Trying not to think of the innocent people who were still locked behind metal doors, hoping the guards really would let them out as soon as the domes were safe.

Nola opened the door to the barracks hall and stepped forward. There were still doctors running between rooms, treating patients. There were still no screams of pain or fear from the Outer Guard, only the precision of orders immediately obeyed. The ten minutes she had been gone really hadn't changed the scene that much. The doctors had moved on to other patients, and there were no more stretchers being carried down the stairs. But smears of blood still marred the floor.

She looked at the door through which Jeremy lay, wanting to walk in and shout that she was staying with him and there was nothing they could do to stop her. But Gentry had said to go. Gentry had promised Jeremy would be all right if Nola left. She walked up the stairs, not daring to look back for fear she wouldn't keep going.

She had to trust Gentry to tell her the truth and Jeremy to heal. She had to trust the guards would let the outsiders go as soon as it was safe and keep Raina where she couldn't hurt anyone.

If I can't trust the domes, there's nothing left for me to hold onto.

Nola turned away from the hospital corridor at the top of the stairs, heading back down the hall to Bright Dome. She shuddered at the sounds of the wounded Dome Guard, but two long corridors later, the noise faded away. Only the steady rhythm of her footsteps ruined the calm of the hall. The others must still be in the bunker below.

Large letters marked the wall: *Bright Dome*. Nola traced the letters with her finger. Home. Bright Dome was her home. She wouldn't be able to get back into the bunker anyway. And her mother would be locked in her lab with the seeds by now.

She walked the rest of the way to her house in a daze. Examining every tree she passed. Trying to memorize the shape of each stone on the path that led her home. Counting the steps it took her to reach her room. The purple-spotted orchid sat on her desk. Jeremy's wonderful gift.

Even thinking his name sent panic surging through her chest. He had to be okay. There was no other choice. Nola climbed onto her windowsill and reached up. Her arms burned as she pulled herself onto the soft moss that covered the roof. She lay down, burying her face in the damp, earthy smell, and screamed. Tears burned in her eyes, and a sob ripped through her chest.

"No!" Nola growled, hating the tears that poured down her cheeks. "No, no, no," she whimpered as panic overwhelmed her.

Curling up on her side under the dark sky, she sobbed. Alone under the glass.

CHAPTER NINE

The sun had already peeked over the horizon when voices from the ground woke Nola. She couldn't make out any words in the sleepy murmurs but blinking away the clouds her tears had left behind, dozens of shapes appeared in the dim light. People making their way home. She rubbed her eyes, feeling their swelling under her fingers.

She watched the group move, waiting for her mother to come toward their house. But Lenora wasn't with them. Digging her fingers into the moss, Nola climbed back through her window and crept to her mother's room. It was empty, as was the rest of the house. Nola stood in the pale darkness.

A void had swallowed her whole. Her tears had dried up. But she had thought that before. When her father died, when Kieran was banished, when the domes were attacked. But it wasn't true. Tears couldn't dry up forever, just until the next terrible thing happened.

Nola walked out the kitchen door and into the dome, brushing her fingers over her curls to get rid of the bits of moss that clung to her from sleeping on the roof.

More people filtered into Bright Dome as she walked down the stairs.

Jeremy.

If people were coming into the domes, it should be safe for her to go and see Jeremy. Breaking into a run, Nola sprinted through the corridors, ignoring the sleepy glares of the people she dodged past.

Through the corridors and down the stairs, no one tried to stop her until she reached the barracks level.

"You can't come down here, Miss." An Outer Guard stepped in front of Nola, holding out a hand to block her path.

"Jeremy Ridgeway," Nola said. "I know he was hurt, and I want to see him."

Pain and sympathy creased the guard's brow.

"He's okay." Nola's voice shook. "Please tell me he's okay."

"He's alive," the guard said, "but I don't have authorization to let you see him."

"Ask Captain Ridgeway," Nola begged, letting the news that Jeremy was, in fact, alive embolden her. "He'll say I can see him. I promise, I'll wait here."

The guard stared at Nola before waving another guard over. The woman limped as she approached. "Ask Captain Ridgeway if Magnolia Kent can see Jeremy."

The other guard nodded and limped away toward Captain Ridgeway's office.

It's not that bad. If his dad's not with him, it can't be that bad.

But the blood and the terrible wounds.

"How did you know my name?" Nola asked, seizing the only thing her mind could cling to aside from Jeremy being so terribly hurt.

"You're the one the Vampers captured," the guard said. "We sent a crew into the city after you, organized a whole mission to find you. I was on the failed rescue mission in Nightland. It's hard to forget a face you go into battle for, especially if you fail to save the person you're after."

An all too familiar shadow passed across the guard's face.

"You didn't fail," Nola whispered. "I'm here, aren't I?"

The guard nodded and gave a pinched smile.

"The captain said she can go in." The limping guard returned. "But she's not to wake Ridgeway or disturb the wound dressings."

Wound dressings.

Nola exhaled shakily. "I just want to see him."

The limping guard nodded and beckoned for Nola to follow her. "He's a lucky guy. Keep a good watch on him for us."

"I will," Nola said, so softly her words barely made a sound as the door to Jeremy's room swung open.

He lay on a bed, needles and tubes attached to his arm. He slept peacefully, no pain marring his face nor any trace of blood on the white gown that covered him.

Nola walked toward Jeremy, not noticing the guard had followed her into the room until she pulled up a chair for Nola to sit next to the bed. Before Nola could thank her, she slipped back out, leaving her and Jeremy alone in the room.

The white gown and sheet of the bed couldn't diminish Jeremy. He didn't look smaller or weaker. Only peaceful. If it hadn't been for the tubes in his arms, he could have simply fallen asleep after a long day of work in the domes.

She watched his chest rise and fall with each breath. No rattle came from the terrible hole that had pierced him. She reached for his hand before stopping herself. She wasn't to wake him. Instead, she curled up on the chair and stared at him.

The tiny lines from his constant smile showed even in sleep. But the newer lines, the ones made by worry, were gone. He hadn't shaved in a few days. Stubble marked his chin. Nola wanted to touch his cheeks. To feel their roughness on her skin. To feel the warmth that meant life still filled him.

Wrapping her arms around herself, she fought the urge to hold him. Trying to content herself with watching his chest rise and fall, rise and fall. Each breath was another victory. Another moment of life the cruel outside world hadn't stolen from them.

Inhale, exhale. Inhale, exhale.

How many millions of breaths would mean they had made it through another year?

Inhale, exhale.

How many breaths until it counted as a long, full life?

She didn't know she had fallen asleep until fingers grazed her palm.

"Nola," a gravelly voice whispered.

She blinked, trying to see in the dim light of the room. A hand lay gently in hers.

"Nola," the voice said again. She looked up to Jeremy. His eyes were open, and a faint smile curved his lips. "Are you all right?"

She choked on her laugh, tears tightening her throat. "Am I all right?" Nola repeated, tenderly twining her fingers through his. "You almost died, and you're asking if I'm all right?"

"Always." Jeremy reached toward her.

"Don't." Nola moved closer as a shadow of pain crossed Jeremy's face. She leaned in, kissing his palm and pressing it to her cheek. "You have to stay still and rest so you can heal."

"I'll heal just fine." Jeremy grinned. Only his eyes betrayed his pain and fatigue. "I just want to hold you."

"If your dad thinks you aren't resting because I'm here, he'll kick me out." She glanced toward the door. "I don't want to leave."

"Come up here then." Jeremy patted the bed next to him. "Then I can hold you without moving."

"I don't want to hurt you. You were wounded in the city. Really, really badly and..." She didn't have the words to say how close to losing him they had come.

"I know." He took her hand, coaxing her toward the bed. "I was there, and it hurt like hell. But I'm going to be fine. And I'll sleep a lot better if I can feel you safe beside me."

She sat gently on the bed, easing her weight down slowly and watching his face for any sign she was causing him pain.

"I was safe, you know." Nola lay down next to Jeremy. He drew her in so her head rested on his shoulder. "I was in a bunker. You were the one out fighting."

"It doesn't matter where you are, Nola." He kissed the top of her head. "I'm always going to worry about you. I love you too much not to."

"I love you, too." She tipped her chin up and brushed her lips against his. "You have to rest and get better. I need you whole and healthy."

"I'll be fine." He smiled, and this time his joy touched his eyes as well. "As long as I've got you."

"Sleep," she whispered. "I'll be here when you wake up. I promise."

"Don't let them make you leave," Jeremy said, and in a moment, he was asleep.

Closing her eyes, she could feel the steady rise and fall of his chest as it timed with her own breaths.

He was alive, and he loved her.

I love him.

A smile still on her lips, Nola drifted to sleep.

CHAPTER TEN

L ights flashed on. With a squeak, Nola fell, thudding onto the concrete floor.

"Nola!" Jeremy shouted.

"I'm fine," she groaned.

"Sorry to wake you," Captain Ridgeway said from his place by the door. While he didn't look sorry, he didn't look angry either, which Nola took to be a good sign as she pushed herself off the floor. "The doctors are ready to check on you, Jeremy."

The captain stepped aside, letting a doctor dressed in a white uniform enter the room. The tag on the front of her uniform read *Doctor Mullins*.

"I feel great," Jeremy said, taking Nola's hand in his as soon as she stood.

"I need to check your wounds, nonetheless." Doctor Mullins glanced at Nola before looking back at Captain Ridgeway.

"Nola, if you wouldn't mind leaving while the doctor examines Jeremy." Captain Ridgeway held the door to the hall open.

"Sure." Nola started for the door, but Jeremy held tightly onto her hand.

"I don't need to be examined," Jeremy said. "I'm fine, and Nola can stay."

"You are an Outer Guard," Captain Ridgeway said, his voice leaving no doubt that he was speaking as Jeremy's commander, not his father. "You were wounded in the line of duty, and you will receive medical treatment."

"I'll wait outside." Nola kissed Jeremy's cheek. "I'll come back as soon as they're done."

Nodding to Captain Ridgeway, she went out into the hall to wait. The brightness of the lights in the hall meant it was nearly midday.

All the tunnels were lit according to the time of day to ensure the people of the domes would stay attuned to the sun even while working underground. But the false brightness bore into Nola's eyes, a garish contrast to the soothing light of Jeremy's room.

Even the few hours Nola had slept made a huge difference. No hint remained that patients had been treated in the hall. No blood marked the floor. The scent of fear and fighting had left the air. The door to one of the long barrack's rooms swung open. Half the beds Nola could see were filled with sleeping Outer Guard. The other half were empty.

Were the beds empty because the guards with families were in their homes aboveground or already out working? Had more been lost in the city?

But it wasn't Jeremy. I didn't lose him.

Self-loathing welled in Nola's chest.

Is it so terrible to want the person I love alive?

"Nola." Captain Ridgeway stepped out of the door and stood next to her, following her gaze toward the empty beds. "We lost two."

She looked up at Captain Ridgeway and felt like a little girl again. As terrified and small as the night he had come to tell them her father had been killed in a riot.

"I'm so sorry," Nola said. Her words sounded hollow, unbearably inadequate.

It had been winter when her father died. The air in the domes had been chilly. She remembered staring at the goose bumps on her arms while the captain told her mother how brave her father had been. How his act of heroism had saved lives. But all Nola could think was how badly she wanted her father brought back inside where it was warm. She didn't want him to sleep in the cold. Even if he was to sleep forever.

"What happened?" Nola asked, not really expecting an answer.

Captain Ridgeway rubbed his chin for a moment before speaking. "Follow me."

Without looking to see if she obeyed, he turned and strode down the hall to his office. Before she could take a step, he held the door open for her.

Feeling as though she were being led to a teacher's office for disobedience, Nola walked down the hall and through the open door.

It was a small room with only a desk, two chairs, and a filing cabinet. One picture sat on the desk. Jeremy and Gentry smiling together, back when Jeremy was shorter than his older sister. A faint hum permeated the air but did nothing to lessen the horrible quiet while Nola waited for the captain to speak. She expected him to sit behind his desk or offer her a chair, but he stayed just inside the door, standing right in front of her so she had to look up to see his face.

"It was the wolf packs. Since Nightland cleared out, there's been fighting to see who controls the city. Vampers don't naturally like to live together. A community like Nightland may very well have been the only one of its kind in the world. Now they're out of the city, and there isn't another Vamper group to step in and take power." Captain Ridgeway ran his calloused hands over the graying stubble on his face. "At least not one that can stand up to the wolf packs. The packs started by picking off Vampers, and now they've moved on to fighting each other to see who will end up in power."

"But why did all the guards go into the city?" she asked, unsure if she had overstepped by speaking. "I know the Outer Guard have to protect the peace in the city, but the Dome Guard have never gone in to stop riots."

"We aren't dealing with riots. It's become an all-out street war. They aren't burning factories, they're burning homes. Taking over whole blocks, and anyone who tries to fight back, or just doesn't run fast enough, dies. Or is forced to join the pack. So, the winning pack gets stronger and stronger—"

"Until they're as strong as Nightland and can come for us," Nola said. "So, you took everyone to try and stop the pack from growing. Did it work?"

"It bought us time," Captain Ridgeway said, "but we didn't stop them. I think the world might have fallen too far for us to actually keep the shadows from spreading."

Fear swelled in her chest. "Then what do we do?"

"Find a way to survive the shadows. Then fight like hell when they come to our door."

"We can't leave the domes." Nola's mind flipped through a hundred possibilities, trying to find a path that didn't lead to more gray smoke rising above the domes. "The food and the plants, they can't be moved. Even if we could find another place for the people."

"We aren't going to leave, we're going to fight. We'll burn the whole damn city if that's what it takes."

Nola froze, frightened by Captain Ridgeway's vehemence.

"I hope—" Nola searched for words in the tangles of her mind. "I hope it won't come to that. But if it's the city or the domes…"

"Then the domes have to survive. We were built to protect the future of mankind. And that's what we'll do, no matter what it takes."

The captain's words hung heavy in the air.

"Why are you telling me this?" Nola asked, wanting to flee Captain Ridgeway's heavy gaze. It felt like he was searching her, trying to find some grain of information that would help the domes survive. But even if she hadn't sworn to

Jeremy that she would lie, there was nothing she knew that could save them from a wolf pack. "Isn't this the sort of thing the Outer Guard always try to hide from the rest of us?" she pressed on after a long moment of silence.

"It is," he said, "but for some reason you, Magnolia Kent, seem to be mired deeper in this bloody muck than the rest of us. And if there's one thing I've learned, it's that when blood and death come for someone once, they'll come back again. And again. The bloodthirsty don't forget."

The captain's words rang over her like a judge delivering a death sentence. She had played with shadows. Now she was condemned to darkness.

"They'll keep coming for me till they kill me." The words came so naturally, so simply, it felt like she had known since the first time she stared into the void of a Vamper's black eyes.

"They'll kill you, or you'll kill them. You can't get away from a monster that has your scent. And Emanuel isn't dead, at least not as far as we can tell. The storm that's brewing carries one word on the wind: *Nola*."

Nola swayed on the spot, and the captain caught her by the elbows.

"Your name is still spoken in the city. The second Nightland took you, you became a symbol of the domes. And until you're not, you aren't safe."

"Why are you telling me this?" she said, her voice stronger and louder in her anger as she pulled away from the captain. "If I'm doomed, why not just leave me in the streets and let the wolves have me? If Emanuel wants me, I'll go. I'm not worth more people dying. Just let it be done!"

"No. You are a citizen of the domes, and the Outer Guard are sworn to protect you. Letting the wolves have you wouldn't make the domes any safer. It would only make you dead. Not to mention my son is in love with you. And I'm not going to let the wolves or Vampers or zombies or whatever else this hellhole of a world throws at us destroy my son's life. He is willing to risk everything for you. It's my job to make sure that *everything* doesn't end up meaning his life."

"Tell me what to do." Her words came out as a plea. "Just tell me what I'm supposed to do."

"Stay safe, Magnolia. I don't know why you're so damned important, but you are. And if you end up in trouble again, my son will be running at the head of a pack of my guards trying to save you."

"I would never ask him to—" she couldn't form the words. "I want Jeremy to be safe."

"I'm glad we both agree on that." The captain's eyes darkened for a moment. "That's the problem with my raising children to be Outer Guard. They got to be really good at it."

"How was Jeremy hurt?" Nola pictured Jeremy running at the front of the guards as they fought the wolves, risking his life to protect everyone else's.

"The same as all Outer Guard get hurt." Captain Ridgeway opened the door to the hall. "Doing his duty to the domes." Without another word, he bowed Nola out of his office.

Nola jumped at the firm *click* of the door behind her as though it had been a gunshot. Part of her wanted to run as far away from the domes as it was possible for a person to go. Out into the wild where even the wolves and Vampers couldn't find her. But the much larger part wanted nothing more than to be with Jeremy. To make sure Doctor Mullins was positive he would to be all right.

Running toward the door, she knocked before anyone could try and stop her.

The instant Jeremy called, "Come in," she swung the door open and slipped into the room, closing the door quickly and leaning against it, her heart racing as though she had just run from the boogeyman.

"I thought you'd run away." Jeremy sat up in bed and had more color in his cheeks than he'd had when he'd woken up.

"Your dad wanted to talk to me." Nola pushed herself off the door and ran the few steps to the bed, anxious to be closer to him. "Did the doctor say you could sit up? You need to be—"

"What did my dad want to talk to you about?" Jeremy cut her off, taking her hand and pulling her down to sit by his side.

"He told me—" Nola began, instinct telling her to lie, to say that Captain Ridgeway had lectured her about not tiring Jeremy and allowing him to rest and heal.

When did lying become so easy?

"He told me he's worried about me," she began again. "He thinks the wolves or Vampers or someone will come after me again. Apparently, I'm a symbol of what the outsiders hate about the domes, so basically I'm doomed. Mostly, I think he's worried you'll get hurt trying to protect me. I can't let anything happen to you because of me." She dug her nails into her palms to keep her hands from shaking.

"Don't worry about me getting hurt," Jeremy said, taking her hands in his. "Turns out I'm really pretty good at this guard thing."

She laughed weakly. "Good or not, I just want you to be safe."

"I will be." Jeremy held Nola so her head rested on his shoulder. "And so will you. I'm not going to let anyone hurt you."

"But what if your dad's right? What if all the darkness and blood really are chasing me?" The words felt foolish in her mouth, but it didn't erase the fear Captain Ridgeway had left lodged in her chest.

"They are." Jeremy wrapped both arms around her. "My dad was telling the truth. People in the city know your name. Wolves, Vampers, they've all heard the name *Nola Kent*."

"But why? I'm no one. I'm not important at all." She buried her face in Jeremy's chest, the stench of chemicals obscured his familiar scent of fresh earth, and she hated it. Hated the one who had torn his flesh and left him stuck in this hospital room. She wanted to fight all of them. Find the people who knew her name and destroy every last one of them, until there was no one left to hurt Jeremy.

"You are important." He held her even closer, as though he had sensed her urge to run. "You're important to me because I love you. And important to the domes because you're brilliant."

"But why in the city?" Nola whispered. "Nightland is gone. Emanuel and Kieran are gone. There's no one I've ever met left in the city."

"You were important to Nightland." He pressed his cheek to her hair. "You were important enough for there to be a battle over you. And if you were important enough for us to fight over you, then you're important enough to be a target. Yours is the only dome name people know in the city. It's the only name they can shout."

"What do I do?" Nola held onto Jeremy as tightly as she dared.

"You don't do anything. We will figure it out. Together."

CHAPTER ELEVEN

"I'll be back soon." Nola leaned down and brushed her lips against Jeremy's, unable to keep a smile from the corners of her mouth as he tried to pull her in tighter. "I have to go."

She had already been given a whole day to spend in Jeremy's room, more than anyone but Lenora Kent's daughter would have been granted. And, as far as Nola knew, none of the other injured Outer Guard had been allowed to have visitors stay in their rooms at all.

Captain Ridgeway hadn't allowed any of the wounded Outer Guard to be moved to the hospital wing, insisting on keeping his men separate from the injured Dome Guard.

The lines between Dome Guard and Outer Guard had always been thick. Two arms meant to be doing the same thing but hating each other all the while.

The Dome Guard alternated between calling the Outer Guard violent and incompetent, depending on how riots ended. And the Outer Guard called the Dome Guard cowards for never going out into the city.

Then half the Dome Guard had been dragged away to help stop the fighting. Some had been injured, and four of them killed. But still the line between the two sections seemed as stiff as ever.

"If you don't get out of my way, I'll bring your name before the Council!" The shout pounded through the door from the corridor.

Jeremy moved toward the edge of the bed and was halfway to standing before Nola put both hands on his chest, trying to keep him still.

"You're not supposed to get up," she said as the shouting voice came closer.

"My men fought alongside yours against the wolves, Ridgeway!" Nola recognized Captain Stokes' voice as his words became crisper, as though he were right outside the door. "And if you expect me to allow you to use *my men* to fight in your damned city again, I want answers!"

Before she could wonder at Stokes' foolhardy courage in shouting at Captain Ridgeway while surrounded by a flock of Outer Guard, stomping footsteps approached.

"If you don't mind"—Nola gasped as her mother's voice cut through Captain Stokes' shouts—"I need to get through this door to collect my daughter. Some of us in the domes are still trying to be productive rather than having pissing contests and shouting in the hall like spoiled children."

Nola was already halfway across the room when a sharp knock sounded the instant before the door swung open. "Nola, it's time to work," Lenora said in a dangerous voice that shot tension into Nola's shoulders. "Jeremy, I hope you're feeling better and can get some rest. That is *if* these cretins who call themselves captains can stop shouting like a couple of common city dwellers."

Nola didn't dare look back as she followed her mother out into the hall.

Captain Ridgeway and Captain Stokes stood ten feet apart, glaring daggers at one another.

Nola ran past her mother and up the stairs, not stopping until the next landing.

"I will not have my authority questioned by a man who knows as little about the state of the city as an earthworm!" Captain Ridgeway's voice carried up the steps.

Lenora made a sound somewhere between a *tsk* and a growl as she strode past Nola and down the hall. "How on earth do they expect to gain anyone's respect by shouting?"

Nola was glad her mother had moved in front of her and couldn't see the look of astonishment on her face.

"In troubling times, we have to stand together, not push away others who should be our allies," Lenora said.

"Was there a Council meeting this morning?" Nola jogged to catch up to her mother whose words sounded suspiciously like Council parroting.

"Yes, there was."

Nola didn't need to ask how the meeting had gone.

"So, where am I going to be working today?" she asked, more for something to say that didn't involve the Council meeting or the shouting guards below than because she really wanted to know.

"You'll be working with the outsiders again." Lenora looked at her daughter with a furrowed brow. "Just because our work was interrupted doesn't mean it doesn't have to be finished. I let you have all day yesterday to sit with Jeremy. But the world keeps turning, and quite frankly we have more to do now than ever. Extra mouths to feed and all."

"Extra mouths to feed?" Nola asked as they reached the stairs to the Amber Dome. She grabbed a gardening uniform off the hooks on the wall.

"The domes need extra help, which means more people to feed." Lenora turned to her daughter, watching impatiently as Nola hastily yanked on her jumpsuit. "Honestly, Nola, you really should think things through."

"Sorry," Nola said, not really sure what she had done wrong.

"You'll be back with your group from before. They seem competent. Just make sure they don't hurt the plants or steal anything." Lenora strode up the stairs and straight to the high platform in the center of the dome, a sure sign the conversation had ended.

"Thanks, Mom," Nola muttered before looking around the dome.

They had gotten a lot of work done the day before. The rows of plants that needed to be condensed were already finished. The existing plants moved to the far end to make room for the new crop.

Lenora had been right. They had needed outside hands to help in the process. The amount of work accomplished during Nola's absence would have taken at least a week for the Domers to do on their own.

One group moved through with carts, harvesting all the food ripe enough to be eaten. The food would be taken down to the distribution center and sent out to the families of the domes. That had always been Nola's favorite part of the work. Taking the food they had grown and sending it away to be eaten.

But the group with the carts weren't Nola's people. She had to make nearly a full lap of the dome, passing a group refitting the underground irrigation pipes, a group on ladders to reach the top of the high rod-like towers where the herbs grew, and another pruning back the dead branches on the fruit-bearing trees before she finally found her group working on a seedling tray.

Three hundred tiny containers of soil lay on a long table, ready to receive the new seeds on the brink of sprouting.

T stood by the seed tray, carefully counting out how many they had. Beauford moved down the row, putting one seed into each container. Catlyn followed behind him, covering each seed and giving it the tiniest bit of water.

"Wow," Nola said, her voice coming out awkwardly bright as she tried to sound encouraging. "You've all done a great job!"

"Thanks." Catlyn gave a quick smile while Beauford only spared a moment to glare at Nola before placing another seed. "It's good to see you back. They didn't tell us where you were. I was worried you had been injured in the evacuation."

"No," Nola said as she tied her hair back, wavering on the point of lying.

Don't add lies. There isn't any reason for it.

"A friend of mine was hurt in the fighting in the city," Nola said.

There was a sharp intake of breath from T's direction.

"Is he okay?" Catlyn asked, pulling Nola's attention away from T.

"It was pretty bad, so they let me sit with him," Nola said, moving closer to T, "but he's doing better now."

"It's amazing what you can do with fancy medicine," Beauford said from down the table. "Save you from all sorts of terrible things."

"My friend was very lucky," Nola said. "But he was hurt trying to help people in the city."

T gripped the edge of the table.

"Are you okay?" Nola asked, softly enough not to be overheard by anyone outside their group.

"Fine, ma'am." T let go of the table and counted another set of seeds into her hand.

"Were...Is your family safe? Did they all make it through the riot?" Nola asked, covering T's hand to stop her working.

The girl didn't brush Nola away, but she didn't look at her either. "I don't have any family in the city."

"And we wouldn't know if they had been hurt anyway." Beauford grabbed the seeds from T's other hand. "We haven't been allowed to leave the damned domes to go back to the city. Everyone we know could be dead, but they'll keep us locked in here to work."

Catlyn hushed him as one of the Dome Guard headed toward their table.

"Is everything all right here, Miss Kent?" the guard asked, narrowing his eyes at Beauford.

"We're fine," Catlyn said. "Things are moving along."

"I didn't ask you," the guard said roughly to Catlyn before turning to Nola. "Is everything all right here, *Miss Kent?*"

"Y-yes," Nola said, taking a deep breath and trying not to let the gruffness of the guard shake her. "I was actually wondering what time the workers were going to be escorted back to the city tonight."

"Transports in and out of the city have been halted," the guard said. "No point in risking guards' safety while the city is eating itself alive."

"But what if they need to go see their families?" Anger crept into Nola's voice. "What if the workers need to get home?"

"They can go whenever they like." The guard glared at Beauford who stood next to Nola, blatantly not working. "Anyone who doesn't want to stay and work for the domes is free to leave. They're used to the outside air, they can walk back to the city."

"We just won't be let back in or paid for our work," Beauford said. "But we're free to go back to the burning city and starve whenever we like."

"Then perhaps you should be grateful for the food and bed we've given you." The guard turned to Nola. "Would you like me to have him removed from your group?"

"No!" she said too loudly.

The guard narrowed his eyes.

"I think we're all just a little stressed from the last few days," Nola said. "Beauford can stay with my team."

The guard nodded. "I'll report him to Dr. Kent. She should be kept informed of workers who cause trouble."

Leaving his threat lingering in the air, the guard turned and strode to the center platform.

"Look busy right now," Nola spoke through gritted teeth, grabbing a few seeds and moving to the closest pots. Even Beauford had the sense to follow her lead.

After a minute or so, she glanced back at the platform. The guard had gone, but Lenora stared in their direction, watching the group work.

Running out of seeds in her hand, Nola moved back to T. "Can I get another handful?"

T passed Nola a little dish of seeds.

"Please be careful with them," T said. "They only gave us enough for the pots. I think they're afraid of us trying to smuggle seeds out. If we ever get out."

Nola worked on the closest tiny seed pot, miming planting since that soil had already been filled. "Do you want to leave?"

"I doubt I'd have any place to go," T said, her voice shockingly calm. "Where I was staying, it was right near Nightland. If the fighting was as bad as it sounds, I can't imagine I'd have a place to go back to. The tunnels are valuable to vampires and wolves. If there was a big fight, it would have been there."

"But the Domers went out to fight—" Nola stopped working as T's eyes widened. "What?" she whispered, moving closer to T, pretending to need more seeds though she hadn't used any. "If the big fight was Domers and wolves, it might not have been near Nightland. The domes don't want anything to do with those tunnels."

"You're right," T said. "Maybe I'm just being pessimistic. I might still have a place to live and a few friends left alive. No way to find out, but I might be that lucky. Or, maybe the world's turned even more inside out. I did just hear a Domer say *Domer* after all."

"What do you mean?" Nola looked back down at the pots, pretending to plant more seeds, grateful her hands didn't tremble and betray her.

"I've never heard a Domer say *Domer*." T moved in closer, so her shoulder touched Nola's.

"Have you known many people from the domes?" Nola asked, carefully not saying *Domer*.

"No." T shrugged, jarring the dish in Nola's hand. "But I've known even more Vampers than you have, Magnolia Kent. And Vampers say vampires, and Domers say whatever the hell name you like to call yourselves that makes you feel better about the whole world hating you."

"The world doesn't hate us," Nola said.

"Of course, they do," T said, switching Nola's full seed dish out for another full seed dish. "You should know that better than anyone. Emanuel would have made sure of that."

CHAPTER TWELVE

The air in Nola's lungs froze. There was no way for her to breathe. Nothing for her to do. Fear had consumed her body.

Emanuel would have made sure of that.

The dome spun for a second before everything went black.

"Magnolia," a distant and unfamiliar voice called. "Magnolia, are you all right?"

No! the voice in Nola's head screamed. *Nothing is all right. Nothing has ever been all right!*

But her lips formed other words as her eyes fluttered open. "I'm fine."

She was in the medical wing, on a bed with a bright light overhead.

Doctor Mullins leaned over her, concern wrinkling her brow.

"What happened?" Nola tried to sit up, but the doctor placed a firm hand on her shoulder, pressing her back onto the bed.

"You fainted," Doctor Mullins said. "In the Amber Dome. Do you remember?"

"Yeah." Shame and fear pinked Nola's cheeks. "Yeah, I do."

"Your levels are all fine," Doctor Mullins said. "You want to tell me what happened?"

"I panicked. I was talking to one of the outsiders. They...they mentioned Nightland, and I just panicked." Nola hoped her answer would be close enough to the truth for the doctor to allow her to leave without asking any more questions.

"You weren't feeling faint or nauseous?"

"No." She shook her head. "I just freaked."

"It's okay." Doctor Mullins took her hand from Nola's shoulder, allowing her to sit up. "You've been through a lot, Magnolia. More than most could handle. If you need to talk to someone, we can make arrangements—"

"I really don't want to talk." Nola pushed herself to her feet and swayed as the room began to tilt again.

The doctor grabbed her elbow, steadying her.

"Thank you, but I'm fine. I just want to do my work and help the domes and..." Nola's voice faded away. She didn't know what else she wanted to do.

"I understand." The doctor took Nola's hand. She was young, probably only ten years older than Nola, and there she was, a doctor. Saving people. "I know what it's like to want to help. But you have to take care of yourself, too. If you want to talk, let me know and we'll arrange something."

"Thank you." Nola hurried toward the door.

"And if you start feeling faint or dizzy, sit down and have someone call for help. If the outsiders brought in an illness, we need to find it."

"Is one of them sick?" Nola asked.

"The pregnant one fainted in the Amber Dome yesterday," the doctor said, the tone of concern she had had for Nola all but gone. "I ran some tests and there's nothing we can find, but it's always best to be alert."

"But what about the baby? Did you make sure the baby was all right?"

"There isn't much to be done." The doctor shrugged. "She's an outsider. We can't give her dome medicine. She's already eating dome food. And who knows what damage the child was already subjected to in utero? I have enough patients with the guards who were hurt in the attacks and the dome citizens who need routine medical care. I can't add another patient who isn't even mine to care for." She opened the door for Nola. "No more work for you today. You need to go home and rest, but make sure you get something to eat first."

"Thanks." Nola was out the door and into the hall in a moment, walking as quickly as she dared.

How could a doctor not care about the health of an innocent child?

It's Nightland's fault.

Nightland had made the domes' existence so precarious. Nightland had made the city so violent. The Vampers and the wolves were the ones to blame for the horrible things that were happening. It wasn't the domes' fault that T and her baby might be sick.

It's our fault if we don't do anything to help.

Nola stopped at the end of the hall. She could go to Bright Dome. Eat, then go see Jeremy. Pretend Doctor Mullins had never mentioned T at all.

She turned around and walked back to the room where she had woken up.

"Actually," Nola said as soon as she stepped into the room, making Doctor Mullins jump, "I've been feeling a little run-down, what with—" She gave a weak smile and, just as Gentry had done days ago, waved a hand as though to say *everything*. "Would it be all right if I got a vitamin pack? Just to make sure I don't catch anything."

Doctor Mullins stared at Nola for a moment, her gaze seeming to take in everything from the slight purple under her eyes to her shrinking frame. The Domers were never given pills unless they were ill. Their diets were carefully controlled so they received all the nutrients they needed from food. Vitamin packs were reserved for the ill and endangered.

"I'm glad you're willing to admit you aren't feeling well." Doctor Mullins moved to a locked cabinet in the corner. "Being in tune with your body is the first step toward staying healthy." She pulled down a little glass bottle and handed it to Nola. "Take these with each meal and come back in a week, we'll see if you're feeling more yourself. In the meantime, remember, whether it's anxiety or just dizziness, come and see me."

"Yes, I will. Thank you." Nola backed out of the room. "I appreciate it." As soon as the door shut, she ran down the hall, the feeling of having stolen from the domes chasing her the whole way.

She headed straight for the Amber Dome, keeping the little glass bottle hidden in her palm. Her heart raced. What she was doing was wrong. A terrible offense against the domes.

No worse than what you've already done.

She climbed the steps to the Amber Dome, nodding at the guards who seemed shocked to see her on her feet so soon.

"Nola," Lenora called from the high platform.

To Nola's surprise, Lenora came down from her perch, hurrying toward her daughter.

"Nola, what are you doing here?" Lenora crossed her arms and examined her daughter's face. "The doctor sent word you needed to rest."

"I am." Nola corrected herself. "I'm going to. I just want to make sure my team is okay, and then I'll sleep, I promise."

"I'll see you at home." Lenora climbed back up to her platform.

For a moment, Nola considered telling her mother she wouldn't be at home, but by the time her mother made it back to their little house, she would have forgotten to worry about her daughter anyway.

She walked over to her group, careful not to hurry, though instinct told her to run.

"Miss Kent," Catlyn said as soon as she caught sight of her. "Are you feeling better?"

"Yes, thank you," Nola said, walking straight over to T.

Fear flashed through T's eyes for a moment before she stiffened her jaw as though ready to be struck.

"T," Nola said, stopping so close to the other girl that her face was only a foot away, "the doctor said that you were shaky, that there might be something wrong with your baby."

T's face paled.

"It's not much, and I don't know if it will help, but take one of these with every meal." Nola took T's hand in hers, pretending to lead her the two feet back to the worktable. "It's only a supplement, but it's the best I could get my hands on without people asking questions."

"I—" T began.

"Don't let anyone find out about these, or we'll both be walking into the city." Nola looked to the other two outsiders. "I'm sure you'll be able to finish without me. I'll see you tomorrow."

"Why?" T murmured, not looking away from the table in front of her.

"Because I'm not like Emanuel," Nola said. "I don't like to watch innocent people suffer."

Without giving T a chance to respond, she turned and walked through the dome and down the stairs.

It wasn't until she had made it three corridors away from the Amber Dome that Nola leaned against the wall. Her heart raced. Sweat slicked her palms, and a pounding pain gnawed at the back of her skull.

I've made a terrible mistake.

She had helped an outsider, gone against the domes again. If anyone found out, she would be banished to a city that had turned into a war zone. And she hadn't helped just anyone. She had helped a girl who knew Emanuel. At least well enough to know Nola had spent time with him. Stayed in his home and helped save his daughter's life.

Taking a shuddering breath, she pushed herself off the wall and forced her feet to move. Biting her lips to keep them from trembling, she nodded to the people she passed. Waiting for one of them to run at her screaming she was a traitor.

The guard at the top of the barracks stairs didn't try to stop her but instead gave her a wry smile as she hurried down the steps.

She knocked on Jeremy's door, hoping there wouldn't be anyone in there with him.

"Come in," he called.

Nola wrenched open the door and was inside in an instant, locking the door before running to Jeremy's bedside.

"What's going on?" Concern coated Jeremy's face as he moved to get out of bed.

"Careful." Nola tried to push Jeremy back into bed, but he threw his legs over the side as though she weren't holding him back at all.

"What's wrong?"

"Please be careful," Nola said, finally managing to stop Jeremy before he actually stood up.

"You just ran in here like there was a Vamper on your tail, and you want me to be careful?" Jeremy took her hands in his. "What the hell is going on? Is there something happening aboveground?"

"Yes—no." She searched for the best words to tell Jeremy what she'd done. "I mean, I passed out. I'm okay," she pushed on when his eyes grew wide. "One of the outsiders in my work group. She knows I know Emanuel. And I panicked. That's why I fainted. What if she tells someone I helped Nightland?"

"No one would believe her." Jeremy pressed his hands to Nola's cheeks. He was so tall even sitting down his face was level with hers. "She's one outsider. They'll think she's crazy, they'll think she's working for Emanuel, trying to infiltrate the domes and cause trouble."

"But what if Emanuel *did* send her? What if he wants to make me help them again, and I already did. Jeremy, I did something stupid. Really, really stupid."

"What did you do?"

"The girl, T is what she's called, she's pregnant," Nola said, begging him to understand, knowing she couldn't blame him if he decided this was the last straw and turned her over to the Dome Council himself. "She hasn't been doing very well. And she might be working for Emanuel, but that's got nothing to do with her baby, so I asked for a vitamin pack and gave it to her."

Jeremy let go of Nola's face and buried his head in his hands.

"I'm sorry." She sat on the bed next to Jeremy. "I'm so, so sorry. I just got caught up, and the doctor said she wouldn't help T because she's an outsider. But that baby has never done anything to hurt anyone. And I didn't think, until I did think, and now...I'm so sorry."

"The doctor was right, Nola!" Jeremy half-shouted, just softly enough not to be heard in the hall. "That girl has nothing to do with us. She is an outsider. One who might be working for Emanuel, You said it yourself."

"But the baby—"

"Isn't your problem."

"But it should be." Nola took Jeremy's hands in hers, kneeling on the bed so she could look straight into his eyes. "I'm sorry, I know I've messed up and keep messing up. I know what the domes stand for is important. We are the future. And maybe it makes me broken. Maybe I should just be banished. But I can't work next to a pregnant girl who needs medical help and not even try to do anything. And I know that's wrong," her voice faded. "But I didn't know what else to do. I'm sorry."

Silence filled the room for a moment, tainted only by the faint humming of the air ducts.

"You aren't broken," Jeremy said. "They founded the domes to give future generations of children a fighting chance in the rotting world we've been left with. But it isn't a perfect system. The founders laid out a whole bunch of rules, and I don't think any of them thought we'd want to break them. The outside world wasn't made up of monsters and starving people when the domes were built. The founders didn't know what we'd be watching happen on the other side of the glass. But you can't save them all, Nola. And helping that girl could mean hurting your own people."

"But it's so tiny to us." Tears welled in her eyes. "And what if it saves her baby?"

"But what about when T has to go back outside?" Jeremy wrapped his arms around her, laying his cheek against her hair. "You haven't been out there, not lately. It's gotten worse. Worse than when there was a riot at the food center. I know you were in Nightland. But the city isn't being run by one psychopath who might actually be able to control his people anymore. There are no more jobs. Give it a few more months and there will be no more food. It might be kinder if that baby wasn't born."

"But if they can find a way to farm, then they could eat," she whispered, letting Jeremy hold her close, sure she would shatter into a million irreparable pieces if he let go.

"For a while," he said. "Until others found out they had food and tried to take it from them. Or there was a bad storm. Or a new sickness came."

"So you're saying everyone outside the glass is doomed?" Nola said, the finality of her words striking her in the chest.

"Eventually, yes." He held her tighter, as though he could sense the terrible pain growing inside her, threatening to send her back into blackness. "Humans won't be able to survive outside the domes, not for a long time."

"But what about Vampers and wolves?" Nola asked. "Are they doomed, too?"

"They'll make it the longest," Jeremy said. "They're the strongest, and some run in big enough groups to take what they need to survive."

"Like Nightland." She remembered the Vampers coming through the glass, the blood that slicked the floors of the halls. "And the ones that do survive will pick each other off. And then they'll come for us."

"Then they'll come for us," Jeremy said. "That girl's baby might survive. But if it lives long enough, it'll end up our enemy."

"But it isn't now." Nola looked into his eyes. "And if we decide someone is our enemy before they can decide themselves, aren't we losing the chance of there ever being peace?"

"I love you, Nola." He leaned down and kissed her. "I love you for always wanting to see the good. But the world has fallen too far. All that's left is survival. It's my job to keep you safe, and I can't let you risk yourself for a girl who might be working for Emanuel."

She wanted to argue. To say that there was still good in the world, and maybe there could be peace between the domes and the outside.

But Jeremy was right. The gap between the desperate and the privileged was too great. The domes had to stay intact to ensure the survival of the human race, and the outside couldn't be saved from burning. If that had been possible, the domes would never have been built in the first place.

"What do I do?" Nola said. "Just wait and see if she says anything else? Let her keep spying for Emanuel if that's what she's here to do? Wait and see if she turns me in?"

"Nola, calm down," Jeremy hushed as her voice rose in panic. "You're going to talk to this girl and see what she knows."

"How? I can't just ask if she's going to turn me in for helping Nightland in the middle of the Amber Dome."

"We'll wait till they're back in the bins tonight," Jeremy said, lying back on the bed and drawing her down with him so her head rested on his shoulder. "I know where they're being kept, and I can get you in. Then we just ask her a few questions."

"And if she is going to tell the Council something that will get me sent away?"

"We convince her to keep her mouth shut."

CHAPTER THIRTEEN

H ours passed with Nola lying in Jeremy's arms. He drifted in and out of sleep, but all she could do was stare up at the ceiling and wait. A guard had brought a tray in for Jeremy a few hours ago. She had the feeling that if Jeremy hadn't been the captain's son, they might not have been so kind about her and Jeremy being alone in his room. As it was, she only had to endure a few obnoxious winks from the food bearer before they were left alone.

The lights had dimmed, and people had stopped passing in the hallway when Jeremy finally kicked off his sheets.

"You should stay here," Nola said one more time though she knew it was useless. "You have to be careful."

"I'm a fast healer." Jeremy laced his fingers through hers as he led her to the door. "And if that girl is working for Emanuel, I'm not letting you anywhere near her without me."

"Jeremy." She stepped in front of him, blocking his path to the door at the last moment. "I love you. And I'm sorry for getting you involved in any of this."

He leaned down and kissed her, wrapping his arms around her, and lifting her so her toes barely touched the ground. She draped her arms around his neck, twining her fingers through his short hair to pull him even closer. The pounding of his heart echoed in her chest, making her own heart race quicker.

She gasped as he pulled away.

"I never thought loving you would be easy." Jeremy pressed his lips to the top of her head. "You don't get something as wonderful as you without having to work for it. And I'm willing to do whatever it takes."

"You're better than I could ever deserve, Jeremy Ridgeway."

"I'll let you keep believing that." He smiled and opened the door.

The dim night setting of the lights cast shadows in the corridor. Two guards stood by the stairs, their backs to the barracks. Jeremy walked calmly toward the door at the end of the hall.

Nola felt like they should run. Or try to hide in the faint shadows that hovered near the walls. But Jeremy walked boldly and silently forward, not hesitating or looking back as he pulled open the door that led to the row of locked rooms.

Letting the door swing quietly shut behind them, Jeremy turned to Nola. "I don't know what the girl looks like."

"What if one of the guards saw us come in here?" she whispered. "If they catch us in here, you could get in trouble. What if they kick you out, too? I never should have let you get out of bed, let alone help me."

Jeremy stepped in and silenced her with a kiss. "I'm going to help you. And if anyone finds us in here?" He shrugged. "It won't be the best, but I wouldn't be the first Outer Guard to have snuck a girl into this hall. No one's supposed to talk about the bins, so it's a dark corner where people won't come looking."

"I had never heard of them." Nola blushed, trying not to think of what Jeremy's father or her mother would say if they were caught in the middle of the night in a forbidden hallway lined with private rooms she shouldn't even know about in the first place.

"Don't let T see you," Nola said, leading Jeremy to the window where she had seen T before. "If she is going to tell the Council about me, I don't want her to know about you, too."

T wasn't in the room she had been in last time. That one had been taken over by men. She moved to the next window, careful to stop Jeremy just out of sight. But T wasn't in that room or the next. Apparently, the guards didn't care about returning the outsiders to the same rooms every night.

She peeked into the second-to-last window. T was there, lying on a bunk, her head in Catlyn's lap. Nola dodged out of sight of the window, her heart racing.

"The fighting." Nola clung to Jeremy's hand. "When you fought the wolves in the city, where were you fighting?"

"It started on the old Vamper row"—Jeremy's face paled—"by Nightland. The strip of falling-down houses leading up to it. But we got penned in by two different packs who wanted to kill each other and didn't hate the idea of killing a bunch of guards in the process. We had to fight all the way back to the bridge."

Nola rose up on her toes, kissing Jeremy before whispering, "I'm so glad you made it home." She let her cheek rest on his for a moment before pushing him back into the shadows.

Taking a deep breath, she tapped on the window.

Catlyn leapt to her feet, looking ready for a fight. When she saw Nola's face in the shadows, her brows pinched together.

"I want to see T," Nola said.

Catlyn cocked her head to the side and moved closer, apparently unable to hear.

Nola glanced at the door that led to the barracks, and then at Jeremy before saying more loudly, "I need to talk to T."

Catlyn heard that time, as did the rest of the women in the room, all of whom now stared at Nola.

"T," Nola said, jumping right in before the girl had even reached the door. "How did you know I've met Emanuel?"

Fear passed through T's eyes before she spoke.

"Everyone in the city knows you were in Nightland." T raised her chin defiantly. "You're the reason Nightland attacked the domes. In retribution—"

"That's a lie, and you know it," Nola said. "Nightland attacked us because they are thieving, murdering cowards who wanted what the domes have."

Jeremy tightened his grip on Nola's hand.

"Now tell me, how did you know I've met Emanuel?"

T studied her for a moment before answering. When she spoke she said each word carefully, as though measuring every impact. "I was in Nightland. My baby's father is a vampire of Nightland. He told me about the Domer who helped Emanuel's little girl. I saw you there, dancing with the Doctor's son, Kieran Wynne."

Nola swayed, but Jeremy didn't let go of her hand.

"So you saw me there," Nola said. "So what? Why would you think Emanuel would have taught me anything?"

"Because he must have." T leaned in toward the window so her breath fogged the glass. "You were there, you know Kieran, you stayed in Emanuel's home. I heard the order shouted by Kieran himself that you weren't to be touched. He loved you. You're helping them."

"No, I'm not!" Nola's voice echoed down the hall. She froze, staring at the door to the Outer Guard barracks, waiting for guards to come running in. A full minute passed before she looked back at T. "I thought I knew Emanuel and Kieran. But they lied to me. They betrayed me."

"But you have to know," T said, her eyes boring into Nola's as though hoping to rip information straight from her mind. "You have to know where Nightland went."

"What?" The absurdity of it forced a laugh into Nola's throat. "Know where they went? Is that really what you're after? I didn't know they were going to attack or leave. They lied to me. They used me. Do you really think they would have told me where they were going? If I knew, the guards would already have destroyed them."

"But Emanuel and Kieran—"

"Used me," Nola said, disgust replacing all fear. "They're monsters just like the rest of Nightland."

"You really don't know where they are?" T's face crumpled, and for the first time she looked like the nineteen-year-old she was. "There really isn't a way to find them?"

"Why would you want to?" Nola said. "Why would you want to find a bunch of murderers?"

"They weren't all like that," T said. "Some of them were good. Charles was good. He never would have hurt anyone."

"Charles is the baby's father?" Nola asked, not needing T's nod to know she was right. "Was he with Nightland when they attacked us?"

"I don't know," T said. "He told me to stay inside. He left me with food and told me to lock the door behind him. By the time I came out, the domes were shattered, and Nightland was empty. But if I can find Emanuel and the vampires, they might know where he is."

Nola's anger splintered.

She's alone and pregnant.

"I'm sorry," Nola said.

"I'm not going to be able to find him, am I?" T said.

Catlyn came up from behind and wrapped an arm around T.

"We'll make it through just like we always have," Catlyn said.

"You need to stay here for as long as the domes will let you." Nola hated to pile more terribleness on top of everything else. "You were right. The fighting in the city a few nights ago, it was near the entrance to Nightland. I don't think you can go home."

Tears streamed down T's face. "Now he won't be able to find me even if he does come back. It really is over."

"I'm sorry," Nola said again. She began to say *If there's anything I can do* but stopped herself. There was nothing she could do. The domes would never allow it.

"Thank you," T said.

Nola nodded, not trusting herself to speak.

"And don't worry." T pressed her hand to the small window that separated them. "I won't tell the guards anything. I guess we both fell in love with a vampire who abandoned us."

Nola felt Jeremy tense beside her but didn't dare look away.

"We both survived the vampires," Nola said, "and Nightland. We just have to keep on surviving."

"Thank you," Catlyn said, taking T by the elbow and leading her away.

Nola stepped away from the window and buried her face in Jeremy's chest. She wished he hadn't been standing there. Hadn't heard what T had said.

"I'm sorry," Nola whispered, so quietly no one on the other side of the door would be able to hear.

"Don't be." Jeremy held her tightly. "You were right, about you both being survivors. Nightland hurt both of you. The way that bastard manipulated you—"

"Don't. Please don't. I don't want to think about that ever again. It makes me feel sick and filthy, and I hate it."

Jeremy kissed the top of her head before tipping her chin up so he could look into her eyes. "I will never, ever let any of them touch you again. I swear to you, Nola. I'll keep you safe."

"I know." She leaned up and kissed him, letting anger and fear flake away at the taste of his lips. "I believe you. But T. What is she going to do?"

"The Vamper should have thought about that before he got a girl pregnant and abandoned her in the city." Jeremy's mouth twisted in disgust. "The domes' rules might be harsh sometimes, but at least we don't have a bunch of fatherless babies starving. And even if there weren't rules, I would never leave you like that." Jeremy's face turned pink as he looked down at Nola. "What I mean is—I mean I wouldn't..." Jeremy mouthed wordlessly for a moment.

Nola pressed her hand to her mouth to dampen her feeble laugh as his face turned from pink to scarlet.

Giving up on words and shaking his head instead, he led her back down the hall.

Pushing the door to the barracks corridor open a crack, he peered through before leading Nola out into the hall.

One of the guards at the stairs turned to look at them, smirking at Nola and winking at Jeremy before turning back around. It was Nola's turn to blush as Jeremy led her back into his room.

"At least we know you're safe. I wish we could have talked to her away from the others," Jeremy said, lowering himself onto the bed. Nola took his arm, trying to help him, but instead, he pulled her to lay next to him.

"I think T and Catlyn will keep them from talking." Nola untied the knot at the end of her hair, shaking her curls free of the tight braid. "If the domes knew T had ties that close to Nightland, they never would have let her in." *Ties that close* seemed an insufficient term for *carrying a Vamper's baby*. "That'll have to be enough for tonight."

She lay down on the bed, letting herself melt into Jeremy's shoulder.

"No matter what T says," Jeremy said, his voice growing fainter with each word, "we're in this together. I won't let them take you from me."

In a minute, Jeremy's breathing was steady and even. But Nola couldn't sleep. What if she had been the one with a child growing inside of her? Abandoned by Kieran, not knowing where he had gone?

She held tightly to the front of Jeremy's shirt, promising herself that he wouldn't run from her.

The outsiders didn't have the same marriage laws the domes lived by. There were no children born without fathers in the domes. In order to gain permission to have a child in the domes, you had to apply to the Council and go through genetic testing to ensure healthy offspring. She knew some people had snuck into the far corners of the glass, or met in dark passages, in the middle of the night. But unapproved children couldn't be allowed. The domes' population had to be methodically controlled. Even with the loss of life in the attacks, they still would have to be careful to repopulate according to dome needs.

But in the outside world, there was no Council to say who was allowed to be the father of your child. Only a young girl in love with a vampire. And now she was locked in a cell, with no hope for a safe place for her child to be born.

Tears burned in the corners of Nola's eyes as she fell asleep. A faint shadow haunted her dreams. A boy she loved, staring down at her as she held their child in her arms.

CHAPTER FOURTEEN

Dazzling blue filled the bright sky. The gray smoke had stopped drifting up from the domes. The last of the bodies had been burned, and as Nola looked out over the hill there was no sign that anything terrible had ever happened to the domes. The glass that had been shattered in the attack had been repaired or replaced. Cleaning the ventilation systems and making the glass stronger than it had been before were the only things the outsiders were still working on in the atrium and the Grassland Dome. But the labor in the Amber Dome was far from finished.

It had been three days since she and Jeremy had visited T in the locked rooms. Three days of nothing. No alarms, no scares. Waking up, working, seeing Jeremy, sleeping. It amazed Nola that three days could now feel like a new normal. After everything that had happened, three days of calm seemed an incredible gift. Jeremy had moved into the large barracks room and would begin duty again soon. Nola had gone back to sleeping in her own room. Peace had settled over the domes.

She didn't even know she had been humming until T poked her in the arm. "Nola. What's going on?"

T had given up on calling Nola *Miss* after their evening meeting. Their brief talk through the glass had forged a tenuous camaraderie between them.

Nola smiled as T cocked her head, examining her.

"Nothing." Nola grinned. "Just having a good morning."

"Well, then." T smiled back before moving down the long line of new seed trays that were their day's work.

Nola reveled in the feeling of the warm earth under her fingers. Planting a seed, knowing it would grow into food that would provide for the domes.

"It's a little strange," Catlyn said from down the row, "that your botanist mother named you after a flower, isn't it?"

"What?" Nola laughed.

"Well, it's a bit strange, don't you think?" Catlyn said.

"Leave it, Catlyn," Beauford said.

"My mother likes plants, so she named me after a flower. Is that weird?" Nola asked.

The guards turned to look over at them. Nola skipped a few pots, moving closer to the others so she could speak more quietly. "I mean, how do they choose names on the outside?"

"The same as anyone chooses a name," Beauford said. "Pick a name, call a kid it, and be done." He stalked back to the front of the row and took an overly long time grabbing seeds.

"I still don't understand why my name is strange," Nola said.

"It's not your name she's worried about," T said. "Catlyn is unhappy with how I want to name *my* baby."

"Naming it after a man who abandoned you," Catlyn said. "Tell her, Miss Kent, tell her that's an awful idea."

Nola froze for a moment as both women stared at her. "Do you know if it's a boy?" she asked, hoping to dodge the name question.

"Charlie could be either a boy's or a girl's name," T said. "Don't you think it's nice, Nola?"

"It's great," Nola said. "If that's what you want."

"A constant reminder of a man who ran out on you?" Catlyn's voice dripped with disgust.

"He didn't run out. It's more complicated than that, and you know it," T said.

Nightland. They were going to talk about Nightland. They were moving from planting seeds and worrying about baby names to Nightland.

Shadows shouldn't be allowed to destroy sunny mornings.

"How did you get your name, T?" Nola asked.

"I don't know." T shrugged. "It's not my real name. At least not all of it. I think it was a nickname, or a shortening of my name. But my parents died when I was little, and the lady that took me in kept calling me T. She died too, though. By the time I thought to ask what T was short for, everyone who would have known was gone. So, I stuck with T."

It felt like someone had punched a hole straight through Nola's stomach. T carried on, working as though she hadn't said anything strange or sad at all. Like having no one alive who could tell you your real name was an ordinary thing.

"And as for you, Catlyn"—T turned back to her, pointing with a dirt-covered finger—"I'm the one carrying the baby, and I'll name it whatever I damn well please. Maybe I'll make it a tradition and call the baby C."

Catlyn *tsked* and flicked T's hand away.

"We should hurry," Nola said, grateful for once for the presence of the ever-watchful guards. Glad to have the excuse to walk away and work on the other side of the tray. A normal day. That was what she craved. A day filled with happiness, untainted by fear. A schedule she knew how to follow, and a task to call her own. She hadn't been able to start back in classes yet. No one had even mentioned when she would be allowed to return to school.

She felt selfish and angry. She was well-fed and had a bed to sleep in.

I want my life back.

A low chime sounded overhead.

At once, all the Domers stopped, calmly waiting for what would come next. The outsiders glanced around fearfully.

Nola ran over to Catlyn and T, who stood frozen as the chime sounded again.

"It's okay," Nola said. "It's just an announcement. It isn't like the sirens."

A voice had already begun to speak.

"Citizens of the domes. In light of the recent tragedies that have been inflicted upon these domes by the troubles in the city, the Council has requested replacement citizens be brought to live in our community. The twenty-five new residents will be transferring from their home domes tonight. While the majority of new residents are going to be moving directly into the Guard barracks, there will need to be a few adjustments to housing. Any domes' citizen whose housing arrangements will be required to change will be notified immediately. We appreciate your cooperation and understanding and hope you will welcome your new neighbors with open arms. They have left their homes to help us in protecting ours."

With a faint *crackle*, the speakers went silent.

More people were coming to join the domes. Twenty-five people none of them had ever met were leaving their own far away domes to come and share Nola's home.

"If they wanted more people to fight for the domes, you think they would have looked to those starving in the city," Beauford said loudly enough for the guards fifty feet away to hear.

Catlyn and T both turned away from him as though wanting to distance themselves from his words. Though it stung, Nola knew he was right. They had workers living in cells in the domes. It would have been kinder to give them a permanent home instead of bringing in others, but it would never have been allowed.

They aren't like us.

They were outsiders. They hadn't been given a dome education and had spent too long in the filthy air, drinking polluted water, and eating the contaminated food to be approved for breeding.

Beauford wasn't the only outsider who seemed unhappy about the announcement. A woman on the other side of the Amber Dome screeched at the Domer in charge of her group.

"You're going to throw us out to starve? You've got extra food and space and you're going to send us out into the city as soon as you're done with us? Let us burn in the riots or bleed for the vampires? Better yet, be meat to feed the wolves? You're worse monsters than any of them! At least when a wolf wants you dead, he's got the courtesy to do it fast with no lies about saving the world or pretending it isn't plain old murder!"

A sharp *pop* sounded from the pack of guards. A tiny silver dart hit the side of the woman's neck, dropping her to the ground.

The dart only contained a sedative to make the woman sleep, but the outsiders didn't seem to know or care.

The others in the screaming woman's group ran forward, stepping between her and the guard that had shot the woman. Shouts echoed from all sides of the Amber Dome as people started to panic.

"They're going to kill us!" A man charged toward the guards, hitting one in the stomach with a shovel before being knocked backward by another guard, who shot a silver dart into his neck.

All of the guards in the dome surged toward the fighting. And the rest of the outsiders ran toward the fight as well.

"Beauford, no!" Catlyn screamed, catching his arm as he moved to join the fray.

A young man had run forward and grabbed a ladder to push back the guards. A dart struck him in the chest, but two women grabbed the ladder, using it like a battering ram to attack the guards.

"It won't help!" T held onto Beauford's other arm, but he was strong. The two women wouldn't be able to hold him much longer.

"Follow me." Nola added her weight to Beauford's arm as she helped Catlyn and T drag him away.

"We can't let them do this to us!" Beauford fought to pull away from them.

"You can't stop it either!" Nola said. "Try and fight if you want, but it'll only be one more dart they have to fire."

Beauford froze for a moment before his arms sagged.

"Good, now come on." Running away from the fighting, Nola led them toward the back of the dome, where thick rows of vines sat low along the wall.

Ducking under the leaves, Nola winced as she felt a vine snap.

More shouting voices filled the dome. Nola glanced back. She could barely make out a dozen black-clad guards running up the stairs to join the fight.

"Get down and be quiet." Nola pushed aside the last of the vines. A set of low, thorny bushes blocked them from the glass. Creating a gap between bushes, she ignored the thorns that pulled at her palms, crouching down and using her weight to ease the way through the brambles for the others.

"Are we just going to hide back here?" Beauford said as soon as he was through.

"Yes, we are." Nola leaned back against the glass.

The sounds of the fighting had already changed.

Guards bellowed orders, and Lenora Kent's voice cut above it all.

"I don't care what you're trying to do, stay the hell off my plants!"

Nola smiled. Of course her mother would be standing in the middle of a fight, screaming about plants.

Blood oozed out of the scratches on her hands. She wiped it onto her gardening suit. She would be able to wash her hands soon enough.

"I didn't take you as the type to run from a fight," T whispered as the last of the screaming stopped. "I figured you for the sort to run in and try to stop it."

"That lady shouldn't have attacked the Domer." Nola closed her eyes against the bright sun. "But the domes shouldn't be using you the way they are. Sometimes I feel like the right thing is too abstract for me to understand."

"How poetic," Catlyn said.

"But I do know that all those people will be put outside on the road before dark, and I don't want that to happen to the three of you. The most right thing I could think of was to keep you three safe. So that's what I did."

"Who the hell's got time for a moral compass when north keeps changing?" T said.

"Nola!" A voice shouted from the center of the dome. "Nola!"

"Back here!" Nola called. "Jeremy, we're back here!" Before she could stand, Jeremy had appeared, leaping over plants and dodging through vines to get to her.

"Nola, are you hurt?" Jeremy took her face in his hands.

"I'm fine." She smiled, her heart flipping at the depth of Jeremy's concern for her. "Really, we all are. The fight started, and we ran."

Jeremy kissed her. "Thank you. Thank you for not trying to stop the whole thing yourself."

T and Catlyn grinned behind him.

"And thank you for taking care of her," Jeremy said to the three outsiders.

"Come on, let's get you out in the open before they think you got into the tunnels."

"Did outsiders get into the tunnels?" Nola followed Jeremy to the center of the dome.

"Some of them tried," Jeremy said.

The outsiders who had been fighting were all laid out on the ground. Some of them were bloody or had swollen faces. Others looked like they might have been sleeping.

"Nola." Lenora ran up to her daughter. "I should have known that of all the people trusted to work with the outsiders, you would be the only one able to manage them."

"I didn't manage them," Nola said. "They didn't want to fight."

Lenora wasn't listening. "Now we'll have more repair work on top of everything else and no one to help. I think we've proven this is a failed experiment."

"It's not failed," Nola said as two guards stepped toward T, Catlyn, and Beauford. "My group didn't do anything wrong. They're good workers who didn't fight at all."

The two guards walked straight past Nola.

"You three have to come with us," a young female guard said, holding her gun at her side.

"Where are you taking them?" Nola wove through the guards to stand between them and her group.

The guard didn't answer.

"Mom, where are they taking them?" she asked again, her voice rising so Lenora couldn't pretend not to hear. "They didn't do anything wrong. They're good workers, and we need them. Where are you taking my group?"

"Having workers from the outside isn't—"

"Yes, it is!" Nola shouted. Heads turned toward her, but she didn't flinch. "It is for these three. Tell me you aren't going to put them out with the ones who fought. Tell me you're taking them back to the cells you call their rooms and feeding them while we clean up in here."

"Magnolia," Lenora said.

"Mom, tell me you're going to do the right thing." Nola balled her hands into fists, her pulse racing so fast warm blood dripped from her cuts.

"Fine," Lenora said after a long moment. "You've managed well enough with them. But let it be known that if there is one toe stuck out of line, they'll be outside in a minute." Giving the group behind Nola a scathing look, Lenora stalked away.

"If you'll follow us then," the female guard said, her gun still in her hand.

"You can put that away," Nola said.

"You don't have the authority to tell me to do anything." The guard glared coolly at Nola.

"Jeremy, will you walk down with them?" she asked.

"Of course." Jeremy didn't look at Nola or question her as he led the group out of the domes.

Other Dome Guard surrounded the group of downed outsiders. Two guards taking each one and carrying them away. Those who had fought against the domes would wake up on the road outside with no choice but to walk the bridge back to the city and hope they found their homes still standing.

If they even make it that far.

Nola shuddered as two guards lifted the woman who had started the fight, grateful the glass between herself and the outside world was solid once again.

CHAPTER FIFTEEN

The heat of the shower stung the skin on Nola's shoulders, but she didn't turn the temperature down. She knew she should hate herself for standing in hot water, washing with fresh-scented soap while the workers who had fought against the guards trudged toward the city. Toward the dark and unknown.

She took a deep breath, letting the steam fill her lungs.

It's their own fault they were sent away.

That doesn't make marching into the darkness less frightening.

She shut off the water. The urge to run filled her again. To find a way outside the glass and just keep running until there was nothing left to run from.

But there was nowhere to run to. There was nothing to run to. She stepped onto the tiny landing that joined her and her mother's bedroom to the bathroom.

"Nola," Jeremy said.

Nola squeaked and jumped back, banging her shoulder on the doorjamb.

"Sorry." Jeremy stepped out of the shadows at the bottom of the stairs. "I didn't mean to scare you."

Gripping her towel tighter, she turned on the light. "It's fine."

Her heart thundered in her chest as Jeremy dashed up the steps and reached for her hand.

"I just needed to see you, and I thought I would wait down here." Jeremy blushed.

"It's okay." She took his hand, leading him into her room and closing the door behind them. "Is my mom here?"

"No." Jeremy sat down on the bed, holding his head in his hands. "At least I didn't see her."

"What's wrong?" she asked, sitting close enough to Jeremy that her arm pressed into his.

"Gentry's leaving." He didn't look at Nola as he spoke. "She might already be gone."

"Leaving? What do you mean leaving? Gentry loves the domes. She's an Outer Guard, she'd never abandon her home."

"She requested a transfer to another set of domes and got approved," Jeremy said. "They're taking her away on the transport that brought the new guards in."

"But why? How?" Nola knelt on the floor in front of him, moving his hands away from his face. "If we needed more people to be brought into the domes here, why would they let her leave?"

"It's"—Jeremy paused, his brow wrinkled as though the thought of it caused him physical pain—"complicated."

"How?"

He pulled Nola up to sit on his lap, resting his head on her bare shoulder.

"Guard stuff," Jeremy said. "With the city and the fighting...she wants out."

"I'm sorry." She pressed her lips to his temple.

"It's not your fault. It isn't anybody's fault. I just, I never thought she'd actually leave."

Nola wrapped her arms around Jeremy, holding him close.

"I mean, I know people have asked to transfer out before," he said, "but I never thought it would be someone I knew. She's leaving for the other side of the world, and I don't know if she'll ever come back. I may never see my sister again."

Nola opened her mouth to say that of course he would see Gentry again, but she couldn't bring herself to lie, even if it might make Jeremy feel better.

There was hardly any transportation between domes. Her mother, who went to conferences once a year, traveled more than anyone else she knew. Transfers were always for things like specialized training. A temporary assignment that lasted a few years. The far south domes had had too many females a few years back, and the spares had been dispersed to other domes. But leaving just because you wanted to, that wasn't a thing people were allowed to do. If Gentry left, there might never be a way for her to come home.

"Dad's a mess." Jeremy's voice was thick with unshed tears. "She had told him she was going to ask the Council for a transfer, but I don't think he thought she would actually go through with it."

"He'll be okay." Nola pressed her cheek to Jeremy's, too afraid to look him in the eye.

She didn't know if Captain Ridgeway would be okay. She didn't know if any of them would be.

"Your dad is tough," Nola pressed on, relieved her voice sounded strong. "You both are. Gentry is a great guard, and she'll be great wherever she ends up."

"You said you wanted to leave," Jeremy said. "Before the domes were attacked, you said you wanted to leave the domes and live on the outside to help people."

"I did." Nola tensed.

Kieran had shown her ways she could be helpful to the people fighting to survive on the outside. It had all seemed worth it. To be out there doing something that mattered. Risking her life to save others had seemed more meaningful than living trapped behind glass, watching the world crumble.

"I would have gone with you." Jeremy twined his fingers through hers. "I would have left everything behind for you."

"I know."

"I would have gone to protect the girl I love, but Gentry's just gone. Do you think she would have forgiven me if I had left?" Jeremy turned to look into Nola's eyes, searching for an honest answer.

"I don't think so." She swallowed the knot in her throat. "I don't think anyone would have forgiven either of us."

"Then how am I supposed to forgive her?"

"I don't know," Nola said. "I don't know if you can, but if she just couldn't take the fighting anymore—"

"It doesn't matter what she could or couldn't take. She shouldn't have left."

She tried to think of something comforting to say that would prove Gentry had been right to leave. But she was abandoning her family and the domes in their time of need.

There is no excuse.

Nola curled up on the bed and pulled Jeremy to lie down next to her.

"You're so beautiful," he whispered, pushing Nola's hair away from her face.

"When I look like a drowned rat?"

"Always." He pulled her closer. Her towel twisted, baring her hip. She reached down to cover herself, but Jeremy was already kissing her.

He smelled like himself again. Like fresh earth, and new life.

"Nola," Jeremy breathed as she pressed herself to him, feeling every curve of his body against hers.

Beep, beep. Beep, beep.

Nola bolted up in bed at the sound, knocking Jeremy to the floor.

"What's that?" Jeremy said, at the same moment Nola asked, "Are you all right?"

Beep, beep. Beep, beep.

PAM *beeped* at her from the wall, flashing a faint blue light. Jeremy scrambled out of sight as Nola pressed the blue light and the screen blinked to life.

Captain Ridgeway's face stared back at her.

"Captain Ridgeway." Nola straightened her towel, blushing to the roots of her dark hair. Her eyes flicked over to Jeremy, who hid pressed into the corner of the wall.

Eyes wide, he put a finger to his lips.

"Captain Ridgeway, is everything okay?" Nola said.

"I'm sorry to disturb you this late at night, Nola." Captain Ridgeway clenched his jaw as he spoke, as though trying not to shout. "But I need you to come to my office as soon as possible."

"Your office?" Nola's voice squeaked. "Why do you need me to come down there?"

He's found out. He's found out you helped Nightland, and now he's going to throw you in the cell right next to Raina's.

"I'll explain as soon as you get here. Do not accept any further communication. Do not let anyone stop you on your way down. Come straight here. Immediately."

"Okay." Nola nodded. "I'll be there in ten minutes."

"Be here in five," the captain said. "And Nola, wear boots and a coat."

The screen went dark.

"Boots and a coat?" Jeremy craned his neck to stare up at the place where his father's face had just been. "He wants you to go outside?"

Before she could think of an answer, the blue light began to flash again.

Beep, beep. Beep, beep.

Nola reached instinctively forward to press the light before stopping herself. "Why would someone else be calling?"

"No idea, but we need to go." Jeremy turned and faced the closed door of Nola's room.

Beep, beep. Beep, beep.

Nola's hands shook as she yanked clean clothes out of her drawers. "What if your dad found out about Nightland? What if he found out you helped me talk to T?"

"He didn't," Jeremy said. "If he knew about that, there would be guards banging on the door to haul you out for banishment."

"That shouldn't feel comforting." She buttoned her pants and yanked on a shirt. "Why does that feel comforting?"

The beeping that had stopped for a moment, resumed.

Jamming on her boots and grabbing her coat, Nola took Jeremy's hand. "You'll come down with me, right?"

"Of course." Jeremy ran with Nola out of the empty house and onto the stone path.

Night had fallen. Only the faint lights coming from the houses lit their way. Overhead, dim reflections sparkled in the glass. Faraway stars, fighting to be seen through the smog and the light of the domes that surrounded them.

Near the stairs to the tunnel, a stronger light came into view. Not the nearby light of the atrium, something much farther away.

A cluster of tiny lights that seemed to be in the wrong place.

"What is that?" Nola pulled Jeremy off the path and toward the glass. Hundreds of lights flickered on the far bank of the river between the domes and the city.

"The bridge," Jeremy said. "It's all by the bridge."

Without waiting for her to stop looking through the glass, Jeremy dragged her at a sprint toward the stairs.

"Why are there people by the bridge?" she panted, running as fast as she could, struggling to keep up with Jeremy's much longer strides.

She had been on the bridge at night twice before. There had been nothing there but wolves and Vampers searching for victims.

A faint *hum* sounded, and Jeremy looked down at the black band on his wrist. "Shit."

"What is it?" Nola asked.

"They want me in uniform." Jeremy pulled Nola to run faster.

Around the next corner, a line of men waited.

Captain Stokes stood in the middle of the hall, blocking the steps to the Outer Guard barracks.

"Miss Kent." Stokes stepped out of line, planting himself in the center of the corridor.

"We have to get downstairs," she wheezed, moving to go around Stokes, but the guards behind him closed ranks.

"I've been called down to the barracks," Jeremy said, danger sounding in his voice.

"You can go down if you like." Stokes gave a hateful little bow. "Miss Kent is coming with me."

"I can't come with you," Nola said, forcing her voice to stay level though her heart still raced. "I have to go to Captain Ridgeway's office. There's something going on by the bridge. He might not have much time to talk to me if he has to go out there."

"That is exactly why you are coming with me." Stokes stepped forward, his guards matching his movement. "We are going up to the Com Room right now."

"Get out of our way," Jeremy said. "Come on, Nola." Leading her by the arm, Jeremy took a step forward.

Stokes stepped right in front of Jeremy. Had Stokes been as tall, they would have been nose-to-nose.

"You think your blood gives you the right to order me around?" Stokes spoke softly. "I will have you out of the domes so fast your father won't even know how he suddenly lost *both* his children."

"You son of a bitch," Jeremy snarled, dropping Nola's arm and punching Stokes hard in the face.

The line of guards descended on him as he hit Stokes in the stomach, leaving the captain sprawled on the floor.

"Nola, run!" Jeremy punched one of the other guards.

Nola froze. She couldn't leave Jeremy fighting one against five. But what help could she be against trained guards?

"Nola, go!" Jeremy kicked another guard in the stomach, sending him flying into the man behind him.

Running as fast as she could, Nola tore down the flight of stairs to the Outer Guard barracks. People sprinted through the corridor, not with the sense of panic that had filled the domes when guards were bloody and wounded, but with practiced urgency.

None of them even seemed to notice her standing at the foot of the stairs, trying to see a way through the pattern.

"Jeremy Ridgeway needs help!" Nola shouted. "Captain Stokes and his men tried to stop us, and now they're fighting him!"

"Carter, Wright, with me," a guard barked to two others before charging up the stairs.

"You should take more!" Nola called after them, but they were already out of sight.

Forcing her way through the corridor, she managed to get to Captain Ridgeway's office. The door swung open the instant she knocked.

"Inside." Captain Ridgeway gabbed Nola's wrist and yanked her into the office, snapping the door shut behind him.

"What's going on?" she asked. Even with the movement of the hall no longer visible, she could still feel the frenetic energy in the air. "We saw lights by the bridge on the way down."

"We?" Captain Ridgeway asked, his eyes boring holes into her.

"I was with Jeremy when you called," Nola said as he pointed for her to sit.

"He was coming down here with me. But Stokes got in the way, and Jeremy punched him."

Captain Ridgeway swore under his breath.

"Some Outer Guard went up to help him."

"We can't worry about Jeremy. There isn't time. Something is happening in the city right now, and we cannot allow it to continue."

"What?" Sweat beaded on her palms as Captain Ridgeway pressed on.

"There is a group amassing by the bridge, more than a thousand people. If that many decided to attack the domes—"

"It would be worse than Nightland." Nola's head spun.

Blood-slicked floor. Shattered glass. Bodies to be burned.

"We don't know if they are planning to attack," the captain said. "So far, they've only given us one demand. They want to speak to Nola Kent."

CHAPTER SIXTEEN

Nola grabbed the edge of her seat as the room tilted. "Who? Who wants to talk to me?"

"We don't know." Captain Ridgeway leaned over her. He was so much taller than she was. A tower of strength larger than she could ever grow to be.

"Emanuel." Nola mouthed the word. There wasn't enough air in her lungs to speak.

"I don't think so." Captain Ridgeway crouched down, speaking to her on eye level as though she were a frightened child. "There is absolutely nothing to indicate Emanuel or any trace of Nightland has come back to the city. What we do know is that if the people out there try to cross the bridge, there will be a bloodbath. We have to stop them from crossing that bridge."

She nodded.

"We need you to go out there and talk to them. They've refused to speak to any of my guards. You have to help us find out what they want."

She shook her head. She couldn't go out there. She couldn't face a crowd of angry outsiders.

"Nola, there isn't a choice." He took both her hands in his. "You have to go out there. I've told them you'd come, and if you don't show up, people will die. Guards will die."

"Why?" The shock of Captain Ridgeway's words jolted air back into her lungs. "Why would you say I'll go out there? What could they want from me?"

"You won't be there alone. You will be surrounded by Outer Guard. I'll be nearby. We won't let them hurt you." He pulled Nola to her feet.

"What do I say?" she begged. "You can't just send me out there if I don't know what I'm supposed to say."

"There isn't time." Captain Ridgeway thrust a heavy vest into her hands. "There is nothing we can do but get out there." He pressed an I-Vent into her palm. "My guards' lives are depending on you, Nola. Don't let them down."

Captain Ridgeway wrenched open the door to the hall. The Outer Guard had already gone.

"Why me?" Nola's hands shook as she pulled on the heavy vest. "I can't offer them anything."

"You're the girl the domes went to battle for." He took her arm, holding on so tightly she could feel bruises forming as they ran up the stairs.

"That doesn't mean I can help any of them." Nola stumbled, but the captain's grip on her arm was so fierce she couldn't fall. Instead, he carried her up a few steps without even seeming to notice.

They reached the corridor where she had left Jeremy fighting with Captain Stokes.

"Jeremy." She scanned the empty hall. "I left him here."

"He'll be with the other Outer Guard. We'll meet them in the atrium."

"But what if Stokes took him away?" Nola wheezed.

"Not an option." Captain Ridgeway didn't even look worried that his son could be in trouble as he ran the rest of the way to the atrium.

The atrium was three times as high as any of the other domes and wide enough to hold at least six of the others inside it. Stored along one side were all the vehicles that belonged to the domes, always seeming out of place between the benches, trees, and paths that filled the rest of the space. In the wall right next to the vehicles was the only door to the outside world.

Work had only just been finished on the glass and on the giant door that had been damaged in the Nightland attack. The trees and grass that had been torn up had yet to be replaced, giving the place a tattered feeling. The trucks against the far wall roared to life and pulled into a line in front of the door.

The Outer Guard had already loaded themselves into the trucks, dressed in heavy riot gear, all carrying weapons.

"The sirens haven't gone off," Nola said as Captain Ridgeway steered her to the third truck in line. "People need to get to the bunkers. Why haven't the sirens gone off?"

"The sirens are under Captain Stokes' command." The captain lifted her into the high front seat of the truck before leaping up after her. "The Dome Guard are staying put. They can evacuate if the bridge gets crossed."

"But people will have more time if—"

"Use the I-Vent," Captain Ridgeway said, ignoring Nola as the trucks rumbled forward.

She held the thin silver tube up to her lips, taking a deep breath and letting the medicine fill her lungs, preventing the impurities of the outside air from contaminating her. Her panic worsened at the metallic taste the medicine left in her mouth. *Nola Kent. They want to talk to Nola Kent.*

"Where's Jeremy?" Nola asked.

"With the guards," Captain Ridgeway answered, his eyes locked onto the bridge that had just come into sight.

It was easier to see the source of the blaze from outside the domes. A thousand figures standing on the far side of the bridge, holding torches, flashlights, and lanterns, making a patch of light the domes had not been able to ignore.

"Are you sure Stokes doesn't have him?" Nola said.

"Positive."

"Which truck is he in?" Her mouth had gone dry, her lips cracking as she fought to form words.

"Fifth truck. The last one in line."

The first truck in line reached the bridge and peeled off to flank the left side; the second peeled off to the right.

"Can he come here?" Nola asked as the truck carrying her and the captain slowed directly in front of the bridge. "Please, can he come with me?"

The captain studied her for a moment before speaking into his wrist. "Send Jeremy Ridgeway to the front."

Thank you. Nola couldn't manage to say the words.

He climbed out of the truck and lifted her to the ground. A line of guards ran in front of them, standing between Nola and the bridge.

Another guard ran up from behind, heading straight toward her.

"What's going on?" Jeremy asked, his voice muffled through the thick shielding of his helmet.

"Nola's going out there to talk to them, and you'll be in the escort." Captain Ridgeway rammed his own helmet onto his head.

"We can't just—"

"We can, and we are," Captain Ridgeway said. "Now you can either be in the escort or get to the back."

"Yes, sir," Jeremy barked, but Nola could hear the worry behind his words. He didn't want her going out there any more than she wanted to go herself. "She needs a helmet, sir."

"No helmet." Captain Ridgeway took Nola by the shoulders and steered her toward the bridge. "They need to be able to see who they're talking to."

He pushed her through the line of guards.

"Don't let her get past the center mark, and rifles up at all times," Captain Ridgeway shouted to the guards that filed onto either side of Nola. "Under no circumstances is there to be physical contact, and if things get nasty, the first priority is to get Magnolia Kent to safety."

"Yes, sir," the voices around them chorused.

The captain nodded and walked forward. Nola followed a step behind as did the guards that surrounded her.

Jeremy stayed right next to her, matching her every step. She wanted to reach out and hold his hand, but he gripped his weapon, pointing it at the people on the other side of the bridge.

Nola shuddered as she took the step that carried her from the road onto the bridge. The metal beneath her clanged with every footfall. The noise of the guards' heavy boots shook the air and rattled her lungs like a vicious tolling bell, counting down the steps she had left before she reached the middle of the bridge.

A line of people approached from the other side, holding torches and lanterns high in the air. They didn't have any weapons Nola could see, but if they were wolves or Vampers, they wouldn't need guns to kill the guards, or Nola.

Finally, Captain Ridgeway held up a hand, and the guards stopped as one.

The silence rang louder in Nola's ears than the clanging of the bridge had.

The group from the city stopped fifty feet away. There were twenty of them in a tight pack, all tense, ready to fight or run.

Run. Please, run.

"We were told we could speak to Nola Kent," the man at the front of the pack said from across the gap.

Torn clothes hung loosely on his frame, displaying his sinewy muscles. Even in the chill night air, the man wore short sleeves and seemed unbothered by the cold. In the dim light, Nola could barely make out the reddish hue of the man's eyes.

A werewolf.

CHAPTER SEVENTEEN

Shaking, Nola stepped forward, using every ounce of willpower she possessed to move toward the wolves.

"I'm—" She was speaking too softly. They would never be able to hear. "I'm Nola Kent!"

The man leaned forward, and Nola had the terrible feeling he was trying to catch her scent.

"Allory," the man barked, and a woman stepped forward.

Even in the darkness, Nola recognized the woman. She was the outsider who had started the fight in the Amber Dome that morning.

"Is it her?" the man asked Allory.

Looking terrified of standing so close to the man, Allory took a step sideways, squinting at Nola.

"That's her," Allory said. "That is Nola Kent."

The man smiled. "I didn't think they would actually let the little butterfly out of her cage to play at night."

"Well, I'm here." Nola took a step forward. A hand reached out and grabbed her wrist, stopping her before she could step in front of Captain Ridgeway. She knew it was Jeremy without looking, the way his pinky draped over her palm. He didn't want her to move away from him. She stepped to the side, closer to Jeremy and where she could properly see the pack in front of her. "What do you want from me?"

The man threw his head back and laughed. "You are better than I had hoped you would be, you wonderful little butterfly!"

The pack behind him rumbled into laughter, and the sound grew like a wave, which lapped back to the horde on the far side of the bridge, who began cheering and jeering.

"I said, what do you want!" Nola's fear dissolved in the fury of her anger.

"What do we want?" the man repeated. "What do you think I want, little butterfly?"

"How would I know?" she said. "I don't even know who you are."

"Lucifer, at your service." The man bowed deeply.

"I don't believe you," Nola said. "You know my name, why can't I know yours?"

"Lucifer is what I am." He smiled. "A fallen angel who brings darkness to all. What is a name meant to be if not a description of what we are?"

"Fine, *Lucifer*," she spat the name, "what do you want from me?"

Get off the bridge. Get off the bridge and get back to the domes. Being locked in the bunker is better than being on this bridge with the wolves.

"We want what all of us want." Lucifer raised both hands in the air, inciting cheers from the people behind him. He tipped his head to the side and sneered, looking like a rabid wolf that wanted nothing more than to bite. "We want food," Lucifer growled. "We want medicine. We want our fair share of the riches you've got in the domes."

"We don't have riches." Nola laughed loudly, though her heart still fought to burst out of her chest. "I don't know why you think we do."

"We don't want gold and jewels, butterfly, we want food. And I know you have that." Lucifer grabbed Allory under one arm, lifting her off her feet. "Allory here told us about your food. Rows and rows of food just waiting to be eaten. Isn't that right, Allory?"

"Yes," Allory whimpered. "I saw it, worked in just one of the domes, and there's more food there than I've ever seen."

"Thank you, Allory." Lucifer let go of Allory's arm, and she crumpled to the ground where she lay shaking, not even attempting to stand back up. "You have food. You are hoarding food and watching the city starve. We'd always thought it, but now thanks to Allory"—he kicked Allory in the stomach, and, with a cry of pain, she rolled to face the sky—"well, now we know that you have stores of food. That you filthy Domers in your glass castle high on the hill just like watching the rest of us starve. Well, we say *enough!*" Lucifer punched the air, and a roar soared from the far side of the bridge.

"So tonight, we eat!" Lucifer bared his teeth, which shone white in the moonlight.

The rustle of the guards behind her sent a shiver up Nola's spine.

"The only question is do we eat your food, or you?"

The snarls of the pack carried over Lucifer's words.

The domes could feed all these people for one week, maybe two, but then there would be nothing left. All of them would starve.

She glanced toward Captain Ridgeway, but his face was hidden behind his visor.

"Me personally?" Nola asked. "I don't think there's enough of me to go around."

The pack howled with laughter.

"Not just you, my beautiful butterfly." Lucifer took a step forward. Each of the guards pointed their rifle at his chest. He spread his arms wide and took another step forward. "We'll eat all of you. Tear the flesh from your bones and have the freshest, tenderest meat any of us has ever tasted."

"But that still doesn't answer my first question." Nola pulled her hand from Jeremy's grip and stepped in front of Captain Ridgeway. The sound of bodies shifting caught her ear, but she didn't dare turn to look. "Why did you want me out here? I have no authority in the domes, I don't know how much food we've got, and even if I wanted to give it to you, I couldn't. I am no one. Why would you want to talk to me in the middle of the night on a bridge over a rancid river?"

"Because I've heard stories about Nola Kent, the butterfly that flew into Nightland." Lucifer's red eyes bore into hers. "The butterfly that didn't want to kill the Vampers, who helped them get medicine."

Nola's breath caught in her chest. If this man knew she had stolen, then she should walk into the city now and save the Council the trouble of having to formally banish her.

"I can't give you anything." The warmth had drained from her body, stolen by the wind. She couldn't feel her hands as they shook, and each ragged breath stole heat from her lungs.

"You wouldn't let the slaves you master fight," Lucifer said. "You protected them, kept them in the warm."

"They are not our slaves," Nola said.

"We are all slaves to the ones who have the food. The babies who cry from hunger and the old that waste away rather than take a crust of bread that might save the young. We are all slaves to the death that lurks over this city, and you in the glass castle have mastered that death. With your food and medicine. The acid rains can't burn you, and the winters can't freeze you. And the ones who have mastered death are masters of us all."

"That doesn't make sense!" she shouted. "I didn't let my people fight, so what? I kept them inside the domes, but why do you care? What the hell have they got to do with you?"

"My beautiful butterfly, you are the only soul in the glass castle of murderers who has ever shown compassion. The rest all turn away from the diseased and the dying. The light from their mythical bright future blinds them to the darkness. But you've seen what lies in the shadows, and we will haunt you for the rest of your days."

"I still can't help you," Nola said as thoughts of desperate children grasped at the edges of her mind. "I wish I could. I wish there was enough for everyone, but there isn't. Even if we wanted to feed the city, we couldn't."

"I think the butterfly is lying. That the only one from the glass who can see truth has turned to lies to survive. Or"—he turned to look at the woman lying on the ground—"Allory has. Are you lying to me, Allory? Stores of food, you said. Long tunnels with places to sleep, you said."

"It's true," Allory whimpered. "Everything is there up the hill. I swear to you."

Lucifer swept his gaze from Allory to Nola.

"One of my girls is lying. And one knows the price of lying," Lucifer snarled, "which makes me think it's probably her." He leaned over Allory who lay sobbing on the ground.

"Stop!" Nola shouted. "There is food. But not enough for everyone. And it takes time, a lot of time, to grow more. If we fed half of you even, there wouldn't be enough for anyone to survive. Please believe me!"

Lucifer grabbed Allory's arm, wrenching her to her feet.

"I wish I could help you, but I can't." Nola reached toward Allory, wishing she were strong enough to run forward and snatch her from Lucifer's arms, but he pulled her closer, tracing the curve of her neck with his nose as he scented her skin.

"The domes can't save the city," Nola said, "but we might be able to do something, figure out something. Nightland had gardens, gardens that grew good food." She took another step forward, pulling Lucifer's eyes from Allory back to herself. "And they had a way to filter the rain water, and keep the acid rain off the plants. I'll bet you knew that, though," Nola shouted as loudly as she could, hoping the people on the far side of the bridge could hear her. "Nightland found a way to feed the children. And they did it on their own without help from the domes. I saw the garden. Maybe some of you did, too. Is that why you're so angry now, because Nightland abandoned you? Because they aren't here to feed you anymore?"

"No one wants the Vamper scum on our streets!" A man behind Lucifer spat on the ground, and as one, the pack tipped their heads back and howled at the sky.

Nola fought to swallow the knot of fear in her throat as the sound vibrated the metal under her feet.

"Fine!" Nola shouted as soon as the howling began to fade. "Fine! You don't want Nightland's help. But what they did was amazing. And I'll do whatever I can to help you rebuild what they had. So you can grow your own food."

"And how many will be dead by the time the food grows?" Lucifer said.

"How many will die if we eat what we can't replace?" She took another step forward. The sound of boots on metal followed her. "I'll find a way to help, but I can't give you anything tonight."

"So we should wait and starve while you go home to your nice bed and full belly?" Lucifer stepped forward, gripping Allory's neck and dragging her with him. "Tell me how that sounds fair, little butterfly?"

"It isn't fair," Nola said. "The world ending isn't fair. Nothing is fair. But you wanted to talk to me, and this is the best I can do."

"No, little butterfly, it isn't." Lucifer smiled. "The best you can do is for my city to be fed. We'll eat our fill tonight, and when there's nothing left of the Domers but bloody bones, we'll have your nice beds to rest in and all the dome food to eat."

"Please don't," Nola said. "How many people will die if you try to fight us?"

"Butterfly"—with a grin on his face, Lucifer leaned down as though to kiss Allory's neck—"we're already dead."

"No!" Nola screamed, but her cry was covered by Allory's. The shriek lasted for only a moment before a spurt of blood sprayed the ground.

Someone wrapped a hand around Nola's arm, but she didn't turn to see who had yanked her backward. The pack rushed forward, hiding Allory behind their surging mass.

Poor Allory.

"Get her out of here!" Captain Ridgeway's voice cut over the screams as she was dragged through the front line of guards. As soon as she was behind the line, they began firing on the mob that had rushed toward them. The people at the back of the bridge were piling on, joining the fight. There were too many of them for the guards to face. Sheer numbers would overwhelm the domes.

Pure light ripped through the night with a *bang*. A weight struck Nola in the chest, sending her flying as someone pulled her beneath them, shielding her from the terrible light. The bridge under her gave an awful lurch and somewhere far away people screamed. The noise of the screams was muted in her ears, tiny bugs trying to cut through the terrible ringing.

"Get up!" Jeremy's voice shouted. The one who had protected her from the light.

Of course it's Jeremy.

"Are you hurt?" he yelled, sounding like he was underwater, his words almost too muffled for her to understand. But he didn't wait for her to answer. People ran toward them, away from a fire at the end of the bridge.

But the bridge now ended far before the other side of the river. Half of the bridge had disappeared leaving only jagged bits of flaming metal reaching toward the city.

A blaze illuminated the far bank of the river. Bodies lay near the shore, some of the corpses on fire.

Jeremy pulled her farther away, into the crowd of guards charging forward to meet the wolves who had made it to their side of the bridge before the light.

Explosion. That's the word for it. I saw an explosion.

They were behind the last truck now. The domes glittered up the hill, looking so perfect. There was no sign of the explosion that had broken the domes. That had been mended. But the burning bodies on the shore could never be mended.

"Nola. Nola!" Jeremy shouted, taking her by the shoulders and shaking her. "Nola!"

"Yes," she said, wanting so badly to take off Jeremy's helmet so she could see his face.

"Nola, I need you to run for the domes."

Guns sounded behind them.

How many wolves had gotten over the bridge?

"I need you to run home and don't stop until you're at the door. They'll let you in."

"Come with me, please!" She grabbed Jeremy's hands. "I can't go without you!"

"You have to, Nola. Keep your head down and run. I'll be at your house by sunrise, I promise you."

"No, please!" She couldn't lose him. She wouldn't.

An agonizing scream cut through the sounds of the fight.

"I love you, Nola. Now run!"

"I love you," Nola whispered before turning toward the glass castle and running up the hill.

CHAPTER EIGHTEEN

Tears and sweat mixed on her face. The sounds of fighting didn't fade as she ran up the hill. They followed her like a demon, keeping pace with her every step.

She had left him. She had left Jeremy in the dark, fighting werewolves.

Home by sunrise. He'll be home by sunrise.

Screams chased her. Terrible, terrified screams. Something like a snarl followed. And then—

Pop, pop, pop.

Such a tiny little noise that could mean the end of someone's life.

Home by sunrise. He'll be home by sunrise.

The air burned Nola's lungs as she ran up the hill. Her legs protested every step. Something warm and sticky dripped down her shoulder. But she didn't dare look to see if it was her own blood that smeared her flesh or someone else's.

The door to the atrium came into sight. Twelve guards stood out front, weapons trained on the darkness around them. The Dome Guard should be down fighting with the Outer Guard on the bridge. Why were they standing in the darkness while others fought?

"Help!" Nola tried to scream, but the words barely made it past her lips. "Help!"

Two of the guards ran toward her, their rifles pointed at her chest.

"They need help down at the bridge!" she panted.

"Freeze!" one of the guards shouted.

Nola ran faster, trying to get away from whatever was chasing her.

"I said freeze!"

She stopped so suddenly she nearly tipped over.

"Please...they need help...at the bridge!" Nola begged between gasps.

"Magnolia Kent?" one of the guards asked.

"There are wolves on the bridge," Nola said as a guard shone his light on her vest.

"Take off the vest," the first guard said.

Nola pulled off the vest and dropped it onto the ground. She didn't need protection. She needed them to listen. "There was an explosion on the bridge. Guards are hurt."

"The Outer Guard can take care themselves." He pointed his light at her shoulder. "You're injured. We need to get you inside."

"I'm fine." Nola stepped back as one of the guards reached for her.

But another guard caught her tightly around the waist and carried her to the door.

"No, please. I'm fine. You have to help them!" Nola fought against the man's grip.

"Our orders are not to leave the perimeter of the domes." The guard punched a code into the door, and it *whooshed* open. Fresh air spilled out of the atrium, and hands grabbed Nola, pulling her inside before the doors had fully opened.

"We found her, sir."

Captain Stokes stood just inside the door, glaring at Nola.

"Keep them from getting near the glass," Captain Stokes shouted as the door lowered.

"But they need to get to the guards on the bridge!" Nola wrenched her arms free from the hands that held her.

"Captain Ridgeway chose to take his men to the bridge. Their blood is on his hands," Captain Stokes said. "I will not have the blood of my men on mine."

"And if the wolves get past them? If they break through the glass again?"

"My men will do their duty and protect the domes," Stokes said. "Fighting the people across the river is not what we have been assigned to do. As Captain Ridgeway has made clear again and again. Get her medical help."

A guard standing next to Stokes raised his wrist to his mouth and began muttering.

"You fought with them in the city," Nola pleaded. "You did it then. Why not now?"

"Because my men are not in the business of slaughter." Hatred twisted

Stokes' face. "We protect the lives in these domes. What the Outer Guard do is on their own damned heads. Get her to the bunker."

"No!" she screamed as two guards reached toward her. "I just watched a woman's neck get ripped open and a bridge explode. I tried to stop this from happening, and I failed. I'm not waiting underground to see if the monsters make it to our door."

Stokes eyed her for a moment. "Let her stay."

A woman in a white coat ran into the atrium, emergency medical bag in hand.

Nola didn't flinch as the doctor tore away her sleeve. Stokes was still studying her, and she wouldn't look away.

"You never could have stopped it, Miss Kent," Stokes finally said, as though he had spent the last five minutes searching for words. "Nothing you could have done would have stopped the bridge from burning." He pushed the words from his throat as if every syllable cost him an enormous effort. Without waiting for her reply, he turned and walked to the back of the atrium, toward the high concrete tower that loomed over the domes.

Nola turned back to the glass. The bridge was barely visible in the darkness, only flames marked the bloody expanse.

"We need to get you down to the medical unit," the doctor said.

Nola didn't register the doctor pulling at her skin until she looked down. The blood on her arm had been hers. A piece of something was lodged in her bicep. The longer she stared at it, the more she realized she was looking at her own arm. Then the pain began.

"We need to get your arm taken care of," the doctor said. "Did you hit your head? Are you dizzy?"

"I'm fine." Nola shook her head as though the movement would emphasize how fine she was.

"We need to run some tests." The doctor shone a bright light into her eyes.

"I'm not leaving." Nola looked back to the bridge. "I'm not leaving while he's fighting."

The doctor swore, unpacking her medical bag, muttering darkly about guards allowing things to interfere with her patient's care.

"Have you at least used an I-Vent?" the doctor snapped as she pulled bits of shining black metal from Nola's arm.

Pain surged through her with each little scrap that was removed. She savored every sting. She deserved to be in pain. People were dying down the hill because she had failed.

"I-Vent," the doctor shouted, as though Nola were deaf.

Fishing in her back pocket with her good hand, Nola pulled out the tiny tube and took a deep breath, never taking her eyes from the bridge.

The fighting had moved closer to the domes in the ten minutes she had been inside. Nola laughed. A panicked chuckle that caught in her throat.

"And she's lost her mind," the doctor muttered.

"I liked that last doctor I saw better," Nola said.

"I don't think you're appreciating—"

"You're fixing a few broken inches of skin on my arm, and wolves could kill us all by morning."

A blaze lit the far side of the bridge. Something large had been sacrificed to the inferno. Like the city had lit a fire to shed light on the sins of the battle.

With a *hiss* from a canister, the doctor sprayed something that burned Nola's arm.

"I am going to have a lot more patients before the end of the night," the doctor said, dry fear crackling in her voice. "I'd really like to be done with you before they get here."

She smeared blue goo onto Nola's arm. As if on cue, a truck rumbled up the hill.

Her heart leapt.

It's over!

But no, it couldn't be. There were still people moving at the bottom of the hill. Still tiny sparks of firing weapons lighting the night.

"And that will be my wounded." The doctor wrapped a bandage around Nola's arm. "I don't care where the hell you go, but if you actually care about the wounded guards who are about to be coming through this door, get the hell out of the atrium. Go to the bunkers, go to your own bed, I couldn't care less. But I will not allow you to stay here and be in my way."

The vents rumbled as the door opened.

"Take care of them." Nola ran to the far side of the atrium and down into the tunnels.

He'll be home by sunrise.

Nola tore through the tunnel to Bright Dome. From her roof she would be able to see if the fighting came closer, even if she couldn't see the bridge.

Bright Dome was empty, abandoned by all the residents who had fled to the bunker. For a moment, she wondered if her mother had looked for her. Had asked the guard who kept them all trapped where Magnolia Kent had gone. But her mother probably hadn't gone to the bunker. She would have snuck away to be down with her seeds, making sure no panicked person or malicious intruder dared damage them.

Nola leapt up the two steps to her door and burst through the kitchen without bothering to turn on the lights. She sprinted up the stairs and into her room. Something soft tangled around her feet, and she fell forward, screaming as her hurt arm took the impact.

"Leave me alone!" Nola shouted, kicking away whoever was trying to trap her. But there was no one hiding in the shadows or pinning her down. The soft, white towel she had dropped what seemed like a lifetime ago lay on the floor, now stained by her boots.

Panting, she pushed herself up. The pain in her arm had become impossible to ignore, but she had to see what was happening. Stepping up on the windowsill, she couldn't stop the scream of pain that wrenched from her throat as she pulled herself onto the roof.

The cool, soft moss, terribly unlike everything happening in the world, cradled her cheek. She shouldn't be sitting on something so gentle and familiar while Jeremy was outside fighting for his life.

The fire on the city side of the bridge had grown, reaching the buildings that sat along the water. The smoke from the flames clouded the sky, obscuring the river's edge.

Nola swore, screaming at the flames, and the smoke, and the wolves and explosions.

There was still movement on the remaining half of the shattered bridge.

How many wolves had made it to their side of the explosion? Surely the fighting would be over soon. And the rest would be stuck in the fires they had created on the far side of the river. There would be no guards going into the city to try and save people from the flames. There was no way across.

The river ran with a swift current, and the water had been contaminated from years of industrial pollution. Even if someone were strong enough to make it from the city to the domes, submerging in the water would be a death sentence.

But would it be a death sentence to the wolves?

Nola shut her eyes against the night, and dark, imagined shapes swam through the water that shone in her mind.

She wouldn't be able to see them swimming. The distance, smoke, and darkness all prevented that.

But if they could. If they swam over. If there are boats hidden in the city...

Then Jeremy will fight them, too.

Nola opened her eyes and looked back toward the river. Trucks drove back up the hill. And bright, fake lights bathed the remnants of the bridge. She wanted to leap off the roof and run to the atrium, to search every truck for Jeremy as they came in. If he was injured, she should sit by his bed just as she had before. But the doctor had told her to stay out of the way. That it would be safer for the wounded.

Digging her fingers into the moss, Nola anchored herself to the roof as though expecting a wind to blow her away.

Her arm throbbed with every beat of her heart.

Home by sunrise. He promised. He'll be home by sunrise.

CHAPTER NINETEEN

Hours passed. Or maybe just a few minutes. She didn't know what time she had been taken to the bridge, so there was no way to know how long the wait for the sky to turn gray would be.

Her fingers went numb from gripping the moss on the roof long before the faint part of the sky visible through the smoke lightened.

Tears ran down Nola's cheeks, but she couldn't brush them away. Her arms were too heavy to lift to her face.

There were still people moving on the bridge. In the dim light she could see them like ants, carrying and pushing things from the broken bridge to the water.

Bodies. They were throwing bodies into the water. If they were disposing of the dead, the danger must be over.

Jeremy was hurt. He must be, or he would have come for her. Unless he was out with the people left on the bridge. Or maybe he thought she was down in one of the bunkers and had gone there. Or maybe...

Nola couldn't let herself finish that maybe.

I'll be home by sunrise.

He promised.

Orange tinted the sky. A sad, dusty orange tainted by the fire, unable to match the crackling brightness of the flames through the haze that coated the world.

A blanket that suffocates us all.

Her breath came in quick gasps. She would suffocate on the roof. The world itself would smother her, and she deserved it.

A heaving sob broke free, and then another. She wept on the roof, staring at the sun, willing it to stop its relentless rise, knowing she would never have that power.

Home by sunrise.

The edge of the sun burst free from the horizon.

"No, no, no!" Nola railed against the sun, but it wouldn't listen. "Stop! Please stop!"

"Nola!" a voice shouted from the far side of Bright Dome. "Nola!"

She had nearly missed the sound in her screaming.

"Nola!"

Painfully, she pried her fingers from the moss and crawled to the other side of the roof where she could see the rest of the dome.

"Jeremy." His name came out as a whisper through her tears. "Jeremy!"

He ran toward her house. His stride long and even. Blood and dirt marked his uniform, but relief brightened his face as soon as he saw her.

Scrambling back across the roof, Nola dropped over the edge and through her window, all pain forgotten as Jeremy's heavy boots pounded up the stairs.

"Nola, are you hurt?" the words were out of his mouth before he was in her room, but she didn't answer. She had already thrown herself into his arms and was kissing him with everything she possessed.

Explosions and blood melted away. Death and fear didn't matter. Jeremy was alive and holding her.

The room didn't sway, and she didn't want it to. She wanted to hold on tighter, to pull herself closer so no one would ever be able to separate them again. There was no more her or him. No difference between them at all.

His fingers found skin at her waist and drifted up her back. She gasped at the warmth of his touch, craving more. Her heart raced as he hungrily grasped her side with his hand. Suddenly, her shirt became a hateful thing, another horrible barrier between them. Nola eased her hold on him only enough to reach for the edge of her shirt but as soon as she moved, Jeremy was there pulling it off for her.

Blood rose to her cheeks not with embarrassment, but anticipation. He let go of her for a moment to take off his heavy guard's vest. But that brief moment felt like an eternity. Like he would fall away from her completely.

She pulled herself closer to him. Kissing him again as though trying to prove he was still alive. With only his thin guard's shirt between them, his heart racing pressed against hers. The taste of him, the feel of his heat radiating through her, washed away all the cold fear that filled her.

"Nola," Jeremy whispered, and her heart soared. He wasn't saying a name, but a prayer that they would always be together. That he would always hold her tight, and the demons of the outside world would never again come between them.

Fingers trembling, Nola undid the buttons of his shirt, letting her chest press to his. She slid his shirt away without looking.

In one movement that sent her heart bounding from her chest, Jeremy scooped her into his arms and carried her to the bed. Laying her down gently, he gazed at her. His brown eyes smiling down at her. She reached for him, pulling him closer. The light from the sunrise shone through the window, casting an orange light on Jeremy's bare chest. A red mark glistened on his arm. Surrounded by dried blood, the cut looked like a weeks-old gash, already through the first horrible stages of healing.

Nola gasped, and her world shattered.

CHAPTER TWENTY

"What's wrong?" Jeremy asked, reaching down toward Nola, but she swatted his hand away, falling off the bed in her desperate scramble to get away from him.

"Don't touch me!" Nola's back slammed into the edge of her dresser, sending a wave of pain through her spine. "Ouch!"

Jeremy reached for her again. "Nola, be careful."

"I said don't touch me!" she screamed, groping her way up the desk, not looking away from Jeremy.

"Nola, I'm sorry." Jeremy's face crumpled. He tucked his hands behind him as though trying to prove he wouldn't reach for her again.

But the movement tightened the skin on his arm, making the red line of freshly healed flesh even more apparent.

"I shouldn't have done that. I shouldn't have pushed you so fast, I'm sorry."

"How could you?" she whispered. "How could you?"

She wanted to say more, to scream and rage, but the words wouldn't come.

"I love you, Nola. I want to be with you." Desperation filled his eyes. "Please, Nola. I'm sorry. I would never hurt you."

"What did they give you?" Nola asked. "Where did you get it?"

"What are you..." Jeremy's gaze followed Nola's shaking hand as she pointed to his arm. He swallowed, his pulse throbbed in his neck. "It's not what you think."

"It's exactly what I think," she spat. "I've seen people heal like that before. I saw it happen to me in Nightland. What did you take? Vamp? Lycan? Or maybe you got lucky and found some ReVamp?"

"It's not any of that," he said, his voice dry and shallow. "I would never take any of that."

"Then what? What name did you decide to call the drug in order to make yourself feel better about using it?"

"Graylock," Jeremy whispered. "We call it Graylock. They gave it to all the men in the Outer Guard."

"What?" Nola stumbled as the room spun.

He lunged forward and caught her an inch before she hit the floor.

She pushed on his chest with both hands, trying to get him to let go, but he didn't seem to notice.

He set her easily back on her feet. "We had to take it, Nola." Jeremy backed as far away from her as the tiny room would allow. "With Vampers and wolves on the streets, the Outer Guard didn't stand a chance without it."

"So you became them." It was all falling away, one sheet of lies at a time, and the shattering rang through her mind, jumbling her thoughts. "You did what you hate the Vampers for doing. You changed your DNA. Made yourselves monsters just like them."

"No. Not like them. We have better scientists here than the outsiders could ever hope for. Graylock makes us stronger and faster. We can heal and fight, but I'm still me. It didn't change anything about my mind. No bloodlust, no anger. I can still eat, and go in the sun, and I still love you."

"How could your father allow this? The domes were built to preserve the human race. Without contamination from the outside world. If this drug changes the way your body works, it changes what you are. You might as well be a vampire!" The words tore from her throat.

"Please don't shout, Nola. People can't know about this. You aren't supposed to know about this. No one can find out that you know."

"Why?" She crossed her arms, covering her bare chest. "Because if the Council finds out what the Outer Guard have been doing—"

"The Council knows," Jeremy said. "The Incorporation itself gave approval for the research."

"No. No, the Incorporation built the domes to preserve humans, not create monsters. They would never let this happen."

"They approved the research and the Outer Guard's use of Graylock. That's why Stokes has been such an evil little varmint. Our guys can do things his can't. The Dome Guard and Outer Guard aren't equal anymore."

"Because the Dome Guard are protecting what the domes were built for."

Stokes' words suddenly made sense. Why should he send his men out to bleed when the Outer Guard could be stabbed and heal without any treatment?

"We take Graylock to protect the domes," Jeremy pleaded. "We couldn't fight the city dwellers before, but now we can. We can fight the wolves and live. They were slaughtering us before. We had to do something."

"My father was an Outer Guard, and he never injected himself with filth to do his job."

"And they killed him," Jeremy said, so softly she could barely hear. His words were without malice or taunt. Just cold, painful truth. "And I would have died, too. I wouldn't have survived the werewolf riot without Graylock. It saved my life."

Nola's mind raced back to a filing cabinet filled with black vials and a needle filled with black sliding into Jeremy's chest.

"They started giving it to the Outer Guard right before the raid on Nightland, and we still lost six men. We would have lost a lot more without it. And the attack on the domes, it would have been a massacre without Graylock."

"If it keeps you strong and healthy, then we should send it to the outsiders," Nola said. "Graylock could be the cure they've been looking for. You could save people!"

"We're saving the domes." Jeremy took a tiny step forward. "If all of those people had it, we wouldn't be able to stop an attack."

He was right. She knew he was right, and she hated herself for it.

"But the domes were built to preserve the future," Nola said. "That's bigger than who can fight better. It's about protecting future generations. None of the Outer Guard will be able to have children now. What's the point of—"

"But we will be able to have children." Warmth filled Jeremy's voice. "They figured all that out. Before any of us were allowed to take Graylock, they took samples from us. We could still have healthy children."

Nola backed into the wall, leaning on it for support as her head spun.

"Not now, not for a long time. But the doctors"—Jeremy ran his hands through his hair—"they have everything stored, and when, I mean, *if* we ever wanted kids, they could do it."

"With doctors." Nola's lips numbed. The feeling drifted down to her fingers, then coated her whole body. "Doctors to put things inside of me, but not Gentry. That's why she left, isn't it? You said they gave Graylock to the men, but she couldn't have it. She needed to be kept *pure for breeding*." She spat the words, hating the feeling of them in her mouth.

Jeremy pressed the heels of his hands into his eyes. "She fought for it. She wanted to take Graylock, but they wouldn't let her. They couldn't risk losing her DNA for procreation."

Bile rose in her throat. An animal for breeding. That was how they had treated Gentry. Strong, trained, brave Gentry. "How could they expect her to let the rest of her family take it and not be strong enough to protect them? But it doesn't matter what the Council wanted. The domes lost her anyway."

"She can be a guard in a different set of domes," he said. "We're the only ones who use Graylock. We're the only ones who have fighting this bad. We had to do it to survive."

Kieran had said nearly the same thing to her on a roof high above the decaying city. He was drowning in his own body, and ReVamp had saved his life. Had given him a chance to help others...and betray Nola.

She shut her eyes tight, shuddering at the thought of Jeremy and Kieran being anything like the same.

"Nola, I love you."

She sensed him moving closer but didn't shrink away.

"I love you more than anything. I took my first dose the day we raided Nightland to try and get you back. I never wanted to take something like Graylock, but I had to do it. I had to do whatever gave me the best chance of protecting you." His fingers brushed the bandage on her arm. "And even with Graylock, I still couldn't keep you safe."

"An explosion can kill Vampers and werewolves." Nola opened her eyes. Jeremy was only a few inches from her. She leaned into his chest, willing it to feel the same as it had a few minutes ago when she hadn't known about the chemicals racing through his veins with every heartbeat. "A severed neck or a broken heart, it'll kill a Vamper or a wolf. It would get you, too." She shuddered and unfolded her arms. Letting her skin press into his.

"I know." Jeremy wrapped his arms around her. "But I still should have been able to protect you."

"They blew up a bridge. There's no way anyone could have imagined they would sacrifice their own people like that."

Nola felt Jeremy stiffen before the words rumbled in his chest.

"They didn't blow up the bridge, Nola. We did."

CHAPTER TWENTY-ONE

The sound began far at the back of Nola's brain. A terrible screaming that had no words. One high-pitched, piercing screech that floated further and further forward, fighting to block out Jeremy's voice.

"The bomb was planted under the bridge a long time ago." Jeremy held her up by the shoulders, pleading and fear painting his face. "To make sure the outsiders didn't cross the bridge and overwhelm the domes. If we had seen Nightland coming, we could have stopped them, too, but they got over some other way. If we hadn't blown up the bridge, those people would have come across and attacked us. We had no other choice."

The screaming in her head had grown too loud now. She couldn't hear his words at all. He was talking fast, his lips forming important phrases she couldn't hear over the terrible shrieking. Nola watched his lips, trying to find something in the pattern of their movement that would make sense. That would mean her home hadn't just blown up a bridge filled with people.

Bile shot up into her mouth. Shoving past Jeremy, she ran for the toilet. Her stomach threw up the revulsion that overwhelmed her, but the screaming in her head wouldn't stop.

Jeremy knelt next to her, holding her up as she trembled and heaved. The noise told her he was shouting something, but it didn't matter. What he was shouting about didn't matter. How could it matter more than...than.... How many people had been at the edge of the bridge when it exploded? Fifty?

No, more. It was more.

The shriek in her head had learned to speak words.

You saw them running toward you. More than a hundred. Running toward you. Running toward your home until they were burned up in an instant.

"I was a diversion," Nola said as the screaming in her head stopped, leaving her with deafening quiet. "Your dad knew I wouldn't be able to talk to them. He knew I wouldn't be able to stop it. I was just supposed to buy them time. So they could be sure everything was in place." She seized Jeremy's face. "Tell me I wasn't a diversion. Tell me I didn't help you kill those people."

"They would have killed us." Jeremy pressed Nola's hands to his cheeks. "They would have come over here and killed all of us. Ripped out our throats, you heard him."

"They lied to me. They used me," Nola whimpered as the room swayed.

"Nola..." Jeremy reached to pull her closer, but she pushed herself away, falling backward onto the floor and hitting her head hard on the corner of the shower.

"Nola."

"Don't touch me!" she shouted, jumping to her feet even as the room around her swam dangerously.

"Nola, you're bleeding." Jeremy reached again to steady her.

"Get out of my house. Get the hell out of here. And you and your Graylock and your lies and your bombs stay the hell away from me!"

He looked as though she had slapped him hard across the face. Blinking dazedly, he stared at her like he thought she might come to her senses if only he froze long enough for her to sort out what it was she might be thinking.

"Get out," Nola growled. "Get out, get out, get out!"

But he wouldn't move. He stood like a confused statue in her bathroom, which smelled of sour and blood. She pushed around him, snatched her blood-stained shirt from the floor, and ran down the stairs, leaning heavily on the walls as her head spun. She didn't stop to close the door behind her or wonder how long it would be until her mother came home and found blood on the corner of the shower.

Half-formed plans swam in her head. Her feet carried her out through the grass of Bright Dome, off the path, and behind a willow tree. The hole in the glass had been sealed. There was no way out here. But she would have to find one. The ones left to suffer had come for the glass castle, and they wouldn't stop until the river ran red with blood. When that day came, she would not be left in the domes to watch it.

Smoke covered the skyline of the city, blocking out the places where families would be mourning. And where wolves would be plotting their revenge.

Nola pressed her head to the cool glass. The morning light still hadn't stolen the chill of the night away. Warm blood trickled down her neck. There were things to be done, and she knew where to go first.

CHAPTER TWENTY-TWO

Nola waited in the hall of the medical wing for nearly an hour. There were no doctors or Outer Guard in sight. It would have seemed strange or even ominous just a short while ago. But the deep, black Graylock couldn't be injected where Domers could see, and the Outer Guard would be able to heal on their own anyway.

The hall lights had gotten bright before Doctor Mullins finally arrived in the corridor, looking tired and pulling on a fresh, white coat.

She looked at Nola for a moment, blinking as though batting away fatigue. "Magnolia, how can I help you?"

Nola let go of the bandage she had been pressing to the back of her head. "My head won't stop bleeding." She gave a crooked smile.

Doctor Mullins rushed over. "Why on earth didn't someone see you already?" Glancing briefly at Nola's head, she took her arm and led her to the door of one of the examining rooms, punching in a code before the door slid open.

"Someone looked at my arm," Nola said, deliberately not looking at the glass cases in the corner. "But when I got home, I got dizzy and hit my head. I didn't want to interrupt while all the doctors were downstairs helping the injured Outer Guard."

"Well, that was considerate of you, but head wounds are nothing to be trifled with. Especially with..." Doctor Mullins paused for a moment, then spun to face the cabinet in the corner. "Well, those who have had so much physical trauma to deal with lately."

"I'm sorry," Nola muttered, watching as Doctor Mullins punched in yet another code to open the cabinet.

3733

The cabinet popped open.

"I didn't think it mattered that much. I just couldn't get the bleeding to stop."

"We'll get you cleaned up in no time, but you really do need to be careful."

She waited patiently as Doctor Mullins shined a light into her eyes, sprayed things that stung onto her flesh, and tugged at the broken skin.

"I'm so sorry," Nola said as the doctor rubbed cool goo into her hair, "but could you maybe ask my mom to walk me home? I'm just..." She waited, hoping the doctor would sympathetically interrupt her. She didn't. "I'm not feeling great about being alone. I'd like it if my mom could come and get me."

Nola held her breath as she waited.

The doctor's stern face finally crumpled. "I'll go and grab your mom. She'll be down in seeds?"

"Yes." Nola smiled. "I'd call for her, but I'm sure she won't answer, not after having to go back to the bunker."

"I'll go find your mom." Doctor Mullins wagged a finger in an unintimidating way. "But don't let it get around that I'll run all over the domes looking for truant parents."

"Thank you!" she called as soon as the doctor was out the door.

3733

Nola jumped off the bed and ran for the cabinet. Her fingers shook as she punched in the number, but as soon as the final three was pressed, the metal doors popped open.

She stood frozen for a few moments, staring at the vast array of vials and tubs, bottles and packages. She tried to read the names, but she didn't know what half of them meant.

Hands shaking, Nola reached into the very back of the rows, careful not to disturb the order of the perfectly aligned front bottles.

Three bottles of nutrient pills, five I-Vents. Three familiar-looking silver vials she had been injected with when a flu swept through the domes four years earlier. Tubs of the goo the doctors spread on wounds to help them heal. A few packs of bandages.

She shoved the vials into the ankles of her boots, the bandages into the waist of her pants, and the bottles into her pockets.

How much more could she fit into her clothes without the doctor noticing? What would she need? She grabbed three vials of blue pills her mother had given her before for headaches and closed the cabinet.

Kieran would have done it better. He would have known what each of the names on the bottles meant and what they were used for. But Kieran had left her and betrayed her. Jeremy had lied to her and used her.

Her whole body shook as she moved back to the bed in the middle of the room. There was no one left to trust, only people to save.

Nola stared at her hands as she counted the seconds before Doctor Mullins would return. Lenora Kent wouldn't come easily. She wouldn't hear that her daughter had been hurt and come running. She would hem and haw. Be sure to check all of her specimens one last time. Assign a person to watch her computer and make sure it didn't shut down while she was away. The automatic computer alerts from PAM were never enough for her. She would want someone there watching, protecting her precious seeds.

The vials in her boots seemed to burn her skin, shouting to the domes that Nola Kent was a traitor. But the sirens didn't sound, and the lights didn't flash. So she counted until her mother arrived.

"Nola." Lenora burst through the door, looking harassed after 672 seconds. "What happened to you?"

Nola smiled to herself, swallowing the urge to laugh. "I almost got blown up on the bridge, and then hit my head really hard at home. So, a little blood and a lot of trauma."

"What?" Lenora looked at Dr. Mullins as though expecting her to say delusions were a symptom of Nola's head wound. "You were on that bridge? How in the ever-loving hell did you get out there? And what do you mean *blown up*?"

"Can I tell you at home?" Nola said.

"How did you get outside the domes? And where did you hit your head?"

Nola smiled apologetically at Doctor Mullins who stayed plastered to the side of the room as Nola's mother led her out into the hall.

"And you can't possibly tell me you had anything to do with what happened outside. I've been told there were werewolves." Lenora took Nola by the arm and dragged her up the stairs. "How could you have gotten to the bridge in the first place?"

"Captain Ridgeway set me up." Nola expected a shot of pain to fly through her chest. But there was nothing. Only a vast emptiness in the place where the pain should have been. "He made me negotiate with the wolves. Made me think there was a chance to make sure no one died. And then he blew up the bridge with me standing on it. With a hundred people running across it. He's a liar and a killer, and I never want to see him or Jeremy again."

"What?" Lenora stopped in the middle of the hall.

Nola sidestepped her and kept walking toward Bright Dome. "They used me to buy time to kill people. And I hate them for it." She didn't look back to see if her mother was following.

She had reached the steps to Bright Dome when heavy running footfalls caught up to her.

"Nola, honey..." Lenora grabbed her daughter's arm. "That can't be what they meant to do."

"It was, Mom." Nola took her mother's hand. "Please don't pretend you don't believe me. I think you knew what the Ridgeways were capable of long before I did."

"I'm so sorry." Lenora shook her head, her fingers pressed over her lips. "What can I do?"

"Keep Jeremy away from me, and let me live my life away from him." It sounded so ridiculously simple when she said it like that.

"The Ridgeway family is no longer welcome in our home." Lenora chased Nola up the stone walkway to their house. "And I'll be sure to talk to the Council, too, though I don't know how much good it will do since even the Incorporation seems to be on the Outer Guard's side these days."

"Thanks, Mom." She turned to her mother, tears burning in her eyes. "Thank you for believing me and standing up for me, even if you think it won't work. I love you, Mom."

Lenora pulled her daughter into a tight hug. "I love you, too, Magnolia."

As soon as the words had left Lenora's mouth, the moment ended. The deep, tender feelings of a mother protecting her only child disappeared.

"Now that we're home, what can I do for you?" Lenora asked as Nola walked up the steps to the house.

"Nothing, Mom. But can you make sure my work team is up in the Amber Dome and ready in fifteen?"

"Of course." Lenora beamed up at her daughter. "It's always good to turn to your work, Nola. The seeds always make sense. And they will never hurt you."

Lenora turned and walked away without looking back.

Nola wanted to call after her and ask if that was why she preferred the company of seeds to her own daughter.

It won't matter soon.

The steps creaked under Nola's weight as she ran up them, pulling out her dresser drawer before she had even stopped moving. There was a narrow space at the back, discovered years ago when she and Kieran had needed a place to hide their childish secrets.

Carefully, she packed in vials, bottles, and packages, making sure there was no wasted room before sliding the drawer shut. From where she sat, there was no indication that she had done anything wrong. No blaring signals declaring Magnolia Kent had stolen from the domes once again.

What's next?

Nola crawled onto the bed, clutching the covers so her hands wouldn't shake. She needed a place to go and people to go with her. She knew enough about the outside world to be certain she would die quickly on her own. And she wouldn't leave T, Catlyn, or even Beauford in the domes. There was no bridge to the city anymore. No way for the domes to march them home when they were deemed no longer useful. She didn't want to imagine what the Council would do with them.

Moving to the bathroom in a daze, she stuck her head under the faucet of the sink and watched the red of the blood from her hair swirl down the drain. Her head stung as she pulled her hair into a tight braid. She needed to look normal, even if normal made her want to be sick again.

The walk to the Amber Dome seemed shorter than usual. Nola didn't read the signs that greeted her everyday as she normally did, even though they had been the same her whole life.

Her feet carried her to the Amber Dome without thought. She yanked on the brown gardening jumpsuit, not noticing what she had done until she pulled the zipper on the front all the way up.

People were already at work in the dome. The bloodshed of the night couldn't be allowed to affect the work of the day. There were more Domers working than there had been before, taking the place of Allory and the others who had attacked the guards the previous day.

"Miss Kent!" a voice called hesitantly from the far side of the dome. Catlyn gave a quick wave before dropping her hand and shrinking back into the bushes.

Nola ran over to her group, who were working on salvaging the bits of vine they had pushed through fleeing the fight.

"How are you?" Catlyn asked in a bright tone that sounded like she was merely being polite. But the intensity with which she stared at Nola told a different story.

"I'm fine." Nola smiled. "Doing well. Got a little bumped around on the bridge but nothing to worry about."

"You really were on the bridge?" T looked up from the vine she had been binding to a trellis. Her eyes were red and puffy as though she'd been crying.

"I was."

Catlyn gave a slow exhale through pinched lips. "We heard the guards talking and saw the bridge through the glass. I was hoping I had heard wrong."

"The bridge to the city was destroyed." Nola knelt down next to T, pointing at different parts of the vine without really looking at them. "There isn't a way for you to cross over the river to get home. There was a huge fire in the city last night, the biggest I've ever seen, and the Outer Guard aren't going to go back in to try and keep the peace. Now that we're cut off from the city, I don't know how bad things will get."

"Great," Beauford said from his place on the other side of the vines. "So even if we can get out of here and could find a way home, there won't be anything but wolves, Vampers, and death waiting for us. Glad you could give us that helpful information."

"I can't go back to the city." T shook her head, her face paling so her freckles were the only trace of color left. "How am I supposed to keep a baby safe with wolves running the streets?"

"Can you ask them to keep the baby?" Catlyn whispered, taking Nola's hands in hers. "There has to be a way to convince them. No one with a heart would send an innocent baby into a place where they have no chance of survival."

"The people of the domes don't have hearts," Nola said. She expected the words to hurt, to dig at something deep inside of her, but the void had swallowed the pain of that knowledge, too. "They will use you, then dump you outside. They probably won't even help you get across the river."

Fresh tears streamed down T's face.

"So we have to get out of here before they decide they're done with you. We have to break out of here and find Nightland." Nola ducked under the vines, feigning interest in the work Beauford had done. "You can't stay here, and after last night, neither can I."

"But you don't know where Nightland went," T said, leaning back down to the vines and attaching minuscule braces to the damaged section. "You swore you didn't."

"I don't know where Nightland is," she said, "but I know someone who does, or at least would know where to start looking."

"Can you trust them?" Beauford asked.

"I'll never trust her, but she needs my help if she wants to get out of her cell, and she's as close to Emanuel as we could hope to find."

"The Vamper in the cell," T said, then, seeing the shocked look on Nola's face, added, "I've heard the guards talking about her when they come into the hall."

"I'm sure she'd help us if I can get her out, and you out, and find a way out of the domes." Helplessness flared in Nola's chest.

"Getting out of the rooms only takes a code," Beauford said. "All you have to do is find out what it is. Getting out of the Guard barracks take a distraction."

"And getting out of the domes?" T asked.

"The domes are only made of glass."

CHAPTER TWENTY-THREE

"I need to see my work crew." Nola smiled sweetly at the Outer Guard who blocked the stairs to the barracks. "The ones who are in the cells in the back. It's my fault. I handed one of them a few seeds and asked her to keep them in her pocket while we worked. But I forgot to get them back, and now my mom, Lenora Kent, well, she's running inventory, and I really need to get those seeds back before she murders me."

The guard looked to his companion.

"I know I shouldn't have forgotten something so important, but with everything from last night..." Nola let her voice trail away for a moment, feeling foolishly dramatic. "I guess I'm just not thinking so well today."

"Fine," the guard finally said after a stiff nod from his partner, "but please don't tell anyone we let you in. And you've got to make it fast."

"I will." Nola sighed in relief as he led her through the barracks corridor. "I promise, I don't want anyone to know I made that sort of mistake. I mean, they aren't rare seeds. Just a few food plants, but my mother can be scary sometimes."

"I've heard rumors about Dr. Kent." The guard pushed open the door to the hall of cells and stopped at the first one. "I don't blame you for wanting to stay on her good side. Even if she is your mother."

"Especially since she's my mother." Nola forced a laugh.

The guard tapped on the glass, drawing T, Catlyn, and Beauford's attention. They were all in the room together, just as Beauford said they had been last night.

"Catlyn," Nola called through the glass, "I forgot to get the seeds back from you."

"What, Miss Kent?" Catlyn shouted, looking toward the door. "I don't have any seeds."

The guard raised an eyebrow at Nola.

"Yes, you do," Nola said, her face now only a few inches from the glass. "I gave you the sealed dish to carry. But I never asked for it back."

"You did?" Catlyn patted her pockets a little more dramatically than necessary before pulling out the tray. "You're right! I'm so sorry, Miss Kent."

"It's not your fault. It's mine," Nola said. "But I do need to get it back tonight."

"Leave the dish on the floor and step away from the door." The guard stepped over to the numbered panel by the door.

"Thank you for helping me." Nola laid her hand on the guard's arm.

The texture of his uniform made her skin crawl, but she inched closer to him.

"Of course," the guard said. Pink rose in the guard's cheeks as he punched in the code.

25663

"Stand back." The guard opened the door and, in one swift movement, grabbed the dish of seeds and closed the door again. "And there you go."

"Thank you." Nola beamed. "Thank you so much. After last night, I really don't think I could take any more stress. I'm not built for that kind of thing."

"I was there." Sympathy sounded in the guard's voice. "I saw you talking to that wolf, and you were great. But you can't always talk a crazy person out of doing a crazy thing."

"No, I guess not." They would be calling *her* crazy soon enough. "Is there any way I could talk to Captain Ridgeway while I'm down here? Just for a minute. After last night, I mean, well, I guess I don't understand everything that happened."

"Understanding what drugged-up outsiders do is impossible. I might have only been a guard for three years, but even I know that." He was young. Nola hadn't bothered to look before, but he was only a few years older than she was. And now Graylock had taken over his system.

Nola swallowed her scream. "I'd still like to try."

"We can see if he's in." The guard shrugged. "Just don't mention the seeds or me opening the door, all right?"

"Don't worry." Nola winked. "It'll be our secret."

The guard led her back out into the barracks corridor. There were still guards milling between rooms. It would have been better to come at night when everyone not on duty would be sleeping, but she needed the code.

The guard knocked on Captain Ridgeway's office door.

"Come in." Captain Ridgeway's rumbling voice sounded angry even through the thick metal.

"Are you sure you want to go in there?" The guard shrugged and swung the door open. "Miss Kent here to see you, sir." With a jerk of his head to the captain and Nola, the guard shut the door behind her.

"Nola." Captain Ridgeway stood behind his desk. She hadn't even started speaking, and his eyes had already narrowed suspiciously. "What can I do for you?"

"What happened to Lucifer and his pack?" she asked. "I know the story in the domes is that a pack tried to attack and blew themselves up. I've heard it repeated three times since lunch. But I know that isn't true. It wasn't one pack, it was a thousand people. And we blew up the bridge, not them."

Captain Ridgeway hesitated for a moment before tenting his fingers under his chin. "Fine, we blew up the bridge to cut off the domes from the city before the wolves could become a threat to our people. After what you saw last night, I would have assumed that would be self-explanatory."

"Is Lucifer dead?" Nola asked. "Did any of the Outer Guard see him in the fighting?"

"One thinks he fought him, but we didn't find a body. It's not unexpected. Between the fire and fighting so close to the broken ledge of the bridge, he could have been burned beyond recognition or fallen into the river."

"So, we just hope he's dead?" She wished the thought of Lucifer dead would bring at least a little sadness if for no other reason than the loss of precious life. But she had seen what he did to Allory, and she couldn't mourn a murderer. She could barely stand speaking to the one in front of her.

"We hope he's dead and hope even harder someone worse doesn't take his place." Captain Ridgeway sat back in his chair. "Of course, the city isn't our problem anymore. If they destroy themselves, so be it."

"And if they build boats and come for us again, will you burn the river to drive them away?" Nola's nails bit into her palms.

"I will burn the river and all of them with it. I believe in the mission of the domes with all that I am. And I will defend it with my life and with my children's lives. Don't forget what we're locked behind glass to do, Nola. We're here to save mankind, and if some have to be lost to let the human race survive, so be it."

"So be it." Nola nodded and turned for the door. She couldn't stand to look at him anymore.

"I'm glad you understand, Nola," Captain Ridgeway said.

She turned back around at the hardness of his tone.

"Jeremy seemed upset today," Captain Ridgeway said. "I won't pry into what goes on between the two of you. But you need to appreciate the sacrifices he is making for the domes. And for you."

She took a breath, begging the screaming in her head not to start again.

"I know Jeremy would do anything to protect me and the domes." She gave a pained smile and walked out of Captain Ridgeway's office, closing the door slowly behind her.

CHAPTER TWENTY-FOUR

T he guards still stood at the end of the corridor, facing the stairs.
They were so trusting. Not even watching for the girl who had seen the code. Convinced of their safety behind glass walls.

Nola walked toward the hall of cells, not looking back to see if anyone followed.

Fingers trembling, she opened the door and stepped into the corridor. Closing it as silently as possible behind her, she turned and stared at the solid door to the Outer Guard's hallway.

"One, two, three," she counted. She couldn't afford to try unlocking the cells until she was sure she hadn't been followed. If she were caught, she would be banished without hope of taking the others with her or stealing any of the medicine she had hoarded in her room. "Ninety-seven, ninety-eight, ninety-nine, one hundred."

The door stayed shut. Nola walked to the door behind which T, Catlyn, and Beauford were trapped.

It only took a light tap on the glass for Catlyn to whisper, "Miss Kent."

25663

Nola held her breath as she punched in the numbers, only letting it out when the lock clicked open with a soft *beep*.

"Is everyone ready?" she whispered.

"Ready." Beauford was the first one out the door. He stood facing the exit to the Outer Guard barracks as the girls slipped past.

Nola ran down the hall until she reached the single cells. Raina lay on the floor of her cell just as she had the first time Nola had found her.

"Raina." Nola knocked on the glass.

Raina glanced up for only a moment before laying her head back on her arm.

"Raina, do you know where Emanuel is?" Nola asked.

"Torturing the filthy Vamper didn't work, so sending a lost little girl to ask questions will make me talk? Pathetic Domers," Raina grumbled, as though talking in her sleep.

"You don't have to tell me where he is," Nola said. "I only need to know if you can find him."

"I fought by Emanuel's side." Raina rolled onto her back and stared up at the ceiling. "I will always be able to find him."

"Will you take me to him?" Nola's heart crashed against her ribs. "Me and three outsiders the domes have trapped."

"Take you to him to kill him? To collect a bounty on his head? I'll take torture first." Raina curled back up into a tight ball.

"I'm leaving the domes," Nola said. "I can't stay here anymore. They used me to murder people. I can't live with that."

"Huh!" Raina laughed. "So, he was right all along. The beautiful girl locked in the domes with a heart big enough to want to save the poor ones left out to die."

"Right now, I just want to save the people I'm taking with me," Nola said, her face so close to the glass her breath fogged her view of Raina. "The city is falling, I don't think there's anywhere left we can survive but wherever Emanuel is."

"Not my problem," Raina said.

"One of the girls is pregnant," Nola said. "The baby's father is with Nightland. Raina, please."

"I can't help you." She turned her head just enough to be able to peer at Nola through the matted strands of scarlet and purple hair. "Even if I wanted to tell you, words alone couldn't help you find Emanuel."

"I don't want words. I'm taking you with me."

Raina pushed herself up to her elbows and glared at Nola.

"I'm going to get you out of here, but you have to help us get out of the domes and take us to Emanuel." Nola spoke as though each word were a dart, throwing them at Raina, making sure she had no choice but to understand.

"You want to let the monster out of its cage, ask it for a favor, and hope it doesn't rip your throat out?" Raina pushed herself to her shaky legs and wobbled to the door.

"You aren't a monster," Nola said. "You saved me when Nightland attacked. The knife that got you stuck in here was meant for me. So yes, I am going to let you out and hope we can get out of the glass and to Emanuel without the Domers or the wolves killing us."

"You left out vampires and zombies." Raina gave a grin that didn't reach her eyes. "Fine, better to die on the outside than in this damned room."

"But no killing in the domes." Nola's fingers hovered above the keypad. "I know they hurt you, but we're not going to cut innocent throats to get out of here."

"I think our definitions of innocent might differ," Raina said.

"No killing on the way out. Or I swear I will leave you in this cell to rot." Nola held Raina's gaze, every instinct telling her the vampire was searching her for a sign of weakness.

"Fine," Raina said after a long moment. "I won't kill anyone, unless they try to kill me first. Is that all right with you, oh mighty rescuer?"

"If they try and lock us back up, we'll all fight, Nola," Catlyn said. "We won't have a choice."

Nola scrunched her eyes closed, trying to block out the memories of the domes' floors smeared with blood.

"Fine."

25663

Panic seized Nola's heart for the split second between pressing the 3 and the *beep* of the door unlocking. Raina twisted the door handle and pushed it open, her legs wobbling as she stepped out into the hall. "And here I didn't think I'd ever get out of that cell."

"How are we going to get past the guards to the stairs?" T asked, the twisting of her fingers the only betrayal of her fear.

"*I'm* going to get past the guards by the stairs." Nola walked down the hall. "You wait until there's an opening and run for it. Don't let yourselves be seen. Raina will take you to where the way through the glass used to be. I'm sure she'll remember where it was. She used it before."

"Too right I did." Raina stumbled and tipped forward. Catlyn and Beauford both lunged to catch her before her face hit the ground.

"Is she going to be able to make it out of here?" T whispered to Nola.

"*She* can still hear you," Raina snarled as Catlyn helped her to her feet, "but *she* hasn't eaten in a month. Let's try starving you for that long and see how well you do?"

"They haven't fed you for a month?" Nola asked, louder than she'd meant to. She clapped a hand over her mouth, and the group waited in silence for a moment.

"I think they wanted to see if it would break me," Raina said. "Or maybe they just wanted to see how long a vampire lasts without a food source. Besides,

I don't think they would have found it tasteful to feed a guest of the domes blood."

"You need to eat." T turned to Nola. "Do you have something sharp?"

"What? No."

T reached into Nola's pocket and pulled out the glass seed dish. She took off the top and passed the bottom that held the seeds back to her.

"T, don't," Nola began, but T had already placed the lid on the ground and stomped on it, breaking the glass with a crunch. Without pausing, she reached down and picked up the largest piece of glass, moving it toward her neck.

"T, no." Catlyn grabbed T's hand. "You can't do that with the baby. You need all the blood you have to stay healthy."

"She needs to eat, or we won't make it out of here," T said.

"Then use me," Catlyn said. "You make the cut, and she can drink from me. I'm not growing a human life. I'm sure I have blood to spare."

The two women stared at each other for a moment before T raised the piece of glass to Catlyn's neck, making a small cut right above her shoulder.

Ruby drops formed on Catlyn's skin, sparkling in the artificial light of the hall.

"Thank you," Raina breathed.

"Well, eat up," Catlyn said. "I can't stand here bleeding all night."

Raina licked the first drop of blood that rolled down Catlyn's pale flesh. The hall spun for a second, but Nola couldn't look away as Raina lowered her mouth over the wound and greedily began to drink. Catlyn turned her head away and froze, never moving as Raina drank.

A faint tinkling sound cut through the air as T dropped the bit of glass she had used to slice Catlyn's flesh. Her fingers were bleeding, but she didn't seem to mind. Blood couldn't bother her if she had sold her own to the Vampers of Nightland. Pale scars lined the base of T's neck. Nola had never noticed them before.

I didn't want to look.

"Thank you," Raina said a few minutes later as she pulled away from Catlyn. Blood coated her lips, but rather than making her look like a monster, it made her look glamourous. Like the blood was nothing more than shiny red lipstick.

"Are you sure you don't need more?" Catlyn pressed her sleeve to her neck. The wound had nearly stopped bleeding.

"We can't afford to slow you down either." Raina grinned, showing red-stained teeth.

"Right." Nola spun to face the door. "When the hall is clear, you get out of here. I'll meet you at the way out."

With more confidence than she felt, Nola pulled the door to the cell corridor open and walked out into the barracks corridor. The two guards still stood at the stairs with their backs to her. Faint voices sounded in the barracks, but there were no longer people meandering around the hall.

Keeping her shoulders back, Nola walked toward the stairs, not looking at the guards as she passed them.

"Everything all right then?" one of the guards called up after her. The young one she had spoken to before. He smiled up at her expectantly as though hoping she would stay and talk to him more.

"Everything's fine." She forced herself to smile. "Well, I suppose as fine as things ever get these days. And thank you, for everything."

Nola climbed the steps, ignoring the sounds of the second guard laughing at the first. They were deep down in the tunnels, laughing, secure in their safety. How could they forget fires and blood so quickly?

As soon as she was up the first flight of steps and out of sight of the guards, Nola turned and walked a few feet down the hall leading off in the opposite direction of Bright Dome.

Heart racing, she opened her mouth to scream. "Ahh. Ouch! Help! Can you please help!" She let her voice wobble as she lay down on the floor, hoping her cry had been enough to illicit action but not panic.

"Miss Kent!" the young guard called up the stairs. Two sets of heavy foot-steps came running.

Both guards appeared at the top of the steps, weapons drawn.

"Miss Kent"—the young guard knelt next to her while the other's gaze swept the hall—"what happened? Have you been attacked?"

"No, I just"—Nola pushed herself halfway to sitting before falling back to the ground—"I was walking, and I got so dizzy. I fell, I think I hit my head."

"There weren't any intruders?" the second guard asked.

"No." Heat flooded Nola's cheeks. "I think I just panicked or something. I'm so sorry."

"We need to get you to the medical unit." The young guard moved to pick her up as the other turned back toward the stairs.

Not enough time.

"I can walk." Nola pushed herself to her feet, swayed, and toppled toward the guard who had been walking away.

"Careful!" the young guard shouted.

Nola clawed at the back of the other guard. He spun to face her, a look of fear on his face Nola felt sure he hadn't worn when fighting wolves.

Nothing more terrifying to a strong man than a fainting woman.

Nola hid her smile as she fell back to the floor, gasping for breath.

"I can't—" Nola wheezed. "I can't breathe!"

Both guards stared at her now.

"Please, I can't breathe!"

"Go get a doctor," the young guard said. The other turned to move, but Nola caught him by the front of his uniform, stopping him from turning just as four sets of feet crept by.

"No!" she said. "Home. Please, I want to go home."

"You need a doctor," the young guard said.

"No, I can't go see them again. Please." Nola pushed herself up to her elbows. "I've already been there today. I got hit on the head, and with the bridge..." Tears streamed from her eyes. "I really think I'm all right. I just want to go home."

"Are you sure?" The older guard stood and backed away.

"Really, thank you." Nola smiled wanly when the young guard helped her to her feet. "Please don't tell anyone about this. I don't think I can take being poked by a doctor again."

"Sure," the young guard said, easing his grip on her arm, "but if you keep not feeling your best, you might have to go see the doctor anyway. Don't let yourself get sick. Every citizen of the domes is needed, and needed healthy now more than ever."

Nola nodded and walked up the hallway, feeling their eyes on her. She wanted to rip her skin off, to get rid of every bit of flesh those guards had touched.

Needed healthy now more than ever. Breeding. He was talking about breeding.

Fighting the urge to run with every step, Nola walked up the corridor with a forced calm. She would have to go the long way around to Bright Dome. Stuck for even longer in the tunnels buried in the ground.

I'll never have to walk these tunnels ever again.

The thought stopped her in her tracks, the sheer weight of it locking her feet to the floor.

She was leaving her home. The only place she had ever lived. The place where she was born and learned to walk and talk. The place where her father had read to her at night, where she and Kieran had played in the trees. Where she had watched the gray smoke climb in the sky when her father died in a terrible riot in the city. Where she had watched them banish Kieran to the other side of the glass. Where she had let herself love Jeremy.

"I'm not abandoning the domes," Nola whispered to the empty hall. "The domes abandoned me."

Muscle memory brought her the rest of the way to Bright Dome and up the stone walkway to her house. If she listened hard, she imagined she could hear faint rustlings and whispers under the willow tree, but it wasn't time for her to join the others yet.

The lights in the house were off. It wasn't surprising that Lenora wasn't home. Nola wished for a moment that she were. That she could hug her mother one last time. But it would have made leaving harder, so perhaps the dark house was better after all.

It only took her a few minutes to steal the backpack from under her mother's bed. To pull on the warmest clothes she had and shove a few changes into the bag on top of the vials. She managed to empty the kitchen cabinets and fill the three bottles she could find with water so quickly it hardly seemed like she was moving at all. Only the heavy weight of the pack on her shoulders made it seem real.

"Goodbye," Nola said to the empty house, then walked out the door.

CHAPTER TWENTY-FIVE

Nola stayed off the path as she made her way to the willow tree. Night had fallen, and it was easy to slip unseen through the darkness.

"It's me." Nola stepped around the bushes to the open patch of grass behind the willow tree. The tiny space was crowded with four people crouching in it.

"Took you long enough," Raina said.

"We thought you might have been caught." Catlyn gave Nola's hand a squeeze.

"We all could be if we stay here," Beauford said.

"You'll be grateful I took my time when you have something to eat in the morning." Nola knelt with the others. "Could you get the pane out?"

"Mostly," Raina said, lifting a thin metal bar in her hand, "but it didn't seem right to pull it the rest of the way free without you."

"Where did you get that?" Nola asked.

The thing Raina held looked like a weapon. And sparkling on her hip was a knife, attached to a pair of worn leather pants that matched her leather top.

"Sweet, sweet Nola," Raina said. "Never, ever invade an enclosed environment without stashing a few backup supplies. I must say when I was slowly starving to death, I didn't think my extra bag of goodies was going to do me a damn bit of good, but what do you know? My hoarding paid off."

Raina kicked a bag with the tip of her toe. Dirt covered the canvas bag, as through it had been buried. T held up a small dagger and, now that she looked, Nola could see Catlyn and Beauford had weapons, too.

"Where did you bury them?" Nola reached for the bag. A narrow blade eight inches long was all that remained in the canvas sack.

"Outside your house, of course." Raina shrugged. "Now, if you've finished marveling at my brilliance and foresight, can we get to the escaping part of this escape?"

"Do it." There wasn't a trace of hesitation in Nola's voice.

Raina stood in the shadows and jammed the bar into the crack between the panes. It wasn't like when Doctor Wynne had pried the loose pane out with his fingers. The weakness Doctor Wynne had utilized had been sealed. But Raina was a vampire, and even the small bit of blood Catlyn had given her had brought back some of Raina's unnatural strength.

Nola held her breath, waiting for the pane of glass to move, but the glass wasn't sliding away. Thin lines formed in the pane, making a spider web just before the glass shattered with an ear-splitting *crack*. The sound rattled, echoing around the dome, but Raina didn't stop moving.

"Did you hear that?" a voice called on the other side of the trees.

"Is it the Vampers, Mommy?" a tiny voice asked, before the child started to howl.

Raina didn't pause to listen to the fear of the people who lived in Bright Dome. In seconds, there was another *crack* as the outer pane shattered.

"Go." Raina shoved T through the hole in the glass. Catlyn was out after her in a moment with Beauford close behind.

"You next," Raina whispered as voices drew closer.

"I'm not leaving you in here alone with children and a knife."

"Touché." Raina grinned and ducked through the glass.

"I think there's someone back there!" a voice shouted from not fifteen feet away. "Hello? Hello?"

"Someone call the guards!" a woman shrieked.

Nola dropped to her knees and crawled past the opening. Glass cut into her palms, but it didn't matter. In a few seconds, she was free.

A strong hand grabbed her under the arm, hoisting her to her feet. Nola bit back her scream as she saw Beauford steadying her, and they both ran down the hill, the other three following.

Raina quickly took the lead, tearing through the darkness at top speed.

Nola raced to catch up, her feet pounding against the ground.

She had found the way under the river once before, but it would take her time to do it on her own. They needed Raina if they wanted to beat the guards.

"T!" Catlyn shouted from behind.

Nola turned. T had fallen, panting, to the ground. She doubled back, wrapping her arm around one side of T's waist while Catlyn took the other.

"Keep running," Nola whispered. "We're going to find a safe place for your baby, but you have to keep running."

T swayed even while she ran but didn't stop moving.

A sharp wailing split the night as the domes' sirens blared.

Without speaking, Beauford dropped back to run behind the women, knife in hand. Nola wanted to tell him to run ahead with Raina, that a knife would do him no good against the Outer Guard's rifles, but she couldn't spare the breath.

The crisp, cool night air did nothing to help the burning in Nola's lungs. The shadows of the dead and dying trees looked like hands reaching out to grab them and drag them into some terrifying darkness. Every instinct told her to stop, to turn away from the shadows, but there was no time.

"The woods!" a voice shouted from up the hill. The Outer Guard had found them.

They reached the cover of the trees. Guns fired, breaking away chunks of wood that flew through the darkness, throwing the shadows into confusion. Raina ran ahead of them. Nola could only keep track of her by the shimmering of her hair in the pale light of the domes.

"Leave me," T panted. "They'll catch you. Please leave me."

"Not gonna happen." Beauford shoved Nola aside, lifting T in his arms and charging forward.

"This way." Nola took the lead, weaving through the trees as she followed Raina.

Shots cracked against the trees, but their trunks were too closely packed for the silver darts to find their marks. "Why are they firing at us?" Nola asked, her words coming out in gasps. "They can't hit us."

A string of sharp blasts sounded up ahead.

"They're corralling us," Catlyn said, running forward as fast as ever, a slight hunch of her shoulders the only sign that she knew the shots could hurt her.

They were getting close. With Bright Dome over to the left, they were nearly there. But they were too far back in the trees. They would need to run farther out to get to the way across the river.

"Come on." Nola ducked through the trees, barely making it in time to see Raina disappear into a shadow in the side of a tree.

Nola dived into the darkness, not stopping until she ran into a wall. She knew there were steps beneath her, but there was no way to see them.

Hands closed around her waist, lifting her over and down just as another person entered the darkness, panting. A faint grunt and thud told her Beauford and T had arrived.

"Slowly, down the steps," Raina whispered, so softly Nola could barely hear the words over her own breathing.

Nola reached her toe into the solid black, her hands stretched out in front of her, searching for a wall. She found one stair, and then another.

"Nola!"

Nola froze, teetering between steps.

"Nola!" Jeremy's voice ripped through the darkness. "Nola, where are you? Nola, please come out!"

He wasn't far away. She could hear him as though he were standing just beyond the tree.

Nola held her breath, waiting for lights to beam down on them and tiny silver needles to pierce their flesh.

"Raina, if you give Nola back to us unharmed, we will let you go. You can run off into the darkness and hide, and we won't ever come looking for you. But if you make her go with you, I will tear apart every piece of this planet to find her. When you sleep, I'll be hunting you. Where you feed, I will be tracking you."

There were shouts in the distance, men running the other way.

I hope they don't find a poor outsider.

"Nola," Jeremy called, his voice tighter than it had been before, "I know you're mad at me, at the domes. I know you think what we're doing is wrong, but it's not. You aren't one of them, Nola. Maybe they made you think you are, but you are a citizen of the domes. And whatever they have manipulated you into believing is a lie. I will fight to bring you home, Nola. With everything I have, I will fight for you. I love you, Magnolia Kent, and when you figure out everything they've been telling you is a lie, when you want to come home, I'll be here waiting. I promise."

Pain stabbed through her chest, puncturing the void that had protected her heart. He was shouting to the night that he loved her. That he would wait for her. But he didn't yet understand what she had done. And when he did...

He'll keep waiting for me.

Nola buried her face in her hands to muffle the sound of her tears. A cold hand took her elbow, leading her down the last few steps. A tiny scraping filled the darkness. It should have made her afraid, but she couldn't feel beyond the terrible pain in her chest.

The cold hand pulled her forward again, and the air changed, the chill tingle of outside air replaced by the stench of forgotten darkness.

Shuffling of feet and another faint scraping as the door shut behind them, then a *clink* as the door locked. It was done. Nola Kent had returned to Nightland.

CHAPTER TWENTY-SIX

"Can they get through the door?" Catlyn's whisper broke the silence.

"If they can find it," Raina murmured mere inches from of Nola's face. Nola gasped and stepped backward onto a foot.

"Watch it," Beauford said.

"Sorry." Nola stretched her hands out in front of her, moving away from the group.

"Well, if they can get through the door, don't you think we should get out of"—Catlyn's voice faded for a moment—"wherever it is we are?"

"It won't be easy in the dark. But hey"—Nola could hear the smile in Raina's voice—"who better to lead you through the dark than a creature of the night?"

"Comforting," Nola whispered.

"Take my hand, and follow the leader." Raina's cold fingers closed around Nola's wrist. She wanted to shout at Raina not to touch her, but she needed Raina to lead them.

A warm hand found Nola's other arm and moved down to take her hand.

"Catlyn?" Nola asked.

"It's me, Miss Kent," Catlyn said.

"Let me down, Beauford," T said from behind. "We aren't running now. I've caught my breath. I can walk on my own."

"Are you sure?" Catlyn asked.

"Positive," T said.

After a rustle of movement, Beauford said, "Ready back here."

"Look, an adventure in Nightland, how novel," Raina purred from the front.

"You know, I really didn't think I'd ever come back here. It's not as homey without lights."

"Are we in Nightland?" Catlyn spoke just loudly enough for her voice to carry to Raina.

It hadn't occurred to Nola that the others wouldn't know where they were. She had told them she knew a way under the river. But she hadn't told them how. She was too afraid that, were they given the information, they would leave her behind. Or worse, turn her in. They had slipped through a hidden shadow in a dead tree, and now they were in the dark. Gratitude swelled in her chest, and she squeezed Catlyn's hand. They had trusted her with their lives.

"We are in Nightland," Nola said. "At least a tunnel that leads to the main part under the city. This tunnel will take us under the river to the place where all the vampires used to live."

"Magnolia Kent, tour guide of darkness," Raina snorted.

"I never knew there was a tunnel to the other side of the river," T said. Her voice sounded shaky, but they didn't have time to stop and let her rest.

"It wasn't something Emanuel liked to advertise," Raina said. "Only a handful of people knew about the way to get to the domes. Hundreds of hungry, angry vampires living packed together, and you tell them it's only a short walk to make a meal out of the people they hate? Emanuel didn't think most would be able to resist the temptation. He didn't tell the masses until it was time to attack."

"Massacre," Nola said without anger in her voice. "It wasn't an attack. It was a massacre done by thieves. You weren't just killing guards."

"If you think that was a massacre, you clearly need to spend more time on the streets," Raina said. "Out here we call that a Thursday night."

A low laugh sounded from the back of the group.

"Oh, the big guy thinks I'm funny," Raina said.

"It's Beauford."

"Hmmm." Raina didn't say anything else as the tunnel sloped downward.

Nola shut her eyes against the darkness, trying not to think about the thick layers of dirt looming over her. But the air wasn't freshly filtered here like it was in the tunnels of the domes. The stench was enough to tell her the river above could kill them if it chose to.

"How did you even dig this?" Catlyn asked, as though reading Nola's mind for the question she hadn't wanted answered.

"A few old geologists and a lot of muscle. A few people dying, too, of course, but these things happen." Raina's words turned Nola's spine to jelly.

Each step became harder as her body decided on her behalf that there was no point in walking any farther. That the tunnel was just going to cave in and kill them anyway.

But Raina kept pulling her forward, keeping a steady pace, never seeming to doubt which way her feet should be going.

Then the tunnel angled upward.

"When we get to the other side of the tunnel door, there might be some people around," Raina said. "Try not to get killed or lost. I'm not going to waste my time running around Nightland searching for lost lambs."

"We just have to get through Nightland to the street," Nola said. "Once we get up there, you can take us to Emanuel."

"Absolutely." Raina's pace slowed. "I just have to run one little errand first."

"Errand?" T asked.

"It's only a little out of the way. And besides, you can't go anywhere without me." Raina stopped suddenly, and Nola rammed into her back.

"Fine," Nola said, "but make it quick. If the Outer Guard find the tunnel and figure out where we are, we won't be able to get to the street. Then we'll never find Emanuel."

"Quick as a genetically-modified bunny." Raina let go of Nola's hand.

The high screech of metal grinding against stone cut through the darkness. The air changed again as Raina led them forward. The dampness lessened, replaced by the stench of filth and stale blood.

"This way." Raina took her hand again, pulling her through the pitch black.

Nola knew where they were now. In the main body of Nightland, where tunnels split off in every direction. There were dozens of halls and hundreds of doors.

"Will you be able to find your way in the dark?" Nola asked as the door scraped shut behind them.

"Do you have a flashlight you've been hiding?" Raina said.

"No."

"Well then, I guess I'll have to find my way in the scary dark," Raina said. "Try not to ask stupid questions while I'm concentrating."

Nola bit her lips together and followed obediently. She hadn't packed a flashlight. It hadn't even occurred to her while she tossed what she thought she would need for the outside world into a bag.

What else did I forget?

"There used to be electricity down here," T said. "In all the tunnels I ever saw. More electricity than we had in the houses aboveground. I wonder why it stopped running."

"No one to keep it going?" Catlyn said.

"Or the guards cut it off," Beauford said.

"Not all of it," Nola said, squinting as far up the tunnel as she could see. A dim light glowed in the distance, flickering like some kind of flame.

"Well, shit," Raina said.

"Wha—" Before Nola could fully form the word, a shout sounded from the back of the group.

"Beauford!" Catlyn screamed.

But thudding and grunting were the only response.

"Dammit." Raina let go of Nola's hand and a *swish* sounded, like a knife clearing its sheath.

Someone screamed, but Nola couldn't tell who. Her hand fumbled for the knife in her waistband. Before she could find it, something had grabbed the back of her pack and thrown her against the wall.

"Don't touch me!" T screamed. "I am carrying a child of Nightland!"

Her words made the sounds of the fight change but didn't stop a hand from closing over Nola's mouth and wrenching her head sideways. She kicked back as hard as she could, sinking her teeth into the hand that held her.

The sickening taste of blood filled her mouth, but the person holding her only laughed. With a twist of her arm, she pulled her knife free and plunged it behind her. The thin blade cut into flesh, but the one holding her kept laughing. A high, maniacal laugh accompanied by warm breath that touched her neck and crawled across her skin.

Nola pulled the knife back out and stabbed again, and again. On the sixth stab, she managed to hit higher than before, and the one who held her finally seemed to register the pain. With a howl, he pushed her away. She flew sideways, tripping over something that lay on the ground before hitting the opposite wall. Her knife slipped out of her hand. In the darkness, not even a faint shimmer of metal told her where it might have landed.

"You pricked me!" a low voice growled.

Nola dropped to her knees, feeling frantically around in the dirt. A person lay on the floor, warm blood pooling around them, but Nola didn't have time to wonder who the person might be. Her fingers found something hard as a hand closed around her neck.

"What makes you think you can stab me?" the voice shouted, at the same time another voice that sounded horribly like Catlyn's screamed.

Nola grasped the metal thing as she was lifted into the air by her neck. The sharp blade of the knife cut into her palm. She wanted to drop it, to make the shooting pain stop, to claw away the hand that choked her so easily.

But she grabbed the hilt of the knife with her other hand and swung it down toward the arm that held her. The blade cut deep into the man's flesh, the force of it nearly pulling the knife from her grip. The fingers loosened, and she crumpled to the ground, but she didn't drop the knife this time. She dove into the darkness and stabbed. The man bellowed in pain as she sank her knife into every part of him she could find.

A scream tore from her throat, but she didn't know how to make the noise stop. The only thing she could think was to kill the man. Kill the Vamper so his hand couldn't close around her throat again. She couldn't see where his heart would be, so she knelt and stabbed again and again. Cold hands closed around her wrists.

"I've got it." Raina lifted Nola off the man's chest. "Give me some space. It's not easy decapitating someone in the dark with a knife."

Nola sat back on the ground. Both of her hands touched blood. She was surrounded by it, a sea of unseeable red.

"Is everyone okay?" Nola's voice wavered.

"I'm fine," T said from farther down the hall.

"One of the Vampers bit me," Beauford said. "But I'll live."

"I think," Catlyn wheezed from right behind Nola, "I think I might not."

CHAPTER TWENTY-SEVEN

"What?" T said. Footsteps sounded as she came closer. "What happened?" Nola felt her way toward Catlyn's voice, climbing over a body in the darkness. "Where are you hurt?"

"Too many places, Miss Kent." Catlyn coughed a laugh. "I don't know which bits are bleeding worst."

"Catlyn, you're going to be all right." Beauford's hands brushed past Nola, reaching for Catlyn. A sharp intake of breath told Nola what he felt wasn't good. "We need Vamp. Raina, we need Vamp."

"Give her to me," Raina said, moving past Nola who felt Catlyn's body rise as Raina lifted her. "I know where there'll be some."

"No Vamp," Catlyn said. "If you can't save me, don't give me Vamp. I won't live without the sun."

"We have ReVamp." Raina ran down the hall.

Nola took off after them, charging toward the distant flickering light.

"ReVamp is different," Raina said, not showing any signs of being out of breath, despite carrying a full-grown woman while she ran. "You'll still be you. No personality changes, no violent urges. You'll have to deal with drinking blood and living in the dark, but it's a hell of a lot better than death."

"Not for me," Catlyn croaked.

"Then we'll help you without Vamp or ReVamp," T said. "We'll clean the wounds and bandage you up and you'll be just fine."

"You know better than that, T," Catlyn murmured.

"I won't give up on you."

They reached the light just in time for Nola to see tears streaming down T's face as they ran.

Nola glanced back at Beauford. He ran slower than the rest, barely keeping up as he tried to stop the blood that flowed from a bite mark on his arm.

Torches lined the halls here. The torches hadn't been there when Nola had walked the corridors with Kieran. Someone had left them. People were living in Nightland again.

We can't survive more Vampers.

"Catlyn!" T shouted as Catlyn's eyes drifted shut. "Catlyn!"

But Catlyn didn't open her eyes, and her head bounced with each step Raina took.

"Who's down there?" a voice called from around a corner.

Raina dodged into a side hall and kept running. The electric lights were still working in this corridor though half of the bulbs had shattered.

"Where is the Vamp?" Beauford asked.

"I don't know if we're going to be able to get into Emanuel's house," Nola said. "If there are people living down here, I don't know a place more appealing than Emanuel's."

"That's not where the ReVamp is." Raina turned another corner, ducking into a side passage when the sounds of boisterous laughter carried to them from up ahead.

"She needs it now," Beauford said. His steps had grown uneven, and blood dripped from his fingertips. If it got much worse, Catlyn wouldn't be the only one who needed a dose of ReVamp.

They turned into a narrow corridor. The few doors that lined the walls hung loosely from their hinges. Dark stains coated the ground. Chunks of the stone wall had been knocked free.

Raina slowed to a walk.

"We don't have time for this." Beauford moved past Nola to Raina.

"We're here." Raina laid Catlyn on the ground.

The weight of all the earth above them crashed down into Nola's stomach.

A ragged bite marked Catlyn's neck, a deep wound on her shoulder looked like nails had ripped her flesh away, and a gash that reached from her ribs to her stomach left her entire torso drenched in blood.

Crack.

Raina kicked the wall five feet away from Catlyn.

Crack.

Dust and rocks fell to the ground.

"Please don't." T stepped forward, but Raina kicked the wall again.

Crack!

A two-foot square of wall crumbled away.

Blowing the hair out of her eyes, Raina reached into the wall and pulled out a dust-covered, silver case.

"Out of the way," Raina said, but T didn't step aside.

"Move!" Raina growled, opening the box and pulling out a needle.

"I can't." T's voice sounded like she had been ill for months.

"Do not make me be the bad guy who throws a pregnant girl against a wall."

"I can't let you give her that shot." T raised her chin, staring defiantly at Raina.

"You can't let me save your friend's life?" Raina shook her head and moved to sidestep T, but T blocked her path again.

"She doesn't want the drugs." Tears streamed down T's face. "Not Vamp or ReVamp, not Lycan or anything else. She doesn't want it."

"I doubt she wants to die either," Raina spat. "Take it from someone who just kicked a hole through a stone wall without breaking a sweat. Drinking a little blood is way more fun than dying."

"Not for her," T whispered. "Catlyn has lived a long, hard life. Who are we to take her death from her? She said she would rather die. If that's what she wants, then we have to let her go."

"Let her go? Let her go!" Raina laughed. "And where do you think she'll be going? We certainly won't be able to bury her. We could leave her here in case a wolf gets hungry. If they don't want her, I'm sure the bugs and the rats will have a fine feast."

"Stop." Nola leaned against the wall.

"And where will she be when there's nothing left but bones and rot?" Raina stepped so close to T their faces were nearly touching. "She doesn't want to live in the darkness? Darkness is all that waits for her as she decays into nothing."

"Stop it!" Nola's scream echoed against the walls. "Catlyn didn't want to be a vampire. She wanted to die, so let her do it. She died escaping the domes, let that be her end."

"How poetic." Raina held the needle in her hand up to the dim light. A faint, shimmering liquid, so thin it could barely be seen, filled the needle. In a practiced motion, she rolled up her sleeve and shoved the needle into her vein, sighing as she pressed the serum into her blood. "Fine, more ReVamp for me." She looked at Nola, her eyes shining a darker black than they had a moment before. "Or anyone else who actually wants to survive to see Emanuel." She tossed the needle against the wall, and it clattered to the ground with a finality that shook Nola more than the hand around her throat had.

"Catlyn." T knelt down next to her.

Catlyn didn't look like she was breathing.

She might already be dead.

"Thank you." T pressed Catlyn's bloody hand to her lips. "Thank you for taking care of a lost girl. Rest well, my friend, and never know pain again." She laid Catlyn's hand on her torn stomach and stood. "We should go."

"Is she dead?" Beauford asked.

"Close enough." T wiped her hands on her pants, but it didn't take away the bloodstains. "We have to go. Catlyn wouldn't want us to risk ourselves to watch her die."

"She'll never *want* anything again," Raina said.

"How do we get out of here?" Nola asked. If they were going to leave Catlyn lying in a hall, it was better to do it quickly before the evilness of abandonment set in.

"There's a back way." Raina relocked the silver case. "It'll be easier to get to but nasty once we hit open air."

"Will there be a place for daylight?" T asked. "We can't have much longer until sunrise."

"I know a place," Raina said. "If we're lucky, I won't even have to kill anyone to get us in."

CHAPTER TWENTY-EIGHT

Raina led them farther down the hall where the ReVamp had been hidden, moving past more broken doors and shattered light bulbs.

"In here." Raina lead them through one of the dingiest-looking doors.

Someone had scrawled words onto it. A long string of something Nola didn't take the time to read.

The room was so small, the light from the hall lit the four cracked walls. Not pausing, Raina headed to a tiny closet in the back. Fabric had been tacked to the wall. Raina pulled it aside, revealing a tiny trap door.

"Big guy might have some trouble." Raina knelt and yanked a wooden panel out of the wall. "Anyone who minds a tight squeeze can feel free to head out the front."

"You first," Nola said.

Please let it be caved in.

It was an irrational thought. They needed to get out of Nightland before they were attacked again. They couldn't risk another fight. Not after Catlyn.

Nola's chest tightened. Grief and panic flooded her.

Raina slithered into the hole. In few seconds, all that showed were her feet.

"Come on in," Raina said. "Nothing here but a little vampire."

"I'll go." T knelt next to the hole.

For a moment, Nola was afraid her stomach wouldn't fit, but with little more struggle than Raina, she disappeared.

"You next," Beauford said.

"I can go last." Nola shook her head. She needed a minute, just one more minute outside the terrifyingly small space.

"I'm going last, and I'm not going to argue with you. Get in the damn hole."

Nola nodded, not trusting her voice to work, and knelt outside the tunnel.

A creaking sounded behind her. She spun to see Beauford closing the door. Everything melted into black.

"We can't afford to be followed," Beauford whispered over the sound of footsteps coming toward her.

"Right." Nola reached her hands out in front of her, feeling the edges of the tunnel. Her backpack was too big to fit through the gap on her back. She would have to push it in front of her.

For how long?

She closed her eyes and slipped off her pack, pushing it into the tunnel.

"A little faster if you don't want us to die," Beauford whispered.

Lying down on her stomach, Nola slid into the tunnel. Dragging herself forward with her hands, she moved a few feet before pushing up onto her hands and knees. The ceiling touched the back of her jacket, but she could still move forward. Push the backpack, move forward a foot. Push the backpack, move forward a foot.

"Nola, Beauford?" T said, from what seemed like miles in front of Nola. "Are you coming?"

Yes. Nola thought the word, but it didn't make any sound. "Yes."

"It gets a little tighter up here. Make sure you watch your head."

Tighter. The tunnel got tighter.

She dug her nails into the dirt and stone beneath her.

Catlyn was right to want to die in Nightland. It was better than dying trapped in a tunnel.

Nola's breathing quickened as the blackness around her spun.

"Are you all right?" Beauford said. "Miss Kent, are you okay?"

"I-I c-can't move," she whimpered, fighting for each bit of air she pulled into her lungs. "There's no air. I can't breathe."

"You can breathe. There's air just in front of you. Move ahead, and there'll be air."

Nola didn't think her arms were capable of moving, but Beauford's words made sense. There had to be air somewhere. It couldn't have all disappeared at once.

"Just move up a foot, and there'll be air," Beauford said.

Shaking, she pushed the backpack a foot ahead and crawled after it.

"See, it's better already, isn't it?" Beauford's voice sounded closer now. "Think how good it will be in another foot. Go on. Try one more foot."

The air didn't feel better. It was thick and stale, too fleeting for her lungs to grasp.

But Beauford sounded so sure. "You're nearly to the open air now. If you move just another foot, you'll be able to smell it. Just one more foot."

Nola nodded in the darkness. One more foot. One more foot, and she could breathe.

The process went on and on. Beauford urging her to move, Nola fighting for every inch she gained.

"Nola." The darkness changed as the backpack was pulled out of Nola's path. Shadows replaced the thick pitch black.

A cold hand grabbed her wrist and dragged her out of the tunnel and onto a wooden floor.

"I thought you might have died in there," Raina said, without a trace of concern in her voice.

Nola rolled onto her back, panting.

The air here smelled thick with dust and the scent of decay she had only ever smelled in the woods.

"Is she all right?" Beauford asked.

"I'm..." Nola began but couldn't spare the breath to finish saying she was fine now that there was air.

"I think the Domer might be a little claustrophobic. Funny being afraid of small spaces when there are monsters in the world," Raina said.

"I know there are monsters." Nola sat up, regretting it as her head spun. "But being trapped in the dark with no air feels worse. You can't fight air."

"How...literal." Raina pulled back the thick curtains that covered the window, letting faint light into the dismal room.

The wooden floor was worn, warped, and dirty. Dust coated the peeling wallpaper, which looked far older than Nola. A chair had been broken apart and tossed by the filthy fireplace that showed no signs of having been recently lit.

"Where are we?" Nola stood.

Beauford took her elbow to steady her. "Careful, Miss Kent."

"Nola. Please call me Nola."

"Nola," Beauford said. "Be careful."

"Fantastic." Raina grinned sarcastically. "If we're finished, we should probably get to a safe place before dawn."

"This isn't the safe place?" Nola said.

"You're never safe near the escape. It's too easy to be found." Raina rolled her dark eyes as though Nola were the biggest idiot she had ever met. "What we need to do is disappear into the vastness of the city. The Outer Guard might be able to follow us through the tunnels, but they'll have one hell of a time following us through the streets."

"They'll tear the city apart to find us." Nola picked up the pack and settled it on her back. The weight of it seemed to have doubled while they were in the tunnel.

"I'm sure they will." Raina shrugged. "But it'll take time. And the farther we get from here, the longer it will take them. With any luck, by this time tomorrow night we'll be outside the city and on our way to Emanuel."

"Then let's get going." Beauford headed toward the one door in the room. His own blood coated his arm from the vampire bite.

"Wait." Nola slid the pack off her back. "You need medicine for your arm."

"Later." Beauford shook his head. "When we're safe. I'll survive until then."

"Smart man." Raina pushed past him and opened the door. "Try and stay close. You'll all be scented in a minute, and I really don't feel like fighting a bunch of wolves before dawn." She walked out into the hall. Beauford followed, but T stood behind Nola, carefully rolling up her shirt to show her swollen belly.

"You should go next," T said. "It'll be safer with me in the back."

"Why?" Nola asked. The floor squeaked as she walked across it, every step shouting to the world where they were.

"I know the outside must seem dark and lawless to you," T said, following Nola into the hall, "but there are some rules almost everyone will follow. I'm pregnant. Only the worst wolves would hurt me."

"Because you're carrying a vampire's baby? If you were carrying a werewolf's baby, would only the worst vampires hurt you?"

"Basically," T whispered her answer.

Closed doors lined the derelict hall. The smell of stale food permeated the air, and people spoke angrily behind one of the doors.

Nola took a few quick steps to catch up to Beauford, shoving aside the terrible feeling someone could pop out and grab her at any moment.

A big, wooden door blocked the end of the hall.

She tapped Beauford on the good arm and whispered softly, "What is this place?"

"An apartment building," Raina answered from the front in a carrying, conversational tone. "I'm sure you've never seen one. But out here a lot of people consider themselves lucky to live in a place this nice. Solid walls, sturdy doors. I think there's even running water in this one."

The door at the end of the hall burst open. Five men came in, laughing and staggering. One of them fell face-first onto the ground as he tried to cross the threshold.

"Ah, company!" the man at the front of the pack shouted, holding his arms out wide. "Look, boys, the party isn't over after all!"

"Yes, it is." Raina rested her hand on the hilt of her knife.

"The kitten has teeth!" one of the other men laughed.

"This *tigress* has fangs." Raina stalked toward the men. "And she likes to bite. She even likes blood. Anyone here want to give me a snack?"

"Don't be angry," the first man said, taking a step back and stumbling over his friend who still lay on the floor.

"Watch yourself!" the man on the ground shouted.

"I was only playing." Fear filled the first man's face. "I didn't mean anything by it. You be on your way and enjoy the rest of your night."

Raina backed the man into the wall. "Oh, we'll go." She leaned in so her cheek rested on his. "But what if I hadn't been a vampire? What if the kitty you wanted to play with hadn't had claws? What if I had been a poor defenseless little girl lost in the night?"

"I-I don't—"

"Sure you do," Raina cooed. "You would have taken me into the shadows whether I liked it or not."

She pulled her blade from its sheath and pressed the tip to the man's forehead without looking at her hand.

The man moaned in pain, but his friends did nothing.

"Next time, think before you decide someone is your prey, little pig. You'd make an excellent meal." She stepped back, lifting the blade to her mouth and licking away the single drop of blood that clung to its tip. "And now you're on the menu. Avoid dark hallways, little pig."

Kissing the man on the cheek, Raina turned and walked out the door.

She'd carved *V* into the man's forehead. The mark dripped blood down his nose and into his eyes.

"Come on." T strode through the men, and Nola followed, nearly stepping on T's heels as she escaped the hallway.

The sky was still dark, the faint moonlight leaving the streets as terrifying as the hallway had been. Raina led them down a long row of apartment buildings much like the one they had just left. Most were at least five stories tall, and each was broken down and sad in its own way. One missing a front door. Another with all the widows at the ground level shattered. Another had *Night Filth* scrawled across its bricks in bright red paint.

"You didn't have to do that to him," T said as soon as she caught up to Raina.

Walking behind them, a terrifying loneliness clawed at Nola's stomach until Beauford took his place next to her.

"She was right to do it," Beauford said.

"See, the big one agrees with me," Raina said, no hint in her voice that she actually cared what any of them thought.

"It's only a cut," Nola said. "I'm sure he'll heal."

"It's a v-shaped cut right on his face," T spoke through clenched teeth. "She just marked him as a meal. If he keeps showing his face outside at night, he'll be lucky to survive the week."

"Don't think of it as my limiting the time frame of his disgusting little life. Think of it as my giving him an opportunity to realize the error of his ways and have time to seek atonement in this cruel world."

Raina rounded a corner and headed down a street where the sidewalks had been piled high with trash. The sign on the corner read *Maggot Row*, and Nola didn't have to question where the street had gotten its name.

Raina moved to the very center of the street where a three-foot-wide path cut between mounds of rotting garbage.

The smell of decay hit Nola so hard, bile gurgled into her throat, but Raina and T kept moving forward, arguing about the man. Nola covered her nose with the collar of her jacket and tried to keep from wondering what had created the sticky squish under her feet.

"You condemned that man," T said. "He is going to die because you cut him."

"So I should have killed him in the hall?" Raina rounded on T, blocking the way forward.

Nola shook as the piles of trash seemed to creep closer and closer.

"Or should I have stepped aside and let those monsters do whatever they wanted to Nola? Hell, even big boy might have had a moment to shine with the cretins."

"That's not what—" T argued.

"Then I should have made them walk nicely away and let them find another girl who doesn't have a vampire with a knife trying to keep her alive and see what they do to her? There are far worse monsters in this world than I will ever be, little girl. Don't blame me for getting rid of one." Raina turned and walked through the alley between trash, not bothering to check if any of them followed.

"She doesn't understand," T began, but Beauford cut her off.

"She understands perfectly. You of all people should appreciate that. Now move before someone else comes along and Raina ends up killing them more quickly."

T opened and closed her mouth several times before biting her lips together and stepping carefully behind Nola and Beauford, waving a hand to tell them to move.

"Do you really think those men would have hurt us?" Nola asked as she and Beauford jogged after Raina.

"Yes." Beauford's single, apathetic word sent a shiver down Nola's spine.

She had chosen the outside, left everything she had to join it, to help save the humans in a monstrous world. It had never occurred to her that humans could be the ones she would need saving from.

CHAPTER TWENTY-NINE

They didn't speak as Raina led them through the city. The rows of trash finally ended, leaving them on a street that looked like it had recently seen a battle. The outsides of the buildings here were dented and cracked, like a hundred Rainas had decided they hated the bricks for existing.

No one was in sight, but Nola could sense people waiting just out of view. In the shadows behind rusted and burned out old cars. Lurking in the wooden crates that leaned against the buildings, their fronts covered in cloth as though hiding a sleeping person within.

Raina never paused, leading them down a street that had been taken by fire. The lopsided skeletons of the buildings were completely covered in black ash, but people slept within the ruins, huddled in thin blankets against the cold.

Raina turned onto a street unlike any of the others. A long row of houses with streetlights keeping the shadows at bay. There were no signs of fighting or fires here. The fronts of these buildings were well tended, and the only scent in the air was the perpetual stench of decay that was impossible to avoid in the city.

Six men appeared from the shadows as they approached.

"Stay right there," the first man said. He was tall and broad with a bat resting over his shoulder.

"Oh really?" Raina sauntered forward. "And I suppose you're going to make me?"

"Ma'am, this is a private street." The man with the bat stepped in front of Raina. "We can't have any trespassers."

"You must be new," Raina said. "My name is Raina, and if you want to keep your blood in your pathetic little veins, I suggest you step aside and apologize at once."

The man swallowed hard, his gaze traveling from Raina's black eyes to her scarlet-and-purple streaked hair, finally landing on her knife in its sheath.

"I apologize, Miss Raina." The man bowed deeply, keeping his eyes continually on the knife. "I was told you were dead."

"Death can be so hard to define these days," Raina said. "If you scamper like a good little guard and don't bother me again, I'll let you live. How's that?"

"Yes, Miss Raina." The man bowed again, backing away. "Thank you, Miss Raina."

The other guards followed, never taking their eyes off Raina as they disappeared into the shadows.

"They are adorable." Raina sighed. "Little, naïve things who think they can keep away the boogeymen."

"Who are they?" Nola whispered as they moved down the street. The windows in the buildings were dim, but the streetlights glinted off delicate curtains and plants resting on windowsills. "What is this place?"

"The guards were guards," Raina said, "and this is what we on the outside call a nice neighborhood. When the world falls apart, it doesn't happen all at the same rate. The people who live here own the factories that supplied the domes, are a part of the vague thing we like to call city government, or are just plain rich enough to pretend the city they live in isn't rapidly burning to the ground."

"It's pretty." Nola smiled as they passed a house with a bright blue door. "How many other places are there like this?"

"None," Beauford said. "Not anymore. There used to be a few streets like this."

"But Bellevue is the last one left." Raina ran up the stairs to a house and banged on the door. "Every time something horrible happened, another one of the nice streets would disappear. They'd rot gradually or burn magnificently, but either way they'd be gone. This is the last façade in the dying city."

Lights flicked on in the windows that flanked the door. A silhouette appeared, holding what looked like a handgun.

"Whoever you are, you had better get the hell off my steps and go back to wherever you came from!" a female voice shouted from inside the house.

"Tsk, tsk." Raina leaned into the crack by the doorjamb. "You really shouldn't swear like that. It's completely unbecoming of a lady."

The door swung open.

"You?" The woman from inside stepped toward Raina, pointing a gun directly into her face. "What are you doing here?"

"Is this any way to begin a homecoming?" Raina asked.

"I told you never to come back here." The woman stepped closer to Raina. She looked to be in her mid-fifties. Gray mixed in with her long, dark hair, and fine lines surrounded her full lips. "I told you, you don't belong here."

"I would take you at your word, but the guards backed away so nicely when I told them I'd come to pay a call on my baby sister," Raina said.

"I can call them over here right now," the woman said. "I won't let you bring your fighting and blood into this house."

"We aren't looking for a fight." T stepped forward. She moved with her bare belly pushed out, making her pregnancy more obvious than ever. "There are some bad people who are looking for us, and all we want is a place to sleep out of their way until we can leave. We only need a place for one day."

"You bring a pregnant girl to my house with some blood-covered tramps and expect me to have sympathy for any of you? Gah." The woman swung the door to the house fully open and stepped aside to let them in. "I want to know exactly what fresh hell you have brought to my door, Raina."

"*Our* door, little sister," Raina said as she shut and locked the door behind her. "Remember, sweet mommy and daddy left the place to both of us."

"You really are sisters?" Nola looked from one to the other.

"Of course Nettie and I are sisters." Raina pinched Nettie's cheeks.

"My name is not *Nettie*," Nettie growled.

"Call her Nettie." Raina smirked.

"I don't care what you tell the bloody little girl to call me, but please tell me why you're in my house and—"

"Our house."

"—who the hell is after you," Nettie finished.

"Language, little sister," Raina warned, locking eyes with Nettie in a glare neither of them seemed willing to break.

"The domes' Outer Guard," Nola finally said. "They were holding Raina and the other three…" Nola's voice trailed away. "The other two captive. They found out we escaped, and now they're looking for us."

"Captured by the domes?" Nettie raised a dark eyebrow. "Impressive even for you. But you didn't say where you"—she pointed her gun at Nola—"little bloody girl, come into play."

"She's a Domer," Raina said. "A Domer with a heart of gold who just had to save us poor outsiders locked in cells. Or you could say she's the infamous Nola Kent and has seen too much of the world to pretend it doesn't exist. Too bad poor *bloody girl* doesn't have a better imagination. She could be sleeping in her own bed right now."

"For God's sake, Raina, don't be rude to the infamous Nola Kent. If rumors are true, it's your lot's fault the city's going to shit more quickly than ever."

"Why thank you." Raina bowed.

"And thank you for bringing fugitives into my—"

"Our."

"—house," Nettie spat. "The last thing I need is a load of Outer Guard busting down my front door."

"You really hate that this is my house, too." Raina walked down the hall and rounded a corner. "Come on, you lot, enjoy *my* lavish living room."

"Fine, go," Nettie said, "but please don't get any blood or muck on the upholstery. It's nigh on impossible to replace these days."

"Still keeping up appearances as the world crumbles?" Raina lay sprawled out on a bright red couch in the center of the room, facing a fireplace that took up most of one wall. In one corner of the room sat a marble table, supporting a vase filled with silk flowers, while in another, a matching table held a sparkling decanter filled with amber liquid.

"I like to take good care of my things." Nettie stalked to the corner and poured herself a glass from the crystal decanter. The strong scent of liquor wafted across the room. "And get your feet off the couch."

Raina hesitated before lowering her feet to the floor. "Only because you're being so sweet to our guests."

"Anyone who is mixed up with you will need as much help as they can possibly get." Nettie held her glass in the air before taking a long drink. "The sun should be up in an hour or so. How many can't stand the sunlight?"

"Only me, baby Nettie," Raina said. "The others are human as human can be."

"Well, there is something in that." Nettie downed the rest of her glass. "You get in the dark room. I'll take the rest to get cleaned up before my whole house is covered in bloody footprints."

"How kind of you to worry about our carpet." Raina stood. "You three find me when you've finished washing and sleeping...and dealing with Nettie. If the world hasn't ended by then." With one last glare at Nettie, Raina sauntered out of sight.

"How pleasant," Nettie growled.

"Thank you for your hospitality," Nola said. "Your house is beautiful."

"Thanks." Nettie studied Nola, starting from her toes and moving all the way up. She turned to the decanter and poured herself a fresh drink. "I suppose if I am going to be caught with a fugitive, it might as well be a runaway Domer."

"The men outside," Beauford asked, stepping in between Nola and Nettie, "can they be trusted? If they find out the domes are looking for us, will they tell them to knock on your door?"

"Those men would protect the occupants of Bellevue Avenue with their lives." Nettie waved her drink precariously through the air. "And they have no love for the domes besides. No, the damn Outer Guard will have to track you themselves."

"But won't they know Raina's your sister?" Nola asked. "I mean, if she really is your sister."

"Raina *was* my sister." Nettie smiled ruefully. "A very long time ago. But as for them tracing that colorful-haired Vamper to my home, impossible. The Raina who was my sister is dead."

T stepped forward, reaching out to shake Nettie's hand. "Well then, thank you even more for taking us in."

"Coming from the pregnant girl who I would be a monster to leave on the streets, that means so much." Nettie raised her glass in salute.

"I've been on the street before," T said. "You are being good taking us in, not just avoiding being bad."

"Oh good God, the types my sister drags into this damn house." Nettie rolled her eyes. "Come have a bath and sleep. Wherever Raina is leading you, I doubt they'll have water as clean as I do, let alone warmed for a bath."

"You have clean water?" Nola asked, moving quickly to match Nettie's stride out of the living room. She hadn't noticed the fine blue wallpaper when they had been in the hall a few moments before, or the big wooden staircase that led to the upper level.

"Not clean by dome standards." Nettie shrugged. "But nothing really is. And aren't impurities what make life worth living?" She took another sip of her drink before heading up the stairs. "I'm going to put you all in one room, and, no offense, I'm locking you in. You seem quite nice, but I have met too many of my sister's compatriots to be able to go back to sleep knowing any of them are wandering the halls."

"We understand," Nola said. "Thank you for letting us stay."

"How gracious of me, I know," Nettie said. "I'll send a touch of food, and the water is drinkable. Try not to get blood on anything."

Nettie swung open the door to a bedroom. T went in first, whistling at the sight of whatever waited inside, Beauford followed after her, but Nola didn't want to let Nettie leave. "You said she's your big sister. Raina, I mean."

Nettie took another drink from her glass. "Yes, little Domer covered in blood, she was my big sister."

T's voice came from within the room. "Can I go first? Do you mind if I go first?"

"But she's, I mean you're—" Nola fumbled for the words.

"Older?" Nettie laughed. "Grayer, smaller, and a bit more sane? Yes, that I am."

"How?" But the answer had already formed in Nola's mind. "Vamp. It's the Vamp. It stops you from aging?"

"They don't tell you anything locked behind the glass, do they? You do age once you've turned to Vamp. Only much more slowly. My sister decided to hide in the darkness a long time ago, and so she's stuck living in the night. A long life without sunrises. It's the blessing and the curse of the damned stuff. And why they can't give it to children. Their bodies need to grow but the Vamp won't let them. So child zombies wander until they rot. Charming, isn't it? A life that won't allow living."

"But if it saves people from dying," Nola said, "doesn't that make it worth it? I mean, not for zombie babies, but for adults. Doesn't the choice come down to vampire or death?"

"For most." Nettie shrugged. "And most definitely for you. But some can skate by living under the ever-killing sun. Forgive me, bloody girl, a few sips of this amazing stuff and I become quite philosophical." She waved Nola toward the open doorway. "Go sleep. I doubt anyone will kill you before it's time to wake up. But for the love of all that survives in this cruel, dark world, please wash your face, child."

She shoved Nola into the room, and a moment later a heavy lock *thunked* behind her.

CHAPTER THIRTY

Nola stood by the locked door, unable to move. The bedroom was different than anything she had ever seen before. It looked like something out of an old novel. A canopy of deep red fabric hung over a four-poster bed, which was wide enough for three people to sleep comfortably in and had a fluffy quilt that perfectly matched the canopy. A fainting couch covered in gold fabric sat at the foot of the bed.

Thick carpeting, so beautiful Nola felt terrible standing on it, covered the floor. And T's voice drifted from the back of the room as she hummed to herself over the sound of running water.

"It's"—Beauford chewed his bottom lip—"something, isn't it?"

"We don't have things like this in the domes." Nola unlaced her boots, leaving them by the door. "I mean, I know we have a lot, but this"—she ran her fingers over the quilt—"this is amazing. I didn't think things like this existed anymore."

"They do." Beauford sat on the fainting couch. "The world didn't end when the domes sealed their walls. At least not entirely. Millions and millions of people have died. More than that have turned to things like Vamp and Lycan to save themselves. But some people profit from death. Some can afford those who call themselves doctors. They'll be the last to go. Or the next. It all depends."

"Depends on what?" she asked, silently sliding the pack off her back and carefully unzipping it.

"Who takes over first." Beauford stared down at his hands. "The domes will let the rich ones out here live because they aren't hurting the domes. They don't need help. They don't want trouble. They are above and below the domes' notice all at once."

Nola pulled the tub of thick blue goo out of her pack.

"But the vampires hate the ones who have managed to survive in comfort on the outside without turning to Vamp. The ones who can afford water purifiers and gardened food. They hate them for proving Vamp isn't the only way to live. So, if the vampires or the wolves manage to take power, Bellevue and the last of the outside luxury are gone."

"But the wolves have already won." She knelt on the couch next to Beauford. His sleeve was fairly intact, but the wound on his arm showed through. "The Outer Guard won't stop them, so why aren't they here?"

She rolled up Beauford's sleeve, expecting with every movement that he would push her away and shout that he didn't need help. But he only watched as she scooped blue goo from the jar and dabbed it onto his arm.

"Because the wolves haven't won. Not really," Beauford said. "The Outer Guard could come across the river and kill them. The vampires in the city could band together and rise up, and worst of all Nightland could return and demand their city back."

"But wouldn't it make sense to take care of Bellevue while they have the chance?" Nola screwed the top of the tub back into place. "Then they can tick one thing off their *to-kill* list."

"Do you want them to come kill us?" Beauford asked.

She shook her head.

"Bellevue is here. It'll always be here. A constant target that would be too risky to take until they know they don't need their muscle in other places. Bellevue doesn't hurt anyone, it just...is. A tiny prickle in the side to remind the poor people others survived." He rolled his sleeve back down, covering the skin Nola had tended to.

"It seems to me that would be more dangerous than anything else. The idea that there can be peaceful life in the light."

"That's the difference between Domers and outsiders." Beauford shook his head, and his shaggy hair covered his eyes. "Domers can argue about thoughts and meaning and ideas. Out here it's about what the food source is and who controls it and who has the medicine you need to get patched up. They'll come for the rich as soon as they have the city. Take the food and the medicine and every last thing they own. They'll fight to the last man just for the joy of seeing them fall."

"I can't—" Nola shut her eyes tight as she zipped her mother's backpack shut. "It's...it's hard for me to believe how much I didn't know. It'll probably get me killed first, right? Like the rich people."

"First." Beauford smiled grimly, his lips pulling into a tight line. "Or last. The domes prepared you to outlive us all, not to actually survive."

"But she can't die first." T stood in the doorway to the bathroom, wrapped in a white towel that made her look younger than ever. "Catlyn already did that. So, you'll just have to die last, Nola." Her words hung in the air for a moment. "The bathroom is all yours, and the soap smells better than flowers."

"Thanks," Nola said. "Just promise you won't be gone when I get out?"

"Don't worry," T said. "We're locked in."

"Right." Nola hesitated for a moment with her hand on the top of her backpack. Raina had the ReVamp. She had the medical supplies and food.

My entire worth is in this backpack.

Nola tightened her fingers on the strap. "I'll be right back." She lifted the pack and carried it to the bathroom, shutting and locking the door behind her.

She closed her eyes and leaned on the door for a moment, letting the quiet of the room echo in her ears. There was no one trying to capture or kill her in here.

I'm never going to feel safe again.

When she finally managed to open her eyes, she had to blink a few times to be sure she was seeing everything properly.

The floor was bright white marble. A heavy white ceramic sink matched the white ceramic tub. A small chandelier provided the light for the room, its reflection glinting off a mirror that covered half the wall. A girl was reflected in the mirror, too. Logic told Nola it was her, but it didn't seem possible.

She let the backpack slide to the floor, and the girl in the reflection moved just the same way. She stepped closer to the mirror, drawn to the horror she had become.

Her hands and clothes were caked in blood and dirt. Her hair was tangled and filthy, but it was her face she couldn't look away from. Dried blood covered her mouth, a dark red stain that dripped down her throat. She had bitten the man, she had tasted his blood, and the horrible truth of it covered her face. She looked like a vampire. Tears cut wide, pale tracks through the deep red.

She turned on the water as hot as it would go and scrubbed her face in the sink. It didn't matter if the water was contaminated or filthy. She was worse.

She didn't stop scrubbing her face until it was raw, then she climbed into the tub, crouching under the faucet to wash. There was no shower here, and she couldn't bear the thought of soaking in someone else's blood. She should be sobbing. They had left Catlyn in the tunnels. But the tears came slowly as she scraped the blood out from under her nails.

It felt like an eternity before her hands were finally clean. The girl in the mirror looked like her again. Bruised and cut, but her.

She dragged on clean clothes and rinsed the blood out of everything else, without real hope of it being dry when they had to leave. Finally, she grabbed the pack and headed back out to the bedroom.

Beauford and T sat on the bed, a tray of food between them.

"Eat up." T smiled. "There's plenty for all of us."

"Thanks." Nola put the bag in the corner and climbed up onto the giant bed.

"It's good food, too." T handed Nola a piece of bread. "I mean, not dome good, but..." She blushed.

"It's great." Nola took a bite. It was sweeter than dome food, but her stomach growled greedily at the taste of it. "I haven't had much food made outside the domes. We don't have sugar or preservatives in our food. This is nice, just different."

"We won't have anything this good when we get to Nightland," Beauford said. "If we make it there alive."

"Beauford, don't," T said.

"We already lost Catlyn. And we haven't even made it to the city limits," Beauford pushed on.

"Please stop." Tears welled in T's eyes.

"Catlyn was a wonderful woman," he said, the usual gruffness in his voice gone, "but the last thing she would want is for our grieving for her to hurt our chances of survival."

"If you don't want to go to Nightland, then what do you want to do?" T said. "This city is falling. Even if we could stay away from the Outer Guard, how long do you think we would survive?"

"Not long enough for that baby to be born," Beauford said.

T wrapped her arms around her stomach.

"I don't see how this is helping." Nola set her half-eaten slice of bread down on the bed, resisting the urge to wrap an arm around T.

"Catlyn wanted us to get out of the city," Beauford said. "I know that better than anyone. And if we're getting out of the city, the only place any of us knows to go is Nightland."

"Then why are we talking about this?" T asked. "We have to go. If we die, we die, but there's nothing to do but keep trying."

"Because, if I'm hurt as bad as Catlyn, I want ReVamp," Beauford said, looking into both T's and Nola's eyes in turn. "I promised Catlyn I would do whatever it took to get us to Nightland. If that means becoming a Vamper to keep fighting, then I want to do it."

"Okay." T nodded. "I'll make sure you get the injection."

"But you can't take it." A tinge of fear touched Beauford's voice.

"No." T shook her head. "If I die, I die."

Both of them turned to Nola before Beauford asked, "And if you get hurt?"

"What?" Nola pushed herself as far back as the four-poster bed would allow.

"If it comes down to it," he said, reaching across the bed and gripping her hand, "do you want to go like Catlyn, or do you want to be like Raina?"

"I-I," Nola stammered, her mind racing so quickly she could hardly breathe. "That won't happen. We'll be fine. We'll all be fine."

"Catlyn is dead," Beauford said. "I've known Catlyn my whole life. She'd been looking after me since before I could crawl." Pain shot through his voice, and a thick wrinkle appeared between his brows. "I would have given her the shot. I would have made her into a Vamper, saying it was to keep her alive, but really it would've been for my own selfish benefit. Because I didn't want to lose her. I don't know you, *we* don't know you. We're out here with half the city wanting to eat us and the people with fancy guns wanting to catch or kill us, and the one who knows you best is a crazy Vamper with a knife fetish. So, I'm asking you once and for all, Vamper or corpse: what do *you* want?"

She couldn't move. Panic surged through her. Beauford gripped her hand, leaning across their meal, his eyes bright with held-back tears. T was crying in earnest now, wiping her tears away with her still dirty sleeve, which left filth on her cheek.

"I have a clean shirt." Nola wrenched her hand away from Beauford. "You can wear it and wash out yours." She crouched down by her bag, hiding her face from him while she searched for the other shirt.

"We need to know what you want us to do." Beauford jumped off the bed and knelt by her side. "Nola, we need to know."

The use of her name, the sound of it in his voice, stopped Nola's frantic digging.

"We made it this far." He pulled the bag out of her reach. "And that is amazing. But we have a lot farther to go. I know all of us will fight like hell to survive, but I almost went against Catlyn's dying wish because I didn't know any better. I don't want to risk that with anyone else."

"I don't know." Nola's voice came from a million miles away. "I don't know what I want. I want to eat bread and sleep in a bed. I want to find T a clean shirt."

"Leave her alone, Beauford," T said. "She just left her home. Give her a second to breathe."

"Okay." He tossed the bag back to Nola. "But if the time comes, she'll just have to live or die with whatever choice we make for her." Beauford walked into the bathroom, closing the door roughly behind him.

Silence filled the room for a moment. The only sound was Beauford turning on the taps of the bath.

"You have to forgive him," T said. "He's never been great with people, and losing Catlyn is a lot for both of us."

Nola's fingers finally closed around her other clean shirt. "I didn't know you three were so close. I thought you just got grouped together for work in the domes."

"Thanks," T said, taking the shirt Nola offered. "Catlyn was the pied piper of lost children. She had a strong door and a big floor in her apartment, so she would let all of us stay with her when we needed a place out of the rain or away from the riots. I don't know how she scraped it together, but there was always something to eat. Enough to get by until we could find food on our own. She was devastated when I went down to Nightland, thought I would get myself drained by some Vamper. Took her months to even agree to meet Charles, and then when he disappeared, well, she found us work in the domes. And that kept us from starving."

T pulled on Nola's shirt. It was tighter than what T had worn in the domes, hugging her pregnant belly. T's face crumpled as she stared down at her stomach.

"And now Catlyn's gone." T buried her face in her hands. She'd stopped crying. She just looked exhausted.

Hesitantly, Nola stepped forward and wrapped her arms around T.

"I'm so sorry," was all she could think to whisper as T leaned into her shoulder, sagging with the weight of what lay behind and the unknown they had left to face.

CHAPTER THIRTY-ONE

The daylight faded from the crack in the curtain. Nola had been staring at the tiny sliver of light for hours. Every time she fell asleep for a few minutes, a noise would wake her, and she would lay frozen, convinced the Outer Guard had found them.

T lay in the bed next to Nola, her arms wrapped protectively around her stomach.

Beauford was sprawled out on the gold couch at the foot of the bed, breathing slowly and steadily as though fear were a thing he couldn't understand.

Nola pinched her eyes shut, knowing Nettie or Raina would be coming for them soon. They would be back on the streets, walking far at best, fighting for their lives at worst. She needed sleep. Even the few minutes she had left would be valuable. But she couldn't manage it.

Her mother would be in tears. Or furious and refusing to say Nola's name ever again.

Jeremy was probably still out looking for her, convinced she was a brainwashed captive. She wished she could have told them why she had to leave. That the beauty and safety of the domes weren't enough to cover the lies and blood that lay beneath. But then she never would have been able to leave. They would have locked her up in one of the cells.

She rolled onto her back and stared up at the ceiling. She shouldn't feel guilty about Jeremy wasting his time searching for her. He had lied. He had let her be a part of murder. But her mother...

You had to do it. You had to get out. And you saved four people doing it.

Three, a voice whispered in the back of her mind. *You only saved three.*

Finally, a faint rapping sounded on the door followed by the heavy *thunk* of the lock flipping over.

"Wakey, wakey." Raina swung open the door. "My beloved sister wants to offer you one more meal in our house before we run for our lives, so who's hungry?"

"We should all eat," Beauford said, on his feet before either of the girls could climb out of the sheets. "It doesn't matter if we're hungry."

"What about you?" T asked as she pulled on her shoes. "Do you need to eat?"

"How kind of you, worrying about feeding the vampire," Raina said. "Don't worry, I met a tasty little street guard already. I feel fit as a night-walking fiddle."

"Then let's eat and get out of here." Nola picked up her pack. Her back ached in protest.

"I can carry that for you." Beauford reached for the bag.

"No!" Nola said. "I can carry it. I mean, I want to carry it." Her face flushed at Beauford's suddenly stony expression.

"Smart girl," Raina said. "Now eat before it gets completely dark. We can't afford to waste time."

T followed Raina quickly out the door, leaving Nola and Beauford alone.

"I really do appreciate the offer," she said, "but I can carry it myself."

"I wouldn't steal your pack from you." Beauford examined Nola's face. "But I guess you won't believe that, will you? You've been lied to too much. If we live long enough, maybe you'll trust somebody again."

He strode past Nola and out the door, leaving her head spinning. She moved as quickly as she could, grabbing the still-damp clothes she had washed and stuffing them in the top of the pack, making it heavier still, but by the time she reached the downstairs, the others had nearly finished eating.

"Eat up." Nettie raised a crystal glass in welcome. "I made sure the meal was special, a goodbye feast for my sister. Of course, we've had a few of these before, and the goodbye part never does seem to stick."

"Thank you." Nola didn't know what else to say. She slid into the empty seat left at the polished wooden table. A slice of meat and something that looked like potatoes sat on a china plate.

"You know, it's not like I ever *try* to come back here." Raina kicked her feet up, putting her boots on the table. "It just sort of happens, and I do actually own the place, so I think you should be grateful I let you live in my house, baby sister."

Nola shoveled food into her mouth as Nettie's face turned red.

"Your house? Your house! You can't even live aboveground!"

"That's what curtains are for." Raina's eyes sparkled as her sister's anger grew.

"You abandoned this house when you decided to be a Vamper!" Nettie stood, sloshing the pungent liquid from her glass. "Dammit."

"I didn't decide to be a Vamper. I decided to survive," Raina said. "I decided I wanted to survive without all the terribly strict rules that have kept you alive."

"You wanted to run around on the street. You got yourself sick." Nettie pounded her glass down on the table, shattering the crystal. "Shit! You made your choices, and leaving this house forever is your consequence! This is my house." Nettie wrapped a napkin around her bleeding palm.

"I have no intention of taking it from you, little sister." Raina kicked her feet off the table and stood as Nola shoved the last bite of meat into her mouth. "Just remember when I come knocking, you will answer. Or I'll burn the place to the ground and neither of us will have it."

"You are cruel," Nettie said. "You are cruel and psychotic."

"Half of that is reasonably true." Raina waved the others to stand. "But I always have your interests at heart. And your best interest is never to forget you have a vampire sister in Nightland. It might just save you one of these days."

"I don't need your protection," Nettie said.

Beauford took Nola by the elbow and dragged her to the doorway.

T followed, hiding in Beauford's shadow.

"Of course not." Raina walked over to her sister and kissed her on the forehead before Nettie could back away. "Until you do. Try not to die, Nettie. It'd be a pity for the house to be empty."

"How dare—" Nettie began, but Raina had already pushed past Beauford and out into the hall.

"Don't you dare darken my door again!" Nettie shouted after Raina, chasing Nola, Beauford, and T out into the hall. "I won't be taking in anymore of your friends either. I'm done!"

"That's what you said last time." Raina worked swiftly on the seven locks that ran along the side of the door. "And if I do show up again, you'll open the door. Partly because it's my house I let you exist in, but mostly because you love me, baby Nettie, and you'd never leave me out to die in the sun or burn in the rain."

"I will, I swear it!"

"Until next time, sister." Raina flung open the door and stepped into the darkening night.

"Thank you," T whispered as she followed Raina out onto the street.

"Thanks," Beauford mumbled.

"Yes, thank you for your hospitality," Nola echoed and moved to follow.

"Glad to help." Nettie's gaze followed her sister as Raina strode down the road without glancing back. "But you had better follow Raina before she leaves you behind. Who knows how much harder it will be to get yourself killed without her help?"

As soon as Nola was through the door, it slammed behind her. She ran down the street, chasing Raina, the pack bursting pain through her spine as it bounced with every stride.

"Where are we going?" Nola wheezed as soon as she caught up.

"Nightland." Raina led them past the guards who waited in the shadows, winking at one who wore a conspicuous white bandage on his neck.

"I meant more immediately."

"To the western outskirts of the city." Raina turned a corner and led them out of view of Bellevue Avenue. "Then we head out into the wild. There's no point in my telling you where to go after that. You wouldn't find Nightland anyway."

"And if we get separated?" Beauford asked as Raina led them down a street where torches were lashed to the broken lampposts. A withered-looking man moved down the road, lighting each post in turn as people began emerging from their houses for the night.

"If we get separated, you're on your own. Find a safe place to wait out the apocalypse and try not to die. I'm not stopping until I get to Nightland."

Nola wanted to think Raina wasn't serious, but she knew her too well.

The city is too dangerous for any of us to risk lingering.

"Hey, you!" a man shouted from the side of the street. His long, matted hair framed his gaunt, gray face. "What are you doing here?"

At the sound of his voice, other people on the street began to take notice of them.

"Passing through," Raina said, not slowing her stride as twelve people closed in around them.

"We don't like Vampers on this street." The man stepped into the light of one of the newly lit torches. The dancing flames glinted off his bright red eyes.

"Didn't know this street had been taken by wolves." Raina spoke as though the fact that they were surrounded by werewolves was only vaguely interesting.

"Well, it has been, and we don't just let Vampers and humans wander down our street." The man stepped in front of Raina, blocking her path.

"I'm not wandering." Raina's hand tightened around the handle of the metal box she carried. "Actually, I'm in a hurry. So get out of my way."

The man let out a howling laugh that echoed around the street.

"If you don't move, I'll have to hurt you." Raina smiled and stepped so close to the wolf, it looked as though she might kiss him. "It would be a pain in my ass, but I'd win. And then the Outer Guard would come and kill you all. So, move or die."

"The Outer Guard won't come," the man said. "Maybe you don't know they blew up the bridge, just like you don't know werewolves run the city now."

"One." Raina wriggled a finger over her shoulder, beckoning T forward.

"Oh god, she's counting!" A chorus of laughter surrounded them as the wolves came closer.

"Two." Raina pressed the silver box into T's hands.

"Vampers are so cocky," the man sneered. "You really think you can beat a whole street of werewolves?"

"Three." In one, fluid motion Raina grabbed the knife that had been tucked into T's belt and slit the wolf's throat.

Before the man hit the ground, Raina threw T's knife, hitting the wolf that was farthest away right in the eye as she dove toward another, sinking her own knife between his ribs as though he were made of air.

"Anyone else?" Raina asked politely as she pulled her knife from the wolf's chest and raised it to his neck making an incision just the right size for her to eat from. She lowered her mouth and took a long drink, never taking her eyes from the other wolves as she easily supported the dead man that had become her second supper. "No one?" She wiped her mouth on her sleeve. "I forgot how disgusting wolves taste. Someone bring the pregnant girl her knife."

A girl in the back walked to the man who lay face up on the street with a knife sticking out of his eye. Shaking, she grabbed the hilt and pulled. The faint squelching noise made Nola shiver more than the cooling night air had.

Still shaking, the girl ran forward, placing the knife at T's feet before sprinting away.

T picked up the knife and walked over to the first of the wolves Raina had struck, wiping the blood onto his shirt before sliding the blade back into her belt.

"All set?" Raina asked, turning back down the street. "If anyone follows us, I stab them in the heart and make sure they don't get up."

She led them calmly away, not looking back until they rounded the corner and were out of sight. "We need to run, and no one can fall behind."

"What?" Nola turned to look back at where they had left the wolves. "No one's following us."

"I just knifed three wolves in the middle of the street," Raina said. "We're leaving a trail of body-shaped breadcrumbs behind us along with a pack of pissed off wolves. We need to put as much distance between us and them as we can. So we run." She looked at T. "You need me to carry you, baby machine?"

"I'm fine," T said.

"You fall behind, I'm carrying you. You fight me on it, I'll kill you myself," Raina said.

T's nod hollowed out the last of Nola's courage.

"This way." Raina set off down the street.

Keep running.

Nola took a deep breath and followed. She could easily keep pace with T, and Beauford ran in the back as he had done in the woods. She watched Raina's hair streaming behind her, a shimmering flag Nola had to follow if she wanted to get out of the city. She didn't study the buildings where the fronts had crumbled almost entirely away. She didn't stare at the corpse someone had left to bloat in the gutter during the heat of the day. All she could do was follow the blur of scarlet and purple.

The backpack rubbed her back raw, and every time it slammed into her spine, it seemed to steal some of the precious air her lungs were working so hard to use.

"Give me the pack." Beauford's words were uneven as they ran. "It's slowing you down."

"I can do it," Nola panted, her gait faltering as her body begged her to give up the extra weight.

"It's not about what you can do, it's about surviving." He grabbed the loop at the top of the pack, stopping Nola in her tracks. He pulled the bag away from her and had it on his back before she could catch her breath enough to argue.

"Now run," Beauford said.

Side by side they sprinted to catch up to Raina and T.

The sky was fully dark now, and its darkness was easier to see as they made it closer to the outskirts of town. Here there were no torches or streetlamps to light the decaying buildings. The people who were out in this part of the city didn't roam in packs or sit on stoops. The few people they passed either moved nearly as quickly as they did or shambled in the deep shadows.

When Nola's lungs burned so badly it felt like they might burst, one of the shamblers appeared at the end of a street, moving toward the center of the road as though waiting for them.

Raina pulled her knife and drove it into the person's chest as they ran by. Nola's feet caught the uneven pavement beneath her, and she tumbled forward, catching herself with her hands. Beauford looped an arm around her waist and hoisted her to her feet, not letting go until she was running on her own again.

"She killed him," Nola panted as they ran past the person.

But a brief glance told her that it wasn't a man but a woman. A shriveled woman whose gray hair matched her skin. Angry red splotches and terrible black sores dotted the woman's face. A zombie. Raina had been right to kill the poor woman.

"T!" Beauford's shout pulled Nola's attention back to the road ahead of them. T limped, favoring one ankle as she tried to keep up with Raina.

"I'm fine," T panted.

Raina turned and raced back to T, scooped her into her arms, and was running again without breaking her stride.

They had to be near the end. Surely, the edge of the city would come soon.

Inside her shoes, Nola could feel the skin on her feet tearing. Her legs felt like lead, spots danced before her eyes, but she had to keep running.

"Halt!" the shout cut through the night.

Nola faltered for a moment, just long enough for Beauford to smack into her. She pitched forward again, but Beauford grabbed her, dragging her into the shelter of a stoop as a string of tiny *pops* pierced the night.

CHAPTER THIRTY-TWO

"Magnolia Kent, are you hurt?" a voice shouted.

"The Outer Guard found us," Nola whispered, sure Beauford knew what was happening but needing to say the words aloud so she could feel them in her mouth. They had only been out of the domes for a day, and the Outer Guard had already found them.

"Magnolia Kent," the voice shouted again. "Are you hurt?"

"She's fine," Raina shouted, "but you won't be if you don't get out of our way."

"Magnolia Kent," the voice shouted again. "Are you hurt?"

"I'm fine." Tears stung Nola's eyes. "None of these people hurt me. They would never hurt me."

"Magnolia, come down to the end of the street slowly."

"Promise you won't hurt them!" Nola shouted. "Promise you'll let them leave, and I'll come with you."

"Nola, no." Beauford grabbed her wrist. "Going with them won't make things any better for us."

"But it might buy you some time." Nola leaned around the edge of the steps. "Promise me you won't hurt them, and I'll do whatever you want."

"Fine," the guard called quickly. Much too quickly for an order to have been decided upon.

"Run," Nola said. "I'll try to keep them busy. Get as far away from here as you can."

"We can't just leave you with them."

"You can and will. The Guard's guns can do worse than sedate people. Get to T and get out." Nola stood and walked out to the center of the street. Beauford had the pack. She was glad he had taken it. Maybe it would help the others survive on their way to Nightland.

Moving as slowly as she dared, Nola headed toward the end of the road. Two men in Outer Guard uniform faced her, guns raised.

"Two?" Nola coughed a laugh. "They only sent two guards to take me back?"

"There are Outer Guard all over the city, Magnolia. We're just the ones that found you." The guard's face was hidden behind his helmet's visor, but Nola imagined him smiling. Captain Ridgeway would be so proud of the guards who captured the runaways.

"Two alone won't be able to stop the ones I've got with me." Nola paused in the middle of the street. "You should have followed us quietly, waited for others to come."

"We have guns," the other guard said. "They have none."

"She doesn't need a gun."

No sooner had the words left Nola's lips than a whizzing sound came from the shadows, and two knives sank into the throats of the guards. Both men gasped and gurgled as they fell to the ground.

"Found a way around the coat problem." Raina stepped out of the shadows. "I mean, coats that block weapons, what fun is—"

A howling scream from the end of the street cut off Raina's words.

"You think you can murder us and get away with it?"

A group of thirty wolves rounded the corner, the girl who had given T back her knife at the front of the pack.

"You think you can walk down our street and we'll let you disappear? Shouting to tell us where you were, that was so helpful. Naïve, and deadly, but terribly helpful."

"I'm surprised it took you so long to catch up." Raina smiled, backing away from the wolves toward the downed guards.

"No, you don't get your knives back," the girl growled, crouching in a frighteningly animalistic way before leaping forward with a howl.

Beauford grabbed Nola's arm, pulling her forward as the wolves charged. Raina ran ahead of them. She would reach the knives before the wolves could reach her, but the pack was right on Nola's heels.

"No!" T screamed.

Nola glanced over to see three big male wolves backing T into a corner.

"Please!" T begged. "Please, I'm pregnant."

Nola heard the wolves laugh as something heavy collided with her spine, knocking her to the ground. But the heavy thing was pulled away as Beauford bellowed, "Leave her alone!"

As Nola scrambled to her feet, Beauford punched the wolf in the face, but there were more of them coming.

Nola ran as fast as she could, all thoughts of fear gone. Most of the pack had gone straight for Raina, who fought the snarling mass, a knife in each hand.

Nola ran past the wolves to the two bleeding Outer Guard. Each of them still held a gun in their limp hands. Her fingers trembled as she grabbed them both.

Her father had let her hold his gun years ago, taken her down to the training room to fire it.

The safety was off.

She pulled the trigger, trusting the clip of tiny silver needles would still be loaded.

Pop.

A needle shot from the gun, missing the nearest wolf by a foot.

Pop, pop, pop.

The wolf who had knocked the knife from Raina's left hand fell.

Pop, pop.

Another wolf fell.

She aimed farther away to the wolf that had Beauford pinned to the ground.

Pop, pop, pop, pop, pop.

A silver needle sank into the man's shoulder, and he fell on top of Beauford, who pushed the man off him and ran toward T.

Nola aimed for the wolves that had surrounded T.

Pop, pop, pop, pop.

Needles sank into two of the wolves, but Beauford had closed in. She couldn't risk hitting him.

She looked back at Raina.

Pop.

One of the wolves looked behind as the man fighting next to him fell. His eyes locked on Nola, and he charged.

Nola raised the gun to shoot again.

Click.

The first gun was empty, but before Nola could lift the other, the wolf leapt, striking her in the chest and knocking her to the ground. Her head cracked on the pavement, and stars swam in front of her eyes.

"You stupid little girl." The man pressed on her wrists and dug his knee into her chest. She still clutched the loaded gun, but she couldn't move her hand to aim it.

He let go of her arm and raised a knife high in the air. Nola aimed and pulled the trigger. A silver needle disappeared into the man's neck a moment too late.

The filthy blade sank into Nola's stomach. Pain like fire soared through her as a scream tore from her throat.

The man toppled sideways, wrenching the knife from her flesh as he fell. Nola screamed again as the pain doubled. Her shaking fingers found the warm blood that seeped from her stomach.

"Help," Nola croaked. "Help."

But Raina was still fighting three of the wolves, blood coating her back.

I hope she survives. I hope the three of them survive.

"No. No!"

Someone was screaming from down the street, farther away than Nola could see.

"Nola!"

The stars above shimmered in and out of being. Blackness pulsed at the edges of Nola's mind.

"Raina!" Beauford's voice shouted.

There was a scream of pain, and then another.

I hope that's not me screaming.

"Nola." Beauford's face swam into view as he pressed hard on the part of her stomach torn by the knife. The pain tripled.

She wanted to tell him to stop, there was too much damage to press it away, but the pain had made it impossible to form words.

"Nola," Beauford shouted. "Stay with me, Nola."

"You're okay." T was there, her face bruised, but she was alive and breathing. "You're going to be okay."

Nola smiled.

There was more shouting, more fighting. They needed to run.

"Nola!" Beauford shouted again.

It took Nola's eyes a moment to focus on his face. He looked frightened and pale in the moonlight.

"Nola, we need to know," he spoke slowly as though determined for her to understand. "Nola, ReVamp or death? We need to know what you want us to do. Do you want the shot? Nola, Nola!"

The sound of her name being shouted followed her into darkness.

"Nola!"

NIGHT OF NEVER

Book Three

CHAPTER ONE

"Nola!"

Cold. She knew only cold. Unrelenting, irredeemable cold.

Pain grew deep within the ice.

The cold held no power to hurt her. The pain came from something else.

A ragged, itching ache that blossomed at the center of her stomach, tingling like a thousand bugs burrowing inside of her.

If the bugs were going to eat her away, it would be best if they worked more quickly. If there were nothing left of her, there could be no more cold.

Maybe.

Maybe it will all end.

She formed the words in her mind.

More words existed, fighting through the fierce frost that enveloped her.

"If we don't move now, we'll never make it out."

The words faded from her ears before she could think of their meaning.

"She would never, not in a million years..."

A million years. The cold will keep me for a million years.

The pain in her stomach changed as the insects fought for territory.

Endless nothing would be better than a million frozen years.

"She would understand. You don't have to do this."

Agony seared through her chest and shot through her spine as something wrapped around her. The torment flooded air into her lungs.

My lungs. There's air in my lungs. Pain in my spine.

I'm alive.

Nola fought to speak the words.

I'm alive!

No sound came. The frozen part of her that was her mouth wouldn't move.

"I don't care what you want, I'm staying with her."

The air tasted of blood, rot, fresh earth, and something else. Something with a tinge of chemical. A scent she'd smelled before.

Before the cold took me. Before the knife cut me.

"I'm too damn tired to fight you. You want to follow, follow."

"Then let me carry her."

"You will not touch her again, Domer."

Domer.

The word had meaning that brought pain beyond the burning in her stomach.

She had been a Domer. Lived trapped within glass, safely hiding from the end of the world.

Then she ran away.

Running through the city on her own legs. Legs that now bounced uselessly as the person carrying her ran.

Before the ice had taken her body, she'd broken out of the domes. Saved her friends from being locked in concrete cages.

They'd gone through the abandoned tunnels of Nightland and into the city. They'd almost made it out.

Searching for Emanuel, for wherever the vampires of Nightland had found refuge.

But they didn't make it. Werewolves had attacked.

She'd fought back. But the wolf had won, driving his blade into her stomach.

She gasped at the remembered pain. Arms tightened around her, keeping her safe.

Nola!

The scream had echoed from so far away, but blackness had devoured her before she could see who had screamed her name.

Blackness. Then cold.

Now pain.

Pain radiating from her stomach.

Where he stabbed me. I should have died.

This can't be dying. The pain is getting worse.

A stinging, like fire blazing in her veins, pushed farther from her chest with every breath.

"We need to find a place to rest," a soft female voice spoke.

T. She made it.

Nola wanted to smile, but the notion only spread pain to her face.

"We can keep going a little longer," Raina said, the words close to Nola's ear. "The first bit of sun isn't too bad."

"And if you get sick from it?" Beauford said. "We can't find Nightland without you."

"Too right, so keep up," Raina said.

They made it. They all made it.

Thank you for not leaving me!

"We need to find a safe place for Nola," T said. "She's getting paler. She lost so much blood."

"She'll be fine," Raina said. "The chemicals are changing her. That's never a pretty process."

Chemicals.

Chemicals to change me.

Meaning came as pain bit her frozen fingers.

ReVamp. They gave me ReVamp.

Panic quickened Nola's breaths. Fire surged into her arms. She needed to scream, to move, to do something to break free from the pain.

"We need to stop," a voice spoke from far away, the sound nearly too low for Nola to hear.

"This is as good a place as we're going to find," Beauford said.

"There's a safe place in another mile," Raina said.

"The sun will be too high by then," T said.

"We need to stop for Nola," the far away voice spoke again. "Changing with a wound like that doesn't happen easily."

Changing. I'm changing.

"She can hold on."

A *creaking* echoed in Nola's ears, zapping to the center of her brain, waking up the horrible itching insects that had lain dormant in her head.

"Hold her," Raina said.

Pain shot through every inch of Nola's being as new arms cradled her.

They've made me a vampire. Does it torture all of them this much? Raina, how long until the pain and cold leave me?

Please let me speak.

Her body wouldn't allow her to do anything but breathe.

"Let me—"

"Over your dead body, Domer."

Thumping footsteps carried away.

"You're hurt." The far away voice had come closer. "I'll hold her."

"No," Beauford said.

"I would never hurt her," the voice whispered. "You have to believe that."

"We don't," T said.

Something damp cooled Nola's forehead.

The fire sought the cool, racing up to destroy the comfort, boiling away Nola's thoughts.

"I had to save..."

The words wobbled in and out like lapping waves of sound.

"...didn't need your help."

Flames reached Nola's knees, pushing the hateful cold toward her feet. The ice raged, ferociously fighting back the fire.

Let me scream.

"We don't even know if she wanted this, so you can't say..."

"Upstairs will be the best place..."

"...what she needs anymore."

Embers seared the insides of Nola's ears.

Let me slip away. Let me fall into the black far away from pain.

"I'm not letting her out of my sight. I'll tear down this house if you try and keep me from her."

The pain in Nola's head doubled as she fought her way to the voice.

"If you're dumb enough to think I'm going to let you drag her back—"

"The domes will never take either of us back."

Jeremy.

A swooping ache tore the air from Nola's lungs.

Jeremy here. Jeremy protecting me.

"I'm not going to take her anywhere, but I sure as hell won't leave her," Jeremy said.

Jeremy had been there. Had known the domes betrayed her. Used her to murder hundreds of people.

Then she had taken the others and run. Run through the city. Been stabbed by the knife. Been filled with cold that turned to fire.

"I love her. I'm going to keep her safe."

Traitor.

The urge to hit him, to stop him from speaking, drove past the flames, curling her fingers into a fist.

Pain beyond fire surged through every ounce of Nola's body as a scream tore from her throat and blackness stole her thoughts.

CHAPTER TWO

Heavy weights pressed down upon her, leaving only her face open to the cool air.

The urge to move zinged through her fingers and toes, but the weight brought comfort. And, lying still, nothing hurt.

Voices whispered far away. Sounds of life came from nearby as well. A squeaking floorboard as someone shifted their weight. The soft sound of someone breathing.

Nola lay still, letting her mind arrange everything in an order that made sense. On their way to Nightland, they had been attacked. Someone had given her ReVamp to save her. They were still heading to join the vampires of Nightland, and they had stopped to wait out the daylight. Jeremy was with them.

Nola sucked in a breath as her muscles tensed.

"You're awake," Jeremy said. His voice carried from across the room where the floorboards creaked. "You can lie still for as long as you want. It's going to take your body some time to adjust to the changes. It feels worse before it feels better."

Tears squeezed from the corners of Nola's eyes. The foreign heat of them trickling past her temples gave her the courage to move her lips.

"Worse?" The word crackled in her throat. "Worse than being encased in ice and having your whole body lit on fire."

Heavy bootfalls pounded across the room.

"Don't touch her," T said.

"T." Nola's eyelids scraped open like sandpaper, blurring her vision.

"I'm here, Nola." T knelt by the bed, brushing Nola's hair away from her forehead.

"Are you hurt? Is the baby okay?" Nola blinked, forcing her eyes to focus on T.

The edge of the bed hid T's stomach from view.

"I'm fine." Only half of T's mouth curved as she smiled. Purple bruises covered the left half of her face, swelling her cheek past the point of movement. "The baby will be fine, too."

"Good." Nola sighed.

"Nola." Jeremy stepped toward the side of the bed.

"Stay back." T didn't look away from Nola as she spoke.

Pain shimmered through Jeremy's eyes as he stepped away. "I would never hurt her."

Dried blood speckled his dark blond hair, the shiny pink line of a cut in the final stages of healing marked his jawline. The arm of his black Outer Guard uniform had been torn. The marks of fighting weren't as startling as the worried lines etched between his eyes.

Nola swallowed the instinct to ask if he was okay. "What are you doing here?"

"Protecting you," Jeremy said.

"From what?" Nola asked. "From T? From Raina or Beauford? I trust them. I'll be fine with them."

"I—" Jeremy looked up to the ceiling. "After what I saw last night, I agree. I don't think any of them would hurt you."

"Then go home," Nola said.

Jeremy flinched.

The twinge of regret at her words lasted only a moment.

"I can't go home any more than you can, Nola," Jeremy said. "Even if I made it as far as the glass, they'd never let me in. I betrayed them."

"You should drink." T heaved Nola's backpack onto the bed. Blood stained the material.

"She won't need—" Jeremy began.

"I don't remember asking you anything." T dug a water bottle from the depths of the pack. She pulled back the worn gray blankets that covered Nola.

A dark stain marked the center of Nola's shirt, surrounding the tear in the stomach.

Nola's head spun, her thoughts wrenching her back to the moment the knife had plunged into her flesh.

"Breathe, Nola," Jeremy whispered.

T lifted Nola's head, gently pouring a trickle of water into her mouth. The water tasted of minerals with a hint of chemical, like someone had tried to clean the contaminates from the water by adding other contaminates.

"Thanks, T." Nola pushed herself up onto her elbows. Her muscles shook from the effort.

"Careful." Jeremy reached for her.

"Go home, Jeremy." Nola fell back onto her pillow. "Tell them you were trying to capture me. Tell them you killed me when it didn't work. Your father won't be too angry I'm dead."

"I doubt my father will admit to having a son anymore."

"Why? Because you disappeared with Vampers for a night?" Nola clenched her fists. Her fingers moved without pain, the cut on her palm from two days before had disappeared. "I'm sure you can talk your way out of it."

"I don't think so." Jeremy stepped forward.

"Don't touch her." T sat on the bed, glaring at Jeremy.

"They gave an order over the coms," Jeremy said. "Capture if possible, kill if necessary."

"For who?" Nola's heart raced, faster than a heartbeat should have been able to go.

"For you," Jeremy said, "and the ones you took from the domes."

"They wanted me dead?" Nola could picture it. Jeremy's father, the Captain of the Outer Guard, giving the order to kill her.

Did my mother know? Did she try and stop it?

Nola couldn't answer for sure. Tears coursed down her cheeks.

"I was in a search party in the city when the order came down," Jeremy said. "I couldn't let them hurt you. I knocked out my partner and started looking for you on my own. I found some downed werewolves in the street. Knife wounds in each of them. I knew it had to be Raina, so I started tracking the pack. If I had gotten there a little bit sooner, I might have stopped the wolf from stabbing you." Tears trickled down Jeremy's cheek. "I will never forgive myself for not getting to you faster."

"I'm sorry," Nola said. "You shouldn't have—"

"Shouldn't have what?" Jeremy said. "Shouldn't have come after you? Shouldn't have saved you?"

"Shouldn't have given up your home for nothing," Nola said.

"You aren't nothing, Nola. You're everything."

T held up a hand as Jeremy reached for Nola again.

"And I couldn't go back there anyway." Jeremy didn't lower his hand. "They wanted you dead. My father gave the order for your murder. I could never go back to the domes."

"And it wasn't for nothing." T took Nola's hand. "He—we weren't sure if you wanted the ReVamp. Beauford tried to ask you, but you were already fading. The case was caught in the middle of Raina's fight. Beauford was going to try and get it, give you the injection and screw what you wanted. But..."

"I got there first." Jeremy's hands shook. "There was so much blood. You wouldn't open your eyes. I gave you the shot before Beauford managed to get near Raina's case of ReVamp."

"A shot of what?" Nola pushed herself to sit up, ignoring the swaying of the room. "Jeremy, a shot of what?"

"Graylock," Jeremy said. "I had a triage kit on my belt. You were bleeding out. I didn't know what else to do."

"Graylock?" Nola looked to T. "He gave me Graylock?"

"He betrayed the domes as much as you ever have," T said. "Raina's furious he didn't wait for Beauford to give you the ReVamp."

"Graylock is better." Jeremy dragged his hands over his hair. Flecks of dried blood drifted to the ground. "Nola is healed and can still go out in the sun, eat food, and—"

"And is stuck with dome medicine coursing through her body," T said.

"I saved her life, which is what you were trying to do," Jeremy said.

"No. We're her friends. We were making a decision for her she had been too scared to make for herself. You weren't there when we asked Nola if she'd prefer death over being a vampire." T's cheeks flushed as she spoke. "You betrayed her, chased her through the city, and made the decision to drug her. Maybe you love her and wanted to save her life, maybe you just felt guilty for being such a screw up. Either way, sticking her with that needle is the last decision you'll be making on Nola's behalf."

T and Jeremy glared at each other for a long moment.

"My eyes." Nola took T's hand. "Do my eyes look different?"

"No," Jeremy said.

Ignoring him, T examined Nola's eyes.

"You look just the same." T smiled.

Nola nodded. The room didn't spin this time.

Jeremy opened his mouth to speak.

"Where are we?" Nola asked, looking to the one window in the corner. Boards had been nailed across the broken glass in a haphazard fashion, letting the red light of the setting sun filter through.

"In an old house six miles west of the city limits," Jeremy said.

"Raina wanted to push it farther toward Nightland. Apparently there's a safe house, but we had to get her out of the sun and you someplace to rest." T bit her bottom lip. "It was rough for a while. I think you were in pain."

"I was." Nola squeezed T's hand. "But I'm fine now."

"It shouldn't have hurt." Jeremy shook his head. "An oppressive cold—"

"I had that for sure," Nola said.

"And then some unpleasant tingling while the Graylock got in deep," Jeremy said. "There shouldn't have been pain."

"Says who?" Raina asked, leaning against the doorjamb. "Life is full of pain. Why should a chemically enhanced life be any different?"

"Says me." The ridges of Jeremy's neck bulged. "I was given the shot. It felt like I'd been dunked in ice, but it never hurt."

"Had you been stabbed?" Raina asked.

"No," Jeremy said.

"Well, I think we've found the difference." Raina stepped past Jeremy, her black eyes fixed on Nola. "You going to make it?"

"I think so." Nola straightened her spine. Embers sizzled in her stomach where the slash cut through her shirt. "I may not be able to run too far tonight, but I'm breathing."

"I can carry you again," Raina said. "Just don't get too used to the special treatment."

"I'll carry her," Jeremy said.

"I don't think so, Domer," Raina said.

"I gave up my home to protect her. I love her. I would do anything for her." Jeremy paced the room, his boots thudding on the wooden floor.

"I'm hearing a lot of *I* from you." Raina dumped Nola's backpack out on the foot of the bed. "And I think we need to move forward with what Nola wants and needs. I mean, since she is the one who almost died."

"I—" Nola's heart pounded in her chest, the thump of it so strong it seemed ready to break through her ribs. She took a shuddering breath. Raina smelled of blood. Not of fresh blood, or even like the dried blood on Nola's shirt. Her very essence held the scent of blood. Bile rolled up Nola's throat. "I want to eat, put on a new shirt, and get ready to leave." Nola tossed back the blankets. "The farther we get from the city, the safer we'll be."

"Nola," Jeremy began.

"You can come with us. There's nowhere else for you to go because of me. And I can't believe you'd hurt any of us." Nola stared into Jeremy's eyes. "But you aren't in charge here. You don't make choices for me or for anyone else."

Jeremy nodded.

"And if there's even a hint of you trying to turn us in to the domes or betray any of us in any way, Raina has permission to kill you," Nola finished.

"Yippee," Raina whispered.

"She won't need to," Jeremy said. "But Nola, we have to talk."

"It's almost dark." Nola tossed her legs over the side of the bed. Fire ants gnawed at her knees. "We can talk in Nightland."

"This can't wait." Jeremy pulled a silver syringe from a hard-sided leather case on his belt. Black liquid showed through the glass.

"Graylock." The word tasted foul in Nola's mouth.

"I gave you one shot," Jeremy said. "It was enough to heal you, but the medicine is meant to be given in a series."

"Funny how Graylock is medicine and Vamp is a drug that should be destroyed," Raina said.

"You need to be given another shot tonight and one in two weeks," Jeremy said. "After that, it's just a matter of booster shots when something really horrible happens."

"Like when your chest was ripped open." Nola blinked back tears at the memory of Jeremy lying helpless in a hospital bed. "What happens if I don't take the shot?"

"The work the medicine has started will begin to reverse," Jeremy said. "The wound in your stomach will stay healed, but the rest of it—the changes to your immune system, nervous system, ability to heal—will all disappear."

"And then?" A chill that had nothing to do with Graylock shook Nola's shoulders.

"It'll kill you," Raina said. "Your body won't remember how to function at normal capacity, and you'll just stop."

"Okay then." Nola held out her arm. "Give me the shot."

"And then the next shot in two weeks, then again when you get hurt," Raina said. "You're chemically tied to Jeremy Ridgeway."

"How many shots do you have?" Nola asked.

"Five," Jeremy said. "Each guard is sent into the city with two. I stole two off each of the guards—"

"If you say anything other than who tried to murder Nola," T warned.

"—off the guards who didn't need them anymore," Jeremy finished.

"Then give me three and you keep two." Nola held out her hand.

"The injections have to be done carefully," Jeremy said. "To work best—"

"Then give me one shot now, and I'll hold my other two," Nola said. "I'm sure I can find someone in Nightland to give me a booster in two weeks."

"I would never keep the Graylock from you." Jeremy pulled two more syringes from his pouch. "But they would be safer with me. The case is built to pad them."

"I don't want to be tied to you, Jeremy." Nola took the two black-filled syringes from him. "If your conscience says to kill some people I don't want dead, I don't want to be stuck chasing you because you have a fancy pouch."

"Then take the one you need—"

"I need both." Nola held up her arm for the injection. "If I don't have a full syringe, what am I supposed to give Dr. Wynne to study?"

"Nola, you can't..." Jeremy sagged, his whole frame crumpling. The giant Outer Guard, with shoulders broad enough that once upon a time it seemed like he could fold himself around Nola and keep her safe forever, shrunk to nothing more than a boy filled with horrible sadness. "Take the whole thing then." Jeremy unfastened his belt, sliding the case free. "Give Dr. Wynne as much as you like after you've taken your booster. If he's still half the doctor I remember him being, he should be able to do some good with it."

"Thank you." Nola took the black leather case. Inside, padded ridges separated the vials, keeping the glass from breaking and the precious liquid from being lost. Nola slipped the two extra syringes into the case. "Give me the shot and be done with it."

Jeremy looked to Raina.

She helped T to her feet, and both women moved to the head of the bed.

Nola held up her arm.

"That's not—" Jeremy looked to Raina again.

Raina raised her dark eyebrows.

"That isn't where the shot has to go," Jeremy said.

"Then where?" Sweat beaded at the nape of Nola's neck.

"In your heart." What little color Jeremy had drained from his face. "It would be better if you lay down."

"You're kidding." Nola looked to Raina. "Tell me he's kidding."

"Most vampires don't do it that way since aiming is a bitch and it hurts like hell," Raina said, "but yeah, Domer's right."

"Okay." Nola lay back on the bed, the sheets puffing up dust in protest. "Okay, that's fine. I can do this."

"The ice is going to come back," Jeremy said.

"And the fire?" Nola's voice trembled.

"I don't know." Worry creased Jeremy's brow. "Just breathe and know I won't let anything happen to you."

"And know once the shot is in he doesn't get to touch you again," Raina said.

Nola nodded. Her jaw had locked shut in fear.

Jeremy pressed a button on the side of the syringe. The needle grew, tripling its length.

"Close your eyes," Jeremy whispered.

Nola clenched her eyes shut. Her pulse thumped in her ears. Other sounds cut through the pounding. Footsteps downstairs. Jeremy's ragged breaths. Raina's hard-soled boots stepping closer.

A sting pierced her chest. Ice cold pain flooded her heart, racing out into her veins. A scream tore from her throat as everything went black.

CHAPTER THREE

A rms wrapped around Nola, holding her tightly.

Nola didn't have to open her eyes to know it was Raina's shoulder her head bounced against. The scent of blood both old and new cut into Nola's nose. The soft squeak of leather against leather punctuated Raina's every step. The heartbeat stayed steady beneath Nola's ear, despite the extra effort of carrying a full grown person.

Vampire.

The definition didn't bring fear, but all Nola's instincts told her she was right.

Ice still filled Nola's limbs, warning her with every throb that moving would be agony.

She let her mind explore, moving where her limbs didn't dare.

Behind Raina's left shoulder, that was T. Her feet fell heavily on the crisp ground, and her breathing didn't reach the bottom of her lungs. Behind her walked Beauford, his shoes crashing through the brush on the ground without any hint of grace.

Jeremy moved at the back of the group, his faint steps taking him from side to side. Not staggering. Searching.

A twig snapped up ahead.

Nola tensed. Ice stabbed every piece of her. Tears welled in her eyes as she bit back her scream.

"Give her to me," Jeremy whispered.

"Not a chance." Raina lowered Nola to the ground.

Movement rustled in front of them. Like dry leaves crumpling underfoot.

"There," Nola croaked, the single word tearing at her throat as she pointed toward the sound.

"I'll stay with them," Beauford said.

Nola forced her eyes open at the sound of his knife clearing its sheath.

Raina and Jeremy looped to the sides of the sound, creeping through the trees, which towered in the darkness.

Scars marked the wood. Pockmarks from the acid rain that plagued the city, but this wasn't the forest near the domes. These trees had young branches struggling to survive.

Nola turned her head, ignoring the screams of the cold as she squinted at the trees.

The nobbles on the branches were clear. Tiny protrusions where leaves would soon fight to grow poked through the thin bark.

I can see it.

Night darkened the forest with barely a hint of moonlight to give the world shape, but she could see the tree. Not as though a new light existed, her eyes simply no longer required the assistance.

She locked her gaze farther into the trees where Raina and Jeremy had disappeared.

Trees dotted the hillside, quickly forming a wall of wood Nola couldn't see beyond.

The sounds of movement in the decaying leaves carried from the darkness. Coming from three places. But the size of what moved was impossible to tell.

Gritting her teeth against the inevitable pain, Nola pushed herself to sit up.

She swayed as her brain rejected the agony of her limbs.

"I've got you." T wrapped her arms around Nola.

"Get her up." Beauford held a knife in each hand, his eyes flicking between the trees.

"They're up the rise," Nola said through gritted teeth as T helped her to her feet. Or rather the two ice blocks that had at one point been her feet.

"It shouldn't be taking this long," Beauford said. Bruises marked his face and neck. A chunk of his shaggy hair had been torn out. "Not if it's an animal."

"It's okay. They'll be okay." Nola felt her belt for her knife. The black case had replaced the blade. Someone had changed her shirt, too.

The scrape of bark peeling off a tree cut through the dark overhead.

"Raina!" Nola screamed as black eyes caught the moonlight.

A lopsided mouth twisted into a smile. The expression stayed on the Vamper's face as he flung himself out of the tree at Nola.

Crashing carried from up the hill, but the Vamper landed ten feet in front of her. His eyes flicked from T to Nola as he bared his sharpened teeth.

Beauford leapt forward, a knife in each hand.

The Vamper grabbed the knife from Beauford's left hand. Blood dripped from his fist as the blade sliced his palm, but the Vamper didn't seem to mind as he tossed the weapon into the trees.

Beauford lunged, his remaining knife grazing the Vamper's ribs before the monster punched him in the back, sending him sprawling to the ground.

"Beauford!" T screamed.

The Vamper's eyes fixed on T. He opened his mouth to laugh, baring his fangs.

"No!" Nola dove at the Vamper's knees as he reached toward T's throat.

"Nola!" Jeremy shouted as Nola and the Vamper tumbled to the ground.

The ice in Nola's veins shook as she crumbled into the decaying leaves. Pain blinded her, sending bright spots dancing in front of her eyes.

A thump shook the ground. Then a bellow and a *snap*.

"Nola are you okay?" Jeremy's arms wrapped around her, lifting her to her feet.

"Don't touch her." T's voice shook.

"Shut up." Jeremy brushed the curls from Nola's face.

"Where's Raina?" Nola blinked away the spots. "Is Beauford okay?"

"I'm fine." Pain filled Beauford's voice as he pushed himself to his knees.

"Raina went up and over the hill," Jeremy said. "There was another Vamper heading that way. I was tailing him with her when I heard you shout."

"We have to find her." Nola swayed.

Jeremy wrapped an arm around her waist, holding her upright.

"You need to slow down," Jeremy said. "You've still got Graylock working in your system, and Raina will be just fine."

"If she's not, we all die," Beauford said. "You understand that, right?"

"Why don't you sit?" Jeremy said, his hands moving to take Nola's.

"I'll help her." T took Nola's elbow.

"I'm really fine." Nola's legs gave out halfway to the ground, landing her in the leaves with an undignified *thud*. "Shouldn't I be all strong and agile now that I've had Graylock?"

"Sort of." Jeremy knelt in front of Nola.

"Back off," T said.

"Do you want to explain the effects of Graylock?" Jeremy asked.

T didn't answer.

Beauford moved over to the Vamper, driving a knife into his heart with a sickening *squish*.

"Your vision and your hearing should already be getting better," Jeremy said.

"They are." Nola looked up to the trees. "I can tell it's dark, but I can still see. I heard the Vamper in the trees. I can smell the dirt from the domes on you."

"Good." Jeremy gave a small smile. "It means the Graylock is working."

"Was there a chance it wouldn't?" T asked.

"It's never been used on a female before," Jeremy said. A hint of a blush crawled up his cheeks, peeking through the stubble.

Nola wanted to touch the red. To see if it held heat. To know if his face still felt the same as it had only a few days before when they had been nothing more than a boy and a girl who loved each other.

"Why not?" Beauford asked.

"Breeding," Nola said, sparing Jeremy from explaining as the red swallowed his whole face. "In the domes, women have to be kept away from chemicals to make sure they can bear healthy children. They'd never let a woman take something like Graylock."

"Not even to save them?" T asked.

"They wouldn't be worth keeping in the domes." Nola searched Jeremy's eyes.

"No, they wouldn't. Nola, I'm so—"

"When do I get my super strength?" Nola cut across him.

No pity. Don't let yourself feel pity.

"It all comes in stages." Jeremy's voice returned to normal, all hint of pleading gone. "The first shot fixes what's wrong with you. The second improves you. The third locks the changes in. The others—"

"Bring you back from the brink of death," Nola said. "I saw, remember?"

"Of course I remember," Jeremy said. "I could have healed without the injections. But it would have taken weeks for me to regain consciousness while my body tried to fix that much damage. Better to get an injection and be able to fight again."

"You mean almost die again," Nola said.

"Sometimes they're the same thing," Jeremy said. "And sometimes you don't care if there's not a difference."

Nola's stomach flipped, twirling itself up to the blissful place where reaching out to hold Jeremy would be the most natural thing in the world.

"When do I get to be strong and fight?" Nola asked.

"Your strength and reflexes should start getting better in the next few days," Jeremy said. "It'll come on slowly, so don't push things too fast. Graylock makes you stronger, but bones can still get broken, so can skin. And you won't be fighting anytime soon."

"Why not?" Nola narrowed her eyes.

"You've never been taught," Jeremy said. "Strength doesn't always help if you don't know what you're doing. I was trained in the skills needed to fight long before I was given Graylock. The medicine just helps me do what I was taught... better." He gave a wary smile.

"Then teach me," Nola said. "If I'm going to survive out here, I need to be able to fight."

"Nola, you shouldn't have to fight," Jeremy said.

"I also shouldn't have been used as a prop to murder people or stabbed in the stomach, but we don't always get to choose how things should be," Nola said. "Jeremy, you owe me this much."

"You're right." Jeremy rubbed his hands over his face. "Once we get where we're going, I'll teach you."

"Or she could learn from a lioness instead of a kitten." Raina sauntered out of the darkness. "Do you want to line up body counts and see who's the more experienced teacher?"

"Was there another vampire?" T asked.

"Yes, there *was*." Raina held up her knife. The blade dripped red. "I think they were a mated pair, two hunting in the wild so close together. I'll bet you all are the best meat they've scented in weeks."

Raina crouched, cleaning her blade on the leaves.

"Do you think there's more of them?" Nola's eyes flicked through the shadows between the trees. The dark shapes held magic in them. Details she had never imagined before. The back of one of the youngest trees had been smoothed by something rubbing across it time and again. Whether a person or animal, she didn't know.

Raina stood, examining her knife before sliding it into the sheath on her belt. "I don't think they had any others in their group. Probably holed up in a little cave, having sex and waiting to kill things. But there could be more. We're still close enough to the city that vampires out here could run in to grab some Vamp and a snack."

Nola shivered at the thought of being a human snack.

"We should keep moving," Raina said. "The sooner we get to Nightland, the better. Can you walk?"

Nola pushed herself to her feet.

Raina growled as Jeremy reached out to steady Nola.

"I'm fine." Nola shifted her weight from one leg to the other. Tendrils of cold wound around her veins, throbbing with every movement. The pain set her teeth on edge but didn't steal her sight. "I can walk, but I might not be the best at running."

"I don't think I can run much more anyway." T took Nola's hand.

"I can carry Nola, and Raina can carry T," Jeremy said.

360   MEGAN O'RUSSELL

"I don't want to be carried," Nola snapped. She swallowed the bubble of anger that rose in her chest. "We need to keep moving, and my legs work. Why don't you keep an eye out for anything that wants to kill us?"

Jeremy stared at Nola for a long moment, his eyes drifting from her face to her hands. "Just take it easy. Your body is still changing."

"I'll walk carefully." Nola turned to Raina. "Lead on."

"Right this way, campers," Raina said. "We're starting our stroll through the woods. On the list of sights today: dying trees, a few boulders, and the possibility of meeting some fine folks who want us dead. Keep up. You won't want to miss the fun."

CHAPTER FOUR

How much longer?

The question balanced on the tip of Nola's tongue, but she didn't dare ask. Aside from Jeremy's unavoidable offer to carry her and Raina's inevitable snarky response, no one had spoken in the last few hours. The silence seemed like a truce with the woods. A pact that kept their party safe as the trees thinned out, leaving them in an open field.

Brambles clung to Nola's legs, picking away at the fabric of her pants. She walked with her arms over her head, keeping her bare hands above the reach of the thorns.

The protests of the ice had begun to fade. A frozen stream ran through her veins, but the cold had lost its ability to cut.

High silhouettes blocked the stars as mountains rose up in the distance. Nola had always known there were mountains west of the city, but she'd never seen them before. They'd always been hidden behind crumbling buildings.

Is that where Nightland is waiting? Are Kieran and Dr. Wynne high up in the peaks?

Nola took a few quick steps.

Raina turned before Nola could tap her on the shoulder.

Nola pointed up toward the mountain.

Raina winked and kept walking.

"If we're going that far, we won't make it before sunrise," T whispered in Nola's ear.

Raina shot a scathing look over her shoulder.

"How did they evacuate Nightland out this far?" T asked. "All those people trampling through the woods, and the domes didn't follow them?"

"We didn't have the chance." Jeremy stepped up to Nola's other side. "By the time we managed to get out to look for them and establish they weren't in the city, they must have been miles away."

"And you didn't keep looking?" T asked. "Not that I think the domes have any right to come after Nightland, but it seems weird they didn't."

"It's complicated." Jeremy's jaw tightened, and his eyes locked on the mountain in the distance.

"The domes haven't patrolled beyond the city in twenty years," Nola said. "I doubt they'd know where to start."

"Who knew freedom was so close?" T rubbed her belly.

"Not really freedom for people like you." Raina's words carried over the field. "You would starve and die out here on your own."

"Not necessarily," Jeremy said. "These brambles are growing, other plants could grow, too. Set up a water filtration system. Find a way to protect your plants when the clouds turn acid. Build a place with enough shelter to protect you and you could make it."

"Funny," Raina said. "Nightland figured out the same thing."

"And if they hadn't broken into the domes to rob us and kill our people—"

"Us?" Raina asked. "Don't make me question your allegiance, Domer."

"The domes would have been happy to let Nightland go if they'd gone quietly," Jeremy finished.

"Would they?" Nola looked up to the sky. "Would they have just let them leave? Not knowing if they were building up power out here? Letting a big group survive outside the control of the domes?"

"Of course," Jeremy said.

Nola rounded on Jeremy. Brambles tore at her skin as she dropped her hands to her sides. "Think about it, Jeremy. Actually think about everything that's happened. They wanted me dead. They blew up a bridge with people on it. Everything that isn't serving the domes is a threat to them. And the survival of the domes is all the Outer Guard and the Council care about!"

A flock of birds burst out of the trees, frightened by Nola's yelling.

"You aren't an Outer Guard anymore, Jeremy Ridgeway," Nola said. "Stop thinking like one."

She turned and shoved her way through the brush toward Raina, who began clapping.

"You know"—Raina started forward—"the first time I saw you, I really wanted to kill you just for a snack. I hate to admit it, but I'm glad you're not dead."

"Thanks." Nola smiled. The cold didn't punish her face.

"Shouldn't be too much longer," Raina said, speaking as loudly as Nola had when she'd frightened the birds. "We all need to stay together. Remember, I'm the only vampire in our little pack, and that means more out here than a shiny Domer coat in the city."

"Raina, is there a reason you're talking so loud?" Chills that had nothing to do with Graylock floated up Nola's neck.

"Because it's better to make noise and let them know we're coming from far away than to sneak up on them and let them act without time to reason," Raina yelled.

"Who's *them*?" Beauford asked.

"Whoever Emanuel's decided is meant to guard the path."

A stand of dead trees grew out of the darkness, swallowing the base of the mountain. There were no new branches sprouting from these trees. Thick trunks with knobby lumps that no longer held the promise of growth blocked their path like ill-formed columns sculpted by a clumsy giant.

"Are we almost there?" Hope filled T's voice.

"Almost to the first place we need to reach," Raina shouted. "Not quite to Utopia."

Raina kicked free from the last of the field of brambles and stomped into the trees.

"She wanted them to see us coming." Jeremy pushed the thorns out of Nola's path with his arm. "I was hoping she had a reason for taking us through such open territory."

Nola hesitated, tempted to fight through the last foot of brambles rather than take Jeremy's help.

"Why does it matter if she wants to cut through a field?" She stepped through the gap.

"Because it's a dumb move." Jeremy held the path open for T and Beauford.

T gave a murmur of thanks. Beauford ignored Jeremy entirely.

"If we were trying to get to a secret location, knowing the Outer Guard might be coming after us, leaving a trail through a field would be just about the worst plan I could imagine." Jeremy jogged a few steps to walk next to Nola. "But if you want to give the people we're heading toward plenty of warning so we don't startle them, and make sure anyone who follows us will be visible to Nightland's guards and not able to sneak up, then letting ourselves get torn to pieces by thorns is a great plan."

"You know," Raina called back from twenty feet ahead, "if you weren't a filthy, murdering Domer, you'd make a great vampire. If you had found your way into Nightland as one of us, Emanuel would have found great uses for you."

"I don't know if I could agree to any use Emanuel would want me for," Jeremy said.

"You'd be surprised what desperation makes possible," Beauford said.

Jeremy opened his mouth to answer, then clamped his jaw shut and shook his head.

"Will we arrive in Nightland tonight?" T asked.

"If we're allowed," Raina said. "But don't get your hopes up for finding baby daddy tonight, little pregnant girl. I think you're in for a few surprises."

"Surprises?" The barren trees kept Nola's voice from carrying.

"I've been alive for quite a while." Raina banged her fist on the trunk of a tree. "I've been a vampire for most of that time. Since before any of you were even thought of at least."

"I didn't know Vamp had been around that long," Nola said.

"It wasn't," Raina said. "Not the way you'd think of it. Not the way it is now. Hundreds of different hack chemists brewing batches with no real knowledge of what the chemicals are meant to do and without the equipment to make untainted Vamp. More than half the people who try to become one of us turn out as zombies these days."

Nola shuddered as visions of men and women with sores on their skin and their minds destroyed sent sour soaring into her throat.

"You're okay, Nola," Jeremy whispered. "That can't happen to you."

"Obviously," Nola said.

"But that's because most people don't have access to ReVamp." Raina ignored them. "See, Nightland has Dr. Wynne, and he makes the good stuff. The kind that makes you all vampy without the *delightful* mental changes Vamp gives you."

"I know about ReVamp," Nola said.

"Of course you do. That's what we gave your beloved Kieran." Raina turned to walk backwards, her black eyes sliding from Jeremy to Nola. "Sorry, was that offensive?"

"Kieran used her and betrayed her," Jeremy spoke in a low voice.

"Seems like a theme," Raina said.

"Stop it," Nola said.

"Do you think the only thing Emanuel had planned was a new form of Vamp to build our ranks?" Raina winked and turned away from them, climbing up the steep hill.

"I know he had more planned than that," Nola said. "Kieran helped him find a way to garden—"

"A garden? How fancy," Raina cooed.

"They had more than that planned," T puffed, one hand on her stomach while Beauford held the other, dragging her uphill.

"Let me help you," Jeremy said.

T ignored him. "Charles told me there were plans. A place where the baby and I could be safe. Where we could live and not have to worry about food or werewolves, or the domes."

"Smart Charles," Raina said. "After all, what's the point in ruling a society of vampires if there's no plan for the future? Nightland isn't a street gang. We are the beginning. We are a better hope for the future than the domes could ever be."

"And what sort of future would that be exactly?" Jeremy asked. "A world ruled by thieves and murderers."

"Yes." Raina clapped her hands and looked to the sky. "That is the question. You've finally gotten to it! If thieves and murderers rule, how is there hope for anything but death?"

"Then the domes would have been right to destroy Nightland," Jeremy said.

"Wrong!" Raina shouted. "The domes are the ones who are the killers. Leaving people to starve in the street. Letting children die when they have the medicine that could save them—"

"There aren't enough resources—"

"And where do they get the resources to run the domes?" Raina asked. "The glass for your walls, the fuel for your trucks?"

"The city," Nola said. "They get everything from the city."

"A new prize pupil," Raina said. "All the things the domes need to create their perfect society come from the city."

"They paid for the glass—"

"Not a fair price," Beauford said. "You could work in a factory every day of your life and still have to choose between food and a safe place to sleep."

"You have some competition, Nola," Raina said. "The big guy is right. Work for the domes and you work for nothing. You work yourself to death without even a proper meal to show for it. And it was no better when they brought outsiders into the domes to work."

"They fed the workers," Jeremy said.

"They kept us locked up," T said. "Nola was the only one who even bothered to tell us what was happening in the city."

"Think about it, Jeremy." Nola tucked her hands behind her back, fighting the old habit of reaching for him. "We lived in the domes, sure we were the answer to saving the world. Never questioning the cost of our own survival. The domes only care about protecting human DNA. They stopped caring about people a long time ago."

"It's not all bad," Jeremy said. "You're making it sound like the domes are filled with serial killers."

"They blew up a bridge with people on it," T said.

"People who were going to attack the domes!" Jeremy said. "There were no non-combatants on the bridge."

"Except for me," Nola said. "I was on that bridge."

"And then they gave the order to kill her." Raina's teeth glinted in the faint moonlight. "And isn't she supposed to be the love of your life? First, you let them use her to slaughter all those wolves."

"I didn't have any say in that," Jeremy said. "Nola, you know I never would have wanted you out there."

"And then the people you still seem to be under the delusion are good ordered her death," Raina said. "Think about it, little boy. Really think. About the unforgivable suffering they turned their backs on. About all the lives they ended. About them letting your girlfriend face a pack of wolves and forcing her to watch them burn. Imagine the reception they would have given the guard who managed to kill her."

"I—"

"Don't talk," Raina said. "Just think. As deeply as that dome-crafted head of yours is capable of. If what they've done doesn't make you sick, then turn around and lead your Guard friends to Nightland. There would be no hope for you outside the glass castle of murderers anyway."

CHAPTER FIVE

"Let me help you." Nola wrapped her arm around T's waist.

"You're still healing." T shook her head.

"I feel all right," Nola said.

I feel better than all right.

The thought held as much terror as relief.

As they tramped up and down through the curves of the mountain, the sky above began to lighten with the rising sun, and the ice melted from Nola's veins. Her legs didn't feel tired, though they'd been climbing for hours. Her breath came easily and evenly, as though she were strolling through the halls of the domes.

Even in the dim light, the edges of the trees held crisp lines in Nola's sight. The faint scent of T's sweat filtered past the stench of decaying undergrowth and tinge of blood wafting from Raina.

I could run up this mountain.

The urge to sprint up the slope tickled Nola's feet, but she wouldn't leave T and Beauford and couldn't risk getting ahead of Raina.

"Raina," Beauford said.

"Yes, big guy?" Raina spoke loudly.

The muscles in Nola's neck tensed at the noise.

"If you're lost, I think it might be time to admit it," Beauford said. "The sun's coming up and we've got to get you to ground."

"Are we lost?" T's voice wavered.

"We're not lost," Raina said.

"We've looped up past this rise twice," Beauford said.

Nola looked to Jeremy. He hadn't spoken in hours, but he nodded at Nola's glance.

"Raina, why are we going in circles?" Nola studied the rocks to their left and the downed trees to the right. She had been so busy wondering at the changes the ice had brought, she hadn't been watching where they were going.

"I'm going in circles because it would be unwise to wait in one place." Raina didn't slow her pace.

"Wait for what?" Nola asked. "You either know the way in or you don't."

"Knowing the way in and being able to make it through alive are two very different things," Raina said. "We have to be welcomed in, and that welcome sure as hell had better be coming soon."

"What if they didn't make it?" T leaned heavily on Nola. "What if something happened and none of the vampires made it out this far?"

"They did," Nola said. "You've got to believe they did."

Tears rolled down T's face.

"That's it." Nola took a deep breath, filling her lungs with the chill morning air. "If someone is out there watching us, waiting to let us in, now would be a really great time!"

The cawing of frightened birds echoed from over the next rise.

"We've come from the domes, and for all we know there are Outer Guard chasing us—"

"Maybe not the best thing to mention," Raina said.

"My name is Magnolia Kent," Nola shouted. "I have Raina with me, and T who is carrying a child of Nightland. I have an Outer Guard who abandoned his post to come with us. If you're fool enough to think Emanuel won't want to see me, then I pity the punishment waiting for you if you leave us out here to die!"

Raina leaned against a tree, her face caught somewhere between amusement and disgust. "You just had to push their hand didn't you?"

"Push whose hand?" Nola asked. "You say this is the entrance to where Nightland is. You're from Nightland, T's got a Nightland baby. Emanuel owes me after the hell he put me through—"

"Does that mean we should leave the other two to die?" A low voice carried from above.

A dark-skinned man holding a long staff stood on a ledge ten feet above them. Bald headed with scars dotting his skin, the man smiled as he looked down at Raina, showing his sharpened fangs. "I thought you were dead."

"Desmond." Raina grinned. "I thought you were smarter than to listen to such nasty rumors."

"Hmm." Desmond's black eyes turned to each of the other four in turn, leaving Nola for last. "Nola Kent, none of us ever imagined we'd see you here."

"I never imagined it either." Nola kept her voice steady.

Now is not the time to fight, Nola.

She forced her hands to unclench.

"But I didn't think the domes would order my execution either," Nola said. "So, I guess it's been a really surprising few days for me."

Desmond laughed, the low sound more like a lion than a man.

"Desmond, you know me," Raina said. "How many years did I fight by your side?"

"Too many to count."

"Then you know I would never betray Emanuel. I've come home, old friend. Let me in." Raina and Desmond stared at each other for a long moment. "I've got tons of fun stories about being locked in a concrete cage, and I'd hate to die in the sun before I can tell them."

"What do you want me to do with the Domer?" Desmond pointed his staff at Jeremy. "Hang his entrails out for the birds? Bleed him for a snack?"

"No." Nola stepped in front of Jeremy. "He saved my life, and he can't go back to the domes."

"And?" Desmond said.

"And..." Nola glanced behind.

Jeremy stared at her with sadness in his eyes. He didn't open his mouth to defend his own life.

"And he has information for Dr. Wynne," Nola said. "About the drugs they've been giving the Outer Guard. If you leave him out here to die, the information dies with him."

Raina raised an eyebrow at Nola. "See, massively important information."

"Do you trust him, Raina?" Desmond asked.

"I trust my ability to kill him if he steps a toe out of line." Raina shrugged.

"Good enough." Desmond stepped back, disappearing behind the edge of the ledge.

"And in we get." Raina strode over to the slant in the mountainside.

From below, it didn't look like the ledge should be able to hold a person's weight. Covered entirely in moss, it seemed like nothing more than an overgrown lump of foliage.

Raina jumped, grabbing the ledge and pulling herself up in one easy motion. "Domer, give us the baby maker."

Jeremy nodded. T didn't argue as he led her to Raina, or as he took her waist, lifting her high overhead and into Raina's waiting arms.

Beauford walked up to the ledge.

Jeremy held out his hands, offering to lift Beauford.

"Not a chance." Beauford stared at the ledge.

Jeremy shrugged and made a step with his hands.

"Fine." Beauford stepped on Jeremy's palms. Raina grabbed his wrists before he could reach for the moss, lifting him straight up.

Nola laughed as Beauford's feet wiggled in the air before he disappeared.

Jeremy looked to Nola. Her laugh dissolved.

"Are you mute now?" Nola strode over to the ledge.

"I don't know what to say."

The hollow tone of Jeremy's voice slammed into Nola's gut. Like someone had punched her right where the wolf's knife had pierced her flesh.

"Let me help you." Jeremy reached for Nola's waist.

"I can do it myself." Nola looked up to the top of the ledge.

"Thank you," Jeremy whispered. "For vouching for me. For not letting them leave me out here. It's more than I deserve."

"I—" Nola dug her fists into her eyes. "Wanting you to not die and forgiving you are two very different things."

"I know."

"And I don't..." Nola's words faded away as she looked at Jeremy. The lines of worry etched in his face were more than any seventeen-year-old should bear. His shoulders were rounded, like someone had shattered the strong Outer Guard he had been. Dark blond stubble coated his cheeks.

Nola knew what his face would feel like against hers. Where on his shoulder her head fit so perfectly.

"I don't want you dead, Jeremy. I've never wanted anything bad to happen to you. I don't know if I could stand it."

"Nola—"

"So don't pull any asshole guard moves with Emanuel," Nola said. "I know you're strong, but so are they. And he'll do whatever it takes to protect his people. He already murdered people in the domes. I don't think he'll mind killing you."

"Are the two formerly known as lovebirds done?" Raina said. "Some of us would like to get moving."

"Right." Nola didn't look away from Jeremy.

He nodded, offering his hands as a step as he had done for Beauford.

"I want to do it on my own." Nola turned to the ledge.

"Aim a little higher than you think you need to. Try and get your palms on top, not just your fingers on the edge. Use your momentum to push up from there." Jeremy stepped back.

Nola stared up at the moss, feeling foolish.

I'm not strong enough to do this on my own.

"Don't think, just go," Jeremy said.

Nola bent her knees and jumped, sure she would fall flat on her face.

But the strength in her legs carried her up into the air. It wasn't until she neared the ledge that she remembered she was meant to grab hold. Her fingers tangled in the moss at the very edge.

"Yes!" Jeremy said. "That was great, Nola."

The moss she clasped in her fingers shifted, tearing from the stone beneath, as she pulled herself up.

With a *crack*, the moss ripped free. Before she could fall, Jeremy grabbed her feet, lifting her so her torso landed on the rock.

"Graceful." Raina stared down at her, shaking her head.

Nola crawled forward onto the ledge. A gap cut deep in the rock leading to an entrance that had been invisible from the ground below.

"It was my first try." Nola leapt to her feet. Her hands didn't ache from trying to cling to the side of the ledge.

Jeremy jumped up in one smooth movement as Raina had. "She did great." A smile flickered across his face.

Nola searched his eyes for the twinkle that should have been there. The joy of being with her.

"Come on then, super girl." Raina bowed them toward the cave.

Nola walked into the darkness, grateful she couldn't see Jeremy anymore.

"Nola?" T said.

Even in the darkness of the tunnel, Nola could see T's silhouette.

"I'm right here." Nola took T's hand, walking next to her, trailing her free hand along the rock walls.

The path sloped up, leading them deeper into the mountain.

A hint of panic seized the edges of Nola's heart.

You've already died. The middle of a mountain can't hurt you any more than the world already has.

"Are you the only welcoming committee?" Raina asked.

"Don't be offended," Desmond said, his voice rumbling from up ahead in front of the shadow that was Beauford. "We didn't think it was really you. Once I knew it was, too strong a greeting—"

"Seemed likely to get whatever hot headed children Emanuel put this far out on the perimeter killed?" Raina said.

"It's good to see your time with the Domers didn't change you," Desmond said.

"Some things never change, old friend. It would take more than concrete walls and starvation to break me."

Light glimmered in the tunnel up ahead. Nola squinted, trying to decide if the light was electric or only torches like the ones she'd seen in the tunnels of Nightland far beneath the city.

"How is he?" Raina asked.

"Triumphant."

Nola could almost hear the smile in Desmond's voice.

They rounded the corner, and the source of light came into view. Neither of Nola's guesses had been right. A section of the tunnel wall had been cut away, giving a view of the valley beyond.

Far below, at the bottom of the mountain's slope, the limbless trees met the field of brambles. Then the woods with trees fighting to survive where they had met the Vampers hours before.

Beyond the trees, glinting in the light of the rising sun, the city peered up.

"It's still burning." T tightened her grip on Nola's hand.

"It's been burning for a few nights," Desmond said. "We thought the whole place might be done for."

"It almost was." Nola watched the gray smoke twisting into the sky.

"It looks so small from here," Beauford said. "I lived my whole life there, never even crossed the river until the domes came for workers."

"I can't see the domes behind the smoke," T said.

Nola squinted through the gray. A glint touched the hill on the far side of the river, but she couldn't see the sweeping glass domes that had been her home.

"They're still there," Raina said.

"They were built to survive the end of the world," Nola said.

"Like warts from a disease," Raina said. "Awful to get rid of."

"Come on." Desmond moved beyond the light.

The path continued, stretches of darkness broken by swatches of light where windows had been made to view the outside world.

As the sun grew strong, Raina and Desmond hugged the inside edge of the tunnel, carefully keeping out of the light.

"What would happen if you stood in the light?" Nola asked as the bright beams warmed her face.

"Have you ever seen someone with an allergy be stung by a bee?" Raina said. "It's like that, but with a lot of bleeding."

"It won't be like that for you." Jeremy stepped up behind Nola's shoulder, speaking softly though there was no chance of Desmond and Raina not hearing. "You'll always be safe to be in the light. I promise."

Desmond's footfalls slowed. "I'm sure Dr. Wynne will be interested to hear what's left your blood smelling so strange."

"I smell?" Nola sniffed the back of her hand. "What do I smell..."

The question drifted from her mind as the tunnel in front of them widened to an open door leading to a cavern large enough to swallow Bright Dome whole.

CHAPTER SIX

The roof of the cavern towered forty feet overhead. Electric bulbs strung together with thick black wires shed light on every corner. A few tables with chairs and a few dozen cots lined the sides of the great room. Cages filled with weapons from Guard guns to crossbows and swords had been cut into the stone walls. The center of the cavern had been left open. Painted squares marked the floor, boxing in sparring pairs.

All sparring stopped, and sixty vampires stared at them as Desmond led them into the cavern. All had black eyes. All held weapons.

"This is more like it," Raina said.

"Desmond." A woman with platinum blond hair sauntered forward, a sword held in each hand. "Did you make some new friends, or find us a snack?"

Jeremy stepped in front of Nola, his hands raised and ready to defend.

"Friends," Raina said. "I'm surprised they've started letting you touch the pointy objects, Stell. Weren't you just meant to be a pretty face?"

Stell growled.

The other vampires moved in toward their group.

"Raina, you're alive?" asked a man with blood dripping from a cut on his head.

"Yes, I know, quite a miracle." Raina stepped in front of Desmond. "I'm alive, and I've brought some presents for Emanuel. You"—Raina pointed at a reedy-looking boy who didn't appear old enough to have survived being given Vamp—"run ahead to the library. If Emanuel isn't there, find him and bring him to me."

The boy bowed and ran toward the back of the cavern.

"Bring a snack, too!" Raina shouted after the boy.

"Where have you been?" the bleeding man asked.

"Hell," Raina said. "And I'll tell everybody all about it, just as soon as I've told Emanuel. Now, give it up, lover boy." Raina reached for Jeremy's belt.

Hs face flushed bright red, but he didn't fight as she unfastened his belt and took both holstered guns.

"Make a little stash for me." Raina tossed the holstered weapons to the bleeding man.

He bowed and headed for the weapons cages on the side of the room.

The crowd parted as Raina led them forward. Not even Stell stood in her way.

Nola kept her eyes front as they passed through the vampires. All of them held weapons. Any of them could kill her if they wanted to.

Jeremy won't let them. Even without weapons he'll protect me.

She didn't realize she had drifted closer to him until the back of her hand brushed against his.

Don't be stupid, Nola.

She tucked her hands behind her back.

New blood shone red on the floor, spattered across the brownish-black of dried blood from older fights.

"Back to work!"

Nola jumped at the shout. Before they'd made it to the far side of the cavern, the *clang* of steel on steel echoed off the walls.

"What are they training for?" Nola whispered.

"We're not naïve enough to think the domes will leave us alone forever," Raina said. "The domes will try and attack, or the wolves, or a hoard of zombies will catch the scent of blood and come looking for a feast. Arriving in Utopia doesn't end the battle. It only gives you more to lose."

A thick metal door set into the stone wall waited open at the edge of the cavern. The metal was four inches thick, and the wall had been carved to receive six heavy bolts to fasten the door in place.

"How long have you been building this?" Beauford asked. "You didn't decide to dig these tunnels right before you attacked the domes, or even in the last year."

Desmond took the lead through the tunnel. Electric lights had been set into the ceiling, bathing the smoothly carved stone walls in an even glow.

"I'm really starting to like you, big guy," Raina said. "Emanuel has been planning for a better world for a very long time."

"Then why is he just now coming here?" Nola said. "He could have left the city ages ago. There would have been no fighting with the domes—"

"And you'd still be safe behind glass?" Raina said.

"It would have been better for everyone." Pain cut through Jeremy's words.

"They didn't move into the domes until the final pane of glass had been sealed in place," Desmond said. "We couldn't move until everything was ready."

"And that took a very long time," Raina said. "I'm so glad I didn't die before I got to see the wonder of the true Nightland."

"Where is everyone else?" T said.

"If you're hoping for a cafeteria, you're out of luck." Raina glanced over her shoulder. "Don't worry, baby machine, I'll put out a call for the sperm donor and see who can find him."

"Thank you." T dragged her fingers through the tangles in her hair.

"How many people live here?" Nola took T's hand.

"I think I missed the census," Raina said.

"Over a thousand, including vampires, non-changed humans, and children," Desmond said.

"There are humans here?" Beauford asked.

They reached a fork in the tunnel. Desmond led them down the right hand side.

"Some," Desmond said.

Lambs living amongst the lions. Normal people sleeping in the safe haven made for those who would use them as a meal.

"Are you keeping them locked up?" Jeremy asked. "Are you keeping the humans caged as food?"

"Yes, little piggy, and you'll be next," Raina said.

"Emanuel wouldn't do that," Nola said. "Vampires in Nightland aren't allowed to drink from unwilling humans. Most live off animal blood. If humans are bleeding to feed vampires, they're making that choice themselves."

"Well done, Nola," Raina said. "Emanuel will be pleased to know all his work on you wasn't wasted."

"Was this work leading up to Emanuel blasting away part of the domes and killing innocent citizens, or was it some other thing?" Jeremy said.

Desmond tightened his grip on his staff.

"Something quite different." Raina laid a hand on Desmond's shoulder. "Emanuel had a strange notion that Nola might be proof there's hope for humanity. One heart that hadn't been so frozen by privilege it could no longer bleed."

"Well, he should congratulate himself then." Tears stung the corners of

Nola's eyes. "My heart keeps getting torn apart again and again, and it always bleeds like hell."

T squeezed Nola's hand.

The tunnel branched off three ways. Desmond took a sharp left into a wider tunnel. Wooden doors dotted this corridor, and people moved through the hall.

A man so tall he had to bow his head to walk through the tunnel sniffed the air as he passed, looking from Nola to Jeremy.

A green-eyed woman led four children down the hall, holding a fifth in her arms. She spotted T's belly. "Congratulations," the mother said with a smile.

"Thank you." T watched the children until they were out of sight, trusting Nola to guide her. "Did you see them?" Tears rolled gently down T's face. "They all had color in their cheeks, and so much hair."

"They were beautiful," Nola said.

"They were healthy," Beauford said.

"I wish Catlyn had seen this place," T whispered.

"You made it here," Beauford said. "That would have been enough for her."

"What happened to her?" Jeremy asked.

"Do you actually care?" Beauford said.

"The domes wanted Nola dead, and Catlyn helped keep her alive," Jeremy said. "I absolutely care."

"*All lives have value* would have sounded better, lover boy," Raina said.

A hollow pain swelled at the center of Nola's chest. "We were attacked before we ever got into the city. Catlyn didn't make it."

"I'm so sorry," Jeremy said. "She seemed like a really nice woman."

"She was," T said. "Maybe if the baby's a girl, I can convince Charles to name her after Catlyn."

"Catlyn would like that," Nola said.

Desmond stopped in front of an intricately carved double door.

"Only the best for Emanuel." Raina shoved the doors open.

Four stained glass chandeliers cast colorful light on the room, which was big enough to hold the largest house in the domes. Bookcases lined the walls with paintings and tapestries hanging above. A single door at the far side of the room was the only other exit.

"It's just like Nightland." Nola's throat tightened.

A lifetime ago, she had stood in Emanuel's library, desperate to know if Kieran was alive. She had thought the tunnels of Nightland were destroyed, a casualty of attacking the domes. But Emanuel had remade his sanctuary, preserving his precious proof of what being human used to mean.

A stuffed red armchair, which looked like something out of an old gothic novel, sat in the middle of the room. The seat hadn't been in the library in

Nightland. Nola kept her eyes focused on the chair, ignoring the rumble of voices behind the door in the back of the room and Jeremy inching closer to her.

"Raina." Emanuel's voice carried from the door behind them. "I thought I had lost you."

"Not so lucky." Joy filled Raina's voice. "I've come home, Emanuel."

"Thank you for fighting your way back to us. Who have you brought with you?"

There were swirls in the stitching of the chair. A twirling pattern that held no meaning.

"Jeremy's a disgraced Outer Guard who wants to see Dr. Wynne. Beauford was taken to the domes as a worker, so was T—she's carrying a child of Nightland. They helped Nola and me escape."

"Nola." Emanuel stepped in front of Nola, blocking the chair from view.

Curling black hair hung around his shoulders. His eyes were so dark, they moved beyond a given color and into a void of nothing. The natural tanned tone of his skin had been only slightly paled by years away from the sun.

"Nola, you've come back to us." Emanuel reached for her.

"You son of a bitch." Arms locked around Nola before she could launch herself at him. "You made me trust you. You convinced me to help you!"

"You saved an innocent child," Emanuel said.

"And you killed innocent people in the domes. Look at all you built here. Why break in? Just to prove you could? To spit in the face of the domes one more time before you disappeared?" Nola fought against the arms that held her. She would scratch his eyes out, then punch through his chest until she could rip out his heart.

"We needed supplies," Emanuel said.

"You could have asked for them in the trade." Nola's shout echoed off the walls. "Remember that? The time you handed me over to the domes when I wanted to stay with you. Why bother trading? Why bother sending me back if you were just going to break in anyway?"

"There were things we couldn't ask for," Emanuel said. "What we took from the domes will keep the children of Nightland healthy and safe for a hundred years. Is it not worth a few Domer lives to save four generations of children?"

"You sick bastard."

"This is a war, Nola Kent," Emanuel said. "You've known that since the first time you knocked to get into Nightland. It's a war the domes hide from their people, and yet one of their soldiers stands behind you."

Nola glanced down. It was Jeremy who held her in his vise-like arms.

"All I want for my people is to live in peace," Emanuel said. "But one final battle had to be fought. And I did everything I could to minimize loss of life on both sides."

"Tell that to the civilians killed in the domes. And what about the vampire that bit me? Huh? Was he just aching for a snack?"

"They scented blood and a frenzy took over," Emanuel said. "Not all of my soldiers were as strong as I believed them to be. Bringing the weak ones in was a mistake."

"A mistake that got people killed," Nola said.

"That isn't the first blood on my hands I regret, and I doubt it will be the last." Emanuel examined his impeccably clean palms. "It's the burden of power, and the plague that touches all at the end of the world who refuse to go gently into the dark night."

"You can justify anything, can't you?" Nola said.

"Anything that gives my people a better chance of survival. The domes were wrong to lock themselves away and hoard every resource the rest of us need to survive, but they got one thing right. You can't save everyone. You can't make them all follow you to salvation," Emanuel said. "I gathered those I could, as many as I could, and I found them safety. The few who perished along my path are nothing to the number I have saved."

"Tell that to the families they left behind," Jeremy said.

"I'm still comforting my own who lost loved ones to the domes," Emanuel said. "And now you're here. That either makes you enemies in my halls, or my own family to protect. I will leave that choice to you."

"Are you going to attack the domes again?" Jeremy asked.

"What would I gain tactically from attacking the domes from this distance?" Emanuel sat in his red chair.

"Nothing," Jeremy said. "They would be ready, they would destroy you, and they would follow the stragglers home."

"Then you have your answer." Emanuel spread his hands.

"Nothing about how you have what you need and causing any more bloodshed is a horror you won't risk?" Nola asked.

"That's more true than you know," Emanuel said. "But you won't believe me. Jeremy knows the truth of tactics. That he can believe."

"It would be suicide for them to attack again," Jeremy said.

"Good," Nola said.

"Are you past wanting to attack me?" Emanuel asked.

"No," Nola said. "But it wouldn't be a *tactically sound* decision."

"I think you can let Nola go, Jeremy," Emanuel said. "Learning to live in Nightland won't be an easy transition for either of you, but know you are welcome and will find safety within my home."

"Just like that?" Nola said. "You'll welcome us with open arms?"

"You helped Raina," Emanuel said. "The least I can offer you is a chance at a home."

"What sort of home are you offering?" Jeremy eased his grip on Nola, though he didn't let her go. "A bunker in a mountain, is this really the hope you've been waiting for? How are you going to feed a thousand people? What plants can you grow in the dark to feed the children, and where are you getting blood from?"

"I always suspected the Outer Guard were smarter than their uniforms let on," Raina said.

"I would be happy to give you a tour of our gardens and farm, but it's better to wait for nightfall," Emanuel said. "We have plenty to do in the meantime. Find you a place to rest—"

"And Charles." T stepped forward. "My baby's father is Charles. He fought with you at the domes."

Emanuel's brow wrinkled. "Desmond, find Julian and have him search the records for Charles."

Desmond strode toward the door at the back of the library.

"We'll do what we can to find him," Emanuel said.

"Thank you." T gave a small bow.

The door at the back of the library swung open before Desmond reached for the handle. A boy with dark hair and a pale face stepped into the library.

"We need to get her fed, too," Raina said. "I pushed her hard to get here."

The boy's eyes weren't the green they should have been. Black had swallowed the color.

"Nola."

The boy's voice was the same. She would recognize the way he said her name even after a hundred years.

"Nola, how did you get here?"

The room swayed as he came toward her, worry and joy marking his face in equal measure.

She didn't know how she broke free of Jeremy's arms, didn't feel her feet carry her toward Kieran, couldn't hear the words his mouth formed.

Nola didn't know anything until pain shot through her knuckles as they met his face.

CHAPTER SEVEN

"Nola!" Jeremy's shout echoed off the walls as Nola punched Kieran again. "You filthy traitor!" The scream tore from Nola's throat as Jeremy's arms locked around her again, lifting her feet from the floor. "You knew them. The people you helped Nightland kill in the domes, you knew them!"

"Nola." Kieran's eyes were wide with shock.

"How could you?" Nola kicked back, catching Jeremy in the knee. "I trusted you. Was everything a lie? Did you ever even give a shit about me?"

"I have always loved you," Kieran said.

Jeremy's grip loosened.

Nola launched away from him, tackling Kieran to the ground with strength she didn't recognize.

"Don't you dare!" She punched him in the chin. "Don't you fucking dare. You led them into our home." She hit him again. "I got bit, Jeremy almost died. So many people did die." She hit him again and again. Hands forced her arms to her sides, lifting her away from Kieran. "No, let me go. You let me go."

Desmond kept her arms pinned.

Kieran stared up at her from the ground. Blood trickled from his nose, and bruises covered his face.

"You were my best friend." Tears coursed down Nola's cheeks. "I loved you. I mourned for you. How could you?"

Kieran sprung to his feet like she hadn't hurt him at all. "We had to go into the domes. There was no other way. I'm sorry."

"*Sorry* doesn't bring people back to life." Nola kicked and squirmed, desperate to break free, to hurt Kieran. To make him feel every ounce of agony he had caused. "You made me believe in you, and then you ruined everything."

"I'm so sorry." Kieran took a step forward, both hands out as though approaching a wounded animal. "I wish there had been another way to get the medicine to save Eden. I wish I had never led you to Nightland and we hadn't needed the supplies from the domes. I wish my dad and I had never gotten kicked out of the domes and you and I were still living there safely, the two of us together, like it was meant to be."

The will to fight left Nola's limbs. Desmond loosened his grip on Nola, setting her back on the floor.

"Nola, I'm sorry," Kieran whispered. "I never, ever wanted to hurt you."

"Well, you did." A sob hitched in Nola's chest. "You broke my heart. I trusted you, and loved you, and…" There were no more words, just tears.

Arms wrapped around Nola. Not holding her back but comforting her. Jeremy held her close to his chest, his scent of fresh earth filling her lungs.

Nola pushed away from him, smacking him hard across the face.

Jeremy blinked wide-eyed at her.

"Don't pretend you didn't hurt me too." Every inch of Nola's body shook as tears streamed freely down her face.

"It's okay, Nola." T took her hand. "You're okay. We'd like to find a place to rest, please."

Nola couldn't see past her tears as T led her out the double door of the library and down the hall.

Emanuel and Raina spoke softly at the front of the group. The sound of Jeremy's boots echoed far behind.

"How?" Nola asked. "How did all of this happen?"

"The end of the world sucks," Beauford said. "Surviving is hard, and it makes people hard. Death is common, pain is normal. When finding a way to live to the end of the day is a battle, it's easy to think of everyone as a casualty of war."

"Big guy is smart." Raina stopped at a wooden door. 113 had been carved at the top. "In you get. I'll bring some food around later." She swung open the door, bowing them in. "Nola, do you still eat?"

"Yes, she eats," Jeremy said.

"Don't speak for me," Nola growled.

T dragged her into the stone room.

"I don't think so, lover boy." Raina blocked Jeremy at the door. "We'll find a different place for you to rest your weary head."

"I—" Jeremy began.

Nola stopped him with a glare.

Jeremy shrugged and stepped back.

"Get some rest." Raina shut the door, leaving Nola with T and Beauford.

Four cots and a table took up most of the room, leaving barely enough space for the three sets of drawers crammed between the beds. None of the furniture matched, and all of it had been patched up in some way.

"They must have scavenged all over the city." T pulled out one of the four chairs and sat, hands draped over her belly.

"How many carved out rooms are there in this place?" Beauford asked. "How long did it take them to dig, and how did the whole thing not collapse?"

"No idea." Nola's voice shook.

"Come sit." T nudged a chair with her toe.

"I don't want to sit." Nola buried her face in her hands. The pain in her knuckles from punching Kieran had already begun to fade.

"Then what do you want to do?" T asked.

"Punch some more people is my guess." Beauford sat on the bed nearest the door.

"That would be nice. Or I could run until my legs fall off. Or grab a pick and smash the walls until this whole place caves in." Nola paced in front of the door.

"You're stronger now, but I think the mountain might still win," T said.

Nola examined the skin on her knuckles. She hadn't even noticed she'd been bleeding, but drying blood coated her hand, surrounding freshly healed skin.

"I hope I'm strong enough that it actually hurt him." A tremble of shock stung Nola's heart at her own words. She sank into a chair.

"I didn't know you'd really been in love with him," T said. "Kieran, I mean."

"Maybe I wasn't," Nola said. "I mean, I thought I was, he was my best friend for forever. I trusted him…"

T squeezed Nola's hand, ignoring the blood on her skin. "You can't always pick who you love."

"It's not supposed to be like this." Anger flushed Nola's cheeks as she said the childish words. "You should be able to love people. To trust people."

"And no one should be hungry, and clean water should fall from the sky," Beauford said.

"How did this happen?" Nola swiped the tears from her cheeks. "How did I end up in a dug out cave with vampires? How did this become the good idea?"

"You got betrayed by a lot of people, and there's nowhere else you can go and stay alive," Beauford said.

"Beauford," T shushed.

"He's right," Nola said. "Living with the devil is better than death."

"See? Start with *better than death* and work your way up from there." Beauford stretched out on the bed.

Footsteps passed in the hall. T sat up straight, staring wide-eyed at the door, but the person on the other side kept walking.

"They'll find him," Nola said.

"They will." T gave a faint smile. "They have to. I came too far to find him."

A minute passed, then another.

"What happens if they can't find him?" T whispered.

"Then you'll still be okay." It was Nola's turn to squeeze T's hand. "You're strong and brave."

"And you're not alone." Beauford spoke with his eyes closed. "Nola and I will be here."

T looked at Nola.

"He's right," Nola said. "We're all here together. And we'll all make sure your baby is safe."

"Thank you."

A cluster of footsteps passed through the hall, the sound rumbling through the door.

Nola wanted to prop open the door to see who was passing by or, better yet, go find Julian and help find Charles herself. But wandering the tunnels would only get her lost.

"What if the baby isn't born healthy?" T whispered. "What if I find Charles, but our baby doesn't survive?"

"Breathe, T," Beauford murmured. "The best thing you can do for the baby is breathe."

"What if the baby hasn't got lungs to breathe or a brain?" T said. "What if the baby already has a terrible disease from my living in the city?"

"Dr. Wynne is the best doctor on the outside," Nola said. "He'll make sure your baby is okay."

Please let Dr. Wynne be able to help her.

Nola held onto T's hand, examining the room to keep from staring at T's belly.

These walls hadn't been carved as smoothly as the walls of the hall. Three bulbs hung from the ceiling, linked together by a red cord that ran through the top of the wall on one side of the room and out the other. There was no window in the room, but the air didn't have the stifling quality she would have expected. Nola searched the walls for the vent pushing in the cool air. Only a four-inch hole in the ceiling gave any hint as to where the air might be coming from.

Emanuel built a good home.

Nola hated herself for being impressed almost as much as she hated herself for being in Nightland.

"Make a count," Beauford said. He'd turned to lie on his side, his brow wrinkling as he watched Nola.

"What do you mean?" Nola asked.

"If you can't decide which is worse, being here or in the domes," Beauford said. "Maybe you're even thinking you would have been better off in the city."

"I wouldn't last a night in the city," Nola said.

"You've had Graylock." T's gaze stayed fixed on the door.

"Okay, a week then," Nola said.

"It's bigger than you surviving, and you know it," Beauford said. "If you want to know who the real monsters are, count bodies. How many has Nightland killed, how many have the domes killed?"

Nola's mind raced through blood and shattered glass. "I don't know all the numbers."

"But you can guess," Beauford said.

"It all changed on the bridge," Nola said. "It would have been Nightland before that."

"But the domes slaughtered wolves and outsiders," Beauford said.

"They were attacking," Nola said.

"The domes attacked Nightland," T said, "and Nightland attacked the domes. And the domes decided to put down the riots and everyone in them, and the wolves decided to fight back. What they put you through on the bridge never should have happened. Outsiders locked up in cages under the domes never should have happened. Needing Vamp to survive never should have happened. Charles leaving me never should have happened. When everything is dark, a lot of *never should haves* happen. This is the only chance we have to survive. They're keeping children alive here. If Nightland will protect my baby, then I don't care who else they've hurt. The domes would have dumped us outside to die at best, killed us themselves if they felt like it. That decides it all for me."

"You're right," Nola whispered. "You're absolutely right."

"There is no right, only the least bloody path to survival." T leaned forward in her chair, staring at the door as though willing it to open.

The room slipped back into silence.

A little girl ran past their door, laughing, and a woman chased her, scolding.

Seventy-two Domers killed when Nightland attacked.

At least a hundred on the bridge when the domes set off the bomb.

She didn't know how many vampires had been killed when the domes had raided Nightland.

Nola gasped as a sharp knock sounded on the door.

"Come in." T tightened her grip on Nola's hand.

Julian stepped into the room, his dark shining hair perfectly in place. His sword sheathed at his hip.

"Nola." He bowed. "It is an unexpected but truly pleasant surprise to see you again." The words rolled perfectly out of his mouth, the inflection different from anyone else Nola had heard speak in the city or the domes.

"I'm just as surprised as you are, Julian," Nola said.

"Julian?" T stood, still clutching Nola's hand. "You're the one who was going to find Charles."

"T?" Julian said.

T nodded.

Nola's heart shattered at the pain that drifted through Julian's black eyes.

"I'm so terribly sorry," Julian said. "I'm afraid Charles didn't make it to our new Nightland."

T's knees buckled. Nola caught her under the arms before she hit the floor.

"What do you mean he didn't make it?" Beauford pushed the chair behind T, helping Nola to lower her into the seat.

"I'm not sure how much you know," Julian said. "Charles came with us to the domes. He was an excellent fighter, one of the best we had."

"Then where is he?" T said.

Nola held onto T, keeping her in the chair even as her whole body shook.

"He was wounded in the fighting at the domes," Julian said. "His group made it out of the glass, but the werewolves had seen the explosion. They were waiting across the bridge. They picked off the wounded before we could stop them. Charles died fighting for a better future for Nightland."

A wail tore from T's throat as she crumpled in Nola's arms.

"I know it won't seem like much now," Julian said, "but Charles wanted Nightland to reach its new home to protect his child. He died ensuring your baby's future. I know he would be happy you found your way to us."

Nola wasn't sure T could understand Julian's words through her sobs.

"You should leave," Beauford said.

"Of course." Julian bowed again. "If there's anything I can do—"

"We need water and food for her," Nola said.

"Right away."

Nola didn't bother to watch the door shut behind him.

Beauford lifted T from her chair.

Nola pulled back the sheets on the nearest cot.

"He's gone," T sobbed. "We came all this way, and he's gone."

Nola pulled up the covers, tucking T in. "Shh, you're okay. We're safe now, and it's going to be okay." She curled up behind T, holding her tightly as she cried. "It's okay. You're going to be okay."

The lie soured in her mouth.

CHAPTER EIGHT

A day had passed. Or maybe only a few hours. It was hard to know when Nola didn't need sleep. Not the way she used to at least.

She made T eat and drink some water. The fruit, bread, and cheese were more than Nola had expected. The water didn't taste of chemicals, or numb her mouth with unknown contamination. A hint of earth was the only thing that set it behind dome standards.

She'd curled up in the same bed with T, holding her while she cried herself to sleep. Beauford snored quietly in the bed across the room. But Nola couldn't sleep. Neither her body nor her brain were tired.

Closing her eyes against the light coming from under the door, she tried to clear her mind. But shadows climbed into her thoughts, unwilling to let her go.

Her mother sitting in her seed laboratory, refusing to acknowledge Nola was gone. Or maybe refusing to admit she'd had a daughter at all. Captain Ridgeway, Jeremy's father and the head of the Outer Guard, pacing in his office, plotting a way to find his son.

Will he be finding him to save him, or to protect the Graylock?

Tears squeezed from Nola's eyes.

It wasn't right. Jeremy shouldn't be out here. He should be safe at home. Raina would have saved Nola.

And I'd be a vampire. And I'd never see Jeremy again.

Nola bit the inside of her lips, willing her tears to stay silent.

The domes would give up on trying to find them soon, if they hadn't already.

Even Captain Ridgeway wouldn't risk his men going out beyond the city limits to find his son.

Her tears passed, but still Nola couldn't find sleep.

She'd climbed a mountain, she should be exhausted. She considered each part of her body, from her toes up, looking for pain or strength. Any sign that she had nearly died and chemicals had altered the way her body worked to save her. Everything felt the same.

I'm never going to sleep again.

Nola lifted her arm off of T, hating herself for her choice even as she made it.

The cot squeaked as she stood. Nola froze, waiting for T to wake. But exhaustion and grief trapped her in sleep.

"I'll be back soon," Nola whispered.

Checking the case on her hip, Nola opened the door a crack and slipped out into the hall, closing the door behind her.

"Nola."

She jumped, her heart throttling her throat. She spun to see a boy in jeans and a red shirt sitting on the floor.

"It's just me," Jeremy said as Nola finally looked at his face. "Raina thought it best if I ditched the uniform."

"Probably."

"I feel naked without it." Jeremy stood. The foreign brightness of his shirt didn't diminish his size, but rather made him seem bigger and younger at the same time.

"What are you doing here?" Nola asked.

"I knew you wouldn't be able to sleep." Jeremy shrugged. "And I didn't think you'd want to lie still for very long."

"Do we not sleep?" Nola asked, her head spinning at the concept of never sleeping again. "Does Graylock make it so you can't?"

"You will sleep," Jeremy said. "Just not as much or as often. I only do about six hours every three days."

"Is it awful?"

"Not once you get used to it. Give it a couple weeks and you'll be all right. If we can find you a watch, it'll help. Keeps the meaning in time."

Nola rubbed her eyes, testing them for fatigue. "How did I never notice you not sleeping?" Nola asked. "I slept beside you in your hospital bed. Or was that a lie? Were you only faking?"

"I would never lie to you, Nola."

She made a sound between a growl and a laugh.

"I never lied," Jeremy pressed on. "There were just some things I wasn't allowed to tell you."

"Like that you were taking a drug to change the way your body works or that there was a bomb planted under the bridge?"

"Yes."

Nola turned her back on him, striding down the hall toward Emanuel's library.

"Nola." Jeremy's bootfalls thumped after her. "Nola." He took her arm.

Nola stopped, glaring at Jeremy's hand touching her.

"Sorry." He tucked his hands in his jeans pockets. "I couldn't tell you about Graylock. The whole thing was classified, and the Council had banned normal domes citizens from knowing about it."

"Because sane people would know it was wrong," Nola said.

"But you were willing to forgive it, remember?" A line wrinkled Jeremy's brow. "The Graylock saved me. I would have died without it."

Nola dragged her hand through her hair, catching her fingers on her tangled curls. "Fine, Graylock I can forgive, but using me to kill people—"

"I never thought they'd actually take you out there," Jeremy said, his tone shifting as his desperation grew. "If I had known my dad was going to send you out to face a pack of wolves, I would have told you to hide until it was all over. It wasn't until I saw you by the bridge that I even knew you were there."

"But you knew about the bombs," Nola said. "You knew they were going to wait until the bridge was packed and then blow it up, with both of us still on it."

"Yes. I knew about the bomb."

Nola turned away, unwilling to look at Jeremy's face and see a murderer.

"But I had no control over when the explosives went off." Jeremy stepped around to stand in front of Nola again. "It shouldn't have happened the way it did. They should have blown the bridge as soon as they could. Part of Lucifer's group might have been killed, but it would have been worth it to block the rest of the mob, you've got to be able to see that."

Nola willed her mind back to the bridge. To Lucifer promising to kill and eat the Domers if they wouldn't give up their food supply.

A massacre of the people who hid in the glass castle.

Nola nodded.

"I don't know why my father waited until the bridge was full," Jeremy said. "Maybe he thought you could talk them down, or at least wanted to seem like he'd tried to end things peacefully. Maybe the explosives weren't ready. I don't know. It wasn't my choice. If it had been, you would have stayed inside, and the bridge would have been blown before any Outer Guard set foot on it. I don't know why the guards were ordered to kill you, and I don't know what they would do to me if they found me."

"They'd catch you and stick you in a concrete cell or kill you on sight." Nola wrapped her arms around her chest, trying to squeeze out the pain of thinking of Jeremy dead.

"Nola, when you told me what you'd done to help Nightland, I forgave you."

Nola looked up to the light on the ceiling, willing the brightness to burn away the image of Jeremy's pleading face.

"I was angry, but I knew you were only trying to help people. And those people used you, and lied to you."

"I've been lied to a lot." Nola pushed the words past the knot in her throat.

"I was lied to, too," Jeremy whispered. "The Outer Guard are supposed to protect the citizens of the domes and they used you. They hurt you. I didn't think my father or any of the other guards were capable of that."

"So you want me to just forgive you?" Nola blinked away the spots from the light. Tears trickled down her cheeks. "To just say, 'Oops, I watched a hundred people get blown up, but that's okay, I still love you?'"

"No, I don't." Pain echoed in Jeremy's voice. "I want you to not hate me. I want you to be able to walk next to me without cringing at the sight of me. I need to protect you, Nola."

"I don't need—"

"Because protecting you is all I have. And whether you ever love me again or not, I will spend the rest of my life loving you." He reached out, gently brushing the tears from Nola's cheeks. "I have to keep you safe, because not knowing if you're okay hurts a lot more than getting shot or stabbed, and I don't know if I can take it."

"Jeremy..."

"You don't have to be in love with me," Jeremy said. "But at least trust me to be your friend. I swear to you, Nola, I will never hide anything from you again, even if I think it'll scare you. And no matter what it costs me, I promise there will be no more secrets. Just let me be near you, that's all I need."

"I don't need a bodyguard."

"Then let me teach you to fight," Jeremy said. "Since I've promised honesty, it felt really good to see you pummeling Kieran."

Nola coughed a laugh.

"But your form was bad." Jeremy grinned. "You could have done a lot more damage if you knew what you were doing."

A twinkle glimmered in the corner of his eye. Like the old Jeremy, the one who had always known how to make her laugh, was waiting right below the surface.

Either way it'll hurt.

"Fine," Nola said. "You can teach me how to fight. But you don't get to fight for me, or speak for me, or make choices for me."

"Deal." Jeremy held out his hand.

"Deal."

The warmth of Jeremy's hand spread up Nola's arm. It would be so easy to twine her fingers through his. To lean into his chest and feel safe and secure, like being so far from home didn't matter because home had come with her.

"It's probably best we're on speaking terms anyway." She dropped Jeremy's hand but let him keep step beside her as they continued toward the library. "I have no idea what Graylock is doing to me, we're the only two on Graylock outside the domes' control, and the only two Domers in Nightland."

"It'll be good to have you watching my back," Jeremy said. "I have a feeling the Vampers will be a lot friendlier to you than they will to me."

A smile curved Nola's lips before she could stop it. "First rule: don't call them Vampers. Go with vampires. It's more likely to keep their teeth from your neck."

"I'm learning already."

The doors to Emanuel's library were shut. Nola had never been left on her own to wander the tunnels of Nightland under the city. She'd only been alone as she fled the blood and screams of the Outer Guard's attack on the club. She raised her hand to knock. Flakes of blood still marked her knuckles.

She shoved the doors open. Her heart skipped a beat as she waited for someone to scream at her for barging in or to attack her for being in a forbidden place.

But the library was empty and unguarded.

"What are we doing here?" Jeremy asked. "Not that I'm questioning your decision."

"In the tunnels, Dr. Wynne's laboratory was right behind the library, in Emanuel's house. We need to see Dr. Wynne, and this seems like a good place to look."

A painting hung over the door at the back of the room. Nola studied the picture as they neared. A girl in a garden, sitting in a sea of flowers, surrounded by trees dripping with fruit.

Emanuel's dream for Eden.

Nola paused with her hand on the door. To enter the throne room was one thing, to enter a home another.

Knock, knock, knock.

The sound thudded through the thick door.

The door swung open a few seconds later.

Raina, her hair re-dyed to its scarlet and purple streaked glory, leaned against the doorjamb. "Have you come to punch Kieran some more?"

"He would deserve it if I had," Nola said.

"Aren't children adorable with their little temper tantrums?" Raina cooed.

"We're here to see Dr. Wynne," Nola said. "I'm assuming his lab is back here."

"Keep the jewels close to the keeper." Raina stepped out of their way. "Be gentle with the doctor."

"How is he?" Nola asked.

"His eyes are turning a nice shade of black." Raina led them down the hall, past a kitchen and four closed doors.

"He had to take ReVamp?" Grief pressed into Nola's lungs.

"His genius bordering on madness had turned more to madness," Raina said. "His memory started to slip when Kieran was almost killed by the Outer Guard who raided Nightland."

"And what good is he to Emanuel without his brain?" Nola said.

"What good is he to himself if he can't think?" Raina said. "He injected himself, no one pinned him down."

"At least there's some mercy in that," Jeremy said.

"Oh, are we letting lover boy speak?" Raina stopped at the only metal door in the hall.

"My name is Jeremy."

"So says you." Raina tapped on the door, not waiting before she swung it open. "Company, Doctor."

"Company?" Dr. Wynne looked up from the papers on his desk. His hair had gone fully gray and stuck out at odd angles, as though each of his thoughts blew his hair in a new direction. His pale skin had been nearly translucent the last time Nola had seen him, but the ReVamp had thickened it, hiding the trails of blue. The drugs had begun turning his eyes black, but as they found Nola's face, they held a sharper awareness than Nola had seen from him in a very long time.

"Magnolia." The doctor was on his feet in an instant, crossing the lab in a few strides to pull Nola into a hearty hug. "I'm so happy you're safe."

"Dr. Wynne," Jeremy said.

Dr. Wynne let go of Nola. "Jeremy Ridgeway. I thought Kieran must have made a mistake when he said you were here." Dr. Wynne shook his head and Jeremy's hand. "Well, as surprised as I am that you've sought refuge here, I'm glad you made it in one piece."

"Thank you." A hint of something between fear and disgust flitted through Jeremy's eyes as he looked at Dr. Wynne.

"You'll both be assets to Nightland, of course." Dr. Wynne smiled, either not noticing or not caring about Jeremy's coldness. "There is so much work to be done. The gardens are still expanding, and so many vampires are undisciplined. You need discipline to be prepared to defend your home."

"You also need discipline if you're going to invade someone else's." Jeremy spoke through clenched teeth.

"Actually"—Nola stepped in front of Jeremy—"we were hoping you might be able to help us."

"Help you?" Dr. Wynne squinted at Nola's face. "You don't appear to be ill."

"I'm not." Nola opened the black case at her hip, pulling free one precious syringe. "But only because this saved me." She held the black liquid up to the light.

CHAPTER NINE

"Will you thank Dr. Wynne again for me?" T's soft voice bounced off the stone walls of the corridor.

"Of course," Julian said.

T, Beauford, and Nola clustered around him as he strode down the hall, Jeremy trailing ten feet behind. "He is the best doctor Nightland has to offer. And quite frankly, I think it was a relief for him to do something as joyful as check on a mother and baby. A nice change from other tasks."

Like finding a way to make more Graylock. Nola chewed on her bottom lip.

"And it'll be a nice change to get all of you outside as well. I'm sure it'll be quite healthy," Julian pressed on. "Dr. Wynne recommends it, and I must say my own mother would have thought the same." Julian led them down a flight of roughly hewn stone steps. "A task to perform. Something important to do."

Fresh air wafted up from below.

"Of course, I won't pretend we don't need the help. Especially from you, Nola. We don't have anyone as qualified in botany as you are."

The stairs ended at a doorway to the open air. Two different doors had been left ajar. One with thick metal bars like a cage, the other solid metal like the door through which they had entered the mountain.

"Of course, I don't know if there's anything that truly requires your specialty to be done this evening, and Kieran has been doing an excellent job of maintaining the gardens," Julian said.

Jeremy took a few quick strides, catching up to Nola and walking right behind her shoulder.

"We wouldn't be able to maintain our non-vampire population without him," Julian said. "But when resources are scarce, every innovation possible is needed to produce food."

"Happy to help," Nola said. "Is everything set up the way it was in Nightland, or have…"

The rest of her question faded from her mind as they reached the open air.

They hadn't arrived in another brief opening before a new set of tunnels, but in a valley carved out between the peaks of the mountains.

Terraces had been cut into the slopes, creating steps of soil supporting rows of crops. Disks of fabric, larger than any Nola had ever seen, had been placed around the tops of the mountain. Though the half-moon gave the only light, Nola could imagine the parasol-like fabric blocking out the worst rays of the sun.

Julian led them to the far side of the narrow valley toward the steps that cut up the terraces.

"How do you block the rain?" Nola asked.

"We don't usually need to." Kieran wound his way through a row of greens, dirt coating his clothes.

Nola's hands instinctively curled into fists as he stopped in front of their group.

"The pollution that causes the acid rain usually stays pretty low over the city," Kieran said. "Most of the rain at this elevation is clean. And when it looks like we might get bad rain, we cover everything by hand. I'd love to have a tenting system, but keeping the sun from scorching the crops had to be the first priority."

"Good evening, Kieran," Julian said. "I've brought four more to help with the gardens."

Kieran looked to Nola. "I need all the help I can get."

"It looks like you've done well all on your own," Nola said. "This is huge compared to the garden on the roof above Nightland in the city. Were you running up to the mountains to plant things on off days? Why did you even bother taking the plants you'd been working with in the city when you had so much here? You could have left them behind. People could still be eating from that garden."

The people working in the rows around them stood, watching Nola as she shouted.

She couldn't bring herself to care. "What the hell did you need from the domes if you have all this out here?"

"Nola, I don't know if this is the venue for a lovers' quarrel," Julian said.

"Maybe we should go dig something," Beauford said.

"We have less than twenty crops we can grow out here, Nola," Kieran said.

"Do the math. That isn't sustainable. Bugs, bacteria, we could lose everything, and people would starve. The domes aren't the only ones planning for the future."

Jeremy stepped forward to stand next to Nola. "When plans involve killing people, they're usually bad plans."

"Weren't you an Outer Guard?" Kieran asked. "Did you get through that without hurting anyone?"

The gardeners crept closer, whether for entertainment or to defend Kieran, Nola didn't know.

"Just tell us what work you want us to do." Beauford pointed to a barrel holding shovels, hoes, and rakes. "Let's stop talking and shovel things."

"What did you take?" Nola asked. "What did you need that you couldn't ask for in the trade? Remember the time you traded me for seeds and medicine? What was so precious the domes wouldn't pay it to get me back?"

"They would have paid anything," Jeremy said. "Between your mother and my father, there's nothing the Council wouldn't have given to get you back safely. I was waiting outside the meeting with the ice from the Graylock taking over my veins. I heard it all. The domes would have done anything to get her back."

Nola laid her hand on Jeremy's arm. He stopped shaking at her touch.

"What did you steal, Kieran?" Nola asked.

Kieran looked up at the stars. "You'll have to ask Emanuel. I was only a guide to get them in and out as quickly as possible while meeting as few guards as possible. I was trying to keep as many people safe as I could."

"By betraying your home?" Jeremy said.

"The domes kicked me out," Kieran said. "Nightland is my home. Nightland saved me and my father. Nightland took care of us when the domes left us outside to die."

"Kieran—"

He spoke over Nola. "I didn't know when we gave you back that Emanuel needed more from the domes before we could leave the city. I couldn't stop the raid, so I went to the domes to try and get in and out as fast as we could. If the vampires who went in hadn't known exactly where to go, how many more people would have died? Did I really do something so terrible?"

"Yes!" Jeremy spat.

"You told them not to hurt me," Nola said. "You led them into my home. You let them kill people all around me, but I had to survive."

"I couldn't let them touch you." Kieran spoke softly. "It was the only protection I could give you, and the thought of anyone hurting you is more than I can stand."

"It wasn't mercy." Nola dug her nails into her palms, refusing to let tears come. "And it wasn't kindness. And it didn't work anyway. I got bit, Kieran. Raina saved me, not you."

"Who bit you?" Kieran said. "Tell me who it was and—"

"And what?" Nola asked. "You'll kill him?"

"Nola, I'm so sorry." Pain creased Kieran's face.

"Can we just work on the garden? It would be a lot more useful than apologies." Nola studied the nearest greenery, unwilling to look at Kieran any longer. Leaves from a potato plant peeked up through the dirt.

"We have some squash ready to harvest down the row," Kieran said, his voice even and unreadable. "We're almost to the end of what we can grow out here for the season. With the nights getting cold, there's not much we can keep alive."

"And then what do people eat?" Beauford asked.

"What we've stored, and what we can grow below," Kieran said. "I want to build a way to grow in the cold season aboveground, but that will have to wait until next year."

"Just don't try stealing glass from the domes." Jeremy moved out in front of their group. "The guards would destroy you."

"There's plenty of glass to salvage in the city." Kieran stepped forward. "Just because the domes demand fancy glass doesn't mean it's the only way things can work."

"Nola, I'm sure you're up to harvesting some squash," Julian said loudly. "Why don't you lead Beauford and T down that way? I'm sure Kieran has work to get back to, and Jeremy can help me transfer the new soil from below."

"I should stay with Nola." Jeremy's fiery gaze stayed on Kieran.

"I can harvest some plants without supervision." Nola stalked down the row, her brain pounding with all the things she wanted to scream.

The path ended before the edge of the slope, blocking the area beyond with a fence. Edges cut through the soil and grass, the first round of digging to build more steps for growing. Goats wandered through the grass, grazing without caring for the vampires working nearby.

"Nola."

She jumped at T's quiet voice.

"Just pick the dull-colored ones with no green." Nola knelt next to the long, prickly vine.

"The squash in the domes were bigger." T began lowering herself to the ground, pain wrinkling the corners of her eyes.

"Careful." Beauford took her arm, helping her the rest of the way.

"Is it the baby?" Nola asked.

"No, I just climbed a mountain." T's smile lasted for only a second. "Are you all right?"

"I'm fine." Nola's stomach twisted. "Please don't worry about me."

"Better than worrying about me." T took Nola's hand. "You're going through a lot, being asked to forgive a lot."

"I just…" Nola grabbed a heavy gourd, twisting the vine until it broke. "I just don't know if some things should be forgiven."

"Some shouldn't," T said. "Maybe there have been too many lies, and too much blood spilt, and too much hurt to ever forgive." T reached to twist a squash free.

Beauford moved her hands, doing the work for her.

"The thing is"—T sat back on her heels—"I had this whole speech planned for when I found Charles. I was so mad that he left me behind to go fight with Nightland. He left me alone in a city on the edge of burning itself to the ground with no way to keep a baby safe. And then he didn't come back when he was supposed to be right home. And I had to go to the domes, and be locked in a cell, and break out, and I shouldn't have had to do any of it." Tears streamed down T's face. "He should have stayed in the apartment with me, and waited for whatever Nightland was doing to be done. Then he should have brought me here himself. I was going to scream at the top of my lungs if I had to, to make sure he understood all the things he had done that had hurt me. And now he's dead."

"I'm so sorry." Nola wrapped her arm around T's shoulders.

"He's dead, and I still want to scream at him. But I would go through the hell he left me in all over again to see him alive. I'm not saying you have to forgive them, Nola." T took Nola's face in her hands. "I don't know if what they've done is so horrible forgiveness is impossible. Maybe you can't ever love either of them again, and that's your choice. But at least you have a choice. You can decide if you forgive them or love them or never want to see them again. I would do anything to have that."

Nola hugged T tightly. She didn't know what words to use to say how grateful she was T had come into the domes to work and trusted Nola enough to follow her out.

"Think about it, Nola," T whispered. "Think about what you really want."

"How?" Nola sat in the dirt, studying the terraces.

Kieran worked three rows below, digging up plants that had passed for the season. Jeremy and Julian were nowhere in sight.

"I barely know where I am." Nola pinched a vine with her fingers and spilt the rough fibers apart. It should have been hard, tearing at her skin and making her wish she had a knife to do the job. But the vine snapped without her really having to try. "I don't know what I'm capable of, or turning into. How am I supposed to choose?"

"Choose between Kieran and Jeremy?" Beauford lifted the squash Nola had split from the vine. "Who says you have to? You're strong and capable. You'll be just fine on your own."

"You really think so?" Nola asked.

"Got out of the domes without either of them, didn't you? Catlyn always used to say, 'Never need someone more than you love them.'" Beauford's smile didn't reach his eyes. "You don't need anyone. If you decide to love someone, that's your choice. But you don't have to. The world is ending. The only mandatory thing is survival."

CHAPTER TEN

The simple tasks of working in the garden helped. Laboring side-by-side with T and Beauford felt normal. Like they were back in the safety of the domes. Nola's shoulders relaxed as she made her way down the row. Dirt clumped under her nails, giving her hands the familiar look of productivity she knew so well from her years harvesting in the domes. Years spent feeding people who now wanted her dead.

Tension crept back into Nola's shoulders.

She focused instead on the people around her. T and Beauford worked as a team, Beauford never letting T lift anything. Part of Nola wanted to tell T to go rest, but most of her knew better. Sitting alone in a room with nothing but time and grief would do more damage than kneeling in the dirt.

Jeremy and Julian had gone back into the tunnels and had yet to return. Kieran worked at the base of the terraces, placing tall metal stakes into the unplanted ground. Strangers worked around them as well.

A woman with dark green eyes mingled with the goats as they chewed their way through the grass beyond the fence. On the terraces facing Nola, fruit trees hid beneath the disks of fabric. An older man wove his way between the trees, inspecting the progress of their bounty.

Kieran had done a wonderful job.

My mother would be proud.

Or disgusted.

Orange touched the sky, burning the night away.

"We should start heading in," Nola said.

T looked up at the sky. "I've been out in the sun before."

"But you shouldn't be, none of us should," Nola said.

"It's so easy for Domers to say things like that." Beauford stood, brushing his hands off on his pants. "But if it's let the sun bite your skin or starve, you can live through the rays well enough."

"But it isn't live through the sun or starve," Julian said. "Not here."

Carrying an empty crate in each hand, he walked up the row toward them. Jeremy followed behind, more crates perched on his shoulders.

"We work at night," Julian said, "which means our work day is ending. If you'll put the fruits of your labor into these, we can get inside."

Beauford took a crate from Julian and passed it to Nola, then took Jeremy's extra for himself.

Nola carried her box to the end of the row.

A goat hollered at her as she carefully placed the squash in the bin.

"These aren't for you," Nola said. "I doubt you'd even eat the leaves anyway."

It took only a few minutes for her to fill her bin. She stared down at the loaded crate. In the domes, everything would have been placed on a wheeled cart.

"Do you want help?" T asked.

"No," Nola said.

Julian and Jeremy had both moved their crates to the bottom of the terrace. Beauford had hoisted his up. His muscles strained the fabric of his sleeves as he carried his load down the steps.

Jeremy looked up at Nola. Without saying a word, he started up the stairs toward her.

"It won't do any harm to let him help," T said.

"I can do it myself." Nola crouched next to the crate. There were no handles to grab onto. Her only choice was to get her fingers under the bottom.

"Nola." Jeremy jogged down the row.

She shoved her fingers under the bottom and lifted. She waited for pain to shoot through her fingers, or her balance to sway at the weight. But the crate lifted like it weighed no more than it had empty.

"Careful." Jeremy stopped in front of her, his hands reaching for the crate.

"It doesn't feel like it weighs anything." Nola shifted the weight back and forth in her arms.

"Don't push it," Jeremy warned.

"It has to be, what, sixty pounds? It doesn't feel like anything."

"The Graylock is working," Jeremy said.

"If this is how Graylock is supposed to work, why are you telling me to be careful?" Nola narrowed her eyes.

"I kept breaking things my first few days." A hint of pink crept up Jeremy's cheeks. "I destroyed about five doorframes before I relearned how to close doors."

"I'm sure your dad loved that," Nola laughed. The bounce of it loosened the pain in her chest.

"He wasn't too mad." Jeremy stepped aside, letting Nola and T pass, then followed them down the row. "He'd had a whole pack of guards breaking things for a while. Your mom freaked when I broke the door to your house."

Nola turned at the edge of the steps. "You broke a door in my house?"

"Yeah." Jeremy ran a hand over his closely cropped hair. "When you were out for a couple of days. Your mom made maintenance fix it right away. She didn't want you to feel like your home had been broken."

Tension gripped Nola's jaw. "Our home was broken. A door wouldn't have made it any worse."

"I—" All hint of laughter faded from Jeremy's face. "Nola, I'm sorry."

"For breaking a door?" Nola walked down the stairs. "Don't be. You took the medicine to try and help me. You broke a door when you were worried about me. I just can't believe my mother's priorities were so skewed, and the domes went along with her."

"But at least she noticed the door was broken." Jeremy leapt down a few steps to walk by Nola's side. "The whole thing is too messed up to riddle through, but at least in all the chaos, and your mother freaking out about protecting the seeds, she took a minute to worry about you. Maybe she was worrying about the wrong thing, but she noticed something and cared enough to fix it."

"This way, if you will." Julian gave one last glance to the rising sun and headed toward the tunnel.

The gardens were nearly empty. Only the green-eyed woman with the goats remained outside.

"Do you think they hate us now?" Nola asked.

"Close the door behind you, if you please," Julian called from the front of the line.

"What about the woman outside?" T squeezed to the back of the group, leaning with all her weight to close the metal door. Locks clicked into place as soon as the door shut.

"She'll be out until nightfall," Julian said. "Don't worry, it's her own choice to stay with her precious goats. It's a rather strange affinity she has for them, but the goats are healthy and breeding like mad, so we find it best to let her be."

"Ha." Beauford's monosyllabic laugh echoed off the walls.

"Nola, who do you think hates us?" Jeremy asked.

The tunnel widened as they reached the main level.

"Our families," Nola whispered.

"I don't know," Jeremy said. "The best we can hope is that they've given us up for dead."

Nola tightened her grip on the bin, the wood cracked in protest.

"Careful," Jeremy said.

"The best we can hope for is that they're comforting themselves that we're dead," Nola said. "We're their children."

"Children who ran away from the domes," Jeremy said. "They spent time and a ton of resources raising and training us."

Julian turned left into a side corridor, which slanted down, cutting deeper into the mountain.

We're a waste of resources.

"What's the worst?" Nola asked.

"Huh?" Jeremy stepped behind Nola as their path narrowed.

"If us being dead is the best, what's the worst?"

"They're considering us rogue assets," Jeremy said. "They know our training. They know how useful we both are, and they don't want anyone else to have us. You know enough about botany to help build greenhouses out here that could produce enough food to allow the humans of Nightland to thrive. I'm a trained Outer Guard who knows all the domes' security procedures. And all that's without us having Graylock."

"Is that why they wanted me dead?" The words didn't sting as much as she thought they would. "Not because they wanted to punish me for the crime of helping people escape, but because if they couldn't have me no one could?"

"Yeah," Jeremy said, "which made my leaving a really easy decision."

A wide door blocked the end of the corridor.

Julian balanced his bin on his hip and knocked with his free hand. "Produce from the garden."

Nola waited for a voice to call back through the wood.

Julian peered into his bin, as though checking the squash for instantaneous spoilage as the seconds ticked past.

"Should we just go in?" Nola asked.

Julian looked up from his crate as the door swung slowly open. An old woman peeked her head out.

"Bea?" Nola stepped forward, recognizing the woman's wrinkled face. "You used to work in Emanuel's house. You cared for Eden."

"We all care for Eden." Julian slipped through the door. "And all of this is Emanuel's house."

Bea stayed in the doorway, glancing into each of their bins as they passed.

"It's good to see you again," Nola said. She forgot to listen for an answer as she entered the room beyond.

Wooden barrels lined the walls. Dried herbs and meat hung from lines above. Tables laden with food took up the center of the space. On the far wall, rows upon rows of glass jars filled ceiling-high shelves, surrounding a smaller door, which stood ajar. The scents of smoke, meat, and hot sugar drifted from the room beyond.

"What is this place?" T reached for the apples lined up on one of the tables.

Bea slapped her hand away.

"The pantry," Julian said, "and it is controlled by the fiercest woman in all of Nightland. So best to leave the crates on the floor and be on our way."

Bea peered into each of their crates as they placed them on the ground then stared at them until they were through the door and safely in the corridor.

"How long have the gardens here been growing?" Nola asked.

"This is the first full season." Julian led them back up the way they'd come. "We'd been trying to farm up here for quite a while, but with little success. Kieran's plans for the garden changed things. Without his insight, we wouldn't be able to feed our non-blood drinkers."

"But he was in the city," Nola said. "I saw him."

"He had been here when he took ill," Julian said. "We barely got him to his father in time for the ReVamp to be effective. After that, Dr. Wynne refused to be separated from his son, and the doctor's presence was required in the city."

"To care for Eden," Nola said. "Where is she?"

"Safe," Julian said, "healthy, and turning out to be a very bright little girl."

"Good." Pictures of the tiny girl with big dark eyes flitted through Nola's mind.

"How long did it take to build this place?" Jeremy ran his finger along the stone wall. "You said you've been harvesting for a season. This construction took a lot more than a year."

"Quite right." Julian headed down the main corridor that led to the room Nola shared with Beauford and T. "The expansion to the natural cave system began years ago. Long before I found my way to this corner of the world. It took a long time to build our true Nightland, but I have to believe it was worth every year of labor and hardship to have a place to reimagine the future of those fighting for survival in this world."

"I thought Nightland was the tunnels under the city?" Beauford said.

"Nightland is a people not a place," Julian said. "We were Nightland in the city, and now we are Nightland here."

They stopped in front of the door marked 113.

"What would have happened if the tunnels up here weren't ready yet?" Nola hung back as T and Beauford went into their room, both slumping with fatigue.

"We wouldn't have come here," Julian said. "If we had attempted the transition before everything was ready, the endeavor would have failed."

"But if the domes had gone after Nightland a little sooner," Nola said, "or if the city had eaten itself alive, what would have happened then?"

"We would all have died," Julian said. "Whether here or in the city. There would have been no hope for long term survival."

"What I don't get is how you pulled it off," Jeremy said. "This wasn't done by Vampers—"

"Vampires," Nola hushed.

"—with pickaxes," Jeremy finished.

"It was built by the architects," Julian said. "They spent years on our home, and now they've moved on to building another refuge for another group. They're working nearly a continent away from what I understand."

"The architects? Who are they?" Jeremy asked. "Why did they decide to build here?"

"Emanuel is very old, has lived a life of many marvels, and is owed many debts," Julian said. "There are some debts that can't be repaid even by building a village under a mountain."

Nola shuddered at the mere thought of what debt could be so great.

"They just travel and build?" Jeremy crossed his arms, his eyes narrowed. "So, you're saying there are other settlements hiding underground?"

"Most definitely. And not all of them were built by the architects," Julian said. "I've heard of a settlement out west in a long forgotten military shelter. The people who built the domes found the structure to be unappealing for their purposes, but that doesn't mean the space can't aid in survival."

"That's a lot of people," Nola said. "I thought it was only the domes that could survive."

"Of course that's what you were taught." Julian smiled kindly. "Swearing allegiance to the domes is much simpler if they are the only available path. There are many truths the domes have dismissed. Too many to be discussed this morning. Rest, both of you. I'm sure I can rattle your world views a bit more when the sun sets."

Julian gave each of them a nod and headed down the hall, leaving Nola to stew in her thoughts.

"They lied to us," Nola said. "The domes must know."

"They don't know about this place, and it's right on their doorstep." Jeremy dug the heels of his hands into his eyes. "Are you tired yet?"

"No," Nola said. "I wish I were. I wish I could fall asleep and forget about the mess my life has turned into."

"I have a better idea." A hint of a smile played at the corners of Jeremy's lips.

"What?"

"Your strength from the Graylock is kicking in," Jeremy said. "Want to go test it out? I'll teach you to throw a proper punch."

Nola bit the insides of her cheeks, willing her face to stay passive. "No time like the present to learn to defend myself."

CHAPTER ELEVEN

T he sparring room hadn't been cleared out by the rising of the sun.
     A few had taken refuge in the cots along the side of the space. A man with his teeth filed into sharp fangs slept with his mouth dangling open, though Nola didn't understand how anyone could sleep through all the noise in the room.

Pairs matched up in the squares painted on the floor.

One pair sparred with staffs, while the match next to them was fought with swords. The center four blocks had been taken over by a group of six, who had no weapons but their own hands.

Vampires stood around the periphery, cheering and stomping their feet as the fight heated up.

A girl no older than Nola with bright blond hair dove into the middle of the fight, kicking a man twice her size in the stomach with enough force to send him flying out of their squares.

The bystanders laughed and jeered as the man hit the ground. Two women grabbed him under the arms, throwing him back into the fight. He hit a younger man in the back, knocking him over.

The blond girl twisted the larger man's arm behind his back with a knee to his neck, pinning him to the ground.

"We're not going to be doing that, right?" Nola asked. "I don't think I'm ready for that."

The young man knocked the blond girl aside, dragging the fallen man to his feet only to punch him in the face and knock him over again.

"No," Jeremy said. "We aren't going to brawl."

"Good. Not brawling is good." Nola kept close on his heels as they moved toward an open square on the far side of the room.

"We're going to start nice and slow." Jeremy stopped in the center of a green square. "Just how to throw a proper punch."

"Is that how they start the guards?" Nola asked.

"Kind of," Jeremy said. "First, they run you till you feel like you can't breathe anymore. Then it's strength training until you can't lift your arms anymore. Then you learn how to hit things."

"But I don't have to run until I can't breathe?"

"You've already had Graylock." Jeremy rolled up his sleeves. "Honestly, we could run through the tunnels for a couple of hours to see if you get winded, and go lift some barrels for strength, but I'd rather you learn to defend yourself. Just in case...well, in case you need to."

"To punch a vampire?" Nola asked.

"Or someone on Graylock," Jeremy said. "You should be able to defend yourself against everyone."

Nola grinned, the expression slipping too easily onto her face. "What should we be called? If people who take Lycan are werewolves, and people on Vamp and ReVamp are vampires, what does that make us?"

"Superheroes." Laughter glimmered in Jeremy's eyes.

"Okay, Captain Domer, how do I punch things?" Nola widened her stance, planting her hands on her hips.

"Not things," Jeremy laughed. "People. Punching is only for people."

"Can you imagine Pillion teaching self-defense in school?" A laugh bubbled up from Nola's throat. *"Punching is for People and Other Basics."*

Tears streamed down Nola's cheeks as Jeremy gave a comical frown, looking shockingly like Mr. Pillion himself. "Your skin and bones will never be stronger than stone or metal. Punching is a skill only useful for defense against assault by other people. If a wall or a door is attacking, kicking is a much more useful tactic."

Nola brushed the tears off her cheeks. "No wonder they never taught us any of this in school. None of us would have been able to take it seriously."

"They should have though." The joy vanished from Jeremy's face. "They should have made all of us learn to defend ourselves and basic first aid. If they had, things would have gone differently when Nightland attacked. They're just too cocky. Living safely behind the glass and assuming nothing can hurt them. Not the sun, or rain, or thousands of desperate people. How could they have been so stupid?"

"They." The word rushed from Nola's lungs, stealing all the air from her.

"What?"

"You said *they*." Nola looked up to the stone ceiling, so different from what she had grown up with in the domes. "They and them. That's what you said. Not us and we."

"We aren't them," Jeremy said. "Not anymore. It's just us, Nola."

"Two superheroes alone in the world?"

The clattering of the fighting around them drilled into her ears, shaking her breath as she exhaled.

"The only ones of our kind. Then I'd better learn to fight," Nola said. "You can't do all the fighting. I have to be able to pull my weight or we won't survive."

"Then punch me." Jeremy held up his hands. "Go on, punch."

"Just punch your hand?" Nola glanced around. All the other pairs were sparring full force. Heat crept up her cheeks.

"Come on," Jeremy said. "Don't think about it."

Nola drew back her hand and punched, hitting Jeremy's palm.

"Okay," Jeremy said. "That's a good start, but don't pull your arm back. If someone sees you prep, they'll know exactly what you're trying to do. Keep your hands in front of you."

"Okay." She balled her hands into fists, holding them in front of her chest.

"And don't put your thumbs on the inside your fists." Jeremy took Nola's hands, moving her thumbs to sit safely on the outside of her fingers. "Now try it again."

Nola punched again, hitting the tips of Jeremy's fingers.

"Try for—"

"Aiming?" Nola cut him off, striking the middle of his palm.

"Good." Jeremy nodded. "But even as strong as you are, you've got to put the force of your body into it. Use your shoulders to rotate—"

"Nola, if you want to learn to fight, you could ask someone who's actually good at it." Raina sauntered into the green square.

Kieran hovered outside the lines, a knife in each hand.

"The child was a guard for what, a weekend?" Raina asked.

"Jeremy knows what he's doing," Nola said.

"Show me." Raina tipped her head, her hair shimmering as it swished to the side.

"Okay." Nola squared off to Jeremy and punched his palm again.

Raina tossed her head back and laughed. "I take it back lover boy, keep her until she gets past Kindergarten."

"At least I'm trying to learn." Nola pulled her fist back and punched again.

"Not like that." Kieran stepped forward, his eyes darting from Jeremy to Nola. "You have to keep your wrist straight. If you let it tip to the side, you'll break your wrist. It doesn't matter how fast you can heal, broken bones still suck."

"I can teach her to throw a punch," Jeremy said. "Try it again, Nola."

"She's going to break her wrist if she keeps going like that." Kieran stepped forward.

"And I'll make sure she doesn't." The muscles in Jeremy's neck tensed, forming root-like ridges. "The only time she's ever thrown a punch is at your face. I'm starting her from the beginning."

"I'm just trying to help," Kieran said.

"She doesn't need your help," Jeremy said.

"Don't speak for me," Nola said softly.

Raina let out a low whistle.

"Nola, do you want to break your wrist, or do you want my help?" Kieran said.

"I'll make sure she doesn't get hurt," Jeremy said. "I'm the trained guard, not you."

"And dome training is the best?" Kieran said. "Have you seen the vampires of Nightland fight hand to hand? Outer Guard rely on trucks and guns and things we don't have out here. If she wants to survive, she's going to have to do it the Nightland way."

"I can teach her. I can keep her safe." Red had taken over Jeremy's cheeks.

"You're not the only one who wants to protect her," Kieran said.

"And what a great job you did!" Jeremy flung his arms wide, stepping toward Kieran. "She snuck out into the city because of you. Because you lured her out there."

"I never wanted—"

"Never wanted what?" Jeremy spat. "To steal her I-Vent? To convince her to steal from the domes? You almost got her killed!"

"To be fair," Raina said, "I'm the one who actually stabbed her."

"Nola can handle herself," Kieran said. "She's stronger than you give her credit for."

"Then let me learn to punch people!" Nola stepped between Kieran and Jeremy.

The boys stared at each other.

"I'll be happy to keep teaching you," Jeremy said.

"I don't know if you're the best person for the job," Kieran said.

"I have an idea." Raina took Nola's shoulders, pulling her outside the green square. "You both want to teach Nola, and no one can agree on who's the more qualified. So let's have a demonstration."

"Raina, no," Nola said.

Raina ignored her. "No better way to see who's the better teacher than finding out who's the better fighter. It's not like you two don't want to beat the hell out of each other, and I could use the entertainment besides."

"Raina, this is a terrible idea."

Jeremy and Kieran glowered at each other.

"They don't have to if they don't want to." Raina grinned.

Kieran tossed his knives on the floor. "You want to hit me, fine. Give it your best shot, and we'll see how well that Graylock of yours actually works."

"A lot better than ReVamp. I can still walk in the sun." Jeremy took a step to the side.

Kieran matched him, moving in the opposite direction.

"See? They wanted to fight," Raina whispered. "They're prowling like angry kittens. It's cute."

Nola balled her hands into fists as they kept circling each other.

"My father created ReVamp without any of the fancy resources the domes have. He's the only hope you have for getting more Graylock."

"Then I hope he's up to the task." Jeremy charged forward, plowing his shoulder into Kieran's ribs.

Kieran kicked out, catching Jeremy behind the knee and sending him stumbling to the side.

"What if he's not?" Kieran said. "What if he can't replicate it? What if you gave Nola something you don't have more of?"

"We have enough to finish her dose."

"And then we just hope no one tries to kill her?" Kieran darted forward, punching Jeremy in the jaw and ribs, then catching him in the chin with his elbow.

Jeremy stumbled back.

Kieran lunged to strike again, but Jeremy blocked the blow, hitting Kieran hard in the stomach.

"I'll keep her safe." Jeremy wiped the blood from the corner of his mouth.

"She would have been safer with ReVamp," Kieran said. "Even you've got to know that. Better supply, being a part of the strongest group the outside has. You made a mistake."

Jeremy charged forward, fists raised.

Kieran swung, but Jeremy ducked, dodging the blow. Jeremy kicked low, knocking Kieran's legs out from under him. Kieran hit the ground hard.

"I saved her life," Jeremy growled.

"Raina could have done it." In one fluid movement, Kieran sprung to his feet. "She could have given Nola the ReVamp. Did you not think, or are you just that selfish?"

"She was bleeding out," Jeremy said. "I had Graylock on me, and I saved her life. You know who wasn't there to give his opinion? You."

Kieran jumped five feet into the air, launching himself at Jeremy and bringing his elbow down on Jeremy's shoulder with a sickening *crunch*.

Jeremy stumbled back, sweat slicking his brow.

"Your precious guards were trying to kill her," Kieran said.

"And I made sure they didn't." Jeremy ran forward, knocking Kieran to the ground, pinning him down with his knees pressed into his chest. "When your precious Vampers blew up part of the domes, it was me who took care of her. You weren't there to wash the blood out of her hair." He sunk his knuckles into Kieran's eye. "You weren't the one who held her when she was sobbing like she would break apart." He hit again. "She was bleeding in the middle of the street." He struck again. "She wouldn't open her eyes. I thought she was gone."

He sprang to his feet, lifting Kieran with him. Kieran didn't fight as Jeremy slammed him to the ground.

"I've made some mistakes," Jeremy said. "Graylock wasn't one. Nola's breathing. If you don't like how I did it, go walk in the sun."

The air went still. The ones sparring around them had stopped. All eyes were on Jeremy.

Raina clapped, the sound bouncing off the stone walls. "Now wasn't that therapeutic?"

"Don't." Jeremy ran his hands over his hair. Blood marked his knuckles. His eyes met Nola's. "I just..." He shook his head. Without another word, he turned and stalked back toward the tunnels, ignoring the stares of everyone he passed.

"Kieran," Nola said. "Are you okay?"

He rolled onto his back. Bruises covered his face, and blood trickled from his nose.

"Kieran?"

"Whose blood was in your hair?"

"What?" Nola stepped closer.

The vampires around them had lost interest in the green square. *Clangs* of weapons and *thumps* of fists rumbled around the cavern.

"He said there was blood in your hair. Whose was it?"

"I don't know." Nola stood over Kieran. "Mine, the man I killed, probably some other people's. I don't remember all of it. I don't think I want to."

"We never should have sent you back." Kieran sat up, wincing as he moved. "You wanted to stay with Nightland. Emanuel should have let you."

"And what, locked me in a room while he attacked the domes? It happened. It's done." She stepped back as Kieran stood. "Fighting about who should have done what to protect me is pointless. I need to be able to protect myself. That's what I was trying to do before you and Jeremy started beating each other up."

Kieran's shoulders sagged. "I'm sorry."

"I'm so tired of *sorry*. Sorry doesn't bring people back to life or rebuild walls. I'm here because it's the only way I know how to survive, not because I want an apology."

"Then what can I do?" Kieran asked.

"Keep people alive and leave Jeremy alone. If Emanuel wants to hurt people, find a way to convince him to stop. Prove that you're worth being alive when other people aren't." Nola pressed her thumbs into her eyes. "I don't know what else to say."

"My dad will find a way to make more Graylock," Kieran said. "I'll do whatever it takes to help him."

"Who knows what else he can make of it?" Nola said. "Maybe he can find something in it to make ReVamp better for everyone. Maybe the next generation of vampires won't have to hide from the sun."

"What's the fun in being a creature of the night if you have to work during the day?" Raina shook her head. "I think vampires are perfect just the way we are. Also, I think I'll teach you to fight from now on. As entertaining as the boys' spat was, you still can't throw a decent punch."

Nola wavered between laughing and yelling at Raina for starting it all.

"First, I'll teach you to hit, then we'll move on to throwing knives." Raina's eyes sparkled with glee.

"I don't know if I'm a knife—"

The ground shook under Nola's feet.

The weapons hanging on the walls clanged as they bounced off the stone.

Nola squinted, trying to hear past the questioning voices of those around her. "What was that?"

"Nothing good." Raina ran for the tunnel that led toward the mountainside.

CHAPTER TWELVE

The ground rumbled again as Raina shoved open the giant metal doors.
"Was that an earthquake?" Kieran asked.

Nola's heart tumbled in her chest. She had read about earthquakes but had never felt one. The earth had spared their area from that curse, even as the sun's rays scorched and the rain hung heavy with poison.

"I don't think so." Raina ran down the tunnel, Nola and Kieran at her heels.

Nola's legs didn't mind the pace, nor did her lungs scream for air. Only when she looked at the tunnel walls sweeping past them did she realize how fast she was actually running. What felt like a gentle jog was really a full-blown sprint.

"I'm fast," Nola said, the words coming out easily. "I'm really fast."

"Welcome to the good life, Domer." Raina stopped, pressing her back to the wall as they reached the first window. The sun shone brightly through the gap, barely leaving enough space for Raina and Kieran to hide in the shadows. "Well shit."

"What?" Nola stepped in front of the other two, leaning toward the window.

Smoke billowed up from the city, rising in a thick shroud of black. Flames lapped at the buildings below, their brightness startling even in the morning sun.

"What happened?" Kieran said. "The riot fires have never been that big."

A light flashed in the city. Flames soared into the sky.

Tears streamed down Nola's face as the ground beneath her feet rumbled. "I don't understand."

"It's the Domers," Raina said. "They've finally had enough of their trashy neighbors."

"What?" Nola leaned out the window, desperate to see if any of the buildings in the city were still standing.

"The factories have shut down," Raina said. "The city is of no use to them. It's just a cesspit filled with people who want them dead. Why wouldn't they bomb the city?"

"Because there are children in the city," Nola said. "There are innocent people."

"Like Nettie?" Raina asked.

Nola froze.

"My baby sister is in that burning city, and the only crime she ever committed was being an alcoholic brat. I warned her for years, and she wouldn't listen. The house is gone, my sister is probably dead. And if not now, she sure as hell will be soon. Why? Because the domes want to live out the end of the world in peace, and the city is nothing more than a disease to be eradicated."

"We need to get out there and help people," Nola said. "Nettie could still be alive. There could be other survivors."

"You think the domes will let anyone out alive?" Raina said.

"We don't know what happened," Nola said, "but there are people out there who need our help."

"Or they're all already dead," Raina said.

"Nettie could be alive," Nola said. "We have to go find her."

"And do what?" Kieran watched the smoke rise. "We could rescue Raina's sister. But what about all the others you'd find. We couldn't bring them here. The domes would follow us back. They'd know where we are, and they'd attack. We don't have enough food to take in hundreds more people, and—"

"You sound like them," Nola said.

"I hate the domes, but they didn't get everything wrong." Pain pinched Kieran's brow. The bruises from the fight had already begun to fade.

"Kieran's right," Raina said. "Noah didn't load his ark with every living thing. He took what he could keep alive."

"You're supposed to be different." Nola shook her head. "Nightland is supposed to be different from the domes, to save everyone."

"If Emanuel could, he would," Kieran said. "That's the difference."

Another rumble shook the ground.

Nola spun back to the window. The flames that leapt into the sky were deep within the smoke, on the dome side of the city.

Will the glass even survive?

"We at least need to know what's going on," Nola said. "You say it's the domes, but it might not be. It could all be a huge accident. Or the werewolves destroying everything, or—"

"The domes," Rain cut across her. "No one else would be able to coordinate this."

"It could be someone we've never even heard about!" Nola shouted. "We need to go see."

"We'll talk to Emanuel," Raina said. "If he wants us to go, we can do it at nightfall."

"That's so long from now," Nola said. "How many more people could die in that time?"

"The Outer Guard could come slaughter us," Raina said. "They could come blast our tunnels and bury us alive. But it doesn't matter. We can't go until nightfall."

Kieran studied Raina's face.

"I'll go," Nola said. "I can run fast now."

"No," Kieran said.

"The sun would kill both of you, but I'll be fine," Nola said. "Even if I get burned, I can heal now."

"If you want to commit suicide, there are easier ways," Raina said.

"Jeremy will come with me," Nola said. "He won't let anything happen to me."

"Such confidence in lover boy," Raina said.

"We can't just sit in a tunnel while the city is blowing up," Nola said. "How far away is the city?"

"Thirteen miles," Kieran said.

"Okay." Nola nodded, the magnitude of the distance hurtling through her mind. "That's not too bad, right? I've had Graylock, I can do it."

"Absolutely not," Kieran said. "What if something happens to you? How would we find you? How are you going to find your way back?"

"He's right," Raina said. "You were knocked out for most of the trip. You'd get lost on the way back and die in the wild. *If* you made it to the city, and *if* you don't get attacked by any more rogue vampires. Or do you not remember the two who wanted to tear your throat out?"

"And Jeremy stopped them," Nola said. "What if the domes did attack the city? What if they're on their way here now?"

Kieran looked to Raina, who glared at Nola, her mouth twisted in a frown. "Fine, you get to go and play scout. You don't go into the city proper, and you get back here by nightfall. You drag lover boy out in the sun, see which group is running through the burning city in triumph and get out."

"We should ask Emanuel," Kieran said.

"Emanuel will agree with me," Raina said. "If she's going to go, she needs to go now."

"I'll get Jeremy." Nola took off back up the corridor, not waiting to hear the argument Kieran called after her.

She didn't know where his room might be, or if he even went back to where he had been sleeping.

The door to the sparring room burst open before Nola could reach for the handle.

"Nola!" Jeremy charged into the hall. "Are you okay?"

"The city is exploding. We have to go see what's happening." Nola took Jeremy's hand, dragging him back into the cavern.

"What?"

"The ground shaking—"

"Bombs are going off in the city?" Jeremy said.

"Yes." Nola stopped in front of the sparring vampires. "I need a backpack with water and food," she shouted over the fighting.

The sparrers turned toward her.

"Please."

No one moved.

"Raina said so."

The blond girl ran toward the back of the room, pulling a pack down from a shelf. "Ritchie, grab water and food."

The man she had pummeled less than half an hour before ran up the hall toward the main corridor.

"We don't keep those things in here," the blond said. "The water drinkers don't come to the sparring room very often."

The girl moved to hand the pack to Nola.

"I'll take it," Jeremy said. "You're strong, but you're still adjusting. We don't need anything throwing off your balance."

"Did you want any weapons?" the girl asked Nola as she handed the pack to Jeremy.

Nola's cheeks flushed. "Do you have any Guard guns? I know how to shoot those."

The girl nodded to a boy near her age. He opened the weapons locker and pulled out two belts with Guard guns and a slim silver box of darts.

"I'll take a knife, too," Jeremy said.

"Good," the girl said. "Keep to that if you can. Darts are worth more than blood."

"Thank you." The weight of the belt was no more than an egg in Nola's hands, but the reality of holding it took her breath away.

Where did they get this? Which guard's body did they take it from?

Jeremy strapped on his gun and tucked his knife into the side of his boot.

"I hope this is enough." The man who'd run down the tunnel returned, four bottles of water, five apples, and a loaf of seedy bread in his arms.

"It's plenty," Jeremy said. "We're not going far."

"We're going to the edge of the city." Nola strapped on the gun belt. Clasped as tight as it would go, the belt still hung low around her hips.

The man loaded the food into the bag.

"Is there anything else you need?" the girl asked.

"No," Nola said. "We'll tell Raina how much you helped."

Nola headed toward the door to the outer tunnel, Jeremy's boots thumping behind her.

"Are you sure about this?" Jeremy asked. "I can go on my own. I'll find out whatever we need to know and come right back."

"I'm going, Jeremy." Nola shoved the door open. "Either you can come with me and do the punching, or I can go by myself. It's up to you."

"No, it isn't." Jeremy stayed close on her heels. "If you're going, there's no choice in my coming along. You know that."

"You're right, I do." Nola ran down the tunnel. "Maybe next time don't argue with me."

"Trying to talk you out of doing dangerous things is as much a part of keeping you safe as punching duty."

Raina and Kieran came into view, both still pressed into the shadows, watching the window.

"Has anything new happened?" Nola asked. Her mind told her she should be out of breath, panting from running down the hall, but the words came easily.

"A few more bangs," Raina said. "The domes are leveling everything."

Kieran glared at Jeremy. "Do the domes have the explosive power to pull that off?"

Another rumble shook the ground.

Jeremy peered out the window. "I wish I could say no."

A plume of fire danced in the air.

"I don't think they do," Jeremy said. "It was never in my training. I never saw a stash of explosives anywhere in the domes."

"Did you ever see the explosives they used on the bridge?" Nola asked.

"No," Jeremy said, "but we knew there was a plan. That's why the Dome Guard freaked out when Nightland broke in. They were never supposed to get across the river."

"But a plan to end the whole city?" Nola said. "How would they hide it, or pull it off?"

"Never underestimate what desperate people are capable of," Raina said. "How do you think Vamp happened?"

"Does Emanuel know what's going on?" Jeremy asked.

"I'm sure he does," Raina said. "He'll be hiding Eden by now."

"We need to go." Nola's fingers and toes tingled. "We need to know if anyone's coming after us."

After Eden.

"Jeremy can go alone," Kieran said.

"I've already tried that," Jeremy said.

"I'm going, so let's move." Nola stepped through the patch of sunshine.

"Don't play Pied Piper," Raina said. "If you let rats follow you back, you'll sink the ship. You save a pack of strays, you kill us all."

Dread settled into the pit of Nola's stomach.

"But if you find Nettie, bring her here," Raina said.

"I will." Nola nodded and started down the tunnel.

"Promise you'll take care of her." Kieran's words froze Nola in place.

"I will always take of her," Jeremy said. "Keep the door open for when we get back."

"We'll be waiting," Kieran said.

"Come on." Jeremy stepped up next to Nola. "If we're going to get back by dark, we're going to have to run."

"Let's run."

CHAPTER THIRTEEN

The gun thumped against Nola's hip, smacking her with every stride. *Will it leave a bruise? Or do I heal too quickly now?*

The questions seemed absurd, but wondering about her hip kept away the thoughts of what the gun was meant to do.

"Do you really think it's the domes?" Jeremy said.

They passed another window in the long corridor. The city had disappeared behind the smoke.

"I don't know," Nola said. "Every time I think I know the line someone won't cross, they do it. Can the glass even withstand blasts like that so close by?"

"Yeah. The only way Nightland managed to blow a hole in the domes was by planting the charge on the glass itself. The domes were built to survive this sort of thing."

"Then it really could be them." Nola ran faster, her feet barely skimming the floor. She didn't bother slowing to look out the next window she tore past.

"Who's coming?" a voice shouted from around the bend.

"Nola and Jeremy," Nola called. "Raina's sent us to go and see what's happening in the city."

As they rounded the corner three vampires came into view.

Twin women, heads shaved and breasts barely covered by their artfully torn tops, flanked a gangly man with freckles coating his face.

"Raina wants you to go out there?" the man asked. "Is she trying to kill you?"

"That would be fun." The left twin smiled, baring her teeth.

"We're just trying to get information," Nola said. "We'll be right back."

"You'll burn without a sunny," the right twin said. "And no one gets to touch the sunny."

"What?" Nola shook her head. "We'll be fine in the sun, but you need to let us pass."

"Sun walkers who run like vampires." The freckled man tipped his head to the side. "What wonders have come to Nightland?"

"If you don't move right now, we're going to have to tell Raina you got in our way." Nola puffed her chest out and planted her hands on her hips.

The right twin and freckled man looked toward the left twin. The left twin's smile slipped away, her lips covering her teeth. Rolling her eyes, she stepped aside. The other two followed her lead, leaving a path down the middle of the hall.

"Thanks." Nola took off at a run, glancing behind to see the three glaring at her.

"Nola, watch out." Jeremy seized her arm.

Nola squeaked as Jeremy pulled her back from the ledge. Her lungs fought to reclaim the air fear had forced from them.

"Running faster means getting places faster." Amusement wrinkled the corners of Jeremy's eyes. "Super running lesson one: look where you're going."

"Lesson learned." Nola peeked over the edge. A patch of wilting grass waited ten feet below. "How do we get down?"

"Jump." Jeremy stepped up to the edge. "It's not too far. Hold your core for balance and don't forget to bend your knees."

He jumped off the edge like it was nothing more than the last step on a staircase, landing on the ground below with barely a sound.

"Right." Nola inched forward, placing her toes at the end of the moss-covered shelf.

"Don't worry, Nola," Jeremy said. "I'm right here. You'll be okay."

Nola pushed off the edge. Her heart vanished from her chest as reason told her pain awaited her on the ground.

She stumbled as she landed, tipping to the side and into Jeremy's arms.

"I've got you." He held her close to his chest. His heartbeat thundered next to Nola's ear.

"It didn't hurt." She stepped away from him. "I thought it would hurt."

"Your muscles are strong enough to cushion you now." Jeremy shrugged. "Don't try and push it too far, though. Jump from high enough, and even Graylock can't help you."

"You've never been scared of falling. You jumped out your bedroom window before you had Graylock." Tingles surged through Nola's chest at the memory of Jeremy jumping down to hold her, his face still creased from sleep.

"It was the fastest way down, and I wanted to get to you as quickly as I could," Jeremy said. "I won't lie, jumping out my window got a lot easier after I'd been given Graylock."

Nola stared into his eyes. Their color was the same brown it had always been, but lines of worry marked the corners, taking the place of the constant twinkle of joy that should have been there.

"We should go," Nola said. "It's going to be a long day."

"Yeah." Jeremy turned toward the city. "Run side-by-side, okay? I don't want you running into something I can't see, and I don't want you behind where I can't keep an eye on you."

"You don't trust me to take care of myself?" Nola tipped her head to the side. "I do know how to use the gun."

"Anytime I can't see you to know you're safe, it's like someone's lodged a stone in the back of my lungs. It hurts. And it steals my breath away. You've lived through things that would have killed some of the best Outer Guard." Jeremy took her hand in his. "Just stay where I can see you so I can breathe."

His fingers were warm and so familiar. It would be so easy to lace her fingers through his. They would run toward the flames together, their pulses keeping time.

"Okay." Nola pulled her hand away, adjusting her gun belt. "As long as it's not because you think I'm incompetent."

"I would never be that stupid."

Nola looked down the slope. The trees blocked the bottom of the mountain from view.

Down will be easier than up.

Rolling her shoulders back, Nola started to run.

The sloping ground made for longer strides, but her legs didn't tire. Keeping her gaze focused on the trees rushing past, she dodged between branches and ducked under low limbs.

Even running at top speed, she could see the details of the bark. Claw marks where an animal had mauled a tree, cracks where lightning had split a trunk open, decay where acid rain had worked its malice.

A waist-high rock protruded from the earth. Nola leapt onto the stone and down on the other side without breaking her stride.

"Now you're getting it." Jeremy beamed at her.

"This is amazing." The bottom of the mountain came into view. "No wonder they didn't want all the Domers to know what the Outer Guard were doing. Running this fast, it's like flying."

"It's pretty great," Jeremy said.

"But what?" Nola asked, hearing the hesitance in his voice. She looked over to him. "Ouch." They'd reached the bramble field, and the thorns tore at the back of her hand.

"Careful." Jeremy ran with his hands high over his head.

Nola did the same, feeling foolish as the brambles pulled at her pants like a thousand fingers searching for purchase.

"What's bad about being able to run this fast?" Nola asked.

"We're not wholly human anymore," Jeremy said. "We're different. If everyone took Graylock, there wouldn't be a next generation of humans."

She stumbled, her legs forgetting how to move for a moment. "There's T's baby. And Eden. We're not the end. We're not the last people who will live in this part of the world." Tears stung the corners of Nola's eyes. She pushed herself to run faster. "The fighting and fear are going to end. Somehow, someway. And children will be born, and this monstrous world will be nothing more than a scary story to them. I have to believe that, Jeremy."

The field ended, tossing them into the barren trees.

"If I don't believe there's going to be something good after all this, I don't know if I can keep going. I don't want to hurt people just to keep myself alive. But I can do it to protect T's baby. I can fight if it means keeping her baby safe."

"There will be something good after this." The gaps between the trees widened, and Jeremy moved to run right next to Nola. "I don't know what it's going to look like or who will be there to see it. But there will be people who do. And I'm going to do everything I can to make sure you're one of them."

"You have to be there too, Jeremy." Nola kept her eyes front, though she wanted more than anything to look at him. "I can't be the only superhero. I can't lose you."

His hand brushed the back of hers.

She didn't pull away.

Neither spoke as they ran past the body of the vampire who had attacked them such a short time ago. A dozen birds had found the corpse, taking advantage of the feast in mass.

The ground shook again, and again. They turned out onto a road whose surface had been cracked by weather and time. Leaping over the potholes took more concentration than jumping over the roots of the trees.

"That one." Jeremy pointed between the trees to a two-story house whose red front door hung loose on its hinges. "That's where we spent the daylight. If something happens—"

"Nothing's going to happen."

"If it does, that's a safe place," Jeremy said. "Raina likes you enough, she might even come looking for you there."

"Looking for us," Nola said. "Say looking for *us*."

"She might come looking for *us*."

Nola hurtled over an eight-foot pothole.

"You can't go back to the domes. You know that, right?"

"They tried to kill you." Jeremy dodged around a rusted out, old car. Someone had driven sharp metal spikes into the sides. "I would never go back there. Not for anything."

"Then you have to promise you're coming back with me," Nola said.

"I promise."

A knot of fear Nola hadn't noticed melted, trickling down the back of her spine.

More houses lined the road as they neared the city.

The homes had all been built symmetrically. Fractured sidewalks met cracked driveways at regular intervals. These houses were so different from the crumbling stone apartment buildings in the city, Nola couldn't imagine what life in one of them must have been like. A little lawn all her own. A car to drive into the city. The peaceful life the domes strove to create. But this idyllic outside had failed.

What if the domes are failing right now? What if the domes are under attack as well?

Nola shoved the thought aside. There would be no way for her to cross the river to help, even if the domes didn't want her dead.

The road twisted around the bend, giving them a level view of the city.

Fire lapped at nearly every building in sight and lunged toward those that had been left unscathed by the flames.

Dense smoke settled on the wide track of road that led out of the city.

"We need to get off the road." Jeremy veered left into the thin line of dead trees that covered the fronts of the tumbled down houses.

"Why?" Nola followed him even as she asked the question.

"There are people on the road down there." Jeremy pointed to the wide highway at the edge of the city. "We don't want them to see us coming."

Nola squinted, trying to make out what Jeremy had seen. Dozens of tiny ant-like things moved around on the highway. As she watched, one ant charged another, sending the other dots scattering to the sides of the road.

Pain sliced through Nola's face as she tumbled backwards. The ground pummeled the air out of her lungs as she landed in the dirt.

"Nola." Jeremy knelt beside her.

"What happened?" Nola touched her cheek. Blood stained her fingers.

"You hit a branch." Jeremy pulled off the pack and took out a bottle of water. "Running into things hurts more when you're moving faster."

"I think there's a fight on the road."

Jeremy ripped off part of his sleeve. "Hold still."

Nola gritted her teeth as he poured water onto the gash.

"Sorry." He dabbed at the wound.

Each touch sent stars dancing in Nola's eyes.

"We have to get the tree bits out before you start to heal." Jeremy trickled more water onto her cheek. "Your body can work foreign objects out, but it hurts like hell."

"Thanks." Nola gasped as he pulled an inch-long splinter from her cheek.

"I think that's it." He trickled water onto her face again, peering into the wound. "You should be able to heal fine now."

"Is it really bad?" Nola cringed at her own whimper.

"You're still beautiful," Jeremy said, "and in an hour it'll be like it never happened at all."

He passed Nola the water bottle.

Nola took a long drink. The water trickled coolly down her throat, washing away the gritty dryness she hadn't noticed before.

Jeremy stood and looked out toward the road.

"Should we cut around the fight?" Nola asked.

Jeremy rubbed his hand over his face. "I say we head right toward it. That many people, someone is bound to know how all this started."

"Right." Nola sprang to her feet, a jolt of joy flipping in her stomach at the ease of her movement.

"We should go a little slower though." Jeremy pointed at the road. "People are starting to come up."

A group of ants had indeed moved beyond the fighting and up the road, all bunched together like they were afraid of being attacked at any moment.

Jeremy took a drink and tossed the bottle back in his pack.

"What if it was the domes?" Nola asked.

Jeremy started jogging, always choosing the path that allowed Nola room to run by his side.

"Jeremy?" Nola said when no answer had come for more than a minute.

"I just can't believe it could be them. That I served as a guard and never knew we had access to those sorts of weapons. That my father would give an order like that."

"He gave the order to kill me."

Jeremy flinched at her words.

"I thought that was the lowest," Jeremy said. "The worst thing my father could ever do, and to me it is."

"But if he ordered the destruction of an entire city—" Nola began.

"Then he had a lot further to fall than I ever imagined."

CHAPTER FOURTEEN

Nola peered out from her perch twelve feet up in a dying tree. Her arms didn't ache from the climb, and her fingers had no trouble clinging to the crumbling bark.

Four men and three women marched up the road. Two of the men supported a third between them. The fourth man leaned heavily on a woman's shoulder, while the other two women carried children in their arms. Soot stained all their faces. Blood and dirt marked their tattered clothes.

Nola shifted carefully on the branch that held her weight, ignoring the open air beneath her as she leaned toward Jeremy's ear.

"Where are they going?" she whispered.

Jeremy loosened his grip on the limb he dangled from, pressing his shoulder into Nola's. "I'm not sure they even know. They might not be running toward anything, just away from the city."

The urge to call out and stop the group, to tell them to hide in the house with the broken red door until she could lead them safely to Nightland, fought to burst from Nola's mouth.

The rats will sink the ship.

Anger tensed Nola's fingers. The bark cracked beneath her grasp.

"We should talk to them," Jeremy said, "find out what they know."

"We should help them," Nola said.

"We can't."

"We can go without eating for a day," Nola said. "We can at least give them the food."

Jeremy chewed his lips. "We keep an apple for each of us and give them one bottle of water."

"Deal." Nola let go of the tree branch and dropped to the ground, her legs holding steady as she landed.

The group looked toward her as Jeremy landed by her side.

From twenty feet away, the fleers looked even more pitiful than they had at a distance. Dark bags marred the skin under their eyes, and fatigue from years of survival marked their faces.

One of the children twisted to look at Nola. His tiny frame was no bigger than a toddler's, but his face made him appear at least seven.

"Stay away from us." One of the women pulled a rusted kitchen knife from her belt.

"We don't want to hurt you," Nola said. "We just want to know what happened in the city."

"How could you not know?" the man being supported by two others croaked.

"We were far away when the ground started shaking," Jeremy said. "We saw the explosions, but we don't know why they're happening."

"The fire came down from above," the youngest of the women said. "I was inside when the windows shattered."

"I heard buzzing overhead," one of the men said. "I looked up to see where it was coming from. A black and silver thing fell from the sky, then the street exploded."

"Do you know who was doing it?" Jeremy asked.

"I didn't bother trying to find out," the young woman said. "I saw Outer Guard though, swarms of them. They'll know."

"Do you think it was them?" Cold rushed through Nola's veins. "Do you think the domes did this?"

"Does it matter?" the wounded man asked.

"Where are you heading?" Jeremy asked.

"Away," one of the women said. "There's no place left to go but away."

"Here." Nola dug in Jeremy's backpack, pulling out the loaf of bread, apples, and a bottle of water. "It's not a lot. But maybe it can help until you find a place to rest."

The man who leaned heavily on the woman reached into his pocket, pulling out an old fashioned revolver, cocking it with a *click*.

"We're trying to give you something." Jeremy stepped sideways, planting himself in front of Nola. "Take the food and water and go."

"Your pack isn't empty," the man said. "You've got more in there and guns on your hips besides. Take off the belts and toss them over. Then drop the pack and food and walk away."

The man's hand didn't shake as he pointed the revolver at them. Nola wished it would. Wished he would show some hesitance at threatening their lives.

"Don't do this." Jeremy inched forward. "I'm asking you to walk away."

"We'll walk away once you've given us your supplies," the man said. "You can hand them over yourselves, or I can take them off your corpses. I don't care either way."

"I'm giving you one last chance to leave," Jeremy said.

"I'm the one with the gun drawn, and you're out of chances to listen."

Too many things happened at once.

Jeremy launched himself at the man, knocking his gun aside with one hand, and punching him in the face full force with the other. At the same moment, a *bang* shook Nola's lungs.

"Jeremy!" the scream tore from Nola's throat.

Her fingers fumbled as she pulled the gun from her belt, aiming it at the rest of the group, while Jeremy rolled off the man, revolver in hand.

Jeremy was on his feet a moment later. Blood dripped from his thigh, but his hands held steady as he pointed the revolver at the nearest man.

"We wanted to help you," Jeremy growled. "He shouldn't have had to die."

Nola glanced at the ground. The man who'd shot Jeremy lay still, his eyes wide, his neck twisted at an unnatural angle.

"You're going to run up the road," Jeremy said. "I'm going to give you one minute to get as far away from here as you can. If any of you are still in range after that minute, I shoot."

All six adults stared at him, a mix of horror and anger staining each of their faces.

"Go!"

At Jeremy's shout they ran. After ten seconds, the two supporting the injured man dropped him on the ground, picking up their pace to run in front of the women.

"No!" the man shouted. "Don't leave me, please!"

"Put the food back in the bag," Jeremy said.

"You're hurt." Nola tossed the supplies into the pack, pulling the top tightly shut. "You need help."

"I'll heal," Jeremy said.

Nola crouched by his leg. A hole dripped red on the front of his thigh. "There's no exit wound."

"The bullet's still in there."

"We have to get it out," Nola said. "How do I get it out?"

"You don't." Jeremy winced as he put his weight on his leg. "We have to keep moving."

"But it'll be awful." Nola glanced up the road.

The group had disappeared, leaving the injured man to crawl after them.

"You said healing with something stuck inside you is terrible. We have to get the bullet out."

"We need to move." Jeremy took Nola's elbow, leading her down the road at a run. "I don't know if any of the others have guns, and I really don't want to fight them. We need to get away from here."

They wove back into the trees at the side of the road.

Jeremy's gait had become uneven, but still his strides were longer than Nola's as they ran.

"Promise me you're going to be okay." Nola took Jeremy's hand.

"I promise," Jeremy said. "I can take a bullet in the leg."

He held her hand as they ran toward the highway.

Others passed on the main road, moving in the opposite direction. Toward the land of vampires they didn't know existed.

Some moved on their own, others in pairs or groups.

Nola cringed every time they were spotted. Her fingers itched to reach for her gun. Jeremy still held the revolver in his hand.

The revolver had scratches on the barrel and could hold only six bullets. A relic of another time.

"How do people still have guns like this?" Nola said. "Why didn't the Outer Guard take them all away years ago?"

"Officially, they did." Sweat trickled down Jeremy's brow. "But my dad runs into a few every year. Most of the time, the fools who held onto them for protection ended up dead."

"Like the man you killed," Nola said.

"I didn't want to kill him." Jeremy's face turned an unnaturally pale shade. "But he was pointing a gun at us. He would have hurt you."

"Jeremy." Nola tugged on his hand, stopping his limping run. "I don't blame you. We tried to help them, and he threatened to kill us. He had a gun."

Jeremy's eyes slipped down to the revolver in his grip.

Nola took his face in her hands. "Jeremy, he shot you. He could have killed you. If somebody had to die, I'm grateful it was him and not you."

Unshed tears pooled in Jeremy's eyes.

"You can't feel guilty for defending yourself. You kept us safe."

Jeremy nodded. In a moment, all trace of tears had vanished from his eyes, replaced with the determination of an Outer Guard.

"We've only got about a quarter mile until we reach the city limits," he said. "We need to see if whatever dropped the bombs is still in the air."

"Wolves don't have planes or helicopters." Nola took Jeremy's hand, leading him through the trees. "Neither do vampires. Something like that is beyond everyone's power. I don't even think the domes could pull that off."

"They couldn't." Jeremy tightened his grip on Nola's hand. "We've only got the skeleton helicopter, and that can barely lift two people."

They reached the edge of the woods.

The highway in front of them had been built for six cars to be able to travel down at once. The crumbling river of concrete separated the houses on the tree-lined street from the edge of the city.

Fires burned in the apartment buildings across the way. The tallest structure reached up seven stories, and flames danced high above the roof. Cutting between the buildings, a road four lanes wide with faded white dashes running in parallel lines provided the exit from the inferno of the city.

Evacuees funneled onto the path between the flames, all heading toward the six-lane road beyond.

Some stopped when they reached the old highway, turning back to gape in horror at the destruction of their city. Others, like the group they had met before, kept moving up between the tumbledown houses, heading into the wild unknown.

"There should be more coming out this way." Nola stepped out onto the wide road, craning her neck to see in either direction. The sweeping bend of the river that surrounded three-quarters of the city trundled downstream, caring nothing for the fires that torched the city its banks caressed.

"There's no other way out. The survivors need to come this way," Nola said. "Where is everyone else?"

"I don't know." Jeremy moved slowly across the road, weaving through the clumps of people who had stalled on the concrete.

"Mama!" a little girl cried, tugging on the sleeve of a weathered old man. "We have to go back and find mama!"

"She'll find us here." The old man didn't look away from the flames. "We have to wait here, and she'll come."

Nola looked back, willing herself to be strong enough to see the desperate child's eyes.

The girl had sores on her cheeks. Some illness had taken hold of her tiny body.

"We should have taken the food." A woman leaned against her husband's shoulder, tears coursing down her cheeks.

"What food did we have?" The husband pressed his lips to his wife's hair.

"We had six cans of beans, two cans of corn, meat stew," the woman said, ticking the list off on her fingers, "a filter for water, and one Nightland apple. We should have taken it all with us."

"The walls fell down, Dora." He held her tight. "We couldn't have gotten to the food even if we thought about it before we ran. All our supplies were destroyed before we left the doorstep."

"But I worked so hard—"

"We've got each other. Let's just be grateful for that."

Nola threaded her fingers through Jeremy's, pressing his palm close to hers.

"How could this happen?" A young man Nola's age turned his back on the city to rage at the crowd. "Years of complacency and servitude. Working for the domes for money, for the Vampers to keep them from stealing the blood from our veins. Working for the wolves who promised us riches of food. But none have ever cared for us. None have ever wanted to keep the people who struggle everyday to have food and a place to sleep at night healthy. They only wanted us alive for their own benefit. This is what happens when our use is gone." The boy spread his arms wide. The flames of the city danced behind him like a cape of fire. "They've left us to burn with their trash. Our time of usefulness has ended. There is nothing left but fire."

The boy dropped his arms. He scanned the crowd, though what he was searching for Nola didn't know.

With a nod, he turned and ran back toward the city, not down the lane where the survivors drifted out, but straight toward the tallest building. With a *crash* the boy threw himself through the front door, disappearing into the flames.

CHAPTER FIFTEEN

"We have to help him!" Nola dove forward.

Jeremy caught her around the middle, lifting her off her feet. "There's nothing we can do, Nola. He's gone."

"But—"

"He's gone." He set her down, holding her tight.

Nola buried her face in Jeremy's chest. Tears streamed down her cheeks. A sob burst from her throat. "How?"

"I don't know." Jeremy pressed his lips to the top of her head. "But we're going to find out."

"We have to go in there." Her words came out between coughed sobs. "There have to be more people alive. We have to lead them to the way out."

"We can't," Jeremy whispered. "Going into the city is suicide."

"We can do it." Nola tipped her head up, looking into Jeremy's eyes. "How far away is Bellevue? That's where Raina's sister lives. If we can get to the street, we might be able to find her."

Jeremy shook his head, his arms tightening around Nola. "If I say *no*, will you listen to me?"

"No." Nola glanced toward the flames. The top floor of one of the buildings collapsed. Sparks shot into the air, cascading down in a rain of deadly fire. "I don't think I can live with myself if we don't try."

"If I say it's time to head back, you can't argue." Jeremy took Nola by the shoulders. "No matter how close we are, or who you want to help. If I say run, you run, and you don't stop till you're back in Nightland."

She nodded, wrapping her arms around Jeremy's waist and pressing her cheek to his chest for one more moment.

"How far to Bellevue?"

"Not far." He took Nola's hand, holding on tight as he started for the flames. "Only about ten blocks. We should be able to get in and out in a few minutes."

They reached the far side of the road. The heat from the flames pulsed against Nola's face. Her skin ached in protest, warning her to back away from the fire.

"Get out your gun." Jeremy let go of her hand. He pulled out his own guard weapon, keeping the revolver held tight in his other hand.

Nola pulled her gun free from her hip, checking the chamber and making sure the safety was off.

With a nod, Jeremy ran into the flames.

The heat lapped at them from all sides, but it was the sound Nola hadn't expected.

Screams echoed in the distance, far behind the *crackle* of flames. Before they had made it a block, a *crack* sounded behind them. A *screech* of crumpling metal sliced into Nola's ears as the building behind them collapsed.

Two figures ran out from the flames. A cape of fire trailed behind one. The flames consumed her body, a horrible wail carried through the blaze. Nola turned back to help.

"No!"

She froze at Jeremy's shout. The other figure stopped by the girl on fire.

For a moment, Nola thought the man would help. Stamp out the flames, find a way to heal her.

But the man looked up at the sky, his dark matted hair falling behind his shoulders. Black eyes glinted in the faint sun fighting to break through the smoke.

A groan poured from his mouth, but it was more than a sound. Blood followed the noise, trickling from his jaw. His shoulders shook as he dropped to his knees, raising his hands to shield his face.

He was too late.

Pink boils formed on his cheeks one moment only to burst the next, sending blood streaming down his face.

A scream echoed through the street. Nola knew the sound came from her throat, but she had no power to stop it.

The man clawed at his cheeks, as though to rip away the boils. His flesh tore free. Blood streamed freely down his chest. Blood leaked from his hands, dripping down his arms. He fell sideways, mauling his own face.

The girl coated in flames had long since stopped moving. But the man still writhed, tearing himself to pieces without seeming to know the damage he'd done. His nails found his neck, clawing a gap in his flesh. Blood spurted from the wound, coating the street in a rain of red.

He twitched on the ground, reaching to claw at his own legs. The plume of blood trickled out, and the man finally went still.

Nola's scream ended in a retch.

Jeremy's arm wrapped around her waist, guiding her forward though she could barely see through her tears.

"There's nothing we could have done for him." Pain crackled in Jeremy's voice. "He was dead the moment he went outside."

"They did it on purpose." Nola coughed, sucking more smoke into her lungs. "They're driving all the vampires out into the sun. They'll all end up like him."

"We can't do anything to help him." Jeremy pulled Nola to run, pushing his weight unevenly off his wounded leg. "If we can get to Raina's sister, we might be able to save her, but there's nothing we can do to protect vampires from the sun."

"Get to Nettie." Nola wiped her tears away. "We're going to get to Nettie."

Jeremy let go of her, though he kept right by her side as they ran.

Smoke seared Nola's lungs. The foreign ache of it in her throat was enough to tell her she shouldn't be able to breathe. The smoke coating the street should have been enough to kill her. But the Graylock kept her lungs working, allowing her legs to pound against the cracked pavement with ease.

The farther into the city they ran, the more bodies they found of those who hadn't made it out of the flames in time. A scorched corpse lay in the middle of the street, splayed out as though they had jumped from a window, seeking a swifter death than fire would allow.

Another vampire, her black eyes the only part of her not disfigured by sores, stared up at the murderous sun even in death.

"I didn't know that was how it would look," Nola said.

"You shouldn't have to." Jeremy turned onto another road, down a row of houses that had yet to catch fire.

A group huddled in the middle of the street, staring at the inferno waiting on either end.

"You need to get out of here," Jeremy shouted to the group.

They all spun to face him.

"The Domers said they would come back." An older woman shook her head. "There was a whole swarm of them, and they said they would come back."

"They aren't coming. The fires are all over the city," Jeremy said. "Get to Main and then to the old highway."

"But the guards said to stay." A teenaged boy stepped in front of Jeremy, puffing his chest out though Jeremy towered five inches over him.

"The guards lied," Jeremy said. "You can stay here and burn or get out. If you wait much longer, there won't be any way out at all."

"Then where are you going?" a little girl asked.

"We're looking for a friend," Nola said. "But you've got to go."

"So do we." Jeremy walked past the cluster of people. "Go as fast as you can!" He called back as they ran down the road.

"Why wasn't that street touched?" Nola asked as they ran around the corner. "The fire should have spread that far by—"

"Nola!" Jeremy seized her arms, tossing her into the air.

Pain shot through her shoulder as she hit the ground ten feet behind Jeremy. In a second, he landed on top of her, covering her head with his chest.

"What?" Nola mumbled the question into Jeremy's shirt. "What!"

"Get up slowly, and stay behind me." He eased his weight off of her, kneeling in front of her until she scrambled to her feet.

"What was that about?" Nola rubbed her shoulder. The pain had already begun to fade.

"I know why this street isn't on fire."

Nola peered around Jeremy's shoulder. A silver and black metallic canister rested in the middle of the street. The pavement hadn't even cracked where the thing had landed.

"Is that a bomb?" Nola whispered, her voice stolen by the foolish feeling that speaking too loudly would cause an explosion.

"It's a fire pack." Jeremy took a step closer.

Nola grabbed his arm, pulling him back. "I don't know what a fire pack is, but please don't go any closer."

"It's pre-domes Incorporation tech. When blight started spreading, fire packs were used to purge the fields," Jeremy said. "Drop them from up high and torch everything below. A bang at the start of the cascade, then pure flames. The fire burns away whatever fungus or bacteria is killing the crops to keep it from spreading."

"Or wipes out the city to stop the people from spreading." A void enveloped Nola's chest. "The domes did this. Our home did this." She had no anger or tears. The void had swallowed the place where rage should have lived

"How did they get them?" Jeremy asked. "This many fire packs, there's no way they were stored in the domes, that's too dangerous. And how did they get them in the air?"

"We have to get to Nettie and get back to Nightland." Nola skirted around the fire pack, pressing her back to the buildings as she crept past.

"I don't understand." Jeremy followed Nola. "I just...how?"

"We're going to find out," Nola said, "but we've got to get Nettie."

They kept their backs to the buildings all the way around the corner until bricks blocked the fire pack from view.

"We're almost there." Jeremy took off down the street, glancing sideways to be sure Nola kept pace.

This street hadn't been burned either, but smoke hung heavy in the air.

Turning onto the next road, flames soared up in front of them. The stench of burning rubber singed Nola's nose. Fire had decimated the houses. The fronts of the buildings had caved in or toppled onto the street, leaving only burning skeletons of homes behind.

"We have to find another way." Nola gagged on the stench. "If we cut around—"

Jeremy took Nola's shoulders, turning her from the blaze. "There isn't another way, this is Bellevue."

"But..." Nola's protest faded as she looked back at the flames.

The twisted forms of melted lampposts dotted the street. The remains of stone stairs lead up to houses that no longer existed.

"No." Nola knew the word couldn't help but she shouted it anyway. "No, no, no!"

"We have to go."

She didn't fight him as he kept an arm behind her back, guiding her away from the blaze that was the end of Bellevue.

The fire pack still sat in the middle of the street.

How can a thing so small cause so much death?

No larger than her torso, the fire pack didn't look deadly at all. It could have been built to transport water or fuel for one of the domes' trucks.

But it's killed a city.

The group they had told to flee was gone.

"Do you think they made it?" Nola asked.

"We can hope." Jeremy didn't slow their pace, even as he favored his injured leg.

The smoke had thickened in the time they'd been in the city. Destruction that had been easy to see on the way in now hid beneath a sheet of smoke, as though the fire itself felt the disgrace of what it had done and wanted to hide the horror of its actions.

A boy lay in the middle of the street. Crumpled up like he'd been tossed aside. The slight rise and fall of his chest was the only thing that separated him from the other corpses they'd seen.

"He's breathing." Nola knelt next to the boy, rolling him onto his back.

It was the boy they'd spoken to only a few moments before. The one who truly believed the Domers would come for him.

"We can't leave him here." Nola slipped her arms under the boy. Gritting her teeth, she straightened her legs. She could feel the weight of him pulling her off center, but her arms didn't scream in protest.

"Give him to me." Jeremy reached for the boy.

"You're hurt. I can do it." Nola stepped back.

"He's bigger than you." Jeremy holstered his Guard gun, keeping the revolver in his other hand. "If we walk out of here with you carrying him, what will people think? They can't know we're different."

Nola helped Jeremy sling the boy over his shoulder.

"Are you sure you can do this?" Nola asked.

A gray tinge had taken over Jeremy's face, and sweat slicked his hair.

"We need to move."

Nola took the lead, weaving their way out to the alley between the walls of fire.

More buildings had collapsed, leaving flaming rubble coating the street. Something that looked like a couch or a bed burned like a bonfire in the center of the path. Two charred corpses lay next to it.

With a wail and a *crack*, the façade of a storefront toppled onto the street in front of them.

"Is there another way out?" Nola shouted over the rumbling *crash* of an apartment building crumbling in on itself half a block behind them.

"No. Run, Nola."

"Not any faster than you." Nola pushed Jeremy in front of her, running right on his heels as he dodged between debris.

A glimmer of sunlight shone through the smoke ahead of them. A stretch of concrete filled with people.

"Almost there!" Nola shouted.

The top floor of a building sagged in on itself, showering Nola with sparks and catching the tip of her braid on fire. She patted the flames out with her palm, barely feeling the pain as her lungs seared, trying to find usable air within the shroud of smoke.

A *boom* sounded from far away, shaking the ground under her feet as they burst onto the highway.

"Out of the way!" Jeremy called.

He didn't stop until he reached the far side of the road.

"Help me," he said.

Nola grabbed the boy's shoulders, easing him carefully to the ground. The boy was still breathing, but his eyes stayed closed.

"Can you hear me?" Nola patted the boy's cheek.

"Nola." Jeremy grabbed her shoulder.

"He needs a doctor."

"Nola."

She looked up. Jeremy had his head down, his chin tucked to his chest.

Behind him, the street teemed with people. Some covered in soot. Some in the black uniforms of the Outer Guard.

CHAPTER SIXTEEN

"Oh no," Nola whispered.

Jeremy knelt in front of her, pulling the pack off his back. "Give me your gun belt."

Nola's fingers shook as she undid the clasp.

"Keep your head low." Jeremy slipped his own belt into the pack with Nola's and pocketed the revolver.

"Why are they all here?" Nola pulled her hair out of her braid, fluffing her unruly curls to hide her face. "How did they even get here?"

"No idea." Jeremy glanced back over his shoulder. "How many of them are there?"

Nola scanned the street through the curtain of her hair. "Two hundred, maybe three."

"Way too many." He shook his head. "A week ago, the domes were down to eighty-seven guards. Even with new people coming in we couldn't break one-fifty. The domes aren't built for it."

"Then who are they?"

"If you're in need of water, come over here," a voice shouted over the crowd. "Only one bottle per person. They are equipped with filters. Find a water source that isn't the river and the bottle will make the water pure enough to drink."

"They're giving out filters?" Nola stood, trusting in the crowd surging toward the voice to cover her.

"Why would they burn a city and help the survivors?" Jeremy said.

"It doesn't make sense."

"We need to get out of here," Jeremy said. "If they recognize us—"

"You mean you don't think your dad rescinded his kill order on me?" Nola knelt next to the boy. "We can't just leave him like this."

"His own people abandoned him in the middle of a burning street," Jeremy said. "We can't take him to Nightland, and I don't know the first thing about saving someone who's inhaled that much smoke."

"Please line up in an orderly fashion," a guard called from the center of the throng.

"What did they think was going to happen when they offered water to a few hundred desperate people?" Jeremy ran a hand over his face.

Guards surrounded the mass of outsiders. All had guns drawn.

"Remember to save these bottles," a guard instructed the crowd. "Keep them with you, and you'll be able to get more clean water."

"From where?" an angry voice shouted. "If we can't use the river, where should we go?"

"Where are we going to sleep and care for our wounded?"

"Why haven't you brought food!" a woman shoved a guard hard in the chest.

Two guards grabbed the woman, pinning her to the ground in an instant.

A *clap* like thunder sounded an instant later, pounding out from the center of the crowd.

Nola clamped her hands over her ears a moment too late. The sound throbbed through her brain, shaking away all thoughts but wanting the pounding to be gone.

The crowd scattered. Some falling to the ground and covering their heads, others stumbling away from the noise.

Only the Outer Guard in their heavy helmets didn't seem to mind the brain-shaking sound.

As the whooshing in Nola's brain settled, a man climbed up onto a set of crates. His limbs looked almost too long to be allowed, like the world had forgotten the difference between man and spider in his creation.

The man pulled off his helmet. His bald head glistened in the sun. "We have come out here in your time of need to offer aid. The domes are under no obligation to assist any of you."

Nola studied the man's face, wracking her brain to remember when she had seen him in the domes.

"We will leave in two minutes," the man continued. "If you would like a water bottle, calmly claim it now. Any unclaimed bottles will return with us to the domes." The man lifted his wrist, speaking into the cuff of his uniform.

The crowd surged forward, pushing each other out of the way to get to the center of the pack.

"We need one of those bottles," Jeremy said.

"I'll go." Nola stood.

"No, some of those guards could be from our domes."

"I have hair camouflage, you don't." Nola pulled more hair to cover her face, and ran toward the crowd.

She shoved her hands between two men, prying them apart, and slipped through the gap. Someone stomped on her foot. Stars danced in her eyes, but she pushed forward, shouldering past people until the crates came into view.

Rows of shining silver bottles sat in the crates. There were dozens of bottles in every crate and dozens of crates in the pile.

They were expecting more survivors.

Keeping her body smashed in the crowd, Nola reached her fingers out, barely managing to close them around a metal cylinder.

A fist swung for her face and nails scraped the back of her hand as she pulled her prize from the crate.

The punch connected with her forehead. She stumbled as arms wrapped around her chest, pinning her arms to her sides. She kicked back. A *crack* of breaking bones sounded the moment before the person holding her bellowed, their arms slipping away from her.

Cradling the bottle to her chest, Nola plowed her way through the crowd, back toward Jeremy.

The rumble of engines shook the air. The mob scattered, all moving in the same direction as Nola, knocking each other over in their haste to flee.

Heat licked the back of Nola's neck.

"Load them out!"

Nola glanced back at the shouted command. A helicopter large enough to hold all the crates landed on the street.

The guards pushed through the crowd, loading the crates onto the aircraft, then formed a line in front of it. All the guards' guns pointed at the crowd.

In less than a minute, the helicopter had been loaded and, with a whine of its engines, soared straight up into the air.

As soon as the helicopter had cleared, the guards turned, running down the highway toward the river beyond. Four dark boats had arrived on the riverbank, waiting to ferry the soldiers home.

An arm wrapped around Nola's waist. She jabbed her elbow backwards, catching the person who grabbed her in the ribs.

"Ouch." Jeremy coughed.

"Sorry." Nola stopped running, but Jeremy kept a hand on her back, pushing her forward. "I didn't know it was you."

"Then I'm glad you defended yourself."

Angry shouts took over the street as the sound of the helicopter faded.

A dozen brawls broke out in a matter of seconds as everyone fought for the bottles.

"How could they just leave like that?" The question barely made it through her gritted teeth. "They had to know everyone would fight to keep more bottles."

Footsteps pounded after them. Jeremy let go of Nola, catching their pursuer in the ribs with a punch.

"Run faster." Jeremy took Nola's hand.

"What about the boy?"

"He's still breathing and I moved him into the shade," Jeremy said. "There's nothing more we can do."

Nola bit the inside of her cheek, tasting her own blood.

Helping got Jeremy shot.

At least you didn't leave him to the flames.

They didn't bother sticking to the trees but sprinted up the center of the street.

Nola kept at Jeremy's side.

I could run faster.

But Jeremy's breathing came in rattling gasps, and his gait became more uneven every minute.

"We need to stop." Nola tugged on Jeremy's hand.

Jeremy didn't argue as Nola veered off the road and into the trees.

Others had followed their path, but none moved half so fast.

"We have a few minutes before they can catch up." She led him to a tree, pushing his shoulders to make him lean against the trunk.

"Give me the bottle." Jeremy coughed. He turned his head to the side and spat black into the brown grass.

"Are you okay?" Nola took his face in her hands.

"My body is purging, just give me the bottle."

Nola handed the silver bottle to Jeremy.

He didn't unscrew the top as she had expected, but flipped it over, examining the base.

"Do you want water?"

Jeremy ignored her. He dug his fingers into the seam at the bottom of the bottle.

"What are you doing?" Nola said.

He swayed as he reached down, pulling the knife from his boot.

"Jeremy."

"There has to be a reason." He dug the tip of the knife into the seam. With a *pop* the bottom came loose.

Another layer of metal waited beneath, as smooth and shining as the outside. A blue triangle run through with tiny lines had been stuck to the very bottom.

Jeremy pulled the triangle loose and held it up to the sunlight.

"What is it?" Nola whispered.

"It's a beacon. They're in the wrist cuffs the Outer Guard wear. It's how the domes track guards when they're out in the city."

"And they've planted them on all the survivors." Nola took the water bottle, unscrewing the top before looking back to Jeremy. "Can I drink it?"

Jeremy nodded. "No use in tracking dead people."

Nola took a long drink of the cool water, letting it dampen the fear rising in her chest.

"The domes destroyed the city and gave trackers to the ones who made it out alive." Her mouth went dry. She took another long drink. "They're trying to find Nightland. The guards are banking on some of the survivors making it to the vampires, and Emanuel taking them in."

"He won't." Jeremy pushed himself away from the tree. "No one will find Nightland. We'll warn Emanuel. We won't let the guards find them." A groan of pain slipped from him as he put weight on his leg.

"We have to get the bullet out." Nola pushed him back to the tree.

"It's already working its way out." Jeremy pushed himself up again, not seeming to notice Nola's hands on his chest.

"What do you mean working its way out?"

"It's like getting shot, but really slowly, and in reverse." His mouth narrowed into a thin line, and pink splotches blossomed on his forehead.

"We have to get it out." Nola grabbed his arm, trying to pull him back, but he kept walking toward the road, dragging her along behind him.

"We have to get back and tell Emanuel what the domes have done." Jeremy spoke through clenched teeth. "We have to warn them not to take anyone in, we need to tell Raina we couldn't find her sister, and I need to get you safely into those caves before the desperate people who just lost their homes catch up to us. I'm not sure if you noticed, but I'm not in fighting shape right now. Our best bet is to keep ahead of the crowds, so we have to move."

He stared into Nola's eyes, fierce determination pushing past his pain.

"Okay." She laced her fingers through his. "We'll get back to the caves."

Jeremy dropped the blue triangle onto the ground and downed the rest of the water.

Nola let him set the pace back to the road, keeping right by his side and scanning the tress for more guards with gifts or men with revolvers.

Jeremy tossed the bottle back onto the road.

No point in risking more trackers.

Nola opened her mouth to say something, anything to distract him from his pain. She couldn't think of any words.

She glanced behind.

A group of survivors had reached the spot on the hill where they'd stopped. Jeremy had been right to make them keep moving.

The caved in houses gaped at them as they passed, as though judging the world that had let safety deteriorate. The run down old buildings were the closest things to home the survivors would be able to find.

They passed the house with the red front door.

"They're going to fight over the houses aren't they?" Nola asked. "Even if they can find water and food, they'll start fighting each other."

"Or the vampires and werewolves will come for them when the sun goes down. There might have been some hiding deep enough down that they survived. If they did, they'll come out when the sun sets, furious and ready for a feast."

The incline of the road steepened as they neared the trees. Jeremy glanced behind then pushed himself to run faster.

Nola looked back. The groups behind them were nearly out of sight. A little faster and no one would be able to see where the two first up the hill had disappeared.

They stayed silent as they ran through the trees. The only sounds the thumping of their feet and the branches clawing at their clothes.

The sun had begun to sink when they reached the field of brambles.

How many sunsets since I've slept?

A wave of unbearable fatigue swept through Nola, adding a hundred pounds to each of her limbs and sand to her eyes. But Jeremy kept running.

All the color had faded from his face. Pink and gray had disappeared, replaced by sickly white.

"Almost there." Nola lifted her arms over her head, away from the thorns that clawed at her legs. "We're almost there, and then Dr. Wynne will get the bullet out. We'll sleep when we get there, and then you'll feel better."

"Will you stay with me?" Jeremy's forehead furrowed with pain. "You could have burned to death today, can you just stay where I can see you're safe?"

Nola coughed a laugh. "I'm fine, Jeremy."

"It's hard to remember when I wake up."

They reached the stripped trees, and the path grew steeper still. Nola wrapped her arm around Jeremy's waist, helping to propel him up the mountain.

"I've almost lost you so many times," Jeremy said. "When I wake up, it's hard to believe you still being here isn't just a dream. I always have this second of panic. I have to go through all of it, just to make sure I haven't lied to myself. That you really are alive. I hate that second. It's worse than any bullet."

Tears stung the corners of her eyes. "I'll stay where you can see me. You won't have to panic. I'll be right there with you."

"Thank you."

Jeremy led them up the mountain, though Nola didn't know how he could see the path through the sweat that dripped into his half-closed eyes.

"Here," he wheezed as the sun kissed the tops of the mountains.

Nola searched the slopes around them. The moss-covered ledge peered out overhead.

What had seemed like an impossible leap a short time ago looked easy now.

"I'll boost you up." Nola made a step with her hands.

"You just go." Jeremy shook his head, stumbling at the movement. "I'll be fine."

"You first then." Nola took a step back. "I'm not jumping up there without you."

Jeremy turned in a slow circle, scanning the trees around them. He looked back at the ledge, squaring his shoulders, and pushed off.

A moan escaped him as his fingers caught the ledge.

"Let me help you." Nola reached for his legs, but he had already begun to pull himself up.

His arms shook, and his breath hissed through his teeth.

Nola covered her mouth with her hand, biting back the urge to shout for help from above. Her palm smelled like smoke.

With a feeble kick, Jeremy's legs disappeared from view.

"Come on up." His voice sounded like he'd been sick for a week and the dome doctors had decided to ignore him.

Nola bent her knees and aimed her weight for the ledge. Her palms landed on the soft moss. Pushing with her arms, she leveraged her weight up and over the edge. She stumbled on the stone ledge, but stayed on her feet.

Jeremy sat, propped up against the tunnel wall. "You're a pretty quick study."

CHAPTER SEVENTEEN

"Nola!" Kieran's voice carried out of the tunnel. "Nola, are you hurt?"

"I'm fine." Nola looped an arm around Jeremy's waist, hoisting him to his feet. "Jeremy's hurt. He's got a bullet stuck in his leg."

"Shit." Footsteps ran up the tunnel. Kieran stopped in the shadows ten feet down the entrance. "Can you get him this far?"

"We've gotten all the way up from the city," Jeremy wheezed. "We can make it to Emanuel."

Jeremy leaned on Nola's shoulder. The weight felt heavier than it should have. Whether from fatigue or knowledge of the horrible pain that weakened him, Nola didn't know.

"Lover boy got a bullet in the leg and you didn't pull it out?" Raina appeared by Kieran's side.

"Didn't have time," Jeremy said. "It's been a bad day out there."

One shuffling step at a time, they reached the shadows.

"Let me see it." Kieran knelt by Jeremy's leg.

"I'll go to your father," Jeremy said.

"How long has it been in there?" Kieran asked.

"Too long for a few more minutes to make a difference," Jeremy said.

"What's going on in the city?" Raina asked.

"I..." Nola searched for the words.

"There is no more city," Jeremy said. "We tried to find your sister. Bellevue is gone."

Raina nodded, her face betraying no grief at hearing of her sister's end. "We need to get you to Emanuel."

Jeremy limped a step forward.

Kieran raised a hand to stop Jeremy. "I'll carry you. It'll be faster."

"No chance in hell," Jeremy coughed.

"*I'll* carry you." Raina walked up to Jeremy and scooped him over her shoulder. "Don't argue and don't kick. I'm in a bad mood."

Jeremy mumbled a response as Raina ran down the tunnel.

Say that you ran into the fire to look for Nettie. Say you tried but the flames were stronger. Tell them about the guards and the fire packs. Tell them about the beacons in the water bottles.

Nola could only form thoughts as they ran up the tunnel. No speech would come.

Raina slowed at each of the windows, carefully keeping her skin in the shadows.

The sunset tinted the sky brilliant, lively colors, filled with the promise of a brand new tomorrow. But the smoke of the city stained the horizon, tainting its grandeur.

Kieran ran in front of Raina, wrenching open the metal door to the sparring room.

Every match stopped as Raina entered the room. A chorus of shouted questions echoed off the walls.

"Are they coming for us?"

"What have the Domers done?"

"Were the wolves finally slaughtered?"

"We have to talk to Emanuel first." Raina didn't slow her pace as she shouted over the crowd. "Once we've talked to Emanuel, he'll let everyone know what's going on."

"Is the sun runner dying?"

Nola spun toward the voice.

The blond girl stared back at her.

"He's not dying," Nola growled. "He's going to be just fine."

"Good." The blond winked.

Nola curled her hands into fists as she chased after Raina.

"He shouldn't have left a bullet in this long," Kieran said.

A group of six women carrying mismatched baskets plastered themselves to the wall as Raina ran past. One dropped her load, sending clean sheets spilling onto the floor.

"*He* can hear you," Jeremy said, "and *he* didn't really have many options."

Kieran reached the double door to Emanuel's library first. He only managed to knock once before Raina shoved him aside and flung the door open.

"Raina!" a little girl squeaked, running toward their group.

Eden.

Nola's heart melted at the sight of the child.

Black curls surrounded her round, rosy cheeks. Her big, dark eyes sparkled as she reached up for Raina.

"Go get your father and Dr. Wynne," Raina said.

A flicker of hurt wrinkled the child's forehead before she ran for the library door, calling, "Daddy! Doctor!"

"What's happened to Jeremy?" Julian stepped away from the bookshelf, a mug clasped in his hands.

"Bullet," Nola said.

Raina eased Jeremy off her shoulder and laid him on the floor. "Take off your pants like a good boy."

Jeremy shook his head.

"The world is ending," Raina said. "It's not like we've got pants to spare."

Planting a foot on Jeremy's chest, Raina undid his pants. "Do you want the honors, or should I?" Raina winked at Nola.

Heat flashed in Nola's cheeks.

"Oh for heaven's sake." Julian knelt by Jeremy's feet and pulled his pants down in one swift tug.

"I didn't know your talents in this field were quite so impressive," Raina said.

"Years of practice." Julian untied Jeremy's boots.

Instinct told Nola to help him, but she couldn't move. Couldn't think beyond anything but Jeremy's bare legs.

He still wore his dome-issued briefs, but they only reached halfway down his thigh. Nothing covered the wound on his leg.

Red streaks spread out like a spider's web over his thigh, surrounding a bump that moved with each of Jeremy's heartbeats, pulsing up as though fighting to break free.

"We have to get that out of him." Nola shook her head. Her body didn't know what else to do. "It's infected."

"If Graylock is as good as it's supposed to be, he'll be fine," Kieran said.

Emanuel came through the back door, a confused Dr. Wynne on his heels.

"Nola, what's happened?"

"Jeremy needs help." Nola pointed a shaking finger at Jeremy's leg.

"What did the two of you get into?" Dr. Wynne knelt by Jeremy.

"He got shot, and the bullet—"

"Leaving those sorts of things in there really isn't a good idea, you know." Dr. Wynne fished in his pockets, first pulling out a spray bottle, then a metal case.

"I tried to convince him to let me try and get it out, but he didn't think we had time."

Dr. Wynne popped open the metal case. Three scalpels waited inside.

"What did you find out there, Nola?" Emanuel asked.

"The domes dropped fire packs on the city," Nola said. "They destroyed the whole thing. I don't think there will be a building left standing when the fires go out."

The doctor sprayed foam onto the pulsing lump on Jeremy's leg.

"Why?" Julian asked. "That many fire packs so close to the domes, it seems like an unreasonable risk. With the bridge destroyed, the city is hardly a threat."

"They think it is," Nola said. "There were Outer Guard in the city, and not just from the domes here."

"Salinger," Jeremy groaned. "It was Salinger."

"What?" Nola knelt beside him, taking his hand.

His eyes flickered open. "The man who spoke. I couldn't remember why I recognized him. Salinger."

"This might sting." The doctor sliced into Jeremy's thigh.

Jeremy clamped his mouth shut, swallowing his shout as white leaked from the wound.

"You're okay." Nola squeezed his hand. "This'll make it better. Soon it'll feel better."

"Might need to go a bit deeper." Dr. Wynne wrinkled his brow.

"Who's Salinger?" Kieran asked.

"He's from the Incorporation." Julian pinched the bridge of his nose. "An evil man whom I had hoped to never hear of again."

"The Incorporation's here?" Raina tipped her head, her mouth pinched as though trying to reason through why a joke might be funny.

"Just a bit deeper and I should have it." Dr. Wynne pressed the scalpel into Jeremy's leg again.

Jeremy shut his eyes. A groan rumbled in his chest.

Blood trickled from the wound.

"You're okay." Nola pressed her forehead to his. "Just breathe, you're okay."

"The domes we have dealt with for so long are but one of many," Julian said. "They were all incorporated under the same project. All meant to trade people, supplies, and knowledge as the world dwindled to nothing. And, of course, all spread out in an appropriate manner for repopulating the world once the planet has found a path back to sustainability."

"Salinger is from another set of domes?" Emanuel asked.

"Yes," Julian said, "but the more worrisome and deadly part of the equation is his place as head of the guards. All of the guards, in all of the domes."

"Just another moment." Dr. Wynne tipped the scalpel into the wound.

"Shh," Nola hushed. "You're okay."

"Why would the head of all the guards be here?" Raina asked. "They blocked themselves off. The fight is over."

"They want Nightland," Nola said.

"Gah!" Jeremy shouted as Dr. Wynne pulled the bullet free.

"There you are." Dr. Wynne held the hunk of metal up to the light. "Such a tiny thing to cause so much pain. I would offer to stitch you up, but a nice lie down and you'll be fine."

"What do you mean *they want Nightland?*" Emanuel pressed.

"Salinger wasn't there shooting people," Nola said. "They were waiting for survivors and giving out water bottles complete with filters that will make anything but the river water drinkable."

Julian whistled. "That is a gift I had never thought the domes would consider giving."

"They had beacons hidden in the bottoms," Nola said. "They're tracking where all the bottles go. They destroyed the city and are making the survivors lead them anywhere people might be hiding and surviving. People like Nightland."

"Damn," Julian whispered.

"Raina," Emanuel said, "double the guards at every entrance. There is to be absolutely no one entering or leaving Nightland. If anyone has any qualms with my ruling, send them directly to me."

"Yes, Emanuel." With a nod, Raina ran out the door.

"Julian, check the gardening tiers and the air shafts. Make sure we can't be seen from below."

"Or above." Nola looked to Kieran. "They had a big helicopter, big enough to fly over the mountain. If they see the garden, they'll know we're here."

Kieran's black eyes widened in fear. "We have to take all the sun disks down. We can pull brush to cover the tiers."

"Do it."

Kieran and Julian were out the door before Emanuel could speak again.

"Is there anything else we need to know?" Emanuel stood with his hands behind his back, his shoulders relaxed even as terror filled those around him.

"I don't think so. It's going to be bad out there. None of the survivors have anything, and..."

"And you can't believe the domes would do such a thing?" Dr. Wynne patted Nola's shoulder, leaving behind smudges of Jeremy's blood. "I *can* believe it. Each dome is a part of a greater plan. Our dome has been struggling with the city for some time. If the Incorporation had to become involved, there is nothing they would consider unreasonable for the protection of the domes."

"So they fly in on their fancy helicopter and fix the problem? Captain Ridgeway couldn't control the city so just kill everyone to clean up the mess?" Nola looked from Emanuel to Dr. Wynne, waiting for one of them to tell her how wrong she was.

"The Incorporation believe their mission is the only hope for the world," Dr. Wynne said, "and only those chosen to save the world can truly matter. Everyone else is already doomed and none of their concern."

"The domes are monsters." Nola's hands shook.

Jeremy pressed them to his chest, his eyes still closed.

"I'm afraid so." Dr. Wynne stood. "I saw it many years ago. A simple vaccine could have stopped so much illness in the city. I was reprimanded for wasting my time in saving those outside the glass. For years I sat in the sterile domes, pretending the children out in the world who were suffering and dying had nothing to do with me. But they did. I failed to serve them when I had the knowledge and resources. I let them die because I didn't know their names. When I couldn't stand it any longer and found a way to help the outsiders, the domes found out and left me and my son out to die. They are kind only to those they need and killers to everyone else. I can think of no better definition of *monster*."

"You hated us for breaking into the domes." Emanuel knelt in front of Nola.

Tears streamed down her face as she looked into his black eyes.

"To the Nola Kent who lived safely in the domes, we were monsters seeking destruction," Emanuel said. "To the Nola Kent I see now, the monsters surrounded her the whole time. I led freedom fighters into the demons' lair to protect children the domes would gladly burn."

Nola coughed a sob.

"I ask your forgiveness for the blood we've shed to build our home," Emanuel said. "The path to salvation has led us through many dark and terrible places. I never wanted to fight the monsters. I only wanted my child to survive."

"Am I a monster for living with them for so long?" Nola said.

"Not at all." Dr. Wynne packed away his scalpels. "If that were true, Kieran and I would be monsters as well. And I hope you don't think that of me."

"No," Nola said. "You're a hero and a healer. I just..."

Jeremy lifted Nola's hand, pressing it to his cheek.

"I thought I knew which direction was up," Nola said. "And I don't know what to do now that I can't even pretend I wasn't wrong."

"You forgive yourself," Emanuel said. "You forgive others, and you work."

"The work is the part that helps most," Dr. Wynne said.

Jeremy's hand slipped from Nola's, falling gently to the floor.

"We need to get him someplace to sleep," Nola said.

"His room is right down the hall." Emanuel lifted Jeremy, carrying him like a small child.

"What happens if they find us here?" Nola followed Emanuel into the hall.

"They will attack us," Emanuel said.

"Can the fire packs get down this far?" Nola asked.

"If they come for my family, they will bring far worse than fire packs." They stopped three doors away from the library. "If you would?"

Nola twisted the nob. The door opened without a *creak*.

A single bed waited along with a desk and a chair.

"Is this where he's been sleeping?" Nola pulled back the sheets on the bed.

"It seemed right." Emanuel laid Jeremy carefully down.

"To keep him so close to you and Eden?" Nola said. "Not that he would ever hurt you."

"Keep your friends close and your enemies closer," Emanuel said. "My grandmother always used to say that."

Emanuel stepped around her to the open door.

"Do you think he's your enemy?" Nola asked before the door could shut.

"No." A weary smile curved Emanuel's lips. "But shattered hearts are the enemies of all men, and that boy has been broken. I can only hope that somehow my friend's heart will be pieced back together."

The door closed with a *click*. The tiny noise seemed louder than the *bang* of the revolver.

Every muscle in Nola's body screamed for sleep. Her legs longed to collapse.

Jeremy lay in the bed, his chest gently rising and falling. Color had already begun returning to his face.

Tears slipped down Nola's cheeks. She didn't bother drying them, or untying her shoes before wriggling her feet free.

Jeremy's arm splayed out to the side, as though even in painful sleep he'd remembered to leave a place for her.

She curled up next to him, tucking her head onto his shoulder. His chest rose and fell with each breath. Another inhale, another victory. Another moment the end of the world hadn't stolen from them.

Sleep came for her before she could wonder how close the end might be.

CHAPTER EIGHTEEN

J eremy's arm moved, pulling Nola out of sleep.

"Don't," Nola mumbled, burying her face in his chest. "Don't move."

Beneath the stench of smoke, he still smelled like him. Like fresh earth. *I hope that smell never goes away.*

"You don't want me to move?" His words rumbled in his chest.

"No." Nola wrapped her arm over his stomach, pulling herself closer to him. "If you move, then I have to open my eyes."

"You don't want to?"

Nola could hear Jeremy's smile shaping his words.

"No, I don't," she said.

He leaned his cheek against her hair.

They lay silently for a long moment. Footsteps passed in the hall. Life in Nightland continued without their aid.

"Does your leg still hurt?" Nola asked.

"It feels fine. I'll stretch it out a bit and be good as new."

"I should let you get up then."

Jeremy held her tight. "You shouldn't."

A child ran past in the hall, laughing about something.

"If I open my eyes, then we have to go out there." A tear leaked down Nola's cheek. Her hands started to shake. She balled them into fists, gripping the front of his shirt. "If we go out there, then I'll know yesterday wasn't just a nightmare. And the domes murdered people, and Nightland is in hiding, and I don't know if I can deal with all of that."

He pressed his lips to the top of her head. "I wish I could tell you it was all a bad dream."

"You promised not to lie to me again," Nola said.

"I know."

Nola wiggled up higher on the bed, pressing her forehead to Jeremy's cheek.

"Remember before all of this started, when the zombie woman made it to the outside of the domes?"

"Yeah."

"I thought she was terrifying," Nola whispered. "I thought the kids in the food lines on Charity Day were the saddest thing I would ever see. I was so stupid."

"Not stupid. You were never stupid. Maybe a little naïve, but we were kids. We weren't supposed to know how messed up everything is."

"It wasn't that long ago, you know?"

"A lot's happened."

"Yeah."

They lay still for a long while. Nola's breaths matched Jeremy's, their chests rising and falling in time.

"Promise me we'll both make it out of this?" Nola whispered. "You and me together."

"Nola..."

"You've never broken a promise to me." She found Jeremy's hand, lacing her fingers through his. "So promise we're going to get through this."

"I would never let anything happen to you." Jeremy's lips brushed her cheek as he spoke.

Nola opened her eyes, turning so her face was a breath from his.

"I don't need you to protect me. I don't need you to fight my battles or pretend everything is okay just to make me feel safe."

"I know. I just"—a shudder shook his shoulders—"the idea of anything happening to you, it kills me."

Nola leaned in, brushing her lips against his. A tingle squirmed at the bottom of her toes.

"I love you." She rested her forehead on his. "I can fight for myself, but I need as many things worth fighting for as I can get. I need to know at the end of all this, you'll be by my side."

"I promise you, Magnolia Kent, when all this is over, I'll be with you." He brushed the curls from her face. "As long as you let me, I'll be by your side."

Nola pressed her lips to his, letting the warmth of their kiss flood her chest, sweeping away all thought of fear and worry.

Jeremy wrapped his arm around Nola's waist, pulling her closer.

She separated her lips, deepening their kiss. Her pulse thundered in her ears, but beyond the steady thumping off her own heart, she could hear Jeremy's blood racing through his veins, his pulse keeping time with hers.

His fingers found the skin at her hip. Heat throbbed from the trail his fingers traced up her spine.

Nola found the bottom of his shirt. His hands joined hers as she pulled it up, snaking the fabric over his head.

No scars marked his chest. All of the blood and pain had left his skin unharmed.

She pressed her lips to his chest. Never had she been so grateful for the simple sound of a beating heart.

He took her face in his hands, kissing her cheeks, her lips, trailing his kisses down her neck.

She shifted her weight, twisting to sit.

He lay on the bed beneath her. His short hair tousled from sleep, the lines of worry fading from around his eyes.

His hands slid up her sides as she pulled off her shirt.

She lay down, pressing her chest to his.

"Nola." Her name fell from his lips as she kissed him.

Their limbs twined together as they searched for every inch of flesh they could share.

All thought of where she ended and he began disappeared. All fear of what lay beyond the moment vanished.

There was nothing left in the world but them and the darkness.

CHAPTER NINETEEN

The thick smell of fertilizer filled the air. Even with the cloth tied over her face, the inside of Nola's nose itched from the scent. Footsteps echoed dully in the cavern, and water trickled down the back wall.

While no glamour could be found working in the mushroom field, Nola welcomed the peace.

Kieran had banned visitors from entering the lowest cave in Nightland without his permission, and his consent was not easily given.

Nola pulled a glass vial from her bag. Carefully, she dug the vessel into the dirt. Fumbling in her thick gloves, she worked the stopper into the vial. She plucked the mushroom nearest where she had taken the sample, and wrapped the two in a rag before placing them in her bag.

The task she'd been assigned was simple enough. Find the best fertilizer for the different growing conditions in the mushroom field.

She chuckled to herself at the absurdity of calling this place a field. Buried deep in the mountain, the mushrooms were grown in a cavern the architects had barely altered. Most of the field consisted of random patches of growth rather than rows of crops to be harvested.

Lights hung from the ceiling at odd intervals, doing little more than casting strange shadows. Nola didn't mind. As long as a trace of light existed, Graylock gave her the power to see. Only absolute darkness could blind her now.

Humming faintly to herself, Nola wandered down the twisting paths of the cavern. Tucked up under a ledge, a patch of mushrooms fed off the water dripping from a crack in the wall. She scraped a bit of soil away from the base and plucked a mushroom sample as well.

None of the food eaters in Nightland relished the thought of living off of mushrooms for the cold months. In the week since Nola had started working in the caves, some had even gone so far as to question if she really needed to work on growing *more* mushrooms.

They'll be grateful if the other supplies begin to run out.

If they come for us.

Nola shivered, the chill of the cavern suddenly biting her to the bone.

She worked her way farther down the path, squeezing between a set of stalagmites to reach a growth of mushrooms that clung to the wall.

There had been no news from the city in more than a week. Raina said the smoke had stopped rising, and the stench had finally left the air. Emanuel had put her in charge of the ones set in the windows to watch the woods.

Nola would never dare say it, but she knew Raina spent her time scanning the outside world through that open window, searching for her sister.

Nola clasped her hands together, waiting for their shaking to stop before she pulled another glass vial from her bag.

A few lost survivors had been spotted at the base of the mountains wandering aimlessly. Searching for the safety and supplies they couldn't know were so close by.

She pulled down a half-moon shaped mushroom from the wall and tucked the sample safely in her bag.

The helicopter hadn't been spotted, but the tiered garden on top of the mountain still stayed covered. Only vampires were allowed out at night to silently tend the crops in the darkness.

At least the growing season is over anyway. And there was time to protect the animals. And the domes haven't dropped fire on us.

Slipping back through the stalagmites, Nola moved on to the main chamber of the cavern, to the part of the mushroom farm constructed by Kieran. The ceiling towered fifty feet overhead, and the space reached two hundred yards before meeting a pool. Then who knew how much farther until it ended?

We should try and farm fish in the water. There has to be a species that would thrive.

The domes hadn't trained her in animal husbandry. Just like they hadn't trained her in fighting or first aid.

She shook off the flare of anger that bubbled in her chest.

"Do the work you know how to do, Nola."

Each of the plots had been built of heavy-tarred wood filled with soil and fertilizer. Mushrooms blossomed at odd angles, thriving in the damp air. She worked quickly, moving from bed to bed, taking the samples that would help them expand the mushroom farm.

What Kieran had built didn't take up even a tenth of the space, and there was more room between beds than necessary. If they figured out the most efficient soil, condensed the beds, and spread out the operation...

Kieran and I will be the most hated people in Nightland.

Nola laughed. The sound bounced around the cavern.

A face appeared from behind a stalactite. A scowling, weathered old man with black eyes.

"Sorry," Nola whispered, knowing the man would easily hear her even at a distance.

Carefully dusting off her gloves, she tucked them into her bag with the last of the samples.

The face disappeared.

Nola rolled her eyes and headed for the pool. She could understand the man's love of the quiet. The peace was part of what made working in the mushroom fields worthwhile.

The tension above held nearly as strong a scent as the fertilizer in the cavern. Hardly anyone ever chose to venture outside Nightland, but now that it had been banned, stir crazy vampires roamed the halls. Between all the brawls that had broken out and the constant threat of hundreds of guards swooping in on them, the cavern was the only place that could truly be considered quiet.

Kneeling by the pool, Nola stared down at her reflection.

My eyes still look the same.

She smiled. Her eyes didn't brighten as they should.

Nola splashed her hands in the water to rinse them, swishing her fingers around vigorously enough that her reflection couldn't reform. Letting her hands drip dry, she jogged through the cavern to the tunnel that led to the main corridors of Nightland.

The tunnel had been left mostly to its own devices just as the cavern below had. Swatches were pure, left as the mountain had created them. Then the walls would be carved smooth for a few feet as the architects guided the path to the farm below. The steep and winding climb would have tired her legs before, but jogging up the tunnel with her bag bouncing at her side didn't even change her breathing.

Bright lights from the main corridor poured into the last few feet of the tunnel. Nola pulled the cloth from her nose, relishing her first breath of clean air.

"I was just about to send a search party down after you." Jeremy leaned against the wall, a plate of food in his hand.

Nola's mouth watered at the scent of fresh bread and cheese. "Am I running late?"

"Only about an hour." Jeremy shook his head as Nola took a giant bite of the bread.

"Sorry." She covered her mouth with her hand. "I'm not very good with time down there."

"Well, if I can ever find one, I'll snag you a watch." Jeremy winked.

Nola rose up on her toes, pressing her lips to the stubble on his cheek. "Thanks."

He wrapped an arm around her, letting her lean on his side as she downed the food.

"How was it down there?" he asked once she'd emptied the plate.

"Fine." She wrapped her arms around his waist, laying her cheek on his chest. "Stinky, quiet, I got all the samples I needed."

"Good."

"Was it not supposed to go well?"

Nola smiled as a rumble of laughter shook Jeremy's chest.

"I'm just always surprised is all." He tipped up her chin to look into her eyes. "You used to hate being underground, and now you march into the middle of a mountain every day. I'm just impressed." He kissed her gently.

Her heart skipped a beat as he lifted his face away.

"You never cease to amaze me, Nola Kent."

Nola took his hand, keeping her arm pressed to his as they walked down the hall.

"There is no aboveground here," Nola said. "Except the gardens, and only vampires are allowed out there. Besides, after everything we've seen and survived, and after that last trip through the Nightland tunnels, I guess my definition of *scary* has changed a bit."

"Last trip through the Nightland tunnels?" Jeremy asked.

"When we were running from the domes," Nola said. "Before you found me in the city. After the tunnel I had to crawl through, the mushroom field seems huge."

Jeremy's shoulders tensed. "You went through Nightland?"

"Yeah." Nola stopped, stepping aside to let a man with a crate of food pass. "How did you think we got into the city?"

"Boats," Jeremy said. "The same way Nightland crept across to attack us."

Nola furrowed her brow, trying to remember if Jeremy had ever asked how she had gotten into the city. "There were never any boats. At least not that I saw. There was a tunnel that started in a dead tree and cut under the river. I thought the Outer Guard had found it. I thought that's how you knew we were in the city."

"We just knew Nightland had gone back over the bridge after they attacked the domes and assumed Raina would take you into the city," Jeremy said.

"You were so close to us. I heard"—a lump pressed into Nola's throat—"I heard you say you'd never stop looking for me."

Jeremy closed his eyes. "I could have found you before you got hurt."

"Shh." Nola wrapped her arms around his neck, pressing her cheek to his. "Please don't. You saved me, and we're together. And even if you had found me, the domes would have locked me up. And Salinger and the Incorporation still would have destroyed the city. And I know you, Jeremy. You wouldn't have been able to help them do that."

"No, I wouldn't." He held her tight, like he was afraid the domes could still come and rip her away.

"Then we're where we should be." Nola kissed him, letting his taste flood her mouth. "And we're together."

"I love you." He kissed the top of her head. "More than anything that has ever existed, I love you."

Nola's heart swelled, sending heat rushing to her cheeks. "I love you, too."

We could sneak away, hide where no one will find us.

"I need to turn these samples in," Nola whispered.

"We must work for science." Jeremy took her hand. "What the world needs is more mushrooms, and I think you're just the one to deliver."

"Stop it." Nola knocked her shoulder into his arm.

"Then we spar?" Jeremy asked.

"Oh yes," Nola said. "Raina laughing and telling me I'll never properly gut someone is my favorite time of day."

"It brings her inside," Jeremy said. "That's something."

Nola's joy faded away, popped like a bubble of soap she had been foolish enough to think she could hold in her hand.

"It is good for her to come in for a while," Nola said. "We all have a job to do, but..."

"Her sister isn't coming," Jeremy said.

"No, she's not."

They walked in silence until the crackling of remembered fire grew too loud in Nola's ears.

"How was Emanuel today?"

"Fine. We talked about organizing everyone for training sessions and working on drills for evacuating non-combatants in case Nightland is attacked."

"And?"

"And there's nowhere to go," Jeremy said. "Everyone could run to the mush-room farm, but there's no way to reinforce or create an exit. The survivors would end up in a siege with the guards, and there's no way Nightland would win."

Nola bit her lips together, holding her question as four children ran past. Each of them held a book in their hands.

A hope for the future if the domes will allow us to have it.

"So there wasn't any progress?" Nola stopped in front of a metal door.

"Well"—Jeremy glanced up and down the corridor—"a helicopter was spotted in the sky."

"What?" Nola squeaked. She clapped a hand over her mouth as her voice bounced down the hall.

"It took off at daybreak and flew away. There's been no sign of it since."

"What does that mean?" Nola held Jeremy's hand with both of hers, clinging on like she already knew what he was going to say.

"Not sure. Emanuel and I agree, if we don't see any movement, in two days we send scouts down to see what's happening."

"No," Nola said. "Why would anyone go down there? The only information we could gain is that we don't need to hide anymore. It's past season for the garden, we can wait—wait a month even—then see what's going on."

"What if they've brought in more guards?" Jeremy asked. "What if they're rallying guards from all over the world to attack us?"

"Does it matter?" Nola asked. "There's nowhere else for us to go. We have to stay here, so we should just stay hidden."

"If they're going to come for us, we could disband," Jeremy whispered. "Head out in small groups. They wouldn't be able to find us all, and some people might make it. If they attack while we're all here, we all die."

Nola pressed her forehead to his chest, searching for a reason to tell him he was wrong.

"If we have to run—"

"We run together," Jeremy said. "There's no question of that."

"And T and Beauford come with us," Nola said. "I won't leave them."

"I wouldn't ask you to."

"And if you go on the scouting mission to the domes"—Nola squared her shoulders—"I'm going with you."

"Absolutely not," Jeremy said.

"Then you don't go either," Nola said. "The only reason you'd be a better choice than Raina or Desmond is because you can go in the daylight. If you have to go in the daylight, you aren't going alone, which means I'm coming with you. I'm the only other superhero we've got, remember?"

Jeremy stared up at the ceiling for a long moment. "We'll just keep our fingers crossed that something will change in the next two days that will keep Nightland safe and you in the tunnels."

"Why two days?" Nola asked.

"That's when you get your last dose," Jeremy said. "I won't risk either of us going far from Dr. Wynne before you get that injection."

Pain raced through Nola's veins at the thought of the ice flooding her again.

"Right." She nodded, feeling like her head was bobbling uselessly around. "Right. Mushrooms. I should get these in to him."

"Want me to come in?" Jeremy asked.

"Better not," Nola said. "I'll meet you in the sparring room?"

"I'll be the one with the bow staff." Jeremy kissed her and left her in front of the metal door.

Nola turned the handle without knocking and stepped into Kieran's lab.

CHAPTER TWENTY

B eakers bubbled on the table, sending puffs of steam into the air. Vines grew up the far wall, their color gray though the plants thrived. Terrariums of insects lined one side of the room, while cupboards and a heavy sink stood along the other.

Kieran sat at the center of it all, hunched over a scraped up microscope that looked older than him or Nola. He glanced up for only a second when she entered his laboratory.

"I've brought all the samples," Nola said. "Things are still going well. Too bad people can't live on mushrooms alone or we'd be set for the whole winter."

"The animals can eat the extras." Kieran kept his eye pressed to his microscope. "Better to have too much than too little."

"Of course." Nola dropped her bag on the table, careful to let it fall with a *thump*.

Kieran's jaw tensed, cutting into a line that looked more statue than living.

"Do you want me to test the samples?" Nola opened the far cupboard, pulling out the giant binder that held all the data from the mushroom field experiments.

"I can do it," Kieran said. "You should go meet up with him."

"Him?" Nola dropped the binder onto the table. "You mean Emanuel, Beauford, Julian?"

"Jeremy." Kieran gripped the table, his knuckles turning white from the pressure. "You know I mean Jeremy. I could hear his voice through the door."

"You're right." Nola pulled the samples from her bag, laying them out in a long line. "Jeremy walked me here, and he's waiting for me in the sparring room. But he has practicing of his own to do, so I have time to do the work myself."

She unwrapped the first set of samples. A young button mushroom from one of the beds. "We should look at putting in more places to grow in the cavern. There's plenty of room, and it's going well."

"He could have come in with you." Kieran stood.

For a moment, Nola thought he would walk toward her, but he headed to the cupboards, pulling out a green file. He didn't say anything else as he walked past her back to his seat.

"Did you want Jeremy to come in with me?" Nola asked.

"I'm sure he'd be happier if you weren't alone with me." He scratched out notes on his paper.

"I'm surrounded by vampires all the time. I don't think you're any more likely to try and hurt me than the rest of them," Nola said.

"That's not what I mean."

"I know." Nola pulled an oyster mushroom from its wrapping. "Jeremy trusts me."

"Hmm."

"Don't *hmm*, Kieran." She pulled the glass vial from its cloth. "Just because you live in a warped little world where trust is something most people don't bother to understand doesn't mean it doesn't exist." The vial snapped. Nola gasped as shards of glass cut deep into her palm. "Dammit."

Kieran took her hand, his cold fingers touching her skin before she even knew he'd stood up.

"We need to wash out the dirt." He moved toward the sink.

"The dirt won't hurt me, Kieran."

He closed his eyes, nodding to himself before opening them again. "Right, you're right. But we at least need to pull out the glass."

His black eyes didn't turn up to her face as he ran water over her palm.

The water in Nightland held no heat. It matched the cool of the vampires' skin. Graylock hadn't stolen Nola's warmth. It had left her maddeningly close to human. Her flesh warm, feeling every chill of Kieran's touch.

"I know you trust Jeremy," Kieran said, his tone barely above a whisper. "And I want you to be right about him. I just..."

"Just what?" Nola held her hand still as Kieran pulled free the first shard of glass.

"I've loved you for a very long time, Nola. You were my whole world. Dead mom, crazy dad...you were everything to me. If I hadn't left the domes, we'd probably still be together." A smiled touched Kieran's lips.

"I never wanted you to leave." Blood dripped from Nola's hand, falling to the stone floor. "I mourned for you. It was like you died."

"Sometimes, I wished I had," Kieran said. "But Dad had a mission. He had to save people, and I had to make sure he didn't die doing it."

"He did save a lot of people."

"That's just it." Kieran finally met her gaze. "Half of Nightland wouldn't be here without him, without ReVamp. Some of the humans would be dead, too."

"And without you, what food would there be?" A tingle of something itched at the center of Nola's chest.

"Not enough to keep our people fed." Pleading filled Kieran's eyes. "The day we got kicked out of the domes was the day I lost you. And then when you came to Nightland, for one crazy moment, I thought I could have you back."

"So did I."

"But it was already too messed up, Nola. You never could have walked away until the domes made you. And you had Jeremy waiting for you and protecting you in ways I couldn't, because Nightland is my home. These are my people. They have been for a long time." He ran her hand under the water again. "But the thing is, if I could go back, I wouldn't change it. If Dad and I had stayed in the domes, a lot of people would have died because we wouldn't have been there to help."

"Kieran—"

"I love you, Nola. I will always love you, and maybe I'll never love anybody else. But I can't regret what's happened. I can't regret the Nightland I helped to build."

"What you've done is amazing." Nola touched Kieran's cheek. "If this place didn't exist, I don't know what would have happened."

He held her hand to his face. "I know I've messed up a hundred ways, and I don't know if you're ever going to be able to forgive me or trust me. But I don't think I can survive in this tomb with you hating me. And Jeremy hating me. Jeremy and I used to be friends, and...I don't know if I can be happy for you yet, but I'm going to try. And maybe someday—"

Nola wrapped her arms around his neck, laying her cheek next to his. "We'll all work on it. On trusting each other. There are only five ex-Domers here. We can't afford to hate each other."

"We can't." Kieran held her tightly. "I've really missed you, Nola."

"I've missed you too." A tear fell from Nola's cheek, mixing with the blood she'd dripped on Kieran's shoulder. "Sorry I bled on you."

"A snack for later." Kieran gave a tiny smile. "Too much?"

"Maybe a little." Nola shrugged.

The tiny tingle in Nola's heart had turned into a painful tear. "Is this supposed to hurt?"

"It hurts me," Kieran said, "but I won't keep fighting it and make you hurt more. That's all it would do, and I can't take that."

"Right." Nola rubbed her fingers over her palm. The cuts had already disappeared. "How long do you think it'll hurt?"

"For me?" Kieran turned back to his worktable. "Forever."

CHAPTER TWENTY-ONE

"You've got to pay attention," Raina growled. "Your work is sloppy."
Nola wiped the blood off her cheek. "Well, my face is bleeding."
"You'll heal." Raina prowled the inside of their sparring square.
"I also don't know what I'm doing," Nola said.
"You're distracted." Raina flipped her blade back and forth in her hand. "Distraction gets people killed. Not paying attention gets people killed."
Raina threw her knife at Nola's thigh. Nola dove to the side.
"Hey!" The shout came from behind Nola. She rolled over to see a man hopping on one leg, Raina's dagger protruding from his calf.
"What the hell do you..." his voice trailed away as his eyes found Raina's face. "Sorry." He grimaced as he pulled the knife free, carefully wiping his blood from the blade as he hobbled over to Raina. "Sorry." He passed her the blade with a bow, leaving a trail of blood behind as he limped back to his own square.
"See what happens when you don't listen, Domer?" Raina held her blade up to the light as though inspecting it for any damage the man she stabbed might have done to it.
"I *am* listening," Nola said. "I promise I'm listening. I'm just not very good at fighting."
"Sure you are," Raina said. "Your heart just isn't in it. I heard from a little birdy you even stabbed yourself a vampire in the domes. You have to want to kill, Nola. You can't just want to learn to swing a knife around. You have to learn to *want to kill*. Now let's go again."

Raina tossed her knife into the air, letting the blade spiral before catching the hilt with a grin.

A flicker of red moved behind Raina's shoulder as Jeremy stepped away from his match to watch.

"Don't look at lover boy. Look at the one holding the knife," Raina said. "If it comes down to a fight and you worry more about where he is than who's trying to kill you, you'll end up dead. Then he'll probably end up dead because he's distracted by your death. So get your shit together and focus on not getting sliced and diced."

"Fine." Nola tightened her grip on her own blade. "Let's do this."

"Don't you sound fancy?" Raina leapt forward before she finished speaking.

Nola spun out of the way.

The hard touch of metal brushed her shoulder before she could face Raina again. Nola sliced in, aiming for Raina's thigh. Raina grabbed her wrist, smashing the knife from Nola's grip with the hilt of her blade.

"You've got to do better." Raina sauntered back to her side of the square.

Nola shook her hand out, trying to get rid of the tingling Raina's blow had left behind.

"Are you sure—" Jeremy began.

"Do you want me to be nice or do you want your lover alive?" Raina asked.

Heat flooded Nola's face. "It's fine, Jeremy. No killing each other in the sparring room. That's Emanuel's rule, right?" The powerful assent Nola had been hoping for didn't come.

"I won't kill you," Raina laughed, "but those poor people who've been assigned to the laundry, they are starting to hate all the blood stains I've been making."

You can do this, Nola. You are more than just another bloodstained shirt.

Nola took a step forward.

"Here kitty, kitty," Raina cooed.

Nola dove forward, slashing at Raina's arm.

Raina knocked her hand aside, but Nola held onto her blade.

Nola aimed for Raina's forearm. Her blade touched Raina's sleeve before Raina swung her left arm, hitting Nola hard in the elbow.

Stars danced in Nola's eyes as she stumbled aside. The glint of Raina's knife cut through her vision. Nola kicked back, catching Raina hard in the shin.

"Yes!" Jeremy's shout carried around the room.

Raina swiped a kick at Nola's ankles, knocking her face first onto the ground.

Nola coughed, dragging air back into her lungs.

"Better," Raina said. "You'd still be dead, but I'd be a little less ashamed to have known you."

"Thanks." Nola rolled onto her back. "Are you sure I shouldn't just practice with the Guard guns. I'm pretty good at those."

"We don't have the ability to manufacture the fancy little darts those guards love so much, so no." Raina kicked Nola's toes. "There will be no target practice in this apocalypse, Domer. We can sharpen blades, and, if we get really desperate, we could even make some knives. So let's stick to things your incompetence won't waste, shall we?"

"You don't have to be mean about it," Jeremy said, glaring at Raina as he lifted Nola off the floor. "She's doing really well."

"Then let her fight her own battles." Raina snatched Nola's knife from the ground. "Like it or not, we can't always be there to protect the people we care about. Better to make sure they can fight on their own."

Jeremy opened his mouth, but Nola covered his lips with her fingers.

"Leave it," Nola said. "What's the point in being a superhero if I can't take care of myself?"

Jeremy shook his head and left their square.

"Superhero?" Raina raised an eyebrow and handed Nola back her knife. "How fancy."

"Can we just get to the bit where you cut me again?" Nola asked.

"How did you know that was my favorite part?" Raina strolled back to her side of the square. "This time I want you to try and get my knife out of my grip. Don't worry about inflicting damage. Focus on disarming me."

"Right." Nola focused on the blade in Raina's hand.

Raina didn't grip the hilt as Nola clutched hers. She held her blade tenderly, like the knife was a treasure to be cherished. An extension of her arm.

Nola loosened her grip on her own blade, willing the tension out of her hand.

"Come on, we don't have all night," Raina said.

Nola lunged, swiping her blade up toward Raina's stomach. Raina's palm crashed into Nola's forearm, knocking Nola's knife hand aside.

Nola sliced her other hand up, striking Raina's wrist from below.

Raina grabbed the wrist of Nola's knife hand, twisting her arm, and pinning her blade behind her back. Pain burst from Nola's shoulder, radiating down her arm.

"And we have a dead Domer." Raina tapped her knife on Nola's jugular.

"But it was better." Nola spoke through gritted teeth. "You have to admit I'm getting better."

"Not good enough," Raina whispered in her ear. "Don't make me regret letting you out of the domes."

"I helped you escape." Nola gasped as Raina let her arm go.

"I could have left you behind," Raina said. "Let them keep you locked in a glass cage where it's safe."

Nola shook blood back into her fingers. "You wouldn't have done that. Mostly because you keep your word, even though you like to pretend you're all rogue, but a little bit because for some weird reason you like me. And you don't like many people."

Raina stared at Nola, her lips twisting into a sneer.

Feet planted and ready, knife in her hand, Nola waited for Raina to laugh or to charge and stab her in the heart.

"If you think my considering you worthy of the oxygen you consume means you're any more likely to survive with subpar fighting skills, then we might as well light your funeral pyre now," Raina said. "You can collect the wood yourself. It will save the rest of us the trouble."

Nola kept her chin up and her gaze locked with Raina's.

"Let's go again," Raina growled.

"Good." Nola softened her knees, waiting to see which direction Raina would attack.

"Raina." The young blond vampire burst through the tunnel door. "Raina, you need to come right now."

"What is it?" Raina slid her knife back into its sheath.

"I'm not sure," the girl said. "But there's a pack of them coming up the hillside."

"Dammit." Raina was through the door before she finished her curse.

Nola hesitated for only a moment before running after Raina.

"Nola!" Jeremy's footfalls thundered behind her. "What are you doing?"

"If the guards are coming to kill us all, I'd rather see what's happening than wait in the dark to die."

Jeremy slipped his fingers through hers, still holding his staff in the other hand. "If things go badly, and I say—"

"If you say run, we run," Nola said. "But if they were going to drop fire, they wouldn't be sending their own people up the mountain."

"They sent them into the city," Jeremy said. "We can't predict what they're going to do, not anymore."

Four people waited at the first window. Raina stood in front of the opening, arms crossed as she stared out into the moonlight.

"What is it?" Nola whispered.

"Zombies." Raina shook her head.

"What?" Nola peered out the window.

Halfway down the mountain, a group of six shuffled up the slope in the darkness. They didn't climb with deliberate steps as an Outer Guard, vampire, or werewolf would, nor did they stumble tiredly up the incline. Their gait lurched as they wove closer, barely avoiding ramming into the trees, their movements more like sleepwalkers than people who had deliberately chosen a path.

"I've never seen them travel in packs like that," Jeremy said. "You usually find them one at a time."

"Why are they coming up here?" Nola asked.

"Scent." Raina leaned on the window sill. "At least that's what we've found. Blind them, plug their ears, and the zombies hunt by scent."

"They're smelling Nightland?" A wave of bile surged into Nola's throat.

"Yep," Raina said. "But they can't get up here, so let the chompers hunt."

"We can't," Jeremy said. "Six moving that quickly. Most zombies make it, what, a week after taking a bad batch of Vamp or Lycan?"

"Some make it two," Raina said. "I've seen one at three weeks, couldn't move though. Mostly just a pile of snarling goo."

Nola covered her mouth with her hand, swallowing the vomit that burned her tongue.

"If they're moving that well, chances are they injected after the fire in the city," Jeremy said. "They could still be carrying bottles with trackers hidden in them."

"And six moving together might be enough to get the domes' attention." Raina pulled her knife from her belt. "Come on, kids. Let's go kill some zombies."

"I'll come." Jeremy stepped between Nola and Raina. "Nola can go tell Emanuel what's happening."

"She comes, and that's final. She needs to start fighting for herself, and what better way to learn than with the undead?" Raina said.

"She's right," Nola said.

"You don't need to go out there and kill people, Nola," Jeremy said. "I know you need to learn to fight, but killing is different."

"They're already dead, Jeremy," Nola said. "Their bodies just haven't stopped working yet."

"You." Raina pointed to the blond who had come to the sparring room. "You've been all antsy. You get to come and be our runner."

"Really?" The girl's face lit up. "I mean"—her smile disappeared into a façade of cool indifference—"if you need someone fast, I can help you out."

"Oh joy." Raina walked down the hall, twirling her blade in her hand. "Remember, it's the head and the heart, kids. And avoid the teeth. Zombies give a nasty bite, and we don't want anyone to bleed all the way to the library on the way home from our field trip."

The weight of the blade in Nola's hand grew as they neared the exit of Nightland. She had killed before. Her hand remembered the strength it took to drive a blade into a person's heart.

It'll be easier now. I'm strong enough to break through bones.

Her hand shook.

"You don't have to do this," Jeremy said.

"Yes, she does," Raina said.

"You can go back," Jeremy said. "Three against six is fine numbers for zombies. I'll be back in no time."

"I'm coming," Nola said. "Hiding won't stop it from happening."

"But it will keep you from remembering doing it," Jeremy said.

The back of Nola's hand brushed Jeremy's.

Agree with him. Go back.

"She needs to practice. End of discussion." Raina stopped at the ledge. "If she gets killed the first time she fights, bad memories won't matter for long."

Nola nodded, not trusting herself to say anything other than *I can't do this.*

"Keep together, and keep quiet." Raina looked to the blond. "If this is a trap and the Guard come for us, we die before we give up the location of Nightland. If anyone slips and lets the Domers know where our home is, the blood of every man, woman, and child of Nightland will be on their head."

"Death before betrayal." The blond nodded.

"Good." Raina winked at Nola and Jeremy. "Now let's get some exercise." She jumped off the ledge and moved down to the tree line.

"Why didn't she question us?" Nola whispered.

"We saw the fire packs work," Jeremy said. "Neither of us would let the domes do that again."

Nola nodded and leapt off the ledge. Her feet met the ground without bobbling. Jeremy landed at her side a moment later.

The night air held the chill of frost. The cold tickled her skin but had lost the ability to freeze her fingers. The ground crunched under her feet as they crept toward Raina.

She didn't look at Nola and Jeremy as they approached but kept her gaze toward the base of the mountain.

Raina signaled them forward.

Jeremy stepped behind Nola as the group moved down the mountainside.

Nola wanted to glance back to be sure he was still there. His boots made no noise as they crept onward.

There were no shapes moving through the woods. Nothing but the shadows of the trees.

Anything could be hiding out there.

Images of a hundred Outer Guard lurking just out of sight flashed through Nola's mind. Sweat slicked her palm. Her knife slipped in her grip.

Jeremy.

She tried to keep her eyes focused on the woods, but she still couldn't hear his boots.

She glanced back. He walked four feet behind her, his forehead tense as he searched the shadows.

Her heart slowed as she looked back to her own path.

A flutter of movement cut through the trees beyond.

Do I say something?

An arm reached out from behind a tree.

"There," Nola whispered, pointing to what she had seen.

Raina turned around, giving Nola an eye roll before following her pointing finger.

A woman with bright red hair stumbled out from behind the tree. Black and red sores covered her face and bare arms. She swayed in place for a moment, then tipped her head, her blank gaze finding Nola.

CHAPTER TWENTY-TWO

"Go on." Raina shooed Nola toward the redheaded zombie.

"I can—" Jeremy began.

"We've got a bigger one for you." Raina grinned as a man even larger than Jeremy lumbered out of the shadows. His face had been burned, whether before he injected himself or after, Nola didn't know.

Jeremy ran toward the towering zombie, his staff raised over his head as a slender female appeared from the shadows.

"Go, Domer." Raina charged toward the female.

Not giving herself time to think, Nola ran toward the redhead. The woman stumbled in Nola's direction, her jaw snapping like an animal determined to bite. Nola kept her knife near her center, ready to strike the woman in the heart.

She swiped at the woman's chest. The woman didn't try to bat the knife away or even seem to notice when the blade sliced into her skin. She seized Nola's arm in her grip, and dove her face toward Nola's wrist, gnashing her teeth.

Nola swallowed her scream and punched with her left hand, hitting the woman in the side of the head. She wasn't sure if the woman could register pain, but she stumbled at the blow. Nola kicked, swiping the woman's feet out from under her.

A rasping snarl rattled from the woman as she fell, rolling down the mountainside.

Nola chased after her.

The woman slammed into a tree with a *thud* that would have meant broken bones for a normal human. Her arms shook as she pushed herself up to her knees.

Nola kicked her, slamming her back to the ground. She raised her knife, aiming for the heart. Nola had expected her knife to meet bone and stop, or for muscle to slow the blade's momentum. But the knife sunk through her back like she was nothing more than soft earth.

The woman stopped struggling and lay limp on the ground, her red hair covering her face.

A gurgling growl sounded behind Nola's shoulder.

A man in a black coat dove toward her. His teeth found her shoulder, digging deep into the muscle.

Nola screamed before she could stop herself. She grabbed the man's forehead, trying to push him away. He wrapped his arms around her, his vise-like grip pulling her closer. She stabbed, slicing into his stomach. Warm blood rained down on her leg, but her knife couldn't reach his heart.

Her fingers found his face. She pulled up, fighting to free herself from his jaw.

A flash of movement, and the man fell to the ground.

"Nola." Panic filled Jeremy's eyes. He tore the sleeve from his shirt, pressing the fabric to the bite on Nola's shoulder. "You're okay. You're going to be okay."

"Where are the others?"

Jeremy wrapped an arm around Nola as she swayed.

"We got all six," Jeremy said. "We're done here, we can go inside. Raina will deal with the trackers."

"He tried to eat me." Nola looked down at the man.

Blood covered his mouth, but the rest of his face still seemed human. Only three small sores marked his skin.

"We'll take you to Dr. Wynne, but you should be able to heal on your own." Jeremy had his arm around Nola's waist, trying to lead her back to the ledge.

Her feet wouldn't move.

The man didn't have rings under his eyes or lines on his face from a hard life on the outside. The cut of his chin, the shape of his cheeks....

"He's a Domer." Nola moved to kneel by the man, but the blood from his stomach had pooled on the frozen ground. She turned around, vomiting on the roots of a dying tree.

"Really?" Raina strolled up. "You get a little bit of blood on you and you puke?"

"He's from the domes," Nola coughed.

"Are you sure?" Raina tipped her head to the side.

"He looks familiar," Jeremy said. "I never worked with him, and he's too old to have been in our classes."

"Maintenance." Nola leaned against the tree. "He worked in maintenance. My mother hated him. He used to hum while he mopped."

"Check the others. See if you recognize them." Raina unzipped the man's shredded coat.

Nola looked away before Raina flapped it open.

Jeremy took Nola's arm as they walked toward the red-haired woman. He held her up as though he thought she might pass out at any moment.

She wanted to say thank you but couldn't find the words.

Jeremy rolled the redhead over with his foot.

Her eyes were as haunting and blank in death as they had been when she'd attacked.

"I don't recognize her," Jeremy said.

Nola shook her head, too afraid to open her mouth.

They moved on to the next. A man with dark skin and a crooked nose. Neither Nola nor Jeremy had ever seen him before.

Jeremy steered Nola away from the giant burned man. "I would have known someone that large from the domes."

"What about this one?" The blond held up a severed head.

Nola covered her eyes with shaking hands.

"No," Jeremy growled. "Now put the head down."

"Just making sure the zombie doesn't come back," the girl said.

Jeremy took Nola's hands from her face. "Last one."

A girl with blond hair lay face down on the ground, a gash sliced through her back.

Jeremy rolled her over with his foot. Her bare arm flopped to her side. There were barely any sores on her either. Only two marked her round face.

"Lilly."

Jeremy's arms wrapped around Nola before she even said her name.

"How did she get out here?"

Nola wanted to reach down and shake the girl, smack her until she woke from death and ask Lilly why she had left the domes with nothing but a bad batch of Vamp as a hope for survival.

"You know this one?" Raina said.

"She was in our class." Nola's voice shook, not with grief, but with anger. "She was in the domes when we left, and she wasn't the kind to get kicked out."

"Maybe she decided to become a rebel and left." Raina bent down, considering Lilly's corpse.

"Lilly wasn't the type for that either," Jeremy said. "She never made waves or a fuss."

"So why are they out here?" Raina asked.

"Love affair gone wrong?" the blond asked. "No one wanted them to be together so they ran away?"

"With the city burnt to the ground?" Raina pointed between Nola and Jeremy. "Not even those two are that dumb."

"Then why are they out here?" Nola asked.

"No idea," Raina said. "We need to tell Emanuel. You"—Raina turned to the girl—"search the bodies for trackers. Anything that looks strange, take it with you down to the row houses. Dump it and get back before dawn. I'll send a group out to salvage."

"Salvage?" Nola followed Raina up the slope.

"The world is ending, Domer," Raina said. "Never let a pair of good shoes pass you by."

"You're going to strip them and leave them to rot?" Nola said.

"They won't rot," Raina said. "The scavengers will eat them long before rot gets them."

"Can't we burn them?" Nola ran a few steps to catch up to Raina. Warmth squished between her toes.

"All of them or just the Domers?" Raina stopped below the ledge and rounded on Nola. "It's the circle of life. We burn our own, the rest are food for the animals. Or do those two deserve extra pity for having lived a life of privilege? Should they get better because they come from the place that just burned an entire city?"

"No." The syllable rattled in Nola's ears.

"Let's get inside," Jeremy said. "We need to talk to Emanuel and figure out what the hell is going on."

"I'll talk to Emanuel," Raina said. "You get the bloody girl cleaned up before she has a break down."

"What do you..." Nola looked down at her feet.

Blood coated her legs. Her shoes shone strangely as the red reflected the moonlight. Her fingers were stained crimson, as was the knife she still held in her hand.

The blade slipped from her grip, tumbling end over end to the ground.

"And she's gone." Raina crossed her arms.

"Nola." Jeremy tipped Nola's chin up, making her look into his eyes. "Everything is going to be okay."

"No it won't." Nola wanted to reach out and touch him, but she couldn't taint him with the death that coated her hands. "Lilly is dead, the other five are dead.

Domers have gone zombie, the city is burned, and we don't know why any of this is happening."

"But we're going to figure it out," Jeremy said. "You and me together. We'll work it out, and we're going to be fine."

"You and I will." Nola stepped around Jeremy to line herself up with the ledge. "But just because we're going to be okay doesn't mean the rest of the world will be."

She jumped up, leveraging herself to land on her feet on the ledge above. Blood squelched in her shoes. She leaned over the side of the ledge and vomited again, the acid of it throttling her already raw throat.

"Are you serious?" Raina growled.

Jeremy jumped up behind her. "Let's get you inside. We'll get you into fresh clothes and—"

"Am I supposed to be good at this?" Nola searched her sleeve for a clean bit of fabric to wipe her mouth. "Do you want me to be okay with blood between my toes?"

"Never." Jeremy brushed away the curls that had pulled free from her braid. "It's not who you are. You care too much to be cold and indifferent to the pain and death around you. I will do whatever I can to make sure the world never pushes so hard you lose the ability to care for people."

"How sweet." Raina jumped up.

"Let's get you to Dr. Wynne," Jeremy said.

"Don't bother the doctor. She just needs to wash up. The skin on her shoulder's already healed. Try not to puke on anything on your way." Raina headed down the tunnel, leaving Jeremy and Nola alone in the cool night air.

"I'm not weak." Nola stared into the shadows as Raina disappeared.

Jeremy took Nola's hand, ignoring the blood on her skin. "You're the furthest from weak I could ever imagine."

They started down the hall. The wet slosh of Nola's shoes resonated off the stone walls.

"Then why do I feel like the world is going to swallow me whole?" Nola's words came out in an odd spurt as she lost the fight to keep her breathing calm.

"It won't. The world won't swallow you, Nola. It needs you too much." He kept his voice low and steady. "We need someone whose heart can still care. Still hurt for people she doesn't even know."

They walked in silence past the windows. Nola wanted to hum or scream. Anything to be sure she wouldn't hear the sounds of the girl searching through the pockets of the dead.

The door of the sparring room heaved open before they could reach it. Two men with empty crates squeezed past them in the hall.

Lilly's shoes will be worth something. Life in the domes won't have given them much wear.

Silence overtook the sparring hall in a deafening wave as Nola stepped into the room. All eyes found her, taking in her bloody legs, torn up shoulder, and deathly pale face.

Nola kept her head high as she walked through the room, carefully avoiding looking anyone in the eye.

"Her shoes." The whisper prickled the back of Nola's neck.

She turned to see who had spoken, but the path behind her drove every other thought from her mind.

Dribbles of blood stained the floor everywhere she'd stepped.

Jeremy wrapped an arm around Nola's waist, half-carrying her out of the room.

"I have to clean it up." Nola struggled against Jeremy's grip.

"Someone else can do it."

Tears blurred Nola's vision.

Raina's voice carried through the library door as they passed.

Jeremy didn't stop at the door to his room. He led her farther down, barely knocking before swinging open the door to the shower.

The small room smelled like damp stone and silt. A tap hung high on the wall.

Jeremy took the bottom of Nola's shirt, pulling it over her head before she could blink the tears from her eyes. She kicked off her shoes and socks, unwilling to touch them with her fingers.

He turned on the tap. Cool was the only temperature Nightland had to offer. Nola stepped under the water, grateful for even that thin comfort as she scrubbed her hands.

"I'll go find some clean clothes," Jeremy said.

Nola grabbed his hand before he could reach for the doorknob.

"Stay." Nola pressed her forehead to his chest. "Please stay."

Her lips found his as she pulled him into the water, grateful for the racing beat of his heart. Proof she couldn't ignore that life still existed.

CHAPTER TWENTY-THREE

"We need to know." Jeremy stood in front of Emanuel's red chair. "If there are Domers roaming outside the glass, we can't afford to hide here anymore."

Nola glanced from Jeremy to Emanuel. The tension in the air pressed against Nola's lungs. Emanuel sat with his fingers tented under his chin. Raina's hand rested on the hilt of her knife. Kieran stood with his arms crossed, looking anywhere but at Jeremy. The only one who seemed at ease was Julian.

"What would there be to find out?" Kieran asked. "If they're coming for us, they'll come. If they've kicked out some of their own people, it doesn't affect us."

"It does." Nola tucked her damp curls behind her ears. "Something is wrong with the domes. Salinger may be a demon, but he wouldn't go around kicking people out. They're needed to maintain the population. The guards that were killed threw off the numbers. Jeremy and I leaving did, too. They wouldn't just let people leave."

"They've just brought in a massive amount of Outer Guard," Emanuel said. "Perhaps they've decided they have no further use for a civilian population."

"Even in Nightland someone cleans the floors and does the laundry," Raina said. "You'd have to be desperate to get rid of the guy who mops."

"Fair enough," Emanuel said. "But if the domes have lost their minds and started getting rid of their own, it only gives me more reason to keep my people safe within Nightland's walls."

"Not if Salinger has taken over." Jeremy glanced around the room. "Is there someplace else we could talk about this?"

Emanuel's gaze traveled from Julian to Raina and Kieran before fixing on Nola. "We could go to my kitchen if you like, but all of these people will come with us."

Jeremy bit his lips together. "There's a reason people don't talk about Salinger. I barely know anything about him, and I was a guard. He's the side of the domes none of the Domers want to talk about. He's basically the boogey man. He's vicious, was vicious enough with the outsiders at his home domes he got a reputation for being brutal. The Incorporation wanted to send him here a few years ago when the riots started to get bad. My father said no."

"What?" Nola stepped up next to Jeremy.

"It was right after your dad died," Jeremy said. "We needed help, but my dad knew Salinger would just make things worse. He told the Incorporation he had his own plans."

"Graylock," Kieran said.

"A way to keep the Incorporation and Salinger as far away from here as possible." Julian leaned against a bookcase, mug in hand. "It's rather brilliant. Where I come from, they welcomed Salinger with open arms. He was much younger then, though I'm not sure if time will have made him better or worse. He stripped down the community outside our domes to the bare minimum for keeping the useful factories running. Everyone else was given three days to clear out of the area or risk the wrath of the domes. I left the domes and blended in with the others who were fleeing. Most of those poor people didn't last two weeks once the city had been closed to them. The man has no mercy."

"We already figured that out when he slaughtered a city full of people," Raina said. "So why are we still talking about this?"

"Because it doesn't make sense," Jeremy said. "Either Salinger is in control of the domes and is kicking people out, in which case we need to get as far away from here as we can. Or there's something else wrong with the domes."

A knot of fear pinched between Nola's shoulder blades.

"What do you mean *wrong*?" Raina asked.

"If the domes have fallen." Julian set down his mug. "The domes are a delicate ecosystem. Everything must be in perfect order for life to continue. When I was part of the domes, I was an asset manager. Every item the domes utilized had been decided long before I took my post, and there was no room for error or short falls. Maintaining the operation of the domes was a worry constantly haunting all our dreams."

"The domes were built to run for generations." Fear twisted a path down Nola's spine.

"Absolutely," Julian said. "If everything goes well, the domes could be self-sustaining for hundreds of years. But if the population were to decrease or increase too drastically, there would either be a work shortage or a food deficit. A fungus could wipe out the food supplies, an issue with the cooling systems could destroy all of the seeds."

"If life in the glass is always on the verge of collapse, why didn't they tell us?" Nola asked.

"We were kids," Kieran said. "Why would you tell kids they might not get to grow up?"

"The domes demand certainty," Emanuel said. "You started to doubt, and look where it led you."

"How much harder would it be to invest yourself in the mission of the domes if you weren't sure the mission would succeed?" Julian asked.

"So the two theories we're going with are a psychopath has taken over the domes," Nola said, "or the domes have fallen?"

"Can you think of another option?" Emanuel asked.

Nola's mind raced, searching through every possibility. "What if Lilly decided she couldn't stay in the domes after they burned the city? What if she couldn't live with the guilt?"

"Do you really think Lilly would have done that?" Pity filled Jeremy's eyes.

Nola rubbed her hands over her face. "No, she wouldn't."

"Emanuel," Jeremy said. "Something is going on out there. We need to know what it is."

Emanuel stared at Jeremy for a long moment. "The five of you go. Take the sun suits and whatever weaponry you need. Find out what you can, and come back alive. Don't let anyone follow you home."

"Nola should stay behind," Jeremy said.

"I'm going." Nola laid her hand on his arm. "Don't fight me on it."

"Not until you get your last dose," Kieran said. "Dad won't allow it."

"Then I'll take it now." Nola walked toward the back door of the library. "One day early can't hurt, right?"

"Nola, we don't know what will happen if you take it early." Jeremy chased after her.

"You got a shot in the stomach when you almost died," Nola said. "That was less than two weeks. They did it for you. Dr. Wynne can do it for me."

Nola strode through the door.

Eden pouted at the kitchen table. Bea sat across from her, glowering at Eden as she pushed food around her plate.

"Eden." Nola stopped in the doorway, the desire to hold the child just to prove the little girl was alive pressed painfully in her throat. "What's wrong with your food?"

Eden looked at Bea, then back down at her plate. "Daddy said he would sit with me while I ate."

"We had to talk to him in the library." Nola knelt next to Eden's chair. "It's hard when your parent has a lot of responsibility."

Eden's bottom lip trembled. "I want daddy."

"I know." Nola tucked Eden's dark hair behind her ears. "But you know what we were talking about? Keeping you and everybody who lives here safe. I'm sorry he missed dinner, but he's trying to take care of you as best he can. Okay?"

Eden nodded.

"You know how you could help him?" Nola asked.

Eden shook her head.

"Eat up all your food so you can stay nice and strong." Nola pushed Eden's plate toward her. "That would be a really big help."

Eden narrowed her eyes at her roasted mushrooms and squash. "I want to help." She picked up a mushroom and tucked it into her mouth.

"Good job." Nola stood and walked out into the hall.

"Nola?" Eden's voice pulled her back. "My daddy will take care of you, too."

"He will." Nola nodded, pressing her face into a careful smile.

"Nola," Jeremy whispered behind her shoulder.

"What?" She stopped at the big metal door.

"We could wait another day," Jeremy said. "If you're really determined to go—"

"How many more people could take bad Vamp in a day?" Nola asked. "I don't want to have to stab someone I know in the heart. You said I'm strong, Jeremy. I don't know if I'm strong enough for that."

She knocked on the laboratory door.

"Come in," Dr. Wynne's cheerful voice called back.

Before Nola had pushed the door fully open, Dr. Wynne was on his feet.

"Nola." He held out his hands in greeting. "I was told you had been bitten, but I don't think there's anything I can do for you. Jeremy." He added the less enthusiastic greeting as Jeremy stepped into the room.

"I'd like my last injection." Nola sat on the table. "It's only a day early, and I need to leave for a little while."

"Leave?" Dr. Wynne blinked at her. "Leave for where?"

"It's a long story," Jeremy said. "We shouldn't be gone long, in fact we can wait—"

"Jeremy." Nola spoke his name as a warning.

"I can give you the shot now." Dr. Wynne moved to his table in the corner where a cold storage box hummed dully. "I'm not sure if it will reduce its effectiveness, though it certainly shouldn't damage you."

"Reduce its effectiveness?" Jeremy asked.

"Healing and the like," Dr. Wynne said. "I'm not sure if the dose will remain as effective in the long run. I'm afraid I just don't have the data to make an accurate assessment."

"We already know I heal just fine from zombie bites." Nola unbuttoned the top of her shirt. "If I get really hurt, we can give me another dose then."

"Well, yes." Dr. Wynne lifted a black-filled syringe from the box. "We are working with a limited supply, of course. We've only got two full doses after this. I've been using one to study the formula."

Nola gripped the edge of the metal. The bottom lip of the table hadn't been filed down. The sharp edges dug into her fingers.

"You can't make any more?" Jeremy asked.

"I could," Dr. Wynne said. "It's not that difficult, really. I could make more of it right here, if I had the formula. Right now, I'm working my way backwards. Think of it as baking bread, if you will. I know I need flour, leavening, salt, but the exact recipe is very difficult to find. That's how we end up with so many bad batches of Vamp and Lycan. Without the exact details, the results can be deadly. In time, perhaps I would be able to come up with the right process, but it could take years."

"Then you can't go." Jeremy took Nola's hands. "You have to stay here and safe."

Nola pressed her fingers to his lips. "I can heal. We've seen it. If someone ripped out one of our jugulars, we'd still heal. It would take time, but I could keep you safe. And I know you would do the same for me."

"But—"

Nola leaned into Jeremy, pressing her lips to his.

"This makes going to the city even more important than before," Nola said. "The city is one small river away from the domes. Graylock was made in the labs there. If the domes really are falling apart, the formula could be lost forever. Let's find the bread recipe and bring it back."

"And if Salinger is still there?" Jeremy asked.

"We let Raina kill him," Nola said.

"I would suggest taking one spare dose with you and leaving the rest here for me to continue my work." Dr. Wynne stepped up to Nola, needle in hand. "Then, if this doesn't work as planned, you can give Nola the extra dose."

"I won't need it." Nola closed her eyes as Dr. Wynne opened her shirt.

She didn't gasp as the needle pierced her heart or scream as the ice raced down her veins.

Her blood greeted the cold as an old friend, welcoming it into every part of her.

"You'll be as strong as the drug can make you now." Dr. Wynne's words floated from far away. "So do try not to break anything."

"Breathe," Jeremy said.

Nola inhaled. Air flew into her lungs, sending power through her muscles like zaps of electricity.

The sound of crumpling metal came from beneath her.

"Oh dear," Dr. Wynne said.

"Careful." Jeremy's hands touched hers. The texture of his fingers sent chills flying up her arms.

She gasped and opened her eyes.

Blood dripped from her fingers. She let go of the table. Handprints dented the metal, and blood stained the edges.

"Here you are." Dr. Wynne passed her a wet towel.

She wiped the blood from her fingers with the cool cloth. The prefect skin on her hands held no trace of where she'd sliced open her fingers only moments before. She grabbed the edge of the table, squeezing the place where she'd already left handprints until she felt the metal cut her skin.

Holding her hands up to her face, she watched the skin knit back together as drops of blood trailed down her palm.

"This is amazing," Nola said. "I really am like a superhero."

"Superheroes can still get killed." Jeremy caught her hands as she reached toward the edge of the table again. "You have to remember that, Nola. There are some things we can't come back from."

Nola wiped the blood from her hands. "I know we can get hurt, just the same as vampires and wolves, but this is still amazing."

"Quite." Dr. Wynne handed the black case to Jeremy.

"Thank you." Jeremy slid the case onto his belt.

"Try not to need the dose, either of you." Dr. Wynne waved them toward the door.

"Dr. Wynne." Nola turned back as Jeremy stepped into the hall. "Thank you for trying with the Graylock. Your helping us means a lot."

"Well"—Dr. Wynne fluttered his hands in the air—"it is my duty as a doctor, and it could help save many more lives. Besides, you're both good people. The world needs as many of those as it can come by these days."

CHAPTER TWENTY-FOUR

R aina had cleared the sparring room, sending the fifty-odd fighting vampires scurrying into the tunnels of Nightland.

Julian pulled open the weapons cage, narrowing his eyes as he touched the hilt of each sword.

Raina reached into the other side of the cage.

"Here." She tossed Nola a belt with two knives in leather sheathes and an Outer Guard gun hanging off the side. "Remember, the pointy end goes into the people we don't like, and the bang bang stick doesn't get pointed at our friends."

"Thanks." Nola wrapped the belt around her middle.

"You almost look a little dangerous." Raina smiled.

"I'll take that as a compliment," Nola said.

"Good." Raina dug deeper into the weaponry. "Looking the part is half the battle. And for lover boy." She pulled his own Guard belt from the depths of the shelf.

"And here I thought you'd burned it." Jeremy's face betrayed no emotion as he fastened his belt around his waist.

"It still fits." Raina winked.

"I need more ammunition," Jeremy said, "and some knives wouldn't go amiss either."

Raina pulled out two smaller knives in sleek leather sheathes. She tossed one to Jeremy before tucking the other into her boot.

"Do we need packs?" Nola asked. "If we're going to be hiding during the daylight, Jeremy and I will at least need food and water."

"Who said anything about hiding?" Kieran came in from the tunnels, two wooden boxes balanced in his arms.

"I've seen what happens when vampires go into the sun, Kieran," Nola said. "None of you can risk that."

"We'll be fine." Kieran yanked the lid off the first, larger box.

"Sun suits?" Jeremy peered down at the wide brimmed hats and neatly folded stacks of tan material. "Those are sun suits from the domes."

Nola pulled out one of the jumpsuits. She'd never held one before. The coarse material itched her skin and, even with her new strength, weighed twice what she'd expected.

The sun suits were only used by the maintenance workers of the domes when they had to spend hours outside working on the air ducts, cisterns, and other external assets. Normal Domers were never outdoors long enough to need the suits, and Outer Guard uniforms had their own sun protection.

"How did you get these?" Nola asked.

Kieran opened the second smaller box. Ammunition packs of the tiny metal darts needed for the Guard guns filled the crate.

Jeremy whistled.

"You wanted to know what we couldn't ask the domes for," Kieran said. "This is what we needed."

"You broke into the domes for sun suits and ammunition?" Nola dug her fists into her eyes. "How many people died so you could have these?"

"So we could defend ourselves in the daylight?" Raina asked. "Far fewer than the domes would kill if they found us here."

"We gained a few other assets as well," Julian said. "Emanuel planned very carefully for the things we would need."

Raina took the suit from Nola, curling her lip as she shook out the fabric. "Leave it to Domers to make something so horribly unattractive."

"They'll keep us alive." Kieran pulled his suit on over his dark pants and shirt. The baggy tan fabric made him look younger, softening the hard lines the outside world had carved into him.

An old pain tugged at Nola's chest.

"Are you sure they'll work?" Jeremy asked.

"Of course." Julian tucked his brown gloves into his sleeves and took a wide-brimmed hat from the box. A tube of fabric hung from the hat, ready to cover everything but the vampires' eyes.

"I really hate these things." Raina fastened her belt on the outside of her suit. The effect was comical, like a child playing in grownups' clothes.

"So, you really are going?"

Nola spun toward T's voice. She and Beauford stood in the tunnel, Emanuel right behind them.

"We have to." Nola reached for T as she crossed into the sparring room. T stopped to look in both boxes before taking Nola's hands.

"Why?" T asked.

"We need to know what's happening," Nola said. "We'll be back soon."

"I want to believe you," T said.

"If they say they have to go, they have to go." Beauford laid a hand on T's shoulder. "Fussing won't help anything."

T opened her mouth, then chewed her lips together and shook her head.

"Do you have everything you need?" Emanuel stepped forward to join the group.

"Weapons, sun suits, Domers." Raina counted them off on her gloved fingers. "We should be set."

"Go in and come back," Emanuel said. "If you don't have to go near anyone, don't. If you do—"

"Kill them?" Raina said.

Nola gripped the knives on her hips.

"If you have to." Emanuel took Raina's hands in his. "You have my trust, old friend. You command with my voice."

Raina bowed her head.

"Don't let them take you from me again," Emanuel said.

"I won't," Raina said.

"We should let them leave." Emanuel turned to T and Beauford. "There's only a few hours left until morning."

Tears pooled in the corners of T's eyes. "Don't let her die, Jeremy. You have to bring her back here."

In two quick steps, Nola threw her arms around T's neck. "I'm coming back. I'm going to be with you when the baby's born, I promise."

"Good." T squeezed Nola, then stepped back, looping her arm through Beauford's.

"See you soon." Beauford gave a quick nod and led T back into the tunnel.

"I expect you back by tomorrow morning." Emanuel gave each of them a long look before walking away.

Nola stood frozen, watching them all disappear from view.

"That bastard," Nola said.

"We'll be back soon." Jeremy wrapped his arms around her.

"Yeah." Nola swiped the tears from her cheeks. "Using a pregnant girl to make sure we don't jump ship. That's a really low blow."

"Would you have left?" Kieran asked.

Jeremy's arms tensed around Nola.

Nola dug her fingers into her curls. "I'm a superhero, you're a vampire, and I'm in borrowed shoes because mine got soaked through with zombie blood. Let's just go and find out if the boogey man is hiding in the domes."

"Sounds like a good time." Raina shoved open the door to the outer tunnel. "We run fast and we run silent. Last one to the city limits is zombie food." With a grin, she took off down the tunnel.

"I'll take the rear." Julian bowed the rest forward, checking the sword he'd fastened over his tan suit.

"You next." Jeremy pointed to Kieran.

"Then Nola?" Kieran asked.

Jeremy gave a nod so small it looked like a twitch.

Kieran nodded back, his eyes sweeping over Nola before he ran down the tunnel.

She chased after him, exhaling all the air from her lungs, wishing she could squeeze the air from her whole body. That she could freeze in a void with nothing to fear and nothing to care for.

Kieran ran twenty feet ahead of her, slowing and hastening his pace to match hers. Jeremy's boots thudded steadily behind her.

She had lost her dome clothes and shoes. Everything she wore had been someone else's, but Jeremy still wore his boots.

Raina dropped from the ledge as it came into view. Kieran leapt out of sight. Nola didn't hesitate to jump when her turn came.

Hitting the ground didn't break her stride.

She kept her eyes fixed on Kieran's back as they ran past the bodies of the zombies they'd ended only a few hours before.

Ended. So simple. So true.

Everything would end.

Her legs moved faster than they had when she and Jeremy had run into the city. The Graylock had finished its work. Her toes barely touched the ground as she sprinted down the mountain. She longed for her lungs to burn or her legs to ache.

End. If the domes had ended, then anything could.

The gleaming beacon of safety. The hope all the world had been told to look to as a future for the human race.

Or Salinger had stayed, ruling the domes with a fist drenched in blood. Destruction or contamination.

Which would leave more survivors?

She left her hands at her sides as she ran through the field of briars, relishing each tear of her flesh. Knowing she would be healed before she could lift her hands to see the cuts.

Death for many, or power for a devil.

Either way, the world is ending.

Raina led them out of the field and into the trees. Fresh footprints marked the dirt, leading north, away from the mountain to somewhere Nola had never seen.

I hope they survived. Wherever they are.

A voice that sounded terribly like Jeremy's echoed in the back of her mind. *If they survive, they'll live to be our enemies.*

Tears touched Nola's cheek, freezing in the cold night air.

The plants will be dead by now. T will have to live off mushrooms for the winter.

Anger burst into flames in Nola's chest, pushing her legs to run faster. But the speed didn't hurt. Running couldn't burn away her rage.

Rundown houses came into view, like slumping giants sagging from years of sadness.

Someone had built those homes. Lived in them. Children had been raised and deaths mourned within those walls.

None of it matters now. It's all just rot.

Kieran reached back, wrapping an arm around her waist before Nola could run past him.

He clapped his hand over her mouth before she could speak.

"Look." His breath whispered over her ear.

A light burned in the window of the house in front of them.

Raina stood in the middle of the road, a knife in each hand. Her head swiveled slowly from side to side as though she were scenting the wind.

Nola nodded and stepped away from Kieran, reaching for her own knives.

Jeremy's fingers grazed her wrist.

Nola glanced over her shoulder.

Jeremy shook his head.

Julian's sword rasped as he pulled the long blade from its sheath.

Jeremy let go of Nola, pulling his gun from its holster. He touched the black case on his hip before raising the gun, pointing it toward the house with the light.

Raina stalked slowly toward the house, placing one foot in front of the other as though she were walking on ice.

Like people used to do on the outside. When the world would freeze them for months at a time. When life could disappear with a crack in the ice.

Raina stopped in front of the porch.

Jeremy slunk in front of Nola, pressing his back to the doorjamb, gun raised and pointing toward the closed door.

Kieran leaned against the other side, his daggers poised to strike.

Julian took Nola's shoulders, pulling her to Jeremy's side of the door as Raina nodded and leapt forward, kicking through the door with a *crack*.

Screams echoed from inside the house.

"Don't move and I don't slice, got it?" Raina said.

Nola leaned toward the door. Jeremy shot one arm back, pressing her against the wall.

"Please don't kill us!" a woman shrieked.

"That's a good start," Raina said. "Now let's get to the bit where you all stand against the wall with your arms over your head and we'll be in great shape."

"I won't be told what to do," a young man shouted.

Be good. Do what she says and be good.

Nola leaned into Jeremy's arm.

"Just do it, you fool," a woman said.

"That's better," Raina said. "See how easy it is to get along when you all do what I say?"

Kieran nodded toward the door.

Jeremy moved his arm, freeing Nola from the wall. Gun steady, he walked into the house.

Nola stepped forward to follow him.

Kieran shook his head and disappeared through the door.

"We're not here to hurt anyone." Kieran's voice carried from inside the house. "All we want is to ask a few questions and we'll be on our way."

Raina's laugh shook the cracked window panes.

Nola looked behind to Julian. He scanned the street before nodding.

She hadn't noticed she'd been holding her breath until she stepped through the doorway.

A table with four candles threw a flickering light across the room.

Four people stood pressed up against the wall: the young boy Jeremy had carried from the flames, flanked by the three women from the group that had attacked Jeremy.

Nola pulled her knives from their sheathes. "There should be more."

CHAPTER TWENTY-FIVE

"What do you mean *more?*" Raina held the tip of her knife to the boy's heart.

"When we saw those ladies last time, they had kids and two other men with them," Nola said.

"He'd been with a group in the city." Jeremy pointed to the boy. "We told them to run for it. Found him on the ground on our way out and carried him from the smoke."

"That was you?" the boy cocked his head to the side. "Where's the rest of my family?"

"We didn't see any of them," Nola said. "They left you in the middle of the road. I don't know where they went from there."

"You're lying." The boy shook his head so violently Raina's knife pierced his chest. Red blossomed on his filthy shirt. "They would never abandon me."

"People are shit, kid. Get used to it," Raina said. "Now where are the others?"

"There's no one else here," one of the women said. Her gaze darted through the shield of her dark scraggly hair toward the stairs.

"Liar," Raina whispered. "Kieran, Jeremy, sweep upstairs. If anyone is hiding up there, kill them."

"Wait!" the gray-haired woman yelped.

"Something you want to tell me?" Raina raised her other blade to the woman's neck.

"There's a little girl up there, but no one else," the gray-haired woman said. "She's just a child, please don't hurt her."

"Go." Raina nodded to Kieran and Jeremy.

"Please," the gray-haired woman murmured. "Don't kill my baby."

"I'm a vampire, not a Domer," Raina said. "I'm not in the habit of murdering children."

Kieran disappeared one way at the top of the stairs and Jeremy the other.

"What about the two men and the other child?" Nola asked, keeping her ears focused on the sounds of Jeremy's and Kieran's footsteps overhead.

"Jeffy died," the red-haired woman finally spoke. "Got into a fight that first night. Lou took the other kid and bolted. We tried to look a bit, but there were too many people running around out there. We had to stay hidden."

"Next time you decide to hide, don't leave a light on," Raina said.

"We can't see in the dark," the scraggly woman said. "We aren't like you."

"Pity," Raina said. "You'd be more likely to survive."

"It's okay," Kieran cooed from the top landing. "I'm not going to hurt you." Sniffles sounded under his words.

He stepped onto the landing, holding a tiny girl in his arms. "We're going to take you down to sit with the others, that's all. We're making sure you're nice and safe."

"The rest is clear." Jeremy stepped out of the shadows.

"Make sure there's nothing else of interest," Raina said.

Jeremy slipped back out of sight.

"Please don't take our supplies." The redhead tipped her chin up, as though preparing to be hit. "We barely have anything. If you take our food, you might as well kill us."

The little girl began to cry.

"Shh." Kieran rocked the child. "You're okay."

The child buried her filthy face in his shoulder.

"We aren't interested in your food," Raina said. "We want information. Tell us everything we want to know, and we'll walk right back out of here, and you can go back to sitting around your candles like a pack of fools."

"What do you want to know?" the gray-haired woman asked.

"What's happened since the city burned?" Raina asked.

"We were up the hill by the time most made it out of the city," the gray-haired woman said. "That's when your friend upstairs killed one of us."

"Your friend pulled a gun on us when we were trying to help you." Nola tightened her grip on her knives. "Your *friend* shot Jeremy. You're lucky we let the rest of you run away."

The gray-haired woman glared at Nola.

"What happened after your failed attempt at murdering Jeremy and Nola?" Julian asked from his place in the door. He had his sword drawn as he faced out into the night.

"We went into one of the houses to hide," the redhead said. "We stayed in there for a couple of hours. Wanted to make sure no one was coming after us. Then we heard people coming up the road in groups."

"What kind of groups?" Kieran asked.

"Some people alone, a few groups of fifteen or twenty," the scraggly woman said. "Probably saw about three hundred people pass."

"Some of them tried to come into the house where we were hiding," the gray-haired woman said. "Jeffy tried to get them out. That's when he got killed."

"We ran," the redhead said. "Came up here to the end of the houses. Most of the ones closer to the city already had people holed up in them. Some people went into the woods, but I don't know what they think they'll find there."

The floor upstairs groaned. Jeremy stepped back out onto the landing. "Where did you get these?" He held up two dome-issued water bottles. "You were away from the city before the Outer Guard started handing these out."

"Pulled them off some bodies," the scraggly woman said. "Found a few that had been killed but still had bottles and a bit of food. It wasn't stealing. The dead don't need water."

"Have you seen any Outer Guard?" Nola asked.

"Not since I was in the city," the boy said. "I saw the ones who told us to stay put, then I woke up on the old highway. There were some people left around me. Told me the Outer Guard had taken off back across the river."

"How did you end up with them?" Raina asked.

"Knew his mother and saw him trying to go off into the woods to find her," the gray-haired woman said. "No one who's gone into those woods is still alive. People can't survive out there. It's just not possible."

"You're very clever," Raina said.

"I've heard rumors," the scraggly woman said. "Met two children headed out to the forest. They said the guards have been lurking around the city. I don't know what they're looking for, but no one in their right mind would go back in there. Took nearly a week for the smoke to stop. There's nothing of worth left in the city. Going in there is as close to suicide as going out into the woods."

"They're in there looking for more people to kill." Anger filled the boy's sallow face. "They told us to stay on that street so we would burn. Now they're going through killing anyone the smoke didn't get."

"The men who told you to stay put, what exactly did they say? How many of them were there?" Jeremy came down the steps, his gun still in his hand.

"There were five," the boy said. "One of them shouted at us, told us to follow.

That was a girl, but the four men, they all did as she said. Some ran in front of us and some in back. It felt like they were trying to protect us. We ran with them for a bit. Then guns started firing. The woman told us to run down the street and wait, said she'd be right back for us. They never came back. They left us there to die. I didn't think she'd do that. She seemed nice."

"Who was firing the guns?" Julian asked.

"The female guard, did you see her face?" Jeremy stepped closer to the boy.

The boy leaned back against the wall. "All of them had helmets on. She was taller than me. I only knew she was a girl because of her voice. Even her name didn't sound like a girl's. But I've never heard of any kind of a Gentry before."

Nola stepped between Jeremy and the boy before she knew she'd asked her feet to move.

"Where did she go?" Jeremy bumped into Nola, knocking her into the boy as he reached forward to shake him.

"Back down." Kieran grabbed Jeremy's shoulder.

Jeremy glared at him.

"Jeremy," Nola whispered.

He looked into Nola's eyes. His anger changed to fear as he saw her mashed between him and the boy. He shook Kieran's hand off and stepped back.

"Where did she go?" Jeremy said.

"Toward the shooting." The boy held his chin high.

"Where was the shooting?" Nola asked. "Which part of the city were they heading toward?"

"The old Vamper section of town," the boy said.

"Did you see any other guards while you were waiting for Gentry to come back?" Kieran asked.

The boy shook his head. "Just the ones who left us to die."

"She didn't—"

"Don't." Nola pressed her hands to Jeremy's chest.

"What about the others around here?" Raina asked. "You've just been playing decaying house for a few days. No one's come by? No more people hunting for a nice place to stay?"

"There were whole streams of people the first few days," the gray-haired woman said. "It's died down a bit. I think either folks are already dead or they've found a place to settle."

"Maybe some have found their way to you," the scraggly woman said. "Wherever you are has got to be pretty nice. Vampers and humans living together. All of you look fed and healthy. Where have you been hiding out?"

"Don't even bother," Raina laughed. "You're not invited to the party."

"What about my baby?" the gray-haired woman asked. "You had food before, you're still doing well. Surely you can help a little girl."

The little girl turned her head, pressing her cheek to Kieran's chest.

"We can't help you." Kieran set the child down.

"I would advise you put your lights out," Julian said. "And stay here as long as your supplies will last. The longer you hold out before searching for a more sustainable option, the fewer you'll have to compete with."

"You're just like them," the boy said. "Leaving us in the middle of a fire."

"Gentry wouldn't do that," Jeremy said.

"Don't start that pity party with me," Raina said. "You aren't ours to care for. One of yours tried to kill one of mine. You should feel pretty damn lucky I'm walking away without having a snack. So all of you scurry up the stairs and lock yourselves in while we wander away. If you're really lucky, I won't tell any creepy crawlies where you're hiding."

"How long do you think we'll make it?" the redhead asked. "Would it really make a difference if you killed us now?"

"Probably not," Raina said. "But I'm giving you a chance to fight. Believe me, that's something."

"It's really not," the boy said.

"We should be on our way," Julian said.

"Go," Raina ordered the group.

The gray-haired woman snatched up the little girl and ran up the stairs. The other two women were right behind her, and the child began to cry as they disappeared from sight.

The boy didn't move.

"Get upstairs," Kieran said.

"Or you'll kill me?" the boy said. "You could light the house on fire as soon as you step outside."

"I carried you from the city," Jeremy said. "I could have left you there to die, but I didn't. Don't make me regret saving you."

"Why not? I do." The boy stepped toward Jeremy.

"Raina, we need to go," Julian said.

"I don't have time for this." Raina ran her blade along the boy's shoulder, slicing through his shirt and into his skin.

The boy howled with pain.

"Run," Raina growled.

The boy dodged around her and tore up the stairs, pressing his hand to his bleeding arm.

"I hate teenagers," Raina said.

"Thanks," Nola said.

She started for the door, lining up behind Kieran.

A *thwack* and a grunt sounded from in front of her.

"Kieran!" Her shout was swallowed by Kieran's voice.

"Get him inside! Raina, come on!" Kieran leapt over something and ran into the night.

"Shit." Raina knocked into Nola as she followed Kieran out the door.

"Nola, get back." Jeremy shoved her against the wall and reached down, seizing Julian's hands and dragging him into the house.

Blood pooled on Julian's stomach, surrounding an arrow that had pierced his suit and body.

"How?"

Jeremy ignored Nola, pulling Julian away from the door before grabbing the shaft of the arrow and yanking it from Julian's stomach.

Julian coughed. Blood spattered his veil. "I suppose I should thank you for that."

CHAPTER TWENTY-SIX

"We need to put pressure on it." Nola leaned over Julian, pressing her hands to his wound.

Julian grunted in pain, his eyes rolling back in his head.

Jeremy slammed the remains of the shattered door shut and crawled to the window, peering out into the darkness.

"What happened?" Nola asked.

"I was shot with an arrow," Julian wheezed.

"By who?" Nola asked.

The arrow lay on the floor where Jeremy had tossed it aside. Blood slicked the arrowhead and the start of the wooden shaft. The tip of the arrow had been carved from rock and faded feathers adorned the end.

"I'm almost impressed." Julian reached for the arrow. "You remove all hope and still life finds a way."

"Just breathe, Julian." Nola kept her hands pressed to the wound. "You're going to be just fine."

"I'm sure I will," Julian said. "But in the meantime, this is a bit excruciating."

"Did you see which way they went?" Jeremy kept his eyes focused on the darkness beyond the window.

"No, I was too busy looking at the arrow in Julian's stomach."

"Blow out the candles," Jeremy said.

"I can't move," Nola said.

"Don't worry about me." Julian shooed her away.

Nola crawled toward the candles, blowing each of them out in turn.

Her heart forgot to beat for a moment as the last candle went out and sense told her darkness would envelop her. But the faint light coming in from the window was enough for her eyes to see a face appear at the top of the stairs.

"Get back in the room or Jeremy shoots you," Nola said.

The boy glared at her for a moment before running away.

"They should be back by now," Jeremy said. "One person with a bow, that shouldn't give Raina any trouble."

"Unless there were more of them." Nola wiped the blood from her hands on the side of the couch, leaving streaks of red across the frayed fabric.

They sat in silence for a long moment. The faint shuffle of footsteps creaked upstairs.

"Should we go out after them?" Nola whispered.

"We're not splitting up," Jeremy said. "And we can't leave Julian behind."

"How very kind," Julian said.

"How long until you can move?" Nola asked.

Julian shifted his weight from side to side. "A few more minutes, and I should be able to stand. Might be an hour before I can fully run."

"If he can stand, you can carry him," Nola said.

"I don't believe that's the best idea," Julian said.

"Fine," Nola said. "I'll carry you. Jeremy's better with a gun."

"But where would we go?" Julian grimaced as he eased himself up onto his elbows. "I don't think there's anything to do but wait for them to come back."

"And if they don't come back?" Jeremy asked.

"They will," Julian said. "You need only give Raina time."

"How much time?" Nola asked. "They could be hurt."

"Shh," Jeremy hushed. He tipped his head, leaning closer to the windowsill.

Nola froze. Even her heart seemed to slow as she stared at Jeremy.

The floorboards above them creaked. A bedspring squeaked as someone sat down.

Outside, the dead leaves rustled, a branch cracked, someone grunted.

"Jeremy!" Nola screamed his name as the window shattered.

He covered his face as glass showered over him. A rock thumped onto the floor, rolling and settling by Nola's hands.

"Stay down!" Jeremy leapt through the broken window and out of sight.

"Help me up." Julian rolled over. His hands fumbled on the shattered glass, but still he pushed himself up to his knees.

"He said to stay down." Nola crawled to Julian's side.

"If we're being attacked, I'd prefer to be on my feet," Julian said.

Nola wrapped her arm around Julian, hoisting him up.

A *pop* sounded from the street followed by a scream of pain.

"Jeremy." Nola moved toward the shattered window.

"No!" Julian reached for her arm a moment too late.

A *whizzing* cut through the darkness. Nola twisted away from the window. Pain cut deep into her back.

"Nola!"

A *crunch* and a *thud* sounded on the street.

"Are you injured?" Julian grabbed her hand, pulling her away from the window.

"I'm fine."

An arrow stuck out of the wall right behind where Nola had been a moment before.

"Nola." Jeremy's boots thundered up the porch steps.

She twisted out of Julian's grip.

Jeremy leapt through the window and had Nola's face in his hands a moment later. "You're safe." Blood marked his cheeks, remnants of wounds that had already healed.

"It just got my back," Nola said.

Jeremy stepped around her, examining the place where the arrow had grazed her. "Dammit."

"Is it bad?" Nola asked.

"It was very nearly worse." Julian leaned against the wall.

"What happened out there?" Nola asked.

"Two new dead bodies." Raina stepped through the window, sunhat in hand, her windswept hair and the blood dripping from her blade the only signs she'd been fighting.

"Where's Kieran?" Nola asked.

"Stashing the dead men's loot to carry home." Raina wiped her knives clean on the curtains.

"Who were they?" Nola asked.

"Two outsiders who picked a really bad time to raid this house," Raina said. "You hear that up there? If we hadn't paid you a visit, you'd all be dead."

"I can't believe it's gotten this bad so quickly," Nola said. "Breaking into people's houses?"

"If they have candles, what else might they have?" Kieran stepped through the window, a bow in hand and a quiver of arrows over his shoulder. He grabbed the bloody arrow from the floor and pulled the other from the wall, adding both to his supply.

"But then they're just killing each other," Nola said. "There won't be anyone left."

"Exactly," Raina said. "Soon, only the strong and the sneaky will be alive. Welcome to the end of the world."

"We should go." Julian pushed away from the wall, giving his shoulders a tentative shake.

Raina stepped out through the window.

"We need to find Gentry," Jeremy said. "She'll know what's happening."

"We'll just walk right on up to the domes and knock on the door," Raina said. "Ask if we can talk to your sister."

Nola stepped out into the night. The cold tickled her back. She reached behind. Her shirt had been sliced open, and blood slicked her fingers.

"Damn." She reached back through the window, wiping her fingers on the curtains.

"Kieran, keep an arm around Julian," Raina said. "If he starts to fall behind, carry him."

"Nola." Kieran held out the bow and quiver. "Can you take these?"

"I don't know how to use them." Nola let Kieran pass her the hand-carved weapons.

"I just need you to carry them." Kieran winked.

"I can do that part." Nola looped the quiver over one shoulder and the bow over the other.

"Lover boy with me." Raina walked out through the grass, ignoring the two bodies crumpled on the lawn. "And keep your gun out. We might have made a bit of noise."

But you won. They'll leave us alone because you won.

Nola swallowed the childish sentiment as they reached the cracked road. The time for speaking seemed to have ended, though no one gave the order.

She examined every shadow as they moved down the street. Every rustling leaf was a killer aiming an arrow at her heart. Every house held a dozen people waiting to attack.

They moved more slowly, keeping to a human running pace.

A wide circle of ashes and debris covered the center of the road. Three unburnt bodies lay nearby. The animals had already begun their work on the corpses. Nola shuddered and focused on staring at the back of Jeremy's head. Blood stained his hair, and tiny flecks of glass sparkled in the strands.

Raina didn't slow her pace until they reached the edge of the highway.

Tents and huts had been built in a clump in the center of the wide road. Soot stains covered the fabric of the tents. Nola's eyes watered at the stench of human filth wafting from the ramshackle village.

"Stupid." Raina shook her head. "Do they think the Domers are going to help them? Do they think the city being gone is going to get rid of the acid in the clouds before the spring rains?"

"Let them believe what they like," Julian said. "The illusion of safety is the best they can hope for."

"We could raid it," Raina said. "Force them into safer dwellings."

"No time." Kieran pointed east.

Gray tinted the sky.

"We've got the suits," Raina said.

"We should get to ground," Jeremy said. "Julian's suit already has a hole in it, and he's still recovering."

"Where do we go?" Nola looked toward the city. There wasn't a single building in sight that hadn't been ruined by the fire. There would be no way to know which buildings were stable.

"If we're going to play in the city, we're going home." Raina threw one last glare at the tents and strode across the highway.

"Might it not be better to go somewhere a touch more discreet?" Julian asked.

"The tunnels of Nightland were made for us," Raina said. "We're going to ground there."

"The Outer Guard know where the entrance is," Jeremy said. "If I were stuck patrolling a burned out city, that's where I'd shelter."

"Weren't you just asking for a family reunion?" Raina said.

"They'll have the advantage if they've barricaded themselves in there," Jeremy said. "We don't know how many of them there are, what sorts of weapons they have—"

"So what's your plan, lover boy?" Raina asked. "Wait around for the end of the world to come? Head on over to the tunnels and sit on the sidewalk, waiting for someone to come out with a roll call and supply list?"

"I go check and see if the tunnels are clear," Nola said.

"No," Kieran said at the same time Jeremy said, "Absolutely not."

"I know the tunnels well enough to be able to find out if anyone's down there and get back out," Nola said. "I can be quick."

"I'll go in," Jeremy said. "If the Outer Guard are down there—"

"Then you're a deserter," Nola said.

"And they put out a kill order on you," Jeremy said.

"I've got a great idea," Raina said. "You both go in, poke around, and see what there is to see. Then if you're not dead, you come back up and give us a wave."

"Who's to say they won't kill them on sight?" Kieran said. "It's too dangerous."

"We're going into the tunnels, and someone has to go first," Raina said. "They won't hesitate to go for the heart of a vampire, but maybe Gentry and her little guard friends will be a bit slower to kill her brother and his girlfriend."

"We could go some—"

"Jeremy and I will go." Nola interrupted Kieran. "We'll go see who's down there and come right back out."

Raina turned off of Main, following a narrow alley between blackened ruins. "Perfect. We'll find a place to watch the exit. Nola and Jeremy, go in and scout."

Kieran shook his head but didn't argue as he and Julian followed Raina.

"Nola." Jeremy walked right behind her shoulder. "I can go in on my own, or take Kieran with me. He knows the tunnels better than you do."

"I want to stay with you," Nola said. "You jumped through that window and I didn't know where you were going or if someone had hurt you. I hated that feeling, and I don't want to do it again. You don't just get to worry about me, Jeremy. I get to worry about you, too."

"I love you," Jeremy said.

"Good," Nola said. "Because you're stuck with me."

"That's what I'm hoping for."

Nola could hear the smile in his voice, but the burned out buildings stole the joy from her heart. Melted metal twisted up from the charred remains of the city. Piles of brick and stone littered the street.

The scent of smoke, burned rubber, and decay sent sour rolling into Nola's mouth. She pulled her shirt up over her nose, but the stench penetrated the thin fabric.

There were no street signs left or any landmarks Nola could recognize, but Raina steered them through the city without hesitation.

A *clatter* and *crash* sounded in a nearby building. Nola wrenched her knives from their sheaths, her heart racing. Before the blades were fully free, a cat ran across the street.

Most of the poor creature's fur had been burned away. The cat hissed as it ran across their path and dodged out of sight.

Run before someone eats you.

The ground crunched beneath their feet as they moved deeper into the city. Nola didn't look down to find out why. She was too afraid of what the answer might be.

She looked up to the lightening sky instead. Orange tinted the horizon.

Hurry, Raina.

As if Raina had heard her thoughts, she waved the group toward a tilted building. The roof had burned entirely away, leaving only a shaft of brick behind.

Raina held up a hand, stopping the others as she stalked silently up the steps.

The quiet of the dawn pounded in Nola's ears. She reached for Jeremy. His hand found hers. A minute passed. Then two.

Finally, Raina stepped back out onto the stoop. She pointed to Julian and Kieran, waving them into the house, then to Nola and Jeremy, pointing the two of them across the street.

Kieran turned to Nola, a line creasing his brow. She could hear his voice in her mind. *Don't go. It won't be safe.*

I know you too well, Kieran.

Nola shook her head and passed the bow and quiver to Kieran. Her hand lingered on his for a moment.

He looked to Jeremy and gave him a nod, then turned and disappeared into the shadows of the bricks, Julian right behind him.

Pain scratched at Nola's chest.

Call after him. Tell him to be careful.

But silence filled the city, muting her voice.

Words don't belong on the streets anymore.

Jeremy laid a hand on her shoulder. She turned away from the leaning bricks, following the warmth of his touch across the street.

The building in front of them had collapsed entirely. Not even the stone steps stayed standing. A giant hole in the ground had eaten the stoop.

Twisted and torn metal stairs reached into the hole and out of sight.

Jeremy held up three fingers then pointed into the ground with his gun.

He lowered one finger at a time, counting down.

One.

Nola's heart quickened as she watched his first finger fold. This is where it had all begun, at the door to Nightland.

Two.

The sun found its way over the horizon, giving depth to the shadows of the devastated city. The world had crumbled so quickly. Soon there would be nothing left but stone and ash.

Three.

Together, they jumped into the ruins of Nightland.

SON OF SUN

Book Four

CHAPTER ONE

S hadows pressed in around her, snapping the thin thread of her courage. The scent of old blood and rancid rot hung heavy in the air.

Jeremy's silhouette moved in front of her, broken bits of concrete crunching under his feet.

Nola followed his gaze as he squinted into the darkest corners of what had been the club at 5th and Nightland. Not so very long ago, the room would have been packed with vampires dancing as though the world weren't ending.

How many of them are dead?

Jeremy reached into his pocket and pulled out a flashlight, holding the beam level with the barrel of his Guard gun.

Nola pulled her weapon free from her belt, holding her breath as Jeremy shone his light into every crevice. Portions of the walls had caved in, whether from the fire that had destroyed the city above or from the domes' raid on Nightland, Nola didn't know.

Jeremy froze as his light fell on a human form on the floor. A woman with long blue hair, half-buried under a giant chunk of fallen ceiling. A length of rebar stuck out of the woman's head. The rodents of the city had feasted on her flesh.

Nola bit her lips together, blinking back the tears that burned in her eyes.

No life should end like that.

"Which way?" Jeremy whispered.

Nola stepped around him, heading toward the door that led to the main tunnel of Nightland.

Jeremy held out a hand, blocking Nola's path. "Let me stay in front."

"It's that way."

She stayed close behind Jeremy's shoulder as they wound through the debris toward the broken archway. The steel door that had once been heavily guarded lay on the floor to one side. Rubble had been dragged away from the passage as well, leaving a clear path to the corridor beyond.

"Somebody put a lot of effort into clearing this," Nola whispered.

"Let's just hope it's someone we want to see," Jeremy said.

Nola touched his arm with her free hand. "We'll find her, Jeremy. We'll find Gentry."

"Keep close." Jeremy stepped through the archway, sweeping his light across the hall.

Shattered remnants of light bulbs hung uselessly from the ceiling. A section of wall had crumbled, spilling dirt into the hall. Dozens of footprints leading in both directions marked the ground.

"Keep going forward," Nola said. "I only know one path to Emanuel's old house."

They crept down the hall, Jeremy setting a slow and deliberate pace, stopping every few feet to listen and sweep his light over the corridor behind them.

The plan had seemed so simple aboveground. Kieran, Raina, and Julian would hide from the sun in the ruins near Nightland. Nola and Jeremy would check the tunnels to be sure the domes' guards weren't patrolling. The Outer Guard would kill a vampire on sight, but two people who had, until a few short weeks ago, lived in the domes might give them pause.

Now, moving silently through the tunnel, the idea that Nola could face an Outer Guard and hope to survive became unforgivably naïve. The thought that Jeremy could fight against Gentry, his own sister, lost all reason.

He'd do it for me. He'd fight her to protect me.

What if I can't protect him?

A hollow ache gnawed at Nola's chest.

Ahead, another section of the tunnel had collapsed. A chest-high pile of rocks blocked their path.

"Stay back," Jeremy whispered.

"No."

Nola stepped up next to him, aiming her Guard gun at the debris.

Jeremy shook his head but didn't fight Nola staying at his side as they approached the barricade.

Her heart thudded in her ears. There could be nothing behind the mound. Or a rat. Or an Outer Guard waiting to kill them.

Jeremy picked up a fist-sized rock and backed toward the remnants of the wall, keeping Nola pressed behind him. He tossed the rock over the mound and into the shadows beyond, where it landed with a *clatter*.

Nola's nerves zinged as she waited for vampires to spring over the barrier, werewolves to howl their rage, or guards to fire their weapons. But nothing came, not even the scurrying of frightened rats.

Keeping his flashlight and weapon pointed toward the hall beyond, Jeremy moved closer to the barricade, sidestepping to block Nola from walking next to him.

Nola barely caught the quick movement as Jeremy bent his knees and dove over the fallen rocks, landing on the far side with barely a sound. His flashlight's beam darted around the tunnel before he beckoned Nola across. She bent her knees, trying to judge the height and distance of the obstacle in front of her and the amount of space she had between the barrier and the low ceiling.

A few short weeks ago, such a leap would have been completely impossible. But she wasn't human anymore. Graylock had changed her, granting her the ability to survive the contamination outside the glass and giving her body unnatural strength.

"Are you all right?" Jeremy barely voiced the words, yet she could hear him perfectly.

Nola bent her knees and dove over the pile of rubble. As she cleared the mound of dirt and rock, the floor on the far side became horribly real. She pulled her legs forward, trying to get her feet under her. The ground came too quickly, and she stumbled, landing on her knees.

"Are you okay?" Jeremy glanced at her, his eyes quickly flicking back to the dark corridor ahead.

"I've never tried that kind of jump before." Nola stood, shaking the pain from her legs.

"You did great." A hint of a smile touched the corners of Jeremy's eyes before vanishing. "Let's keep moving."

The stillness of the corridor devoured the muffled noise of their footfalls as they moved farther down the hall. Away from light and fresh air. Away from escape.

A door came into view, hanging off its bottom hinges.

"There," Nola said. "Through that door."

She had run through it before. Fled from her own people and locked the door behind her. But the door couldn't be locked now. There would be no hope of blocking danger with something as simple as a door.

Shadows from a different life drifted across the doorjamb. Faint shapes moving as though Nightland had found a way to survive the dome-made massacre in the city.

"Turn off the flashlight," Nola said.

Jeremy flicked it off without question.

Shadows moved across the doorway, cast by a light source Nola couldn't see.

She stilled her heart, listening to the sounds around her. Whispers filtered through the doorway.

Jeremy leaned close to Nola's ear. "Stay here."

"No." Nola met Jeremy's gaze, willing him to understand that she would no more let him walk through that door alone than he would let her.

Jeremy's neck tensed with unsaid words, but he nodded and didn't try to block Nola as she followed him toward the door.

The light from the tunnel beyond flickered, like someone had lit torches or lanterns. The whispered voices grew stronger, as though the speakers waited just out of sight.

"I don't want to be a meal," a male voice said. "I didn't spend this long fighting for survival to become a meal for a Vamper or wolf."

"I don't know what else you want me to do," a female spoke. "We're out of the weather. We've got some water and a bit of food."

"No enough to last," a second female said. "We're going to need help. There has to be someone in this nightmare who has food to spare."

"And what kind of angel would swoop in to save us?" the man said. "There is no help. No one is coming to save us. You've got to understand that."

A sniffle of stifled tears tugged on Nola's heart.

Nightland's home in the mountain had food, water, and solid walls.

The rats will sink the ship. Raina's words echoed through her mind.

"We need weapons," the man said. "If we can fight, we might be able to take what we need."

"I never thought stealing would sound like a good idea," the first female said.

Jeremy crept closer to the door. The nearer they got to the entry, the clearer the shadows became. One of the people sat in front of the light source, while the other two stood near the wall.

Two against three isn't bad.

Jeremy leaned against the wall right next to the door, keeping his eyes focused on the shadows.

"Stay out of sight," Jeremy mouthed.

Nola shook her head.

"I don't want to play our whole hand." Jeremy pressed her against the wall.

She wanted to refuse. To insist on walking through the door by his side. Danger for him should mean danger for them both. But Jeremy had been training as an Outer Guard when he abandoned the domes, had been raised by the head of the Outer Guard.

I was trained in growing food, not fighting.

Nola nodded, hoping she was right to trust Jeremy's instincts.

Squaring his shoulders, he stepped in front of the door, leveling his weapon at the corridor beyond. He took a step forward, moving through the door and out of sight.

Her heart rocketed into her throat. She strained her ears, trying to hear the sound of his footsteps.

"I don't want to be sitting ducks when the Vampers come for a meal," the first woman said.

"What the—"

A terrible *shriek* of metal against stone cut through Jeremy's words.

"Jeremy!" Nola leapt forward as a sheet of steel crashed down, blocking the doorway.

CHAPTER TWO

"Nola, run!" The metal barrier muffled Jeremy's shout.

"Jeremy." Nola stumbled in the pitch black of the hall, falling into the steel door that separated them. "Jeremy!" She pounded on the metal.

"Get out, Nola!"

She ran her fingers along the steel, searching for a handle or lock. Dents and scratches marked the barrier, as though it had slid into place many times before.

"I can't find a way to move the door." Nola's hands trembled as she reached up to the corners of the doorjamb.

"It's a trap. The voices came through a speaker," Jeremy said. "Nola, get out. Go back to the others."

"I'm not leaving you." Nola kicked the door.

"Nola you have—"

"I said I'm not leaving you!" Nola kicked the door again.

"I think there's gas in here," Jeremy coughed.

"Make the other people help you look for a way out." Nola knelt, digging her fingers into the dirt under the metal door.

"There are no other people," Jeremy said. "They're dead. They're all dead."

Her fingertips found the edge of the metal. Gritting her teeth, she lifted with all her might. A scream of rage and fear escaped her.

"Nola," Jeremy's voice rasped.

"Cover your face," Nola said. "I'm going to get you out."

"I love you."

Panic and outrage sliced into Nola's chest, stealing the strength from her limbs. "You're going to be okay." She pushed herself to her feet. "You promised you wouldn't leave me. Don't you dare break your promise, Jeremy Ridgeway."

She needed a light and a crowbar. Or explosives to blast away the door. A hundred impossible ideas raced through her mind.

She tore her fingers through her curls.

Jeremy trapped with dead people. Jeremy dying.

"Stop panicking, Nola Kent. You can't help him if you're panicking."

The people who built the door wanted her to panic, wanted Jeremy to die. What kind of monster would be evil enough to build such a trap?

The domes.

"Jeremy, the other people, are they just dead on the floor?" Nola leaned against the metal.

"No, staged like they're alive." Jeremy's words slurred. "Ropes. Puppets."

"Then they had to open the door." Nola pushed away from the metal, fumbling toward the wall beside it. Starting at the base of the wall, she ran her hands across the packed dirt and stone. "Please," Nola begged the darkness. "Please, please. I will not lose him."

She moved to the other side of the steel, feeling the outline of the broken door that hung off its hinges, her heart racing faster with every second that passed. The tips of her fingers caught on a ridge in the wall, a metal square packed with loose dirt.

"I found something," Nola shouted through the door. "Jeremy? Jeremy!"

"I'm here." His voice barely carried through the door.

"Hang on." She dug into the loose dirt. Her fingers found something hard and metallic. A lever packed in with the dirt. She tried to push the handle up, but it wouldn't budge. "Come on." She shoved the metal down, but again the lever stayed firmly in place. "Open, dammit." She planted both feet on the wall and pulled backward with every ounce of strength Graylock had granted her. The handle moved a fraction of an inch.

A slit of light appeared at the bottom of the door.

"Move!" Nola yanked harder, ignoring the pain in her hand as a bone cracked under the strain.

The door slid up farther. Fingers appeared, reaching through the gap.

Nola screamed as another bone snapped. The door raised a foot.

Jeremy dragged himself through the gap and lay gasping on the tunnel floor.

Nola let go of the handle and ran to his side. The door snapped shut, leaving them in darkness.

"Jeremy." Nola fumbled blindly for him, not caring about the pain in her hands as she felt his chest rise and fall.

"I'm okay." Jeremy's voice came out as a rasp. "I can heal, I'll be okay."

"The shot of Graylock, you need it." Nola reached for his belt, for the case that held the one dose of the medicine they carried.

"No." Jeremy rolled over, moving the case out of her reach. "I just need a minute, I'll be okay."

Nola felt his face. Sweat slicked his clammy skin. She leaned down, pressing her lips to his. His breath tasted of chemicals.

"What was the gas?" Nola said.

"I don't know." Jeremy clicked on his flashlight.

Deep purple patches mottled the skin on his face and hands. Bright red veins marked the whites of his eyes.

Nola swallowed her tears. "Are you sure you're going to be okay?"

"I can breathe better already." He pressed Nola's palm to his lips.

"Why would the domes build something like that?" Nola asked.

A part of her expected Jeremy to argue. To say the domes would never build something so terrible. But they'd seen the city burn, run into the flames that killed thousands. People who were willing to slaughter an entire city could build a trap to kill underground.

"Trying to round up vampires, I expect." Jeremy pushed himself to sit up.

Nola wrapped an arm around him, steadying him as he swayed.

"Lure blood drinkers in with the promise of a good meal then trap them." Jeremy's voice came out stronger than it had moments before. "There was solid metal on the other side, too."

"And the people?" Nola asked.

Jeremy shuddered. "Too far dead to be a meal for anyone."

Nola swallowed the bile that shot to her throat. "That's sick. Absolutely disgusting."

"We should get away from here." Jeremy knelt. Nola took his elbow, helping him to his feet. "The domes might have a way to track when the trap is tripped."

"Should we search for another way to Emanuel's?" Nola asked. "I don't want to have to try coming down here again."

"It's not worth it." Jeremy kept his arm over Nola's shoulder as they started back the way they'd come. "If they put a trap here, they put in others. There isn't a way to hide in the Nightland tunnels. Not anymore."

"Raina is going to be so pissed," Nola said.

"Yeah."

The steady pace of Jeremy's steps eased Nola's worry.

Graylock saved him again.

Chemicals blended as medicine to save them from the chemicals contaminating the world that had killed so many humans. The domes had hated the vampires and werewolves for turning to drugs like Vamp and Lycan to survive.

Then the domes made Graylock, their own version of altering the body, exchanging human DNA for survival.

Nola had despised them for betraying the mission of the domes: to preserve human life in the dying world. A person who could heal from being stabbed in the stomach with no more than a little rest couldn't really be called human anymore. But Graylock had saved Jeremy. And her.

She leaned in closer to him, listening to his rattling breaths.

They reached the barricade of debris.

"Let me go first." Jeremy lifted his arm from Nola's shoulder.

"I don't think you'd make it." In one swift move, Nola leapt up, landing in a low crouch on top of the pile. Nothing waited in the shadows beyond to attack her.

"You can't blame me for trying." Jeremy reached for her hand.

Nola grabbed his wrist and hoisted him up to sit on the pile. Even though he was tall and had the broad build of one born for fighting, his weight didn't strain her muscles.

"My hands." Nola let go of Jeremy and jumped down on the other side of the rocks.

"What about them?" Jeremy jumped after her, tipping forward as he landed.

Nola caught his arm and held him on his feet.

"I broke my hands opening the door, but they don't hurt anymore," Nola said.

"Probably a hairline fracture," Jeremy said. "Those don't take very long to heal."

"Wow." Nola opened and closed her fists. "I could get used to this superhero thing."

"Good." Jeremy smiled. His eyes scrunched up at the corners. The red in them had already begun to fade.

Before Nola could reach out to touch the creases, his smile faltered.

"We'll find her, Jeremy." Nola raised her weapon and started down the tunnel. "It might not be as easy as we'd hoped, but we're going to find Gentry."

"We have to." Jeremy stepped in front of Nola, his gait even as they moved toward 5th and Nightland. "If she really did stand against the domes to try and help the people in the city, she can't go back. Not to our domes or any place under Incorporation control. If she's stuck out here, she should be with me."

"I know."

They walked in silence for a long while. The end of the tunnel came into view.

Jeremy slowed and moved Nola right behind him as they approached the open doorway.

Nola strained her ears, listening for the *thump* of heavy boots or the tiny *pop* of silver darts being fired.

The wall on this side of the door hadn't suffered as much damage as the inside of the club. The stone remained intact with only a few cracks taunting the tunnel's ability to crumble and trap them.

The urge to dart around Jeremy and run for the open air tensed Nola's muscles. She tipped her gaze higher, to where light and open space waited just above them.

Words painted above the door caught her eye.

> *There is no life left in Nightland.*
> *Death is all that awaits us.*

The warning had been painted in black, the letters crooked as though the one writing had hurried to their own escape.

"Look above the door," Nola said.

Jeremy froze, aiming his weapon at the words.

"What do you think it means?" Nola asked.

"That someone smart was here." Jeremy stepped up to the door, pressing Nola to the side as he peered through the entry to the club.

A chill tickled the back of Nola's neck.

There is no life left in Nightland.

Did an Outer Guard write the words, or a vampire who had tried to return to the refuge Emanuel built?

Nola stayed close on Jeremy's heels as he stepped through the doorway. There was no *whine* of deadly doors as they passed into the club. Bits of stone clacked under Nola's feet as she skirted around the body of the blue-haired woman. Perhaps she had met a kind end after all. Better a quick blow than a slow death by poison.

A bright shaft of sunlight streamed down from the hole that led to the street. Nola's shoulders relaxed as they neared the path to freedom.

"I'll go up first," Jeremy whispered. "I'll call when you can follow."

"We should go together," Nola said. "You're sick. You almost died."

"If I get attacked, I'll scream extra loud." He put his flashlight in his pocket and jumped to the street above.

"Be okay," Nola whispered. "You have to be okay. You have to be okay."

"It's clear."

Relief flooded Nola's chest as she bent her knees and pushed off as hard as she could. The wind raced past her as she leapt out of the ground, cleared five feet of open air, and landed on what remained of the cracked sidewalk.

She took deep, gulping breaths of the wonderful oxygen that had seemed too polluted to be safe for human lungs when she'd lived trapped in the domes but now granted her blissful freedom.

Jeremy coughed a laugh. "Nice jump." The purple patches on his face had turned a pale pink.

"Thanks." Nola touched his cheek, savoring the roughness of his stubble. "I've had a pretty great teacher."

Jeremy laughed again, his lungs wheezing from the effort.

"Let's get to the others." Nola took his elbow, leading him across the street.

There were no signs of life around them. No humans, vampires, werewolves, zombies, or Outer Guard moving through the burned out skeleton of the city.

They reached a house where some of the bricks had managed to stay upright in the inferno. Jeremy didn't insist on climbing the cracked steps first.

"Raina," Nola said, "it's us."

Nola hesitated on the threshold, counting to ten before stepping through the gap that should have been a door. Most of three walls of the building remained, surrounding piles of ash and scorched rubble that took up the center of the space.

"Raina," Nola said. "Where are you?"

Thin shadows shaded the corners of the walls, but nothing dark enough to protect a vampire.

"There." Jeremy pointed to a gap in the rubble.

The floor had fallen away, leaving a hole where the steps to a lower level should have been.

Nola tightened her grip on her weapon as Jeremy stalked toward the opening and pulled his flashlight from his pocket.

"Raina," Jeremy said. "Julian?"

"They've got to be down there," Nola said. "They wouldn't leave without us."

Jeremy glanced to her, one eyebrow raised. He turned back to the gap, shining his light on the ground twelve feet below.

"What if the domes rigged another trap?" Nola asked.

"We'd still need to go down and see if the others are alive." Jeremy picked up a blackened brick and tossed it into the basement. The brick fell to the ground with a *thud*. "Good enough, I guess."

Jeremy jumped down into the darkness.

Nola bit her lips together as he landed and swept his light around the space below. He beckoned for her to follow.

Checking her grip on her weapon, she jumped down into the hole. The feeling of being swallowed by the earth pressed against her ribs.

Not far down. Not too far down.

She stood in the sunlight, her Graylock-given vision allowing her to see even in the deep shadows.

One side of the basement had collapsed. The charred remains of shelves and tools littered the dirt-packed floor.

A sheet of scorched plaster had fallen from the other side, revealing a wall that had been cracked and singed but otherwise left untouched by the blaze that had claimed the house.

A heavy metal hatch had been built into the wall, and scratches marked the dirt where the door had recently been dragged open.

Nola filed in behind Jeremy as he moved toward the door. A narrow corridor waited beyond, leading toward what should have been the basement of the building next door.

Faint voices carried down the passage.

"It may not be what we set out to find, but that doesn't mean it isn't valuable." Julian's voice came from the far end of the tunnel.

"I'm not carrying any of this," Raina said. "And if someone kills you because you decided to weigh yourself down, I will only feel moderately guilty."

Nola dodged in front of Jeremy and darted down the tunnel. The dim glow of flashlights filled the space beyond, barely lighting the corners of the room where shelves were lined with beakers and bottles.

Three people stood in the middle of the room. Julian holding a rack of vials, Raina playing with her knife, and Kieran clutching a microscope to his chest.

CHAPTER THREE

"The lovebirds are back so soon?" Raina said, her scathing look bordering on comical in her baggy, tan sun suit.

"Booby traps." Jeremy leaned against the wall just inside the door. "There's no one living in the tunnels. The domes made sure of that."

"Those evil bastards." Raina threw her knife at the wall. The blade sunk into the dirt between two stones.

"Are you sure?" Kieran asked.

"Positive," Nola said. "Jeremy nearly died before we even got into the housing tunnels."

"Damn." Julian set his rack of vials on the floor. "I didn't hold much hope of discovering allies below, but I thought we might be lucky enough to find sanctuary."

"Fuck." Raina scrubbed her hands over her face.

"What about the little tunnel?" Nola's chest tightened at the thought of crawling through the darkness. "The one you brought me through before."

"No one we want to see would be able to find that way in," Raina said.

"We need to move," Jeremy said. "If they have a way of knowing when the trap is tripped, this whole area could flood with guards."

"Who will be really mad when they find out Jeremy escaped," Nola said.

"I didn't escape." Jeremy took Nola's hand. "You saved me."

She leaned her cheek against his chest, hating the stench of poison that clung to his clothes.

"So we head up to the streets and then what?" Kieran said. "We came here to get information for Emanuel. We need to know why there were Domer zombies on the mountain."

"Well, our only way under the river to the domes has just been cut off." Raina yanked her knife out of the wall. "We haven't seen anyone in the city. So unless you have a boat you've been hiding or know a great place we can find some secret information, looks like we're shit out of luck."

"It's not as though the trip has been entirely wasted," Julian said. "The things we've found here are incredibly useful."

"You didn't know this was down here?" Nola asked.

"I knew there was a basement," Raina said. "I'd gone to ground here a couple of times when I got home too late and the door to the club had already been barred for the day. The former owner never showed off the giant hidden door or their side business."

"Side business?" Nola stood up straight, examining the shelves. "Doing what?"

"This is a Vamp lab," Kieran said. "And from the looks of it, not the kind that made the pure stuff."

"I'd be willing to wager more than one person who sought salvation from the Vamp made in this lab ended up a zombie," Julian said.

"And here I thought they were just nice people who were willing to save a vampire from the sun," Raina said. "Did they really think having me on their side would save their lives if Emanuel found out they were poisoning people?"

"Some of the equipment can be salvaged," Kieran said. "My father could use these things to make ReVamp."

"So we close the door behind us and come back when there aren't guards wondering how lover boy escaped from their trap." Raina waved them all toward the door. "Maybe we'll get lucky and capture a guard, ask them some very friendly questions." She winked at Nola.

Nola waited for her stomach to squirm at the thought of taking a Domer prisoner.

They're the enemy.

"Fine." Kieran set the microscope carefully in the corner. "But I'm coming back. Dad and I could both use these things for our work."

"You can't work if you're dead," Jeremy said.

Kieran looked up, meeting Jeremy's gaze.

Raina took Nola's shoulders, pulling her out from between the two boys.

"A microscope isn't as useful as your brain," Jeremy said. "So let's get out of here while we can."

Kieran gave a jerky nod. "There are some things I won't risk leaving."

"The doctor and his son. Trying to save everyone as the world burns," Raina said. "If it weren't so poetic, I would laugh."

"Being able to make medicine isn't a laughing matter." Kieran lifted two small jars filled with white powder, one jar of clear liquid, and a metallic tin off the shelf.

"Stash them in your suit and let's move," Raina said. "We have another stop to make before we can head back."

"Where?" Jeremy asked.

"Not the domes if you were hoping for a little trip home." Raina strode past Jeremy and into the narrow corridor, pulling on her sun hat and lowering the veil that protected her face.

"My home is in the mountain," Jeremy said. "My home is with Nightland, but we still need to..." His voice trailed away as Raina raised a warning hand.

Nola gripped Jeremy's arm, unwilling to risk being separated from him.

Raina wiggled her finger, beckoning them forward.

Nola pulled her weapon free as she followed Jeremy into the corridor.

The distant thumping of boots carried through the shadows as they neared the first basement.

Raina stayed close to the walls, out of sight should anyone look down from above.

There were no voices to go with the heavy footfalls as the people moved away, toward the entrance to 5th and Nightland.

Nola pressed herself into the shadows, still clinging tightly to Jeremy's arm.

Julian and Kieran stepped out of the tunnel.

The footsteps stopped.

Raina folded her arms and shot Kieran a glare before striding back down the tunnel.

Nola looked to Jeremy and mouthed, "Do we go back in?"

Jeremy shook his head.

Nola watched the sunlight filter in through the hole in the ceiling above them. Where there had once been a staircase, now only charred bits of wood remained. But someone had lived in this house. Someone had gone up and down the stairs to the basement without ever thinking the whole building could burn.

Someone who had made poison.

Images of people with red and black sores on their faces swam unbidden into Nola's mind. People who had tried to take Vamp or Lycan, searching for a cure as the outside world slowly murdered them. The poorly made drugs changed them into prisoners in their own dying bodies, with no thought left but to attack those who somehow still survived.

Low voices rumbled through the silence. Nola tried to listen but couldn't make out anything beyond the vague sound.

A soft scraping came from the lab where Raina had disappeared.

Minutes ticked by. The voices outside didn't disappear, nor did the footsteps move.

Nola wanted to close her eyes, to curl up and pretend life hadn't led her to a world of tunnels and fear.

Then I'd be in the domes. I'd still be one of them. I'd be a murderer.

There was no way to deny what her former home had become. A glass castle filled with killers.

Raina stepped out of the hallway, two large glass bottles in her hand. She looked to Kieran with a glint a mischief in her eyes, held up both bottles, and winked.

"What?" Nola whispered.

Kieran looked to Jeremy.

Jeremy stared at the bottles in Raina's hands for a long moment.

"What?" Nola stepped between Raina and Jeremy.

Jeremy kept his gaze over Nola's head and nodded.

"Jeremy?" A sense of dread squeezed Nola's throat.

"Stay back." Jeremy stepped around Nola, blocking her from the gap in the ceiling.

Raina handed one of the bottles to Kieran.

He pulled down the veil on his sun hat as she counted down from three on her fingers. Together, the two of them jumped up through the ceiling and out of sight.

The dull creaking of the floor above gave the only sign of the two landing at street level.

Nola waited for shouts or the sound of weapons.

A second ticked past. Then another.

Bang!

The sound itself pummeled Nola's body as the walls around them shook.

"And up we go." Julian ran under the gap and sprang out of sight.

Jeremy grabbed Nola's hand, dragging her forward. Her feet couldn't move. Her mind didn't know how to reason past the *bang*.

Jeremy wrapped an arm around her waist, lifting her as he jumped through the hole and into the open air. Smoke shrouded the other side of the street where the entrance to 5th and Nightland had been. But the chasm had grown, swallowing the sidewalk and half the street.

Raina waited on the steps of the burned out building, a knife in each hand, though Nola couldn't see anyone for Raina to stab.

The others started to run, following Raina away from the smoldering ruins of the club.

Jeremy kept his arm around Nola's waist, carrying her as he sprinted down the stairs and up the street. He ran at an incredible pace, leaving the world to whip by in a blur of destruction.

"I can run," Nola said as sense battered its way through shock. "I can run fast, too."

Jeremy didn't set her down. He kept her pinned to his side as he tore past an open square where a park might have been a long time ago. Past a wide building with a metal fence melted around its ruin.

"I can do it," Nola said.

Jeremy let her feet touch the ground but kept a hand on her hip as they ran.

The speed didn't bring any stress to Nola's limbs. The steady movement soothed her nerves.

I am not helpless.

She ran faster, catching up to Julian.

They turned down a narrow alley between buildings. The reek of rotting flesh stung Nola's nose. They sprinted onto a larger road before Nola could spot the unfortunate cause of the stench.

Raina cut right, onto a road lined with melted lampposts. The fire packs the domes had dropped on the city hadn't spared any of the houses on this street. The wide stone stoops had cracked. The front façade of one home had toppled, leaving debris strewn all the way to the other side of the road.

"Bellevue," Nola said, the word coming out easily despite how far they'd run. "Raina, your sister's house is gone. I'm so sorry."

Raina slowed her pace as she neared the crumbled stoop. "It wasn't Nettie's house. It was mine."

"There's nothing left here," Julian said.

"Of course there is." Raina kicked a chunk of cement the size of a backpack out of the way. "You people, all of you grew up in the privileged society of the domes."

"But..." Nola's voice trailed away. She'd forgotten Julian had once lived in a different, far away set of domes.

"You grow up convinced you'll always have food and a safe place to sleep, and it changes the way your brain works." Raina lifted a burnt slab of something and tossed it aside. "You don't think. You don't plan for what you're going to do if the whole world goes to shit and no one wants to feed you anymore."

She cleared the top of the stoop and stomped hard on the ground. "Not me. Being a kid in the brutal outside world, you learn that nothing is guaranteed. Not love. Not family. Not living to see the damned sunrise." The thumping of the stoop under her foot changed, the sound becoming thinner. "So you learn to plan. To have a backup plan for your backup plan."

Raina kicked down on the steps, pummeling the ground again and again.

"Raina." Kieran ran up the crumbled stairs. "Raina, you're going to hurt yourself."

The stone beneath her cracked.

"Don't worry, kid." Raina tore away a hunk of stone. "I know what I'm capable of."

Jeremy's touch brushed the back of Nola's hand. She laced her fingers through his, fighting the urge to help as Raina dug deeper into the stone.

"The domes have taken too much from all of us," Nola said. "How can they just keep going? Do they not see how evil they are?"

"Evil is in the eye of the beholder," Raina said. "The exterminator doesn't think he's evil for killing the rats. The domes have never seen any of us on the outside as anything better than vermin. There you are, beautiful." She bent low, yanking something free from the hole she'd created.

Raina held a black metal box up to the light. The size of a shoebox with only a latch to hold it closed, the case didn't seem worthy of holding anything that might help them.

"Now we can head for home and find a new plan." Raina jumped off the steps.

"What's in the box?" Kieran asked.

"Wouldn't you like to know?" Raina said.

"Do we just go back the way we came?" Nola squared her shoulders, trying not to look daunted by the thirteen mile run.

"Do you have a better idea?" Raina said. "Or better yet, a hidden boat?"

"No," Nola said.

"We didn't find the information we wanted." Kieran climbed down to the street. "But at least we know the whole city isn't swarming with Outer Guard."

"Which could leave them across the river organizing to attack us." Jeremy rubbed his hands over his face. The purple splotches had disappeared entirely, leaving him looking tired but healthy.

"So let's take a pass by the river on our journey home," Julian said. "It shouldn't be hard to see if the domes falling caused the creation of the Domer zombies who stumbled up our mountain. There's also a good chance of us spotting a giant helicopter parked out front."

"I hate running errands." Raina sauntered down the street, carrying the black box. "It always seems like such a waste of time. Ah well, best view of the river is right this way, ladies and gentlemen." She didn't pick up her pace as the others followed.

Nola kept her fingers laced through Jeremy's as they walked. The feel of his palm pressed next to hers sent warmth tingling up her arm. Even as she searched the corners of burned out buildings for hidden guards and listened for the sounds of impending attack, the delightful warmth didn't fade away.

Jeremy raised their hands, pressing his lips to her wrist.

"What was that for?" Nola asked.

"Saving my life." He kissed the back of her hand. "You never cease to amaze me, Nola Kent."

"Good." A smile curved Nola's lips.

They rounded the corner, and her smile vanished.

The rancid river flowed in front of them, the stink of its water slamming into Nola's nose more fiercely than even the forgotten corpses. And on the far bank, the domes glittered in the sunlight.

CHAPTER FOUR

The domes were perfect, just as they had been designed to be. A series of glass structures centered around one tall concrete tower. No cracks marked the giant door of the Atrium. No smoke or frantic movement signaled distress. The wreckage of the bridge reaching toward the city gave the only sign the domes had ever been attacked.

"Well, that answers that," Raina said.

Nola squinted toward the distant domes. Amber Dome where her mother would be hard at work putting in new plants to feed the Domers. Bright Dome where Nola had lived her whole life.

"Just because the glass isn't shattered doesn't mean there's nothing wrong," Jeremy said.

"If you'd like to swim over and peek in to see if everyone looks like happy little mass murderers, feel free," Raina said. "I, however, am going to report what we do know to Emanuel."

"We can't get across the river," Nola said. "There's nothing more for us to learn."

Jeremy's neck tensed, displaying the thick cords of his muscles. "You're right."

"After me, then?" Julian turned away from the river without waiting for a response.

Jeremy tugged on Nola's hand, guiding her away from the domes. She kept staring at the glass until they turned onto another street and a tower of burned bricks blocked the river and her former home from view.

"Did you ever go back, Julian?" Nola asked. "To see your home domes?"

"I never had the opportunity." Julian led them down a different path toward a part of the city Nola had never entered. "When they cleared out the population of our city, they gave the citizens three days to evacuate the area. By *area,* they meant a thirty-mile radius. Anyone left within that circle without authorization after the three days was to be considered a hostile threat. As I fled the city with those being evicted, I no longer held any authorization."

"That's terrible," Nola said.

"I made it thirty-eight miles before the time passed," Julian said. "I was lucky enough to be healthy from living in the domes. Many of the city dwellers didn't even make it five miles."

"How could they?" Nola said. "How could they even consider..."

"Genocide," Kieran said. "That's the word you're looking for Nola, genocide."

"The domes shift from indifference to slaughter so quickly," Julian said. "Their complacency allows them to feel nothing while they watch others suffer. Their righteousness allows them to kill when murder fits within the domes' cause."

The group fell silent as they passed a row of burned bones laid out on the street. The bones weren't in the shape of the bodies they'd once belonged to, nor were they randomly strewn about as though dragged by animals.

Seven charred and cracked skulls sat in one line above eight femurs and a grid of small bones.

"Domers didn't do this," Jeremy said.

"Too good for organization but not murder?" Raina leaned over the bones.

Nola gripped Jeremy's hand tighter, trying not to lose the hope that came with his touch.

"No," Nola said. "It's not about *too good.* It's just...wrong. There's no reason for it. When have the domes ever put effort into anything that didn't directly benefit them?"

"Sampling the dead for some reason?" Julian asked.

"They'd have to bring the samples back to the lab," Kieran said. "There's no way they'd let anyone as valuable as a doctor or scientist come near the city."

"It feels wrong," Jeremy said. "I know the Outer Guard. I know the domes. This isn't them."

"So who then?" Nola glanced around the buildings, searching for people collecting bones.

"It could be any crazy," Raina said. "Someone who lost their family in the fire. A vampire so far gone with bloodlust they forgot you can't drink blood from burnt bones."

"Please don't." Nola pressed the back of her hand to her mouth. Dirt from the tunnels coated her lips.

"I don't fancy the idea of lingering here," Julian said. "These remains were either laid out by someone with a specific mission in mind, in which case I have no interest in standing in their way, or this is the work of one whose mind is lost—"

"In which case I'd rather not be here when they come back," Kieran said.

"Exactly," Julian said.

"Let's go," Nola said. "Please."

Julian nodded and jogged down the street. He kept to a human pace, like he was simply a rich person, who owned a sun-blocking suit, out for a bit of exercise.

Down one street and onto another. The pavement had been cleared of debris, like someone had hoped to drive a car down the pothole-ridden road.

"Damn." Julian stopped before the others rounded the corner.

Nola opened her mouth to ask what had happened, but before her lips could form the words, her thoughts shattered, leaving nothing but numb horror behind.

A pile of skulls three feet high blocked the middle of the street. Long bones stuck out of the pile like spikes. Small bones littered the ground around the pile, as though daring anyone who wanted to approach to tread on the dead.

Jeremy wrapped an arm around Nola's waist, holding her close to his side.

"Definitely not the domes." Raina pointed to the front of the building nearest the pile. The four walls remained relatively intact even though the center of the building had collapsed.

Words in red paint had been scrawled across the black brick.

It is not the living the killers need fear.
It's the dead who will haunt their every step.
The dead who stand in judgment.
The dead who will form a mountain of bones the living can no longer ignore.

Nola shivered, the feeling of being watched by thousands of eyes setting goose bumps on her flesh.

"This took time," Raina said, "and a hell of a lot of work."

"By whom?" Julian walked as close to the pile of skulls as he could without stepping on the scattered bones.

"Is it bad if I really don't want to know?" Nola said.

"No," Jeremy said.

"Change of plans, kids." Raina pulled her knife from her belt. "We aren't going to pack it up and go home just yet. This city just got a lot more interesting."

Kieran turned away from the painted words. "How are we going to find them?"

"We're not," Jeremy said. "We're not going to go looking for a crazy person. There would be no use in it."

"I do not believe this is the work of one disturbed individual," Julian said.

"Exactly," Raina said, "and a whole band of crazies, that's something I can work with."

"How do you expect to find a bunch of lunatics when we can't find Gentry?" Jeremy's voice echoed off the brick walls.

"We're not going looking for the crazies." Raina laughed. "We're going to make them come to us."

"But—" Jeremy began.

"Feel free to run back to the mountain on your own, if you like," Raina said. "Of course, you would be disobeying your commander since Emanuel placed me in charge. I speak with his voice. And I say we're staying."

Jeremy tightened his grip on Nola. "Yes, ma'am."

"Perfect." Raina clapped. "Now, let's set fire to this pile of bones and see who comes running because we ruined their art project."

"What?" Nola said.

"I liked the *yes, ma'am* better," Raina said. "Kieran, give me your burny bottle."

Kieran placed his hands over his pockets. "I need it. I can use it—"

"I can use it to make a fire," Raina said. "A big fire."

Kieran stared at Raina for a long moment.

Nola wished she could see behind the thick veil that protected his face from the sun.

"Fine." Kieran pulled a bottle from his pocket. "And if this doesn't burn bright enough, or whoever built this doesn't come but the Outer Guard do?"

"Then we get to kill a few Outer Guard," Raina said.

Jeremy stiffened.

"Sorry," Raina said. "We get to kill a few mass murderers to go with the set we blew up by the tunnels. You didn't seem too mad about spilling Domer blood then."

"We weren't looking for a fight then," Jeremy said. "We were trying to get out of a hole in the ground without being penned in and slaughtered."

"We're always penned in." Kieran threw the glass bottle at the base of the skull pile.

Nola covered her eyes as the glass smashed, but no explosion came. A scent of chemicals strong enough to strip flesh from bone wafted over her. She peered between her fingers.

"No big bang this time. Give me your knife." Raina held her hand out to Nola.

"Why?" Nola gripped the hilt of her blade.

"Because I like my knives and know how to use them," Raina said.

Julian walked to the front of the building, yanking a chunk of mortar and brick free.

"Knife." Raina snapped her fingers. "Now."

"I'll keep you safe." Jeremy placed his hand on Nola's back.

She pulled her blade from its sheath, feeling naked as Raina lifted the knife from her palm.

"This should do." Julian passed the chunk of debris to Raina.

"You know me so well." Raina took the hunk and threw it at the base of the pile where the bottle had landed. She flipped Nola's knife over in her hand a few times as though testing the balance, then threw the blade at the stone.

A hint of a spark flashed before a cloud of flames soared five feet into the air, enveloping the skulls.

"And now we hide." Raina skirted around the side of the building where the words had been painted.

"What was that?" Nola covered her nose with her shirt as she ran after Raina.

"One of the base chemicals in Vamp," Julian said. "I suppose it's not a wonder that when poorly used, the results are disastrous."

"The explosion at 5th and Nightland," Nola asked, "how did she do it?"

"Mixed two chemicals together that hate each other," Kieran said.

"Is that kind of stuff in Graylock?" Nola asked.

Raina leapt over a seven-foot high portion of wall and out of sight. Kieran jumped out of view behind her.

"I wish I knew." Jeremy stopped before the wall, waiting for Nola to jump up and in.

Nola bent her knees, judging the height of the wall as she leapt. The freedom of flying sent a thrill through her as she reached the apex of her jump and looked to the ground below.

Raina and Kieran stood together, facing twelve people with arrows nocked in their bows.

Nola couldn't change the trajectory of her jump. Couldn't do anything but land boxed in with the enemy. Stumbling as her feet hit the ground, Nola opened her mouth to scream, but an arrow three feet away pointed at her face kept her silent.

The *thump* of Jeremy landing came an instant later. Nola didn't see his arm move as he grabbed her, shoving her behind his back.

Another *thump* came as Julian landed.

Nola tried to move enough to see the enemy they faced, but Jeremy kept both arms behind him, holding her still.

"Now that our numbers are better balanced," Raina said, "let's have a chat."

CHAPTER FIVE

The heat of Jeremy's back pressed on Nola's face, making it difficult to breathe.

"You don't have anything to say?" Raina said.

The shuffle of moving feet came from the other side of the room.

"You just want to stand there and point arrows at me and my friends?" Danger dripped from Raina's words.

"Perhaps we started off on the wrong foot," Julian said. "We aren't here to hurt anyone. In fact, we had assumed this building to be empty. Our mistake, of course. We're more than happy to be on our way."

"You lit a fire," a female voice said. "You desecrated the dead."

"I think the person who jumbled a bunch of bones together is really the one who started the desecration game," Raina said.

Nola pushed against Jeremy's arm, inching far enough to the side to peer around his shoulder.

The twelve still faced them, pointing their arrows at Jeremy, Kieran, Raina, and Julian. The bows were the only sign the twelve belonged together. Their clothes were a tattered mix of leather like the vampires wore, the scraps homeless city dwellers survived in, and clothes that looked like factory uniforms. The woman in the center of the group wore a black, dome-issued jacket, and stood with the air of a leader.

"We came here to honor the dead," the leader said. "We came to this city to be sure the world would never forget the atrocities committed here. Now murderers have ruined our monument."

"We aren't murderers," Nola said.

"Monsters," a man dressed in leather hissed.

"That is a more accurate description," Raina said.

"You've done enough damage," the leader said, "and you'll never stop." She pulled back her bowstring.

"We haven't done any damage." Kieran stepped to the side, blocking Nola's view. "We set the fire outside, but it was only because we wanted to find whoever built the monument."

"Maybe not my best idea," Raina said.

"Crazies," a man said. "You called us crazies."

"An evidence-based term," Raina said.

"Raina, play nice," Kieran said. "We didn't understand why you'd put the bones together, but it makes sense now. A few hundred years in the future, when people have forgotten about this city and the terrible things the domes did, someone will find that pile of bones, and they won't be able to deny something horrific happened here. Maybe they won't understand the details, but they'll know. Humans lived in this city. They had children and homes. And they all died."

"Because of you," the leader said. "A whole garden of people wiped out by your hand."

"Nope," Raina said. "That's where you're just plain wrong. I can see where the confusion comes from, what with our fancy sun suits and those two looking so healthy and strong."

"Dome blood," a voice whispered.

"Look at my eyes," Raina said. A *rustle* of fabric came from her direction. "I'm straight out of Nightland. So are my other fashionably-dressed friends."

"Vampires? Here?"

"We came to see if the Outer Guard were still in the city," Julian said. "We wanted to know if they were still hurting people."

"That's why we wanted to talk to you," Jeremy said.

"You're not a vampire," a man said.

"No." Nola wiggled out from behind Jeremy, pushing against his arm until he set her free. "We did live in the domes. After they blew up the bridge, we knew we couldn't stay anymore. We escaped and found our way to Nightland."

"You have strong dome blood," the leader said. "Like the ones who slaughter."

"We're not like them," Jeremy said. "They're murderers. That's why we left."

Nola took Jeremy's hand, offering the only comfort she could.

"We'd very much like to talk to you," Julian said. "Perhaps if you could lower your bows—"

"Vampires who are afraid of bows?" a boy said.

"I was shot by one of your people only last night," Julian said. "I honestly don't care to repeat the experience."

"We didn't shoot you," the leader said.

"He was shot with an arrow." Kieran turned, showing the bow he had across his back. "We were attacked in the dark without warning."

"Not us," a man with a white beard said. "We don't do that sort of thing. Them, not us."

"Them?" Nola asked.

"Very descriptive," Raina said.

"We don't hurt people," the leader said. "We only defend, never attack."

"It's a miracle you're still alive." Raina laughed, her shoulders easing.

"It's not about living," the boy said. "It's about what will come after."

"What do you mean?" Nola stepped closer to him.

The ground crunched beneath Jeremy's boots as he moved up right behind her.

"After we're gone," the leader said. "When we're nothing more than bones."

"Ah," Julian said. "I can see why you're so upset with our disturbing your work. You have my deepest apologies." He gave a bow, which the leader acknowledged with a nod of her head.

"I'm sorry," Nola said, "I still don't understand."

The leader lowered her bow, though the other eleven stayed alert.

"Our lives can be nothing but pain," the leader said. "The death that will claim us is the peace of oblivion. When those who come after find this place, they will know our stories. Our work will live on. Our blood and pain will teach those who come after not to commit the same terrible mistakes that led us here."

"You're teachers," Kieran said.

The leader spread her hands toward the sky. "Of students who will live long after we're gone."

"We should leave you to your work," Julian said. "Our task is very different from yours, but we must attend to it nonetheless."

"We will not harm those who do not harm us," the leader said. "We will not have murder be the lesson we leave behind."

"Thank you," Julian said.

"Can we ask you something?" Jeremy stepped in front of Nola.

The leader stared at him for a long moment. "There is no danger in questions, only in answers."

"There's a girl," Jeremy said. "She'd be in a guard uniform but not working with the Outer Guard. She was helping in the city when the fire packs blew, trying to save people."

"We weren't in the city then," the man with the beard said. "We didn't bring our work here until the city fell."

"There are only guards that slaughter left in the city. The man who looks like a spider made sure of that," the leader said.

"Salinger is still here?" Jeremy clenched his hands into fists.

"Don't know the spider's name," the leader said. "Never got close enough to ask. They prowl the city, looking for anyone they can kill. The city's been declared off limits. People are only allowed on the highway."

"The buildings are too dangerous to go near after the fire." The boy's face twisted in disgust. "Anyone found here is considered an enemy of the domes."

"A hostile threat," Julian said, "to be exterminated by the Outer Guard."

"We've been here for two weeks. There hasn't been anyone but wolves and dying lambs on the streets," the leader said.

"If the girl you ask for really is good, she's either dead or gone," the bearded man said.

"Gone?" Nola placed a hand on Jeremy's arm, stilling his trembling. "What do you mean by gone?"

"To the wilds, the waters, or to them," to leader said.

"You all have spent far too long in isolation," Raina said.

"The wilds." The leader pointed west toward the mountains Nightland had made their home. "The waters." She pointed south. "Them." She pointed north.

Jeremy closed his eyes. "You have no idea where she would have gone?"

"Most go north," the boy said. "But most who go north don't last very long. Too many arrows flying."

"Who are the people in the north?" Raina asked. "Refugees from the city?"

"Been there for a long time," the leader said. "Don't know when it started. Don't know where they hide. But you go there, the arrows fly."

"Thank you for your help." Julian bowed again. "And for the good work you're doing."

"And that's our cue to jump on out of here." Raina turned toward the wall, ignoring the arrows still aimed at her.

"Where did you all live?" Nola asked. "Before you came to the city, I mean?"

"Far from the eyes of the domes," the leader said. "Where we can do our work in peace."

"Right. Thank you." Nola gave a little bow.

"I'll go first," Raina said. "Don't follow until I say so. Not to sound like I don't trust these fine people, but I hate to repeat my mistakes too often." Raina jumped over the wall, disappearing onto the street beyond.

Nola held her breath, waiting for the sounds of an attack.

"Come on out," Raina said. "Nothing here but smoke and bones."

"Kieran," Jeremy said, "you next."

Kieran turned to Jeremy. He froze for a moment before nodding and jumping over the wall.

"Nola, you go," Jeremy said.

She grazed the back of his hand with her fingers as she leapt into the air. The feeling of flying held no joy this time. The street came into view with only Kieran and Raina in sight. Both had their weapons drawn as they scanned the block. Nola landed between them and reached for her knife. Her stomach dropped as her fingers found the empty sheath. She pulled out her Guard gun instead.

Jeremy landed four feet in front of Nola, and Julian arrived a moment after. Jeremy moved to Nola's side, a knife in one hand and a gun in the other.

"You in there," Raina called over the wall. "Either run or find a better place to hide. The Outer Guard are coming."

"What?" Nola asked.

"Listen," Jeremy said.

Nola's pulse thundered in her ears. She listened past the thumping, searching for a different sound. The faster beat of running feet pounded under the rhythm of her racing heart.

"Outer Guard?" Nola asked.

"We need to go," Kieran said.

"What about them?" Nola turned back to the brick wall that blocked the twelve from view.

"We warned them. That's all we can do." Julian took off down the street piled with still-smoking skulls.

"Run, Nola," Jeremy said.

She forced her feet to move. "We started the fire. If the guards are coming toward the smoke, it's our fault—"

"Don't," Kieran said.

Nola faltered as they reached the small bones strewn across the ground. The bones reached too far down the road for her to be able to jump across. She gritted her teeth as the bones cracked beneath her feet.

"We should help them hide," Nola said when her feet found clear pavement.

"They can't run like us," Raina said. "We can't slow to their pace, and there's too many of them for us to carry."

"It's wrong to leave them," Nola said.

"If we stay, we'll have to fight the Outer Guard," Jeremy said.

"Jeremy, I—"

"We can't afford that kind of fight," Jeremy cut across Nola. "We have to get back to Emanuel and tell him what we've learned. We risk all of Nightland if we don't get back to him."

"Right." Nola blinked away the stinging in her eyes. "We have to get back."

"They've survived the city for two weeks," Kieran said. "They've got weapons. The Teachers have as good a chance on their own as they do with us leading them to the base of the mountain and abandoning them."

The rats will sink the ship.

They ran down a long row of tumbledown warehouses and onto the wide highway that surrounded the city. A sprawling mass of tents had sprung up in the middle of the road. Few people moved around the makeshift dwellings.

One man dived back into a red patchwork tent as soon as he spotted them. An older woman sat down on the pavement, as though daring them to force her to move.

"We can't head straight up the road," Kieran said.

Raina took the lead, heading toward the path Nola had always followed to the mountain that had become Nightland's new home.

Nola swallowed her questions as Raina led them past the first set of derelict houses. The fire hadn't spread across the expanse of the highway. These homes had been lost to abandonment long before the Outer Guard decided to extinguish life in the city.

Raina led them off the main road, cutting north through the trees.

Toward them.

They had gone to the city seeking information and were returning with a dozen pieces to a puzzle that made no sense.

Traps set in the ruins of Nightland. Salinger still in the domes. People living to the north. Teachers sneaking past the Guard patrols to leave marks for future generations to find.

If Salinger is still in the domes, what is Captain Ridgeway doing?

Nola glanced to Jeremy who ran by her side, determination burning in his eyes.

She needed to talk to him away from the others.

Soon.

They sprinted past dead and dying trees. The marks of human life littered the forest. A tent someone had abandoned. A wooden cross pounded into the ground. Empty food cans rusting in the dirt. After a few miles, Raina headed west, and the signs of life petered away.

"Why would people head north and not west?" Nola asked.

"Easier terrain to cross," Julian said. "That and fear."

"Fear of what?" Jeremy asked.

"Vampires," Raina said.

The ground sloped up, toward the base of the mountain.

"No one knows where Nightland is," Nola said.

"Of course not," Raina said. "But we had to keep people away while the architects built our home. Having angry vampires prowling the edge of the woods kept people away for long enough that legends spread and everyone started avoiding the area entirely."

"A rather brilliant plan," Julian said.

"Well, I am a genius," Raina said.

They kept to the trees as they climbed the mountain, following an unfamiliar path. Even as the incline increased, Nola's breath still came easily, and the exertion didn't burn her legs.

It's not right.

She missed the burning. The feeling of fighting for each step.

But then I'd be dead.

Familiar mountain peaks came into view. The sun sat high in the sky, giving crisp detail to the trees that still grew near the summit, above the reach of the heavy, acid-filled clouds.

They arrived in a basin nestled in the mountainside. A mossy ledge poked out over the clearing. Raina jumped to the ledge and out of sight without pause. Julian sprang up after her.

Nola didn't bother asking if Jeremy wanted to go next before launching herself at the moss. She planted her palms on the surface, and pushed herself up and over the edge into the entrance of Nightland.

CHAPTER SIX

Three guards stood just out of reach of the sun, each with their weapon raised.

"Knock, knock," Raina said. "Guess who's come home."

"You made it back." Stell, a vampire with bright blond hair let her sword drop back into its sheath. "And here I'd bet you'd be gone for good."

"Don't place bets based on wishes," Raina said. "Now get out of my way."

Stell gave a tightlipped smile but backed against the stone of the corridor wall. The other two guards jumped aside without hesitation.

Raina stepped out of the sun and pulled off her hat, shaking her scarlet and purple streaked hair. "As much as not dying is great, I really hate these suits."

Stell growled.

"Don't bother with jealousy, sweetie. You're not important enough to ever get to wear a sunny," Raina cooed as she sauntered down the hall.

Nola resisted the urge to hide her face as she passed Stell's vicious glare.

"You don't have to antagonize her like that," Kieran said.

"Sure I do." Raina unzipped her suit, letting the upper half fall over her belt, revealing her usual black leather top.

The tunnel wound up through the mountain. Every few minutes, they passed a window cut into the rock wall, looking out over the mountain they'd just climbed.

Nola paused at the last window, leaning out to see the city. The blackness of it all seemed like a sore on the land. A horrible blemish brought on by disease.

"Come on." Jeremy took her hand. "We should get to Emanuel."

"You all go ahead," Raina said. "I'll see Emanuel later."

"Of course," Julian said before Nola could ask why.

The giant metal door to the sparring room stood open. Pairs of vampires sparred in colored squares painted on the ground.

The pair nearest the door spotted Raina and froze, the woman with her knife still raised in the air. Each of the matches stopped as a wave of stillness rippled through the fighters.

Raina raised a hand. "Don't even bother asking."

The fighters cleared a path to the door on the far side of the room.

Despite having chosen Nightland as her home, Nola's skin crawled as she walked the alley between the well-armed vampires.

Raina stopped before the door to the interior tunnel. "Silly me, turn in your toys."

"Really?" Jeremy placed his hands on the weapons at his hips.

"Stell's not fancy enough for a sun suit, and you're not important enough to keep weapons inside Nightland." Raina held her hand out to Jeremy.

He shook his head and unfastened his belt. "Do you really think it's smart to keep people unarmed with Salinger still around?"

"If the domes attack, they'll have to come through the front door," Julian said. "You can claim your weapon on the way to meet them. In the meantime, it's best not to pack a thousand people underground with weapons being carried in the halls. You'll find it greatly increases the mortality rate."

Jeremy handed Raina his belt.

"You too." Raina turned to Nola.

"Just tell them it wasn't me who lost the knife." Nola passed over her belt.

A mousy-looking boy took the weapons from Raina with a bow.

Raina winked at Jeremy and sauntered down the hall with her black metal box, leaving them behind.

"Has she always been like that?" Jeremy said.

"For as long as I've known her," Julian said.

They walked in silence through the stone hallways, passing a woman carrying a crate of mushrooms and a man balancing a stack of clean sheets. Even as they arrived at Emanuel's door, Nola stared longingly down the hall toward the bed that awaited her.

Julian opened the door to Emanuel's library without knocking.

A sense of delight broke through Nola's growing fatigue at the sight of the chandeliers hanging from the ceiling, art adorning the walls, and stuffed bookshelves surrounding the room. In the center of the library sat Emanuel in his red wingback chair, with Eden curled up in his lap as he read her a story.

Emanuel looked up from the book as Julian entered the library.

Nola froze on the threshold, uncertain of disturbing such a rare moment of serenity.

"Go to Bea." Emanuel set Eden down.

The little girl shook her head, sending her black curls flying. "You didn't finish."

"Later, Eden," Emanuel said.

Eden crossed her arms, tucked her chin, and headed for the door at the back of the room.

"Where's Raina?" Emanuel asked as soon as the door shut behind his daughter.

"She'll be here to see you later." Julian climbed out of his sun suit. "This one will need a bit of repair, I'm afraid. I was shot by an arrow."

"An arrow?" Emanuel stood.

"Things didn't go exactly as we'd hoped," Julian said.

"Salinger is still patrolling the city," Jeremy said. "He hasn't gone back to his home domes."

"You saw him?" Wrinkles creased Emanuel's brow.

"No," Nola said. "But we met people who had."

They took turns explaining everything that had happened. Starting with finding people holed up in a house on the way to the city and Julian being shot. Then Nola and Jeremy finding the trap in Nightland. Catching a glimpse of the unharmed domes across the river. Then meeting the Teachers.

"I didn't think the fanatics would come back to the city," Emanuel said. "I was sure they'd died out and we had seen the last of their kind a very long time ago."

"You've heard of the Teachers?" Kieran paused halfway through folding his sun suit.

"Not under that name, but yes." Emanuel tented his fingers under his chin. "I'd heard rumors about people heading north as well."

"Why have I never heard about it?" Kieran asked.

"There are many rumors and legends. I don't choose to waste my time on things that cannot be proven as fact." Emanuel sat in his red chair. "There was talk of tunnels under the city for years before we began construction on Nightland's home underground. If I had listened to them, our people would never have had a sanctuary where we could grow strong enough to come to our true home."

"The people in the north," Nola said, "are they really violent? I mean, if they were killing people, wouldn't the domes have noticed?"

Emanuel looked to Jeremy.

Jeremy ran his hands over his face before speaking. "I never heard anything about settlements beyond the city limits. The domes decreed that people could only live in this area if they stayed between the highway and the river a long time ago. I don't know if they chose to ignore the people lurking in the wild or if they were just so damn cocky and sure everyone would follow their laws they never bothered to look."

"What do we do about them, though?" Nola took Jeremy's arm. "If the people in the north like to attack, what happens if they find us?"

"We need to worry about Salinger first," Jeremy said. "We can defend ourselves against bows and arrows. We can't fight fire packs."

"I need to think," Emanuel said. "You've all done very well. Thank you for risking your lives to protect Nightland."

"Of course." Julian nodded and headed toward the door through which Eden had disappeared.

"I want to get these supplies to my dad." Kieran followed Julian.

"We should find T and Beauford," Nola said.

"You need rest first." Jeremy brushed a stray curl from Nola's forehead. They turned to go back out into the hall.

"Jeremy," Emanuel said, "I'm sorry you didn't find your sister."

Jeremy said nothing as he closed the door.

"Be careful," Nola said in a voice too soft for even Emanuel to hear.

"Of what?" Jeremy said.

"Emanuel isn't a person you want as an enemy." Nola held Jeremy's hand as they walked toward the long corridor of sleeping quarters.

"Why did he need to mention my sister?" Jeremy said. "It's not like he cares about her."

"You're right, he doesn't," Nola said. "He'll never think of a rogue Domer as someone he should worry about." She pressed her fingers to Jeremy's lips before he could speak. "But he cares about us because we help him. Letting us make Nightland our home is in the best interest of Emanuel's people. As one person trying to survive on the outside, Gentry means nothing to Nightland. But *when* we find her, we need Emanuel to see how valuable she is so she can come live here with us. It'll be a lot easier to convince Emanuel that having a second Ridgeway under his protection will be best for Nightland if he likes you."

Jeremy wrapped his arms around Nola and kissed the top of her head. "Isn't it good enough that he likes you?"

"He likes me because I stole medicine from the domes to save his daughter." Nola tipped her chin up, brushing her lips against his. "You've risked your life to find information for Nightland twice now. You've done enough for him to consider you a part of his family. Just try to be civil."

Jeremy kissed Nola.

She stood up on her toes, leaning into their embrace.

"I'll play nice with the vampires," Jeremy said.

"Good."

They stopped in front of the door to Jeremy's room. He lived only a few doors down from the entrance to Emanuel's library, where the leader of Night-land could keep a close watch on the Outer Guard who had betrayed the domes.

Nola leaned in to kiss Jeremy one more time.

"Stay," Jeremy whispered. "Please stay."

A rush of heat flooded Nola's face.

"We both need to sleep." Jeremy caressed Nola's cheek. "Let me wake up knowing you're safe."

A little bubble of contentment grew amidst the worry and confusion shouting in Nola's mind. "It would be really great to sleep."

Jeremy opened his door, letting Nola enter first.

The small stone room barely fit the bed, dresser, and chair Jeremy had been provided. One light hung from the ceiling, next to a hole that led up to the surface, allowing fresh air to filter in through the mass of the mountain.

Weight pressed on Nola's eyelids at the sight of the bed. "I shouldn't be this tired. I slept a couple of days ago."

"Your brain has processed too much information since the last time you slept." Jeremy tugged on his bootlaces. "Even superheroes need sleep."

The journey into the city, the time they'd spent there before they'd run back, all of it had taken less than a day. But the running, fear, and pain all blurred together in a swirl that moved too quickly for her mind to focus on one moment at a time.

Nola sat on the chair to untie her shoes, blinking to bat away the excess noise surrounding the failure that hurt most. "We're not going to stop looking for Gentry. You know that, right?"

Jeremy sank down on the edge of the bed. "How can we possibly find her? If she's still alive, which is a big *if*."

Nola sat next to Jeremy, wrapping her arm around his waist. "Gentry is strong and brave. She's had training. She's out there somewhere."

"Where?" Grief filled Jeremy's eyes. "If she left right after the city burned, she could be hundreds of miles away by now."

"I..." There was no argument she could make. With how fast Gentry could move...

We might never find her.

"We'll keep trying," Nola said. "We're not going to give up on her."

"I can't drag you around the wild searching for her." Jeremy dug his knuckles into his temples. "If you had gotten into that room first, if I hadn't been able to figure out how to open the door...I can't risk your life, Nola."

She knelt in front of him, pulling his hands from his face to make him look into her eyes.

"We're in this together, Jeremy," Nola said. "You and me. I love you."

"We can't get to the domes," Jeremy said. "There's no way for us to get more Graylock."

"We can heal without more doses. It'll be slow, but—"

"But what if that doesn't work? Graylock isn't even as old as ReVamp. Our ability to heal could lessen with time. We don't know." He kissed the palm of her hand. "I have to protect you. From Salinger, and whatever drove people from the domes to turn into zombies, and the people in the north, and the vampires here."

Nola sat on his lap. Jeremy laid his head on her chest.

"You can't worry about all of that," Nola said. "It's too much for one person."

"I have to worry about all of it," Jeremy said. "I love you. I have to find a way to keep all of this awfulness from hurting you."

Nola lifted his chin and kissed him, savoring the taste of his lips. She let her mouth linger on his for a long moment.

"You can't protect me," Nola said. "It's not possible. But we can face whatever is coming together. And if that means searching the wild for Gentry, then building a boat to cross the river to the domes, and breaking through the glass to find out how to make more Graylock, we'll do it."

He kissed her again, exploring her lips.

Nola's heart flipped in her chest, shattering the weight the dying world had thrust upon her. She pulled herself closer, wanting to feel the beat of his heart pulse through her.

He lifted her from his lap and laid her down on the bed. Her body throbbed from her toes to the tips of her fingers as she reached for him.

"You should sleep," he said.

"Jeremy."

"We have to sleep." He crawled into bed next to her, staring at the stone ceiling above them.

She lifted his arm, finding the spot on his shoulder that seemed to have been designed as a place for her to lay her head.

"We're going to be okay," she said. "Both of us. We're going to be okay."

He kissed the top of her head but didn't say anything.

Say something. Do something.

She couldn't think of a way to help either of them. Fatigue took her before a plan could form.

CHAPTER SEVEN

"It's really all gone?" T leaned across the table as far as her ever-growing belly would allow, pushing yet another portion of mushroom soup toward Nola.

The scent of the thick soup filled the room Nola shared with Beauford and T.

"There's nothing left in the city," Nola said. "The fire packs got everything between the highway and the water."

Beauford gave a low whistle. "When the domes want a mass slaughter, they do it right."

"I can't even picture it, the whole city just gone. All those people." T brushed a tear off her freckled nose.

"It's awful." Nola fought the urge to lie and spare her friend. "And the people on the highway are in tents."

"They'll be dead soon enough." Beauford pushed away his half-full soup bowl. "One bad sickness, and it'll get almost everyone. Acid rain comes back, and they won't have anywhere to hide."

"There are the houses," T said. "The falling down ones on the little road west of the highway."

"Not enough for everyone," Beauford said. "Unless an illness cuts down their numbers first."

T cradled her belly as she stood and paced the small space between the table and the four beds. "Is there a way we could convince Emanuel to take more people in?"

Nola picked up her spoon and took two bites of soup. Eating didn't make the answer any easier. "We don't have the resources." Self-loathing curdled the food on its way to Nola's stomach. "There are only a few empty rooms left in the tunnels. Those could hold forty people if we packed them in. But then we'd have to feed them."

"Couldn't we make it work?" T said. "Cut down just a bit on how much the humans eat?"

"I—maybe," Nola said, "if we knew when we'd be able to use the garden again. But we can't count on the weather. We don't know how long it'll be before the freezes stop. Forty people could mean the difference of a few more weeks before starvation if it takes too long for spring to come."

"Is it wrong of us not to try?" T said. "There are kids out there. People's children who are hungry and cold. We could at least take in the little ones."

Beauford stood and hugged T. Her shoulders shook with silent sobs.

"I should go," Nola said. "I have work to do."

Neither T nor Beauford said anything to stop her as Nola ducked out into the hall. She closed the door behind her and leaned against the wall.

"I sound like them," Nola whispered.

Which them?

She'd hated the domes for ignoring the suffering in the city. Hated Nightland for causing pain by attacking the domes to steal supplies.

I'm just as much a monster as the rest of them.

Nola walked down the corridor, passing a flock of chattering children surrounding a woman who looked like she hadn't slept in a week. The children had full heads of hair and skin free from sores. They bombarded the woman with questions in voices so loud, the sound could only have been made by lungs undamaged by polluted air.

The children stuck on the outside will never have a chance to bounce around with so much energy.

Nola clenched her fists, letting her nails dig into her palms. She didn't know where her feet were carrying her until she stopped in front of the door to Kieran's lab. She knocked before allowing herself to think.

"Come in," Kieran's voice came through the door.

Nola's hand froze above the doorknob. She worked in the lab, had spent dozens of hours inside.

Don't be an idiot.

She opened the door, stepped into the lab, and snapped the door shut behind her.

"Nola." Kieran looked up from his microscope. "I didn't think you were working on samples today."

"I'm not." Nola's curls bounced around her as she shook her head. "I just needed…"

"Needed what?" Kieran's dark eyebrows pinched together.

"Convince me we're better than them." The words tumbled out. "Tell me why us leaving the people in the tent city is better than the domes leaving the city to rot. Tell me I was right to choose Nightland over the domes. Over my mother. Tell me I'm not a horrible murderer for sitting safely in these tunnels while other people are suffering. That there's a way out that doesn't end with the domes penning us in here and slaughtering the few people Emanuel has managed to save." Nola took a gasping breath. Tears streamed down her face. "A thousand people hidden here in the mountain. And that's it. We're supposed to say this is good enough? The rest of them are just dead whether or not they've stopped breathing?" Sobs overtook her words.

Kieran stood, hesitating before walking over to Nola. "Can I hold you?"

Nola nodded, stepping into the embrace. His body didn't envelope her as Jeremy's broad shoulders did, but a familiar safety came with the feel of his arms around her. She leaned her forehead on his shoulder, letting her tears fall onto his shirt.

"It's not enough." Kieran pressed his cheek to her hair. "The people we've managed to protect in Nightland aren't enough. But we can't take them all in. We can't even get them here without the domes finding us."

"How do we live with that?"

"I don't know. Try to find ways to not feel so helpless. Work to make Nightland sustainable for T's baby so that her child will never understand what we feel like right now."

"I don't want to be like the Domers." Nola wrapped her arms around Kieran. "I couldn't survive being a monster in a glass castle. I don't think I can live as a monster in a stone fortress either. I can't hide and wait for them all to die out."

"I don't think we're going to be doing much hiding."

Nola looked up. Her face was only a few inches from his. Not so very long ago she would have leaned in, finding comfort in the feel of his lips against hers.

"Why won't we be hiding?" Nola asked.

Kieran shook his head and took a step back to the edge of the table.

"Kieran?" She shivered at the hollow feeling growing in her gut.

"Emanuel doesn't like the idea of waiting either. There are too many hostile groups, too many scenarios that end with Nightland being attacked."

"So what does he want to do?" Nola reached for her hip, to where her knife would have rested.

"No idea," Kieran said. "He's planning something. We'll just have to wait for him to tell us what that something is."

"Are you okay with that?" Nola asked. "With waiting for other people to make decisions for us?"

Kieran smiled, and, for a moment, Nola caught a glimpse of the boy she'd once loved.

"I'd rather be in on the meetings." Kieran shrugged and moved back to his microscope. "But then I remember I'm seventeen. Emanuel and Raina have been working to build this place for more than twice my lifetime. Julian's been helping Nightland since before I was born. I want to be a part of the solution, but I have to let them make the decisions."

"And what if you don't agree with the choices they make?"

"We worry about that if the time comes," Kieran said. "In the meantime, we trust them. And we keep working."

"Right." Nola wiped the tears off her cheeks. "Right. I should go get some samples from the field."

"You don't have to," Kieran said.

"I do." Nola moved to her tiny corner of the lab, taking her bag, a case of empty vials, and a stack of clean cloths.

"Is he okay?" Kieran asked.

"Jeremy?"

"Yeah." Kieran pressed his eye to his microscope.

Nola dug her fingers through her curls. "No, he really isn't. My mom is still in the domes, but I know she's not hurting anyone. His dad is still in the domes, but he could have given the order to drop the fire packs. We need to find Gentry, but I have no idea how. He wants to protect me and keep me safe, but I can't protect him."

Kieran laid both his hands out flat on his worktable. "Loving you got him out of the domes. He's here because of you. He's out of reach of the Incorporation because of you. None of us are strong enough to protect the people we love from the nightmares of this world. But he loves you, and you love him. That's a lot."

"Kieran—"

"You should get down to the field." Kieran placed a new slide under his microscope.

"I'll bring some samples back in a bit." The weight of a broken heart pulled against her as she left the lab.

The vials clinked against each other as her bag bounced on her hip. She didn't want to go farther underground. She wanted to be in the fresh air. To stand on top of the mountain under the stars and pretend the human race had never touched the valley below. There would be no city of ash and bones waiting to be found by future generations. No illness, no pollution, no want. Just a rock drifting through space with sparkling stars as its traveling companions.

Nola reached the entrance to the low cave. The door blocking the path had been carved to fit the natural curvature of the stone, leaving gentle waves around the edges.

Just work. The best thing you can do is work.

The door creaked as she opened it, almost as though protesting the existence of the person who had dared to close it.

Nola took one last deep breath and stepped into the narrow tunnel.

The architects who had built the caves had spent years carving out the corridors and rooms that made up the bulk of Nightland. No one seemed to know if the architects had gone looking for the caves toward the base of the mountain, or if they had just stumbled on the path that cut deep into the earth by chance.

Most of the passage had been left in its original state, the floor uneven as the walls bent and twisted to the mountain's will. In places where the tunnel had gotten too tight for a person to pass, the architects had left their mark on the stone, carving out smooth sections to guide the traveler in the right direction, ever downward to the root of the mountain itself.

Nola kept her pace steady, fighting the urge to sprint through the passage and dive into the wide space below.

"I've faced worse than stone. I'm not afraid of you." Even as she said the words, the thumping in her chest beat its disagreement.

At last, the tunnel opened up into a wide cave. Only a few lights had been hung in odd corners, but Graylock gave her the ability to see in the dim shadows. The scent of stone and water filled Nola's lungs, breaking through the hum of her fear. The massive lake at the back of the cavern kept the air moist, allowing Kieran's crops to flourish.

He had carefully placed different types of mushrooms throughout the cave. Some grew by the water constantly dripping down the face of the rock. Others peeped out of crevices where the stone had cracked long ago. But the long mushroom beds built of tarred wood were the real prize for Nightland, even if a few of the residents weren't overjoyed by the thought of anyone feeding them more fungus.

Nola walked the edge of the wide cavern, letting her fingers trail along the cold stone wall. The stalagmites hid troves of mushrooms behind them, but they also provided places for a person to lurk unseen.

Since when am I afraid of people?

She shook her head, trying to fling aside the question.

But the nagging thought remained. If she lined up the evil against the innocent, she didn't know which tally would be higher.

"Maybe the world is right to try and kill us all." Her voice carried around the cavern, but there was no one in the shadows to answer her.

She stopped at the edge of the lake, kneeling down and dipping her hands into the chill water.

Goose bumps crawled up her arms, but the temperature didn't hurt her fingers. Graylock protected her from the cold, as Vamp protected the vampires.

They'd all had to change to fight the disease and contamination that had taken over the outside world.

The domes had locked their people behind glass, relying on technology to filter the air and water and block the worst of the sun's rays.

Nightland had dug deep, relying on the weight of the earth for protection.

"It doesn't make sense." Nola took off her bag and kicked her shoes aside. She stepped out into the water, letting the cold seep through the legs of her pants. She sloshed farther out into the lake. She didn't shiver as the water reached her knees. Her nerves didn't set fire to her skin, warning her to get out of the cold. "It's not right."

She took another step. The ground beneath her disappeared. She plummeted down, falling deeper into the water than she had imagined the lake could reach. The dim light overhead faded, leaving her surrounded by crushing darkness.

Even as her lungs screamed for air, her body cared nothing for the cold.

Graylock protects me.

She kicked up toward the surface, fighting to find the open air above. She kicked again as the horrible thought that she had somehow swum the wrong way pinched her lungs.

A hand reached out, seizing her wrist. Arms she would recognize even after a thousand years wrapped around her, dragging her up. Her head broke through the surface, and she gasped, sucking in wonderful air.

"Nola." Jeremy dragged her onto the edge of the rocks. "Are you okay?" He pushed her mop of sopping curls away from her face.

"I'm fine," Nola coughed. "What are you doing down here?"

"What the hell were you thinking? You can barely swim."

"Of course I can't. We're from the domes. We're lucky they teach kids to tread water in a tank." Nola tried to stand, but Jeremy gripped her shoulders, keeping her sitting in the waist-high water.

"You could've drowned."

"I didn't know there was a ledge." Nola took Jeremy's face in her hands.

"What the hell were you doing in the water?" He pressed his forehead to Nola's. "If Kieran hadn't told me to come down here—"

"Kieran gave you permission?"

"I could've lost you," Jeremy said.

"I needed to see if I would get cold." Nola pressed her lips to Jeremy's cheek.

Even as they sat dripping in the cold water, his skin held onto its warmth. She pressed her lips to his, breathing in his heat.

"Nola," he whispered.

She pulled herself closer, reveling in the faint thumping of the blood pounding through his veins. She wrapped her legs around him, keeping herself pressed to him as her fingers found the bottom his shirt.

He started to speak, but she silenced him, deepening their kiss, only stopping to drag his shirt over his head. His lips found her neck, trailing kisses out to her shoulder as he unfastened the buttons of her shirt.

Flesh met flesh, and the world disappeared.

CHAPTER EIGHT

"We've been thinking about it all wrong." Nola sat at the table in Emanuel's kitchen, Jeremy by her side. "All of us. Nightland, the domes, everyone."

Emanuel leaned back in his chair, but did nothing to silence her.

"In the domes"—Nola looked to Kieran, Julian, and Dr. Wynne—"we always assumed the only way people would be able to survive long term was to lock themselves away from danger."

"It has been a very effective, if morally unsound, solution," Dr. Wynne said.

"The vampires turned to drugs." Nola looked to Raina. "You found a way to change your bodies to survive."

"And it's been grand." Raina raised her tumbler of blood. "Cheers to surviving."

"You copied the domes, Emanuel," Nola pressed on. "You saw them build a home and hide away, and you created your own version here in the mountain. And the domes saw how strong Vamp made you, and they made Graylock to mimic you."

"And now we have two strong opponents pitted against each other," Emanuel said. "The survival of the domes puts us in danger."

"But see what you just did?" Nola said. "You left out the people to the north."

"I'm not too worried about the people with sticks," Raina said.

"I agree they're not the largest of our concerns, but I must say being shot was wholly unpleasant," Julian said.

"I'm not talking about them attacking." Nola gripped the edge of the table.

"I'm talking about them surviving. Emanuel, you made the same mistake as the domes."

"I prefer to think of myself as different from those monsters," Emanuel said.

Nola took a deep breath. "But you're both cocky. I'm sorry, but you are."

Jeremy laid his hand on her thigh.

"You were all so busy thinking you'd found the one path to surviving, you didn't think about there being another way," Nola said. "The way the people up north have been surviving on the outside."

"It's an interesting point," Dr. Wynne said. "In mirroring our enemy, we've been neglecting to look away from our own reflection."

"But you're assuming the people up north are actually living a reasonable life and not starving in a ditch," Raina said.

"If they have enough people to let *arrows rain down*, there's got to be a good number of them," Jeremy said. "If it were only a few archers, it would be easy for people fleeing north to slip past them."

"The person I fought after Julian was shot was human," Kieran said. "No extra strength, nothing like that."

"Which is why you killed him," Raina said. "He's dead, you're alive, so I feel pretty good about our odds of beating the Northerners."

"You don't get it." Nola made herself let go of the edge of the table. She folded her hands in front of her. *Just like Mom.* "I'm not talking about who might come up the mountain to attack us. I'm talking about pure humans surviving on the outside."

"Careful, little girl," Raina said. "Every person in this room would be dead if they had been left as *pure human*. Don't make me think you regret surviving."

"No, no." Dr. Wynne tapped the tip of his nose. "I see what Nola means."

"I'm not sure I do," Emanuel said.

"They've found a way to build some kind of community," Nola said.

"That's got nothing to do with us unless they want to attack," Raina said.

"It has everything to do with us if we don't want to be like the domes." Nola's words echoed around the kitchen. "We can't bring all the people who survived the fire in the city here, I understand that. All our humans would starve if we tried to feed hundreds of extra people. But if we could find out how the people in the north are surviving, we might be able to help the people from the city find a way to provide for themselves."

Kieran pushed away from the wall to pace behind Emanuel.

"I have a thousand people here," Emanuel said. "One thousand lives are depending on my ability to keep them safe."

"I thought Nightland was bigger than that," Nola said. "Do you remember the first time I came to Nightland?"

Kieran froze behind Emanuel.

"You said the domes want to preserve human DNA," Nola said, "but you wanted to protect what it means to be human. Being human means learning and helping. If we ignore the fact that a group of people might be doing what we'd assumed impossible, if we don't take the opportunity to find out if there's a chance to save hundreds of innocent lives, we're no better than the domes."

"The people living on the highway are already as good as dead," Raina said.

"If we accept that, then we're no better than the Teachers," Kieran said. "Giving up on the present and assuming there's nothing left but death."

Nola let a small smile curve her lips. "The second we decide there's nothing we can do to change things, we're nothing more than dust and bones for future generations to find."

"What exactly do you propose we do?" Emanuel asked.

"I want to go north," Nola said.

Jeremy gripped her leg.

"I want to try and talk to the people there." She placed her hand on top of Jeremy's. "See how they've been able to live and see if they'll take in anyone from the highway. They might know something more about the domes, too."

"And when arrows start flying?" Raina asked.

"I'll protect her," Jeremy said.

"How romantic." Raina rolled her eyes.

"What about the Teachers?" Dr. Wynne said. "From what Kieran described, they all appeared to be in relatively good health, and they seem to have been around for a good long while."

"The only direction the Teachers could have come from is south. We can try going south after we're done in the north," Jeremy said.

More chances to find Gentry.

"And how long would that take?" Emanuel asked. "I can't have you away from Nightland that long."

"I..." Nola looked around the room.

Trust them. I have to trust them.

"What if the domes go north and kill the people there before we can learn from them?" Kieran said. "You thought it wasn't possible to have a garden in the city before I built one. We won't know what we could learn unless we try."

Emanuel sat still as a stone for a long moment, his gaze locked on Nola's face.

She held her breath, waiting for his judgment.

"I don't want what my daughter learns from my bones to be that I ignored those who suffered, or dismissed the opportunity to learn when it came," Emanuel said. "One group goes north and one south. You have three nights to gather information and come back."

Three nights.

It was longer than Nola had dared hope for.

"Nola, Jeremy, and Julian go north," Emanuel said. "Raina choose one and go south."

"I'll go," Kieran said.

"No," Emanuel said. "I was foolish to let you go to the city before. I've spent so long building and fighting, I forget it's not only the doctor who does the most good by staying in his lab."

Kieran turned to Nola. She could read the look in his eyes, the words balanced on his tongue. *Then Nola should be left in the lab, too.*

Nola gave a tiny shake of her head.

Kieran hesitated, then nodded. "I'll stay and keep working on the plants. We need to be ready for when the weather warms."

I could help him. I'm better trained in botany. But the tiny voice in the back of her mind, the voice that questioned why she didn't get cold, needed to go north.

"How many sun suits do you have?" Jeremy asked.

"Not enough to spare any more to this venture." Emanuel stood. "Take what supplies you need."

"What if it takes us longer than three nights?" Nola asked.

"You have three nights." Emanuel strode out into the hall, leaving the kitchen in silence.

Dr. Wynne nodded to himself for a moment before wandering out after Emanuel.

"I suppose I should eat a bigger snack before I leave." Raina downed the rest of her blood. "I'm guessing the Teachers won't be very generous hosts. If I even find them while stomping around through the wild." She shot one last glare at Nola before sauntering into the hall.

"We should leave as soon as possible." Julian sat in Emanuel's chair. "Nightfall is in a few short hours. We could cover a good bit of distance tonight, then search for them during the daylight."

"It depends on if we want the element of surprise or don't want to spook them," Jeremy said. "I honestly don't know which would be best."

"We'll have plenty of time to debate the benefits of either course on our journey," Julian said. "I should find nourishment before we leave, and I suggest the two of you see Bea for food to pack. Changed or not, you're going to need to eat a significant amount to run at the pace we'll have to maintain."

"Right." Nola stood, keeping Jeremy's hand in hers. "Let's hope Bea is in a good mood."

Julian laughed as Nola and Jeremy went into the hall. Rooms lined the corridor behind them, but in front, one door blocked the path. Jeremy opened the door with his free hand, ushering Nola into Emanuel's library.

"Why didn't—" Jeremy stopped at the thumping of footsteps behind them.

Kieran stepped into the library and closed the door before speaking. "I can go instead of you."

Both Jeremy and Kieran looked to Nola.

"I'm going." Nola squared her shoulders. "This was my idea, and I'm going."

"You know more about plants than I do," Kieran said. "You run the lab, and I'll go north."

"Emanuel can't spare the sun suit," Nola said.

"Then Julian can stay and just Jeremy and I will go," Kieran said.

"No," Nola said. "Absolutely not."

"We can play nice, Nola," Jeremy said. "It's a good idea."

"I can help him look for Gentry as well as you can," Kieran said.

Jeremy's head snapped up, his eyes narrowing at Kieran.

"I know that's part of why you both want to go," Kieran said. "It's not that hard to see. I like Gentry. She was always decent to me when I lived in the domes."

Nola let go of Jeremy's hand and hugged Kieran. "I know what you're trying to do. But I need to see what's there for myself."

Kieran held her close. "Be careful, Nola. We can't lose you."

"I'm just going for a long walk," Nola said. "Don't let the lab get too messy while I'm gone."

Kieran laughed, but the sound came out forced and wrong. "I won't touch your corner."

"I'll keep her safe," Jeremy said.

"Good." Kieran stepped back. "Nightland needs both of you."

"Keep the path open," Jeremy said.

"See you soon." A lump pressed on Nola's throat. "We should go to Bea."

"I'll let you do the talking." Jeremy held open the door to the hall.

Nola gave Kieran one last smile before going out into the corridor. She reached for Jeremy before she heard the door close behind them. He took her hand, kissing her palm before lacing his fingers through hers.

"You should have warned me," Jeremy said. "Before we went in there to talk to them, you should have told me you wanted to go north."

"I didn't want you to convince me not to talk to Emanuel," Nola said.

"Talking to Emanuel about wanting to learn from the people in the north is one thing. Going north is another. This is too dangerous."

"For me, or for anyone?" Nola asked.

"That's not fair."

"It's completely fair." Nola stepped in front of Jeremy, blocking his path. "I can walk in the sun without protection, so can you. That gives us a unique skill that's valuable to Nightland. Add that to the fact that we need to find Gentry and we can't do it from here, and the two of us going makes the most sense."

Jeremy wrapped his arms around her, enveloping her in a safety she would not allow the horrors of the world to steal. Nola sank into his warmth, a buzz of happiness starting from her stomach and trickling out to her fingers. She rose up on her toes and kissed his neck. "I love you. And it's time for me to help you."

"I know you want to help, and it's one of the reasons I love you so much, but—"

"Don't walk you into a room full of vampires and drop something like this on you again?" She kissed just below his ear. "Okay. I'll make sure I warn you about any crazy plans in the future."

"It's a good plan," Jeremy said. "I just wish you weren't a part of it."

Nola stepped out of his arms, sighing as his wonderful warmth faded from her skin.

"You're just going to have to get used to the fact that your girlfriend is a superhero, too," Nola said.

He took her hand as they headed toward Bea's domain.

"Girlfriend sounds weird, doesn't it?" Jeremy said.

"Do superheroes not date?" Nola raised an eyebrow.

"I think we're making up the rules on that." Jeremy nudged her with his elbow.

"And girlfriend doesn't fit the rules?" Nola nudged back.

"It's just with—"

Nola swallowed her laugh as pink crept into Jeremy's cheeks.

"—it just doesn't sound like enough. I mean, back in the domes, we would have gone to the board, you know."

"We're not of age to have our DNA tested and request to be paired by the marriage board," Nola said.

"There isn't a board here," Jeremy said. "There aren't any rules we have to follow."

"Clearly."

Jeremy's face turned bright red. "What I mean is, we can make up our own rules. You could stay with me in my room all the time. We could decide we want to be a pair without asking anyone's permission."

Nola froze.

Jeremy took another step before realizing she had stopped. He turned to look at her, his face changing from bright red to pale white in an instant. "I'm sorry. I'm sorry, there's too much happening and I always try and go too fast."

"You really want me?" Heat crept into Nola's face. "Just me and that's it forever?'

He gazed down at Nola's hand locked together with his. "With Graylock we might live for hundreds of years. I want to make sure I spend all of them with you."

"I love you. And I want you by my side, no matter what. For as long as we have." She touched his cheek, her heart thrumming as he blushed again. "I pick you as my pair. Whatever the world brings."

"Whatever the world brings."

CHAPTER NINE

T's stomping rang around the pantry. "Again?" She pulled a stack of clean cloths from the shelf filled with jars of preserved fruit. "You're going out there again?"

Nola glanced to Jeremy who shrugged and kept his lips pressed together.

Bea stared at the crates of vegetables along one wall as though she hadn't heard anything.

"We need to know more about the people in the north," Nola said.

"I don't like you leaving like this." T wrapped a loaf of hard seed bread in a cloth and shoved the bundle into Nola's pack. "You should be staying inside where it's safe."

"I'll be fine," Nola said. "I'll be with Jeremy."

My pair.

Her heart flipped and swirled in her chest.

Jeremy smiled at her from across the table where he stored the rations Bea had laid out for him in his own pack.

"We made it through the city to get here, and now you just keep leaving." T shoved apples in after the bread.

Bea banged a wrinkled hand down on the long, wooden table.

"Sorry." T shrank under Bea's glare and placed the dried meat carefully into the bag.

Bea gave a crisp nod that wobbled her sagging cheeks and moved to the barrels in the corner of the pantry.

"I can't just stay here," Nola said. "Not when there could be a way for me to help people."

T *tsked* as she pulled the top of the bag shut with shaking hands.

Nola lifted the pack from T's grip and pulled her into a hug, slouching to reach over the belly between them. "You're not due for another two months. I'll be back in a few days. Beauford will be here with you."

T stepped away from Nola, moving on to the food to be sorted for the humans' evening meal. "If you're going to leave tonight, you should finish getting ready. You wouldn't want to waste any precious hours of darkness staying safe."

"T," Nola said, "please don't be mad. I'm trying to make things better. Make this a better world for your baby."

"I've heard that before." T hid behind the sheet of her hair.

"I'm coming back," Nola said.

T didn't look away from her work.

"I'm sorry." Nola pulled on her pack and headed to the hall, feeling Bea's watchful gaze on her back until Jeremy closed the pantry door behind them.

"I don't want you to think less of me," Jeremy said, "but Bea is terrifying."

"Why do you think Emanuel put her in charge of distributing the food?" Nola gave a laugh that grated against her throat. "No one would dare cross her to steal anything."

"She'll be okay." Jeremy wrapped his arm around Nola, keeping her close to his side as they climbed the hall back to the sleeping quarters. "T, I mean."

"I don't worry about T being safe." Nola leaned her head against Jeremy. "She's pregnant. The vampires here will fight with everything they have to protect her and her baby."

"But?" Jeremy asked.

"Charles, the baby's father, he went to fight in the domes when Nightland attacked."

Jeremy tensed but kept his arm around Nola.

"Charles was injured at the domes and killed by wolves during Nightland's retreat," Nola said. "He left her behind and promised to come back. Now I keep leaving. I can't blame her for being upset."

"She's got Beauford," Jeremy said. "He'll be here."

"Right. You're right."

Nola stopped at the room she'd been sharing with T and Beauford. She knocked before entering. Four beds sat along the walls, with dressers tucked between them. A table and chairs took up the center of the space. Nola went straight to the dresser that held the few articles of clothing she'd brought with her from the domes. Most of them had already needed mending from the few weeks she'd spent living outside the glass.

"What are we going to do when we go through all the factory-made clothes we have?" Nola tucked her clothes in around the food T had packed for her.

"No idea," Jeremy said. "Maybe all of us will just run around naked."

"No," Nola laughed, the sound coming freely this time. "I don't want to spend my life running around a cave of naked people."

"Then I guess we'll have to figure out how to make new clothes. I'm sure Emanuel's made plans for building spinning wheels."

They stopped in Jeremy's room. His drawers held little more than Nola's. Only the few sets of clothes Nightland had provided and his Outer Guard uniform.

"I don't even want to touch it." Jeremy stared down at the folded black fabric.

"Do you need it?" Nola said.

"I have no idea." He rolled the uniform and tucked it into the very bottom of his bag.

"It seems like we should be taking more."

"We're going to get weapons." Jeremy slid his empty drawer closed.

"I know," Nola said. "It just seems like a long time to be gone."

He shrugged on his backpack then took Nola's shoulders. "You can change your mind. You don't have to go."

"Yes, I do." She pressed her lips to Jeremy's cheek. "I just wish I felt a little more prepared."

"Me too." He kissed the top of her head.

Nola waited for something to feel different as they walked out of his room and shut the door behind them. Some sort of finality to the *click* of the lock, since the door wouldn't open for days.

It's not that long. Barely any time at all really.

But how much has already changed in a month?

The fighting in the sparring room didn't stop as they entered. Julian waited by the weapons cage at the side of the space, a sword already strapped to his hip. His pack was larger than Jeremy's or Nola's, and a sun hat had been tied to the back. He waved them over, not bothering to try and speak over the chaos in the cavern.

"It took a bit of work to convince them to trust Nola with another knife." Julian handed Nola a belt with two knives and one Guard gun. "Do be careful with them."

"I'm not actually the one who lost the last knife they gave me." Nola fastened the now familiar weight around her waist.

"Anyone coming to see us off?" Jeremy took his belt from Julian.

"I don't believe so," Julian said. "I don't think Emanuel is to too keen on advertising our mission."

"In case we don't come back?" Dread trickled down Nola's spine.

"In case we find something he'd rather not have people asking questions about." Julian locked the weapons cage. "The peace in Nightland is tentative at the best of times, especially with the threat of Salinger hanging over our heads. The more we can do to keep people calm and grateful for the safety of the caves, the better off we'll all be."

Nola rested her hands on the hilts of her knives as the three of them cut through the sparring pairs toward the exit. No one stopped to bow as they had with Raina. The door at the far side sat open. Chill air swept over Nola's face.

"The temperature's dropped." Nola took a deep breath, feeling the cold rush all the way down to her lungs.

"Hopefully the people in the north will have some fires burning," Jeremy said. "Though, if they've gone this long without being found by us or the domes, I doubt it."

"I hope the people on the highway have a way to keep warm," Nola said.

None of them spoke as they made their way down the tunnel. They passed the first window, and a true gust of cold air blasted against Nola's skin.

She waited for the shivering to start, for her fingers to go numb and her muscles to protest working in the freezing temperatures. But her long sleeve shirt was plenty to protect her from the cold.

Julian stopped by a window halfway between the sparring room and the door to the outside. He pulled a paper from his pocket and laid it on the windowsill under the pale moonlight.

"I don't know how much store we can set by this"—Julian unfolded the paper, revealing a worn and marked map—"but I managed to convince Emanuel to part with a piece of his old collection."

A wide circle on the east side of the river marked the location of the domes. The main streets of the city had been printed on the paper as well. To the far west of the map, the mountains took over the page, though no one had noted the entrance to Nightland.

Gray lines formed the highway that bowed around the city and met up with the edge of the river to the north and south. At the bottom of the map, a set of blue shapes showed the lakes the Teachers had spoken of. By the top, a wide band of green marked a forest Nola had never heard of.

"It's not a very detailed map," Jeremy said.

"The domes took most maps a long time ago," Julian said. "Spread propaganda about the dangers of moving outside city limits. Convinced the citizens to turn in all their maps to protect the youth. The next month they made it illegal to move beyond the highway."

"I can't believe people went along with the domes for so long." Nola traced the circle of the domes with her finger.

"The domes needed supplies from the city," Julian said. "The factories had a reason to run and needed workers. There was nowhere else for anyone who wanted food and money to go."

"Except north," Jeremy said.

"If we are separated for some reason," Julian said, "head east toward the highway. You'll be able to find your way back from there. No matter what happens, we don't risk anyone finding the path to Nightland. Agreed?"

"Agreed," Jeremy and Nola said together.

"Then we begin." Julian folded the map and put it back into his pocket.

Nola's mind wandered as they walked. She'd seen maps before, but never one made of paper. Her father had had a digital map of the city. She had watched him studying the layout of the streets before he went on patrol as an Outer Guard.

I never thought of what lay beyond the city. I was as bad as the rest of the Domers.

They passed the last window. A dull glow glittered in the distance where the domes waited for the world to end.

I was what they made me.

She reached out, twining her fingers through Jeremy's. He squeezed her hand.

We are what we make ourselves now. We make the rules.

The end of the corridor came into view. Three guards blocked the path to the outside. Two twins with shaved heads and Desmond. Even in the dim light, Nola caught shadows of the scars that marked Desmond's dark skin.

"Heading into the world?" Desmond's fangs peeked out from beneath his lip as he spoke in his deep, rumbling voice.

"Only for a little while," Julian said.

Desmond nodded and stepped aside. The twins followed his movement without argument.

"Thanks," Nola muttered as she hurried past the twins.

Julian didn't slow his pace as he reached the end of the tunnel. He stepped off the ledge and out into the open air as though unaware of the drop.

Nola stopped at the edge, looking to the ground beneath before jumping. For the split second while she fell through the air, her heart seized, warning her of the pain that waited when she landed. But her feet touched the ground without shocking the rest of her body. She took two quick steps forward to balance herself and straightened as Jeremy landed behind her.

"If you please." Julian ran up the mountain.

Tightening the straps on her pack, Nola followed, keeping her ears pricked up for the sounds of Jeremy's footsteps keeping pace behind her.

Julian didn't tear through the darkness as Raina did when she led. He kept to a pace that allowed Nola to see the world as she raced by. They ran through the clearing in the basin that surrounded the entrance to Nightland, then up to the ridge that climbed toward the peak of the mountain where Kieran's garden hid. The steep angle to the ridge would have forced humans to use their arms to haul themselves up. But the speed at which they ran made launching herself up step by step easy, almost fun.

Nola reached the top of the ridge and swayed. The ground dropped away on either side of the thin path, leaving nothing but open air and a fall that could hurt even a vampire.

"You okay?" Jeremy asked.

"Fine." Nola kept running, her eyes darting between the path Julian navigated with ease and the view on either side. The dizzying height couldn't mar the beauty of the moonlight on the mountain.

With only the thin sheen of silver, the terrain became a maze of thick shadows, which seemed to swallow chunks of the world, and delicately textured patches of light. Stands of trees that still clung to life despite the torment the weather and toxic rains had let loose. Mounds of rocks where bits of the mountain had crumbled, leaving swatches of sanctuary where shrubs had found a way to survive.

Before they reached the summit, Julian turned north, cutting down the spine of a smaller, neighboring peak. Here, grass and weeds had managed to grow, sheltered from the worst of the sun by their higher neighbor.

Dense bushes clung to the mountainside, their branches bare, whether from the cold or death, Nola didn't know.

They ran down the spine of the mountain, the pounding of their feet the only sound in the night. A wide span of struggling trees covered the slope below.

Nola looked west beyond the mountain she now called home. The range continued below them, turning into rolling foothills in the far distance. No glimmer of light or barren patches gave a hint of human life ever having existed beyond Nightland's sanctuary. To the east, scars of civilization dug deep into the earth. The ruined highway, a gash through the landscape. The burned city, a terrible wound. Nola kept her eyes on the shimmer of the domes until the trees swallowed the view.

CHAPTER TEN

S ense floated in and out of being. They had been running for a long time, that much Nola knew. Down the side of the mountain, through trees denser than any she had seen before. Past a long stretch of fields thick with high grass as though nature had reclaimed the land once cleared by farmers.

Still, her legs didn't tire, and her lungs didn't burn.

Not needing to rest warped the meaning of effort and the ticking of time.

I could run for days.

A sudden longing pulled at her chest. To run faster and farther. To keep racing forward and see just how far she could make it before she dropped.

"Just a moment." Julian slowed in front of her.

Nola skipped a step, teetering forward then righting herself as Jeremy stopped by her side.

"We'll have to move a bit more slowly, I'm afraid," Julian said.

Nola peered around his shoulder. A patchy swamp of frothy water blocked the way forward.

"Too bad this wasn't on the map," Jeremy said.

"Can we cut through?" Nola pressed her sleeve to her nose, blocking out the putrid stench that filled the air.

"I wouldn't recommend it." Julian stepped closer to the edge of the swamp. The ground squelched beneath his feet. "Pity a true freeze hasn't come."

"What do you mean?" Nola asked.

Julian tapped his toe on the surface of the water. The froth swirled in protest. "I forget how little children know," Julian said. "Or rather how old I am." He cut west, skirting along the edge of the water.

"How old are you?" Nola stayed close behind Julian, mimicking his every footfall.

"Old enough to remember snow," Julian said. "And deep freezes. Proper seasons we could predict."

"It used to snow here," Jeremy said. The sound of the ground squishing under his feet stayed right behind Nola's shoulder. "My dad told me about it. How it used to snow in the winter."

"I loved winter," Julian said. "Snow piled up along the bottom of the domes. The whole world washed in pure white. My partner and I would sit right next to the glass to feel the cold against our skin. We don't have that anymore. There's the hot season and the cold season. But the snow doesn't come. The world has given up on a true healing freeze.

"The temperature creeps low enough to kill poor humans left to sleep in the open and frost over the crops we struggle to grow, then wavers so much from day to day it's difficult to know what time of year it truly is. I miss real seasons, the markers that prove time is passing."

"Does it get easier?" Nola asked.

"No." Julian leapt over a fallen tree. "I do forget sometimes what being human felt like. Letting go of that life makes being a vampire less jarring, but I always miss having time mean something."

"Stop." Jeremy grabbed Nola's arm, yanking her behind him.

"What?" She found what he had seen before the word had fully left her lips.

In the starlight, shapes shifted in the shadows to the north.

Nola held her breath, waiting for arrows to fly as the dark figures moved between trees across the swamp.

Julian rested his hand on the hilt of his sword.

Nola's fingers trembled as she reached for the Guard gun at her hip.

The shadows moved again, crackling through the underbrush.

"Come along." Julian waved them onward.

"What?" Jeremy stayed steady, his weapon aimed at the things moving across the swamp.

"Those beasts won't hurt us." Julian clapped his hands. The sound echoed through the darkness.

The shadows froze for a moment, then disappeared into the trees.

"Why did they run?" Nola whispered.

"Not they," Julian said, "at least not people. Deer, I expect."

He leapt a wide patch of sunken grass and continued west.

"How do you know?" Jeremy kept his weapon out as he and Nola followed Julian.

"A person would have the sense to either be quiet or call out," Julian said. "The poor beasts were only searching for a meal and didn't know what to make of us."

Nola tucked her weapon back into its holster. "Animals and people living on the outside, I just..."

"Just?" Julian said.

"Want to tear through the glass of the domes, find every teacher I ever had, and shake them," Nola said. "There are so many things they never bothered to teach us. I was just supposed to learn how to grow plants and get married and have kids. But when my generation had to teach our children, none of us would have known about deer that still eat in the woods."

"That was the point," Julian said. "I was old enough to understand the choice I was making in entering the domes. I believed in the need to protect the ability of humans to bear healthy children, and I knew what sacrifices were expected of me. Those born in the glass never had the chance to decide if safety and a lofty goal for the greater good were worth spending their entire lives trapped in a place the size of a small village. They were never able to choose between a brief, painful, and chaotic life on the outside or a small, regulated life lacking all compassion within the glass."

The domes had never felt small to Nola, had never seemed like a cold and compassionless place. Not until she'd been to Nightland.

"The vast majority of the world's population has died," Julian said, "just as the Incorporation predicted when they built the domes. Most of those who still live in the open have turned to Vamp or Lycan to survive. Despite those horrors, there are some on the outside who would never choose a life behind glass if the opportunity were ever granted them. And there are those who live in the domes who would choose the open air if they knew such an option existed."

"It's wrong for them not to tell us," Nola said.

"I agree," Julian said.

A row of toppled down trees marked the edge of the swamp. Julian stopped, staring at the path ahead for a moment before shaking his head and walking north.

"I can sort of understand it," Jeremy said. "People on the outside get sick and die too easily. Too many babies are born with birth defects they can't survive. Lying to the domes children is wrong, burning cities is wrong, but making sure there will actually be another generation to take our place? I get that."

Nola reached back, taking his hand, trying to think of something comforting to say.

I don't even know if T's baby will be healthy.

"The fate of the last person alive would be a terrible one," Julian said.

"That's not going to happen," Nola said. "We've got a safe place in Nightland. We're going looking for people we didn't think could survive. The human race isn't done yet."

Julian stopped at the north end of the swamp. "Months ago, when Kieran told me of the wonderful girl in the domes he truly believed had the heart to care for those left to die outside the glass, I thought he was a lovesick fool. I'm glad to know he was right. That there are some who have never known hunger who still care for those who have never had a proper meal."

"Kieran said that?" Jeremy said.

"More times than I can count," Julian said. "I'm afraid the rest of us had given up hope of there being anyone worthy of survival inside the glass."

"Then I'm glad Kieran ended up with you," Jeremy said.

Julian turned to face them, one sleek eyebrow raised.

"Whatever Kieran might have done, he was right about Nola," Jeremy said.

Nola squeezed his hand. "And Nightland. I'll never forgive Emanuel for attacking the domes—"

"But it can't compare to what the domes have done," Jeremy said.

Julian smiled. "I never had children. As much as the Incorporation pushed, I refused the procreation orders. At times like this, I don't mind that my DNA was never passed on. I'm simply proud to have been a small part of the story that led us here."

Fallen leaves crackled under their feet as Julian led the way into the forest. The acid rain hadn't torn through their thin membranes. The leaves had fallen to the ground whole, ready to decompose and give nutrients back to the trees.

Julian headed east, toward the place the animals had been hiding in the shadows, and stopped next to a tree where swatches of bark had been torn away. Hoof prints dented the water-logged ground.

"It really was deer." Jeremy shook his head. "How have they survived?"

"The trees help clean the smog out of the air that hurts people so badly in the city," Nola said. "If there's a stream or some other kind of water that hasn't been contaminated like this swamp and the river, they'd have something to drink. The trees are managing to grow, so they have food."

"By keeping people in the city as labor, the Incorporation condemned them to live with the toxins the domes were built to avoid," Julian said.

"They've been killing people from the beginning." Deep lines creased Jeremy's brow.

"I suppose," Julian said, "but even if people had been told to flee the city and create a homestead far away from industrialization, some would have refused to leave. And those brave enough to head into the wilds might not have survived very long anyway. They might have found cleaner water and soil pure enough to farm—"

"But the weather still would have killed their crops," Nola said. "And the sun would have hurt them, and their kids would still have gotten sick."

A pang cut through the numbness in Nola's chest she hadn't even realized existed. She took a deep breath, letting the stink of the swamp burn her lungs.

"It's okay." Jeremy laced his fingers through hers.

The warmth of his palm traveled up her arm, surrounding the terrible ache. The pain didn't ebb away, but the heat of connection transformed the hurt from a hollow hopelessness to a burning desire to fight.

"If the animals have found a way to survive, then people can, too," Nola said. "This isn't the end of the human race. We're just starting over again as something different. We're evolving to survive."

"Adversity has always required adaptation," Julian said. "The penalty we pay for having done so much damage to the earth is having to adapt so quickly, and not being able to change everyone so they can survive with us. Life will never be what it was before, but perhaps it will endure."

They walked in silence for a long while. The ground firmed beneath their feet as they climbed uphill. They didn't run as they had before. Julian kept them to a steady pace a human would have trouble matching but seemed like nothing more than a brisk walk to Nola.

She listened to the crackling of the brush and fallen leaves under their feet. Even in the darkness, she could see the details of the trees and the individual twigs that had fallen to the ground.

The hill crested in front of them, the rolling line of its edge standing out in the darkness.

Jeremy let go of Nola's hand and reached for his weapon. "Julian, I think you should put that sun suit on."

"The sky isn't even gray yet," Nola said.

Julian stopped in front of them, standing still for a moment, then taking off his pack. "I think you're quite right."

"What's going—"

The breeze shifted, blowing up from beyond the rise. Nola gagged as the horrible stench of decay flooded her mouth.

"We don't want to walk into any surprises with Julian vulnerable to the sun." Jeremy wrinkled his nose, his mouth twisting into a frown.

"What is that?" Nola pressed her sleeve over her face.

"What *was* that is probably the more apt question." Julian pulled the sun suit from his pack, quickly stepping into the oversized tan fabric and zipping himself in.

"Nola," Jeremy said, "I want you to stay behind me, and trust me."

"I do trust you," Nola said.

Julian put on the wide-brimmed hat, pulling down the heavy veil to cover his face.

"If I tell you not to look," Jeremy said, "I need you not to look."

"Why shouldn't I look?" Nola said.

"Because, sweet Nola," Julian said, "the horrors of the world hurt those with loving hearts worst of all."

A horrible dread weighed heavy in Nola's stomach.

Julian slung his pack onto his back. "After me, I think."

He started toward the rise of the hill, Jeremy close behind.

Nola moved to walk next to Jeremy, but he sidestepped, keeping her behind him.

I've seen terrible things. What could the world have left to torment me with?

She pinched her nose closed as they reached the top of the hill, swallowing the bile that rose in her throat.

"Damn." Julian stopped on the crest of the hill.

Jeremy reached an arm back, trying to keep Nola behind him.

She dodged to the side, taking her place between Jeremy and Julian.

A wide valley opened up below them. Whatever trees had grown in the valley had burned, leaving nothing but charred stumps and ash in their wake. At the bottom of the basin, human figures lay unmoving on the ground.

CHAPTER ELEVEN

"What happened?" Nola took a step forward.

Jeremy grabbed her arm, holding her in place.

Dozens of people lay scattered across the bottom of the small valley, their bodies twisted and broken.

"How did this many people get out here?" Jeremy said.

"I've no idea." Julian started down into the valley, the movement of his hat giving the only sign of his gaze constantly sweeping the burned out trees for danger.

"The Northerners," Nola said. "Julian, be careful. They already shot you once."

"I hope they will have such poor aim should we meet again," Julian said.

A growl rumbled in Jeremy's throat.

"What?" Nola searched his face for signs of pain.

"I should have convinced Emanuel to keep you in Nightland," Jeremy said.

"Why?" Nola freed her weapon from its holster, her ears straining to hear the *buzz* of flying arrows.

"Because I don't want you to see what's down there," Jeremy said. "I don't want you to have to remember this. But I can't leave you alone up here."

"I can take it," Nola said.

"You're strong enough to take on the whole world." Jeremy brushed a curl away from her forehead. "That doesn't stop me from wanting to protect you."

Nola caught his hand, pressing his palm to her cheek. "Thank you."

Jeremy held her gaze for a long moment before turning back to the valley below.

Nola pressed her sleeve to her nose as she followed Jeremy and Julian down the hill. The crackling beneath her feet changed. The leaves had all been burned away by the fire that had torn through the valley but spared the surrounding four hills. Unburnt trees peered up over each of the ridges, as though the flames had known not to move beyond the bounds of the basin.

The bodies weren't burned.

"This shouldn't be possible?" Nola's eyes watered as the stench grew too strong for her to ignore.

Julian reached the base of the valley where the bodies lay. Soot stained the bottom of his sun suit, giving him the look of a strangely tattered warrior as he drew his sword.

They can't be a threat. They're too far gone.

Nola bit her lips together, swallowing her scream as she approached the first of the bodies.

Whoever it was had been dead for days. Animals had already feasted on the remains. There were no gaping wounds from a battle or sores from illness left behind. They had been dumped like compost and left to rot. The taste of blood and bile filled Nola's mouth.

"Are they Northerners?" Jeremy kept his hand to his face as he leaned over one of the corpses.

"No idea," Julian said.

Nola began to ask a question and gagged on the putrid stink that flooded her mouth. "How did we not smell this from a mile away?"

"The swamp covered the scent until we got close," Jeremy said.

"They weren't killed here." Nola leaned over a tiny corpse.

A child left to decay.

"Why do you say that?" Julian said.

"People run where they're attacked," Nola said. "It happened in the domes, in the tunnels of Nightland, when the city burned. People ran. These bodies aren't spread out enough to have been running from something, and they aren't packed close enough to have been corralled to be killed."

"She's right," Jeremy said.

"But why go through the trouble of moving so many bodies?" Nola said.

"This valley is useless until the plants grow back," Jeremy said. "You can be seen from all sides, and there's no water source. The smell from the swamp covered the stink—"

"But we still found the bodies," Julian said.

"Because they wanted us to, or because they didn't think we could?" Jeremy's gaze swept the hilltops around them.

"We shouldn't stay here." Nola backed away from the body of a person who had been left naked for the animals to consume. "I don't want to be here anymore."

"We should keep heading north," Julian said.

"If this is what the Northerners do, I don't know how much we'll be able to learn from them before it come down to a fight." Jeremy took Nola's arm, guiding her around the corpses.

A glint of metal caught Nola's eye. Sticking out of the torso of one of the bodies, a thin silver dart that had pierced the doomed person's flesh.

"It wasn't the Northerners," Nola said. "The domes did this."

Jeremy and Julian turned toward her.

She pointed to the dart.

"Damn," Julian said. "I think it best if we run." With barely a nod to either of them, Julian took off, sprinting north.

"Stay in front of me." Jeremy drew his Guard gun, ready to fire little silver darts into anyone who might hurt them.

Nola pulled her weapon from its holster as she tore after Julian.

Footsteps thundered behind her. She wanted to turn and make sure it really was Jeremy following her, but Julian dodged through the burnt out trees with such speed, she couldn't spare a glance behind without risking injury.

"The domes didn't leave them like that," Jeremy said.

Nola's shoulders eased at the sound of his voice.

"It's like the bones, it just doesn't fit," Jeremy said.

"The Outer Guard being this far from the city doesn't make sense at all," Nola said.

"It does if they're searching for Nightland." Julian crested the hill. He paused for a split second before veering slightly left as he continued to run.

"The water bottles," Nola said, "the ones they gave people after they burned the city. We found trackers in them."

"It could have been the bottles," Jeremy said. "Or the Outer Guard could have followed those people here."

"Or those could be the Northerners we've been looking for." Julian led them down a rocky curve in the hillside where water would have run after a heavy rain.

"Sending guards out this far is dangerous," Jeremy said. "They'd have to stay on foot, going through the woods."

"The Outer Guard have always relied on their ability to quickly retreat to safety," Julian said. "Attack a nest of vampires, bundle into their trucks, and be whisked away to the protection of the domes."

A rock shot out from beneath Nola's foot. Jeremy caught her under the arm before she could try and right herself.

"That was before Graylock." Jeremy kept right behind Nola's shoulder. "They don't need trucks for speed—"

"But they've never been out of the city," Julian said. "The forest and mountains are an entirely different world. It took Nightland a long time to learn that lesson."

"That's why my dad never ran patrols past the highway," Jeremy said. "Even if he took a hundred Outer Guard into the wild, there's too much ground to cover, too many unknowns."

"Does Salinger care?" Nola asked. "Would a monster like him really care that he's putting his guards in danger?"

"No," Jeremy said. "They'd be collateral damage."

They entered a stand of trees with withered and twisted branches. A few thick leaves still clung to life even as the yellow and orange brought on by the cold touched their tips. Fluttering on their perches in the darkness, the waxy coating of the leaves had dulled in patches, marred by the acid rain.

People aren't the only things to adapt.

"Jeremy," Julian said, "I don't mean to be cruel, but I do need you to remember the guards Salinger is sending into the woods, no matter how doomed and helpless they may seem, are still, in fact, our enemies."

"The guards destroyed the city," Jeremy said. "I'm not dumb enough to think any of them are innocent. The only guard I want to find is my sister."

"We're not going to stop looking," Nola said. "We'll find Gentry."

A skeleton lay on the forest floor in front of them. Nola held her breath, waiting to see what horrible thing the forest hid. But the bones belonged to an animal, perhaps a long dead deer. The white of the skeleton shone unnaturally in the first light of the rising sun.

Nola glanced east.

Through the branches of the trees, the sky had barely begun to turn a pale gray.

"We should find a place for you to hide before the sun gets too high," Nola said.

"I have the sun suit." Julian slowed to a walk.

The forest of twisted trees ended, opening up to a wide and barren field. The expanse reached in front of them, leaving a gap as wide as Bright Dome, and stretched in either direction before twisting out of sight.

"I don't like this." Jeremy stood next to Nola, right behind the last of the trees.

There had been trees in the barren strip. Remains of the stumps still stuck out of the ground at odd angles, as though someone had given up on trying to wrench them from the earth. Patches of fire marked the dirt as well, as though an attempt had been made to burn the stumps away.

"It's like they were trying to clear the land for farming." Nola peeked out from behind the tree. "If the soil is good enough for trees to grow, it might be fertile enough for crops. I think someone was trying to make a field." She leaned farther out to the side.

"We should backtrack," Jeremy said. "Head a bit farther into the woods and hunker down for the day."

"I am well protected by the sun suit," Julian said.

"A sword could slice through your sun suit," Jeremy said.

"I've seen pictures of old plows," Nola said. "You could make one from rocks and wood. It might take time to figure it out, but it could be done."

"If there are Northerners or guards watching this strip, I don't want to get into a fight with them when tearing through the suit could get you killed," Jeremy said. "We can wait and try crossing in the dark."

"It could work." Nola pictured it in her mind, a strip of farmland running between the trees. Protected from wind and erosion by the surrounding forest.

We'd have to build shelters from the rain. Kieran could help me.

"How far from the city are we?" Nola asked.

"I'd say about twenty-five miles," Julian said.

"The guards still made it to those bodies," Jeremy said. "We can't take any chances."

"Twenty-five miles from the city should mean the run off from the factories never made it this far. Or if it did, it won't be as bad." Nola stepped out from behind the tree. "There could be a real farm here."

A *whoosh* cut through her thoughts.

"Nola!"

She spun at Jeremy's scream. His eyes were wide with horror as he reached toward her.

Pain shot through her side, buckling her knees.

Jeremy grabbed her before she hit the ground. He dodged to the side as an arrow hit the tree trunk next to his head. He had her under the arms, dragging her sideways, on top of her pack. The movement sent a fresh wave of burning pain shooting through her. Hands pulled her pack away, and she lay flat on the ground.

A scream tore from Nola's throat, but using the air in her lungs only made the pain worse.

"I think we've found the Northerners." Julian had his back pressed against a tree only a few feet from Nola.

"Nola," Jeremy said. "Nola, I need you to look at me."

Nola blinked, trying to think beyond the searing in her side to find Jeremy's brown eyes.

"I have to pull the arrow out." Black blurred the edges of Jeremy's face. "It's going to hurt, but I promise you're going to be okay."

"Jeremy." Nola reached for his hand. Blood coated her fingers. She looked down. An arrow had lodged in her side. Red seeped from the wound, staining her shirt.

"Just hold still," Jeremy said.

But she needed to touch the arrow. To be sure it really was sticking out of her body. She'd been stabbed before, through the chest. The pain felt the same, but her mind hadn't been stolen from her this time.

Her finger recognized the grooves of the hand-carved arrow shaft. The stickiness of her blood made sense.

I am bleeding. I am hurt.

The horrible pain of her wound didn't panic her. She closed her fist around the arrow shaft and pulled.

"Nola, don't." Jeremy reached for her hand, but she kept pulling, dragging the arrowhead back out of her flesh.

Spots of pain danced through her vision as she wrenched the arrow from her body and tossed it aside.

"Well done," Julian said. "But I do recommend you hold still for a bit."

"Don't move." Jeremy pressed his hands over the hole in Nola's side.

"I'll heal." Nola's voice came out rasping, but strong. The pain in her side began to recede, turning from a horrible red to a dull, throbbing gray. "It's already happening, isn't it?"

Jeremy leaned closer to Nola's stomach.

An arrow thudded into the tree behind him.

"Watch out." Nola coughed, and the pain tore itself back open. "Shit."

"Hold still." Jeremy leaned close to her, sheltering behind the same tree that protected her. "Your skin is already knitting back together, but internal organs are a bit more complicated."

"We can't wait, we have to move." Nola tried to sit up, but Jeremy pressed on her shoulders, keeping her pinned to the dirt.

"Waiting a few minutes now will save us a lot of time in the long run," Jeremy said. "They're firing from a distance. We can hide here."

"Why the hell did they shoot me?" Nola said.

"Because this is where the arrows fly," Julian said. "We came looking for survivors of the apocalypse. I never expected to find a polite society."

CHAPTER TWELVE

An arrow shook the tree behind Nola's head as it landed with a heavy *thud*. "They didn't clear the strip for farming did they?" Nola said.

"It might have started that way," Jeremy said, "but it gives them a clean line of sight for attacks, too."

"No wonder people don't return from the north," Julian said. "I'm not certain even I could make it across the strip alive."

"We can't just turn back," Nola said. The *thud* of another arrow punctuated her words. "Look at what they've done. They have enough people to clear that much land, which means they're managing to feed a real population. We have to talk to them."

"They shot you," Jeremy said.

"Only a little." Nola lifted his hand from her wound. A dull ache throbbed through her side, like a bruise from a bad blow.

"There is no such thing as being only a little shot," Jeremy said.

"We came here for answers," Nola said. "This isn't like the city. The people we're searching for are actually here. We have to talk to them."

Jeremy held Nola's gaze for a long moment.

"I'll go across," Jeremy said.

"Like hell you will." Nola wriggled out from under his grasp to lean against the tree.

"I don't think any of us trying to get across is a good idea," Julian said.

"But—"

"Stop thinking like a guard," Nola cut across. "These aren't wolves on the streets of the city trying to kill you. They aren't mobs attacking the domes. We're invading their home. So let's try and talk to them before anyone else bleeds."

"Okay," Jeremy said, "but you stay behind the trees."

"I think I just learned the value of cover." Nola wiped the blood from her hands onto the cleaner side of her shirt. The red didn't leave her skin. "I don't think I'll forget anytime soon."

"Always good to learn from one's mistakes," Julian said.

Nola shifted to stand, keeping herself behind the tree as she turned to face the strip. Jeremy moved with her, leaving only a few inches between them. The heat from his body radiated toward her. She longed to sink into his warmth and disappear to a place where pain couldn't follow.

An arrow *thudded* into the tree in front of them.

"We didn't come here to hurt you," Nola shouted. She stood frozen, straining to hear any sound beyond her heart thundering in her ears. "I know you don't have any reason to believe that, but it's true. We came here to talk to you. The Teachers told us about you, said you had lived up here for a long time."

She waited again, digging her nails into the bark of the tree.

I will not panic.

She had tried to speak to people who wanted to hurt her once before. That night had ended in blood and fire.

She shifted her weight, letting her back touch Jeremy.

"We found the bodies," Nola called, her voice stronger than before. "Did you move them to the burnt out valley? We know the Outer Guard killed them, but we don't think they moved them. Were they your people, or people from the city?"

"Keep talking," Julian said.

"What the domes did to the city is unforgivable," Nola said. "We have a place where we live away from the city. The domes have tried to come after us. Have they come after you yet? Did they kill your people with little silver darts? If they haven't, if the corpses were just people who fled in the wrong direction, that doesn't mean the domes won't come after you. It only means they haven't found you yet."

"You're one of them," a man's voice shouted across the strip. "I saw the arrow hit. You shouldn't be talking."

Nola closed her eyes, trying to picture the man hiding behind a tree just like her.

Afraid. Desperate.

"I'm not a guard, but I was injected with the same drug that makes them strong. The domes, they'd"—Nola let out a shaking breath—"they'd probably kill me if they knew I'd taken Graylock."

"One of you has a glass suit," the man shouted.

Nola glanced to Julian, whose hat tipped up and down as he nodded.

"He's a vampire," Nola said. "The sun's coming up. He has to wear it to stay alive."

"Prove it," the man shouted.

"Prove that he'll die in the sun?" Nola said. "No. I'm not going to let him leak blood out of his eyes and die a horrible death just to prove a point."

A voice lighter than the man's laughed.

"All we want is to talk to you," Nola said. "We have an enemy that wants to see both of our people dead. There are murderers living on our doorstep. Don't you think having an ally would be a good idea?"

Silence stretched over the gap.

"We need to move," Jeremy whispered. "They haven't had Vamp or Graylock. We can outrun them."

"The entrance to Nightland," the man called. "How do you get in?"

"The tunnels under the city have been rigged to kill," Julian shouted. "There is no entry to Nightland now."

"Not the tunnels," the man called, "the new home of the nightwalkers. How do you get in?"

The subtle sound of Julian's sword clearing its sheath stilled Nola's racing heart.

"You have to jump up," Nola said. "Jumping up is the only way in."

A tree crackled across the strip. A man dressed entirely in brown leapt from the branches, a bow in his hands with an arrow nocked and pointed toward Nola.

"I never thought any of the nightwalkers would come this way." The man squinted in the early morning light, his gaze fixed on the tree sheltering Nola.

"I didn't think we'd be coming here either," Nola said.

"End of the world drives people to all sorts of things," the man said. "I'll let the three of you cross. But there are people in the trees you'll never find. If you show one hint of wanting to hurt us, you will die. Glass drugs in you or not."

"Okay." Nola lifted her pack and moved to step out from behind the tree.

"Me first." Jeremy slipped his Guard gun back into its holster and stepped around Nola. He stood between two trees, facing the man. He raised both hands, displaying his empty palms.

Panic seized Nola's heart. An arrow would fly across the gap and sink into Jeremy's chest.

I won't lose him.

"I was wrong. We shouldn't do this," Nola whispered.

"Just stay behind me." Jeremy stepped out onto the barren dirt.

"I feel it, too, you know?" Nola stepped up next to Jeremy, raising her hands as he had. "The horrible fear when you could be hurt. I hate it."

"You're stronger than I am." Jeremy walked forward. "I've always known that."

Julian stepped up to Nola's other side, his sword sheathed, his gloved hands raised.

"Should things go terribly," Julian said, "find out how they know the entrance to Nightland's new home. More important than how they've managed to survive is how they found us."

"Agreed," Jeremy said.

They were halfway across the strip.

Time stretched as they crossed the barrens. Nola didn't know if it was because she had grown accustomed to moving so quickly, or if dread of the unknown had somehow slowed the seconds.

Nola studied the Northern man. An uneven beard covered his chin, and scars marked the parts of his face not hidden by hair. Not the dots of acid rain burns that marred Desmond's face, or the scratch marks Nola had seen on some of the vampires who attacked humans. These scars were different, varied, as though life had unleashed a hundred unique torments on this man and each of them had left its own individual mark.

His clothes weren't of the make Nola had seen in the city. Baggy and plain, as though someone had made the fabric and fashioned the clothes by hand, their dull brown blended perfectly with the trees, though Nola didn't know if it had been done intentionally or had happened slowly as dirt ground into the fabric.

The man's hands stayed steady, his arrow now pointed at Jeremy's chest, as they reached the far side of the strip

"Thank you for letting us cross," Jeremy said.

"Doesn't mean we won't kill you if you threaten us," the man said.

"I know," Jeremy said, "just like you know we'll defend ourselves."

The man smiled. A gap had taken the place of a tooth in the front of his mouth. "Good to have an understanding."

They all stood silently for a long moment.

"The one who laughed," Nola said, "are they coming out, too?"

"I don't think so," the man said. "It's probably best if we keep our people where they're happiest. *Hidden*."

"Hard to hide when you've made a wide tract around your land," Jeremy said. "We wouldn't have thought we'd reached you if it weren't for that."

"Blight hit the trees." The man shrugged. "Had to kill the bad ones before the whole forest died."

"That was smart," Nola said.

"I know," the man said.

"What's your name?" Nola asked.

"Doesn't matter." The man slid his arrow back into his quiver and his bow over his shoulder as he walked into the trees, giving a wave for them to follow. "I'm not the one you want to talk to."

Jeremy's fingers twitched as though longing to reach for his weapon. Nola took his hand, tugging him to walk with her. He bit his lips together but didn't argue as they followed the man deeper into the trees.

"Not to be old fashioned," Julian said, keeping pace right behind Nola and Jeremy, "but whether or not you think we're here to speak to you, I still feel incredibly rude not knowing your name."

The man laughed. The sound was more like a cough.

Who did we hear laugh before?

Nola's gaze swept the trees around them, searching for people who could be staring at her, waiting to send another arrow into her flesh. She shivered at the remembered pain.

"You okay?" Jeremy glanced sideways at Nola.

"Fine," Nola said, though her skin prickled with the horrid sensation of being watched.

"My name is Julian, if that helps. I'd take off my gloves to shake properly, but I'm sure you understand why that's not possible."

"I've seen nightwalkers before," the man said. "Some made it this far north. Had to kill them before they bled us."

"I don't blame you," Julian said. "Unfortunately, many of my kind are violent. Letting them into your home might have meant the death of your people."

"But the home in the mountains is different," the man said. "At least that's what everyone is meant to believe."

"Nightland is different," Nola said. "I've been living there. I have human friends who are living there, and no one's ever—"

"Human?" The man turned to them. "Your friends are human, but you aren't?"

"I've been changed." Nola held tight to Jeremy's hand. "I was hurt. I had to be given Graylock to survive."

"And that means you're not human?" The man leaned forward, squinting at Nola's face.

"If vampires aren't human—" Nola began.

"Why shouldn't the nightwalkers be human?" the man said. "They were born, and I know they can die."

"But their DNA—" Jeremy said.

"You were bred in the glass, weren't you?" the man said.

Jeremy glanced to Nola. "I was. I left when I figured out they were murderers."

The man combed his fingers through his ragged beard. "I don't know if that makes you smart or plain stupid. Either way, you're just plain human. You were born human. Whatever they shoved in your veins came after."

"How did you know I've had Graylock?" Jeremy's fingers loosened around Nola's.

The man turned and strode away through the woods. "They let you walk in front, and the girl seems fond of you. She wouldn't have let you do that if you couldn't get shot in the gut with an arrow and walk away same as her."

"Nola," Nola said. "My name is Nola."

The man stopped, grinding his toe into the dirt. "You're the one then?"

"What one?" Nola's mouth went dry. Her fingers twitched, longing for the weight of her knife in her hand.

"The one whose name broke through the noise in the city," the man said. "The one the nightwalkers believed in and the pack folk howled for."

"Yes," Nola said. "I don't know why. There's nothing special about me."

"You're a human and you're alive," the man said. "Isn't that special enough?"

"You're quite right," Julian said. "Being alive is, in itself, a wonderful thing."

"Coming out of your mountain to find us," the man said, "that might be dumber than leaving the glass."

"Not if we can find allies," Nola said. "Then it's worth the risk."

The man gave another coughing laugh. "The whispers are right then. There is one pure idealist left in the world." He looked over his shoulder and gave Nola a wink. "If you're trying to call folks who have strayed from the norm unhuman, you're the least human of us all."

Heat rushed to Nola's cheeks. "I just want people to survive. To have a shot at living in peace."

"She'll like you," the man said.

"Who?" Nola asked.

"Rebecca." He waved for them to keep following.

They went down a hill whose base was hidden in the trees. The same orange and yellow-edged waxy leaves hung from these branches, but the trees grew closer together, as though all crowding in toward the most fertile land. Most of the trees seemed entirely wild, but every now and then the bark would carry a mark of human activity. A hefty stick nailed to the side of a tree to help someone climb up into the branches. A nobble where rope had been tightly tied around a branch while the tree grew.

"How long have you been living here?" Nola asked.

The man cut west, following the edge of a dried stream. The rocks at the bottom of the bed carried no moss or grass, almost as though they had been scrubbed clean.

"I've been here long enough not to remember what the river smells like," the man said. "Others have been here long enough they weren't in the city after the stores shut down. Some have been here for as long as there have been rumors of nightwalkers digging deep to build a home."

"How many years ago was that?" Nola asked.

"I'm not good with years," the man said. "The weather doesn't care about years, why should I?"

The streambed branched off in two directions, one cutting up through the trees and heading farther west, the other cutting north. The man followed the northern fork.

The ground by the stream had been worn down, the fallen sticks driven further into decay by the grinding of many footsteps. The dirt around the bases of the trees had been recently turned and carved into sections.

"Are you going to farm around the trees?" Nola stopped to examine the loose earth. The cold of the night still clung to the shadows. Any new plants would be killed by the frost.

They're planning. Preparing to survive another year.

Nola reached down toward the dirt with her free hand.

"Don't touch it," the man said. "The farmers don't like it if you touch their patches."

"I don't blame them." Nola tucked her hand behind her back.

"Come on."

"It makes sense," Nola said as they followed the man farther up the streambed, then turned west and through a patch of newer, shorter trees.

"What makes sense?" Jeremy ducked under a low branch, snaking sideways to keep his pack from getting caught.

"The trees have developed a way to live through the acid rain," Nola said. "The coating on their leaves, they evolved to survive. If you plant around the base of the trees, the leaves will lend their protection to your crops. It's really brilliant."

"I'm glad you approve," a woman's voice carried through the branches right next to Nola.

CHAPTER THIRTEEN

Nola froze, waiting for the voice to speak again so she could find where the woman hid. There was no movement in the trees. No *crackle* of footsteps coming closer.

"I was training in plant preservation in the domes," Nola said. "I would be very interested to see what other ways you've found to grow crops out here."

The man turned to face Nola, his expression bordering on boredom.

"That's part of why we came here," Nola said. "To learn from you."

"Learn from us?" the woman's voice came from Nola's left.

Nola turned toward the sound but couldn't see a person in the trees.

"You've got medicine to keep you strong, and a mountain to protect you," the woman said.

"And you've managed to survive without any of that," Nola said. "Without ReVamp and a home it took years to build, everyone in Nightland would be dead."

"True." The voice had moved to Nola's right.

"There are people living on the old highway right outside the city," Nola said. "They're going to die, and we can't help them."

"But we should?" the voice moved farther to the right.

The man laughed.

"Not alone," Nola said. "The way we're living, the highway people couldn't replicate it. But they might be able to survive the way you have. If you teach us, maybe we could help them survive together."

"What makes you think I care if the street scum live or die?" the woman said.

Nola's heart stuttered. "Because I have to believe there are decent people in the world. Because even though you've made a home out here, your people must have come from the city. You know what it's like to be cold and sick and hungry. You know what it's like to be afraid."

"You don't," the woman spoke from behind Nola. "The glass blocked the whole world from you."

"But I've learned. I don't want to abandon the people whose city has been destroyed by the domes. I don't want to hide and wait for them all to rot." Nola looked to the man. "If you really believe that all of us are just plain human, then you've got to think it's wrong to hide and do nothing."

"What if the kindest act is to kill them all?" the man said. "Put the street scum out of their misery, save them the pain of a slow death."

"No," Nola said, "the world isn't that far gone. Not yet."

"I like you." A woman stepped out of the trees directly in front of Nola.

Nola blinked, trying to find the trick of the light that had concealed the woman. But the shadows of the rising sun didn't reveal any place the woman might have hidden.

"You're wrong about the people on the pavement," the woman said. "They're too far gone to be saved. Still, I like your heart."

The woman crossed her arms and stared at their group, her gaze moving from one to the next as though appraising each of them in turn.

She wasn't old, probably not much more than thirty, but there was a weight to her presence that made the examination unsettling. Nola studied her closely-cropped brown hair that matched the color of her sack-like clothing. Her shoes were made of sewn leather, as were the fingerless gloves she wore. The woman had no weapon Nola could see, yet she stood in front of them, not seeming to mind the Guard guns, knives, and sword Nola, Jeremy, and Julian carried.

"I don't like company," the woman said. "Makes the whole place too damn noisy."

"I'm sorry," the man said.

"It's fine," the woman said. "They're as worth it as the last batch. Get back to the gap."

The man gave a nod and slipped between the trees. Before Nola could think whether to say goodbye or thank you, he'd disappeared without even the sound of footsteps trailing behind him.

I didn't notice how silently he walked when we were following him.

"I'm afraid you might be disappointed," the woman said, "coming all this way just to find us."

"Finding healthy people at all is nothing short of miraculous," Julian said.

The woman snorted. "You've been hiding too long. Come on out."

With a faint rustling of leaves, more figures emerged from the trees. Two men dropped into view from high branches. A tiny woman slipped out from under low-hanging leaves. A set of dark-haired twins stepped out to flank their group.

"Best get moving. Daylight is wasting." The woman looked to Julian. "No offense."

"None taken." Julian bowed.

The woman slipped between the trees, heading farther north.

Nola followed, watching the way the woman twisted and bent to avoid brushing against the leaves, always choosing a path that allowed her to continue forward without making a sound.

"Rebecca?" Nola said.

"Yep," Rebecca answered.

"Thank you for agreeing to see us," Nola said.

"Either that or kill you," Rebecca said. "I don't need more death this week."

"The people in the valley," Jeremy said, "the ones the guards—"

"Guards killed them last week," Rebecca said. "They don't count for this tally."

Jeremy reached forward, taking Nola's hand, his pinky draping across her palm.

"Did the guards find you here?" Jeremy said.

"Turned their trail about four miles east." Rebecca skirted around a wide stand of tightly planted trees. "Moved the bodies to the valley to rot."

Nola's stomach churned. "Why did you move them?"

"They died too close to a healthy stream," Rebecca said. "We can't let that kind of decay touch the water, so we moved them to the valley where they can't do any harm. Their bodies will be helping the brush regrow soon enough."

"What burned the valley?" Nola asked.

"Peter," Rebecca laughed.

Nola waited for Rebecca to continue, but instead she stopped next to the densely packed trees.

"Get the other wanderers," Rebecca said to no one in particular before turning to Jeremy. "Don't forget, I've got the right to have you killed if you try to hurt my people." Rebecca ducked between branches and out of sight.

The twins stood next to the place where Rebecca had disappeared.

"Go in," the left twin said.

"Mind your head," the right twin said.

"Thank you." Julian stepped in front of Nola, bowing low to get the brim of his hat beneath the branches.

"What's in there?" Nola asked.

"Rebecca," the left twin said.

"Right." Nola nodded. "Obviously."

Holding onto the straps of her pack, Nola bent over and followed Julian. The tan of his suit had already disappeared into the foliage. The branches tugged at her shirt, finding the place where the arrow had torn the fabric.

I'm following the people who tried to kill me. Going into a dark place. A closed place.

"Jeremy," Nola said.

"I'm right behind you," Jeremy said.

The knot in Nola's chest eased.

"I must say, I'm impressed." Julian's voice came through the leaves in front of Nola.

"Juli..." His name faded from her lips as she stepped into the center of the trees.

A hint of morning light filtered down through the leaves, helping the candles that hung from the branches to light the clearing. Fifty feet in diameter, the space held tables and chairs, as though the Northerners had been expecting to meet for a morning meal. At the far end of the clearing, Rebecca sat at a square table with candles perched on the front corners.

In the golden-green light, Rebecca lost the look of one who only knew the color brown. The glow softened her, giving a sparkle to her keen eyes.

"Welcome to the Woodlands," Rebecca said. "We're not much on visitors, so consider yourselves lucky to have made it this far."

"Thank you." Nola bowed. "How did you build this?"

"We didn't." Rebecca waved a hand toward the canopy of changing leaves. "The forest built this. We only found it and were smart enough not to destroy it."

"It's beautiful," Nola said.

Rebecca scanned the room. "I suppose. We have better places, but those aren't for people like you."

"Hmm." Julian pressed a palm to one of the trees.

"Just because we know your secrets doesn't mean you get to know ours," Rebecca said.

"And how do you know ours?" Jeremy asked.

"You came here to find out how we survive," Rebecca said. "I can believe that. We're a myth, your interest is understandable, but there's more to it than that."

"Really?" Julian said.

"Of course." Rebecca leaned forward, planting her elbows on the table. "Like you said, the same people are trying to slaughter all of us."

"Fair enough." Julian took a chair from one of the tables and set it across from Rebecca. "The real question is what do you intend to do about it?"

"Us?" Rebecca said. "We do what we have to to keep our area clear. We're not like you. My people don't heal after taking an arrow to the side."

"Most of the Domers don't heal either," Jeremy said.

"So we should attack them?" Rebecca said. "Just rush the glass and hope for the best?"

"Of course not," Jeremy said. "The Outer Guard are well trained and better armed than your people could ever hope to be."

"Then you should attack." Rebecca pointed to Jeremy.

"Not possible," Jeremy said. "We can't get across the river, and even if we could find a way to get every fighter in Nightland over the water, it would still be a slaughter. All they would have to do is hold out until sunrise."

"Then we talk to them," Rebecca said, "form a treaty and live in peace."

"I wish I believed that were possible," Julian said. "The territories of our three peoples don't encroach upon each other. There are no resources we are competing for. In a perfect world, we should all be able to live in peace."

"In a perfect world, children wouldn't be born behind glass," Rebecca said, "and I would be able to give you fairy dust to sprinkle on the street scum so they could all survive."

"There has to be something we can do," Nola said. "I refuse to hide and wait for the domes to come for me."

"My thoughts exactly," Rebecca said. "I'd rather see the glass melt than my trees burn. I'm sure you'd rather not see the mountain brought down on the nightwalkers' heads."

Julian nodded.

"Glad to know we see eye to eye." Rebecca pounded a fist on the table and stood. "I wish your leader had come to see us himself, but I suppose Emanuel doesn't often come out of hiding."

"How do you know his name?" Nola planted her hands on her hips to keep her fingers from trembling.

"I know lots of things," Rebecca said. "Just because the nightwalkers have ignored everything beyond the tips of their fangs doesn't mean the rest of us have been keeping our heads in the dirt. If we're going to be working together, I'd advise you not to underestimate my people."

"Will we be working together?" Nola took a deep breath, trying to stop the feeling of tumbling through the world too quickly for reason.

"Don't know if I'll have to kill you before the end of the day, but it is nice to know we have similar goals. If you had wanted to take my forest"—Rebecca shrugged—"we could have ended this at the blight field, and I wouldn't have had to waste time on you."

"I'm glad our journey wasn't in vain," Julian said.

"I never said that," Rebecca said.

Too fast. It's all much too fast.

"If you don't have an immediate plan to attack the domes, we'd like to see how you've been surviving," Jeremy said.

"Sure," Rebecca said. "I don't think any of it will help you in the mountain, and it certainly won't help the people dying on the highway."

"Why not?" Nola asked.

"Because what we've got can't be built with steel and glass, or by blasting through stone." Rebecca walked to the side of the space. "You can't remake it. You can't demand it."

"I don't understand," Jeremy said.

"You wouldn't. The glass shattered that part of your soul before you learned to talk." Rebecca slipped between two trees. "Keep up if you don't want the twins to get you."

Nola ran a few steps to slide between the trees before Rebecca could completely disappear.

"Nola, wait," Jeremy said.

Nola reached back, taking Jeremy's hand, but not letting her gaze slip from the heels of Rebecca's leather shoes.

"If they wanted to kill us, they would have tried it already," Nola said.

"Not necessarily true," Rebecca said, "but I'm sure your man was about to warn you of the same thing."

"I was," Jeremy said.

"Ha." Rebecca snaked sideways, twisting around a low bush with nobbles on the branches where berries would grow in spring.

"I've been around plenty of people who wanted me dead," Nola said. "None of them ever turned their back to me when I was armed."

"That makes me foolish, not peaceful." Rebecca stopped at the edge of the trees.

The space in front of them cleared, leaving a patch of bright blue sky above. Weeds fought for life on the forest floor, and moss clung to the trunks of the trees.

"Do you hear that?" Rebecca said.

Nola took a slow breath and listened. The bright scent of the trees and the fresh chill morning air filled her lungs. Below the soft *rustle* of the wind through the leaves, a faint *trickle* of running water carried up from the ground.

"What is that?" Nola asked.

"Humans need air, water, food, and shelter to survive," Rebecca said. "The trees helped us find shelter and purged the worst of the city's filth from our air. Water took a lot longer to sort out."

Rebecca pointed to a pile of rocks across the way.

Scanning the trees for the twins or whoever else might be watching, Nola crossed to the rocks, Jeremy keeping step beside her. As they neared the rocks, the sounds of the water became clearer. Not racing like an underground river, but running calmly, like a steady stream.

The rocks weren't a pile as they had seemed from a distance, but a boundary surrounding an opening that led underground.

"Go on down," Rebecca said. "Took long enough to build it, might as well show it off."

Jeremy stepped in front of Nola, pulling out his flashlight and shining the beam into the darkness.

"Used to be a couple streams running through the woods," Rebecca said. "They'd run clean, then the bad rain would drift northwest from the city and ruin all the water."

A dirt path sloped down into the darkness. Nola stayed close behind Jeremy, testing each step as she went.

"Found a spring down here that runs pretty long." Rebecca followed them into the darkness. "Didn't have much water at the time. We dug out part of a stream to make it cut down to meet up with the spring. Dam that stream up and divert the water out of the woods when the rains get bad. Open it up and get as much water running down here as we can when the raindrops are clean."

A spring ran through the rocks on the tunnel floor, the water bubbling and leaping as it cascaded downstream.

"Wow." Nola knelt by the edge, letting her fingers sink into the chill water.

"We store water for the dry seasons," Rebecca said. "That's the hardest part. Boil it all before we drink it just in case."

"It's beautiful." Nola tipped her hand, watching the water dripping from her palm sparkle in the beam of Jeremy's flashlight.

"You spent too much time behind the glass." Rebecca laughed. "If you think it's pretty, good on you. All I care about is not having lost any of my people to bad water in ten seasons."

"Very impressive," Julian said. "I hadn't imagined such a thing to be possible without filters and electricity."

"That rot is what got all of us into this mess," Rebecca said. "I was born in these woods, and I can promise you, we've never had one hint of electricity."

"Can we see where you live?" Nola trailed her fingers through the water. "Are all your homes made of trees like the place with the candles? How do you farm? Do you store seeds for the cold months?"

"Leave it to Lenora Kent's daughter to worry about the damned seeds," a terribly familiar voice growled from the opening above.

CHAPTER FOURTEEN

Nola felt the impact of hitting the dirt before she registered Jeremy tossing her out of view of the opening to the clearing above. Julian's sword cleared its sheath as she sprang to her feet to see Jeremy pointing his gun at the figure silhouetted by the sunlight.

"Back away," Jeremy said. "You may have the high ground, but do you really think you'll get out of this fight alive?"

"I've made it this far, Ridgeway. If that doesn't prove there's more to survival than contaminating your blood with chemicals, I don't know what does." Captain Stokes limped a step down the dirt path toward the spring.

Nola took a step forward, reaching for her weapon.

"You've even trained the botanist to shoot." Stokes eyed Nola. "I'm surprised you let her move beyond a hot house flower."

"What the hell are you doing here?" Nola asked.

"Surviving," Stokes said.

"Pardon me," Julian said, his sword raised, "but I seem to be at a disadvantage. I have no idea who you are."

Stokes' brow furrowed, joining his eyebrows into one dark line. "Who the hell are you, and how did you get a sun suit?"

"Play nice," Rebecca said. "I don't like this sort of noise."

"He's going to kill you, Rebecca," Jeremy said. "You've got to know that. Stokes will lead the domes here, and they will destroy everything you have."

"A Domer then?" Julian said.

"Arthur Stokes, former Captain of the Dome Guard." Stokes took another step forward, his heavy dome boots sinking into the dirt. The boots were the only bit of dome clothing he still wore. He'd traded his black uniform for the brown clothing of the Northerners.

"Captain of the Dome Guard hiding in the woods?" Julian said.

"Domes be damned," Stokes said. "And I really don't need some hopped up, self-righteous fool's opinion on it."

"Such judgment from someone who's never seen my face," Julian said.

"What are you doing here?" Nola said. "These people haven't hurt the domes. You don't have any right to—"

"I didn't come here to hurt the Woodlands people," Stokes said. "Hell, I didn't know they existed when I left the domes."

"Left the domes?" Nola took a step forward.

"Don't trust him," Jeremy said.

"Even out here the Ridgeways assume superiority." Stokes walked down to the stream, stopping as close to Nola as Jeremy would allow. "I'd love to weave you some story of peace and tolerance, but the truth of the matter is the domes have gone to shit, and there are some kinds of hell no loyalty can bargain for."

"What happened?" Nola asked.

"I don't want to talk about this down here," Rebecca said. "Give the water a hint of how ruined the world is and it might not run so pure."

Stokes glared at Rebecca for a moment, then limped back up toward the clearing. One of the twins reached down, helping him up the last, steepest part of the incline.

"You can't trust him," Jeremy said.

"And I should trust a nightwalker and some runaways from the glass?" Rebecca said. "He's given me a better reason to have faith than the three of you have offered."

What happened in the domes?

Nola wanted to shout the question, but the sound of the stream stopped her.

"We need to get moving." Another vaguely familiar voice came from above. "We've got five miles to cover, and we've got to be at the rendezvous point by noon."

Jeremy stepped out into the clearing first, aiming his weapon, not at Stokes, but at another man. One with short hair and an angry sunburn on his forehead.

"You're from the domes, too," Jeremy said.

"Seems to be a theme," the man said.

Nola narrowed her eyes at the man, trying to place his face away from the golden-green light of the glade. "You're a Dome Guard."

"Was," the man said. "Stokes, we've got to get moving."

Stokes. Not Captain Stokes.

"Let's go." Stokes headed east.

"Where are you going?" Jeremy said. "To lead Salinger here to murder these people?"

"Shove your pious drivel up your ass." Stokes rounded on Jeremy, not seeming to care that Jeremy's weapon was aimed at his heart. "You ran away from the domes like a love sick kid, chasing a girl who helped a bunch of strangers slip through the glass, and in that tiny Graylock-altered mind of yours, you can't even imagine why anyone else would have to leave that tyrannical piece of shit prison after Salinger and his men arrived?"

"What are you doing here?" Jeremy said.

"I don't answer to children." Stokes glared at the bloody tear in Nola's shirt and gave a growl of disgust before stalking off through the trees. He didn't slip silently between the branches like the Northerners, or even try to mimic the gentle way Rebecca walked as Nola had. He stomped through the forest as though every tree were under his command and should leap out of his path or risk their captain's wrath.

"If you want to witness this week's count, you should follow him," Rebecca said.

"What are you talking about?" Nola asked even as she followed Stokes and the other guard.

"You wanted to know what we're doing about the domes creeping through our land," Rebecca said. "We might not have the strength of the nightwalkers or the technology of the domes, but we're far from helpless."

"What are you doing?" Nola asked.

"Making a dent," Rebecca said.

Stokes laughed.

"You can't trust him," Jeremy said.

"Coming from a glass child who lives with the nightwalkers, that means so much," Rebecca said. "Stokes has proven his worth. Same can't be said of you."

Nola bit back her questions as Stokes led them through a glade where huts had been built around the trunks of the trees. A fire pit took up the center of the area. An older woman sat near the cold coals, mending a shirt in the shade of the leaves.

Sounds of life carried from a few of the dwellings. Low voices speaking. The scraping of metal against wood, as though someone carved new arrow shafts hidden behind the thin hut walls.

"Is this where all your people live?" Julian asked.

No more than thirty could fit in these homes.

"All the people in this glen live here," Rebecca said.

"Fair enough," Julian said.

Nola wanted to stop and peek inside one of the huts to see how the Northerners kept warm at night, how they made their beds, and what food they kept on hand, but Stokes stomped past the homes and back into the tangled woods.

"Everyone else dispersed as planned?" Stokes said.

"The unit is carrying out your orders, sir," the guard said.

"Unit?" Jeremy said. "You have a whole unit out here?"

"And the rest?" Stokes ignored Jeremy.

"I personally checked last night. Everything is in place," the guard said.

Stokes gave a sharp nod. "You children might as well put your weapons away. We've got a long walk ahead of us, but since you're all hopped up on Graylock, I doubt you'll care."

Nola kept her weapon in her hand. Each leaf hid a person waiting to attack. Every patch of stone led to an underground tunnel filled with unknown enemies.

"What are you doing out here, Stokes?" Jeremy said when they reached a patch of low-lying bushes that left them a clear view of the sky.

The morning sun beat down on Nola's face. The rays would damage her skin cells, but Graylock would heal her before the sun could move beyond causing simple discomfort.

"Had to get out," Stokes said. "It was either that or lose my soul."

"Soul," Rebecca said.

Nola glanced over her shoulder to see Rebecca walking right behind Julian, carrying a bow and a quiver of arrows over her shoulder, though how she'd gotten the weapons, Nola didn't know.

"Funny how glass people ponder things they don't understand." Rebecca looked up to the sky.

"Why were the domes going to make you lose your soul?" Nola asked.

"This coming from the girl the domes sent out onto a bridge they wanted to blow up," Stokes said.

The other guard laughed.

"They used me to kill those people," Nola said, "not you."

"Things didn't get better when you got out," Stokes said.

They reached a creek that cut through the forest. The trunk of a tree lay across the water.

Stokes grimaced as he climbed onto the makeshift bridge. "When the capture or kill order came down on Magnolia, I thought we'd reached a new low."

Jeremy shuddered.

Nola laid a hand on his shoulder. "I'm okay."

Stokes stopped and turned to watch as Jeremy took her hand, kissing her palm.

"Your father should have known you'd chase her," Stokes said. "Maybe Gray-lock scrambled his brain."

"That's not how it works," Jeremy said.

"Then I'm sorry you have such a shit for a father." Stokes limped the rest of the way across the creek. "A father worth his salt would have known he was sacrificing his son by giving the kill order on his own child's girlfriend, but Captain Ridgeway sent down the order anyway."

"He was too afraid of the Incorporation to do anything else," the guard said.

"What did the Incorporation have to do with the Outer Guard being ordered to kill me?" Nola jumped up onto the tree and ran across the creek in a few quick steps. She didn't meet Stokes' gaze as she leapt down on the other side.

"When your disappearance was reported, the Incorporation wanted the situation handled," Stokes said. "By any means necessary."

Jeremy jumped down next to Nola. He pressed his arm against hers, as though needing reassurance she was real.

"Sounds like the Incorporation," Julian said.

"You've dealt with them?" Stokes said.

"Once upon a time, I worked in asset management in a set of domes far, far away from here," Julian said.

"Good to know there are people who have made it long term on the outside," the guard said.

"Well," Julian said, "Vamp did greatly increase my lifespan."

The guard flinched.

"Why would the Incorporation care so much about Nola?" Jeremy said.

"One of their own slipped out of their control," Stokes said. "Those sorts of things can't be allowed. They wanted it taken care of *or else*, so Ridgeway sent out the order. Didn't go so well for him."

"What do you mean?" Jeremy said.

"Instead of taking care of the escapee, he lost his own damned kid." Stokes pointed into the trees, gesturing for them all to follow like they were Dome Guard under his command.

"Is my dad okay?" Jeremy asked.

The growth here wasn't as healthy as it had been by the settlement. Brown spots took the place of orange and yellow on the leaves, and rot had eaten away patches of the bark on the trees.

"Last I saw him, he was as fine as an ass-licking buffoon can be," Stokes said.

Rebecca laughed from the back of their group.

"Once the Incorporation heard Ridgeway had lost his own son, they decided the situation had gone on long enough," Stokes said. "They decided to send in Salinger."

"Because of us?" Nola stopped, swaying on the spot. "Salinger came because we left?"

Jeremy wrapped his arms around Nola, pressing his cheek to her hair. "Breathe, Nola."

"Did Salinger order the burning of the city?" Nola said. "Did all those people—"

"Don't," Jeremy said. "You can't think like that."

"Salinger was called in because you ran," Stokes said, "but the fire had already been started. You were just the first sparks to leap high enough to be noticed."

Tears stung Nola's eyes. "But the Incorporation sent Salinger because of us."

"The second the bridge had to be blown, it was done," Stokes said. "The Incorporation was looking for a gap. The orders were coming, all of them."

"All?" Julian said.

Stokes opened his mouth, snapped it shut, and stomped off into the trees.

The guard looked at them for a moment before following his commander.

"What orders?" Nola chased after Stokes. Jeremy's hand slipped into hers as she ducked between trees. "Stokes, what did the Incorporation do besides burn the city?"

Stokes punched a branch that hung in his path, breaking it and sending the stick crashing away.

Rebecca growled.

The scent of Stokes' blood reached Nola's nose.

"When Salinger came, he brought a hundred Incorporation Guard from different domes with him," the guard said. "After two days, he sent a report back to Incorporation Headquarters, all about how our domes had no leadership. How we had failed to maintain control of the outsiders. How our population had been too damaged by casualties from the fighting."

"But that's why they let us use Graylock," Jeremy said. "We'd already told them the Outer Guard were being slaughtered in the city."

"They used that, too." Stokes crashed through the trees, not bothering to shield himself from the sticks that tore at his skin.

"They've used Graylock?" Julian said. "Are there more than a hundred Incorporation Guard with the power of Graylock in their systems just across the river?"

Fear clawed at Nola's stomach.

"No," Stokes said. "The Incorporation and I see eye to eye on Graylock at least. That filth has no place in the domes. If you're going to build glass walls to keep human blood pure, you can't defend the domes by polluting your DNA. It's hypocrisy at an unforgivable level."

"Then how did they use Graylock?" Jeremy said. "You're not making any sense."

"No," Stokes said. "You're not thinking."

The trees opened up in front of them. They'd reached the rocky edge of a cliff that gave them a view of the lowlands beyond. The forest stretched out before them, but whatever evolution had preserved the Northerners' home hadn't touched the woods below.

The few trees that still clung to life had withered leaves hanging from their knotted branches. The trunks didn't grow as wide and steady either. Instead, they listed to the side like zombies stumbling through the wilderness. Even the breeze carried a scent of rot the Woodlands had avoided.

"The Incorporation decided our domes population needed to be increased." Stokes stared out over the decaying forest. "When I read the first part of the message, I thought they meant for some of the guards they'd brought in to stay with us. We had already received some new citizens. It seemed natural they would leave a few more behind. I read that damned message a dozen times before I could admit to myself I'd actually understood."

No one spoke.

Nola watched Stokes, the man she had feared and hated, gaze out over the trees. The sun glinted off the lines in his face.

How did the world manage to hurt such a hardened man?

"It wasn't a relocation order," Stokes said. "It was a breeding order. Dome females between seventeen and twenty-seven had been ordered to breed. The Incorporation sent a list of assigned partners."

CHAPTER FIFTEEN

"What?"

The trees below the cliff swayed, wavering as the world itself seemed to tip.

"Our male Outer Guard had all polluted themselves with Graylock." Stokes' words pounded against Nola's ears. "Too many domes citizens had been killed. The Incorporation had sent the best of the Outer Guard from all the domes into our home. They couldn't waste the opportunity to spread prime DNA."

"They ordered dome women to breed with the guards?" Jeremy said.

Nola clutched Jeremy's arm, holding him close as though he were the safe place in a game of tag.

"They sent a list of pairings," Stokes said. "The optimal matches to create the healthiest children for the domes."

"That's sick." Jeremy held Nola, blocking the swaying trees from view as he wrapped his body around her.

"All for the good of the domes," the guard said. "The domes were built to produce healthy generations of children. How could a loyal citizen argue with the Incorporation's logic?"

"How were they intending to impregnate the women?" Julian asked.

Nola clenched her eyes shut, pressing her cheek to Jeremy's chest, letting his racing heartbeat thunder in her ear.

"Mating." Hatred filled Stokes' voice. The same hatred Nola had heard when he spoke of the vampires, Outer Guard, and Graylock. "Timed mating for the greatest chance of conception. It was deemed a waste of resources to artificially inseminate the women."

"People didn't go along with it," Jeremy said. "It's a sick plan from the twisted Incorporation. There's no way people agreed."

"Some did," the guard said. "After all the hopeless violence, a chance to bring some good into the world, people thought things were finally starting to turn around."

"And those that disagreed?" Julian said.

"Lilly." Tears streamed down Nola's cheeks. "Lilly was seventeen. That's how she ended up on the outside. She said no, didn't she?" Nola twisted just far enough to see Stokes nod.

"There were a few bold enough to outright say no," Stokes said. "Salinger loaded them onto a boat and took them across the river. After that, no one dared argue."

"My sister," Jeremy said.

"Lost the day Salinger dropped fire packs on the city," Stokes said. "She didn't make it long enough to hear the damned order."

"But you did," Julian said. "Slaughtering the city was acceptable, but treating your women as breeding mares was a step too far?"

"I swore an oath to protect the people of the domes," Stokes said. "When the fire packs blew, my place was inside the glass, making sure that monster didn't turn his wrath on his own people. But when word came down that they would be separating husbands and wives—sending seventeen-year-old girls to the beds of strangers—it got pretty damn clear that I only had three options: Roll over and let the devil himself do whatever he damn well pleased, kill the bastard in his sleep and let the domes banish me, or take who I could and get out. Find a way to stop Salinger from the outside."

"So you took some guards and ran?" Jeremy said. "You just left those women—"

"I took the guards I could trust and got them and their families out," Stokes said.

"A lot of good that does for the people you were sworn to protect who are still trapped with Salinger," Jeremy said.

Stokes stepped up to Jeremy. Blood stained his cracked knuckles.

Jeremy shifted, holding Nola with one arm, while planting himself between her and Stokes.

"I took my people into the woods hoping for salvation," Stokes said. "I kept them alive on the slim hope that we might be able to do something for the people we love we had to leave behind. I don't want to hear shit from you about what a brave Ridgeway would have done. Your filthy father is still in the damned domes kissing Salinger's ass. You haven't done anything to help the people still trapped inside. At least I'm trying to do something. At least I'm trying to figure out how to help the women that wouldn't follow me!"

"How old is she?" Nola's throat tightened, pressing down so her words barely came out.

"Twenty-six." Stokes' face crumpled. "The Domes Council had denied her request for another baby. My daughter cried when she heard the order. At first, I thought she was terrified. I was going to tear down the domes pane by pane to save her. Then I realized how happy she was. The Incorporation gift-wrapped torment with the promise of hope. I knew I had to get out and find a way to do something. I've got two granddaughters. I can't let something like this happen to them."

"How can we help?" Julian said.

"Ha." Stokes blinked, brushing away the brightness in his eyes. "I never thought I'd hear a Vamper suggest anything but murder."

"We prefer the proper term vampire, actually." Julian gave a quick nod.

"Can't do anything about what's happening in the domes," Rebecca said. "They've got a giant helicopter and firepower we can't match. So we make a dent."

"A dent?" Jeremy said.

"Throw rocks at the glass until the whole place shatters." Rebecca stared at Stokes, who had looked back out over the cliff to the crooked forest below. "Move, or you'll miss it."

"Right." Stokes nodded. "Let's move."

He limped along the edge of the cliff, following a faint path.

"Don't judge the captain too harshly," the guard said. "I got my wife and little boy out with me, and my brother's wife is five months pregnant. If I'd left somebody vulnerable behind—"

"Are we moving or are we chatting?" Stokes shouted.

Shaking his head, the guard ran after Stokes. Julian followed them, his tan suit not quite hiding the rounding of his shoulders.

Jeremy held Nola tight, pressing his cheek to the top of her head.

"It was inevitable," Jeremy said.

"What was?" Nola wrapped her arms around Jeremy, memorizing the feel of him, blocking out the notion of ever having to know the touch of another person.

"If they'd given that order while we were still in the domes," Jeremy said, "we'd have had to find a way out. Nola, I never would have let them touch you."

"I know," Nola said. "If Gentry had still been there..."

"She'd have killed them all," Jeremy said.

Nola tipped her chin up, kissing Jeremy. "When we find her, we'll go back to the domes and bring hell to the demons."

"I love you."

"Is this what glass teenagers are like?" Rebecca leaned against a tree, watching them.

"Only the ones who have almost been killed a few times, left their home, and keep balancing on the edge of a dying world," Nola said.

"Children should be raised in the woods," Rebecca said. "We don't have this sort of trouble. Move, or we'll lose the others."

Nola took Jeremy's hand and followed the path Stokes had taken.

A bird sailed overhead, cawing her greeting to the bright new morning.

"Do your people have children?" Jeremy said. "Healthy children?"

The bird twisted in the wind, gliding in a wide circle.

"Some," Rebecca said. "Not enough to replace the older ones who die, and not all of them make it to walking age."

The bird dove into the trees, crashing through the branches and out of sight.

"Our numbers getting smaller isn't so bad," Rebecca said. "Less meat to hunt, less food to grow, less water to boil. Our kind spent a long time driving the trees back to where the forests could barely survive. Might be time for the trees to drive us back so they can take over again. I don't see any sadness in it."

A brief *squeak* of pain marked the end of the life of the bird's prey.

"But what if there are no children left at all?" Nola said.

"The last one alive needs to make sure the cook fires are out," Rebecca said. "World's bigger than humans. It'll keep spinning through space without any of us to mark the passing of days."

The path twisted and sloped down, forming switchbacks along the side of the cliff. The path was small, too narrow to have been made by humans. Nola glanced over the edge. It wasn't a far fall. She could jump it if she wanted to. But Julian picked his way along the crumbling rocks close on the heels of Stokes and the guard.

The stench of the trees below worsened as they neared the bottom. The scent of soil crept through the foul odor, but there was something wrong with it, almost as though Nola could smell the fertility being stripped from the earth.

Stokes didn't pause at the bottom of the cliff. He headed southeast, cutting through the tilted trees.

Julian slowed his pace as he reached the forest floor, his hat tipping side to side as he examined the trees.

"What is it?" Nola ran the last switchback to reach him, twisting to keep Jeremy's hand in hers as they moved single file.

"I don't know," Julian said. "Rather, I know what's wrong, but I can't quite pinpoint the root of it."

"What?" Jeremy's gaze swept the trees.

"The dirt here is wrong," Julian said. "The trees here are twisted but growing. Yet the forest right above seems so much healthier."

Nola knelt, digging her fingers into the earth. A yellowish hue marked the dirt. "Something tainted the soil. I don't know what it is from sight, but I could bring some samples back to Kieran."

"Don't know what good samples will do you." Rebecca walked ahead of them, continuing down Stokes' path. "But I can tell you why it's different."

"Why?" Nola wiped her fingers on her bloodstained shirt.

"Floodplain," Rebecca said. "When the streams go over their banks, this whole place goes underwater. Only difference I've seen between here and up on the cliff."

"I wish I could bring Kieran to see this," Nola said. "I might have more training in plant preservation, but I'm not used to seeing contaminated earth."

"If we all make it through whatever storm the domes might bring, perhaps Emanuel will allow you to take Kieran so far from safety," Julian said.

"Maybe." Nola followed Rebecca, her gaze flicking between the invisible path and the forest around them.

She wanted to run, to reach whatever they were heading toward, but Stokes, the guard, and Rebecca wouldn't be able to keep up, let alone lead.

"Did it bother you?" Nola ducked under a tree that had cracked and tipped to pierce the forest floor.

"Did what bother me?" Jeremy asked.

"When I was still normal," Nola said. "When I was slow and weak."

"You were never slow or weak," Jeremy said.

Nola laughed. The sound sent something scampering away through the grayish crumble of the underbrush. "Me before Graylock compared to you after Graylock? You must have thought of me as an eggshell."

"No. I was worried I might be too strong and hurt you, but I didn't think of you as any more fragile. Wanting to protect you never came from you being weak. You're the most precious thing in the world to me. Graylock made me better able to make sure the world didn't take away the person I love most."

A warm glow of heat blossomed from Nola's chest, soaring up to tingle her cheeks. "I love you, too."

"Good."

She could hear the smile in Jeremy's voice.

They walked on, the bubble of happiness in Nola's chest battling against the decay of the forest, which worsened as they walked farther southeast.

Toward the city.

Where the domes had corralled workers, the humans they had deemed unworthy of salvation. Where the factories had poisoned the water. Where smog hung heavy in the air. Where the streets were lined with filth that spread disease.

"Julian," Nola said.

"Yes?"

"When you traveled here, did you pass places where people still lived in healthy cities?" Nola said.

"Not in the way you're hoping," Julian said. "I would love to tell you that all you were ever taught in the domes was pure propaganda and there are places on this planet where human civilization still thrives. But I will not stoop so low as to feed you a comforting lie. The architects have built other safe havens, and there may be more small communities like Rebecca's that have managed to find healthy land where they can survive, but even if they exist, I doubt you could find them."

"Wouldn't have found us at all if it hadn't been for the blight," Rebecca said.

"And shooting me with an arrow," Nola said.

"Ha." Rebecca skirted the bank of a stream.

They followed the water, Nola trying to ignore the yellow froth bubbling against the rocks.

Time dragged on. The sun rose higher in the sky, its rays cutting through the chill of the morning. They reached the edge of the slanting forest and entered what might have been a meadow. All the plants had died, leaving nothing but cracked earth with a yellowish tint behind.

Stokes tromped through the barren dirt without acknowledging its danger or sadness.

The dull pounding of their footsteps became a lament, a dirge for the dying world. Their trek, a dutiful viewing of all that had been destroyed.

Nola hadn't been able to stand being locked in safety while those outside suffered. She had seen ill humans. Had witnessed the violence of desperation. But there was more to the end than the pain people could feel.

We made everything around us hurt, too.

A heavy stone weighed down her lungs.

This isn't the time to grieve.

Stokes slowed his pace as he moved out of the clearing and into a forest that had rotted much like the trees along the river by the domes.

Shaking her head, Rebecca moved to the front of their pack, slipping silently between the trees.

Stokes drew his weapon. The guard did the same.

As though a silent signal had been given, Jeremy stepped in front of Nola, leaving Julian at the back. The *rasp* of Julian drawing his sword sent Nola's heart racing, anticipating whatever enemy approached them. She drew her weapon, forcing herself to take slow, deep breaths even as the air stung her lungs.

A glint of metal up ahead caught her eye, but Rebecca kept moving forward.

She opened her mouth to shout a warning, but Stokes spoke first.

"Damn fine job you did, boys."

CHAPTER SIXTEEN

Nola's grip on her gun faltered as she tried to decide between aiming at Stokes or the glint of metal in the trees.

"Not too hard," a female voice answered. "We're still waiting on two of the boys though."

"This should be enough." Rebecca stood under the glinting metal. "Sixteen marks all running together. That should scare the spider into coming."

The metal shifted, twisting in the breeze. The thing was tiny, too small to be a weapon.

"What is this?" Jeremy stepped forward, his gaze sweeping the trees.

The *click* of a weapon sounded up ahead.

With enough force to break normal bones, Jeremy knocked Nola to the ground. Something hard slammed into her shoulder.

"Hold your fire!" Stokes shouted.

"What the hell is going on, Captain?" a man asked.

The pain in Nola's shoulder faded as her body raced to heal.

"Found Ridgeway with Rebecca," Stokes said. "He's not an Outer Guard, not anymore."

"You're sure about that?" the female voice asked.

"I left before any of you did." Jeremy stood, lifting Nola with him and keeping her pressed to his back. "I've got more reason to doubt you than you do me."

"Is that Magnolia Kent?" the female voice asked.

Nola peeked around Jeremy. A woman stood between dead trees, her gun pointed at Jeremy's chest.

"I know you," Nola said. "I talked to you in the domes."

"So the Ridgeway boy really did run after you." The woman laughed. "I didn't think Graylock left enough human in a person to love like that."

"It does." Nola stepped out from behind Jeremy. "He gave me a dose, too. Everything I feel is the same as before. My body is just stronger."

"Don't happen to have any extra doses of Graylock around?" A man stepped forward to lean against a tree.

Nola had seen him in the domes too, but his time on the outside had affected him more than it had Stokes. The only color left on his face were the dark circles under his eyes and red patches where the sun had attacked his skin.

"Not enough to change you," Jeremy said, "and we aren't sure how to make more."

"Figures." The man shrugged.

A crashing carried through the trees.

Stokes, the guards, and Rebecca all spun toward the sound, their weapons raised.

Nola followed their gaze, leveling her own weapon. Instinct told her to step away and let the former Dome Guard fight whatever demon they had brought down on themselves.

I'm stronger than they are. They know more, but I'm stronger.

"Get me a string," a voice shouted.

"Neelan." The female guard ran toward the man who puffed into view.

"They're behind me. I tried to meet Cass, but they were already coming," Neelan said. "I caught sight of them a mile back. I don't know how fast they're heading this way." He opened his palm, displaying a tiny square of metal.

Stokes grabbed the square, passing it to the sickly guard who stuck it to the end of a string hanging down from the branch of a decaying tree.

"That's a tracker," Nola said. "Why do you have a dome tracker?"

"We've got more than one." Rebecca pointed at the tiny bits of metal glittering through the trees.

More than a dozen trackers hung from the branches, twisting in the foul breeze.

"The Outer Guard are coming after the trackers?" Nola said.

"We didn't expect them for another hour," the sickly guard said. "Cass should have had more time."

"Shit we can do about it. Take your posts," Stokes ordered, every bit the captain he had been inside the domes. He hurried to the northern side of the trees as quickly as his bad leg allowed.

"What do we do?" Nola turned to Jeremy.

"Come with me." Rebecca beckoned them farther east.

Nola wove between the trackers, keeping close on Rebecca's heels.

"You found the trackers in the water bottles?" Nola said.

Rebecca ducked under a pile of fallen trees. "You don't think we were smart enough to notice that everywhere a cluster of refugees settled, the spider's men came swooping in to rain down hell?"

Nola stooped under the tree, expecting to continue on but finding herself in an enclosed space instead. The downed trees looked to have collapsed in on themselves as the ground beneath them sagged. But the dip in the earth had been hollowed out, allowing room for Rebecca, Nola, Jeremy, and Julian to all duck into the shadows. Gaps had been made between the rotting branches of the trees, creating sight lines in every direction.

"When we kept finding groups of dead, the only thing they all had in common were the bottles," Rebecca continued in a whisper. "Didn't take long to find the false bottom and the beacons."

"Why did you hang them out there?" Jeremy leaned toward the gap in the northern part of their hiding place, peering in the direction Neelan had appeared.

"To make a dent," Rebecca said. "We can't attack the domes, but we're stronger than they are out here."

"You're leading them toward your home," Jeremy said.

"We're far enough away," Rebecca said. "One skill they never thought to pass on to your glass soldiers: tracking."

The dull *thump* of heavy boots caught Nola's ear.

"They're here." Nola inched toward Jeremy to peer out into the woods.

The thumping of the boots slowed.

Nola scanned the trees, waiting for fire and death to surge toward their hiding place.

The thumping came closer, bringing the Outer Guard into view. Their black uniforms blared against the dull brown of the trees. They approached slowly, their faces hidden in their helmets. The one in front kept looking at something in his hand.

Nola wished she could see their eyes so she could know if they'd spotted the trackers in the trees or the people hiding around them.

Rebecca nudged Nola out of the way, claiming a spot at the gap and nocking an arrow.

Nola stooped, peering over Jeremy's head while the Outer Guard drew closer still.

Have I met you before? Or are you very far from home? Were you paired with Lilly?

The rifles in the Outer Guard's hands kept her from calling out.

Rebecca shook her head, working her lips against each other but not saying anything.

The seven Outer Guard stopped just shy of the cluster of trees where the trackers hung.

They know something's wrong.

Nola gripped Jeremy's shoulder, leaning down to whisper in his ear.

But a *buzz* and a *thwap* cut through the air before she could speak.

The Outer Guard at the front of the formation stumbled back as an arrow hit him square in the chest.

"We're under attack!" a voice shouted from the guards' ranks.

A *pop* sounded from the trees to the right, and one of the Outer Guard fell. Another *pop* brought a third guard down, but the guard that had been hit by the arrow had already pushed himself to his feet. His heavy Guard vest did more than block the weather and sun—the armor within the fabric had shielded him from Rebecca's blow. He leveled his gun, shooting into the trees to his right, while another guard fired toward the left.

Rebecca let another arrow fly, hitting one of the Outer Guard in the shoulder. The man cried out in pain.

Another *pop* from an unseen weapon sounded as Rebecca let loose another arrow. Two of the guards started toward the downed trees where Nola hid.

Rebecca shot another arrow, hitting one in the thigh. The other moved his finger to pull his trigger.

Jeremy knocked Nola backwards. She listened while she fell, waiting for the burst of *pops* that would try to kill them, wondering if the chemicals on the deadly darts would be strong enough to kill her and Jeremy.

But a *swoosh* and a *bang* came before the *pops*. The ground beneath Nola shook, and the dead trees above her sent a cascade of rot onto her face.

Rebecca let another arrow fly as a string of *pops* filled the air.

The stench of burning reached Nola's nose just before a triumphant *whoop* carried from the trees.

"Went smoother than last time." Rebecca looped her bow over her shoulder and ducked back out of their hiding place.

"What just happened?" Nola squirmed out from under Jeremy.

"I'm impressed." Julian followed Rebecca.

"Impressed by what?" Nola crawled after them.

The stench of burning was stronger outside the shelter of the trees.

Stokes and his guards had already crept out from wherever they'd been hiding, all heading toward the downed Outer Guard.

Wisps of smoke drifted up from a crater that had appeared in the earth. On the far side, three of the guards lay still on the ground.

"The *boom* should have been bigger." Rebecca pulled her arrow out of the thigh of one of the guards.

He lay still, not flinching as the arrow left his flesh. The sun caught a tiny piece of silver metal sticking out of his neck.

"Helmets off." Stokes knelt next to the first guard who had fallen and yanked their helmet free.

A face Nola didn't recognize emerged. A tiny hitch of panic tightened in her chest as the woman knelt beside the next Outer Guard.

Nola felt Jeremy next to her and reached for his hand without looking.

The next Outer Guard she recognized. She had seen him in the corridor of the Outer Guard barracks.

Nola ran her thumb along the ridges of Jeremy's palm, needing to feel the texture of his skin against hers.

A woman in her forties was next.

"Hmm." Stokes pushed himself to his feet. "Take what we need and dump them all into the pit."

"Dump them into the pit?" Nola stepped forward to stare down into the ditch.

The pit had been dug before the explosion had gone off. Singe marks from whatever the explosive had been lapped the top foot of the dirt. Four Outer Guard lay at the bottom, their clothes charred and bodies twisted.

"I had hoped my arrows would all make it through." Rebecca frowned at the burned bit of wood sticking out of one of the guard's shoulders.

"We can't just drop them down there," Nola said. "They could wake up."

"None of them are waking up," Stokes said. "I left behind the flaccid Dome Guard tranq darts when I took my men and ran. We only carry ammunition that kills now. Neelan, strip the bodies."

"But what about the one with Graylock?" Nola pointed to the man she recognized.

"We stab him through the heart," Rebecca said. "Want the pleasure, Julian? It might be a nice change for a nightwalker."

"You can't just stab him," Jeremy said. "He could have information. He could just be trying to get back to his family that's trapped in the domes."

"Do you really want me to let an Outer Guard who's had Graylock wake up?" Stokes said. "What kind of fool do you take me for? Neelan, get to work."

"Neelan." The female guard turned toward the trees. "Neelan?"

The sickly guard ran faster than Nola had thought possible toward a subtle rise in the dirt. "Dammit." He hopped down on the far side of the mound. "Nee-lan's dead, Captain. Two darts to the face."

"Shit." Stokes scrubbed his filthy hands over his chin. "Shit."

The woman let the Outer Guard helmet fall from her hands as she moved toward the mound. "We're carrying him back to camp. He should be burned."

"We can't move anyone until we take care of these demons." Rebecca knelt next to one of the Outer Guard, unfastening his belt and pulling the weapons free.

"We can carry Rivers back to camp, too," Jeremy said.

Rivers. I should have known his name.

"No," Rebecca said.

"I'll carry him myself," Jeremy said.

"You'll carry him and what?" Stokes said. "Do you have chains strong enough to hold him? Are the Woodlands people supposed to dig a prison? If we carry him back to camp and he wakes up, he could hurt people. If he gets free, he could lead Salinger to the forest. Do you want that kind of blood on your hands? I already have to tell Neelan's damned wife her husband is dead. Don't try and make my day worse by getting more innocent people killed."

"We can't just kill a man in cold blood. We're not the—" A crackling cut Jeremy off.

"Report in." The tinny voice carried from the Outer Guard helmet at Stokes' feet. "North team, what's your status?" Captain Ridgeway's voice asked.

CHAPTER SEVENTEEN

Nola placed a hand on Jeremy's chest, stopping him from stepping closer to the helmet.

"North team, report immediately."

"We knew they'd start watching more closely," Rebecca said.

"North team, report." There was no anger in Captain Ridgeway's voice. No panic either.

"How many times have you done this?" Jeremy asked.

"This?" Rebecca said. "None. Dented their numbers? A few."

"North team, report."

"How many Outer Guard have you killed?" Jeremy stepped forward.

Nola pushed against him. He looked down, his gaze finding Nola's hand on his chest.

"Not as many as Salinger killed in the city." Stokes rolled the female guard into the pit.

"North team, status report now." The resignation in Captain Ridgeway's voice pulled at parts of Nola's heart she hadn't known existed anymore.

The guard who had traveled with them from the forest pulled a sack from his pocket, holding it open as Stokes and Rebecca filled it with weapons, boots, and first aid pouches. She opened Rivers' vest, searching his pockets with a practiced motion.

"Wait," Jeremy said as Rebecca pulled a black case free from Rivers' belt. "Can I have that?"

"Can I kill him?" Rebecca said.

"I need the case." Jeremy lifted Nola's hand away from his chest.

"And I need to not haul a traitor home," Rebecca said.

"North team," Captain Ridgeway said. "We are instituting Beta Protocol. Get the hell out."

Each of them froze as Ridgeway's voice crackled through the trees.

"What's Beta Protocol?" Nola said.

"Time to get the hell out." Stokes kicked an Outer Guard into the pit, leaving only Rivers still above the dirt.

"We don't have time to bury them," the female guard said.

"Blame that on the spider," Rebecca said. "Cut the beacons down."

The female guard darted from tree to tree, tearing the trackers from their strings.

"Rivers might know what Beta Protocol is," Nola said.

"So we carry him, ask him, then kill him?" Rebecca said.

"We don't have time to argue," Jeremy said. "I'll carry him, and if it comes to it, I'll kill him."

"We need to move." Rebecca grabbed the sack of weapons and ran, not the way they'd come but farther east, away from the woods.

"I can't let you do that," Stokes said.

Nola didn't see the steel in Stokes' hand until he'd already plunged the blade into Rivers' heart.

"You bastard," Jeremy growled.

"You'll thank me for that someday." Stokes ran after Rebecca. The other guards stayed close behind, two of them carrying Neelan's corpse.

"We should follow," Julian said.

"Follow murderers?" Jeremy shook his head.

"We're all murderers," Julian said. "The world has become too ruthless to leave any of us innocent."

Blood seeped from the wound in Rivers' chest. The same red that had painted the halls of the domes, had been spilt in the tunnels of Nightland, had coated the streets of the city.

"Come on." Nola grabbed Jeremy's hand, dragging him away from the clearing. "Whatever your—whatever Beta Protocol is, we can't be here for it."

Jeremy followed her, though his gaze didn't leave Rivers until the trees blocked his body from view.

Rebecca and the guards wove through the trees ahead of them, slipping in and out of sight.

"He wasn't a great guy," Jeremy said. "I punched him once."

"Why?" Nola kept her eyes on the trees as they ran, catching up to the guards.

"He made a joke about you," Jeremy said.

"What kind of joke?" Nola asked.

"He said I was lucky to have a girl who wasn't dome prim. Something about you learning to sneak into dark corners from the Vampers in Nightland," Jeremy said. "I broke his cheekbone."

"Seems fair," the female guard said.

"He'd already had Graylock. His face healed before I was called to be reprimanded. Dad said..." Jeremy's voice faded away. "He said if Rivers didn't talk so much, maybe he wouldn't end up accidentally banging his face into a wall."

"Ha." Sweat slicked the female guard's brow. "I didn't know Captain Ridgeway had a sense of humor."

"He doesn't," Jeremy said.

"What's your name?" Nola asked.

"Alice," she said. "Jude is the splotchy one."

"Thanks, Al," Jude puffed.

"Preston." Al nodded toward the guard who had come with them from the woods.

No one tried to say who Neelan had been.

They reached a rocky patch where the twisted trees hadn't even attempted to grow. The rocks slipped out from under Stokes' feet as he tried to make his way across.

"We need to move faster," Julian said, only loud enough for Nola and Jeremy's Graylock-enhanced ears to hear. "If Beta Protocol involves fire packs, I don't want to be anywhere near here."

Al and Preston slid on the rocky terrain, trying to keep Neelan's weight balanced between them.

"Let me take him," Jeremy said.

"We can take care of our own." Preston spoke through gritted teeth.

"Leave him or pass him over." Rebecca leapt from rock to rock, quickly overtaking Stokes. "If the Outer Guard catch us in the open, we'll all be dead and there won't be anyone to carry Neelan back to the woods."

"Let me help," Jeremy said.

"Okay." Al stopped, not flinching under Preston's glare.

Jeremy lifted Neelan, draping him carefully over his shoulder.

"We need to run," Julian said.

A cold dread settled in Nola's stomach. She searched the trees and ground for whatever had made Julian's tone so crisp.

"Not all of us are Vampers." Jude gasped for breath as he moved barely faster than a jog.

The rocky patch sloped up, leading to rolling hills covered in scrub brush.

A *hum* shook the air.

Jude glanced up toward the sky. His foot slipped out from under him.

Nola leapt forward, catching him before his face hit the stone, lifting him back up to his feet, and keeping her arm around him as they ran up the slope.

The *hum* in the air had developed texture in the few seconds it had taken to get Jude running again, a thumping that dug into Nola's ear with every beat.

"Damn," Julian said.

Nola glanced back, following Julian's gaze. A black dot appeared in the sky to the south, heading straight for the point where they'd left the guards.

"I suppose Beta Protocol involves Salinger's helicopter," Julian said.

"Get up here." Rebecca stood at the edge of the bushes on the hill, holding back the thick branches for Al and Preston, who dove beneath the dying leaves and crawled out of sight.

Stokes reached the bushes a moment later. He stopped at the edge, looking back toward the rest. Jeremy stayed behind Nola with Julian, and Nola fought with every step to keep Jude from tumbling out of her grasp.

"Get in, you buffalo," Rebecca said.

"Not without my men," Stokes said.

Nola tightened her grip on Jude, dragging him up the hill, not caring if he kept his feet beneath him. She threw him through the gap in the bushes and dove in behind him.

Jude landed with a *thud*, but she didn't bother to ask if she had hurt him. She scrambled over him, grabbed his arms, and dragged him forward far enough to allow Jeremy to duck under the brush.

Al crawled forward, taking Neelan's shoulders and helping guide his body into an open space under the branches.

Julian dived into the shadows a second later with Stokes at his heels. Rebecca slipped between the branches and let them go. The *swish* of the leaves rustling back into place barely carried over the *thump* of the helicopter's approach.

The branches sheltered them from the sun and hid the trees beyond from sight. If Nola had been a very little girl, she would have felt safe beneath their browned leaves. Hidden beyond reach of danger.

"Do you think they saw us?" Nola whispered, sure no one from the helicopter would be able to hear her but unable to convince herself to speak more loudly.

"If they kill us, we'll know they did." Rebecca sank to her knees.

The bushes were five feet high in places, but the uneven growth left some no more than two feet tall. Each of their group nestled beneath the branches as the thumping grew louder.

"We should keep moving." Julian twisted to crawl.

"Do you really think we can outrun them without being seen?" Jude lay on the ground, sweat glistening on his splotchy brow.

"Not even I could outrun a helicopter," Julian said. "But until we know we've been seen and are being followed, I suggest we keep moving as quickly as concealment will allow. There is a radius to every blast, and I would like to be as far from whatever Beta Protocol might be as possible, even if we only make it a hundred yards."

"Agreed." Rebecca's gaze swept the bushes for a moment before she began crawling north.

"What about Neelan," Jeremy said. "Should we...what do you want me—"

A piercing sound cut across Jeremy's words.

Nola crept toward the edge of the bushes, peeking out between branches.

"We have to move," Stokes ordered.

It's too late.

The helicopter flew in a slow circle around where the dead Outer Guard lay. If the people in the helicopter could see their compatriot's corpses, they didn't seem intent on retrieving them. They didn't drop black and silver fire packs on the dead trees either.

No fire. No blasting. Only a shimmer as they sprayed something into the air.

Nola leaned closer to the edge of safety, trying to get a better look at the mist.

"We have to go." Julian grabbed her arm, dragging her backward through the bushes.

"What is it?" Nola twisted around, gaining her own footing.

"We have to go south," Julian called to the others who had been following Rebecca north. "Leave the body, Jeremy."

"Are you—"

"Do not sacrifice the living for the dead." Julian let go of Nola's arm and stood doubled over to run southeast at a pace the humans would have trouble matching.

Nola glanced back, needing to be sure Jeremy was the one crashing through the brush behind her.

"What the hell is going on?" Stokes ran next to Julian, hunched over and red-faced.

"There are demons in the Incorporation's past even you are too young to remember," Julian said.

"Where are you trying to go?" Rebecca stayed on Julian's heels.

"Against the wind."

Rebecca nodded and took the lead, cutting between bushes as though running doubled over with a sack on her back were nothing.

"Jude," Nola said, "we can't leave him."

"I've got him." Al had an arm around Jude's waist. His face had already turned a bright shade of red.

"Let me." Jeremy looped around, half-draping Jude over his back.

"Are you going to leave me under a bush, too?" Jude asked.

"Not as long as you're breathing," Jeremy said.

The weight of another person wouldn't slow Jeremy, but the size of two people together shook the bushes.

"If they fly this way, they'll see us moving," Nola said.

"If we don't keep moving, most of us will die," Julian said.

Nola ducked under a low branch. "Why? Why are we running from mist?"

"It's not mist," Julian said. "They are using one of the Incorporation's worst mistakes to try ridding themselves of enemies. How quickly they forget what the true meaning of evil is. A little more east."

Rebecca shifted their path.

Nola tried to feel it, the breeze that guided Julian away from whatever had scared the vampire so badly. All she could feel on her skin was the brushing of leaves and scratching of branches.

She took a deep breath, trying to scent the wind. A horrible sting filled her nose and burned its way down her throat.

"What is that?" She choked on her question, muddying the words beyond recognition.

They reached the crest of the hill where the bushes were too thin to hide them completely from view. Nola glanced back toward the helicopter.

The mist had become a haze that hung heavy over the trees. For a moment, Nola thought her eyes had failed her in her panic as the trees beneath seemed to melt into the ground.

CHAPTER EIGHTEEN

Nola stared horrified as the trees shrunk, melting beneath the spray from the helicopter.

"We need to move." Al seized Nola's wrist, trying to drag her away from the hilltop. But Al wasn't strong enough to make Nola's feet move.

Neither was Nola.

She couldn't tear her gaze from the trees slumping to the side in their final death throes before dissolving into the barren forest floor.

"How?" Nola shook her head as her whole body trembled. "That's not possible."

"Nola!" Jeremy's shout cut through the storm of confusion battering her mind.

"What are they doing?" Nola chased after Jeremy, glancing over her shoulder to see the helicopter move on to the next patch of trees, wiping away the forest as though it had never existed.

The bushes tore at her skin, but the rough touch seemed to come from far away. From a dream where trees could disappear.

It's not a dream. Not even a nightmare.

"What's in the mist, Julian?" Jeremy kept right in front of Nola, Jude draped over his shoulder, bouncing with every step.

They sprinted down the far side of the hill, Preston supporting Stokes, Rebecca leading with Julian and Al close on her heels.

"I'm not a chemist." The wind shifted, whisking Julian's voice away and surrounding them with the stench of the mist.

The sound of the helicopter came closer, pounding behind the rise of the hill.

"We're not going to make it," Al said.

"Just keep moving." Rebecca veered farther south. "How much of that stuff can they get in the air?"

"The allotment was 4.35 barrels per acre," Julian said. "If they kept the helicopter to its prescribed load, they should have enough Nallot to clear just under eleven acres."

"That's a lot of forest," Al said.

"Not so much we can't outrun them," Jeremy said.

They reached the bottom of the hill, where the bushes grew thicker with branches unwilling to bend as they ran past. Each *crack* as they crashed through the growth echoed in Nola's ears like a rifle shot.

"That's assuming they spread the shit in actual acres." Jude spoke between coughs. "If they spray in a straight line, they could cut a path from here to the domes."

"Can the mist eat concrete?" Rebecca said.

"Not as quickly as it can eat wood," Julian said. "But given enough time, I'm not sure there's much Nallot couldn't destroy."

"Then we'll just have to hope they don't rain death on us." Rebecca raced farther south, toward a wide expanse of rotting trees.

A million questions jumbled in Nola's mind, but one carried over the din.

Why?

With a grunt, Stokes tipped forward, falling into the dirt. Preston grabbed his arm, yanking him up. Before Stokes had gotten to his feet, Julian wrapped an arm around the captain, lifting him as he kept right behind Rebecca.

"Leave me alone." Stokes pushed against Julian's chest.

"Leave you to die?" Julian said, the sideways tilt of his torso the only indication of carrying Stokes' weight. "Don't tempt me."

The horrible need to laugh bubbled in Nola's throat, but the thumping of the helicopter drawing near killed the urge.

"We need to find cover," Nola said.

"We know," Al panted.

The trees here had no leaves on their branches and didn't grow close enough together for their shadows to offer anywhere to hide.

Nola scanned the dirt, searching for a place they could dig a shelter.

Not fast enough, we couldn't dig fast enough.

The tree line broke in front of them, leaving the terrain even more exposed.

A sound carried beneath the noise of the helicopter—the rushing of water against rocks.

620

MEGAN O'RUSSELL

"They're coming over the hill!" Preston darted behind a tree.

But Rebecca didn't hesitate as she ran toward the water.

The stench of the river broke through Nola's panic and the sting of Nallot in her nose.

Rebecca dodged north and disappeared from view.

Nola ran faster, reaching Jeremy's side as Julian, Stokes, and Al vanished.

A mound in the ground where the entrance to a concrete structure had crumbled poked out of the earth.

"Get in," Rebecca shouted.

"Nola, go," Jeremy said.

She didn't argue. There wasn't time. She dived into the darkness, stumbling on a steep ramp. Hands grabbed her, jerking her out of the way as Jeremy rushed into their shelter.

"Preston!" Stokes bellowed. "Get in here you damned—"

The helicopter blades whirred overhead, their rhythm pounding into Nola's chest.

Jeremy laid Jude on the ground and moved to Nola's side. She threaded her fingers through his, feeling the racing of his pulse as his wrist pressed against hers.

Should I shut my eyes against the end?

If Nallot could melt trees, it would burn through bone. There would be no knife through the heart or slice through the neck to end her second life.

Not even the Teachers will find me.

The thumping of the air changed.

Jeremy pressed Nola to the concrete wall behind her, curving his body around her, sheltering her from the end.

It won't help.

She couldn't bear to tell him, wouldn't take away his final act of shielding her.

A scream cut through the pounding of the helicopter's blades. A blood-curdling cry that shook Nola's bones.

"No!" Julian shouted.

The *thud* of a landed punch punctuated Preston's last painful shriek.

Nola buried her face in Jeremy's chest. She took a deep breath, reveling in his scent of fresh earth, with the hint of something else. Something uniquely hers that hadn't existed when they lived in the domes. Their life together had left a mark in his blood.

I love you.

Jeremy held her tighter, as though he had heard the words in her mind.

The thumping of the helicopter's blades changed, whirring as the craft surged forward across the river and away from their hiding place.

No one spoke as the noise faded away. Silence filled the darkness, leaving Jeremy's heartbeat as the only sound Nola could hear.

"We have to see if he's dead." Al spoke first.

"No one survives screaming like that," Rebecca said.

Nola wrapped her arms around Jeremy's waist, holding him as though the helicopter would come back to rip him away.

"We still have to check," Al said.

"Do you think it wise to go out into the open?" Julian said.

"We don't know if they dumped the stuff right over our heads," Jude said. "Do we want to hunker down here and see if we're melted into nothing, or get the hell out?"

"I'll go up," Rebecca said. "Stay down here."

"Preston—" Stokes began.

"I don't think there'll be anything left of him to carry back," Rebecca said. "I won't lie if I'm wrong."

There was no sound of Rebecca leaving the safety of their hiding place.

"Are you okay?" Jeremy whispered in Nola's ear.

"I'm..." She faltered on the easy lie. "I'm alive."

"I don't want to rain on the beauty of youth," Julian said, "but somedays *alive* is the best you can hope for."

Jeremy stepped back, holding Nola tightly but shifting the bulk of his shoulders enough for her to see the space around them.

Stokes slumped against the cracked concrete wall, nursing a fist-sized bruise that blossomed across his cheek.

Jude struggled to sit up. Bright red patches dotted his sweat-slicked skin.

Al stood at the top of the ramp, staring at the open ground around them, clutching the rusted rebar that poked out from the doorframe.

"What is this place?" Nola's voice wavered.

"I'm not sure." Julian moved toward the far end of the space.

Nola turned to peer past Jeremy's other shoulder, unwilling to relinquish the comfort of contact.

The space stretched back thirty feet. Empty shelves leaned against the cracked back wall.

"Looks like storage," Jeremy said. "But storage for what?"

"Dock maintenance," Rebecca said. "Dock crumbled, but this hole is still pretty sturdy."

Jeremy stepped away from Nola, sliding his hand down to find hers.

"We took everything good out of here ages ago." Rebecca stood in the doorway. The light from behind shone so brightly, Nola couldn't make out her face.

"Did they..." Nola's voice faded.

"There's nothing to carry back," Rebecca said. "We need to get moving."

"Moving where?" Stokes growled. "Back across the hills? Hope they don't come sweeping down on us again? Take a nice walk through the land they just demolished like they were melting ice?"

"We can't stay here." Rebecca hoisted the sack of weapons they'd taken from the Outer Guard over her shoulder. "They spotted Preston, but we don't know if they saw us. They could bring back more guards, more Nallot."

"So we run from here and see how fast they find the Woodlands," Stokes said. "Your people have nothing to protect themselves from this hell!"

Jude wobbled to his feet. "Captain—"

"Don't *captain* me," Stokes spat. "I lost two men today. I don't know where Cass is. He might be melted to nothing right now. What am I supposed to tell the people waiting for him in the Woodlands? I dragged ten guards and their families out of the glass, and for what? To watch them die? To watch their kids get sick?"

"To save them," Julian said.

"My men are dying!" Stokes shouted.

"I didn't say you were saving them from death," Julian said. "You didn't leave the domes in search of paradise. You left for a chance at redemption."

"Does redemption happen to cure whatever the hell is wrong with me?" Jude asked.

"No," Julian said, "but better to die than live as a minion of a monster. Believe me, I learned that lesson a long time ago."

"I have people counting on me," Rebecca said. "I can't stay here mourning for lost men when there are still living people in danger in the Woodlands. I'm going. If you want to come, move fast. If you want to stay, don't come back to my home. I can't risk you leading the Outer Guard to my woods."

"We're coming with you," Jeremy said. "We came here to learn from you. This hasn't changed anything."

"I don't know if I can get very far," Jude said. "But I say we make a break for it. I've still got a few breaths left in me. Don't want to waste them in a concrete hole."

"I'll help you," Julian said. "You won't fall behind."

Jude nodded. Julian wrapped an arm around his waist.

"Stokes?" Al said.

"Where the hell are we supposed to run to?" Stokes said.

"I've spent my life in these hills. Don't doubt me." Rebecca stepped out of view, heading north.

"You two should go next," Julian said. "Don't worry. I'll be right on your heels."

Nola led Jeremy to the door, stopping next to Stokes. "You weren't wrong to help your guards escape. The people I let out of the cells, one died in the first couple of hours. But I know she wasn't sorry we got out."

The left side of Stokes' face had begun to swell. Blood stained his top lip.

"Not all of us get to survive," Nola said. "That doesn't mean you don't have to try."

She walked up the concrete ramp and to the outside.

The fumes of the Nallot pressed on her lungs. Jeremy twisted as they walked, blocking the place where Preston had died from view. She didn't try to look around him.

There are still horrors I'm not ready for.

She kept her gaze fixed north. For a moment, she was afraid Rebecca might have run too far for her to track. But Rebecca waited a hundred feet away, standing at the edge of the trees, staring at the strip of barren land next to the bank of the river. Nola blinked at the blackened ground, wondering what awful thing had stained the dirt such an unnatural color.

"It's a road." Nola walked straight for the strip of black, tapping the pavement with her toe. "Is this the road to the city?"

"Yep." Rebecca pointed south, along the current of the brown river.

Barren islands split the river in places, but none of them blocked the view of the oxbow downstream. The edge of the ruined city peered out over the water, and high on the hill, the domes glistened in the sun.

"They still look perfect," Nola said.

"Looks can be deceiving." Jude leaned on Julian's shoulder.

"Hmm." Rebecca turned north, heading into the barren trees.

"Where are we going?" Nola asked.

"Somewhere we can shelter for the night," Rebecca said. "If the Outer Guard don't find us by morning, we'll start the long way back to the Woodlands."

"Long way," Jude said. "Sounds great."

Just keep running.

The thumping of footsteps pounded up from behind.

Jeremy let go of Nola's hand, drawing his weapon.

Nola glanced back as her fingers closed around the hilt of her knife.

Stokes and Al ran side-by-side, racing to catch up to the group.

CHAPTER NINETEEN

N ola didn't want to look at the forest as they trekked through the trees. Didn't want to think of how easily the domes could destroy everything around her.

Think of better things.

Like what?

Jeremy next to her, healthy and whole.

Julian cradled Jude in his arms. Jude hadn't made it past the first few miles on his own feet. Julian had been carrying him for hours as the sun rose in the sky and began its long journey back to the western horizon.

Better things.

T and the baby.

The baby whose father had already died. The unborn child who could be killed by the domes and their horrible weapons.

"Breathe, Nola," Jeremy whispered. "Just breathe."

Nola took a deep breath. They had stopped running hours ago. They walked up hills and past creeks that smelled of rot. Trudged around a pond covered with a cloud of bugs and through woods so far beyond life, no leaves or needles textured the ground.

But walking, walking and trying to find one hopeful untainted thing, was what stole Nola's breath away.

She clutched Jeremy's hand tighter.

"Why did they make Nallot?" Nola asked.

"Murder would be my guess." Rebecca's uneven words were the first sign of fatigue she'd betrayed.

"No," Julian said, "though Salinger does seem to be making a habit of reusing the Incorporation's mistakes as weapons. As foolish as it may sound, Nallot was designed to combat invasive species."

"What?" Nola stumbled over a rock.

"Not all domes are situated in the same fashion as yours," Julian said. "It's a bit complicated, I'm afraid."

"Well, talk." Rebecca set her sack down and leaned against a boulder, which lay nestled next to the rocky side of a low-hanging cliff. She fished in the folds of her pants, pulling out a leather drinking pouch.

"I've got water for us," Jeremy said.

It wasn't until he said the word *water* that Nola noticed the burning in the back of her throat.

Al sank to the ground, wiping the sweat from her forehead with her sleeve and pulling out a water pouch like Rebecca's. Sun and exhaustion had turned her face a bright shade of red.

Nola took the metal bottle Jeremy handed her, taking a slow sip that washed away the grit in her throat.

"I'd offer you some water," Rebecca said, eyeing Julian, "but I suppose you won't drink it."

"No indeed," Julian said. "Don't worry. I'm just fine."

"Good," Rebecca said, "then talk while we drink."

"Of course." Julian laid Jude on the ground.

Nola crouched by Jude. "Can you drink?"

"If you're offering." Jude gave a wavering wink.

"The location of these domes was chosen for its proximity to a city small enough to be controlled yet large enough to manufacture. The mountain range, river, and high number of streams were also considerations, but not all domes were placed for the same values." Julian paced between trees. "The far south domes were placed for their proximity to an excellent seaport."

"Civilization has fallen," Al said. "Who the hell has goods to ship to a port?"

"You're too young," Julian said. "Even though you were raised in the domes, you don't remember the beginning. The city was needed for manufacturing, but the Incorporation didn't plan on the city surviving in the long term. The world was already too far gone for sustainable urban survival before the first pane of glass was put into place. The Incorporation was looking toward the day when the river would have cleansed itself, the mountains would offer a home to the wildlife the domes have fostered, and the land would be ripe for farming. Placement by a port situated that domes' citizens to be able to travel and spread across the coasts when the ocean has stabilized and become a source of safe food once again."

"That still doesn't explain—" Jeremy began.

"Nallot was created for a set of domes in the southern hemisphere," Julian said. "Farther away than even I have traveled."

"What was so special about the location that the Incorporation wanted to build somewhere that would require Nallot?" Rebecca said. "From what I hear, the world is still pretty damn big even if it has gone to shit."

"The soil around those domes was fertile beyond compare," Julian said. "So much so, farmers had brought in non-native crops. Which inadvertently brought in non-native species and pests. The Incorporation decided purging the area of invasive species and allowing the land to naturally reclaim the region over the course of many years would be the best solution for recreating the ecosystem for a time generations from now when citizens would finally leave the domes."

"They destroyed all the land around their home?" Nola dug her nails into her palms, trying to keep from screaming. "Nallot melted through the trees. The land where they sprayed—"

"Will now be abundantly fertile." Julian tapped his lips through his veil. "On a rudimentary level, Nallot turned those trees into pure fertilizer."

A *crack* shook the air as Stokes punched a tree.

"You said Nallot was a mistake," Jeremy said.

"The Incorporation does seem to forget they are not infallible," Julian said. "They sprayed the area, clearing every plant and animal around the domes."

"And?" Nola shivered.

"The domes were new at the time," Julian said. "The council of those domes became very comfortable in their secluded location. They hadn't been monitoring their systems as closely as they should. The glass in one of the agricultural domes hadn't been properly secured. Fumes were trapped with the workers. Twelve people were killed that day. The Incorporation banned the use of Nallot after the incident."

"Until now," Jeremy said.

"They sprayed the mist miles from the domes," Julian said. "I'm sure the Incorporation set a safe distance for its use."

"The Woodlands are far outside that area," Rebecca said. "They could destroy my entire forest."

"If they have enough Nallot, they could," Julian said. "I don't know how they transferred the Outer Guard here from their home domes. I don't know how much Nallot they brought from the Incorporation's headquarters. I wish I had something comforting to say, but all I can offer is *I don't know*."

Rebecca ran her hand over her head, ruffling her short hair. "Shit we can do about it now." She walked around the side of the boulder and out of sight.

"The barren strip," Nola whispered in Jeremy's ear. "If they saw it from the helicopter—"

"I know." Jeremy nodded. "We could warn them."

"I doubt we could find them on our own," Julian said. "And to travel slowly is to risk being followed."

Stokes glared at Julian, who stared placidly back through the slit in his veil. *Stokes didn't hear me. He can't run to the Woodlands tonight. He's just plain human.*

"Nobody wants to rest?" Rebecca called from around the corner.

"I'll get you inside." Julian lifted Jude from the ground.

Jude gave only a faint murmur of thanks as Julian carried him away.

"Captain," Al began.

Nola tugged on Jeremy's hand.

"I'm not going to lie down for a nice rest when Cass could still be out there somewhere," Stokes said.

"I'm not sure I'll be able to sleep." Nola spoke louder than she needed to, trying to drown out Al's reply.

They rounded the boulder. A gaping void in the cliff greeted them on the other side. Tufts of dead grass waited just inside the lip of the cave where the greenery had flourished until the cold snaps had killed it.

"You're not going to find him, sir," Al said. "This isn't the domes. We can't do a floor by floor search."

"You want me to leave your fellow guard for dead?"

"We should try to rest anyway," Jeremy said. "Who knows how long it'll be until we get another chance?"

"I'm asking you to trust his training," Al said. "Or did what you see in the years of us serving under you convince you of our incompetence?"

Nola scampered into the cave.

Rebecca knelt next to a ring of burned logs. "Want to gather some wood?"

"There is nothing I could have taught any of you to prepare you for this!"

Nola flinched at Stokes' shout.

"I'll get the wood then." Rebecca stood and stormed out of the cave. "Shut the hell up, Stokes."

"Back here." Julian beckoned them toward the far end of the cave.

"Unless you've got a way to sniff out where—"

"Nice to have some cover for the night." Jeremy's voice echoed off the back wall.

The hollow in the cliff side reached less than forty feet. Julian knelt in the shadows where the rock ceiling hung too low for him to stand.

"Glad Rebecca's good at lighting fires." Jude's voice crackled.

"How about another sip of water?" Nola sat, carefully lifting Jude's head into her lap.

"Don't know if you should waste it," Jude said.

Nola's eyes flicked to the leather case on Jeremy's belt.

"We need to look in the bag," Jeremy said.

"Which bag?" Julian said.

"Rebecca's." Jeremy started toward the sack by the entrance of the cave.

"Should we wait for her?" Nola asked.

"There isn't a way out of this." Stokes' shout shook the cave.

"I don't think we have time." Jeremy opened the sack, carefully pulling out the rifles, checking each of them before laying them on the ground in a perfect line.

"I'm impressed she carried the weight for so long," Julian said.

"She's been carrying the weight of hundreds of people for a long time." Jude's laugh turned into a cough.

Nola slipped her pack under Jude's head, braving being closer to Stokes to be nearer to Jeremy.

Jeremy pulled the handguns from the bag, checking the darts in each before placing them in a line below the rifles.

"Which kind of darts were they sent with?" Jude asked.

"The killing kind," Jeremy said. "They didn't even give them a non-lethal option. I don't know why I bothered to check."

"You'll keep checking," Julian said. "The spark of hope takes a long time to go out."

"Mine's gone," Jude said. "Guess it figured it wasn't worth sticking around."

"I've often thought mine had disappeared." Julian sat next to Jude. "The brightness of hope would dissipate for years at a time, only to be revived when a hint of goodness breathed in fresh life."

Jeremy pulled the black leather case from the bottom of the sack.

"Nola survived the domes and came to care for those on the outside," Julian said. "Even if I hadn't had the promise of Nightland's new home, Nola would have ignited the spark again."

Jeremy's fingers shook as he opened the case. Nola held her breath, waiting to see the silver syringes filled with the deep black of Graylock.

"Hope is—"

"Damn." Jeremy gripped the case, cracking the sides. "Damn, damn, fucking damn."

"Jeremy." Nola took his hands, pulling the case low enough for her to see inside.

No glittering syringe waited for her. A thin bottle of white pills was all the padded ridges of the case contained.

We need more Graylock.

A guilty weight sank in Nola's chest.

We can wait. Jude can't.

"What's wrong?" Julian pulled his veil back over his face as he moved toward the mouth of the cave.

"There's no Graylock in the triage kit," Jeremy said. "They were sending every Outer Guard out with two doses."

"A couple of Outer Guard were killed in the city," Jude said. "Their doses were taken. Salinger had a fit about the possibility of outsiders dosing themselves. Graylock doesn't move beyond the glass anymore."

"I took four." Jeremy closed the case and unfastened his belt, hooking the box in place. "It might've just been me."

"Or someone else on the outside could have more doses," Nola said.

"This whole world has gone so far to shit, I don't think you'll ever know." Jude's eyes drifted shut. "Guess Salinger doesn't care how many guards die. They'll just breed more."

"We have to do something," Nola whispered.

"We can keep him comfortable." Rebecca returned with an armful of wood. She dropped the load onto the cold coals. "We'll keep him warm and fed."

"If no one's chasing you," Jude said, "try and bring my body back to the Woodlands. I might not have family, but Stokes will give me a proper send off."

"We'll do our best," Rebecca said.

"There is another option," Julian said.

"We don't have enough Graylock," Jeremy said. "Even if we could get him back to Nightland in time, we don't have three full doses. He'd die without the third injection."

"There were ways to save lives before Graylock." Julian moved back into the deep shadows of the cave, pulling off his hat. "It wouldn't be an easy road, and I don't think you could return to the Woodlands, but there is a way for you to survive."

A chill knot of fear settled in Nola's throat.

"I have one dose of ReVamp with me," Julian said. "The injection would be enough to save your life. We'd have to leave immediately for Nightland. Our doctor would be able to administer the other doses."

"You want to stick him with a needle and run for it?" Rebecca said. "Hope the spider and his men don't follow you home?"

"I mean no offense, but I don't think we would be followed," Julian said. "We can move much faster on our own."

"Move faster to where?" Stokes stepped into the mouth of the cave.

"To save your guard's life," Julian said.

"What the hell are you talking about?" Stokes stomped over to Jude. "Get up, Jude."

"I don't think I can, Captain." Jude didn't open his eyes.

"I know your opinion on vampires," Julian said, "and I will freely admit that some of my kind deserve the revulsion you feel. But this man will not live through the night. If he prefers to die, I will not argue with his choice."

Nola gripped Jeremy's hand.

Julian reached into his pack, pulling out a narrow container. "What sort of a monster would I be if I had a way to save a life and didn't offer to help?"

"He'd never be able to walk in the sun again." Al stood in the entrance to the cave, her hands clasped under her chin.

"But he would still be alive," Julian said.

"He wouldn't be Jude," Al said.

"He would," Nola said. "ReVamp is different than Vamp. He'll be healthy and strong. He won't be able to go into the sun, and he'll have to live off blood. But he'll still be the same person."

"You can't know that." Jude's words came out a rasped whisper.

"I do," Nola said. "My best friend was given ReVamp. It saved his life, and it didn't change him."

Jeremy pressed his lips to the top of Nola's head.

"I don't want to die, Captain," Jude said.

Stokes stood over Jude. His dark brow wrinkled in something between loathing and disgust.

"You've been a good guard, Jude," Stokes said.

Nola moved to step forward, ready to plant herself between Stokes and Jude. Jeremy wrapped his arm around her, keeping her pinned to his side.

"Your work isn't done yet, Guard," Stokes said. "So you take that damned shot, and you get ready. Because we've got one hell of a fight in front of us."

CHAPTER TWENTY

"I t's not a pleasant process." Julian knelt beside Jude. "I'm afraid there will be a fair bit of pain."

"Can't be too bad when you lay it out next to dying," Jude said.

Nola wrapped her arms around Jeremy, trying to push away the horrible memory of ice taking hold of her veins.

The ice has already changed me. It can't happen again.

"Once I've administered the injection, we'll have to leave." Julian took the syringe from its case.

The metal of this syringe seemed somehow less frightening than those that held Graylock. Whether it was from the metal gleaming less brightly, or the faint, shimmering liquid held within the glass, Nola didn't know.

"You're just going to take Jude away?" Al knelt next to Jude, holding his hand.

"He'll have to be protected from the sunlight," Julian said. "Though it won't be completely deadly to him right away, it's unwise to risk exposure."

"So stick him with a needle and run. Go back to hiding in your mountain. Wait to see if the Woodlands are destroyed." Rebecca knelt next to the coals, striking two bits of stone together, throwing sparks onto the crumpled bits of brush. "I'd come to think better of you than that."

"I don't think any of us are dumb enough to think we can hide from the domes," Jeremy said. "But Julian's right, we have to get Jude to Nightland."

"Then what?" Al said. "You keep Jude with you forever?"

"The mountain is the safest place for a vampire," Julian said. "But once his transformation is complete, it will be up to Jude to decide where he wishes to live."

"And if the Woodlands have been melted by the spider before Jude's turned into a full nightwalker," Rebecca said, "you'll just have one more for your ranks and one less to be counted among my dead."

"You'll have one more alive and fighting on your side," Julian said. "Nightland will stand with the Woodlands."

"How?" Rebecca blew life into the embers, sparking a blaze that danced against the backdrop of the setting sun.

"We have to talk to Emanuel before we can do anything," Jeremy said. "He's the one who controls Nightland. He needs to know what Nallot can do."

"He'll never let any of you leave the mountain again," Rebecca said.

"He will," Nola said. "Even if it means breaking every pane of glass in the domes, we have to stop Salinger. There's no other way out. Not for us. Not for the people on the highway. We have to fight."

The weight of Jeremy's arms wrapped around her did nothing to stop Nola's hands from shaking.

"I hate to agree with you," Julian said, "but I don't think there is any other choice. The domes have chosen to wage war on all who survive outside the glass. If we hide, we allow them to slaughter more innocent people. They've proven themselves to be horrible monsters. We can't turn our back on that sort of terror and have any hope of retaining our souls."

Jeremy clutched Nola closer to his chest. "We have to find a way across the river, and a place for the vampires to go to ground close enough to the domes to stage an attack."

"If I can do that, you'll fight with us?" Rebecca stood, dusting the soot off her hands.

There is no way across the river. There is no shelter big enough to hide the vampires of Nightland.

"Fight how?" Stokes asked.

"Emanuel will have to give the order," Julian said.

Jude gave a rattling gasp that shook his whole body.

"Jude." Al gripped Jude's sweat-slicked hand. "We're talking about attacking the domes, Jude, so wake the hell up."

"Give him the shot." The words stole the breath from Nola's body. "We can't stand here talking while he dies."

"No." Julian pulled open the top of Jude's shirt. "Though, from experience, it is easier to inject someone who has already lost consciousness." He raised the needle over Jude's chest. "It might not lessen the pain of changing, but having a still target does make my job much easier."

In one swift movement, he plunged the needle into Jude's heart.

Jeremy gasped, tightening his arms around Nola.

"It's okay," Nola whispered.

Jude took a shuddering breath, and screamed. His pale fists clenched. The muscles in his neck bulged.

"What the hell did you do to him?" Al leapt to her feet, aiming her gun at Julian.

"ReVamp is not a kind drug," Julian said, "but it will save his life."

A moan escaped Jude's lips as he began to writhe on the ground.

"Is this what happened to me?" Nola asked. "I remember not being able to move—"

"You didn't." Jeremy shook his head. "You were so still I thought I was too late."

Nola kissed Jeremy's cheek. "You weren't. I'm still here."

With a gasp, Jude went still.

"Is it done?" Stokes asked.

"He won't wake for several hours," Julian said. "Frankly, I don't envy what he's feeling trapped inside his body right now, but all of our ReVamp is made by Dr. Wynne, who the domes so graciously tossed into the outside world. The batch is good. Jude will wake up. I think it best if we are far from here by that time."

"Right." Al laid Jude's hand on his chest. "You're right."

Julian pulled off his sun suit, carefully folding the material and sliding it back into his pack.

"What if you don't make it by sunrise?" Stokes said. "Are you going to leave him out to die?"

"We'll find a place to hide," Jeremy said. "We aren't the domes, Stokes. We don't believe in murder."

Julian lifted Jude, draping the unconscious man over his shoulder.

"One of my people will come to you," Rebecca said. "The one I send to the ledge will speak with my voice. I'll deliver the path to ending the domes."

"We will be waiting for them." Julian gave a nod.

"If they don't come," Stokes said. "If that bastard gets all of us—"

"We'll still break through the glass," Jeremy said. "Salinger isn't staying in there with your granddaughters."

"Then run," Stokes said. "Get Jude to safety before the sun comes back."

"Travel well." Julian skirted around the fire and out into the night.

"Stokes," Jeremy said, "if you find my sister, keep her with you. Don't let her disappear."

Stokes nodded. "That girl was one hell of a fighter. I'll try to get her on our side."

Say something. Say that I'm sorry for the girls who are still trapped behind the glass. That Lilly was right to leave, even if it got her killed. That Stokes was right to take the people he could. To try and save one small part of the domes, even if the rest are doomed under Salinger's rule.

Say I'll fight even if it's against my own mother. That Jude will be strong and able to fight again soon.

Nola met Stokes' gaze. He didn't say anything as Jeremy led her past the fire and out into the night. Neither did she.

The brightness of the flames hid the inside of the cave from view.

"This way." Julian took off, running through the trees.

Nola tore her eyes from the fire, not bothering to ask if Jeremy wanted to be second in their line.

Running felt better than the slow pace they'd been forced to keep before.

When the unchanged humans ran in our line.

The air moved easily in and out of her lungs. The stars provided enough light for her to be able to see the trees she tore past.

She could keep running for a day, maybe more. She and Jeremy could slip so far away Salinger would never find them, not even with his helicopter.

There would be no hope for T. No way to travel that fast with a baby.

We have to fight the domes.

The thought brought with it a terrifying certainty. There was no other way forward. No other path to a future for anyone beyond her and Jeremy. The Northerners wouldn't be able to defend against an attack on their home and wouldn't be fast enough to run away. The vampires of Nightland were defenseless during the day. Salinger could flood the tunnels of Nightland with Nallot, and, as long as the sun was in the sky, the vampires wouldn't be able to flee.

But Jeremy and I could. I could protect him. Lead him far away where Salinger would never be able to hurt him.

She listened to the steady thumping of his boots on the ground behind her.

They could find a place with water and shelter. She could find a way to grow them food. They could figure out how to hunt.

And we would be the last people in this part of the world.

"Nola," Jeremy said, "are you all right?"

"When it's time to fight," Nola said, "we're going together."

"Nola—"

"I wish I could make you hide." Nola leapt across the banks of a frothy stream. "I wish we could live somewhere just the two of us where there's nothing to be afraid of."

"But neither of us could live with that." Jeremy ducked around a tree to run by her side.

"So when it's time to fight the domes, I'm coming with you," Nola said. "I'm fighting with you."

"I..." Jeremy took her hand, his pinky draping over her palm. "I will do everything I can to keep you safe. But I won't take fighting the monsters from you."

"I never thought I'd want to fight," Nola said. "All I ever wanted was to help people. To make all the awfulness we've been stuck with stop."

"We're going to," Jeremy said. "Maybe not the way we'd hoped, but we're going to get Salinger the hell out of here."

"Hear, hear!" Julian said. "I must say, in the years I've known the horror of what Salinger is capable of, I never thought I would be present at his downfall. I don't know how Emanuel will take the news of Nallot or what his plan will be, but I look forward to ending this particular reign of terror."

A reign of terror. And I was bred to be one of the monsters.

Nola tightened her grip on Jeremy's hand.

They stayed behind Julian as he led them farther west. There was no path for them to follow, no sign of the Northerners living in these decaying woods. Twice they were turned back by cliffs too high to jump. But Julian kept running.

Neither Nola nor Jeremy questioned his route. The helicopter and Nallot had ruled out running to the river and following the path back to Nightland from the city. There was nothing to do but run and hope for a clear way to the mountains.

The heat of friction burned Nola's feet, but the pain never progressed.

I should be bleeding. I should be damaged beyond repair.

Julian paused as they reached the top of a hill.

"Is Jude okay?" Nola asked, stopping next to Julian. "Do you need me to carry him?"

"I can carry the weight, Nola." Julian stared east.

Nola followed his gaze.

In the depths of the decaying forest, a wasteland scarred the earth. A wide circle of death where nothing survived.

"If this is what humans insist on doing, I don't blame the earth for trying to rid itself of us," Julian said.

"It's not all humans," Jeremy said. "There are good people, and that's who we're going to fight to protect."

Jude gave a shuddering gasp.

"If you can hear me," Julian said, "I'm sorry for the bumpy ride, but I'm afraid we must keep going. I don't know which will startle Emanuel more, our returning so quickly, or my jumping into the tunnel with a newly minted vampire over my back. We'll find out soon enough, I suppose."

Julian turned south, heading toward the silhouette of the mountains reaching up into the night sky. "We aren't going to reach Nightland before dawn."

"Then we'll find a place to shelter," Jeremy said. "We've made it far enough. I don't think the Outer Guard are going to find us."

"No," Julian said. "I don't think they will. However, Nightland itself could be found. If the Outer Guard are searching so far north, they may be turning their attention west of the domes as well. We would have had to leave Rebecca tonight even if Jude hadn't been in need of another dose of ReVamp. If the Northerners found the path to Nightland, the Outer Guard could as well. If an Outer Guard were to capture a Northerner—"

"They could give up our home," Nola said.

"I'll get you as close to the entrance to Nightland as I can before the sun starts to rise," Julian said. "You'll have to find your own path from there."

"We can do it," Jeremy said.

"Tell Emanuel everything," Julian said. "Make sure he knows to expect a Northern emissary and understands how much of a threat or ally the Northerners can be."

Nola touched the hole in her shirt where the arrow had pierced her flesh. "We will."

"Good." Julian ran south toward the jagged outline of the mountains.

CHAPTER TWENTY-ONE

Nola stood on top of the ridge, looking down at the uneven mound of earth far below.

"You know," Jeremy said, "when we had all those classes in Green Dome on how to properly plant things, I never thought I would be using those digging skills to bury two vampires."

Nola squinted down at the freshly turned earth. From this height, there was no hint of the two men hiding from the sun beneath the layers of dirt.

"I hope we dug deep enough," Nola said.

"Julian said to go. We have to trust him."

Nola looked toward the summit of the mountain. High above, a familiar divot marked the place where two peaks joined, sheltering Kieran's garden. Taking a deep breath, Nola sprinted up the slope.

A faint fatigue pulled on her limbs.

Sleep. I'll have to sleep soon.

The *clatter* of rocks beneath Jeremy's feet followed her up the mountain.

What if Salinger's found Nightland? What if everyone's dead and we're racing back to a tomb?

"Say something nice," Nola said.

"What do you mean?"

Nola could hear the hint of a smile in Jeremy's voice.

"I need to think about something other than the possibility of Julian bleeding from all over his body, or Nightland being flooded with Nallot." Nola's breath hitched in her chest. She pushed herself to run faster, tearing around the bend in the ridge and twisting to follow a new ridge east.

"Okay," Jeremy said. "When all of this is over, you and I are going to run to one of these peaks just for fun. And we'll lay under the stars and watch the heavens move, and we won't be afraid of anything."

"That sounds really nice." Tears burned the corners of Nola's eyes.

"It's going to be amazing," Jeremy said. "Every night I get to hold you in my arms will be amazing. And we're going to have so many wonderful nights, Nola. We just have to keep fighting for a little while longer."

"We can do it." Rocks shifted under Nola's foot. She leapt forward without thought, landing without breaking her stride. "You and me together, we can do it."

"Absolutely we can."

The ruins of the city came into view, nestled next to the banks of the rancid river. Nola's gaze followed the path up from the city, through the woods and the field of brambles, up to a basin between two steep slopes.

"I see the path." Nola veered off the ridgeline and onto the steep mountainside. Her feet barely touched the ground as she leapt down the slope.

Bang!

The sound caught her ears while she was midair. She twisted toward the noise, forgetting to keep her gaze on the ground beneath her.

"Nola!" Jeremy shouted as she hit the rocks below.

Instinct told her to fight for her footing, but the ground slipped away beneath her. A sharp stone cut into her arm as she tumbled down the slope. Her pack banged into her spine, knocking the air from her lungs.

"Nola."

She caught a glimpse of Jeremy chasing her. She reached out and seized a rock, but the force of her fall pulled the stone from the mountainside, sending a cascade of rocks down on her.

Pain burst through the back of her head, stealing her vision. A *crack* sent a fresh wave of hurt through her leg.

The pain of stones pummeling her skin didn't stop, but the ground beneath her held firm.

"Nola, are you okay?"

Hands pulled the weight away from her chest.

Nola gulped in a breath. Shifting her ribs even that small amount sent the agony in her head spinning.

"I'm okay," Nola said. "I'll heal."

"Just hold still. Let me get the rocks off you."

Nola blinked, pulling the gray stones back into focus. A rock the size of her pack pressed on her pelvis, pinning her to the tree that had stopped her fall. She lifted her arm, pushing her hair away from her face. Blood coated her skin, though the cuts had already begun to heal.

"What was that *bang*?" Nola asked.

"I don't know." Jeremy lifted away the stone that had pinned down her right leg. "It came from the east."

"Nightland?"

"Farther away, I think," Jeremy said. "We have to get to Emanuel."

"I think I can walk." Nola sat up, biting back her scream as pain shot through her stomach.

"I can carry you."

"You have to be ready to fight." Nola gasped as she put weight on her right leg. "We don't know what the explosion was."

I shouldn't know what that noise means.

"Dr. Wynne might have to reset your leg." Jeremy wrapped his left arm around Nola's waist, taking most of her weight as they headed down the mountain. His gaze darted between Nola's face, the path down the mountain, and the city far below.

"I don't see any smoke," Nola said.

"I'm not sure if that's a good thing."

The pain ebbed away from her pelvis as they reached the tree line. Signs of life marked the trees, things Nola wouldn't have noticed before. Dirt piled at the base of a trunk where some small creature had dug its home. Bark torn away in patches large enough to feed a man-sized animal.

The basin appeared in the trees below, as welcoming as seeing the door to her home in Bright Dome.

"Do you think they know we're coming?" Nola asked. "Have the guards spotted us?"

"I've never been sent to guard the tunnel. I don't know what the sightlines are like."

Nola shook her head. The movement blurred the edges of her vision. "As safe as Nightland is, it's still not enough. I don't know if it will ever be enough."

"It won't. Not until the domes are no longer a threat."

Neither spoke as they walked into the clearing below the entrance to Nightland.

Nola scanned the trees, searching for any sign of a Northerner hiding in the branches. She took a deep breath, trying to catch the scent of human life.

"It's Jeremy and Nola," Jeremy said, his voice barely loud enough for vampires to hear. "We're coming up."

They stood frozen for a moment, Nola feeling foolish as she listened for a voice welcoming them home.

"Me first?" Nola whispered.

Jeremy bit his lips into a flat line.

"If there were Outer Guard waiting up there, they would have fired on us already," Nola said.

"Can you jump it?" Jeremy asked.

Nola tested her weight on her leg. The pressure sent pain shooting from her ankle to her knee, but she stayed on her feet.

"I'll be okay." Nola bent her knees and jumped, planting her palms on the ledge and leveraging herself up and into the tunnel. Gritting her teeth against the pain of the impact, Nola staggered forward, pulling her weapon from its holster.

Jeremy landed by her side with only the slightest *thump* from his boots.

"Who's up there?" Nola said. "It's Jeremy and Nola. We're back from the scouting mission Emanuel sent us on."

Stell sauntered into the shadows, a frown pursing her lips. "Where's Julian? I was told you two went with him."

"He was delayed," Jeremy said. "He sent us ahead with news for Emanuel."

"Hmm." Stell pulled her knife from its sheath, twisting the point into her finger. "What about Raina?"

"We weren't sent the same way as her," Nola said. "We don't know where she is."

"Pity." A drop of blood fell from Stell's finger. "I was hoping you'd say she'd blown herself up. Ah well, a girl can dream."

"Can we pass?" Nola said. "We need to get to Emanuel."

"Oh sure, sure." Stell stepped aside. "You're on the list of people I'm supposed to let in, and I do take my duty to Nightland seriously. After all, there's a big difference between hoping someone won't come back and keeping them in the sun to burn."

"Right," Nola said.

Jeremy wrapped his arm around Nola's waist, easing the burden on her leg. "Thanks for watching the path."

Nola didn't speak as they passed a group of five heavily armed vampires a hundred feet down the tunnel. She didn't say anything at all until they reached the first window looking out over the mountainside and down toward the city.

"It's people like Stell we're talking about taking to the domes." Nola searched the horizon for smoke from whatever had caused the *bang*. "The last time Emanuel led vampires into the domes, innocent people were killed."

"You don't think we should attack anymore?" Jeremy said.

"I do." Nola limped down the tunnel, leaning against Jeremy. "I wish there were another way, but the domes have fallen too far. They're wiping out outsiders, torturing their own women—"

A growl vibrated Jeremy's chest.

"But we have to protect the ones who are being hurt," Nola said. "There are little kids, and girls like Lilly."

"And to get rid of Salinger, we're going to have to use people like Stell," Jeremy said.

"There has to be a way," Nola said. "Some plan to get rid of Salinger and his guards without letting the kids get hurt."

"I…" Jeremy paused, facing the line of ten guards that blocked the metal door to the sparring room. Desmond stood at the middle of the line, his bow staff resting against his shoulder.

"Back so soon?" Desmond asked in a low, rumbling voice.

"Found what we were looking for a lot faster than we thought we would," Jeremy said.

"Found it how?" One of the bald twins pointed to Nola's stomach. "By letting them cut you to ribbons?"

Nola looked down at her shirt. Dark, dried blood surrounded the place where she'd been struck by the arrow. Smaller, fresher patches of blood marked the rest of her clothes, matted in with the dirt from falling down the mountain.

"If you wanted to bleed, you could have stayed here and let us help," the other twin said.

"I can manage well enough on my own, thanks," Nola said.

"Julian will be coming at nightfall," Jeremy said. "He's going to have a fresh vampire with him. Try and convince Stell to let them in without a fight."

"And if a stranger comes," Nola said, "keep them alive until you've heard from Emanuel. We made some new friends"

Desmond raised an eyebrow but gave a nod and stepped out of their way.

One of the twins dragged open the heavy metal door. "If you want to bleed more, we'll be out here until nightfall."

"Sure thing." The din of sparring vampires swallowed Nola's voice.

The familiar *clang* of metal on metal and shouting and jeering of the fighters banged into Nola's ears. But rather than bring terror, the cacophony soothed Nola's nerves.

Nightland is home. Even the fighting and blood are part of me now.

A few glanced their direction as they made their way past the painted squares, but no one stopped them to ask questions.

We're not Raina or Julian. No one expects us to lead.

"Straight to Emanuel?" Nola said.

"We need to get you to Dr. Wynne," Jeremy said. "The sooner he resets your leg, the better."

"I can wait a few minutes. Emanuel needs to know what's happening."

The corridors were quiet as they made their way to Emanuel's library. There were no children tearing past or workers chatting as they went about their assigned tasks.

"We'll have to leave some of the fighters here," Jeremy said. "To keep Nightland safe."

"Not us though," Nola said.

"No, not us." Jeremy stopped in front of the carved wooden doors to Emanuel's library.

Nola knocked.

Desmond's standing guard, Raina's in the south, Julian's buried underground. We're already spread too thin.

Nola opened the door and led Jeremy into the library.

The red chair sat vacant in the center of the empty room.

A tingle raced down Nola's spine as her uneven footsteps echoed around the library. She stared at the door to Emanuel's home, waiting for Eden to run through laughing or Dr. Wynne to wander past following some vague and invisible idea. But no one came.

Desmond would have told us if something horrible happened.

She knocked on the door to Emanuel's home, holding her breath until the knob turned.

Bea's weathered face appeared in the crack.

"We're looking for Emanuel," Nola said.

Bea shook her head.

"Julian sent us with important information," Jeremy said. "Nightland is in more danger than we thought."

For a moment, Nola wasn't sure if Bea had heard. After a few seconds, Bea nodded and wandered down the hall in Emanuel's home, leaving the door open behind her.

Jeremy raised an eyebrow at Nola.

She shrugged as much as being half-carried by Jeremy would allow and followed Bea.

Bea waited in the entrance to the kitchen, pointing to the door at the back with one hand while pressing a finger over her lips with the other.

Nola nodded, keeping silent as she and Jeremy maneuvered around the kitchen table.

Dim light and a low voice drifted through the door.

"But the frog didn't want to sleep on the lily pad," Emanuel spoke softly. "'No, no, no,' said the little frog. 'While the glow bugs dance, so will I.'"

Nola peeked through the door.

Emanuel sat at the head of Eden's bed, book in hand, as the little girl's eyes drifted shut.

CHAPTER TWENTY-TWO

The bright lights of Dr. Wynne's lab bored into Nola's eyes.

"It's not that I don't believe what you're telling me is true." Emanuel leaned against the door, his hands tented beneath his chin. "I simply can't understand how such a thing is possible."

"I didn't think I was seeing it right." Nola tried to keep her voice steady as the cold of the table drained her courage. "But the mist from the helicopter melted the trees, and Julian knew what it was right away."

"This isn't going to be the most pleasant task." Dr. Wynne rolled his chair up next to the table. "It will feel better once the bone is properly set, of course."

"Rebecca wants to attack the domes," Jeremy said, "and after seeing what Salinger's weapons can do, I have to agree."

"It's times like this when I miss my equipment in the domes the most." Dr. Wynne pinched and poked at Nola's shin.

"I don't know how far we can trust Rebecca," Emanuel said.

"You trusted me when I came here," Jeremy said. "You knew that after what the domes had tried to take from me, I would never betray you to them. One pass of Nallot from the helicopter and the Woodlands would be destroyed. All of Rebecca's people would be less than ash. Emanuel, I don't know how well they'll do in a battle. I don't know if they have the resources to get us across the river or to shelter your fighters during the daylight. But I do know Rebecca wants to fight. Her people will fight. They've got just as much to lose as we do."

"On the count of three, then," Dr. Wynne said.

"What?" Nola squeaked as he tightened his grip on her leg.

"One, two—"

A *crack* reverberated around the room.

Nola screamed before she knew she was in pain.

"Nola." Jeremy grabbed her hand. "She wasn't ready."

"I sometimes find that's best," Dr. Wynne said.

Nola blinked the spots out of her eyes to find Jeremy glaring at a placid Dr. Wynne.

"Lie still for a moment," Dr. Wynne said. "Don't want to risk the bones slipping out of place and having to do this again."

"Nope," Nola spoke through gritted teeth. "I really don't want that."

"Is there anything else you need from me?" Dr. Wynne rolled his chair back to his desk.

"I don't think so," Emanuel said. "Though we will need to impose until Nola can walk."

"Actually, I wanted to show you something, Dr. Wynne." Jeremy used his free hand to open the dented black case on his hip.

"More Graylock?" Dr. Wynne wheeled back.

"We weren't that lucky," Nola said.

"Any idea what these are for?" Jeremy pulled out the bottle of white pills.

"Hmm." Dr. Wynne opened the bottle, dropping a single pill onto his palm.

With a movement so quick Nola didn't think to stop him, the doctor licked the pill.

"Dr. Wynne!" Emanuel lunged forward, snatching the rest of the pills from Dr. Wynne's hand.

"High grade pain killers," Dr. Wynne said. "It's not the sort of stuff I liked to prescribe even in my dome days." He held his palm up, presenting the licked pill to Emanuel. "Where did you find it?"

"On an Outer Guard who'd been given Graylock. Is there"—Jeremy glanced to Nola—"could there be something wrong with Graylock that would have left him in enough pain to need medicine like this."

Dr. Wynne patted his lips. "My best guess, the pills were given in case of injury. If the guard were to be wounded and not have the time to allow Graylock to heal him, the pills would have kept him from feeling any pain."

"Let him keep fighting while he bled." A horrible twisting seized Nola's gut.

"And these are the men we fight against," Emanuel said.

"We don't have a choice." Nola gritted her teeth as she sat up, expecting pain to shoot from her leg. The mending bone answered with a dull throb.

"How soon do you think the Northerner will arrive?" Emanuel said.

"If Rebecca survived and got back to the Woodlands?" Jeremy said. "Someone could be here in a day or so."

"Ha," Dr. Wynne said, "I sometimes forget how slowly normal people move."

"We need to plan," Emanuel said. "We need to know how we want to attack the domes before the Northerner arrives. We need to be sure those we leave behind are cared for while we're gone."

"And be sure they know what they're to do if you don't make it back," Dr. Wynne said.

Nola held Jeremy's hand tighter.

"I'm not trying to say I doubt any of you." Dr. Wynne fluttered his hands through the air. "But I have worked very hard to keep the children and humans of Nightland alive. I wouldn't be doing my job if I didn't see to their safety."

"You're right, doctor," Emanuel said. "Plans will be made."

"Good." Dr. Wynne turned to the stack of papers on his desk. "She should be fine to walk, best to get moving. Circulation will help you heal."

"Right." Nola rolled down her pant leg and kicked her feet over the side of the metal table.

"Careful." Jeremy took Nola's arms as she stood. "How does it feel?"

Nola bounced on her leg for a moment. "Sore but sturdy."

"When was the last time the two of you slept?" Dr. Wynne didn't look up from his work.

"A couple of days," Nola said. "I think."

"Sleep," Dr. Wynne said. "Both of you."

"We need to plan," Jeremy said.

"Of course you do," Dr. Wynne said. "But the brain doesn't work as well when fatigue has taken over. If you're going to be plotting against the domes, it is my medical opinion that you should do it rested. A few hours now could save lives later."

"Go," Emanuel said. "There is work you can't be a part of. Thank you for finding the Northerners. Now it's my job to prepare Nightland."

"Right." Nola started toward the door.

"Emanuel," Jeremy said, "I know the domes' defenses. I know how the guards work."

Emanuel gave a weary smile. "And I'll need all of that, once I know what my people will be capable of."

"Come on." Nola pulled on Jeremy's hand, drawing him out of Dr. Wynne's lab and into the hall.

Neither of them spoke as they passed the kitchen or walked through the library.

"Does he think we can't do it, or I can't be trusted?" Jeremy asked.

"What do you mean?" Nola's eyes grew heavy as they neared the promise of sleep.

"I'm the best resource Emanuel has," Jeremy said. "I'm good enough to run north, but he doesn't want me to help plan."

"You're not one of his people." Nola stopped in front of the door to Jeremy's room. "Everyone else—Julian, Desmond, Raina—they've all been with him for years."

"Dr. Wynne and Kieran—"

"You're asking him to leave his home and fight," Nola said. "To leave the sanctuary he built for Eden. To him, we're children. He's been working to create Nightland since before we were born. And now we're telling him everything he loves might be taken from him. He's scared and tired. A thousand lives depend on his decisions."

Jeremy wrapped his arms around Nola, pressing his lips to her dirt-dusted hair. "I only have you to worry about, and that's enough to steal my breath when I think about the domes getting anywhere near you."

"He's going to need you," Nola said.

"To tell him how to fight against my father."

"Yeah." She leaned her cheek against Jeremy's chest. "I'm so sorry."

"Don't be." He kissed her head one last time then opened the door to his room. "You aren't the monster, my father is. He gave the order to drop the Nallot."

Nola closed the door behind them. "I wish..."

"Wish what?" Jeremy untied his boots.

"That there was something better for me to say." Nola pulled off her dirt-and-blood covered shirt. "That I could tell you your father wasn't to blame, and the domes weren't evil, and it was all going to be okay, and I wouldn't be lying." The words caught in her throat.

"It's not okay." Jeremy took Nola's hands, kissing both her palms. "None of this is okay. But the only thing I need you to tell me is that you love me. I will fight the whole world, Nola. As long as I'm fighting for you."

"I love you." Nola leaned up on her toes, brushing her lips against his. "More than anything I love you. And whoever we fight, whatever we're fighting for, we do it together."

"Together." Jeremy brushed the tears from her cheeks.

Voices pounded into Nola's ears, but she'd stopped following the thread of the words. They talked in circles over and over again. Emanuel had called them to his library at sunrise. Then the planning had begun. Which direction should they attack from? The likelihood of Salinger being ensconced in the concrete tower that housed the Com Room.

None of it will matter if we can't get across the river. We can't fight if there won't be a place for the vampires to hide during the daylight. We're stuck waiting.

But still they planned.

"If you can't get it done first, there's no point in even trying." Jude's unfamiliar voice shook Nola from her thoughts.

Jude paced in a wide circle around the library. Passing Desmond by the door to the corridor, Kieran by one bookcase and Julian by another, lapping in front of Emanuel who sat silently in his red chair, then Nola and Jeremy who leaned against the far wall.

Nola recognized the need to run burning in Jude's newly strengthened limbs. The way he clenched his hands over and over, the unchanging rhythm of his steps.

He can still feel his second dose running through his veins.

"It can be accomplished." Julian reached his mug out in front of Jude, stopping his circle.

Jude took a deep breath, a look of something between revulsion and bliss taking over his face.

"But if you can't, we're all dead." Jude turned his back on the group to sip from the mug.

"We have enough explosives," Kieran said, "and Raina will know how to do it."

Silence washed over the room.

If she gets back.

She'd missed the deadline Emanuel had given them. She should have come back by sunrise, but she hadn't arrived. Neither had the Northerner.

"And I'm supposed to believe this of someone I've never met?" Jude said.

"Once you meet her, you won't have any doubts," Jeremy said.

"If the Outer Guard don't kill us all before she gets back," Jude said.

"Keep drinking," Julian said. "It will calm you."

"Let me give the unpopular opinion," Desmond said. "We can't assume anyone out there is alive. We can't count on the Northerner arriving or Raina coming back."

"She'll get here," Emanuel said.

"We don't know what caused the explosion yesterday," Desmond said.

"Probably Raina," Kieran said.

"If things are as bad as they seem, we can't afford to keep waiting," Desmond said. "It's only a matter of time before Salinger unleashes some fresh hell."

"What do you propose?" Emanuel leaned forward in his chair.

"We send a scouting party to the river," Desmond said. "See if we can find a way across. Find a shelter on the other side ourselves. Then we take a small team and we fight."

"A small team won't make it back," Emanuel said. "If we go in undermanned, no one will get out."

"Then we don't get out," Desmond said. "There are some things worth dying for, Emanuel."

Nola slipped her hand into Jeremy's.

"I agree with the sentiment," Julian said, "but how would those left behind know if the task had been completed? If we send people out and they don't come back, those left behind will be less protected and still not know if they are, in fact, safe."

"I wish we had coms." Jeremy shook his head. "I never thought about it when I was an Outer Guard. But not being able to check in or give orders in real time, it makes everything harder."

"I can't risk losing you, Desmond," Emanuel said. "Not with Raina gone."

"But we have to do something," Jude said.

And the circle begins again.

Nola shifted her weight to lean against Jeremy's side.

I should be doing something. Helping somehow.

There's nothing to do but wait.

"We have to be sure the humans of Nightland are cared for," Emanuel said. "Their safety has to be our first priority."

Bang, bang, bang.

The pounding on the library door jolted Nola, sending her heart racing.

"Emanuel!" A boy's voice came from the corridor.

Emanuel was up in an instant, wrenching the door open.

Nola reached for the knife on her belt, forgetting she wore no weapons within the halls of Nightland.

A teenaged boy stood in the corridor, his eyes wide as Emanuel stepped toward him.

"Message from the tunnels," the boy said. "There's someone outside looking for you."

"Who?" Emanuel took off down the hall.

"I don't know." The boy chased after him, the rest of the group from the library close on his heels. "I didn't see them. Stell sent word."

"Raina wouldn't wait outside," Jeremy said.

"It's got to be someone from the Woodlands." Jude cut around to run right behind Emanuel. "That means Stokes and Al made it. Rebecca got them back to the woods."

Not everyone gets to survive.

The cacophony in the sparring room stopped as Emanuel burst through the door. The fighters cleared a path, and two men pushed open the door to the outer tunnel before Emanuel made it across the room.

Nola faltered before stepping into the tunnel. It wasn't her place to see if allies or enemies had come.

I went north. I saw Nallot work. I should see this, too.

She tightened her grip on Jeremy's hand as they sprinted down the tunnel.

"Jude, stick to the shadows!" Julian shouted as they neared the first window.

Emanuel turned sideways, skirting the deadly rays of the sun.

Jude slowed, turning to face the interior wall and hunching his shoulders as he sidled by the square of sunlight.

Nola pulled Jeremy through the patch of sun, catching up to Emanuel.

The line of guards came into view up ahead.

"Emanuel," Stell spoke in a hushed tone, "there's someone down there."

"Did you speak to them?" Emanuel asked.

"No, they called up that they wanted to see Emanuel, so we sent for you," Stell said. "They've moved out of view from the shadows. I was told to watch for a stranger, and I'm guessing this is them."

"I'll go see," Jeremy said. "If it's one of Rebecca's people, I might be able to recognize them."

"We don't have weapons," Nola said.

Emanuel looked to Stell, whose pale eyebrows pinched together as she handed her knife to Jeremy.

"I need a knife, too," Nola said.

"You don't—"

Nola silenced Jeremy with a glare.

Stell pulled another knife from her boot and handed it to Nola. "Don't lose my knife."

"I'll do my best." Nola gave a sarcastic smile.

"If it's not who we're expecting, get back in the tunnels," Emanuel said.

Jeremy nodded and stepped out into the sunshine.

The heat of the rays tingled Nola's face. The world seemed to have forgotten how cold it had been only a couple of days before.

Jeremy moved silently out to the edge of the ledge. Nola stepped up by his side to look below.

A woman with a long black braid down her back sat on the ground, staring up at them. Her dark skin had no hint of sores or damage from the sun. She wore Northern brown, and a bow and quiver full of arrows lay by her side.

"Who are you?" Nola asked.

"I'm here to see Emanuel," the woman said.

"That doesn't answer my question," Nola said.

"Rebecca sent me," the woman said. "That should be good enough for you."

"She made it back to the Woodlands?" Jeremy said.

The woman stared at Jeremy.

"What made your people create the gap?" Nola asked.

The woman looked to the struggling trees that surrounded her. "Blight. Took months to get rid of the patch, but we kept it from spreading."

"She's from the north," Jeremy said.

"Bring her up." Emanuel's voice came from the shadows.

Jeremy stepped off the ledge and landed by the woman's feet. If the woman was shocked, she gave no sign as she stood, carefully dusting off her clothes before slinging her bow and quiver over her shoulder.

"If I may." Jeremy reached for the woman's waist. When she didn't protest, he lifted her into the air.

Nola reached down and grabbed the woman's hands. A familiar sense of trepidation tickled Nola's stomach as sense told her pain would come from hoisting the woman's weight. She widened her stance and lifted, feeling nothing but the shift in her balance as she brought the woman up to the edge of the ledge, setting her down on her knees.

"You should build a ladder for guests." The woman stood, peering into the shadows over Nola's shoulder.

"We don't generally allow guests," Emanuel said.

"I suppose I should be grateful you made an exception," the woman said.

"I do not wish for your gratitude," Emanuel said. "Though I do hope you came with information."

"I did," the woman said. "Rebecca wouldn't have sent me otherwise."

"Then please follow us," Emanuel said. "We have food and drink for you."

"I'm not going into your mountain." The woman reached into her pocket.

Jeremy jumped up onto the ledge behind her, gripping Stell's knife.

The woman looked over her shoulder, staring blandly at Jeremy as she pulled a leather scroll from her pocket. She passed the scroll, not to Emanuel in the shadows, but to Nola.

"I've been sent with a map," the woman said. "Be at the blue in two night's time. Get there with enough time to cross the water and get to the black before sunrise. You'll shelter there for the day, and we'll attack at nightfall. Rebecca will bring twenty-three of our people. The black can protect thirty of yours."

"Only thirty?" Jude asked.

The woman looked to him. "Huh. You really aren't dead."

"Nightland has more fighters to offer," Emanuel said.

"We don't have more dark," the woman said. "Bring any more than thirty, and their deaths are your responsibility when the sun takes them. Do you have any messages for Rebecca?"

"Only my thanks for her offering shelter to my fighters and a path across the river," Emanuel said.

The woman nodded and turned back to the ledge.

"That's all?" Nola said. "You came all the way here and you're already leaving?"

"I trust Rebecca," the woman said, "but I don't trust nightwalkers enough to stroll into a mountain filled with blood drinkers. You have the information I have. Our people will bring arrows and knives and fight to the death. Bring what you will to help stop the spider. My people have chosen their sacrifice. Bring yours to the blue."

The woman stepped around Jeremy to sit on the ledge. Grabbing the rock, she twisted, lowering herself before dropping to the ground so softly unchanged ears wouldn't have noticed the sound.

Trying to ignore the feeling of a hundred eyes watching her, Nola stepped into the shadows, handing the scroll to Emanuel. "I'd like to see the map."

Emanuel untied the thin cord that held the scroll shut.

Jeremy leaned over Nola's shoulder as Emanuel unrolled the map.

Their mountain marked the southwest corner. A red line laid out a path that wound east of the rancid swamp marked in gray paint. The Nallot wasteland had been marked in yellow. The red path led them west of the damage to a blue triangle on the bank of the river.

"What is that?" Nola pointed to a black square on the far side of the river across the hills from the domes.

"I have no idea," Emanuel said. "But I hope it will provide enough shelter."

Nola leaned closer to the map, studying the series of circles that made up the domes.

Home.

CHAPTER TWENTY-THREE

"It's not right," T said.

"What's not right?" Nola peered into the box of apples T had been counting through. The fruit was ripe and undamaged, though none of the produce in Nightland would live up to Lenora Kent's expectation of perfection.

T glanced to Bea's door in the back of the pantry and to Kieran working by the barrels along the wall. "This whole project is pointless," T whispered.

Kieran's neck stiffened.

"We're spending all this time preparing food packages, and for what?" T said.

"Emanuel is being careful," Nola said. "He wants to make sure everyone is protected."

"Protected?" T pulled a bundle of empty sacks from under the table. "He wants to lead an attack on the domes. Fine, I get it. But pretending that, if things go badly, sending the human survivors scattering into the wild with a bag of food will somehow magically keep them alive is nothing more than a fairytale he's feeding the children."

We don't leave for the north until tomorrow night and people are already scared.

"If people have supplies—" Nola began.

"You don't get it," T said. "You've never been hungry. You've never wondered where you were supposed to sleep, or if there would be any water safe enough to drink. We're budgeting out food for people to carry, but if there isn't a way to get more, everyone who takes one of these sacks will die."

"We're giving everyone enough for a week," Kieran said. "That's as much as most will be able to carry. And we're going to put a couple of seeds in each package."

"We'll all be long dead by the time any seeds can grow." T banged her hands on the table. "We don't need pretty promises of safety, or packages of food so it will take us longer to die. This was supposed to be a place where we could survive and it's all just shit!" Hands trembling, T stormed out of the pantry, slamming the door behind her.

Nola stared at the door, her mind warring with her feet's urge to run after T. *There's no truth I can give her that will make this better.*

"Well," Kieran said as the sound of T's heavy footsteps faded, "I don't suppose you going after her before she upsets any of the others would help."

"She's scared," Nola said. "Everyone is. T's due soon, and now she's packing food in case she has to deliver her baby on the side of a mountain."

The tang of fear had filled the tunnels of Nightland for the last day, ever since Emanuel had ordered Nightland to begin preparations for battle and evacuation.

"My dad will look after her," Kieran said. "In Nightland or in the wild. He's got his medical bag packed. He'll stick with T and do everything he can to help her."

Nola picked up a sack, shaking it out and starting a neat stack. Hundreds of food sacks had to be packed and distributed.

In case.

We're abandoning them to wait in the dark. Leaving them without any way to know what happened if we don't come back.

"I hate it," Nola said. "I should be staying with T. I'm abandoning her just like Charles did."

Nola shook another sack, sending dust flying into the air.

"Do you want to stay here?" Kieran moved the pile of sacks out of Nola's reach.

"I can't." Nola pinched the bridge of her nose. "I can't send Jeremy without me, without anyone else who can go into the sun unprotected. Emanuel can only bring thirty vampires, adding Jeremy and me makes the number thirty-two. And I don't think I can live with myself if I let Emanuel go after the domes without me."

"Because you'd be ashamed not to fight or because you're afraid of what he'll do?"

Nola looked into Kieran's black eyes. Eyes she'd caught a glimpse of as he fled from the domes, leaving blood and pain behind him.

"I know what the domes did to you and your dad is unforgivable. What they did to me on that bridge is unforgivable. Using fire packs in the city is unforgivable. Spraying Nallot is unforgivable. Making us even consider leaving Nightland to attack them is unforgivable." The table cracked beneath Nola's grasp. She stared down at the ruined wood. "Sorry. I'm sorry."

"You don't have to apologize for being angry, or for being right." Kieran took her hands in his.

"Nikki died, Kieran." Nola blinked the haze of tears from her eyes. "She was shallow and couldn't remember which dome classes were supposed to be held in, but she never hurt anyone. She lived in the domes, but she never understood the harm they were doing."

"None of us did."

"How many more Nikkis are there going to be when Nightland attacks?"

"Emanuel will do everything he can to make sure people who aren't fighting aren't hurt."

"But we get rid of Salinger and then what?" Nola pulled her hands from Kieran's grasp as the need to run seized her lungs. She paced by the table, wishing the pantry were large enough for her to sprint in circles. "We can't just ask him to leave nicely. We're going to have to kill him or force him out. Either way, we'll have to damage the domes."

"You're right." Kieran leaned against the table, his gaze tracking Nola's movement.

"So we shatter the glass and decimate the Outer Guard," Nola said. "Then what?"

"We come back to Nightland."

"But what about the Nikkis we leave behind?" Nola said. "You've heard Julian. The domes are a delicate ecosystem. If we shatter the glass, how will they fix it?"

"We live without glass."

"But what if they can't? Do the pregnant women Salinger will leave behind deserve to die? Because they could. And justified or not, it will be our fault."

"So you think we shouldn't attack?" Kieran leaned on the table, a line creasing his forehead.

Nola recognized that look. The reasoning Kieran. Sorting through a problem that would give their classmates trouble. Sorting through his father's jumbled thoughts to find the spark of genius.

"We have to." Nola leaned against the other side of the table, focusing on Kieran's face.

Get rid of the wrinkle in his brow. Solve that problem first.

"If we don't attack, the domes won't stop until all of us are dead," Nola said.

"But if we destroy the domes, we kill innocent people."

"I don't know if any of us are innocent," Nola said. "But people who have never tried to hurt anyone will die. Even if Emanuel could keep his fighters from killing anyone but the guards, the domes survivors won't be able to keep everything running with the glass shattered."

"Break the glass, and you can't keep the domes functioning," Kieran said. "The entire system relies on technology."

"If the survivors leave the domes, they'll die." Nola dug her knuckles into her eyes. "When the domes kicked you and your father out, your lungs couldn't handle the outside world. You didn't have the immunities you needed. It would be the same for them. And, even if Emanuel would agree to it, we couldn't even take in the domes' children."

"We're doing fine on food, but not well enough to support a few hundred extra food eaters."

"I just can't accept it." Nola dug her fingers into her curls, relishing the pain it brought. "To save people, we have to kill people. I want to survive. I want T and her baby to survive, but I don't want blood on my hands."

"Then we find another way."

"What other way? We can't just hide in these caves and wait to be slaughtered."

The crease disappeared from Kieran's brow as the crinkle of a smile appeared at the corners of his eyes.

"What?" Nola leaned farther across the table. "What?"

"Make it impossible to justify the cost of the fight." Kieran grinned.

"What do you mean?" Nola asked.

"We don't have to win," Kieran said. "We just have to make it impossible for them to."

CHAPTER TWENTY-FOUR

Nola gripped the edge of the bed as her gaze darted from Jeremy to Kieran. "It makes sense," Jeremy said. "I'm not an expert on how the dome computers work—"

"But the domes have their own experts." Kieran leaned against the door to the hall as though trying to sink through the stone and back out into the corridor. "It's not our responsibility to fix it. We're just trying to leave them with something salvageable."

"Getting in won't be easy." Jeremy ran his hand over the scruff on his face.

"None of this is going to be easy," Nola said. "There is no easy plan, but at least ours might not end with a thousand dead Domers."

"How many dead vampires are we going to have on our hands?" Jeremy met Nola's gaze.

If people die, it will be because of our plan.

"No matter how we attack, not all of us are making it back to Nightland," Kieran said. "Every one of us going knows that."

"You're going?" Nola stood.

"I have to," Kieran said. "I know the domes. None of the others do."

"Emanuel won't allow it," Nola said. "He has to keep you here to grow food."

"He already agreed to let me go. It only took about an hour of me reciting the layout of the domes for him to admit he needs me." Kieran gave a half-hearted smile. "That was before you and I even started on our plan."

"Does he want Nola to stay here?" Jeremy asked.

"I won't." Nola stepped across the tiny room to lay her hand on Jeremy's chest. "If you go, I go. And they'll need both of us to pull this off."

"But he wanted one of you here to make sure the gardens—"

"We've packed up food bags for the survivors to take," Kieran said. "If this doesn't go well, there will be no garden to tend. He needs all three of us at the domes. I spent the time you were gone writing out everything I know about the gardens."

"Kieran." Nola searched his black eyes for a hint of fear.

Kieran shrugged. "Honestly, it didn't take as long as I thought it would. Dad has the papers. He'll keep them safe, and if he has to run, the papers will go with him."

"And he'll be with T," Nola said.

"We can't be everywhere and protect everyone," Kieran said. "All we can do is our best and hope people are strong enough to survive without us."

"He's right." Jeremy wrapped an arm around Nola's waist, letting her lean against his side. "Yours is the best plan we've got."

"Do you still have your uniform?" Kieran asked.

Jeremy kissed the top of Nola's head before letting go of her to open his dresser drawer. His black Outer Guard uniform lay perfectly folded inside.

"It's been torn," Nola said.

"As long as they don't see me in it until after the fighting's started, I don't think any of them will notice," Jeremy said.

"We should go to Emanuel," Nola said.

"See if he'll even agree," Jeremy said.

"Emanuel may be desperate to protect Nightland," Kieran said, "but he's still logical. He'll understand."

"We hope." Jeremy reached for the doorknob.

Kieran placed his hand on the knob first. "Thank you. For listening even though I helped come up with the plan."

"I never said I didn't think you were smart," Jeremy said. "I'll listen to whoever has a plan that will keep Nola safe."

Nola froze, watching Kieran and Jeremy stare at each other.

"It's good to be on the same side." Jeremy offered his hand.

A crack in Nola's chest mended as the two shook hands.

"You get to be the one to talk to Emanuel," Jeremy said. "You know him better than either of us. He's more likely to listen to you."

"Best get to it." Kieran opened the door to the hall. "It's probably good Raina hasn't gotten back yet. She'd fight us on every detail."

"Why?" Raina leaned against the wall in the hall. "What on earth is so important that Kieran and the lovebirds would lock themselves in a room together? Unless the plan *was* to lock yourselves in the room together." Raina winked at Nola.

Heat rushed to Nola's cheeks.

"When did you get back?" Kieran asked. "Were you hurt? What took you so long?"

"Asking too many questions at once bores me," Raina said.

"When did you get back?" Nola asked.

"Not long ago," Raina said. "But I had to talk to Emanuel, tell him all about my southern excursion before I came to find you."

"Do you have any news?" Kieran said.

"Not that has to do with your mushrooms," Raina said. "Though from the looks of it, your interests are branching out."

"Does Emanuel want us in the library?" Nola asked.

"Not as much as I want to know what the three of you are chatting about that I'll hate so badly," Raina said. "Come on, give me a clue."

"We shouldn't keep Emanuel waiting," Jeremy said.

"Sure." Raina tossed her scarlet and purple streaked hair behind her shoulder. "That could be fun too. It's not like I just spent days stomping all over creation. Let's do what you want to do." She sauntered toward the library.

"What kept you out so long?" Nola said.

"This and that," Raina said.

"Did you blow something up a couple of days ago?" Jeremy asked.

"Wouldn't you like to know?" Raina opened the doors to the library, stepping aside to let Nola and Jeremy pass.

"Jeremy," a female voice spoke from inside the library.

"And boom," Raina said.

A streak of black raced across the room, pummeling into Jeremy.

A head of short, dark blond hair blocked Nola's view of Jeremy's face.

"Gentry?" Nola said.

"You're actually alive." Gentry stepped back, taking her younger brother's face in her hands.

"Like I'd lie." Raina stepped into the library, heading toward three others dressed in filthy and worn Outer Guard uniforms.

"How did you get here?" Tears rolled down Jeremy's cheeks.

"We spotted Raina, and I knew she'd been with Nola when she disappeared," Gentry said.

"That's not really how it happened, but sure," Raina said. "Took me a little longer to get back since even fancy trained Domers are still slow as hell. But it seemed like you might want to see her."

Jeremy stepped away from his sister, reaching Raina in a few quick strides.

Before she could speak, he'd pulled Raina into a hug, his mass covering everything but her brightly colored hair.

"Thank you," Jeremy said.

"Don't get mushy." Raina backed away from Jeremy's embrace. "I'm morally opposed to feelings, and you'll make me regret hauling four lost humans all the way to Nightland."

"Right." Jeremy nodded. "Thanks." He turned to the other three Outer Guard.

Nola recognized the woman from the domes, but she'd never seen the two men before.

"Thanks for sticking with my sister," Jeremy said.

"She's a pretty convincing leader," the woman said.

"And you'll all be an asset to Nightland," Emanuel said.

Nola turned toward his chair for the first time.

Emanuel stood, his gaze drifting from Jeremy to Gentry. "I'm afraid you've arrived at a difficult time. I built Nightland to be a safe haven for vampires and humans, but the domes and Salinger seem determined to destroy everything outside their control."

"Yeah," Gentry said, "that's the gist of it. They wouldn't even let us give an evacuation order before they started dropping fire packs on the city."

"We're going to attack," Jeremy said. "Things have gotten worse since you left. Salinger sent down a mandatory breeding order."

"What?" Gentry said.

"We can't let him stay in control," Jeremy said.

"We have a plan." Nola turned to Emanuel. "One that might end better for everyone."

"Does it involve lots of blood?" Raina grinned.

"Hopefully not," Kieran said, "but it would take some explosives."

"I'm moderately intrigued," Raina said.

"You can't attack the domes." One of the male Outer Guard stepped forward.

"I haul you all the way here, and that's what I get?" Raina said. "A *sorry Salinger is killing people, but don't attack the domes?*"

"It's not that you'd be wrong to do it," the female guard said. "He means it can't be done. Salinger has made them too strong."

"You have no idea who you're dealing with," Raina said. "Spill the plan, Kieran."

"We should go to the kitchen," Emanuel said. "Let our new friends find food and rest. You'll have to forgive us." Emanuel bowed to the guards. "First generation vampires like Raina and myself often forget how immediate the needs of humans can be."

"We can wait," Gentry said.

"I insist," Emanuel said. "Jeremy, Nola, take them down to Bea. She'll feed them and arrange a room for them to share."

"We should stay," Nola said.

"It's okay," Kieran said. "I won't leave out any of the details. Take care of the Domers."

"Thanks," Jeremy said. "Come on, we'll get you fed."

"Sure." Gentry turned to Emanuel. "Thank you for your hospitality."

"In a world where allies are hard to find, we must make the best of those who come our way," Emanuel said.

"This way." Jeremy opened the door to the corridor. "If you've been outside since the city burned, you probably need a good meal."

"Eating would be nice," one of the men said.

Nola watched Emanuel lead Kieran and Raina into his home.

"Does he not trust you or not trust us?" Gentry said.

"You," Jeremy said.

"It's okay," Nola said. "Kieran will convince them."

"Convince them of what?" Gentry said.

Jeremy glanced to Nola. "Nothing that will happen before you eat."

Shaking her head, Gentry followed Jeremy out into the hall. Nola walked at the back of the group.

Am I protecting them, or guarding against them?

"How long have you been here?" Gentry trailed her fingers along the stone wall as they walked toward the pantry.

"We got here two nights after I left," Jeremy said.

"*Left* is a hell of a way to put it," the female guard said.

"That's rich coming from you, Bishop." Jeremy glanced over his shoulder, a grin on his face. "You ended up here, too."

"Shit happens," Bishop said.

"None of us planned on leaving," the older of the two men said. "But when they plant you at the perimeter of a city and start dropping fire packs on it, your day doesn't go according to plan."

"The world isn't split into dome citizens and Vampers," Gentry said. "I swore I would give my life for the domes. I never promised them my soul."

"And how can you let innocent people burn and claim you still have one?" Bishop said.

"We were in the city when it burned," Jeremy said.

"We?" Gentry said.

"Nola and I. We were looking for someone. We found one of the groups you'd tried to save. You left them near Bellevue. The people, they got out."

"Good." Gentry's voice tightened. "We tried to go back for them, but there wasn't a path through the flames."

"The important thing is that you tried," Jeremy said. "The domes decided to slaughter people, and you tried to help. Even if they hadn't made it out, it wouldn't have been your fault. It's the domes."

"It's Salinger," the younger of the male guards said. "I was in the first batch the Incorporation sent. This was going to be my new permanent placement. I thought everything was going to be okay. Then he came in, and I couldn't see anything in my future but blood and death."

"It'll be—" Jeremy cut himself off. "Don't give up. We aren't done yet." He stopped in front of the door to the pantry, knocking loudly before speaking. "Emanuel sent me down with some new people who need food and a bed."

Silence answered.

"Should you knock again?" the young man asked.

"Hungry, Dave?" Bishop raised a singed eyebrow.

"It's best if we wait," Nola said. "No one rushes Bea."

"What sort of food do you have here?" Dave asked.

"I hope you like mushrooms," Jeremy said.

The door to the pantry opened, and Bea peered out into the hall, her already wrinkled forehead furrowing into thick lines.

"Sorry to bother you, Bea." Jeremy gave a polite nod. "This is Gentry, Bishop, Dave, and..."

"Jefferson." The older guard reached out his hand, which Bea stared at without speaking.

"Emanuel wanted us to bring them here to get food and said you could find a place for them to sleep," Nola said.

Bea shuffled away from the door, leaving it open behind her.

"Don't touch anything she doesn't give you," Jeremy said.

"Really?" Gentry mouthed to her brother.

Jeremy nodded and bowed the others into the pantry.

The sacks of packed food waited at the bottom of the shelves.

Only a day before we leave.

I may never know if Bea had to use the sacks.

Nola ended up by Jeremy's side without knowing she had made the decision to move. He wrapped his arms around her, kissing the top of her head as Bea laid out beans, dried beef, and seedy bread.

With a sigh Bea headed for the door at the back of the pantry.

"Eat up," Jeremy said.

"Thanks," Dave said.

Nola twisted, keeping her back pressed to Jeremy.

While the other three guards ate, Gentry stared at Jeremy and Nola.

"You really did leave because of her," Gentry said.

Jeremy tightened his arms around Nola. "They were going to kill her."

"Right." Gentry ruffled her short hair. "Right."

"I didn't ask him to," Nola said. "Everything just sort of spiraled, and we ended up here."

"With everything that's happening in the domes, I'm not sorry we left," Jeremy said. "Gentry, none of us would have been able to stand by and let Salinger burn a city or treat the domes women like animals to be bred."

"I want in," Gentry said.

"What?" Jeremy said.

"However Emanuel is planning on attacking the domes, I want in." Gentry stared at Jeremy, every bit the Outer Guard her father had raised her to be.

"You can't," Jeremy said. "With how fast we're going to be moving, it would take being a vampire or having Graylock for you to keep up."

"So I'm just supposed to sit here?" Gentry said. "After how far we came to get here, I should just relax in a cave? Bond with Nola, since you two are apparently a real thing now."

"I won't be here," Nola said. "I'm going with Emanuel."

"Gonna ride piggy back?" Gentry said.

"Nola's had Graylock," Jeremy said. "When I found her, she was dying, and I had my triage kit."

"What?" Gentry said.

The other guards turned to stare.

"I can run it on my own," Nola said.

"Nola's like me," Jeremy said. "I made her like me."

CHAPTER TWENTY-FIVE

I should sleep.

Nola pinched the bridge of her nose, willing her eyes to find some hint of fatigue. The sun had risen outside the caves hours ago. As soon as the day ended, they would be leaving for the north, running toward the plan Nola and Kieran had built.

If people die, it will be my fault.

Jeremy had taken refuge in the sparring room, fighting away the words Gentry had shouted at them.

Is she mad that he saved me, or that he followed me?

Nola shook her head, trying to break away from the awful thought.

Gentry wanted to take Graylock from the beginning. Now I've had it, and she hasn't. I'm stronger than she is.

T had refused to look her in the eye ever since she stormed out of the pantry. Beauford had taken the same approach, staying close to T's side, as though the evacuation order might come down at any moment.

I'm hurting everyone. All I want to do is help, and I keep hurting everyone.

"I don't want to do this anymore." Her words rang dully around Jeremy's empty room. "Our room. This is our room, in our home, which I'm trying to save so we can have a life." Nola looked up to the stone ceiling. "And now I'm talking to myself."

She yanked on her shoes, giving one last, longing look to the bed before heading out into the hallway.

A strange scent caught her nose as she moved toward Emanuel's library.

Fresh blood.

Nola shivered but kept moving toward the door. One drop of red stained the handle on the library doors.

"Emanuel?" Nola stepped into the library.

The room was empty. Everyone else in Nightland was either sleeping or preparing.

"And I'm wandering," Nola said. "And still talking to myself."

The scent of blood thickened in the library. Red dots marred the floor, leaving a path to Emanuel's home.

"Eden." Nola sprinted for the door, wrenching it open before knocking. The trail of red didn't lead to the kitchen, but farther down the hall, stopping at the metal door to Dr. Wynne's laboratory.

Nola banged on the door. "Dr. Wynne, are you okay? Dr. Wynne?"

"I'm fine." Dr. Wynne's voice carried through the door. "Quite unharmed. You have no need to worry."

The false brightness of his tone shot fear into Nola's stomach that screaming couldn't have managed.

"I'm coming in." Nola twisted the knob, half-expecting the door to be locked. But the handle turned easily, and Nola stepped into the laboratory. More spots of blood shone on the floor, leading to the metal table where Gentry sat, eyes closed, jaw clenched.

"What happened?" Nola reached for Gentry. "Did one of the vampires attack?"

"No." Dr. Wynne fluttered his hands through the air. "No sort of attack. No harm at all, really. Gentry is extremely healthy."

"But there was blood," Nola said, "down the hall and leading here. Gentry, what happened?"

"Perhaps it's best if we leave her to a nice rest." Dr. Wynne shooed Nola toward the door. "Not long left to get everything ready, and our new, former guard friends have just arrived."

"But—" Nola took a breath to begin arguing with Dr. Wynne, but a scent caught on her tongue. Something more familiar than the fragrance of stone and more frightening than the smell of blood. "What did you do?" Nola rounded on Dr. Wynne.

"It wasn't him." Gentry spoke through gritted teeth. "I did this."

"Did what?" Nola smacked the table where Gentry sat. "Gentry, what did you do?"

Gentry shivered as she looked at Nola. "I will not be left behind while my baby brother fights."

"I didn't think," Dr. Wynne said. "She asked to see the samples. I only turned my back for a second, and then it was too late."

"What do you mean *too late*?" Nola said.

"I've been a guard for two years longer than my brother," Gentry said. "I've fought Vampers and wolves. I've watched my friends die, and I've watched them be changed so wounds can't kill them. I will not sit back and let my brother go up against Salinger."

"We're not—"

"You're going to the domes, and I'm coming with you." Gentry held up a blood-covered palm. The wound on her hand had been completely healed.

"What did you do?" Nola said.

"Asked to see a dose of Graylock and shoved the venom into my veins," Gentry said.

"I really didn't consider she'd do anything of the sort," Dr. Wynne said.

"We don't have enough!" Nola banged the table again. "We don't have three full doses. You're going to die!"

"We all have to go sometime." Gentry stood, her legs shaking beneath her. "You and Jeremy are going to the domes, and I'm coming with you. If I don't get in the glass and find more Graylock, then I die. Do not try to sideline me, Nola Kent. I will do whatever it takes to win."

"It's not worth—"

"Do not tell me what my death is worth." Gentry pushed her shoulders back, showing no fear of the ice that raged through her veins.

"We're leaving soon," Nola said. "We're running north, and you have to have another dose tomorrow."

"I stabbed myself in the heart once. I can do it again." Gentry stepped toward the door.

Nola planted herself in the way, refusing to cower in front of Gentry.

"I need to see Emanuel," Gentry said. "No point in waiting to tell him he's got another fighter running with his pack."

"And if he forbids you from going?" Nola said. "He doesn't know you. He doesn't trust you. He might not want you running right back to your father. Did you even think about that?"

"I am going to fight," Gentry said. "I am going to stop that monster from destroying everything good about my home. If I have to find my own way across the river, so be it. I'm coming."

"And if Emanuel locks you up?" Nola said.

"Then I'm glad I made myself strong enough to fight back."

"If I may?" Dr. Wynne waved timidly. "I have known both of you since you were too young to remember being brought to me for medical treatment. I cared for you during your early years, just as I've cared for Eden. I knew your parents, just as I know Emanuel."

"Thank you for taking care of us," Nola said.

"It's not about thanks," Dr. Wynne said. "I simply want to offer a bit of advice."

"If it involves me not taking Graylock, you're a little late," Gentry said.

"When you speak to Emanuel, don't lie," Dr. Wynne said. "Don't pretend you're going for his good, or for the good of Nightland. Tell him the truth. A monster has taken your home, and you intend to slay the beast."

"With my bare hands if I can."

"Show him that," Dr. Wynne said. "That is a truth he can believe without knowing the teller."

"You think he'll say yes?" Gentry said.

"No," Dr. Wynne said, "but it's the only way I can imagine him not saying no."

"We need to find Jeremy," Nola said. "He should be in the sparring room."

"I'm not asking my baby brother's permission."

"He should know first," Nola said.

He should know the clock is ticking down on your life.

"Where's Emanuel?" Gentry turned to Dr. Wynne.

"I have no idea. Kieran would know, but I'm honestly not sure where he is right now either. He came in a few hours ago to say goodbye." The doctor's voice cracked.

"Not goodbye," Nola said. "Kieran will be back soon. You made him to survive."

Dr. Wynne nodded, puffing his hair into even more of a cloud than usual. "So I did."

"Someone in the sparring room will know where Emanuel is," Nola said.

"Then let's get to it," Gentry said.

"Wait." Dr. Wynne reached into a cabinet, pulling out a syringe filled with deep black Graylock. "Good luck, both of you."

Tears burned Nola's eyes. She nodded to the doctor, not knowing what words to say, and opened the door to the hall.

There were no voices coming from the kitchen or stories being read in Eden's room. The only sign of recent human habitation was the lingering scent of Gentry's blood. Nola breathed through her mouth on the way through the library, trying not to wonder what Gentry had done to her hand to leave such a trail behind.

"I didn't do it to spite you," Gentry said after she'd closed the library door behind them.

"I believe you."

"There has to be a part of this secret plan I can be used for," Gentry said.

Nola stopped in the middle of the hall, closing her eyes and trying to picture actual people carrying out the plan she and Kieran had formed in the pantry.

"You can be," Nola said. "Every vampire in Nightland could be used if there were a way to bring them all."

"Then be grateful for my help," Gentry said. "You've got one more trained and capable person fighting by your side."

"If Emanuel allows it." Nola stopped at the entrance to the sparring room. The thick metal door blocked the path forward. "Why is it closed?"

"I've never walked this direction in this tunnel, so how the hell should I know?"

Gritting her teeth to keep from speaking, Nola raised her hand and knocked on the metal door.

A dull *thunk* carried down the hall.

What if the Outer Guard are here? What if they blocked the passage to save us all?

But the heavy bolts hadn't been slid into the wall.

The door whined as it was pulled open a crack.

"What?" Raina glared out at them.

"We're looking for Emanuel," Gentry said.

"Why?" Jeremy asked from the corridor behind Nola.

Nola spun to face Jeremy. "I thought you were sparring."

"I was." Jeremy's brow furrowed as he glanced between Gentry and Nola. "But we're leaving soon, so everyone who's going is being called to the sparring room. I went to our room to get you."

Heat rose in Nola's cheeks.

"Perfect," Gentry said. "If this is where the squad is rallying to fight, then I've found the right place."

"What are you talking about?" Jeremy said.

Nola backed toward the sparring room door, ducking under Raina's arm and into the giant stone room.

"What the hell were you thinking?"

Nola winced at Jeremy's shout.

The weapon cages were open. Desmond and Julian worked together, pulling out swords, staffs, knives, and guns, making one long line along the far wall. Kieran worked near the outer door, checking the sun suits for damage, preparing them for the vampires who would defend Nightland if their attack on the domes failed.

Emanuel stood in the middle of the room, staring at the door to Nightland.

"I'm going to fight." Gentry's voice rang around the room.

"What's happening?" Emanuel asked.

"Gentry tricked Dr. Wynne and dosed herself with Graylock so she can come with us," Nola said. "She wants to fight."

Emanuel nodded. His face betrayed neither anger, nor amusement. A mask had taken the place of his usual knowing determination.

"Are you okay?" Nola asked.

"I said goodnight to my daughter," Emanuel said. "I won't be here when she wakes up."

"You're coming with us?" Nola said.

"I have yet to meet Rebecca. There are decisions to be made on Nightland's behalf that I would not lay on anyone else's shoulders," Emanuel said.

"Besides," Raina said, "what kind of king doesn't ride into battle with his people?"

The door from the corridor pushed open. Stell and the twins entered, all of them glancing back at Gentry and Jeremy, who stood close together, speaking in hushed voices while glaring daggers at each other.

"If you want to say goodbye to anyone, now's the time," Raina said.

"I"—Nola tried to swallow, but her mouth had suddenly gone too dry—"I don't have anything to say to anyone that would make leaving any easier."

"For you, or for them?" Emanuel asked.

"Neither," Nola said.

"For what it's worth," Raina said, "T and Beauford made it a long time without you. If you die tomorrow, it'll just be another sad blip on their radar of tragedy."

"Raina, don't," Kieran said.

"I'm not a blip," Nola said. "And neither are you, Raina, even if that's all you want to be."

"I'm not a blip." Raina grinned. "I'm a boom." Tossing her hair over her shoulder, she sauntered toward three large black packs lined up by the far wall.

"Is there anything I can do to help?" Nola turned her tear-brightened eyes away from the door as three large men entered.

"I don't know," Kieran said. "We're traveling so light, there isn't really anything to pack."

"Jeremy and I will need food and water," Nola said, "and maybe Gentry, I guess."

"T made up a pack for you," Kieran said. "She packed enough food for a week. I didn't have the heart to tell her you didn't need that much."

"Then Nola and Jeremy will have enough to share." Gentry strode up to them, the pink in her cheeks the only hint of her anger.

"We should talk," Emanuel said.

"I have to go with you," Gentry said, her gaze level with Emanuel's black eyes. "Salinger is a demon inside my home."

"And when we have to shatter the glass?" Emanuel asked. "When we have to fight against those whom you very recently called comrades in arms? Will you turn against us, or stay the course? I can't allow you to run by our side if you will turn your weapons on my people the moment Domer blood begins to fall."

"I won't," Gentry said. "Salinger needs to be stopped."

"We won't be fighting one man," Emanuel said.

"Sometimes you have to cut down part of the forest to stop the blight from spreading," Jeremy said. "Gentry understands that."

CHAPTER TWENTY-SIX

The pack weighed heavy on Nola's back.

Faint whispers drifted up from the back of the line. Thirty vampires waited behind Jeremy, Nola, and Gentry, anticipating the setting of the sun.

Jeremy stood closest to the open air, beyond the shadows that protected the vampires, his gaze scanning the forest below. He wore a large black pack and his torn Outer Guard uniform. The sight of him dressed as the enemy sent shivers down Nola's spine.

She looked down at her own clothes. Bishop's shoes had been too large for her to wear, but Nola had pulled on the rest of the former guard's uniform without argument, trying not to let the unfamiliar feel of the oversized clothes swallow her courage.

Jeremy and I are not a part of the domes.

Nola wanted to touch his hand, to feel the warmth of his skin against hers. To say his name and watch a smile twinkle into being at the corners of his eyes.

We don't have time. We're racing the sun itself.

The sky turned from red to gray as the sun dipped behind the mountains.

Gentry inched closer to the opening, standing shoulder to shoulder with her brother.

Nola's heart raced in a way running for hours could no longer achieve.

Jeremy glanced behind to Nola then stepped off the edge of the ledge. Gentry dropped from view a split second later, not even pausing to consider the fall.

Nola stepped off the ledge, her hand instinctively reaching for the knife at her hip.

Jeremy and Gentry had moved to the north side of the basin. Nola darted to Jeremy's side as Julian jumped down from the ledge. He looked up to the sky before clicking his tongue.

Nola sensed rather than heard the vampires surge toward the mouth of the tunnel.

Julian didn't wait for the vampires to assemble before he ran up the ridge. Jeremy nodded to Nola and took his place as second in the long line with Nola staying close on his heels.

Stay right behind him. Stay with Jeremy.

She wanted to run by his side, but their order had been set by Emanuel.

She would be with Jeremy while the vampires hid from the daylight. They would fight side by side when the time came.

I'll be with him when blood starts to fall.

Nola tried to shake the images of blood-slicked floors from her mind. She studied the ridges and trees they passed, listening for the calls of the night birds.

Julian led them down a different path than the one they'd followed before. He held the rolled up map in his hand but didn't stop to check their route as they cut down the side of the mountain onto a path surrounded by trees tainted by black moss.

He doesn't have time to be uncertain. We're racing against death. Running toward blood and pain.

I've never run toward violence before.

Nola's hands shook, but she kept running.

It's too late for second guessing.

The pounding of the vampires' footsteps chased her north. Somewhere in the long line, Kieran ran behind her. And Emanuel, and Raina. The twins, and Stell. Jude and the blond girl who hated being trapped in Nightland.

I don't know her name. I should know her name.

There wouldn't be as many people running with her on the return trip to Nightland.

If I make the run back.

Nola tipped her chin down, grateful no one could see her face. No moon had risen to replace the burning sun, but the darkness wouldn't have kept the others from seeing the tears in her eyes.

We'll be able to see better than the Domers when we attack. Did Rebecca pick tomorrow night for the darkness?

But Rebecca's people wouldn't be able to see in the dark as Nola could.

They've chosen their sacrifice. They aren't planning on bringing anyone home. They don't know our plan.

The need to hear Jeremy's voice, for him to say something reassuring, pressed against Nola's chest.

She kept her gaze locked on his back as they passed the barren earth left behind by the Nallot.

A faint whisper of murmurs fluttered through the line.

Did Rebecca lead us past this place on purpose? To make sure Emanuel would see what Salinger had done?

Breathe, Nola. Just breathe.

Julian's pace didn't change as they ran parallel with the river and the ruined road, traveling farther north than Nola had ever been.

Movement shifted in the shadows far ahead.

Let it be Rebecca.

Julian didn't slow until he was within a hundred yards of the figures. He moved his hand to the hilt of his sword as the group of shadows turned toward him.

The people wore the brown of the Woodlands. Each had a bow and quiver full of arrows strapped to their backs.

Rebecca stepped to the front. A heavy Outer Guard rifle had joined the bow across her back. "I was hoping you'd make better time."

"It was quite a long journey." Julian bowed.

"I'll cross first and then the nightwalkers follow." Rebecca waved the Northerners out of her path. "Took us damned near a day to get the thing right, but it should hold for all of us."

"What should?" Nola asked. The feeling of speaking felt foreign to her mouth after the long hours of running in silence.

"Our bridge." Rebecca pointed to a pair of ropes hanging over the water.

The two ropes, one six feet above the other, reached from the trunk of a tree on the near bank to another on the far side of the river.

"I'm impressed," Julian said.

"How did you manage it?" Jeremy asked.

"Some damn fine shooting and a raft big enough for one," Rebecca said. "It's not our first time crossing. We're just smart enough not to leave a trail behind."

Jeremy took Nola's hand, lacing his fingers through hers.

Rebecca turned to the vampires. "If anyone falls in, we won't be swimming out after you. One at a time to keep the weight down." She headed to the tree where the ropes had been anchored, patting the trunk before gripping the higher rope and stepping up onto the lower.

Nola clutched Jeremy's hand tighter as Rebecca side-stepped out over the water, moving only a foot at a time as she crossed the raging current.

Emanuel stepped up to the end of the rope.

"Let me go first," Raina said.

"Rebecca and I have much to discuss and no time to spare." Emanuel gripped the top rope.

"Emanuel—"

"If this were a ploy to kill me, there would be much simpler ways than luring me out over the river." Emanuel watched as Rebecca climbed down on the other side, then stepped up and began his own journey.

"This is going to take too long," Gentry said.

"Well, if they had been able to build a nice, big bridge like the one the domes so foolishly blew up, I'm sure they would have." Raina kept her gaze fixed on Emanuel's back until he reached the far bank.

"I'll go next." Stokes stepped up to the rope.

"No chance in hell," Raina said.

"You think I should leave Rebecca alone with a pack of vampires?" Stokes said.

"You think you could do a damn thing against us?" Raina pulled herself up and started over the water, leaving a red-faced Stokes behind.

"We should let the vampires go first," Nola said. "Give them more time to get to ground."

"You're coming, are you?" Stokes eyed Nola. "Where's Jude?"

"I'm here, Captain." Jude stepped up beside Julian, his eyes cast toward the ground.

"Good to see you alive," Stokes said.

"Thanks, Captain."

"Jude." Al appeared at Stokes' side. "I'm glad you made it."

"You too, Al," Jude said.

"Get across the river, Jude," Stokes said. "I didn't send you to get saved just for you to die in the sun. I meant what I said. We need you fighting."

One of the twins stepped up to the ropes.

"We're getting the monsters out of our home." Jude turned his dark eyes up, meeting Stokes' gaze.

"Too right we are," Stokes said. "And now I'll have one guard that won't complain about working nights."

Jude smiled. "I'm your permanent volunteer."

"Go." Stokes waved Jude to the ropes.

"You really did leave," Gentry said.

Stokes blinked at her for a moment before cursing under his breath and turning toward the water.

"Nice to see you, too," Gentry said.

They stood watching while the other twin and Jude made it to the far side.

"Are they going to run on without us?" Nola said.

"They should," Jeremy said. "We can catch up after sunrise. Our job begins in the daylight."

Kieran grasped the top rope.

"Kieran." Nola stepped forward, taking his arm.

Kieran turned to her, a sad smile touching his black eyes. "See you on the other side."

"Stay safe." Nola gripped his hand.

Kieran leaned in, kissing her forehead. "You too, Nola." He looked to Jeremy. "Keep her safe."

"Always," Jeremy said.

Kieran nodded and stepped up onto the rope.

Jeremy took Nola's hand, kissing her palm. "He'll be okay."

"I would have punched him and tossed him into the river, but whatever." Gentry glared across the water.

"And have one less person trying to protect Nola?" Jeremy said.

Nola shrugged out of her pack and leaned it against a tree.

"I can carry that across the river," Gentry said.

"You're not used to Graylock yet," Nola said.

"I've been training for Graylock my whole life," Gentry said.

"Graylock didn't exist our whole lives." Jeremy gave a low laugh.

"Doesn't matter," Gentry said, "it's still what Dad was aiming both of us for even if he didn't know it."

Jeremy took off the black pack Raina had prepared for him, carefully leaning it next to Nola's.

One of the big men stepped up onto the rope. A chip of bark cracked off the tree.

"Got any water in that pack?" Gentry asked.

Nola knelt next to her bag, dug past the bundle of green beans, and reached for the water bottle in the bottom. Something around the metal crinkled as she pulled it free. A folded piece of paper had been tied to the bottle with a thin string.

"What's that?" Jeremy asked.

"No idea." Nola untied the string, pulling the paper loose before passing the bottle to Gentry.

Nola

Her name had been written on the outside of the paper in an unfamiliar hand.

"Crazy how little water you need on Graylock," Gentry said.

Nola unfolded the paper.

Dear Nola,

I hope you read this before you break into the domes. I don't know if you'll make it back to Nightland, or if Nightland will even exist much longer. I don't know if I'll survive having my baby, or if my baby will be healthy enough to live. I don't know anything except that I want my baby to grow up someplace safe.

Thank you for finding us a way to get to Nightland. For trying to help me find Charles. No other Domer would have bothered with outsiders, and you saved us from those awful cages.

I need one more thing from you. I need you to come back to Nightland, and I need you to promise to take care of my baby.

If it's a boy, I'm naming him Charles Catlyn. If it's a girl, she'll be Charlotte Catlyn, but call her Charlie when she's good. If something happens to me, you have to remember her name. Paint it across the mountains if you have to, but never let her forget.

Take care of Charlie and Beauford,

T

Tears fell from Nola's cheeks onto the already smeared paper. Jeremy lifted the note from her trembling hands.

"Did you just find out our plan has been sabotaged?" Gentry asked.

"No," Nola said, her voice thick with tears.

"Then stop crying, we're going into a fight," Gentry said.

"The world is ending," Nola said, "the only mandatory thing is survival."

Jeremy knelt next to Nola, wrapping his arms around her and letting her bury her face in his chest.

She didn't fight the tears that streamed down her cheeks. Didn't care how many of the vampires and Northerners saw her cry.

There are too many people to say goodbye to. Too many people I don't want to lose.

"You're next," Stokes said.

Nola looked up, expecting to find Stokes glaring down at her. His dark eyebrows had pinched together, but there was no anger on his face. "You two go and run after the Vampers. Gentry can follow with the Woodlands group."

"Like hell I'll go with you." Gentry stepped onto the rope. "Sorry, Stokes. Both Ridgeways are running with the fast folk tonight."

Stokes watched her until she had reached the halfway point over the river. "I thought you said you didn't have enough Graylock to save Jude."

"We didn't," Jeremy said, "and we don't. Gentry..." Jeremy dug his knuckles into his temples.

"We're going to get enough to finish Gentry's dose from the domes," Nola said. "No matter what it takes."

"I always knew Captain Ridgeway's kids were going to turn out crazy as hell," Stokes said. "I'm glad they're fighting on my side."

Jeremy gave an almost real smile. "Glad I'm fighting with the evil old bastard Stokes."

Gentry jumped off the rope on the far bank.

"You next," Jeremy said.

"Right." Nola pulled on her pack. "Right."

"Your arms are more than strong enough to hold you," Jeremy said. "Just keep a tight grip and you'll be okay."

"Better than a tiny tunnel." Nola's words came out steadier than she'd dared hope. She gripped the top rope with both hands. The coarse texture of the fibers bit into her palms.

"Keep breathing," Jeremy said.

Nola nodded and stepped up onto the bottom rope. The line bowed beneath her, swaying as she shifted her weight. She leaned farther forward, trying to balance her pack, and the ropes curved backward, away from her body.

"You can do this," Jeremy said. "Nola Kent, I have no doubt in my mind that you can do this."

Centering herself on the rope, Nola slid her right foot sideways. The rope jiggled beneath her but didn't snap and fall away.

No doubt. I will not doubt.

She slid her foot sideways again, stepping out over the river. Though she knew it was impossible, the sound of the racing water seemed infinitely louder once there was no longer solid ground between her and the current.

Ten seconds, Nola.

She took another step sideways.

You get ten seconds to panic.

She stepped again and again.

Then you're done.

She reached the center of the river. The stench of the water pummeled her nose.

That's all you're allowed.

The skin on her palms tore as she slid along the rope, but she didn't ease her grip. Keeping her eyes fixed on the horizon, she repeated the action: move right hand and foot, move left hand and foot.

Her right hand banged into something hard. Nola gasped, preparing to fall into the river. She glanced sideways and found herself nose to nose with the bark of a tree.

"Get down," Rebecca said. "I've still got to get my people through the hills."

Nola stepped down off the rope, taking a moment to convince her hands they really could let go. The pink of her palms was the only sign of the skin the rope had torn away.

She turned east. An empty forest of decaying trees waited for her. The vampires of Nightland had disappeared.

CHAPTER TWENTY-SEVEN

E ven as the sun sank over the horizon, its rays burned Nola's neck. She didn't mind. Pain meant life. Life meant a chance at success.

The only sounds of movement around her came from Jeremy, Gentry, Al, and Stokes. The Northerners made no noise as they wound their way through the dead forest in the hills, moving ever closer to the domes.

A pinch of worry prickled the back of Nola's mind even as she focused on the hilltops around her, searching for signs of Salinger's guards.

They're okay. They made it. They all made it.

Rebecca hadn't led the Northerners to the shelter where the vampires had taken refuge, and Julian had left Nola and Jeremy without a map.

A finger pointed toward the woods hadn't been enough for Jeremy to risk striking out to follow Nightland, so they stayed with Rebecca, hoping Nightland had made it. Hoping they wouldn't stand alone at the domes.

Hope is the hardest thing in the world to kill.

Stokes and Al moved at the front of the group, keeping close to Rebecca, as though afraid of getting lost. The Northerners didn't move in one long line as the vampires had, but spread out amongst the trees, winding their way through the forest, as though hoping to leave a maze for whoever might try to follow their path.

Nola walked between Gentry and Jeremy. For the first time since she'd had Graylock, her limbs didn't burn with the need to run. Whether it was the rise in front of them or the one just beyond, soon the domes would take over the horizon.

Then there won't be any choice but to dive in and hope enough of us survive.
Nola studied Jeremy's profile, the slant of his nose, the stubble on his chin.
I love you.
A smile curved Nola's lips.
I love you.
The sounds of movement in front of them stopped. Jeremy's brow furrowed.
Nola tore her gaze from his face to look south. The first glint of the domes' glass peered through the trees ahead of them.
Nola held her breath as she followed Jeremy forward, toward Rebecca.
They'll see us.
They won't look on this side of the river.
Rebecca waited, leaning against the trunk of a tree and peering through its branches. "At least the helicopter's not in the air."
On the east side of the domes, the helicopter waited. A tent had been erected next to the landing pad, though what might be inside, Nola couldn't guess. Two guards stood in front of the tent, facing the helicopter.
"We'll make sure it stays on the ground," Jeremy said. "If Salinger can send Nallot into the air, we're dead before we start."
"What about the guards?" Gentry said.
"We're fast," Nola said. "We can make it."
"Without being caught?" Rebecca asked.
"I'll go," Jeremy said.
"We're going together," Nola said.
"Can you do it?" Gentry eyed Rebecca.
"I'm used to the way the woods work," Rebecca said. "That doesn't make me invisible."
Gentry turned her gaze back to the guards. "If we get caught and the guards send up an alarm, they'll get us with Nallot before we can get back over the river."
"If we don't get to work soon," Jeremy said, "we won't be ready in time."
Nola glanced west. The sun had already begun to sink out of sight.
"If you have to go, then try making a run for it," Rebecca said. "But, if you want my advice, wait for a nice opening before you go sprinting at the armed men."
"What kind of opening?" Nola said.
"I'm not sure," Rebecca said. "But I like you well enough, I'll try and come up with something."
"Thanks," Nola said.
"We'll be listening for you." Rebecca gave a nod and turned north, heading farther into the trees.

"I wish the ground weren't so open." Jeremy bit his lips together, glaring at the domes. "A hundred and fifty yards of open space? No matter how fast we run, it's too far to hope we won't be spotted."

"Leaving cover right next to the domes would make them harder to defend," Gentry said.

"I didn't say it would have been smart, just convenient."

"Touché," Gentry said.

Jeremy took Nola's hand as he headed east, keeping within the tree line.

Nola willed her shoulders to stay relaxed and her breathing to stay even. "Last time I was in these woods, the Outer Guard were shooting at me."

"I'm sure they'll be shooting at us again soon," Gentry said.

"Gentry," Jeremy warned.

"If she's not ready for it, she can wait in the woods," Gentry said.

"I'm not letting Jeremy go in there without me," Nola said. "Besides, neither of you would know what to save."

"Fine," Gentry said. "Just do me a favor and try to look brave."

They stopped level with the helicopter. Nola peeked around the side of a tree, studying the tent and the guards.

Both guards wore helmets and full gear. Both held rifles in their hands.

"I'll take right, you take left?" Gentry said. "You two should grab their helmets and vests."

"If we can figure out how to get there," Jeremy said.

"Jeremy, let me take your pack." Nola slid off her pack of food. "If you two are fighting, then I can set the box."

"Nola—"

"Give her the pack," Gentry cut across Jeremy.

"Promise me you'll get clear," Jeremy said. "No matter what happens, even if you have to pitch the bag and run, you have to get clear."

"I've got it," Nola said. "I promise."

Jeremy took off his black pack, passing the weight to Nola.

"We're going to have to make a break for it." Gentry looked up to the cement tower at the center of the domes, toward the maintenance ladder too small for even Graylock-changed eyes to see. "I'm running out of time."

"How will we know when Rebecca creates a window for us?" Nola leaned forward against the tree, trying not to think of what she wore on her back.

"Do you trust her to come through?" Gentry asked.

"I trust her to do whatever it takes to win," Jeremy said.

Gentry pulled her weapon from its holster, checking the loaded darts.

Nola gripped the hilt of the blade on one hip and the gun on the other.

Hurt to protect. Fight to defend.

A *crack* sounded in the trees to the west.

All three spun toward the noise. Six brown blurs darted out toward the domes. With a faint *buzz* and *thwack*, an arrow hit a tree near the slowest of the brown things, steering the creatures farther east toward Nola.

"Are those deer?" Nola took a step toward the animals.

"They're our opening." Jeremy took Nola's hand and raced to the very edge of the woods.

The deer charged out of the trees, heading toward the eastern side of the domes.

"Damn she's good," Gentry whispered.

The guards spun, their weapons raised, as the deer raced toward them.

"Wait," Jeremy said. "Wait."

The guards turned, watching the deer run south.

"Run."

Still holding Nola's hand, he sprinted into the open.

Nola looked away from the guards, locking her gaze on the helicopter. Halfway across the clearing, Jeremy let go of her hand.

The horrible feeling of emptiness lasted only an instant. Nola veered away from the others, heading for the far side of the helicopter.

A *thump* and a *grunt* punctuated her footsteps, but she didn't dare look to see who had been hit. She skidded to a stop next to the side door of the helicopter. The doors had been closed, but Nola's aim wasn't inside the body of the craft.

Crack.

Nola yanked off her pack.

Not Jeremy. Jeremy is fine.

Three boxes waited inside the bag. Nola pulled out one of the two smaller boxes. Heavy, gray, and made of soft plastic, the box felt like nothing more than a toy. A red beacon poked out of one side of the box. Nola slipped under the helicopter, ripped a hunk of fabric from the base of the box, and stuck the exposed goo to the underside of the helicopter.

In a moment, it was done. Nola rolled away and sprang to her feet, grabbing the pack as she darted to the tail of the helicopter, peering out toward the tent.

Two guards lay on the ground. Blood pooled around the first, while the other's bare head twisted at an unnatural angle.

Gentry stood over one guard, wiping blood from the side of her neck, while Jeremy stared into the tent.

Nola ran from the shelter of the helicopter toward Jeremy. "We have to keep moving," she called as loudly as she dared.

"Give me the pack," Gentry said.

"Shit," Jeremy said.

"Are you hurt?" Nola removed the second small box from the pack.

"How flammable is Nallot?" Jeremy asked.

Nola passed the pack to Gentry and stepped into the tent.

Nallot.

Large white letters marked the fifteen barrels that waited in the shadows.

"We need to move faster." Nola grabbed Jeremy's hand, dragging him out of the tent.

Gentry had already pulled on the half-empty pack. "See you soon." She ran around the far side of the domes, heading for the back of the cement tower.

Jeremy yanked free the undamaged guard vest while Nola pulled off the other guard's helmet. She didn't let herself look at the guard's face.

Jeremy passed Nola the clean vest and pulled on the second helmet.

Taking a deep breath, Nola settled the helmet on her head. The scent of the dead guard's sweat filled her nose. Sour rolled into her mouth as she slung on the vest.

They'll keep me safe. Protect the heart and the neck, that's all I have to do.

"Ready?" Jeremy tightened his blood-covered vest and lifted the box from Nola's hands.

She couldn't see his face beneath the helmet.

He's not one of them. He's Jeremy. My Jeremy.

"Let's go." Nola took the lead, following the same path Gentry had run moments before.

They ran past the Aquaponics Dome and Leaf Dome.

How many people will see us running?

She waited for the *crackle* of a warning in her ear. For someone to have seen the two fallen guards and sounded the alarm.

They rounded the corner and neared the edge of Green Dome. The lights hadn't been turned on for the evening, but still a figure moved on the other side of the glass.

Jeremy sprinted in front of Nola, tearing the fabric from the box before he reached the dome. He planted the box on the glass wall and kept running.

Nola glanced up to the cement tower. A black figure climbed toward the Com Room.

The last of the sunlight faded from the sky.

Move faster, Gentry.

They reached the far side of Green Dome where an open patch of earth separated it from its neighbor.

Jeremy pulled Nola to the ground at the very edge of the glass, planting his body between her and Green Dome.

How long?

Every breath seemed too fast and too slow at the same time.

Raina, it's time.

Her heart raced. Her pulse thundered in her ears.

Bang!

The explosion shook Nola's lungs. Jeremy yanked her to her feet before she could remember how to take a breath.

Boom!

The sound came from beyond Green Dome. A pillar of fire soared into the air. Blue marred the orange of the flames. Nola couldn't tear her gaze from the blaze as Jeremy led her around the side of Green Dome to the newly made break in the glass.

Raina had planned the charge well. A ten-foot hole had been blasted into the side of the dome.

Not so big they can't find a way to fix it.

But how hot will the Nallot burn? Will the fumes kill or be burned away?

Red lights had already begun flashing on the inside of the domes.

Mrs. Pearson stood between the planting trays in the middle of the dome, swaying and staring at the hole in the glass.

"Get to the bunker," Jeremy shouted. "Go. Go!"

Mrs. Pearson started toward the stairs, but Nola and Jeremy were faster. They reached the corridor below before Mrs. Pearson's footsteps clattered on the stairs behind them.

The helmet dulled the blaring of the sirens and shouts of terror, but the tunnel itself shocked fear into Nola's spine.

The whole thing could collapse. What if the tower falls? What if Gentry didn't make it off the tower before the explosion?

The shouts of the panicked Domers grew louder as Nola raced past the corridor that led to the Guard barracks and the bunker near seed storage. Jeremy turned out of the corridor and ran up the stairs to the Aquaponics Dome just as a family with two small children raced by, the toddler sobbing onto his father's shoulder.

The flashing lights seemed out of place in the Aquaponics Dome, where fish swam in slow circles beneath the crops that fed the Domers.

Nola leaned against the wall just out of sight of the staircase. She found Jeremy's hand without tearing her gaze from the fire that still burned by the helicopter.

"We said we'd keep it out of the air," Jeremy said.

Nola nodded, sending her oversized helmet bobbling. Peeling herself away from the wall, she crept farther into the dome, going down the steps that led to the base of the tanks. High above the domes, a faint glow came from the top of the Com Tower.

"She did it," Jeremy said. "All the communications systems will be out. The guards' coms won't work. They won't be able to contact the Incorporation. All of it's gone."

"You'll have to congratulate her when we get back to Nightland." Nola was grateful the helmet hid the fear on her face.

The screaming in the corridors faded. The pounding of the guards' boots racing toward the threat destroying their home never even passed by the entrance to the Aquaponics Dome.

"Is it time?" Nola asked.

"I don't think we can afford to wait," Jeremy said. "Raina and Kieran will be here soon."

Letting go of Nola's hand, Jeremy led the way back to the steps, pulling his gun from his belt.

Only the flickering red lights moved in the hall.

The dome names painted on the walls were the same as when Nola had called the domes her home, but she felt no welcome at reading them as they ran down the corridor.

Jeremy slowed as they rounded the corner, holding his arm out to keep Nola from passing him. The stairs leading farther down were empty.

Nola pulled her Guard gun from her hip as they ran down the steps at a human speed. Her throat tightened as they rounded the corner and went down another flight of stairs, then another, winding deeper into the earth.

An empty corridor lined with frosted-glass doors waited for them. Her gun slipped in her grip as sweat slicked her palms.

Jeremy stopped next to a glass door, checking to see that Nola was at his side before shoving the door open and stepping into the seed storage room.

The familiar cold tingled Nola's skin. She should have felt safe surrounded by the rows of shelves where seeds waited for the day the world would be ready for the Domers to leave their glass castle, but the sight of the useless bounty sent a surge of anger racing through her limbs.

"What a waste." She turned toward the computer panel in the wall.

"What the hell are you doing down here?" The familiar voice froze Nola's finger an inch above the screen. "I have made it abundantly clear—I will not abandon my seeds, no matter what Captain Ridgeway says."

Nola turned to find her mother glaring at her.

CHAPTER TWENTY-EIGHT

More lines creased Lenora Kent's face than Nola remembered. Lenora pointed toward the door. "Out of my seed storage, now. Whatever this fresh round of hell might be, I'm sure you'll be much more useful somewhere else."

Nola's hand shook as she tucked her gun back into its holster and removed her helmet. "Mom."

"Magnolia." Lenora shook her head, sending her graying hair fluttering around her shoulders.

"Mom, I need you to go to the back of the room."

"What are you doing here?" Lenora said. "You left. You broke those outsiders out of the cells, and you left."

"Yes, I did." Nola took a step toward her mother. "I left because it was the right thing to do. Now I'm here because it's the right thing to do."

"You betrayed your home," Lenora said.

"No, Mom."

"Don't *Mom* me," Lenora spat. "My daughter died the day the Vampers kidnapped her."

Nola flinched, trying to hide the stab of betrayal in her gut. "No. I'm alive, and I'm doing more to save the human race now than I ever would have accomplished locked in here."

"Get out," Lenora said.

"Mom—"

"My daughter is dead."

Jeremy took of his helmet. "Get to the back of the room, sit on the floor, and don't move."

"Filthy traitors, both of you." Lenora stepped forward.

"Don't." Jeremy raised his gun.

"I will not let you harm my seeds," Lenora said. "They are worth more than my life."

"And more than your daughter," Nola said.

"Yes." Lenora met Nola's eyes.

"Make sure she can't stop me." Nola turned back to the screen.

She punched in her mother's passcode without having to think. The whole system pulled up. Inventory, files, climate control. Nola tapped on the climate heading. In three quick strokes, she quadrupled the temperature in the room.

"It'll ruin everything," Nola said. The vents turned on, blasting hot air into seed storage. "These seeds were meant to provide for generations."

Jeremy laid a hand on her shoulder. "So is Nightland, and the spring in the Woodlands."

Nola turned away from the panel. Lenora lay unconscious on the floor. The hateful twist of her face had faded, leaving Lenora looking almost like the mother Nola remembered.

"She's still alive?" Nola asked.

"Yeah."

"Move her to the hall." Nola didn't watch as Jeremy carried Lenora out of the room. Instead, she raced down the rows, pulling slim packets of seeds from the different bins.

The door to the hall closed.

"Jeremy?" Nola called.

"It's just me." The sound of Jeremy's boots pounded toward the far side of the room.

Nola stopped at each of the most precious seed bins, loading her pockets with treasures from root vegetables to healing herbs.

A *whine* sounded from the wall as Jeremy pulled the vent free.

Nola stopped in front of the bin labeled *Ficus Carica* and pulled out a packet.

"Nola," Jeremy whispered.

"Coming." Nola shoved the packet into her pocket with more than two-dozen others and ran for the vent on the far side of the room.

There will be no treasure left in the domes.

Jeremy had already pulled the vent free and kicked open the path to the other side. Still, Nola held her breath as she crawled through the few feet of metal vent and pulled herself out into the medical storage room.

Unlike seed storage, closed cabinets lined the walls of medical storage.

"I have no idea where it could be," Nola said.

"Start looking." Jeremy ducked back into the vent, pulling the grate to seed storage closed behind them.

Nodding to herself, Nola ran to the nearest case and wrenched it open. Vials filled with bright blue took up all of the shelves. Snapping the doors shut, Nola moved on to the next. Bottles of pills waited for her. She grabbed four vials of clear fluid and a handful of I-Vents from the third cabinet, shoving them all into the pockets of the dead guard's vest.

A *click* sounded from behind her as Jeremy began searching his half of the room.

Please, even if it's only one dose. Let me find one full dose.

The next case held closed tubs. The next, dishes of golden goo.

We can't have found Gentry just to lose her. Not after everything we've been through.

Cabinet by cabinet, she made her way around the room, dashing on to the next as soon as she was sure she hadn't found any of the deep black Graylock.

"Oof." Nola ran into something hard and glanced over to find Jeremy staring at her.

"Nothing?" Dread filled Jeremy's eyes.

"I'm sorry," Nola said.

"My dad's office," Jeremy said. "You said you saw some Graylock in his office."

"In the cabinet behind his desk," Nola said.

Jeremy raced to the vent, cramming his helmet back onto his head.

Only a floor up.

Nola had made the climb before she'd been given the strength of Graylock. Getting to the next floor would be easy now.

Jeremy tore the vent free with his fingers and began climbing before Nola reached the grate.

She ducked into the shaft, watching as Jeremy pulled himself onto the thin ledge near the Outer Guard barracks and kicked the grate to his father's office free. In one swift movement, he shifted his weight across the shaft and pulled himself through to the other side.

Nola pulled the grate to medical storage closed and put on her helmet. She took shaking breaths, trying to convince her lungs there was still air in the world.

Hot air aiming toward seed storage rushed down on her.

It'll contaminate medical storage, too.

Better than dumping Nallot onto a living person.

"Come on." Jeremy reached down into the shaft.

Nola jumped, grabbing hold of his hands. She closed her eyes as he lifted her up the shaft and dragged her onto the floor of Captain Ridgeway's office.

Everything was as it had been before. Captain Ridgeway's desk with the one chair behind it, a photo of Jeremy and Gentry from years ago when Jeremy was still shorter than his sister. A humming cabinet against the back wall.

Nola sprang to her feet while Jeremy moved to the cabinet and wrenched the drawer open.

"Shit!" He punched the side of the cabinet.

Nola leaned over the drawer. Cool air filtered up from the empty space.

"Where would Salinger's office be?" Nola asked.

"It could be anywhere." Jeremy dug the heels of his hands into his eyes. "It could be a house in one of the domestic domes. He could have taken over the damn Com Room for all we know. The formula could be in the computer encrypted under any of the doctors' files, and we wouldn't have a damned way to open the files even if we could get them."

"We can figure this out." Nola lifted Jeremy's hands away from his face. "You and me together, we can figure this out."

"Gentry's going to run out of time. There's nothing we can do."

"If I needed Graylock, would you give up?"

"Never." Jeremy gripped her hands.

"Then we have to keep looking. We'll go to the medical wing. There's got to be a triage kit somewhere."

The walls rumbled, shaking with the chaos of a far away explosion.

"Raina," Nola said.

"We have to get to the Atrium." Jeremy shoved on his helmet.

"But the medical—"

"If Salinger is hoarding the Graylock, he won't be keeping it in the medical wing. We're supposed to be in the Atrium. If we don't get there, Gentry won't need Graylock." Jeremy stepped toward the door to the corridor. He waited a moment before pulling the door open a crack.

The red lights flashed, but there was no sign of any Outer Guard.

Again, they both drew their weapons as they ran into the hall.

Jeremy looked every bit the Outer Guard, from his boots to his helmet. If his clothes hadn't been torn, the illusion would have been perfect.

Nola ran by his side in shoes that had once belonged to someone else, and Bishop's pants and shirt, both of which were far too large for her.

I'm playing dress up in the middle of a battle.

Signs of chaos didn't litter the domes as they raced through the tunnels. No wounded being carried to help. No guards charging toward the new break in the glass.

Where are the guards?

They found the first signs of true fighting as they reached the corridor below the Atrium. A smear of blood marred the otherwise perfect cleanliness of the tunnel floor.

Around the next corner, a guard lay on the ground, a pool of blood surrounding him.

Nola skirted the red and kept right by Jeremy's side, not allowing herself time to wonder if the man was already dead or only waiting for Graylock to revive him.

Shouts and the *pops* of Guard guns being fired carried from up the steps.

It should be louder. There should be more people fighting.

Unless something went wrong and the vampires were beaten before they started.

Jeremy slowed as they reached the top of the stairs to the Atrium.

The scent of smoke cut through the stench of sweat inside Nola's helmet.

The domes had been working on replanting the trees and grass damaged by Nightland's first attack. The new growth that had replaced the barren patches was now scarred by footprints and blood. A line of twenty Dome Guard stood around the base of the Com Tower, surrounded by shattered glass and chunks of concrete that had fallen through the dome from the blast on top of the tower. A dozen Outer Guard fought the vampires on the far side of the Atrium where all the vehicles were parked.

"Where's Gentry?" Nola asked.

"Stay behind me." Jeremy ran up the last of the stairs and charged straight for the Guard trucks.

Raina fought two guards at once, her knives flashing in her hands as she sliced the gun from one of the guard's grips. The twins fought side-by-side, tackling a guard and ripping his weapon from his hands. By the shattered glass, vampires lay still on the ground near guards with arrows protruding from their bodies.

Nola scanned the unmoving fighters, searching for Kieran and Gentry.

Jeremy charged into the fight, knocking over a guard who had his weapon aimed at Julian.

Nola raised her gun, firing a dart into the shoulder of an Outer Guard who barreled toward Jeremy.

Raina sprinted through the opening toward the trucks, her pack disappearing from view as the guard she had been fighting rounded on Nola.

He struck down, pummeling her wrist to knock her gun from her grip. Nola pulled her knife from its sheath with her other hand, sinking the blade into the man's thigh.

The helmet dampened the man's scream as she wrenched her knife free.

Before she could swing her blade again, Jeremy stabbed the man under the bottom of his vest. The guard gagged as Jeremy tossed him aside.

"Are you—" A *pop* cut across Jeremy's question. A thin silver dart glanced off the bottom of his helmet. Nola spun toward the shooter.

The Dome Guard had turned their weapons toward the fight by the trucks. Whether they no longer cared about hitting their own men, or had decided enough Domers had fallen to make shooting worth it, didn't matter as darts pummeled the fighters.

Jeremy yanked Nola sideways as another round of *pops* sounded from the Dome Guard's guns.

A shrill whistle blasted from behind the trucks. As one, the vampires ran, not toward the opening in the glass or for the shelter of the trucks, but for the far side of the Atrium and the stairs that led farther into the domes.

"Stop them!"

You're too late.

Jeremy grabbed Nola's shoulders, knocking her to the ground the moment before a *boom* shook the Atrium. Heat lapped Nola's skin. The glass above them shattered, raining fragments down on them as a series of *pops* and *bangs* carried over the roar of the fire and the shouts of the guards.

"Are you okay?" Jeremy grabbed Nola under the arms, hauling her to her feet.

"I'm fine." Nola scanned the faces around them.

Raina blew her hair out of her eyes and wiped the blood off her hands. Kieran stood behind her, his hair singed, but looking otherwise undamaged as he stared at the inferno that had been the domes' vehicles.

"Did you get all the ammunition?" Julian looked to Kieran.

"I set the blast on the weapons locker door," Kieran said. "It was the best I could do."

The flames had swallowed the guards they had been fighting before. But the Dome Guard near the Com Tower were getting back to their feet. Wounded and bloody as they were, they turned toward the stairs where the people of Nightland had fled the blast radius.

"We need to leave." Julian raised his sword.

"Salinger," Nola said. "Has anyone seen Salinger?"

"We've only seen the guards in here," Julian said. "The rest must be on Emanuel's side of the fight."

The Dome Guard raised their weapons.

"Go!" Jeremy shoved Nola toward the wide opening in the glass.

We can't leave. We have to stop Salinger. We have to save Gentry.

She didn't have time to speak as a string of *pops* punctuated the air.

Most of the Atrium wall had fallen, leaving a wide gap for them to escape. Open air waited just in front of them.

An arrow flew in from the night, landing right in front of Julian.

"Shit." Raina raised both her knives, her gaze fixed on the darkness beyond the shattered glass.

Captain Ridgeway ran toward them, a pack of Outer Guard by his side.

CHAPTER TWENTY-NINE

A rrows chased the Outer Guard as they ran into the ruined Atrium, their weapons leveled at the vampires.

An arrow struck one Guard in the back and another in the leg, but still the pack moved closer.

"Guards hold your fire!" a voice shouted from beyond the glass. "All of you, hold your damned fire."

Stokes limped in from the darkness. He held his arm to his chest, and his bad leg dragged through the shattered glass. But as he glared at the Outer Guard, he seemed as terrifying as Raina.

"What are you doing here?" Captain Ridgeway turned his gun on Stokes even as his men kept their weapons aimed at the vampires.

"Trying to keep the rest of my Guard from dying." Stokes pointed to the Dome Guard by the Com Tower. "There's enough blood on the ground. Back away and let these people go."

"I'm not taking orders from a traitor." Captain Ridgeway pointed his gun at Stokes' unprotected chest. "I'm not letting these murderers walk out of my home again."

"Dome Guard." Stokes spoke over Ridgeway. "I trained you to protect the people of the domes. Salinger and Ridgeway have turned you into demons. Have made you sit by while they use the women of these domes for breeding. Salinger needs to be stopped."

"You've lost your mind," Ridgeway said.

"He hasn't."

Captain Ridgeway turned at the sound of his son's voice.

"Salinger is a murderer." Jeremy stepped forward, removing his helmet. "He has to be stopped."

Ridgeway stared stone-faced at his son.

Nola joined Jeremy, pulling off her own helmet and taking his hand.

"You've destroyed our home." A guard stepped up next to Ridgeway.

"Think of it as leveling the playing field," Raina said.

"Dad"—Jeremy took another step forward—"where is Salinger? He's the one we came here for. I don't want to fight any of you. None of us can afford more blood on our hands."

"Run," Captain Ridgeway said. "Now."

"We can't," Nola said. "We have to find Salinger. We have to stop him before he kills everyone on the outside. He's trying to wipe us out."

"He is defending the domes," Captain Ridgeway said.

"By dumping Nallot in the woods," Stokes said. "That's bullshit, and even you're smart enough to know it."

"Let us stop him," Julian said. "The demon is damning you as he murders us."

"I cannot let you—"

"We need more Graylock." Nola stepped in front of Jeremy.

"What the hell—"

"We need more Graylock, or your daughter will die!" Nola shouted over Captain Ridgeway.

The *crackle* of the blaze gave the only sound. No boots crunched on the broken glass. The dead had already given their final gasps.

"She took Graylock, but we don't have a third dose," Nola said. "Gentry left because she couldn't be a part of Salinger slaughtering the city. She took Graylock so she could come here to fight. To try and save whatever bit of decency the domes have left. If you don't take us to wherever Salinger has hoarded the Graylock, Gentry will die."

"Where is she?" Ridgeway scanned the faces of the Nightland fighters.

"Captain, she abandoned the domes," an Outer Guard said.

"I did not give you permission to speak," Ridgeway spat.

"She set the blast on top of the Com Tower," Jeremy said. "She's probably fighting Salinger right now."

"If the coms were working, you might have known the prodigal daughter had returned to fight," Raina said. "But I made a little bomb, so whoops."

"Salinger isn't fighting, Captain Stokes." One of the Dome Guard stepped in front of the rest. "None of the Incorporation Guard are."

"We blow a couple holes in the domes and they don't bother showing up?" Raina said. "How disappointing."

"Captain Ridgeway, where is Salinger?" Nola said.

The Captain looked at his son, shaking his head.

"Dad," Jeremy said, "I don't want to lose Gentry. Please."

"Captain—" one of the Outer Guard began.

"Stand down," Captain Ridgeway said. "All of you. I am the Captain of the Outer Guard, the ranking Council Member outside the bunker, and I am ordering you to stand down."

Nola's breath caught in her chest as both Outer Guard and Dome Guard lowered their weapons.

"Salinger and the Incorporation Guard are in the Iron Dome," Captain Ridgeway said. "The order came down from the Incorporation after we lost a guard unit in the northern woods. The people of these domes are disposable. Salinger and the guards he brought in are necessary to the Incorporation and must be protected."

"They're just sitting in there, watching everything burn?" Anger coiled in Nola's stomach.

"I knew this was too easy," Kieran said. "We should have been outnumbered from the start."

"They closed the dome," Captain Ridgeway said. "Lowered the metal."

Jeremy shut his eyes, tipping his face toward the sky. "Where's the Graylock?"

"In his housing unit," Ridgeway said.

"I need you to get us in," Jeremy said. "Open the door, and we'll take care of Salinger and his men."

"Listen to your son," Stokes said.

The pounding of footsteps approached the shattered wall of the Atrium. Emanuel, flanked by Gentry and Rebecca, stood with fifteen fighters at his back. Only three dressed in Northern brown were still standing.

"Dad." Blood covered Gentry's uniform, but she stood straight-backed and proud as her father turned to her. "I've come to take my home back from the monster."

Captain Ridgeway nodded. "We go in, and we don't come out until that bastard is dead. We fight to the last man, and if the Incorporation blows us all to hell, at least our deaths won't come from cowardice. Anyone who doesn't want to fight, get in the Com Tower now."

Two of the Outer Guard moved toward the tower.

"Leave your weapons," Captain Ridgeway ordered.

The guards laid their guns on the floor and walked through the door at the bottom of the tower. Only one Dome Guard joined them.

"Lock them in," Ridgeway said.

Gentry strode forward, grabbing a piece of metal from the ground. The Dome Guard scattered as she reached the door and rammed the metal between the door and the frame.

"With me." Captain Ridgeway walked past his son and down the steps away from the Atrium.

The guards stared at the vampires and Northerners, unwilling to join their ranks.

Gentry cut through the crowd to Jeremy's side. "You good?"

"Fine." Jeremy smiled. "You?"

"Got a little bloodied up jumping from the damned tower," Gentry said, "but only a handful of Outer Guard showed up on our side to fight. I thought maybe the Nallot fire had scared them away. We waited until we heard the blast."

"And Salinger and his men were hiding the whole time," Jeremy said.

"Cowards," Gentry growled.

"I wonder how hard it would be to blow a hole through the fancy metal dome bits," Raina said.

"I didn't know you were so fond of explosives," Jeremy said.

"Back in the days of my renegade youth, I had a father in construction and a love of chaos." Raina winked. "Took more than shovels to dig the tunnels for our fancy home, lover boy."

Nola held Jeremy's hand tighter as they passed the arrows to Bright Dome. *What will my mother do when she wakes up to find her world shattered?*

Captain Ridgeway stopped at the base of the stairs to the Iron Dome. A metal door blocked the entryway.

"You should stay out here, Nola," Jeremy said.

"No." Nola squeezed his hand.

"I always have to try." Jeremy's smile didn't reach his eyes.

"All of you should stay out here," Captain Ridgeway said. "Salinger is our demon, not yours."

"He is a plague on both our houses," Emanuel said. "He's an enemy we both must face."

Captain Ridgeway flipped open a panel on the wall. "Salinger has taken over Stokes' house. Gentry, Jeremy, get in there and get the Graylock."

"We can get it once Salinger is dead," Gentry said.

"I trained you better than to argue with your captain, Guard." The Captain punched in a long code. "Anyone who fires on you is an enemy."

The lock *beeped.* With a grinding sound that cut into Nola's bare ears, the metal door lurched up. Nola took one last deep breath before placing the helmet back on her head.

Before the door had risen halfway, Captain Ridgeway charged up the stairs,

Emanuel right behind him. A shout carried from above as Nola raced up the steps by Jeremy's side.

The first *bang* sounded before they reached the inside of the Iron Dome.

Lights burned bright, beaming down from the dome high above. Metal panels surrounded the glass, blocking the night sky from view, trapping them with the line of Incorporation Guard who surrounded the staircase.

A knife whizzed past Nola's ear, hitting a guard in the eye. Another Incorporation Guard took his place, firing his weapon at the stairs. One of the Outer Guard fell. Something hit Nola hard in the stomach, knocking the wind from her, but her body didn't register any pain as she leveled her gun and fired a tiny silver dart into the shoulder of an Incorporation Guard.

Another *bang* shook the air. The person running to Nola's left fell from view, toppling to the ground. Nola tried to see who had fallen, but the helmet blocked her line of sight.

A scream of rage burst from behind her, but Jeremy had reached the line of Incorporation Guard and was fighting hand-to-hand. Gentry leapt high into the air, kicking one of the guards and leveraging herself over his body to land on the other side. Jeremy drove his knife into the neck of the guard he'd been fighting.

"Nola!" he shouted, twisting to look for her as a scream of pain came from Nightland's fighters.

One of the Incorporation Guard turned, aiming his rifle for the bare skin on Jeremy's neck. Nola leapt forward, sinking her blade into the guard's chest.

She felt a scream tear from her throat but didn't pause as she ripped her knife back out of the man's flesh.

"This way." Jeremy sprinted toward the far side of the dome, maneuvering to run behind Nola as a long string of *pops* sounded from near the stairs.

Gentry ran ahead of them, racing toward Salinger's stolen home on her captain's order.

The five guards waiting outside the house turned toward Gentry as she approached.

Nola raised her weapon, firing a string of darts at the guards. One was hit in the arm and crumpled to the ground. The others shifted their attention to Nola.

Gentry lunged forward, punching one of the guards in the side of the head with a sickening *crunch*. Jeremy slashed through another's stomach, taking the doomed man's body and tossing it at his comrade before turning to the final guard.

Nola leapt onto the downed guard, driving her knife into his side before he could struggle to his feet.

Silence fell around the house. Nola's own breaths rattled in her ears over the sounds of fighting by the stairs.

"Nola?" Jeremy kept his gaze toward the house.

"Is Salinger inside?" Nola said.

"One way to find out." Gentry stepped up to the door and kicked, shattering the doorframe.

Weapon raised, Gentry stepped into the house.

Nola's heart thudded in her throat as Jeremy followed his sister. She tightened her grip on her weapon and walked into Captain Stokes' former kitchen.

The tiny room had been taken over by a cabinet, which left barely enough space for Salinger's chair behind the kitchen table.

The spider sat, hands folded in front of him, not even bothering to reach for either of the two guns nestled next to his bowl of dome perfect fruit.

"Who are you?" Salinger said.

"Children born in the glass." Nola stepped up between Jeremy and Gentry. "Children who realized that your kind of survival isn't worth it."

"You know nothing about my kind of survival." Salinger gave a weary smile. "You don't understand the lengths the Incorporation has gone to to ensure the preservation of the human race."

"I don't care," Nola said. "We didn't come here for explanations. We're taking the Graylock."

Salinger looked to the cabinet. "I knew that filth would lead to dark places."

"I don't care what you knew," Jeremy said. "You're done here. We aren't going to let you hurt anyone ever again."

"How?" Salinger said. "Are you going to lock me up in the cells below? The Incorporation will come for me. The women, the children, the damned infants and incompetent guards will be left to rot. But I will not be abandoned by the Incorporation. I, unlike the rest of this failed cesspit, am worthy of rescue."

"Every person is worth saving," Nola said. "The second the Incorporation lost sight of that is the second they failed."

"Well"—Salinger shrugged—"if you aren't going to lock me up, you'll just have to kill me in cold blood."

"What?" Nola said.

"I'm not fighting you," Salinger said. "So you can murder me in cold blood or hold me until the Incorporation comes to collect me."

"Your men are out there dying," Gentry said.

"For the greater good," Salinger said. "For the survival of mankind."

"Defend yourself," Gentry said.

Salinger smiled. "I am saving the human race. I—" Salinger's head tipped back as a silver dart struck his forehead.

Nola spun to find the towering figure of Captain Ridgeway behind her, his weapon raised and aimed at Salinger's corpse.

"Dad," Jeremy said.

"Get the Graylock." Captain Ridgeway kept his gaze and weapon locked on Salinger as a trickle of blood ran down the spider's face.

Jeremy pulled open the cabinet. Dozens of syringes of black filled the chilled drawer.

"The formula," Nola said. "Dr. Wynne needs help with the formula to make more."

"I don't know anything about the formula," Captain Ridgeway said. "Take what you need, as much as you can carry."

Jeremy lifted the precious medicine from the drawer, filling the pouch at his hip before placing extra doses in his pockets.

"The others—" Nola began.

"It's done." Ridgeway turned away from Salinger and led them back out of the house.

Figures moved by the stairs, but the urgency of the battle had faded.

Bodies lay still on the ground.

Nola ran forward, her eyes locked on a head of black hair.

"Nola!" Jeremy called after her.

Kieran knelt next to a bloody corpse.

"Kieran," Nola said.

"I hated him. Even when I lived here, I hated him." Kieran lay Stokes' lifeless hand on his torn chest. Kieran's chest had been torn open, too. His shirt slashed by a blade, but the wound had already healed, leaving blood as the only true mark of the damage that had been done.

They didn't get his heart.

"We hate lots of people until they die for something decent," Raina said.

"And sometimes the good die as well." Emanuel laid Rebecca's body next to Stokes.

Nola tore her gaze from the ruined body of the woman of the Woodlands. Black-clad corpses littered the ground.

Only a few minutes for a hundred people to die.

Torn and twisted, the humans hadn't stood a chance in a fight meant for those who had adapted to survive.

Julian helped Jude limp to Stokes' side.

"Is Salinger dead?" Jude didn't look away from Stokes' bloodied face.

"He is," Jeremy said.

"That's it?" Jude whispered. "After everything we went through, it's over."

"Not yet." Nola looked up to the metal sky.

CHAPTER THIRTY

The bunker door slid open. The wave of whispers that swept up from the Domers swallowed the *swish* of the door's movement.

Nola stepped into the doorway, Jeremy right behind her shoulder, the warmth of his arm against hers washing away her fear.

"Salinger is dead." Nola's voice rang through the bunker. "His guards are dead. Your time under the protection of the Incorporation has ended."

Murmurs sprang up around the room.

Nola waited until silence fell.

"You have no vehicles. No weapons. No seeds. Your communication with the other domes has been severed. Your medical and food supplies are limited. Your population has dwindled. These domes are redundant. The Incorporation isn't coming to save you. We offer you peace. You stay on your side of the river, you try to survive and leave us alone, and we will not attack again. If you threaten Nightland or the people of the Woodlands, we will come back for you. And we will not stop until the threat you impose on the world has been ended for good. We want peace, but we are ready for war." Nola turned away, feeling the gaze of all the people she had known upon her.

"But what are we supposed to do?" a woman asked.

"Survive." Nola turned back to the bunker.

"What about the babies?" A young woman stepped forward, her hand pressed to her stomach. "The Incorporation wanted the babies."

"Not anymore," Nola said. "You've been contaminated by the outside air. You're on your own. What you do from here, that's your choice."

"You've taken everything from us." Dr. Mullins laid a hand on the young woman's shoulder.

"No, we haven't," Nola said.

"We don't know how to survive unprotected," Dr. Mullins said.

"Welcome to the end of the world."

EPILOGUE

The last of the evening's stars glimmered in the sky.

Nola tucked her head onto Jeremy's shoulder, savoring every moment of the night chill before the relentless summer sun would rise. Their view from the mountain's peak let them see as far as the Woodlands and the domes, two tiny places in the world where people still managed to survive.

No smoke marred the horizon. No hint of death or blood ruined the peace of the night.

There was work to be done. The gardens of Nightland had to be protected from the sun. Messages had to be run to the Woodlands and the shattered domes as Emanuel fought to foster their tenuous peace.

Jeremy and Nola would run the messages for the domes together, meeting his sister at the eastern edge of the river to hear news of the new order within the glass.

Before they left, Nola needed to check on sweet little Charlie and make sure T and Beauford had eaten and stolen a few hours' sleep. Kieran would be asking for samples from the mushroom farm. Dr. Wynne would want to tell her about his latest experiments in improving Graylock. The library would be busy with Emanuel and Julian planning some ambitious project to help those struggling to survive on the highway while Eden ran circles around their feet. Raina would be waiting, knives in hand, to train Nola in the sparring room.

But Jeremy held her tight as the stars shone above them, and for a few perfect moments, saving their tiny piece of humanity could wait.

DEATH OF DAY

A Girl of Glass Story

CHAPTER ONE

The buzzing beat of the music cut through the pounding in her head. Sweat slicked Raina's skin as she wove through the dancers. The sweet smell of booze filled the dark room. Even the stench of the rotting city couldn't compete with that of the club. In the Rev there was nothing but the moment, and flesh, and the thumping stronger than a heartbeat.

A man snaked his arm around Raina's waist, drawing her toward him. She didn't bother turning to see his face as his stubbled chin brushed against her cheek and his teeth nibbled the edge of her ear.

Let him have a taste.

She swayed with him for a moment, feeling the aging wooden floor bend beneath the weight of the crowd.

The man slid his hand from her waist to her neck. He closed his fingers around her throat. With a laugh, Raina elbowed him in the stomach and ducked under his arm. She didn't turn to look at him as he cursed over the music.

"You okay?" a man with hair spiked high shouted in her ear as she stepped up to the bar.

"Fine." Raina pulled bills from her bra, waving them at the bartender.

"He should be kicked out for that," the spike head said. "I can go get the bouncer."

"Don't bother."

She caught the bartender's eyes.

His chest shook with laughter, though she couldn't hear the sound. He grabbed a full bottle from the shelf and tossed it to Raina.

"Planning on a good night?" spikey asked.

"Sorry, I don't have enough to share." Raina slipped past him to the far corner of the club.

A hand reached for hers, luring her back into the dance. She brushed it aside, not caring who had offered to be her partner.

The vibrations of the music shook her lungs as she neared the wall of speakers. Raina gulped down air like a child swallowing pills for the first time.

A man as wide as the door she sought blocked her path.

Raina pulled more money from her bra before the man had time to ask for it. With a bow he stepped aside.

She rolled her eyes and gave a little curtsy before pressing the metal bar and stepping out into the night.

The city's stink filled her nose at the same moment the chill air sent goosebumps bristling on her skin.

Raina kicked the door closed behind her just in time to keep the bouncer from hearing her cough. Blood splattered the back of her hand. Her lungs cramped, and the coughing didn't stop. She leaned against the poles of the fire escape, waiting for the fit to pass.

"If you want me dead," Raina spoke to her lungs between coughs, "you can stop working whenever you like."

She unscrewed the fresh bottle of liquor, holding it up to her nose. The pungent smell of pure alcohol burned past the scent of her own blood. Taking a sip, she swished and spit the mix of blood and booze over the fire escape railing.

"What a waste." She poured some of the precious liquid over her hand, washing the blood away. She wiped her hand on her pants, trusting the black to cover any unsightly hints of red.

She'd given up on colored clothing two years ago when her lungs had started to go and coughing blood in public had become part of her daily routine.

The first real sip of the fiery liquid cleared her throat. The second fortified her for the climb to the roof. The rusty metal steps clanged under her boots in a pathetic way. Her footsteps couldn't compete with the thumping of the Rev or the shouts of the city below.

One flight up, she could see past the buildings around her. Another flight and Main Street came into view.

Raina took a drink from the bottle and leaned against the crumbling brick wall. Her breath rattled in her chest.

I sound like a corpse.

Her laugh shook free a fresh round of coughs.

A horn honked on the street below. The driver leaned out the window, shouting at the pedestrians walking down the center of the road.

The walkers shouted back. A young man jumped onto the hood of the car, strolling up and over the roof as though the car weren't there.

The driver leaned on the horn. He should have known better than to veer off the main streets. Only the richest in the city had money for gas anymore. The streets had been taken over by the poor, who had nothing but their feet to get them from one point to another.

The fire escape door opened, gushing sound out of the club into the night.

Raina grabbed the railing and dragged herself up the last flight of steps. "What is the point in bribing a bouncer for access if he lets other people bribe him, too?"

Speaking the words aloud to herself took the last bit of breath she could muster. By the time she reached the abandoned rooftop, her lungs had begun to panic. Her heart told her she was suffocating. The liquor made it clear she needn't care.

Tarpaper crackled under her feet. She passed a cluster of sturdy chairs and headed straight for the far edge.

Construction lights shone on the hill across the river.

"The end of the world stops for nothing." Raina sat on the brick ledge, dangling her feet over the ground six stories below, waiting patiently for her lungs to remember how to breathe.

Footsteps crunched across the roof behind her. "Going to jump?"

Raina's neck prickled at the sound of the unfamiliar voice.

"I just bought a bottle." Raina held the liquor high in the air. "What do you think?"

"That you're expecting to live until the last drop." The voice came closer. The footsteps stopped right behind her shoulder.

"Going to push me?" A cough cut through Raina's words. Blood speckled the back of her hand.

Let him see. If he wants to push me, let him know he's killing a corpse.

"Wouldn't dream of it," the man said. "Someone as important as you? What a waste your death would be."

"I'm important?" Raina took a gulp of liquor, burning away the taste of her own blood.

"You're a McNay," the man said. "Your family's the most important this side of the river."

"That's me, the Extinction Heiress." Raina passed the bottle over her shoulder. "Daddy dearest owns the lights and the machines and all the fancy things working to build the domes across the river."

He lifted the drink from her hand.

"If you're looking to hold me hostage, have fun trying to get me out of the building. Daddy pays the bouncers to keep me safe."

"And you pay them to let you sit on the edge of death?" He set the bottle next to her.

"I like to watch the domes at work," Raina said. "Keep an eye on the salvation of the world."

"Do you really believe the domes are our salvation?" The man stepped up onto the ledge.

His boots were worn leather, made in the same hearty fashion as those of the soldiers who patrolled the streets.

"I've read the billboards," Raina said. "*To protect the children. For the future of mankind.*"

"And you believe them?"

Raina took a long drink before speaking. "Do I believe sealing a group of people in a set of glorified greenhouses is going to save the world? Do I believe my father's construction is going to be well built enough to survive whatever horrible thing wipes out the city? Or do I believe that it's an elitist ploy to give the few who are lucky enough not to be dying of disease, malnourishment, or chemical contamination a spa-like extinction experience? I'll be dead long before they seal themselves in the glass, so I really don't give a shit."

"You don't care that they're abandoning you and your family out here to die?"

"We've been dead for years." Tears stung the corners of Raina's eyes. "Just like everybody else who lives in the city."

They'd drunk the water that had been contaminated by chemical dumping, breathed the air tainted by smoke from the factories. No one from the city was pure enough to be taken into the domes. The domes would be built right across the river so the sick city dwellers could stare at their pretty glass bunker, but they didn't get to survive. Only the privilege of staring at hope as they died.

"And your father accepts his family being denied salvation?" the man asked.

"They pay him well enough the domes could be slaughtering children instead of saving them and he'd still invite them to a dinner party."

"And the domes can't do anything to help you?"

Raina dug her nails into her palms, the knowing in the man's voice setting her nerves on edge.

"The dome people won't help anyone but their own." She took another long drink. The fire of the liquor steadied the trembling of her hands.

"And the doctors?"

"Blood's too infected to survive a lung transplant. Daddy paid good money to get a black market set, but the doctors still wouldn't do it. My darling Daddy threw the lungs into the dumpster."

"How long have you got?"

Raina took a rattling breath. "A year if I live like a nun, six months if I do anything worth living for, a few minutes if I jump after I finish the bottle."

"Do you want to jump?"

Raina looked up at the man.

He was only a few years older than she was. Curling black hair kissed his shoulders. His dark eyes held neither sympathy nor anger.

"I'm tired of drowning in my own body." Her words carved a hollow in her chest. "What am I going to see in six more months that I haven't seen already?"

"What if there was another choice?" The man lifted the bottle from Raina's hand. "What if you could live for decades more? With a strong and healthy body, capable of doing amazing things."

"Do I get to ride a unicorn, too?" Raina grasped for the bottle.

He raised it out of her reach. "No magic, only medicine."

"You're offering the rich girl a miracle cure?" Raina asked. "Couldn't you try and be a bit more original?"

"I'm offering to help you. After all, what have you got to lose?"

Raina stared at the street six stories below.

"The ground will still be waiting to catch you tomorrow," the man said.

"Fair enough." Raina pushed herself to her feet. "Slice me up and call me a miracle."

"No knives involved."

"How boring," Raina tried to sigh, but a cough cut through her sarcasm. "Fine, give me the miracle pill or whatever."

He shook his head, looking out toward the glowing lights of the construction. "I need something from you first."

"Of course you do." Raina snatched the bottle from him. "Just back the hell off and let a girl drink herself to death in peace."

The blow caught her in the back before she had lifted the bottle to her lips. Her feet launched over the open air at the same moment pain stabbed through her arm.

"I can deliver on my promise," he spoke over Raina's scream.

"You're insane." She looked up to her wrist.

"And you are the perfect mix of desperation and hope."

The man gripped the bottle in one hand and Raina in the other, dangling her over the street as though she weighed no more than the liquor in her stomach.

"What the hell!" Raina shrieked.

"What the hell am I, or what the hell am I doing?" The man smiled. "What I am is more than humans were ever meant to be. What I am doing is proving I can make good on my word. I need a favor from you, Raina McNay, and in exchange, I offer your life."

Raina glared into the man's dark eyes, the feeling of absurdity melting away the longer he held her casually in the air. "What do you want?"

"Supplies," the man said. "The domes aren't the only ones planning a path to survival, but your father's prices are too steep for some to pay."

"You want me to negotiate prices with my father?"

"I want you to steal supplies from his warehouse and deliver them to me. I want you to tell no one of our arrangement. And once you've procured the necessities, I want you to join me and others like me as we build our own path to salvation."

"Path to salvation?" Raina hacked up the words. "You're going to bomb the city, level it all and save us from our suffering?"

"No." He smiled. Wrinkles formed in the corners of his eyes. "I want to build. I want to dig and fortify. I want to create a home better and stronger than the glistening glass domes."

"And who better to help than the Extinction Heiress whose daddy owns all the tools?" Raina pursed her lips, stamping down the tiny bubble of hope that teased the hollow in her chest. "What do you want me to do? I don't know how to drive a back hoe."

"Nothing like that." He raised his arm, lifting her over the ledge of the roof. He held her up until she was over the solid, flat tarpaper before letting her go. Her legs crumpled beneath her. She gasped for breath, her lungs fighting to keep up with the adrenaline coursing through her veins.

A piece of paper appeared in the man's hand. "I want you to get everything on the list. Load it into a truck and drive it all the way up Park Lane to the dead end by the forest."

"Great." Raina snatched the paper, quickly reading down the list of supplies. "You came prepared, didn't you?"

"You have no idea," the man said. "I wouldn't ask a question if I didn't already know the answer."

"Then you've got to know, desperate or not, I won't be able to get all of this on my own. I'll need help loading the truck. Can your construction crew come help with the heist?"

"No one can know where the materials have gone," he said. "What we're building has to be kept secret."

"So"—Raina tucked the paper into her pocket—"find the supplies to build, not blow up the city. Magically get them into a truck. Drive the truck out to the woods and trust that you're going to save my life, not murder me? Sounds like fun. When do I start?"

"When you're ready." He gave a small bow. "You have a little time left to live your normal life. I wouldn't want to steal the last of those days from you."

"I'm really sick of dying." Raina wiped the blood from the corners of her mouth. "Meet you at the woods in the morning."

Her legs shook as she pushed herself to her feet.

"I can only meet you at night." He took her elbow, steadying her as she yanked the bottle from his hands.

"Cloak and dagger, I like it. Better hurry to steal from Daddy if I'm going to make it in the next few hours, huh?"

She started toward the door, the haze of the city swaying with every step as sense and adrenaline tried to make amends.

"I can take you down a faster way than the stairs." He scooped her into his arms, not seeming to notice as she pushed against his chest.

"I can make the stairs on my own two feet," Raina said.

He took the bottle from her hand and dropped it, letting the glass smash on the rooftop.

"That was a real dick move." Raina kicked, fighting to wriggle free from his grip as he stepped up onto the brick ledge of the roof. "I thought you didn't want me—"

The wind stole her words as he jumped, plunging them both into the open air below.

Terror silenced her scream as they neared the ground. She didn't shut her eyes against the end. She had no fear of dying. Death was nothing more than an old friend she had been waiting to kindly stop for her.

With a thump that shook her teeth, he landed on the sidewalk, not even swaying as he took two steps before setting Raina back on her feet.

"What the hell was that?" Raina leaned against the brick wall, digging her fingers into the cracked masonry to hide the shaking of her hands.

"A taste of what you'll be able to do soon enough." He smiled. "What I have to offer is a lot better than death. All I ask in return is your help in building a future you'll actually live to see."

Raina nodded, not trusting her lungs or her voice.

"I'll see you by the forest." He turned and walked up the street, not looking behind as he rounded a corner and strode out of sight.

"I'm so drunk." Raina pressed her forehead to the bricks. "Fact one: I'm dying. Easy one, Raina. Fact two: he just jumped off the roof and I'm not dead. Fact three: he says he can make me like him."

She tried to picture it. The strength not only to run up the stairs to the roof but also to jump to the ground unharmed. To walk without needing to stop and catch her breath. To never have to taste her own blood in her mouth again.

"Fact four: I've done worse than this shit before, and Daddy's never kicked me out." Raina's lips curved into a smile as she started toward the far side of the city. "This might be even better than a night at the Rev."

CHAPTER TWO

No one bothered her on her way through town. Her clothes were too plain for anyone to guess her father owned half the city and was a traitor helping to build the domes besides. A little rebel roaming the streets. There were so many people out wandering at night the city was far safer than in the daylight.

The sun had stolen the day from the people. Its rays were strong enough now that a few hours outside unprotected could leave blistering burns. Get burned often and cancer would take over the skin. And protective sun suits? Her father only sold those to his richest clientele.

The air might stink and rot the lungs. The food and water poisoned slowly. But none of those things could be avoided. The only thing the people of the city could control was hiding from the light.

Darkness is our refuge.

A gang of teenaged boys catcalled her as she passed their stoop. Raina rolled her eyes, not wasting any precious breath on shouting back. An older woman stuck her head out the fourth-floor window.

"I may not be able to chase you off the steps, but I won't let you steal my sleep!" The woman poured a bucket of water onto the boys.

Raina bit her lips together and ducked down a side street, hurrying along the warehouse row.

The streetlights here were brighter than on the main roads. The owners of the warehouses paid for this street to be maintained.

There was something sick about the road between the hulking buildings being the most normal-looking part of the city.

Her father's warehouse stood at the end of the street along the edge of the abandoned highway. Raina grinned as she banged on the warehouse door, swallowing her glee at the mere thought of driving a giant truck.

"What do you want?" a snapping voice came over the speaker above the heavy metal door.

"Well..." Raina tipped her chin up to the domed camera. "We can start with you being polite to the boss's daughter and move on from there."

"So sorry, Miss McNay."

The lock *beeped*.

Raina wrenched open the door and stepped into the vast space. Crates stacked up against the right-hand wall, each baring a name Raina cared nothing about. Construction equipment from trucks to cement mixers took up the middle of the room. Red and blue barrels peeked through from the back, and packed shelves lined the left side of the warehouse.

"What can I do for you, Miss McNay?" A well-built man jogged toward her from the security booth. His chest pushed against the buttons of his shirt.

Did he ask for one too small, or is he actually getting healthier?

"Miss McNay?" the guard repeated.

Three others appeared from the depths of the warehouse, all looking somewhere between scared and annoyed to have Raina paying them a late-night call.

"Daddy screwed up." Raina pulled out the list the man had given her. "He was supposed to send these supplies to the far side of the river. They're needed for construction immediately."

"He could have just called it in." The guard took the paper from Raina.

"And admit he was too drunk to remember to do his job?" Raina laughed, the sound caught in her throat. "Just put everything in a truck and I'll drive it over."

The four men stared at her.

"Now!" Raina shouted. Her voice echoed around the space. Like she was strong, strong enough to give orders. "Actually, double everything on the list. No point in wasting room on a truck, and I'm sure they'll need it over there eventually."

"Load up truck sixteen," the guard said.

The men huddled around him for a moment before scattering to the corners of the warehouse. More voices joined theirs as they shouted to workers Raina couldn't see.

"I'll radio over to the work site," the guard said. "Make sure they know to expect you."

"Don't," Raina said. "Let them be surprised. I like watching all of you scramble."

"If they know to expect a truck, they'll have men ready to unload," the guard said.

Twelve men were now working on loading the truck.

"Does Daddy dearest know you let people sleep during the night shift?" Raina trailed her fingers along the front of the guard's shirt, landing on his stitched name tag. "Chad."

"I'm just in charge of the door." Chad flashed his straight, white teeth. "I don't know what they do in the rest of the warehouse."

"Well, Chad"—Raina trailed her fingers up to his neck—"I want to surprise them on the other side of the river. So unless you want me to tell Daddy dearest men are sleeping here, I think you shouldn't ruin my surprise."

"Whatever you say, Miss McNay." Chad squared his shoulders as though he were a soldier taking orders, but a hint of teasing played in his eyes.

"Maybe we should go to your office and make sure you've been doing a good job." She traced the outline of his lips with her finger.

"I'd be thrilled to show you my workspace, Miss McNay." He turned toward the small glass office in the front corner.

"I want that truck loaded in ten minutes!" Raina shouted to the warehouse ceiling. Her stomach purred at the frantic sounds of workers scurrying behind her.

"As you can see, I work very hard to protect your father's property." Chad held open the office door.

A line of monitors displayed an overhead view of every inch of the warehouse and surrounding streets.

"How fancy." Raina eyed the computer in the corner. "Such a small machine to monitor so many cameras. You must have seen some very interesting things."

Chad shook his head. His thick hair ruffled around his face, another boast of his health. "I've seen some funny stuff. But nothing fit for your ears, Miss McNay."

"You'd be surprised what I'm fit for." Raina stepped toward him, ignoring the twinkle in his eyes as she traced the ridges of his chest.

The hard lines of his muscles teased her fingertips. Her breath quickened. Her head spun from the lack of air.

"I bet you could tell me a few stories." She leaned her weight against him, pressing him toward the narrow door in the back corner of the room. "Secrets nobody else needs to hear."

She ran her fingers through his hair, trailing her nose up the curve of his neck.

He shuddered a sigh as she nipped the bottom of his ear.

He opened the closet door before she knew he'd reached for the handle. The glowing lights of the fuses and control panels gave depth to the shadows.

"I like it." Raina tugged open the buttons of his shirt, backing him farther into the room. "Now close your eyes."

He shut his eyes and wrapped his arms around her waist, pressing her to him.

"Shh," she hushed in his ear, wriggling against him for a moment before stepping back. "Count to three."

"One, two—"

Raina slammed and locked the closet door before he reached three.

"Asshole." She seized the wires connecting the computer to the walls and wrenched them free.

"What are you doing?" Chad banged on the door.

"Hush now, the boss is working." Raina snatched a pen and paper, scrawling a quick note.

"You have to let me out of here! I'm supposed to be guarding your father's property."

"Yeah, well, you suck." Raina taped the note to the door.

I tried to screw the boss's daughter.

She twisted the center of the knob on the door to the warehouse, locking the office from the inside.

"Is my truck loaded yet?" Her voice rang around the space.

"We need a few more minutes." A red-faced man puffed past, carrying a crate filled with wire spools.

"You have three minutes to get the rest of the supplies loaded, or I'll tell Daddy you want the construction of the domes to fail."

A moment of silence followed Raina's words.

A murmur of growled curses and bangs came next as the men scrambled to finish.

A forklift loaded a palate of crates into the back of the truck with a heavy *thunk*. Before it had fully backed away, barrels were being heaved in behind.

"That's more like it." Raina strode over to the truck, her heart racing against her slow pace.

Sense told her it wouldn't work. Someone would tell her the handwriting on the list wasn't her father's. Or tell her she wasn't authorized to remove assets from the warehouse.

She reached for the handle of the truck door. Her fingers closed around the metal.

"Are you sure you want to drive this over?" A gray-haired man blocked the door with his shoulder.

"You think I can't drive?" Raina touched the man's shoulder with one finger, shoving him aside with minuscule force.

"I'd be happy to drive the truck across and we can make sure you get safely home." Worried lines creased the man's brow.

"I'm not Little Red Riding Hood." She swung open the truck door. "Finish loading so I can get the hell out of here."

The keys waited in the ignition, swinging lazily like there was no danger in letting just anyone touch them.

The garage door in front of her rumbled up.

"And you're all set," a voice called from behind.

"You loaded in everything Daddy asked for?" Raina's voice came out bright and chipper.

"Doubled the whole list, Miss McNay," the voice said.

Raina's heart leapt into her throat as she turned the key and the engine jumped to life.

"Good work, boys," she called out the window.

Raina hummed to herself as she drove toward the highway. The power of riding high above the ground, of moving quickly without pain surging through her chest, filled her with a foreign sense of joy.

A bump in the road jolted the tires as she turned onto the highway. The cargo in the back banged around.

"Oops." She slowed down, weaving around the largest of the splits in the concrete.

Two figures scattered out of range of her headlights as she reached the road heading up the hill.

Houses sat along the narrow street. Light peered through the windows of some of the homes while others had been abandoned, the glass in their windows long since shattered. She didn't know if the people living this far from the city were brave or just plain stupid.

She slowed as she neared the end of the road and the shadows of the forest loomed in front of her. The sense of someone watching her from the darkness sent her heart racing. Spasms shook her lungs. She coughed red onto the steering wheel.

"Dammit." She tried to wipe the blood away with her sleeve but only succeeded in making the smudges larger.

Brush grew waist high in front of the truck. There wasn't a curb to mark the end of the street. The pavement just ran out, like they'd meant to go farther into the woods, but the end of the world had ceased the construction.

Raina stopped the truck. Her fingers sat frozen on the keys.

After a minute the fear of the truck being mobbed by dozens of super strong men disappeared, replaced by the sinking feeling of being fooled.

"You're an idiot, Raina. Met a guy in a bar and stole from your father."

Her father would forgive her. Cut off her money for a week, but then everything would go back to normal. She would be able to die in peace.

A pathetic, whimpering end to a meaningless life.

"Nope." Raina pulled the keys from the ignition and kicked open the truck door. "Hey, you! I brought you what you want, now stop being a chicken shit and come out and get it."

Her gaze swept the trees. A hint of gray had begun to kiss the sky, but the forest in front of her stayed shrouded in shadow.

"Look, you said be here by dawn and I made it in time," Raina shouted. "Do you want everything from your shopping list or not?"

"Did you get it all?" He stepped out from behind a tree, two other men flanking him.

"I got double what you asked for." Raina gave a cocky smile. "It's a big truck, and I didn't want to waste the space."

He nodded to the two men who moved toward the back of the truck.

"You want to do a check before you save my life?" Raina ran through the list in her mind.

They loaded everything. Those assholes better have loaded everything.

"If there was something you couldn't get, I would still save you." He walked toward Raina, pulling something from his pocket she couldn't see. "It means more to me that you would do everything in your power to help me than how well-stocked your father's warehouse currently is. You did well back there." He stopped two feet in front of Raina, his black eyes locked on her face.

"How do you know?" Raina fought the urge to look away.

"I have ways of watching that aren't housed in security booths." He smiled. "I'm very grateful for what you've done for me tonight."

"Then can we get to the part where you save me?" Sweat slicked Raina's palms.

"If that's what you want." He raised his hand.

Raina's heart flipped.

He's going to slit my throat.

A metal syringe filled with milky white fluid lay in his palm. "This is your salvation."

Raina reached for the needle.

"But"—he closed his fist—"you have to understand, there is a price."

"I've paid the price." Raina spoke through gritted teeth. "The stuff in that truck is the price."

"The price isn't a payment for me," he said. "There are side effects. Your lungs will be healed, you will be stronger than you've ever dreamt of—"

"Sounds great." Raina reached for the syringe again.

He tucked his hand behind his back. "You won't be able to go out into the sun anymore."

"The sun isn't safe for anyone," Raina said.

"One dose of this and a minute in the sun could kill you. You won't be able to eat normal food anymore."

"I don't care what I have to eat," Raina said. "I'm tired of choking on my own blood."

"Blood will be your only food."

Raina blinked. "You're shitting me."

"It's the only nourishment the medicine will allow you to metabolize." He took Raina's hand. "You won't be able to go back to your family, not until you've fully adjusted."

"Because I'll want to drink their blood," Raina laughed. "You just sent me to steal from my father so you could save my life by making me a vampire?"

"Vampires are myths. What I have is sound science," he said.

"Yeah right."

She spun toward the truck. He was in front of her before she could take a step.

"You know I'm not a normal human," he said. "The medicine saved me, changed me. It can do the same for you. But I won't lie to you about the side effects. You'll be alive, but your life will never be what it was before."

"Why should I believe you?" Raina's eyes burned, her desperate need to trust him battling with her desire to claw out his dark eyes.

"Because I jumped from the roof and landed alive." He held the needle out to her. "Because if I'm lying, then all you have to lose is a few more months of dying. Because you have great potential, Raina McNay, and I would hate to see it rot with you in the ground."

She snatched the needle from him. "So I just inject it?"

"I can do it for you."

"Trust me, I'll be fine." Raina pulled a foot long band from her back pocket.

"You should aim for a vein."

She tightened the band around her arm with her teeth, squeezing her hand into a fist. "I said I'll be fine."

In the beams of the truck's headlights, she searched her arm for a vein.

"How soon do I get to be cured?" Raina asked.

"By tonight your cough will be gone," he said. "Give it a few weeks, and you'll be jumping from rooftops without a scratch. We'll take you someplace safe to wait out the sunlight."

"Thanks." She pushed the needle into her arm and pressed the milky fluid into her veins. She gasped as ice raced through her blood. "It is supposed to be that cold?"

"The ice will last a few hours."

He took Raina's arm, steadying her as the syringe slipped from her grip.

"Just relax," he said. "The frost is saving you."

The ice reached the backs of her eyes, sending white spots bursting through her vision.

"Am I dying?" The world tilted as her legs gave out, but she didn't hit the ground.

He lifted her, carrying her to the back of the truck. "You aren't dying, Raina. You're being born into your new life. I'll stay with you until the ice melts. I'm building a new world, and you're going to be with me at the center of it."

The ice froze her lungs, but the lack of air held no pain.

"I don't"—Raina fought for an ounce of air—"Who are you?"

"Emanuel." His voice carried through the darkness. "You and I are going to build a new world."

CHAPTER THREE

Nothing existed beyond the edges of the ice. No air. No sound. No pain.
Only cold to keep her trapped for all eternity.

Emanuel had promised to heal her, to fix her lungs. Raina hadn't thought to ask if the cure was spending the rest of her days frozen.

This couldn't be death, not as she had spent so many years expecting the end to come. True death would be more peaceful.

A perfect nothing.

Because, as the ice ebbed away from the edges of her flesh, Raina found something beyond the nothing.

Soft sheets tucked tightly around her. The hum of tools working not far away. Voices laughing at a joke she hadn't heard.

Raina discovered she could move as she opened her eyes.

A single light bulb hung from the stone ceiling over her bed. The bulb swayed slightly.

Raina let her eyes fall shut, feeling for movement in the bed.

The room didn't seem to be shaking or rocking, but as she opened her eyes again, the bulb still swayed.

"Should have hired a better builder." Raina's voice came out as a rough croak.

She listened for a long moment, waiting for someone to come running now that she'd made a sound.

The noise coming through the door didn't change.

"Great." She pulled her arm up and over the covers.

Her hand seemed to have gained a hundred pounds in weight while the ice encased her. She pulled her other arm free from the sheets, holding her hand up where she could see it.

Her fingers looked the same. The ice hadn't left any scars.

She kicked the covers aside, gritting her teeth against the unbearable weight of her legs.

They'd left her in her clothes from the club. Even her black boots remained firmly on her feet.

"How courteous." Her voice crackled again.

Raina took a deep breath, listening for the rattle in her lungs. The air moved freely in and out through her nose.

She took another breath, sucking in as much as her lungs would hold. Seconds ticked past as she waited to exhale. Her lungs didn't tremble in revolt. She let the air out slowly, expecting to hack out blood any second.

Nothing.

She took another breath just to be sure.

"Wow."

The word crackled again, not from her lungs but her throat.

The moment she thought of her throat, it burned with thirst.

She pushed herself to her feet, lurching across the dirt-covered stone floor to the door. She tried to turn the handle, but the knob wouldn't move.

"Hey." She pounded on the door. "I'm awake, let me out."

The voices on the other side of the door stopped talking.

"Let me out! I'm thirsty." She pounded on the wood. A dull *thump* answered her fists.

They've locked me in where I can't break out.

"Tell Emanuel I'm awake," Raina said. "Tell him if he leaves me trapped in here there is going to be hell to pay when I get out."

Voices spoke on the other side of the door, their words too soft for Raina to hear.

A man gave a low, rumbling laugh.

"Let me out!" Raina pounded on the door.

The outside voices drifted away.

"Next time you take a miracle cure from a stranger, make sure you add freedom to the life-saving bargain," Raina chided herself as she leaned against the door.

Her father would be looking for her by now. They would have found the guard and let him out.

Daddy will be looking for me and *angry.*

Raina allowed herself the comfort of a smile. There were very few things an angry McNay couldn't accomplish.

She turned to examine the room. Roughly carved stone surrounded her.

"No wonder they need Daddy's equipment if this is the quality they're working with."

They'd left her with only a bed and a chair. A stack of printed paper lay on the seat, a yellow note perched on top.

"Been sent to my room to study?" Raina pressed her cheek to the crack in the door. "If I die of thirst before you let me out, I will find a way to haunt you from death."

If there was anyone on the other side of the door to hear her, they gave no sign.

She picked up the stack of paper and note, taking them to the bed where she could sit facing the door.

In case you doubt the end of the world.

The note had been scrawled in cramped script as though the author had been in a great hurry.

"No one doubts the end is coming."

Raina set the note aside to read the first page of the pile.

Resource Assessment – North Eastern Section

It has come to our attention that, given the population expansion and level of chemical contamination within the area, a reverse of the current course of extinction within the region is not possible. It is therefore our recommendation that all Incorporation resources currently assigned to maintaining the lives of those in the region be reassigned to a more sustainable project.

"Giving up on saving people and building the domes. Wonder if the people sitting on that board of directors still like to pretend they have souls?"

She flipped to the next page in the packet.

The work needed to build and initially maintain the domes is beyond the capacity of those who will be housed within the glass. For the materials needed for initial building and long term maintenance, it is approximated that a population of ten thousand should be allowed within easy working distance until life inside the domes is sustainable. After all long term resources are stored and the domes have reached sustainability, the city dwellers will no longer be useful as there will be no room within the domes for additional resources to be housed.

Raina crumpled up the page, tossing it into the corner with a shout.

"People are more than resources." Her words bounced around the room.

She moved on to the next page.

The necessity for the Incorporation to maintain a military force to protect the domes is undeniable. However, we cannot recommend calling the force soldiers. Should the outsiders consider them a threat, the danger to our armed men and women of the domes would only grow. Our greatest hope for a gentle path to the end of relations with the outside world is for those in the city to believe the existence of the domes themselves is in the outsiders' best interest. We suggest community outreach to ensure good will.

She flipped to the next page.

At the point when it inevitably becomes disadvantageous to allow outsiders to remain so close to the domes, plans must be made for the evacuation of the area. We request each Domes Council submit an external clearing proposal to the Incorporation, to be reviewed and filed for eventual use.

With the varying topography amongst the different domes there is, unfortunately, no unilateral answer to securing the regions.

"Securing the regions," Raina muttered the phrase, swiping angry tears away from her eyes. "Securing the regions? Securing the regions!" She screamed the words over and over, knocking the rest of the papers from the bed.

It didn't matter what the rest of the pages said. The Incorporation had planned for everything. From using the city dwellers as laborers to getting rid of them when they were no longer of use.

She launched herself across the room, her legs easily jumping the five feet, and slammed into the thick, wooden door.

"Let me out of here!" She pounded her fists on the door. "Emanuel, let me out. I will not sit in this cell while those bastards put together paperwork about this entire city dying. Emanuel!"

She grabbed the handle, twisting as hard as she could. The metal warped, rotating beyond its normal capacity.

Taking a deep breath, she raised her hand, then brought her fist down on the handle.

Pain shot through her arm, but the metal gave, tipping down at an odd angle.

Bellowing in rage, she pounded on the knob, pummeling the metal without care for the pain or the blood dripping from her fist.

With a *crack*, the knob fell away, bringing the innards of the lock with it.

She stuck her fingers through the hole the knob had left behind, swinging the door toward her.

Emanuel leaned against the wall outside, waiting alone in the long dark hall.

"Why the hell did you lock me in?" Raina wiped the blood from her knuckles onto her pants.

The skin beneath had already begun to heal.

"Am I supposed to be able to heal like that?"

Emanuel pushed away from the wall, holding his hand out for Raina's.

Her hand shook as she placed it in his palm.

"You're further along than I expected." He examined the shining patch where the skin had been broken only moments before. "That's a good thing. Some don't react as well to the medicine. You're lucky."

"Thanks." Raina pulled her hand away. "Is that why you locked me in, to see if I could break out?"

"More to see what you'd become," Emanuel said. "But we've been speaking, and you haven't tried to kill me."

"Ought I have?"

"There isn't an ought," Emanuel said. "But you're thirsty and angry, and you haven't tried to claw through my jugular."

Raina's eyes flicked to the pulse in Emanuel's neck. The tiny movement of blood rushing just beneath his skin. Thumping so deliciously and enticingly close to her reach.

"We should get you fed before you give in to your new instincts."

She heard Emanuel's words but couldn't drag her gaze from the pulsing in his neck.

"Come." He walked down the hall without giving Raina a backwards glance.

She teetered between screaming at him and running away, finding a path out of the tunnels and beyond his madness.

But a scent wafted in Emanuel's wake. The sweet smell of blood and a hint of something familiar, something that mirrored the inner most makings of her.

Raina's feet were moving before she'd made the choice to follow.

A few doors lined the hall, each made of the same heavy wood that had kept her trapped. More openings had been carved into the walls, and the beginnings of hollowed out rooms lay beyond.

"How big is this place?" Raina asked.

Emanuel slowed his pace until Raina walked by his side.

"Right now?" Emanuel said. "Not large enough. A few rooms and a couple of halls won't help our cause."

"Cause?" Raina said. "I thought this was about survival."

"Is there a better cause than survival?"

They turned at the end of the corridor, moving into a hall that slanted steeply up.

"So you're building a bunker?" Raina asked. "Going to hide out down here when the people from the domes decide that having the city rabble as neighbors isn't advantageous anymore?"

Emanuel stopped. "You read that far?"

"What kind of monsters would think the world is so disposable?"

"The kind who build a glass bunker with an excellent view of the chaos and pain as society ends." Emanuel strode down the hall, leaving Raina to jog behind him.

"We can't let some *Incorporation* do this," Raina said. "Who the hell do they think they are to decide who gets thrown out with the trash?'

"The ones with the money," Emanuel said. "Money your father happily takes."

Raina stopped in her tracks.

Anger won out over shame.

"Those bastards are lying to him!" She kicked the stone wall.

Sense told her pain and broken bones would follow, but her body didn't find either. She kicked the wall again and again, watching the stones crumble away.

"Those evil, manipulating, cruel"—she punctuated each word with a kick.

"Murdering," Emanuel offered. "They might not have reached that level yet. But if the domes exist long enough, they will."

Raina buried her face in her hands. Her pulse raced, flashing white lights before her eyes.

"You need to eat," Emanuel said.

"Screw you."

"Now."

Raina glared past the white lights and into his dark eyes.

He didn't back down.

"Fine," Raina said. "Direct me to the nearest jugular and I'll tear it out. Do we have a virgin offering?"

"Don't be crass." Emanuel led her forward to a narrow side passage, barely wide enough for him to walk down.

It would have seemed like a narrow alley to nowhere if the walls hadn't been the smoothest she had seen. Lights hung every few feet, giving the passage a bright glow. She hadn't realized how dark the other hall had been until light surrounded her.

Emanuel stopped at the first door they came to, entering the room beyond without hesitation.

Six people sat on worn furniture scattered around the room.

All of them turned to Emanuel, falling silent as he entered.

"We have a new member of our group," Emanuel said. "This is Raina."

The six gave murmured welcomes and greetings.

"Hi." As Raina exhaled the word. The scent of the six caught in her mouth, flooding her with a need she didn't recognize.

"Careful." Emanuel reached out, blocking her path.

"My turn." A pale girl around Raina's age stood.

"Thank you," Emanuel said.

The girl walked toward him, pulling her mop of brown hair aside.

Scars marked the base of her neck. Emanuel pulled a knife from his pocket, slicing across the girl's skin so quickly, Raina almost missed the flash of the blade.

The girl winced but didn't cry out as blood trickled down her neck.

Raina gasped as the scent of fresh blood hit her lungs. A clawing need unlike any she had ever felt before tore at her from the inside out.

"She's really thirsty," the girl whispered.

"Drink carefully." Emanuel seized Raina's shoulders, guiding her forward to the girl's neck.

"No." Raina clung to the doorway. "I can't do this. People shouldn't do this."

"This is the price of survival," Emanuel said. "She gives her blood willingly so we can be strong enough to fight against those who would destroy the city."

Raina dug her nails into the stone.

"No."

"Do you want to stop the domes from discarding the city?" Emanuel said. "Do you want to build a future people like you will actually get to see?"

"Yes." The word came out with a sob.

"It's okay," the girl said. "You need to drink."

Raina let her fingers fall slack. Emanuel guided her, facing her toward the girl's neck.

The girl tipped her head to the side, exposing her blood-stained skin.

Instinct took over. Raina lowered her mouth to the wound, sucking greedily.

Better than liquor, for the liquid held no burn. Better than sun, because the joy of it flooded through her veins in an instant.

Emanuel's hands held her shoulders, anchoring her to the world, as she floated into the bliss of blood.

CHAPTER FOUR

T he stench of the city reeked worse than Raina had ever imagined a foul
    scent could. The sweat and grime of every person who had wandered
through the streets during the deadly day clung to the air even in the shadows of
the night.

Raina moved quickly through the streets, keeping away from the main roads,
dodging past the packs of drunken men.

Her legs longed to run. To let her feet pound against the pavement as hard as
they could.

I could fly across the river if I tried.

The absurd thought curled Raina's lips into a grin.

"It's better if you just dive in," a voice carried up from the shadows of a basement apartment staircase. "Don't think about it, just do it."

Don't think about it, just do it.

"I promise you'll have fun," the voice said.

Raina shivered. Knowing the voice wasn't trying to convince her to do something foul didn't stop her revulsion from setting her teeth on edge.

Raina turned down a side street, heading straight for the calming lights of
Bellevue Avenue.

Little had changed in the three months since she'd walked the all too familiar
street. Each lamppost had been decorated for the festive season. Proof that
while the world ended, the rich would still have their fun.

The urge to build a bonfire of the spangled bows curled Raina's fingers. But
the flock of bought security guards kept the impulse at bay. They roamed the

center of Bellevue Avenue, mingling between houses, the weapons they carried the only vague sign they knew the perils of the surrounding city. None suspected the danger that strolled past them, her gaze locked on the front door of home.

"Miss McNay?" A security stooge jogged from the far side of the street.

James. Jeff?

The tag on his shirt read *John.*

"Miss McNay?" John repeated her name.

The jog had kick-started his pulse. His heart pumped blood through his veins, beating a gentle rhythm at the base of his neck.

Focus, Raina.

"Did my parents move?" Raina asked. "Has there been a warrant issued for my arrest?"

Is there anyone left to do the arresting?

"I, umm." John glanced up and down the street. His hand dropped to his weapon.

Tear the weapon from his hand, break his leg, you'll be down the street before the rest can react.

"If I could escort you to your door," John said. "I don't want to ask too much, but maybe you could say I helped you get here?"

Raina smiled, her body relaxed, leaving only the itching thirst to bother her.

"How much did Daddy offer as a reward for my safe return?" She draped her hand over John's elbow.

"Enough to get my wife and daughter clear of the city," John said.

"Promise you'll take the money and get as far from here as you can?" Raina asked.

"I've heard of places out west where people have figured out how to farm," John said. "Never had an interest in growing anything, but I could learn."

"You found me at rehab," Raina said. "Too embarrassed to come home. You convinced me my family wanted me back."

They climbed the steps to the house. Raina banged on the door.

"I hope you have a nice end of the world, John."

"Thank you, Miss McNay."

The door swung open. Nettie leaned against the doorframe.

"Well, damn," Nettie said. "Mom, Dad, Raina's not dead."

Nettie's breath reeked of booze, the stench strong enough to carry over the scent of the feast of blood that lived in the house.

Raina focused on Nettie's face. Nettie's seventeenth birthday wouldn't be for a few more weeks, but anger and distrust had already marred her brow.

She's a person. See the person, not the meal. Emanuel's voice echoed in Raina's mind.

"Raina?" Her father lumbered down the stairs, moving as quickly as she'd seen him in years.

"Hi, Daddy," Raina said.

"She's still not dead." Nettie ducked away from the door.

"Raina." Her father pulled her into a tight hug. "Where have you been? Were you kidnapped? Are you hurt?"

"I'm fine." Raina buried her nose in her father's shoulder, willing herself to find his familiar scent of engine grease and smoke. "I'm better than fine. I feel great."

"That's..." Her father stepped back, holding Raina at arm's length as he studied her. "That's wonderful."

"I think it's time I join the family business, Daddy." A bubble of hope rose in Raina's chest as joyful tears formed in her father's eyes. "I want to help build things."

NOLA'S STORY HAS ENDED. LANNI'S WAR HAS JUST BEGUN.

One will betray her. One will save her. One will destroy her world.

Do the work, steal the goods, keep her sister alive—a simple plan Lanni has been clinging to. With the city burning around her and vampires hiding in the shadows, making it until morning is the best she can hope for.

But order in the city is crumbling, and the thin safety that's kept Lanni alive won't be enough to protect her family. The people who live in the glittering glass domes—lording over the city, safe from the dangers of the outside world—have grown tired of the factory filth marring their perfect apocalypse.

When the new reign of chaos threatens her sister, Lanni faces a horrible choice—accept the fate she was born to, or join the enemy she's sworn to destroy.

Read on for a sneak peek of *Heart of Smoke*.

CHAPTER ONE

The scent of ash blew in through the window, joining the stench of burning oil that always filled the factory. The foreman had been pushing the machines faster for the past week, so a hint of scorched rubber added its stink, too.

I tightened the bandana that covered my face as I waited for the next rack of syringes to rumble down the line.

The outside doors banged open, letting in a fresh plume of smoke.

The foreman greeted the next shift of workers by shouting at them.

I let the hum of the machines drown out his words.

The new rack of syringes slid toward me. I flipped them all into the tray, moving quickly so the heat from the glass wouldn't burn my hands. I patted them all flat as the belt carried the tray past my station, waiting until the last moment to slip one syringe up my sleeve.

The packaging machine ate the tray, hiding the gap I'd created. I reached up to tighten my bandana again, letting the syringe fall farther up my arm. I gritted my teeth as the heat stung my elbow.

With a rumble, the next batch headed down the line.

Three solid taps on the shoulder and I stepped out of my place, gladly giving my station to the worker for the next shift.

I stretched my arms toward the ceiling, letting my back crack as the hot syringe slid down to the base of my spine, landing where my shirt tucked into my pants.

I'd only managed to snag six during my shift. Not a great day's work by any means.

Better than any of the others could manage.

"Check out," the foreman shouted, like he thought we didn't know what we were supposed to do at the end of our shift. Or worse, he was foolish enough to think we wanted to stay.

All of us rushed toward the booth by the door. I didn't run. I couldn't risk a sharp ear catching the faint clinking of my hard-won treasure. By the time I joined the line, there were already six others waiting to be checked out by the foreman's wife.

Mrs. Foreman sat in the booth, scanner in hand, frowning at each person who dared ask for their belongings back and to be paid for their time.

Or maybe it wasn't our wanting to be paid for our labor that she found so offensive. Maybe it was our dirty faces and rounded shoulders. Or the stink of sweat and rubber that had gotten permanently stuck in all our clothes. Maybe she didn't like the reminder that her husband's factory really produced two products—syringes and broken people.

I leaned out of line, peeking through the door to the courtyard.

The smoke hadn't fully blocked out the sun, but the ash came down thick. The fires were burning close to the city again.

A knot of panic twisted in my stomach as the line shifted forward. My nerves sent tingles from my fingertips to my toes.

Don't panic. You can't afford it.

I pressed my shoulders back and stood tall, making sure not even Mrs. Foreman's keen eyes could spot the lumps on my back from the pilfered goods.

"Trip Benson." Trip held out his wrist, offering his chip band.

Mrs. Foreman narrowed her eyes at him, like she wasn't sure if he was the same Trip Benson she'd been checking out after his shift six days a week for a dozen years.

"Trip Benson." He held his wrist right in front of her face, like he wanted her to lick the tarnished metal bracelet instead of scan the chip it held.

Mrs. Foreman turned in her chair, taking her time gathering Trip's bag and jug, before handing them over and finally scanning his chip.

"Thank you." Trip snatched his things and strode out the door.

I took a deep breath, filling my lungs till they ached, pulled off my bandana, and stepped up to the counter, holding out my wrist.

"Name?" Mrs. Foreman pursed her lips at me.

I leaned over the counter, holding my chip band right under her scanner.

"Name?"

I held her glare even as my lungs started to tense.

Mrs. Foreman made a sound between a growl and a sneeze before turning to grab my bag and three jugs. She lingered, enjoying tormenting me, lining the jugs up perfectly on the counter and trying to balance my bag so it wouldn't tip over. When my lungs had started to burn and my brain had started to scream that I needed air, she finally scanned my chip, transferring over my credits and ration for the day's work.

I grabbed my things, making myself walk calmly to the bare patch of wall where I could set everything down. My fingers fumbled as I tied my bandana back around my face. I took a deep breath, and the familiar stink of the thick fabric pummeled my nose. My head spun as oxygen raced through my veins, leaving bright spots dancing in my eyes. Snatching my things back up, I headed out into the square.

My shoulders relaxed as soon as I stepped outside, though walking through the square between the four factory buildings was hardly more cheerful than working the belts.

Litter and ash stirred with the chill wind that swept between the brick buildings. A crumpled, blue pamphlet rolled across my foot.

I grabbed the paper and tucked it into my pocket as a wave of laughter came from the men smoking in the back corner of the square.

They were right to laugh. There was no use in reading the kep-made pamphlet. Even if I was foolish enough to trust anything the glass guards said, weak words of comfort wouldn't offer me any protection.

I glanced up at the sky. To the east, evening light peered down, but to the west, thick, gray smoke blocked out the sun.

"Dammit." I bolted across the square toward the most rundown of the four brick buildings.

The ash must have been falling the whole day. The thick layer of it muffled my footsteps and puffed up around my boots.

"Where's your coat, honey?" one of the men in the corner called.

I tossed up my favored finger rather than waste air shouting back.

The men laughed again.

I flinched as one of the men's laughs dissolved into wracking coughs that made me wonder how much longer I'd have to deal with his daily taunts.

The sound of his hacking followed me into the kids' factory.

There were no machines to offer a blissful, mind-numbing hum on the kids' work floor, where they scrubbed and sorted bolts and scraps. Everything had to be done quietly so the teacher standing on the scaffold could be heard as she shouted her lessons to her three hundred students.

I stood on my toes, trying to catch a glimpse of Mari's shiny, black hair.

A kid started wailing in the far corner.

The foreman strode toward him, but the teacher didn't pause her lesson on the decimation of the oceans.

I tried not to wonder if the kid was wailing because he'd cut himself or because he couldn't stand the misery of knowing that something as beautiful as a sea turtle had once existed and he'd never get to see one in real life.

One of the minders finally caught sight of me. "Mari Sampson."

I gave the minder a nod of thanks as Mari hopped up from her place at one of the back tables and ran toward me.

"Slower, Mar," I whispered, though I knew my sister couldn't hear me.

"I thought you'd never come." Mari grabbed the jugs from my hands, setting them on the ground while I dug through my bag.

"I come at the same time every day." I pulled out Mari's hat, coat, and gloves.

"But some of the other kids have already been collected." Mari spoke so fast she sucked a bit of her bandana into her mouth and had to spit it out before continuing. "I got stuck on bolt scrubbing today, so you'll have to dig the metal bits out for me."

She held up her hands. Slivers and scratches deep enough to bleed marked her fingers.

I shoved down my sympathy and held out her coat.

Mari sighed before letting me dress her.

I didn't blame her for hating the coat. The ratty outer and inner layers hid the dense material that was worth its weight in credits and would make any decent thief drool. But knowing you were lucky to have a bit of protection from the lethal sunrays and liking to wear the damn thing were two different matters.

I fastened her coat and held out her gloves.

"My fingers already hurt." She tucked her scratched hands behind her back. "I won't get burned. The sun's almost gone, and the sky's filled with smoke. I don't want to wear them."

"Hmm." I tugged Mari's wide-brimmed hat onto her head and tied the rope beneath her chin. "I heard a rumor that someone's been hoarding peaches. I was going to nab them as a treat for you, but if you don't *want* to wear your gloves—"

Mari snatched her gloves away from me and tugged them on.

Biting back a smile, I pulled my own layers from the bag and dressed myself in a quarter of the time it had taken me to dress Mari. I slung my bag on and passed her one of the jugs, keeping two for myself.

"We're going to jog today," I said.

"Why?" Mari tipped her chin up so I could see her eyes below the brim of her hat.

"Smoke's coming in from the western side of the city."

"Oh, reef bleachers!" Mari cursed, grabbing my hand and running out the door.

I let her set our pace as we cut through the litter-strewn square and out onto the street beyond the factories.

The streets themselves had been kept clean of trash—the kep laws made sure of it—but not even the sweepers could keep up with the ash coming down from the sky.

Most of the people we passed had covered their heads, trying to keep the falling grit from settling into their hair. Some held cloths over their mouths or had tied rags around their faces. All of them wore the same painful air of resignation.

We all knew the city could drown in ash, and there wasn't a damn thing any of us could do about it. But watching hopelessness smother us when the ash was only a few inches thick...it almost seemed worse than letting the whole city burn at once.

I glanced up. The smoke had drifted farther in, close enough to coat the western edge of the city. I ran a little faster as we reached Generation Way, trying not to grip Mari's hand tight enough to make the scratches and slivers any worse.

The thumping of a club's music pounded through the air as we rounded the corner onto Endeavor Avenue. The handful of daytime bars that had been allowed to stay open had all been packed into the same few blocks with the shops that still sold non-essential goods. Cheers came from the nearest bar as a singer started a new song.

Mari took the lead, weaving a path through the customers eager to spend their credits.

Before we managed to break through the shoppers, I caught sight of the end of the line. It already stretched a block back from the tanks.

We dodged around a few of the slower people carrying jugs and claimed a place in line behind a man who stank with a tang exclusive to chem plant workers.

"The line's too long." Mari gripped my hand.

"We'll be fine," I said.

"What if the fires get too close and they call the kep away? What if the smoke stays in tomorrow?" She stood on her toes, trying to see between the adults in front of her. "What if they can't push the fires back?"

"Everything is going to be fine. We got here in time. We'll make it to the front." My guilt at lying to my little sister crashed into the hunger rumbling in my stomach.

"Two tanks," a woman a few people ahead of us shouted. "Smoke's coming in, and they're only running two tanks!"

I caught a glimpse of the start of the line as we all shuffled forward.

The woman was right. They were only distributing from two of the three tanks. The kep had only bothered to send twelve glass guards in fancy black uniforms to deal with the thirsty masses.

"Keep to a single line," a kep guard shouted. "If you all keep to a single line, we can get you through faster."

We won't all make it.

I turned my gaze up to the edge of the overhang that protected the tanks, choosing loathing over worry. Years of smoke and soot hadn't managed to destroy the image some idiot had painted to loom over the city scum.

Pictures of a happy family and a blooming tree flanked the words *For the Future of Our Children.* Like the kep cared about Mari's future or mine.

I kept my gaze fixed on the painted family until Mari started bouncing.

There were only five in line ahead of us.

"Come on," Mari muttered. "Come on." She pressed her cheek to my waist, tilting her hat.

I unfastened my coat and draped the side over her, covering the bit of her neck the hat had left exposed.

I glanced west.

The smoke had shifted again. The entire western side of the city would be covered.

One jug. If we can fill just one, we'll be fine.

A grating beep came from the front of the line, near one of the two working green tanks.

"I'm sorry, ma'am. Your chip shows no ration." The guard with the scanner turned away from the rationless woman.

"That's not possible." The woman stepped in front of the guard, holding out her wrist. "I did my day in the factory. They added my ration to my band, I know they did."

"Next."

The chem worker walked past the woman to the other running tank.

"Check it again." The woman shook her wrist at the guard. "I have a ration."

"The factory may have placed the ration on your chip," the guard said, "but fresh fires sparked to the west. Water was diverted from this station for the protection of the city. We have to make sure everyone is provided for."

"I'm part of everyone." The woman edged closer to the tank. "I need my ration."

"We've had to prioritize, ma'am." The guard held up his hand, blocking her path. "You are not in the approved group."

"I will die." The woman clutched her jug. "You are throwing my life away."

"Difficult decisions had to be made," the guard said. "We thank you for your sacrifice."

The woman threw her jug at the tank and leapt toward the guard, reaching for his neck like she thought she could choke him.

Another guard lunged forward, cracking the woman over the head with his club before her fingers had even grazed his fellow's neck.

The woman crumpled to the ground and lay still. She wasn't even breathing.

Mari started to shake as the woman's blood stained the ash on the street.

"Next," the guard called.

I held Mari close, guiding her around the growing patch of red sludge. We stopped in front of the tank. I raised my wrist for the guard to scan my chip band. My heart froze as I waited for the beep.

"Cleared for three jugs," the guard with the scanner said.

The other kep took Mari's jug.

My heart didn't start beating again until he turned on the tap and water began filling the container.

I let go of Mari to open the other jugs.

The guard passed the first back to Mari and had started filling the second before all the kep tipped their heads to the side at once, as though listening to a voice only they could hear.

I reached forward, bracing the still-filling jug the moment before the guard let go of it and bolted for the side of the overhang.

Mari squeaked as I caught the jug, managing to keep it upright so it wouldn't spill. I twisted the top back on, taking the second to protect the slim bit of our ration we'd claimed before grabbing Mari's hand.

"Run." I didn't have to say it.

Mari darted for the corner of the overhang as the high whine of the closing gates began. We slipped into the narrow alley beside the tanks before the crowd still waiting in line started to shout.

The water station would be closed while the glass guards hid, or fought the fire raging to the west, or whatever it was the kep in black guard uniforms did when they abandoned their petty attempts at helping the city scum.

Everyone left in line would have to go without.

Thank you for your sacrifice.

Order your copy of Heart of Smoke *to continue the story.*

ESCAPE INTO ADVENTURE

Thank you for reading Girl of Glass: The Complete Collection. If you enjoyed the book, please consider leaving a review to help other readers find Nola's story.

As always, thanks for reading,

Megan O'Russell

Never miss a moment of the danger or romance.

Join the Megan O'Russell mailing list to stay up to date on all the action by visiting https://www.meganorussell.com/book-signup.

ABOUT THE AUTHOR

 Megan O'Russell is the author of several Young Adult series that invite readers to escape into worlds of adventure. From *Girl of Glass*, which blends dystopian darkness with the heart-pounding danger of vampires, to *Ena of Ilbrea*, which draws readers into an epic world of magic and assassins.

With the *Girl of Glass* series, *The Tethering* series, *The Chronicles of Maggie Trent*, *The Tale of Bryant Adams*, the *Ena of Ilbrea* series, and several more projects planned, there are always exciting new books on the horizon. To be the first to hear about new releases, free short stories, and giveaways, sign up for Megan's newsletter by visiting the following:

https://www.meganorussell.com/book-signup.

Originally from Upstate New York, Megan is a professional musical theatre performer whose work has taken her across North America. Her chronic wanderlust has led her from Alaska to Thailand and many places in between. Wanting to travel has fostered Megan's love of books that allow her to visit countless new worlds from her favorite reading nook. Megan is also a lyricist and playwright. Information on her theatrical works can be found at RussellCompositions.com.

She would be thrilled to chat with you on Facebook or Twitter @MeganORussell, elated if you'd visit her website MeganORussell.com, and over the moon if you'd like the pictures of her adventures on Instagram @ORussellMegan.

ALSO BY MEGAN O'RUSSELL

Myth and Storm

LANNI

The cold wind gusted over the top of the mountain, sending her scarlet and purple streaked hair flying behind her.

Raina sat for a while, staring out at the vast darkness that surrounded Nightland. She listened for sounds of attack, scented the wind for fresh blood and fear.

Nothing.

She unfastened the latches and opened the black box.

The radio inside hadn't been damaged by its years hidden beneath the stone steps. She flicked the switch, and the screen blinked to life. A tiny black bar streaked back and forth, searching for one of the satellites still capable of carrying messages.

The radio beeped, and the words *Relay Found* glowed bright.

She took a long breath before pressing the button to speak. "Nettie, it's me again. You're probably dead. You've probably been dead for weeks. But if you're not, if you're just being a shit and hiding in the woods someplace, it's time to come out."

Raina stared at the radio, waiting for a voice to crackle to life.

No answer came.

She pushed the button again. "The fight's over, Nettie. We won. The domes have fallen. They can't hurt us anymore. So get your ass out of the woods, and come find me."

Lanni clutched the cracked radio, her hands shaking as she listened to the unknown voice.

"*The domes have fallen. They can't hurt us anymore.*"

She ducked between the splintered boards that covered her window and out onto the fire escape.

"*So get your ass out of the woods, and come find me.*"

The metal stairs clanged under her boots as she ran up to the roof. She leapt over the sleepers, ignoring their grumbles as she reached the railing.

Across the wasteland, the domes glittered in the distance.

"*The world isn't over,*" the voice crackled out of the radio. "*Not for us.*"

Not all the domes have fallen.
Lanni's battle has just begun.